Facing the Future

She did love Nathaniel, but she just couldn't count on him being there when she needed him. After he left for Montana for a couple of months, Fionna allowed herself one good cry, then drying her eyes, she looked to the future—a future she'd build with her own hands.

Fionna went to Portland, leaving the children with Nell. It was time she started handling her own investments instead of leaving them to Jacob.

Although she'd told herself her purpose was all business, the moment she walked into Jacob's office, she admitted that she'd had another reason for coming to Portland, one she had to face.

"I just got your letter day before yesterday," Jacob said, crossing the room to take her hands in greeting. "It's wonderful to see you, Fee."

"Yes," she said, thrilling to his touch through her gloves. "It's good to see you, too." *How could I have forgotten his eyes?* she thought.

She hadn't prepared herself to face this now. Her thoughts had been so focussed on business and family, that she'd foolishly ignored the needs of her own heart.

"I hope my visit isn't inconvenient. I can stay at the St. Charles—"

"Not at all. It's just what Ruth needs. She's been excited ever since your letter arrived. Besides," he added, his gaze resting gently on her face, "I want you in my house."

FIONNA'S WILL

Lana McGraw Boldt

BANTAM BOOKS
TORONTO · NEW YORK · LONDON · SYDNEY · AUCKLAND

FIONNA'S WILL

A Bantam Book / May 1987

ISBN 0-553-25542-8

Published simultaneously in the United States and Canada

Bantam Books are published by Bantam Books, Inc. Its trademark, consisting of the words "Bantam Books" and the por-
trayal of a rooster, is registered in U.S. Patent and Trademark
Office and in other countries. Marca Registrada. Bantam Books, Inc.,
666 Fifth Avenue, New York, New York 10103.

Dedication

Not the cry, but the flight of the wild duck, leads the flock to fly and follow.—Chinese Proverb.

To Mom and Dad—
whose flight has been straight and true.

Acknowledgments

In the beginning, when the first threads of an idea began weaving the plot of this book in my mind, I brimmed with confidence. Because it was set in Oregon, I would have very little research to do. Surely, all the details and colorful events ever needed for such a book were mine by virtue of how and where I grew up. Wandering hidden wilderness trails in my father's footsteps would count for something. Growing up on my uncle and aunt's ranch would certainly stand me in good stead. Then there were all those cherished and wondrous tales, heard while sitting at the knees of my grandfather, grandmother, uncles, aunts, and parents.

I was wrong. As in life, the further I went with this book, the more I learned of my own ignorance. Because of this I want to acknowledge the kind and generous help afforded me by others.

Historical facts are sometimes hard to come by. Homely historical details are often impossible to find. I was fortunate to have several institutional resources, all staffed with personnel who could help me find both. The Oregon Historical Society Museum and Library in Portland had much of the information I needed from all sixty-three years covered in this book. Klamath Historical Society, Klamath Falls, Southern Oregon Historical Society, Jacksonville, and Marion County Historical Society, Salem, also were of help, as well as the staff at St. Paul's Episcopal Church, Salem. The libraries at the University of Oregon, Eugene, and Southern Oregon State College, Ashland, were indispensable. I found good information concerning 19th Century musical instruments and early furniture at the Metropolitan Museum of Modern Art in New York City.

Many individuals also gave unremittingly of their time, skills, knowledge, and encouragement.

Rabbi Aryeh Hirschfield, Dr. Florence Schneider, and William Schneider very graciously answered questions about Judaism, especially in relation to Oregon's history.

It is important to be accurate about various illnesses and

accidents and their treatment. I strive to be accurate in depicting what is physically happening to a character as well as depicting medical treatment that would have been administered from sixty to one hundred years in our past. I had three professionals who sympathetically answered some very strange questions. Jean Keevil, M.D., used understanding and thoroughness in answering my questions concerning symptoms of various maladies and physical reactions to bodily injuries. Martin Osterhaus, N.D., has a wonderful collection of 19th Century medical texts and most generously gave me access to them, answering a multitude of questions about herbal therapy. Mark Heller, D.C., not only answered many questions but was able to direct me to other resources.

Benjamin (Kip) Lombard gave generously of his time and legal expertise while indulging his historical curiosity. It is because of his conscientious research that I can rest assured that Fee's will actually could have been written and really would have stood up in an Oregon court of law circa 1924.

Jessie Beaulieu McGraw offered her meticulous editing eye, as well as answering innumerable questions dealing with historic and genealogic details, dialect, and many other bits of information known only to native Oregonians. Likewise, her faith in her daughter exceeds even motherly norms.

Merle E. McGraw was helpful far beyond the call of fatherly duty. His vast reservoir of historic knowledge, Indian lore, woodsmanship, and natural history was only the beginning of his help. He patiently drove the car and played detective as we traced the Oregon Trail from Fort Boise to Oregon City, mile by mile, rut by rut. He was always on call for verification of details, answering questions about mills, ranches, lumber, cars, guns, or wildlife. When he didn't know the answer, he searched until he found it.

Wendy McGraw-Cowan offered her editing skills as well as unbounded encouragement.

(I could ask for no better friends than these three people, but to have them also be my parents and my sister is blessing beyond deserving.)

Dr. Margaret Evans of the Southern Oregon State College Music Faculty is not only a staunch friend but was endlessly helpful with all my music questions. Her colleague, Dr. Frances Madachy, was also a delightful source of information.

Ron McUne has a wealth of knowledge concerning the Oregon Trail, wagon trains, wagons, and many other pertinent subjects, all garnered through his experience driving two wagon trains over the Oregon Trail with his late father, George McUne. His conscientious restoration and preservation of wagons actually driven over the Oregon Trail in the 1800's was a historical treasure for us all. His good-natured answers to my many questions were most appreciated.

Eulice Mitchell was a happy discovery. His long-time experience as a mule skinner was unmatched. His mule team was patient and cagey in tolerating my inexperienced hands on the reins and Eulice's good humor and thoroughness made the learning experience a happy one. By the time I left, I knew more about mules, wagons, and tack than I could ever use in one book. And I'm grateful for it.

Paul Phol of the QX Ranch was wonderful in answering my questions about antique cars, especially the Stutz Bearcat and the Duesenberg, as well as letting me sit behind the wheel of his own beautiful Stutz.

Frank and Leilla Sparks always answered my questions concerning local history, farming practices, and dialect with good patience and understanding, certainly more than you could expect from an ordinary aunt and uncle.

Dr. Joel Summerhays, criminologist and gun expert, enthusiastically provided me with accurate information about firearms. Thanks to him, none of my characters fire a gun before it was manufactured—and they fire it correctly.

Harry Thompson was also a joy to work with. He pridefully showed me the team of horses he still uses for working the farm. He gave me enough background for a multitude of books and I thank him.

Nyla Guthrie Yuzon has the unique and dogged skills of a born researcher. A call to her would send her on the trail of even the most minute detail. The result was accurate information, loaned historic photos, and my gratitude. Moreover, her friendship has seen me through the best and the worst of times.

Jean at the Medford Department of Veterans' Affairs was able to find four spirited and helpful World War I Veterans. I thank her for her efforts and Bill Baker, Fred Hunt, Ray Wakeman, and Robert Wright for their help.

Andrea Cirillo deserves a bouquet of thanks for her support, encouragement, and professional skill. Her rare combination of talents make the mixing of profession and friendship seem natural and easy.

Barbara Alpert used her keen eye for editorial winnowing, catching the grain while blowing away the chaff. She also has the uncanny ability to remain honest, cheerful, and friendly after hours on the phone. For both she is appreciated.

Most of all I want to thank my family. Darrell, my husband, listened to my ideas, read my manuscript, and offered his astute observations. My daughter Katrina traveled the Oregon Trail with me, keeping notes, taking pictures, and being a stern accountant. My daughter Kirsten cheerfully agreed to read and critique a full chapter—using her keen eye to make sure that I was ever faithful to the viewpoint of a twelve-year old girl. All three have given me support and encouragement without which this story would never have been written. For that and their love, I am grateful.

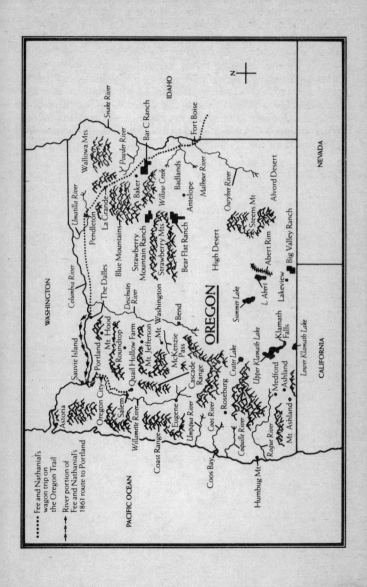

Prelude

May 1924

Jacob had to keep reminding himself that Fee was dead. Lost in memories, he paced across his law office, his hands clasped behind his back. Fee, that gracious, witty, and powerful woman, had woven her influence through every phase of his life, through so many lives. Then, before she died, she gave him the burden of her most peculiar will, insisting he would make it work because he knew her so well.

Now today—today she would reach beyond the barrier of death and impose her will upon her heirs. And Jacob would be her instrument.

He halted in his pacing and turned to the window. From there he could look beyond the buildings of Salem to the rolling fields of the fertile Willamette Valley. A fine gray mist cloaked the afternoon but he could still make out part of the land that Fionna Barry Coughlin had dominated for over sixty years. Fee, as her loved ones called her, had been a powerful woman. Now what was to become of them all?

As if on cue, a large black Duesenberg pulled up to the curb. He recognized it as the one he'd seen Hannah riding in with her new beau.

"Miss Andersen," Jacob called through the open doorway to his reception room. His plump young secretary appeared immediately. "Please have the Coughlin heirs wait in the reception room until they've all arrived. Hannah Balfour, the daughter, is outside, but the others aren't in sight."

As she closed the door, he turned back to the window.

Hannah was still sitting in the car. Jacob could see her tightly folded arms on the passenger's side. Although he couldn't see her face, he noted a man's hand gesturing emphatically across the seat from her. He didn't need to see her to know that Hannah wasn't happy.

Duke was the name of the man she'd been seeing. He'd come to Oregon from Chicago, it was said, looking for "investments." He spent money with abandon, and the townspeople openly took it while privately speculating as to its

1

origin. He'd leased some undeveloped property from Hannah, who was managing the old homestead for her mother. She'd told Jacob some sketchy story about how Duke was using the land for an experimental method of hog-raising.

Hannah got out of the car, shaking her head in disagreement. As she started up the steps of the building, Duke executed a quick, illegal U-turn in the middle of the street, causing the wheels to squeal, then parked the car on the opposite side. He was going to wait.

A sinking feeling came over Jacob. If only Hannah were simply unhappy, and not in more trouble than she could handle. He shivered, suddenly overwhelmed by the enormity of the task he was facing. Fionna had inextricably woven his life with the life of her descendants. The weight of that responsibility was oppressive.

Walking back to his desk, he picked up his carefully prepared notes, then returned to the window just as a sleek roadster pulled up. Emmett Balfour, Hannah's son and Fee's grandson, stepped out onto the curb. Jacob could see a lovely young woman slide into the driver's seat, showing a surprising amount of leg. He couldn't see her face beneath her peek-a-boo hat. Only a pert little mouth that Emmett leaned down and kissed before she drove off. It didn't matter what her name was. She was simply one of a long string of devoted, beautiful young women Emmett escorted to dances, speakeasies, parties, and moving pictures.

What was it that made Emmett so irresistible to women? Jacob wondered. Was it his good looks, his quick sense of humor, his money, or the strange allure of adventure that came from a man of action, a man who flew airplanes?

"He just needs to find an outlet for that seeking spirit of his," Fee had said one day. "He's just like his grandfather that way."

Emmett waved as the young woman drove away, then turned and cast an experienced eye at the gray sky. He caught sight of Jacob in the window, and a sunny smile broke across his face.

Next to arrive was Fee's son, Timothy, who parked his big Maxwell touring car directly in front of Jacob's office. Attached to the trunk was a large canvas banner proclaiming in bold red and blue letters, "COUGHLIN FOR SENATOR—A Native Oregonian!"

So that was his campaign slogan, Jacob mused. *Jacta est*

2

alea; the die is cast. If Timothy won the election, Jacob's hands would be full.

Timothy was a large man, grown portly from fifty-two years of good living and indulgence. He climbed down from his car and paused to straighten his tie and coat. He pulled out his pocket watch, attached to his vest with a heavy gold chain, checked the time, then entered the building.

Now there were three waiting in his reception room. One more to go. Jacob returned to his pacing. The clock on the wall ticked off five more minutes. Where was she?

The sound of a powerful engine brought Jacob back to the window. The long nose of a sleek, buff-colored Stutz Bearcat pulled up behind Timothy's car. It was Josephine Barry Balfour, Hannah's daughter and Fee's granddaughter. Jacob watched her, unaware that he was holding his breath.

Her long shapely legs stepped gracefully from the roadster. She ran her fingers through her tousled dark hair, then hastened up the steps. She was alone, and Jacob was surprised by the immense feeling of relief that fact produced.

He turned from the window, then looked back again. His eye was caught by a wisp of smoke curling out of Duke's partially opened window across the street.

Jacob wasn't the only one watching the arrival of the four heirs.

Miss Andersen peeked in the door. "Everyone is here, Mr. Teall."

"Please ask them to wait," Jacob said. "I'll buzz when I'm ready."

He turned to the sealed wooden box behind his desk; the letter written in Fee's hand was still on top. He sat down, read through his notes one last time, then sounded the buzzer.

Miss Andersen opened the door and Fee's family filed into his office.

Timothy offered Jacob a hearty handshake along with an affectionate pat on the back. "How does it feel to be back in God's country after your sojourn amongst the Philistines?" he asked, referring to Jacob's recent sabbatical back East.

"This is where I belong." Jacob grinned and then caught Josie's eye. She smiled and it was all he could do to look at her and nod, remembering with renewed pain her engagement to Ron West.

Hannah was next, her thin face tight, as if she were trying to pinch in all the emotions that were trying to escape, the

3

same way she might pinch the pastry of a pie to keep the juices from spilling out.

Emmett brought up the rear. "Once we get this all settled," he said to Jacob, "you and I are going to have to go out together. You need someone to teach you how to have a good time with a pretty girl."

Just like his grandmother. Nothing escaped Emmett's sharp eyes. But Jacob didn't mind. There was a kind nature beneath Emmett's mischief. It was the same generous nature that long ago had made him claim partial responsibility for a broken window because he'd pitched the ball that Jacob had hit.

When everyone was seated, Jacob nervously cleared his throat and began explaining in great detail the tax and probate laws of the state, going so far as to open heavy volumes to marked pages and read complicated passages to his impatient audience.

Timothy finally interrupted. "No law-school lectures, Teall. We just want to know how Mother divided up the estate. Get on with it."

Jacob put his books away and turned to his prepared speech. "Obviously, with such a large and complicated estate, these laws lengthen the time needed to arrange matters. Fionna knew this and prepared a unique will to make the transition period more tolerable for you all.

"The state has to go over the deeds, accounts, liabilities, and assets. There's the mandatory four months' notice for creditors. It'll take at least eight to ten months for all this to get sorted out.

"In the meantime, Fionna arranged for you each to continue on much as you did when she was alive. Before she died, she set up a 'living trust.' In this interim I will act as trustee of the estate. This is called a 'pour-over' will because Fee's instructions pour over into the period following her death. Some of Fee's securities are set aside for your income during this time. After probate, the estate will be clearly established, and, as Fee's trustee, I will distribute it according to her instructions.

"During this time you will each receive an equal portion of the income generated by the estate and continue living in the house you now occupy. That means that you, Hannah, will stay on the farm; you, Timothy, will remain in the town house near the main lumberyard; Emmett can stay in and manage the apartment house he occupies in Portland; and

4

Josephine, Fionna wanted you to move into the mansion in Portland where she was living—that way it won't be left empty and unused during this time."

There was a murmur of surprise and dissatisfaction from Hannah and Timothy. Jacob quickly went on. "Fionna also chose a personal present for each one of you and wrote a private letter to accompany it. She wanted you to have a special remembrance from her as well as the general inheritance that will follow when this is all sorted out. Before I distribute these items, I'll read a letter from her that she directed me to read at this time."

He took the letter from the box and broke the seal. As his audience settled back in their chairs, he began reading:

My children: When you hear these words, I will have cut the mortal cord that has bound you each to me. Now it is up to you to look to the horizons I have found, to set your feet on the paths I have blazed.

As Mr. Teall has already explained to you, it will be a while before you will know your true inheritance. In the meantime, you will each receive a token of my affection for you.

These are the conditions of my will:

None of the estate can be touched or altered in this interim period.

None of the investments or businesses can be sold, nor can management be changed.

None of the land can change hands.

You will all be cared for from the profits accruing from the normal operations of the estate.

You will be cared for equally while the estate is being sorted out. No one will suffer a loss of income and you might even enjoy an increase. At the end of that time I will speak to you once more, telling you of your inheritance. Until then, be kind to one another and live as you have been taught to live.

Jacob Teall will be your trustee. You will each come to him for a personal accounting of your monthly income.

These are the requirements of my will. I have worked long and carefully to make sure that it will be obeyed. Should any one of you try to alter its directives, you will suffer not only the full retribution of the state laws and the disdain of all society; you will also suffer for your disobedience in the world to come.

5

Farewell, my loved ones. You are each one my most valuable contribution to the world.

Jacob placed the letter on the edge of his desk so that anyone who wished could read it. Josie was wiping tears from her eyes while Emmett patted her hand and stared down at his feet. Hannah was agitated, twisting the handle of her handbag and glancing nervously out the window. Timothy was so upset he could no longer keep his seat. He got up and stood behind his chair as if preparing to make a speech.

"This is preposterous," he declared, hitting his hand against the back of his chair. "You can't do this to me. I'm counting on liquidating assets to fund my campaign this summer. I must have more money. I have people waiting to lease that worthless land up on Round Top. Surely I can at least do that."

"Who, Uncle Timothy?" Josie asked.

Timothy looked irritated and said, "S&R Logging."

"That's the family's main logging competition," Emmett said. "Why would you want to give our timber to them?"

Timothy snickered. "So they'll go broke trying to log on those steep hillsides. It's just worthless land, anyway."

"But if it's logged, it'll be ruined. Erosion will wipe the whole mountain out," Josie protested.

"Well, Hannah and I feel—" Timothy began imperiously.

"I don't know, Timothy," Hannah interrupted. "What the children said makes sense."

Timothy glared. "You just wait, my sour sister," he murmured menacingly. Then, turning back to Jacob, he tried another tack. "I must have more money," he demanded. "Why, I'm her only living son. I'll receive the bulk of the estate. I demand that you make accommodations for my campaign needs."

Jacob smiled politely and made a gesture of helplessness. "I'm afraid the strict admonition of her will cannot be broken. However, before you protest further, I suggest you check with your bank. Perhaps the monthly stipend you'll receive will be sufficient when it is combined with the contributions you'll surely receive from your supporters."

As her uncle fumed, Josie rose to speak.

Jacob thought, *Here it comes. She's the one who can throw this whole thing into chaos.*

"Obviously," she began in her most reasonable voice, "this is the most fair and logical way of handling things until it's all

6

sorted out. Sit down, Uncle Timothy, so we can get Grandmother's letters and presents. It's just like her to remember us this way. Go on, Jacob." Her smile as she turned to him was almost conspiratorial.

"Yes, go on," Emmett added.

Jacob breathed a sigh of relief.

Timothy seemed temporarily mollified, but Hannah kept biting her lips and glancing out the window. Jacob moaned inwardly and reached for the box behind his desk. How on earth did Fee expect him to keep tabs on all this until December?

"Before I give you her gifts," he said as he lifted the box to his desktop, "I must say one more thing. Fee's instructions on this point are clear. You must not read your letter until you're absolutely alone. The letters are Fionna's private communication with you individually and are not intended to be public."

He broke the seal on the box, opened it, and pulled out an inventory list neatly written in Fee's handwriting. First on the list was a legal-size envelope addressed to Emmett; accompanying the letter were nine bulky journals. The first one was shabby and yellowed with age; the other eight were increasingly new, with the top one bound in fine leather.

"Emmett, your grandmother wants you to have your grandfather's journals," he said. "And here is your letter, which I again remind you to read only when you're alone."

Emmett's handsome face beamed as he took the journals. "She knew how much I'd like these," he said, his eyes glistening. "I was always tagging after Grandpa. I sat and listened to his stories by the hour. Now I can do it again," he ended softly. Josie leaned over to look at them, sharing her brother's pleasure.

"Hannah, here's the gift and letter your mother had for you." He reached into the box and pulled out a long, black leather case. Hannah took it, lifted the silver latch, and opened the lid. Resting on a cushion of pale blue velvet was a very old and carefully preserved flute. It was finely crafted from satin-smooth black cocus wood and fitted with sterling silver keys and mouthpiece.

Hannah gasped. With trembling hands she took the flute out of its case and clasped it to her, staring ahead at something no one else could see. Suddenly the room was filled with her coarse, pained sobs, sobs so wrenching they sounded as if they were being pulled from the depths of her soul where they had been imprisoned for years.

Impulsively, Josie reached over and put her arm around her mother. It was all so unlike Hannah that everyone in the room was silent. They must have been as shocked as Jacob when Hannah leaned her head on her daughter's shoulder and gave way to tears. Even Timothy seemed momentarily to forget his impatience.

Josie patted Hannah's head soothingly, and when the sobs began to subside, she handed her mother Emmett's handkerchief. Hannah wiped her eyes. "Please excuse me." Once more she withdrew into herself, but the brief glimpse into her hidden inner torment had left everyone in the room speechless.

Even the seemingly simple tasks were not going to be as easy as Jacob had thought they would be. With an effort he resumed distribution of the bequests, wondering what other surprises Fee had in store.

Jacob handed Timothy his private letter and then a heavy gold watch chain, identical to one on his vest, being made with intricately twisted links and an unusual watch clip fashioned in the shape of a flying bird.

Timothy took the envelope, but when the chain coiled in his hand, he quickly checked his own watch pocket. Feeling his own chain still there, he stared at the second chain. His hand began to tremble, causing the chain to slip to the floor.

Timothy's lips quivered and his face paled as he looked up at Jacob. "You . . . you . . ." he stammered. "What are you trying to do? You had this made to torment me!"

Jacob stepped from behind the desk, picked up the chain, and handed it to Timothy. "I had nothing to do with it. You saw me break the seal. I didn't know what was in the box. Your mother filled and sealed it by herself six weeks ago. As you can see, the chain isn't new; it's worn." Jacob pointed to a broken link on one end. "Your mother obviously thought you would look elegant wearing a double watch chain and saved this one for you from a long time ago. Do you know who it belonged to?"

Timothy looked at the chain in his hand as if he'd just been handed a hissing serpent. "I . . . no . . . no, I don't know whose it was. I just thought someone had stolen mine. It's so similar, you see," he stammered as he dropped the chain onto a nearby table.

Jacob stood waiting, trying to understand Timothy's strange

reactions to what seemed to be a lovely gift. What did it mean?

"Go on, go on," Timothy commanded irritably. "You have one more to go. Let's see her surprise."

Jacob reached for the last gift, a small hinged box covered in dark green velvet. "Remember, Josephine, don't read your letter until you are alone. However, you are free to open your gift if you wish."

Josephine's eyes twinkled with excitement as she took the letter and box from Jacob. "Of course I'll open it. I can't wait." She opened the box, and her smile changed to a look of surprise and delight. "They're—they're beautiful," she exclaimed. Nestled in black velvet was a pair of earrings, each fashioned from a nugget of pure gold and set with a square cut emerald. Resting beside the earrings was a thin gold ring set with tiny seed pearls and a garnet. "I don't ever remember Grandmother wearing these. Do you, Mother?"

Hannah shook her head. "I've never seen them before, but they look pretty old." She leaned over and looked with an expert eye. "The earrings have some value, but the ring isn't worth much. It matches the brooch I got from Aunt Judith when she died. She said it came from her mother, who'd brought it over from Ireland." She looked at the earrings again before turning to Josie. "I don't have the faintest idea where these came from."

Josie took the ring out of the box and slipped it on her finger, obviously pleased that it fit. She held out her hand, along with the earrings, for her uncle to see.

Timothy absently glanced at the jewelry, then reached over to pick up his gold watch chain.

"Maybe your letter will explain where they came from," Emmett suggested. "I'll bet she's giving us each something that has some special story behind it. The letters will probably clear up all the mysteries."

"Maybe so," Jacob agreed. "Your grandmother worked in mysterious ways at times. Or maybe she simply wanted to give you each something to remember her by. Now, unless you have any further questions, we are done for today. I'll see you between the first and the fifth of each month when you come in to pick up your portion of the estate's earnings and see the books for that month. Until then, I'll be available for any private consultations you may need or want."

Timothy roused himself, slipping the chain and letter into his coat pocket. "I'm registering my complaint right now. If you can't release my full inheritance, at least advance me funds against the inheritance that will surely be mine at the end of this legal morass. I think—"

"If you have any further problems with the conditions of your mother's will," Jacob interrupted, "you may make an appointment with my secretary and we'll talk it over. However, I assure you it is iron clad. Before you go to any further trouble, check with your banker and see what your first month's deposit is. It's already been put in each of your accounts in preparation for today's reading. When you've done that, Timothy, talk to your campaign manager about soliciting funds from your supporters. That seems the logical and normal way to conduct a political campaign. If you had to be wealthy to run for office, this wouldn't be much of a democracy, would it?"

Timothy looked startled, began to say something, then simply turned and walked out of the office, his hand in his pocket.

The others stood up and put on their wraps. As Hannah buttoned her coat, she touched Josie's arm. "Josephine, may I ride with you? I need to go to Portland."

Josie looked surprised. "Sure, Mother. The car's outside."

Hannah hesitated, then said, "I have to powder my nose. Would you get the car and meet me behind the office in ten minutes?"

Josie looked puzzled. "Whatever you want. I'll be in the alley in ten minutes."

Hannah smiled with relief and quickly went out the door, thanking Jacob as she did.

A horn honked below the window. Emmet looked out and waved. "There's my ride," he said with a smile, gathering up his grandfather's journals. "Thanks for all your hard work, Teall. I'll give you a call soon and we'll go out on the town. I know dozens of girls who'd give their eyeteeth to go out with a handsome devil like you," he finished, winking impishly at his sister.

Jacob laughed, and Emmett hurried out the door as the car horn honked once more.

He turned to Josie. She was laughing and shaking her head. "I have never heard so much legal gobbledygook in one speech in all my years at law school. I don't know what Grandmother has put you up to, but I can't wait to find out. What is it, a restricted trust? What kind of special provisions

10

does she have? You're just lucky I didn't blow it for you in front of Mother and Uncle Timothy."

Jacob's heart was in his throat. The look of pure mischief in her eyes made him feel like a little boy caught with his hand in the cookie jar. "Thanks for not asking before. Do you think the others suspected?" he asked sheepishly.

"Maybe Emmett. But I doubt he cares," she said with a grin. "Now, what's really going on with the estate? How did she have you set it up?"

Jacob shook his head and smiled. "Your grandmother and I knew you'd probably question this. But the truth is that I can tell you no more under the conditions of the will."

He paused and considered Josie seriously for a moment. "One thing I can tell you: She was pretty worried because you haven't passed your bar exams yet."

"Oh, that," Josie said with a shrug. "I'll get around to it. There's been a lot happening."

"Yes, I know," he said quietly. "But Fionna wanted you to do the most important first. She thought your admission to the bar was the most important thing for you to do."

"Now you're beginning to sound just like her," Josie teased. "Next thing I know you'll be creating mysteries of your own. Frankly, I can't wait," she added conspiratorially. "In the meantime, I'll try to figure out what Grandmother was up to." She pulled on her coat. Then she picked up her letter and jewelry box and slipped them into her handbag. Smiling at Jacob, she said, "Don't look so worried. I won't tell anyone. It's our little secret." With that she stood on her toes and kissed Jacob's cheek, then hurried out the door.

Even though he was startled by the kiss, Jacob was struck by a chilling thought as she walked past Miss Andersen's desk. "Josie," he called after her, "I forgot to tell you something!"

She followed him back into the office and he closed the door. The soft scent of her perfume suddenly filled him with a heady awareness of her presence. It was all he could do to force his feet to walk towards the window. "Look down there."

Josie peeked out. "Is he that jerk Mother's been seeing?"

Jacob nodded. "Duke's been waiting the whole time. That must be why she asked you to pick her up out back. She's trying to avoid him. I don't know what's going on, but I don't like the looks of him. When you leave, drive around the block like you're leaving town, then circle back to the alley.

11

And keep an eye on your mirror to make sure you're not being followed."

"Isn't this a little melodramatic?"

"Maybe, but then again, maybe not. Your mother isn't taking any chances. Neither should you."

"I knew it!" she exclaimed with a little laugh. "Grandmother's influence is already rubbing off on you. You're already creating your own mysteries."

Jacob looked at her laughing blue eyes and dark curly hair. She was the picture of perfect beauty, and beneath that beauty was a mind so sharp it had kept him on his toes through a full year of law school. There could never be another woman like Josephine. "I just don't want anything to happen to you," he said. Then, to his own surprise, he leaned over and lightly kissed her lips.

Josie flushed. "Did Grandmother put you up to that as well?"

He smiled. "I don't think so. It just seemed like a good idea."

"Good," she said, smiling as she turned to go out the door. "I sometimes think Grandmother put too many people up to doing things that were not their own ideas."

"Maybe so," Jacob said, walking her to the door. "But would that have been so bad?"

Josie looked at him soberly. "I don't know, Jacob. I really don't know. There's so much we don't know about Grandmother, isn't there?" With that she touched her hand to his cheek, then turned and went out the door.

PART I

FEE

Chapter I

December 27, 1860

There was a steady crunch as the wagon wheels rolled over the ice-glazed ruts in the road. Fionna Barry pulled her rough woolen coat more tightly about her slender neck and flicked the reins. "C'mon, Fitz-James," she urged with foggy breath, "hurry it up a bit and I'll give you an extra handful of oats."

The horse twitched his ears and maintained his plodding pace.

"Faith, it's cold this morning," she said, looking at the leaden sky. "I never should have talked Father into letting me make the delivery instead of Matthew."

The Barry farm in western Virginia was a depot on the Underground Railroad. Two nights ago Donnell Barry, Fionna's father, had greeted a man who was only a nameless shadow to the Barrys. Hidden under his load of hay was a runaway slave woman. The nameless man left in the dark and the badly frightened woman slipped into the barn, where she could spend the night.

Fee had gone out to take her a blanket and a plate of food but Nilly, which the man had assured them was her name, was nowhere in sight. Fee called, then called again. The haystack rustled, then Nilly emerged, covered with hay and trembling. "They's got men a-followin' the Railroad," she'd confided.

The rumor that the Underground Railroad was doomed had been rampaging through the plantations. Teams of men were said to follow escaping slaves, allowing a few to get through until they learned all the stops and "safe houses." Then they would kill all involved. Nilly had been haunted her whole journey by visions of moving shadows and furtive shapes lurking in the dark.

Fee assured her that it was probably just a rumor started to frighten slaves and keep them from running away. Fionna felt a burst of motherly protectiveness toward this poor shivering

15

slip of a girl, for that was all she was, being merely fourteen—a full three years younger than Fionna herself.

Returning to the farmhouse, Fee announced to her father that this was not a job for a youthful boy but for a mature woman. Not Matthew but Fee would drive Nilly to the next house. She would protect her newfound charge personally. No manner of protest from her father or younger brother would change her mind. In the end, her father gave in and Matthew sulked as Fee drove the wagon out of the farmyard at dusk. Her load of cornstalks was for the Edwards' pigs— and under the cornstalks shivered Nilly, once more on her way out of the slave states into the free state of Ohio and then on up to Canada and freedom.

They'd arrived safely around midnight. She'd taken the quilt Mrs. Edwards had left on her rail, the one with the log cabin pattern with black squares quilted in to indicate that this was a "safe house," and put Nilly in the barn, assuring her that there were no shadowy followers. Then Fee had slipped into the house and crawled into bed with the Edwards' seven-year-old daughter, Della, for a few hours of sleep. Fee had awakened in the predawn dark to return home. Mrs. Edwards gave her some corn bread and a piece of cold side pork to eat on her way. She was cresting the hill above the Edwards' place by first light and was two hills beyond by sunup.

Now, as she shivered in the cold morning light, she was anxious to get back to her father and brother and warm herself by the fire.

To keep her mind off her aching hands and shivering legs, Fee thought about tomorrow, when she'd be riding into town with her father and brother to pick up their monthly supplies, always a social occasion.

She wondered if Mrs. Lane had had her baby yet, if little Rosie Harbrick would remember her this time, and if Mr. Adams would give her a horehound drop. There might be a letter from her sister, Siobhan, who was attending school in Philadelphia, according to their late mother's wishes and legacy.

Fee was going to follow in her sister's footsteps this fall. Her mother had kept aside a portion of her dowry for the education of her children, maintaining in the hard times that it was better to go hungry now so they'd be able to feed themselves for the rest of their lives. Fee should have left four years earlier, but her mother had died. Each year since then her mourning father had kept her on the farm to help out, promising her freedom as soon as he felt back on his feet. Fee didn't mind terribly; she enjoyed the authority she wielded over her brother and father. Still, she'd long ago finished her schooling at the tiny eight-grade schoolhouse, and she was more than ready to go on.

Fee looked forward to her sister's letters, but the postponement of her own schooling made it difficult to hear about Siobhan's latest scholastic triumphs. How could she possibly catch up with her older sister, who had been at school so long? Siobhan had said in her last letter that she'd applied for a position as a teaching assistant for next year. The possibility of having Siobhan as her teacher galled Fee even more.

Her father had tried to continue her education by providing Fionna with all sorts of reading material. They regularly discussed science and history, as well as the literature she loved. She even took care of the accounting for the farm. Still, it was not the same.

A rabbit scurried across the road and Fitz-James shook his head and snorted. "We're about halfway there," she murmured, as much to herself as to her horse. It was lonely in the cold morning mist.

Fee thought again of her night's dangerous errand, and of the angry words she'd read in recent newspapers. Her father believed that the United States was going to be torn apart by war, but Matthew believed that was impossible. Fee hoped Matthew was right, but she tended to side with her father.

For months now they had been part of the Underground Railroad. Her father's Irish sense of freedom led him to assert that no human should be kept in bondage, and his actions followed his words.

Fee agreed. Even Nilly, who had whined the whole trip and risked detection, didn't deserve to be enslaved. She shook her head as she remembered their parting exchange.

"I's just don' know what I's goin' to do," Nilly had cried as Fee helped her to the barn. "See, I's gonna have a baby, an' bein' in Canada all by myself—"

At that Fee had lost her temper and snapped, "You'll just have to make do, like the rest of us. Work." She'd closed the barn door and stormed into the Edwards' house. Yet now in the cold morning light, she felt a twinge of guilt. She understood Nilly's fears.

A sudden noise brought her out of her reverie. The whistle of the chill wind was overlaid with the faint sound of hoofbeats. Someone was coming up behind her, riding hard. She reached under the seat and checked her rifle. It was loaded and in easy reach. Should she stop?

As the hoofbeats came closer, she turned and watched a clearing in the bend of the road below her. She caught a glimpse of the rider through the trees and relaxed a bit. The coppery red hair under the fur cap was a dead giveaway.

It was Nathanial Coughlin, who periodically stopped by and visited her father. Fionna considered him footloose and irresponsible, unduly influenced by the popular accounts written by explorers of the frontier. She thought at twenty-three he should have been thinking of settling down. Instead he'd chosen a wandering life, trapping furs and taking odd jobs logging in the new state of Minnesota.

Nathanial was the one who'd first told them about the Underground Railroad. Fee had listened surreptitiously from the kitchen as he'd exchanged books and ideas with Donnell Barry. He always asked Fee to play the piano for him. Since he'd spent the last nine years alone, tramping the wild frontier, Fee figured his soul hungered for music.

Now why on earth was he in such a lather so early in the day, she wondered as she reined the wagon to the side of the road to let him pass. It wasn't good for a horse in the cold like this.

Then, as he came up beside her wagon, he suddenly leaped from his saddle to the wagon seat, leaving his horse to trot alongside. Without so much as a word of greeting he grabbed the reins from her hands and whipped Fitz-James into a run.

"What are you doing?" Fee cried as she was thrown back on the seat by Fitz-James' sudden lurch forward. "You can't just come up and . . . Slow down, you fool! There's a curve ahead."

Ignoring her protests, he looked over his shoulder, then glanced at Fee as he turned his attention back to the road ahead. "You got a gun?"

"Yes, and I'm thinking I might have to use it on you."

"Get it out and start praying."

Suddenly frightened, Fee pulled the rifle from under the seat and checked to make sure it was primed. The ride was so rough she had to keep grabbing the sideboard to keep from falling.

She looked behind them. Nothing was in sight. Beyond the rolling hills and through the mist she could see a column of smoke rising from just about where the Edwards' farm would be.

18

"What's happening?" she cried.

The wagon swerved around the bend, careening over the rough wagon tracks and suddenly off the road, through the brush, and behind an outcropping of rocks. Before Fee could pick herself up from the floor of the wagon, Nathanial was out and breaking off a branch to use in covering the wagon's tracks.

"What in blazes is going on?" Fee demanded as she shoved her bonnet back over her dark curls and crawled down from the wagon. She checked Fitz-James to make sure he hadn't been hurt by the rough handling. "You'd better have a good reason for—"

"Look down the road," Nathanial commanded.

Fee crawled up and peered over the rocks.

"Seven riders, coming fast. Who are they?"

"Rebel marauders. They burned out the Edwards'. Figure they're heading for your place next."

"But why?"

"Shh. Hold that horse's nose and pray they don't figure out where we've gone."

Fee stroked Fitz-James' ears and gently cupped her hand over his nose, trying to calm him, hoping that he couldn't hear the hammering of her heart.

The riders came closer. Fitz-James reared his head and Fee pulled it down, covering his nose with her coat.

They thundered past, never slowing their pace.

Within a minute Nathanial was in his saddle. "Where are you going?" Fee demanded.

"Got to warn your folks."

"I'm coming, too."

"And slow me down? Can't take a wagon through the woods, and that's the only way to outrun those murderers."

"What'll I do?"

"Wait here. If you don't hear a warning shot, come out in fifteen minutes and go at your regular pace down the road. If anyone stops you, just say that you're heading on into town. Give them some made-up name," he added over his shoulder as he disappeared into the underbrush.

Fee watched the movement of the brush as he urged his horse up over the hill. Within seconds the noise of the horse faded and she was left alone with the early morning winterbird sounds.

She waited, trying to understand what was happening. Why did he call those men marauders? Was it something to do with the Underground Railroad? Was Nilly right? Had they been followed last night? She shivered at the thought. Maybe Father was right. Maybe the whole country was going to explode into a civil war. There was that business of that fanatic abolitionist John Brown who tried to seize the Harper's Ferry armory last year. Maybe this was just the beginning . . .

She looked back over the rocks and saw the smoke from the Edwards' farm. The smoke rose above the hills now, thick and black. What had happened to Mrs. Edwards and chubby little Della, whom Fee had slept with last night? And Nilly? Suddenly Fee realized that these same men were riding towards her home—towards Daddy and Matthew!

She didn't know how long she'd been waiting, but it was long enough.

She grabbed Fitz-James' harness and guided him out of the brush and back to the road. Jumping back up on the seat, she whipped the reins and urged the horse into a run, causing the wagon to careen wildly down the road towards their farm. The speed was soon too much for the old wagon on the rough winter road. With a crack and a jolt a wheel broke off and spun down the hillside. Fitz-James stopped short, halted by the suddenly cumbersome load. He turned a puzzled look at Fee, steam rising from his back and nostrils.

"Damn!" she cried, then grabbed the rifle and ran down the road, leaving the horse and crippled wagon behind.

Running as fast as she could, she soon stumbled, her full skirt tangled between her legs. Panic rose in her throat. Quickly she tucked her skirt into her waistband and continued running, harder and faster. Each breath burned in her throat by the time she saw the lightning-split tree just a mile farther.

Was that a tiny column of smoke curling above the mountainside? No, it couldn't be. Not Daddy and Matthew! Barely able to force her legs to run, she climbed the last hill. Her heart denied what her eyes saw, and her mind knew even before she crested the hill. Thick black smoke was billowing above the land.

Flames consumed the entire farm. The neat two-story clapboard house, the barn, the chicken coop, even the storage shed; all were burning. Seven men were riding around the farmyard, flaming torches in their hands. On the ground lay two lifeless bodies.

Raging, Fionna dropped to her knee and took aim from the top of the hill, her vision blurred by her tears.

Just as she started to squeeze the trigger she was thrown backward. A rough hand clamped over her mouth and dragged her back into the bushes. Seeing Nathanial's red hair out of the corner of her eye, her terror turned to anger. She tried to break his grip and club him with the stock of her rifle.

"Stop it!" he hissed in her ear as he deftly pinned her arms with one hand. "It's too late to save them, but I can save you—if you'll stop fighting me. There's too many, and they're too close. We'd get off two shots, and they'd be on us as we reloaded."

She stopped struggling.

"Promise to keep quiet and I'll let you go." His gray eyes were serious.

Fee nodded, and Nathanial took his hand away. Quickly she scrambled up the rocks cresting the hill. Nathanial followed, his coarse whisper frantically cautioning her to keep down.

She had no intention of giving away their hiding place. Even in her anguish, she'd understood the logic of his words. She just wanted to see, to confirm her worst fears.

Below them, through the smoke, she could see a twisted body. It was Daddy. He was wearing the bright green shirt she'd made for his Christmas present. Deathly still, he lay sprawled where he'd fallen.

Matthew was lying on the ground near the barn. Distance gentled the scene, making it look as if he'd gone to sleep after work.

"No," she whispered. "Not Daddy . . . not Matthew . . ." She smothered her rising sobs in the crook of her arm, hiding her eyes from the massacre, hoping it would be gone when she looked again. Her tears spilled onto the cold rock. She looked up once more to see the horror of flame and blood.

"Daddy . . . oh, Daddy . . ." she cried softly. "Matthew . . ."

The marauders were leaving. The last one turned his horse and threw a torch on the haystack. As it burst into flames, they began riding up the hill toward Fee's hiding place.

She dropped behind the rock, ducking her head beneath a bush and quickly wiping away her tears. Nathanial was to her left, covering the nose of his stallion with his hand. He was hidden from the view of the road by a thick growth of underbrush.

Fee held her breath and watched from behind the rocks as the men galloped by. They wore the leggings of mountain men from back east. One of them was wiping the bloody blade of his long knife on his leg. She shuddered. They were all strangers, but she'd remember their hate-twisted faces until the day she died.

As the sound of their horses faded into the distance, she cautiously raised her head and watched the diminishing figures. They took the right fork in the road. They were going into town. Her pain-numbed brain wondered dispassionately whom they would kill next. Who was the next one on the Underground Railroad? The nameless man who brought Nilly? She didn't even know how to warn him.

"They're gone," she said flatly.

"Where'd you leave the wagon?"

" 'Bout a hundred fifty yards from the fork in the road. They took the town fork. They won't see it."

Nathanial came forward, leading his horse. "I'm sorry."

Fee pulled her skirt out of her waistband, covering her muddied pantaloons. She turned to him, holding her chin high, ignoring the tears coursing down her cheeks. "Could I trouble you to help me bury my kin?"

Chapter II

It was useless to try to put out the fires. Fee didn't even consider it. The stench of burning feathers told her that all the chickens were lost. What livestock was in the barn was gone as well. She could see five cows and the bull milling in confusion near the woods. They'd stay there until she was ready.

With faltering steps she went first to her father and knelt beside him, stroking his cheek with a trembling hand. She'd not heard any shots fired, and now she knew why. He'd been struck from behind as he ran out of the house. He lay in the front yard, splayed across her herb garden, his head oddly twisted from his broken neck. A trickle of blood ran from his bald spot to his bluish colored face.

"Daddy," she whispered as tears washed her cheeks.

Then she got up and went to her brother. His brown eyes were still open, his young face showing more surprise than fear. His throat had been slit, and he lay in a puddle of his blood—soaking the earth, turning the brown soil dark as death.

Fee stooped and closed his eyes, feeling the soft bristle of his unshaven cheek, a promise of manhood never to be realized.

"Oh, Matthew, why?" she cried. "You never hurt a soul . . ." Her well of sorrow overflowed, and she collapsed in great gulping sobs.

Then, deep within, she felt her own stubborn will taking over, filling her with courage and determination. "No," she whispered to herself, "stop it. I can't give in now. Not now. Daddy and Matthew wouldn't want me to." She dried her eyes on the corner of her apron, stood up, and gently lifted Matthew's body to drag him over to where her father lay. "Don't worry," she murmured, "I'll take care of all of us. Don't worry."

Taking a shovel from a corner of the trampled garden, Nathanial began to dig two graves. He chose the precise spot where her father had loved to go in the evenings and smoke his pipe and survey his land, the knoll where her mother was buried.

She nodded her approval, then went to find two boards behind the burning barn. She began carving, stopping only to wipe her eyes when the tears blinded her vision, ignoring the blisters that quickly formed and eventually began bleeding beneath the constant pressure of the knife. After two hours she had written the epitaphs:

Donnell Liam Barry
Born County Cork, Ireland—March 29, 1801
Died Wood County, Virginia—December 27, 1860
A good man and father—murdered by the foulest hand

Matthew Donnell Barry
Born and died Wood County, Virginia
June 21, 1847—December 27, 1860
A good son and brother—murdered by evil butchers

That accomplished, she went to her herb garden and dug up three rosemary bushes. "Don't worry, Daddy," she whispered. "They won't get the best of me. I won't be weak. You always said your little girl must be strong. Now I will be—for your sake."

When her father and brother were buried, she planted two of the bushes by their heads. Then, stepping back, she quoted:

There's rosemary, that's for remembrance;
Pray love, remember . . .
I would give you some violets, but
They withered all when my father died.

And then her voice broke and she fell to the ground, weeping inconsolably as Nathanial stood guard over her fathomless grief.

It was too late to ride into town, so Nathanial made a shelter of pine boughs, hidden from view in the woods above the farm. Then he built a fire and gave Fee some jerky to cook with potatoes and carrots she'd pulled from the garden. When they remembered the broken wagon and Fitz-James left in the road, Nathanial left to make the necessary repairs and bring the horse and wagon back while there was still daylight.

While the stew bubbled over the fire, Fee returned to her garden and dug up a rosebush and eight herbs. She carefully fit them into a wooden box beside the fence and went back to the fire to wait for Nathanial.

When Nathanial returned and the animals were cared for, they ate their dinner by the light of the fire. A steady rain started falling, so Nathanial stoked the fire and they sat hunched under the pine-bough shelter, sipping catnip tea.

As the firelight flickered shadows across their faces, Nathanial did his best to keep Fee's mind from her grief. He told her of traveling part of the Overland Trail his last trip out, of the vast open prairies and the black herds of buffalo stretching as far as the eye could see. He spoke of the rushing rivers and of the towering mountains and the green valleys that lay beyond.

As the wind soughed through the boughs of the trees, he recalled his conversations with her father about slavery and the division threatening the United States. If people were going to kill one another so mindlessly, if they were going to value human life and freedom so lightly, he didn't want to stay. Nathanial could see a senseless war coming and wanted no part of it.

That was why he'd come back, to tell her family good-bye and to urge them to follow him. He was going to follow his dreams and head for the frontier, for the new state called Oregon.

Fee listened to his stories, contemplated his dreams and his decision, and fell asleep on his bedroll.

* * *

The next morning, after a quick breakfast of jerky and hardtack, Nathanial hitched Fitz-James to the wagon while Fee returned to the ashes of her home.

She walked past the barn, avoiding the spot where Matthew's innocent blood darkened the soil in a frost-silvered circle, hearing the lost echoes of their laughter, remembering their nightly milking races, mourning the dreams that would never be.

She walked through her garden where she'd spent long hours tending her herbs and flowers, remembering the afternoons Daddy heard her singing and joined her. Now, as she stepped over the crushed herbs where her father had fallen, she swallowed her tears and turned her eyes to the flagstone walk Matthew had so carefully laid when he was ten.

Taking a deep, quivering breath, she walked through the ashes that had once been the family parlor. The books were gone. Charred keys and bits of melted metal were all that was left of her piano. Only the fireplace was still intact, its mantelpiece blackened with smoke. The chimney of field rock towered over the landscape of death and destruction, pointing to the heavens like an accusing finger.

A cold, thin rain covered the bitter landscape and blended with the tears washing her cheeks. Fee paused, then walked to the right side of the fireplace. Her sorrowing breath caught in her throat as she pulled out the loose stone. Father had showed it to her and Matthew after Mother had died, saying it was the family secret, a secret that protected their most treasured possessions.

She reached into the niche and pulled out a metal box. Looking at the charred ruins of her family and home, she tearfully thought how tragic it was that they hadn't kept the family Bible her mother had brought from Ireland in some secret place. If only they'd saved the books, her sister's letters—Daddy and Matthew's lives . . .

Nathanial whistled from the road. She quickly wiped her tears on her apron and left the only home she'd ever known. She helped herd the cattle and tether them to the back of the wagon. Then they slowly made their way up the hill. Fee pulled Fitz-James to a halt, and turned to look back for one last time.

When she'd burned every detail into her mind, when she'd memorized every curve of the land, every rock and tree, when she'd silently bid farewell to the graves of her mother,

her father, and her brother, she turned and wordlessly drove down the road.

At the fork she reined Fitz-James towards town, the same way she might have been traveling at this very moment with her father and brother on their monthly trip to town—she might have been—but she stopped dwelling on what might have been and forced herself to think of what was to be.

Their pace was slow, and Fee asked Nathanial for more stories about the parts of the Oregon Trail he'd seen. She listened in silence as he told her of the emigrants' bravery and the hazards they faced.

By the time they reached town she was holding her head high, although her face was pale and drawn.

They went first to the magistrate's office and reported the murders. The magistrate told them there was little he could do. He remembered some men riding through town yesterday, but they were long gone now. There were reports of this kind of thing happening all over western Virginia. It seemed the rich land- and slaveowners in eastern Virginia wanted to convince the stubborn, independent small farmers in the western area that it wasn't in their best interest to oppose them on the slavery issue. With all the talk of secession and the trouble stirred up by the abolitionists, it was small wonder more of this hadn't happened. The magistrate offered his condolences, and promised to do what he could to find the men who murdered her father and brother and burned her home. His words held little comfort or promise of justice.

As she left the office, Fee spotted Mr. Campbell's wagon. She found him in Adams' General Store as he stood haggling over the price of a plow blade.

"Mr. Campbell," Fee said as she approached him, "you offered my father ten thousand dollars for the farm last year and he refused."

"Yes, Miss Barry, and a right good offer it was, too."

"Are you still interested?"

"Most likely. Tell your father to come see me and maybe we can strike up a bargain for the both of us."

"My father and brother are dead. They were murdered yesterday, Mr. Campbell. Our farmhouse and outbuildings were burned down."

Mr. Campbell and Mr. Adams both stood in shocked silence, then offered their sympathy.

Fee brushed aside their kind words, fearful of breaking into tears, and went on.

"I am the one you will have to deal with to buy the property, Mr. Campbell. I will accept an offer of seven thousand dollars. That's seventy dollars an acre for cultivated bottom land. A fair price."

"You say the house and barn are gone? Well, I don't think I should pay more than four thousand dollars for the whole lot then."

Fee hesitated, then raised her chin. "I'm sorry, Mr. Campbell, I'm not in a position to haggle. That's a firm price."

Nathanial got up from the cracker barrel and stepped forward, towering over Mr. Campbell. "I don't imagine a churchgoing man like yourself would be trying to take advantage of a helpless young woman in her grief, but I happen to know that you offered the Belmonts eighty dollars per acre for their land on the other side of you and it's not even bottom land. Maybe you just didn't understand the bargain she was offering you."

Mr. Campbell looked at Mr. Adams, then at Nathanial. With all these witnesses, it was best for his reputation that he make a quick and fair deal. He cleared his throat and said he'd go to the bank and get the money. If Fee would meet him back here at noon they could seal the deal, with Mr. Adams and Mr. Coughlin as witnesses.

The mail pouch was due in around noon as well. Fee told Mr. Adams that she'd return at that time to pick up her mail. She would have a package ready to go out on the dispatch when it left.

Before they left the store, Nathanial told her he was riding on up into Ohio, and he'd be glad to escort her to where she could get a stage to Pennsylvania to join her sister. Fee thanked Nathanial for his generous offer and said she'd be ready to leave with him in the morning.

With that, she accepted Mr. Adams' repeated condolences and one of his horehound drops, then set out on her errands.

At twelve noon she returned and signed the paper that turned over the ownership of her family's farm to Mr. Campbell. She then sat down and wrote her sister a letter, put a thousand dollars into a box, and sealed it along with her letter. In her grief she had to reach out to Siobhan, the only family she had left.

Nathanial had the wagon wheel repaired properly at the blacksmith shop. Fee tethered her cattle behind the boardinghouse, watered the plants she'd put in the wagon, and went to bed with her head full of plans. It didn't leave much

27

room for sorrowing, but her pillow was wet before she fell asleep.

A curtain of cold rain veiled their early morning departure. As they drove along the main street, Fee looked longingly at each of the familiar buildings of the little town, gray and still in the predawn light. A single tear slid down her cheek as she silently bid it good-bye.

Nathanial told Fee she was foolish to keep her cattle. Fee had finally compromised and sold two of the older cows, but kept three cows and the prize bull. These four were tethered to the back of the wagon, their ropes attached to the backboard.

She had made carefully considered purchases while she was still in town, knowing that she must prepare for anything, while still hiding her true plans. One of her purchases was already proving valuable—a rubber sheet. Nathanial nodded his approval when she pulled it out and wrapped it around herself for protection from the rain. The pungent rubber smell filled her nostrils as she drove behind Nathanial, who led the way on his horse.

Nathanial's plan was to follow the well-traveled roads and have Fee in Columbus, Ohio, within the week. They could find lodgings most nights along the way. He had no idea that Fee had other plans. It wasn't until they were a full day out of Columbus when Fee casually made her announcement.

"I'm not going to Philadelphia."

"You're what?" he exclaimed, reining in his horse.

"I'm not going to Philadelphia. I'm going to Oregon."

"You're what?" he repeated, his face reddening beneath his fur cap.

"I'm going to Oregon," she repeated blithely. "I considered California. The eternal spring you described certainly was tempting. But I come from farming stock, and the rich lands of Oregon hold the best promise for me."

"But . . . what about your sister?" he stammered. "You should be with your kin."

"We're cut from different cloth. I'm not sure she'll take to this." Fee said. "But no matter. I've written and told her what I'm doing and asked her to join me in Independence by March thirtieth. That was where you said we'd be taking off from, wasn't it?" she asked. Nathanial numbly nodded yes. "Whether or not she comes, I'm going," Fee concluded with a determined set to her chin. She flicked the reins and urged Fitz-James on a bit faster, as if to prove her point.

28

"You can't!" Nathanial shouted from behind as he kicked his horse and caught up with the wagon. He was valiantly trying to regain his composure.

"Of course I can," she said calmly. "I've already purchased some of the provisions I'll be needing. When we get to Independence, I'll buy the rest. You said they have outfitters all around there, and since we'll be getting there early, I should have plenty of time."

"But you can't," he repeated lamely. "They won't let single women on the trail."

"Don't be silly. Who's to stop me?"

"People," he hedged. "Women just can't go out on the trail defenseless and alone."

"I won't be alone. I'll sign up with one of the wagon trains you told me about. And you know full well that I'm not defenseless. And besides, I'll be with you."

"With me?" he sputtered. "I think you should know right now, I have no intention of being hooked up with any woman, much less a blackheaded slip of a girl with iron for a backbone and a tongue that could cut wood. I'm a loner. I've avoided getting hitched—"

"Hitched!" she cried. "Whatever gave you the idea that I was . . ." Indignation made her voice crack, but she was quick to regain it. "Why, I'd shoot you between the eyes before I'd let a redheaded tree of a man like you . . ."

She stopped and gathered a cloak of dignity around her, then added with forced calm, "I'm going west because I've nothing to lose and everything to gain. In Oregon a woman can claim land the same as a man. I'm going to have my own land and take care of myself. Now, if you don't wish to ride with me, you may go on ahead and I'll make my way by myself—but I *am* going."

That ended the argument for a few miles while Nathanial gathered his wits. Then once again he began berating Fee for her obstinacy. It was a heated discussion that continued all the way to Columbus.

Once settled in a boardinghouse there, Fee made sure her animals were well stabled, then set out to find some books on the Overland Trail. Before she settled in for the night, Nathanial once more tried to dissuade her. He even went so far as to say that if he weren't around she wouldn't consider the trip.

By this time Fee knew it was useless to argue with this

stubborn woodsman, so she simply set her mouth, raised her chin, and ignored him. She would prove that she didn't need him.

The next morning before daybreak, Nathanial slipped out of town on his horse and—by himself—headed down the road leading to Independence. Without him around, he reasoned, Fee would see the foolishness of her idea and go to Philadelphia where she belonged.

He hadn't been on the road for more than half an hour when he spotted a familiar caravan: a wagon, three cows, and a bull, stolidly plodding down the road ahead.

It was more than a saint could bear. "What the hell do you think you're doing?" he bellowed as he came up behind Fee.

"I'm going to Oregon."

"Well, it'll be without me!" he shouted. "I told you I won't be burdened with a woman!"

"You don't have to be," she replied calmly. "That's why I left without you. You didn't have to catch up with me, you know."

"Catch up with you? I was . . ." He stopped and glared at her. "I will not have you making me feel guilty."

"That's not my intention. Ride ahead without me."

"Don't you see? I can't leave you, newly orphaned, wandering helplessly down the road by yourself."

"As I told you before, I'm not helpless. I've got my rifle and a hunting knife and, more important, my wits."

They rode on in silence for about a hundred yards before Nathanial tried once more.

"When we get to Independence you can apply for a job as a schoolmarm. I'm sure the folks who are living there will need—"

"Mr. Coughlin!" Fee interrupted, her temper flaring. "I will thank you to desist in your efforts to dissuade me from going to Oregon. My mind is made up. Now, if you choose to ride with me, you will kindly refrain from talking about this subject—"

"Well, you certainly talk like an uppity schoolmarm—"

"And if you can't refrain," she continued pointedly, "please do me the kindness of riding on ahead and giving me some peace."

Nathanial studied her face as she looked ahead and flicked the reins over Fitz-James' back. Her profile conveyed a stubbornness that Nathanial knew was at least equal to her father's

30

and certainly a match for his own. But, she looked delicate and fragile with her dark curls slipping out beneath her bonnet. He knew from past experience that the flash in her blue eyes was real. She probably could take care of herself in most situations.

Still, she would be helpless in the woods. She was ignorant of the ways of the Indians. He couldn't abandon her just because she was pesky and stubborn; he'd never be able to live with himself if he did. On the other hand, how could he stand traveling with a woman all the way to Independence? And if they made it that far, could he abandon her to the uncertainty and dangers on the Oregon Trail? It was an impossible situation.

Then a brilliant idea hit him. Why hadn't he thought of it before? On the trail to Independence, they wouldn't be able to stay in inns all along the way. Although it was a well-traveled, relatively civilized trip, it would be rigorous enough to convince her to turn back to Pennsylvania without his saying a word.

He smiled to himself and glanced once more at her profile, her delicate nose determinedly pointing forward, her dark brows knitted in a stubborn frown. His smile faded. He settled back in his saddle, hoping he was right—that what would deter her would be the trail itself.

Nevertheless, Fee was not in the least deterred by the cold rains, the long nights sleeping on the ground, nor by the thick mud she had to wade through just to get her wagon unstuck. Instead, she threw herself into each new chore and setback as if it were what she expected. She smiled at his intermittent tirades, acting as if they simply were rigors of the trail that had to be endured. Worst of all, she maddeningly persevered in her set course.

In St. Louis there were more things happening and more people in one place than Fionna had ever imagined possible. It was just like the cities of London and Paris and New York that she'd read about all rolled into one. She hadn't been there half an hour before she'd heard not only French but at least three Indian languages spoken; she'd seen sweating black slaves loading wagons, and colorful, albeit foul-smelling, trappers arguing with well-dressed businessmen.

The river was alive with steamboats, keelboats, flatboats, pirogues, and Mackinaws. Carriages and wagons clattered over cobblestone streets, carrying women in beautiful dresses.

There was a bustle in the air that her books had never conveyed. And the noise—that was something else she didn't expect. For a girl used to the lowing of cattle and the cooing of doves, it was overwhelming.

Now there was even more excitement than usual. The latest news was that South Carolina had seceded from the Union and had marshaled its own forces around Fort Sumter. Fee's decision to head west had been the right one.

She accompanied Nathanial to a yellow and gray stone building with deer antlers lining the front façade. It stunk to high heavens from the furs the trappers brought in each year. Nathanial's catch for the winter had been a small one due to the increasing settlement in Minnesota, where he usually did his trapping—a fact that had contributed to his decision to move West. Since it was already afternoon, Fee promised to meet him the following morning in front of the stable where she'd left her wagon and livestock. That way she'd be able to do her errands without his interference.

"You mark my words," Fee told Nathanial the next morning as she harnessed Fitz-James, "the murder of my father and brother was only the early rumbling of a terrible storm that's coming. I can't stay," she said with a shake of her head, "I've lost too much to this insanity already. I owe this country nothing more—but it owes me the chance for a new start. And that's a chance I'll cash in when I get to Oregon and claim my very own land."

She'd thought about it all night and was proud of the way she'd been able to express herself so well. Surely Nathanial couldn't possibly disagree.

He listened to her impassioned speech with troubled eyes, considering her long and hard from behind his burnished copper beard. Then, to her complete surprise, he said nothing but turned to flick the reins of his horse. They were headed for Independence, Missouri—and the wagon trains west.

Chapter III

Independence was smaller than St. Louis, more rough-hewn, with the robust energy of a booming town peopled by those who are looking to live elsewhere. It was a point of departure, a place built on the dust of transition. The stores were hastily built to accommodate the demands of the emigrants. Nearby farmers made a point of raising crops to stock the wagon trains. Gamblers, trappers, and drunks wandered the streets alongside missionaries, clerks, uprooted farmers, and errant gold-seekers. It was a place of rough edges, lacking the refinement that came from having a stable population with its roots in the soil. Still, it was better than what they were going to see from now on.

Independence was in a flurry of news and excitement. Six more states had seceded from the Union. It was February 1861, and that tall, homely newcomer from Illinois, Abraham Lincoln, was to be inaugurated as president of the United States in March, almost a month before the first wagon train of the year was scheduled to leave Independence.

Fee immediately set about making purchases and arrangements for the trip. Resigned at last to Fee's decision, Nathanial signed them both up with a wagonmaster named Ezekial Edwards, a man who'd already led seven wagon trains across the plains.

Fee paid a bargain price for a large wagon left by a discouraged would-be pioneer. Because the forty-niners who went to California looking for gold proved that they were a better and faster means of getting across the trail, the wagonmaker sold Fee six stubborn and hardy mules. She found a stable for her livestock, a room in a boardinghouse for herself, and set to work, filling her wagon for the trip.

It wasn't until the end of February that she learned that Ezekial Edwards thought she was Nathanial's wife.

"What on earth gave him that idea?" Fee demanded.

"I suppose he could have gotten it when I signed us up. I told him that I would work for my passage by scouting and hunting but that you would expect to pay full passage for yourself and the wagon. He took only my name."

"Well, we'll set him straight on that," Fee said, pulling on her coat and heading down the street.

"I wouldn't if I were you," Nathanial warned, catching up with her.

"Why not? You told me you were as anxious to remain unmarried as I am. I certainly wouldn't want any misconception interfering with your precious freedom."

"My freedom won't be hindered by an idea in some wagonmaster's head. And if you go telling him we're not married, you won't be part of this wagon train nor likely any other."

"Why not?"

"They don't want single women alone on the trains. It causes fighting among the womenfolk. People don't want to take care of their own families and some stray female as well. And," he added before she could protest, "some consider it bad luck. It's felt they need all the luck they can muster just to get through Indian Territory. No need to tempt fate."

"Well, I'll take my chances. They'll surely find out sooner or later."

"Listen," he said in exasperation, "I'm willing to pretend we're married as long as you don't expect anything from me. At the end of the trail we go our separate ways. Agreed? You've gotten this far on your gumption. I might as well help out now," he added begrudgingly.

"And you could use a wagon on the trail as well. I mean, you surely didn't expect to stay outside in all kinds of weather, did you?"

"I had planned to. I have a tent," he said stiffly.

"Well, I can't imagine as to how you could do it, sleeping on muddy ground half the time—or how you could carry enough supplies on your horse to see you even halfway. Howsoever, if you're willing to swallow some of your pride, Mr. Coughlin, I'll swallow some of mine and borrow your name for the trip. But if you try anything—"

"That, Miss Barry," Nathanial interrupted indignantly, pulling himself up to his full six feet, four inches, "is the last danger you need worry about on the Oregon Trail."

An uneasy truce established, Fee concentrated her energies on preparing for the trip. However, when Nathanial sauntered up and inspected her work, she bristled with indignation. She'd carefully planned her arrangement for the wagon. Two mattresses, one hair and the other feather, would rest on rubber sheeting Fee would place over the slats of the wagon bed, which she was tarring to waterproof it for river crossings.

"Make sure you tar up the sides," he said. "Water's pretty rough in some places and—"

"If you're so all-fired worried about my work," she snapped, "maybe you'd just better grab a brush and do it yourself."

"If you do it wrong, my food will get wet, too," he explained.

"I didn't think I was," she said fiercely, stifling angry tears as she handed him the brush and tar bucket and stomped off.

She was sitting on the boardinghouse porch stitching her

34

mattress when he returned the bucket to her. "Why didn't you tell me you were almost done?"

"You wouldn't have believed me."

He stood with his hands in his pockets, squinting at something on the horizon. "How'd you know how to do it right?" he asked finally.

"There's lots of people nice enough to explain things. And books. I manage."

"Hmph," he grunted, then nodded and walked away.

She couldn't help a tiny smug feeling that rose like a bubble in her throat. She knew she was doing things right, and she knew that Nathanial Coughlin was surprised. She'd show him. She didn't intend to put up with his Mr. Know-it-all attitude clear to Oregon.

Since she'd lost everything she owned in the fire, she had to buy everything she needed. She explained her problem to Mrs. Burrell at the general store. "I'm starting over in Oregon because there was a terrible fire and my . . . our house burned to the ground. I lost everything."

"Why, honey, you're just lucky you weren't lost, too."

"I did lose my daddy and brother," she said quietly, a sudden lump in her throat and hot tears behind her eyes.

"Poor thing," Mrs. Burrell clucked as she leaned her ample form over the counter. "Do you have anything?"

Fee nodded. "I got my underclothing right away in Columbus. I have a shawl, this coat," she said, ticking items off on her fingers. "There's this linsey-woolsey dress I'm wearing and a calico one for warm weather, and . . . a skirt and blouse," she added. She'd bought a split skirt in St. Louis, which was all the rage on the East Coast, but quite daring for the prairie. Fee remembered how her skirt had hindered her that black day when she was running to save her family, and she knew a split skirt was more sensible for the hard traveling ahead.

Mrs. Burrell nodded. "You'll need some stockings, another gingham dress. I got a couple over there that should fit a little size like you. Then you need sunbonnets and aprons. Two each, white for good, calico for everyday. If you can afford it, you'd best get an extra pair of boots and shoes. Then choose a couple of bolts of cloth—best make one unbleached muslin you can dye later on. Some thread and needles, and you should be fixed up pretty good."

As she talked she bustled around behind the counter, piling up goods and pointing to others for Fee to try on and choose. Before the hour was out, Fee felt she was properly fitted out with dry goods for the trip.

Three days later, Mrs. Burrell greeted her like an old friend and threw herself with bustling efficiency into stocking Fee's medicine trunk.

"I've got some herbs from back home growing in a wooden trough I'll put in the back of the wagon," Fee said, "like lemon balm for calming nerves and hysterics. But nothing for more serious afflictions."

"Don't you worry none." Mrs. Burrell started another pile on the counter. "Quinine, bluemass, laudanum, opium . . . let's see, now. You'll need citric acid crystals to cure the scurvy, and some whiskey and hartshorn for snake bites." She looked at the pile for a moment, then beamed. "There," she pronounced.

Fee was glad she had the income from the sale of the farm. The price of the wagon alone was $350. As she began filling it with Mrs. Burrell's help, she'd spent well over $100 and still had more to do.

Pockets on the double canvas walls of the wagon held toilet articles, twine, an awl, and buckskin strings for mending harnesses and shoes. Hung from the hickory bows of the wagon were a shotgun and powder pouch as well as the rifle she'd brought from Virginia. Fionna also purchased a small pistol for herself, which she wore in a small holster she fashioned to fit around her leg under her skirt.

She bought spare parts and hung them under the wagon— axles, wheels, and boards. On the back she fitted two boards nailed together that could serve as a table and—if necessary—a bundling board for the bed.

Nathanial's curiosity wouldn't allow him to stay away from the wagon long. Since the tarring incident he was more careful about what he said, but she still sensed he was judging her in everything he observed.

"What's this?" he asked as she was installing a wooden mileage meter on her wagon wheel.

"They call it an odometer," Fee explained, feeling a little smug that he didn't know what it was. "As the wheel turns, it measures the miles traveled each day." She wondered if he would mock her for the unusual purchase.

He studied it for a moment, then nodded. "Heard the Mormons invented something like that a few years back. Not a bad idea, if you can afford it."

Fee clenched her teeth and put her tools away. Nathanial

couldn't even give his approval without some kind of reservation tacked onto the end of it. "Have you bought your food supplies yet?" she asked, coming back around the wagon.

"No, but I got a list made up. Figured I'd give it to you to take care of."

"Well, I have a list, too. You'd best come along with me and make sure we agree on what we're to eat," she said. " 'Sides, half the food cost is coming out of your pocket."

For each person it was recommended that they take 200 pounds of flour, 150 pounds of bacon, 10 pounds of coffee, 20 pounds of sugar, 10 pounds of salt, and various other items. Mrs. Burrell started with these basic goods, then stood back, waiting to see what they wanted to add. What she didn't expect was an exchange that sounded like two opposing bidders at an auction.

"I want five of those," Fee said, pointing to the large hams, all crusted with salt and wrapped for keeping, hanging from the rafters.

"I'll take ten pounds of chipped beef," Nathanial said.

"I need rice," Fee said with a stubborn thrust of her chin.

"Fifty pounds of potatoes for me," Nathanial said.

"Dried vegetables and fruit."

"Dried beans."

"Vinegar," Fee said defiantly.

"Mustard," Nathanial said just a little too loudly.

"And this and this and this," Fee said, going behind the counter and choosing some spices.

"Don't forget the tallow."

Mrs. Burrell was writing frantically, stealing apprehensive glances at Nathanial with each item he shouted at her.

"And some pipes and tobacco," Nathanial said finally, turning to go.

Fee raised an eyebrow. "Food?" she asked quietly.

Nathanial glared, slammed some coins on the counter, and stomped out, saying, "Bring the bill for the rest when you deliver it to the wagon."

"Now," Fee said to Mrs. Burrell, who was looking at her wide-eyed, "I'll need some basic kitchen utensils—pots, tin plates, knives, forks, cooking spoons, candles, matches, and the like."

Mrs. Burrell dropped her pad and pencil on the counter and leaned back against the shelves. "Not many women could keep up with the likes of your man," she said, pushing a loose strand of hair out of her eyes and shaking her head. "But it's right good to see a little gal of your ilk handling him just fine."

Fee tried to keep from laughing out loud but couldn't. "Yes, it is, isn't it?"

At the wagonmaker's suggestion, she purchased two rough locks, which were sled-shaped devices made from wood and metal and attached to the wagon by chains. When the grade got too steep for the brakes alone to hold the wagon, the rough locks could be dropped down in front of the rear wheels. The wheels then rolled onto them and they became skids, augmenting the braking action and helping to keep the wagon from running away.

Fee remained infinitely practical in all her purchases until the day she saw a flute in the window of Mr. Striley's store. Someone had brought it all the way from Germany but had sold it for supplies. Mr. Striley showed her the fine workmanship and blew a note as pure and clear as a mountain stream. When he added that it came with a chart showing how to finger the notes, she was helplessly caught in its spell. She ran her fingers over its satiny smooth black wood, admiring its delicate dark brown grain and the smooth, shiny sterling silver mouthpiece, molded to fit so comfortably to her lips. Mr. Striley showed her how to place it to her mouth and blow. It sounded like the call of a lonely whippoorwill. It was irresistible.

From then on, she spent every spare minute she could find sitting in the stable, learning to play the flute. She was terrified that Nathanial might find out about her extravagance and she would never live it down, but the solace she found in the music she made was worth the risk.

Fee also bought something for Nathanial as a kind of peace offering: a bound journal, complete with a real metal clasp.

"What's this?" he asked suspiciously as she handed it to him.

"It's for you," she said awkwardly, "so you can keep a journal of our trip."

He turned it over in his hand, examining it. "What for?"

"I thought you might like it. It might prove useful, having information about the trail, mileage, weather, and all."

He thought for a moment. "Maybe so, but you needn't go spending your money on me."

This was too much for Fee. "Nathanial Coughlin," she exclaimed, "you're an ungrateful wretch and it's a wonder any human being puts up with you."

"Well, it was your idea!" he called after her as she stormed away from him.

Besides spending her days preparing her equipment and organizing her supplies, Fee was learning to drive the wagon with her team of six mules. It was no easy task for anyone, much less a girl who'd grown up with only a good-natured horse to pull her wagon. They were six ornery, independent, stubborn creatures with six different ideas about how they should be treated and where they should be going and who was in charge. Still, as Fee assured them when they were alone on the roads, they couldn't be more stubborn than she. She was cold, wet, and muddy at the end of each day's drive, her shoulders and arms ached, and she was exhausted, but she felt that they were making progress. Within a month she'd won the cooperation of Smokey, the big gray lead mule. After that, she knew the others would eventually give in and be more cooperative. She'd have a working team by the time the wagon train was ready to go—and she would be able to handle them.

Nathanial was not so sure. His expression said as much as he watched her drive back into Independence one afternoon.

"What's the largest team you've driven before this?" he asked as he followed her into the stable.

"Why?" she said evasively as she busied herself unhitching the wagon.

"A single team is hard enough, but you got yourself six mules here. Fitz-James the only thing you've ever driven?"

"Yes," she admitted quietly, slapping the wheeler mule's flank to make it move forward.

"You'd better trade these in on some oxen. They're slow, but they're a lot easier to handle. They don't try to outthink you, and you can—"

"The mules are strong and much faster. In a tight place you can count on a mule to—"

"I know the advantages of mules," he interrupted. "I also know that they're harder to learn to drive. We don't need you holding up the train with a team that keeps acting up 'cause you don't know how to handle it."

"They won't. I promised you I wouldn't be a burden. My word is good."

"A team of six mules running off out in the middle of nowhere is dangerous—"

"I said, don't worry. Just today Smokey was as good as gold, and I know the others will fall in line real soon because she's a good lead mule. Just wait and see."

As she spoke, Powder, one of the middle mules, absently reached up with her hoof to scratch her stomach and in the process got her hoof caught in the belly strap. "Here, cut that out," Fee said, slapping her on the side and bending over to pull her foot out of the strap before she broke it. Just as she bent over, Smokey slyly stepped to the side and backward, forcing the other mules to bump into Fee, knocking her to the floor, much to Nathanial's ill-concealed amusement.

"Good as gold, eh?" he said, laughing as he helped her up.

"I know what I'm doing," she said, yanking her arm out of his grasp and brushing herself off.

"Well, you can still change your mind. Doesn't take much to learn how to handle oxen," he said as he started out the door.

Fee turned her back and finished taking off the harness until he was gone. When she was sure she was alone in the dusty light of the stable, she dropped the harness and kicked it.

"Damnation!" she swore. Then she leaned against the stall with tears streaming down her cheeks.

Smokey stepped forward and gently nuzzled her cheek. "Sure, now you want to make up," Fee said, smiling through her tears. "But where were you when I needed you?"

In the evenings Fee found time to visit Mrs. Pringle, the Danish lady who ran the boardinghouse. Two of Fee's heifers had been bred before the massacre in Virginia, but she got up every morning to milk Daisy, the one remaining milk cow. Mrs. Pringle took the milk as part of Fee's board and room payment. She also taught Fee how to make cheese as she'd made it in Denmark. Mrs. Pringle gave Fee some rennet to take along with her, and Fee left some of her cheese with Mrs. Pringle in exchange. Before long, Fee had added cottage cheese and hard cheese to her culinary skills. She also had two large wheels of unripened cheese packed in her wagon.

Fee counted the days until she would be leaving for her new life. Organizing her supplies and packing the wagon kept her busy. Each thing had to be as light as possible and tightly

40

packed. The only heavy items she allowed herself were her cast iron Dutch oven and ten books she felt she couldn't live without.

Fionna waited impatiently for the weekly mail deliveries. Granted, Siobhan was of a different temperament, but Fee was counting on her sister joining her. Sisters should stick together, she told herself. Fee was certain that they could establish a small school and make a fairly comfortable living while cultivating their farms. Besides, it would be so lonely there by herself.

Nathanial seemed to have forgotten all about Siobhan in the shock of Fee's announcement to go west, and she didn't remind him of the possibility. Each week she secretly went to the General Delivery box to see if there was any word from Siobhan. Fee also met each stage coach, searching the debarking passengers for a familiar figure. Perhaps her sister could help stop the undercurrent of sorrow. She felt the loss of her father and brother greatly; her dreams were haunted with their bloodied images, and an aching sadness at being alone in the world.

Fee had great plans for her cattle. With the two calves to be born in September and the three milk cows and bull, she could establish a well-bred herd. Now that she'd learned cheesemaking, she'd begun to think she should establish a first-rate dairy instead of a beef herd.

Her dreams were shattered one afternoon as she was oiling her harness.

"You'll have to sell the cattle, you know," Nathanial announced.

"I know no such thing. They'll help feed us on the trail, and when I get settled, they'll be my livelihood."

"Not likely. I've been checking around. There are great expanses of land out there with no feed or grazing. You expect them to make it over two thousand miles, eating air and with only occasional drinks of water? And even if you got fodder for them, there are places with very little water for humans. If there is water, it's often miles away from the trail, and it has to be hauled. You willing to haul buckets half the night to slake the thirst of three cows and a bull plus the six mules you got pulling the wagon? I'm not."

Fionna's eyes glistened with tears as she saw her dream crumbling. "There's got to be a way," she blurted out. "I'll haul water all night if necessary. There's got to be a way to feed them."

Nathanial shrugged. "It's better to get some cash now than to feed vultures later on."

Fee sat down next to Daisy, her favorite cow, and wept. It was hard enough knowing that she'd soon have to sell dear old Fitz-James and the farm wagon, her last connection with home.

"What's the matter, Mrs. Coughlin?" a kindly voice asked.

At first, Fee didn't understand that the person was talking to her. Then she quickly wiped her eyes and looked up. It was Mrs. Gould, a lady from one of the other wagons in their train. Full of concern, her hazel eyes peered out from under her calico sunbonnet. "Anything I can do to help?" she asked.

"Oh, I don't think so." Fee sniffed. Mr. Coughlin just told me that I can't take the cattle because there are places with no feed. If only I could figure out a way to feed them—they'd give us milk and butter along the way and there'd be a start for my herd in Oregon. But I just can't—"

"Isn't that your farm wagon there?"

"Yes, but I have to sell that, and the horse as well."

"But if you could find some hay and fill the wagon and take it along?"

"I can't drive two wagons at once. Mr. Coughlin's going to be working as a scout and hunter, so he can't drive a wagon."

"Ah," Mrs. Gould said thoughtfully. "Is the horse an easy one to control?"

"Yes. Why?"

"Well, I was just thinking that my boy Harley is only ten, but he's a fair hand at driving. If he would sign up to drive your load of hay, perhaps you could pay him with milk and butter along the trail? I got six children, and—"

Fee brightened. "That's perfect. I'm much obliged to you. I can even get two rubber sheets to cover the hay so's it won't spoil."

Fee went immediately to the blacksmith and placed a peculiar order, then spent the next two days driving to neighboring farms seeking surplus hay. On the second day she struck a bargain with one of the farmers, and by that evening she had the wagon loaded with hay and covered with the rubber sheeting. Attached to the side of the wagon was a cleverly contrived trolley to hold several buckets with lids for hauling water. Even the blacksmith told her she was one clever woman.

The next morning she was milking her cow when Nathanial came to tell her that they would be pulling out the next day.

42

He stopped in his tracks when he saw the load of hay, and his mouth gaped open. "You're not going to—"

Fee looked up from her milking and smiled brightly. "I most certainly am. I told you that I plan on using these cows for my herd in Oregon. I've struck up a deal with Mrs. Gould. Her son'll drive Fitz-James and the wagon in return for milk and butter for her children. We'll have a surplus, so it's a good bargain."

Nathanial simply looked at Fee in wonder, turned, and walked off in silence, shaking his head.

That afternoon she went to check one last time to see if Siobhan had come in on the stage. Three men got off, the door closed behind them, and her heart sank.

With a heavy heart, she went to check the General Delivery box. The store clerk handed her a thick white envelope. Happily, she paid him and hurried out to read it.

It was from Siobhan. She wasn't coming. She'd met a wonderful young man, and she was using her thousand dollars as a dowry. Her intended said there'd soon be a war between the states and he wanted to serve his country and make a fortune by building a textile factory to supply the Northern armies. Siobhan wished her sister all the best and thanked her for sending her the money. She enclosed two miniatures, one of her and one of her fiancé, and requested that Fee find a photographer and send her a likeness in return.

Fee looked at the pictures. Her beloved sister, familiar yet strange in coppery tones, looked out at her. Would she ever see her again? Slowly, Fee folded the letter, put it back in the envelope, and sighed. She was leaving everything and everyone. She was alone.

Fee fought back tears as she slowly walked back to her wagon. She would take her last bath at Mrs. Pringle's boardinghouse and then spend the night in the wagon to be ready to leave at first light with the rest of the train.

The next morning they waited patiently in line to be ferried across the Missouri River, running wide and brown with winter silt. They were the second wagon train to leave this season, but the train that left the previous month had to turn around and come back. There had been a group of five young men who'd left two weeks earlier, but they'd been headed for the mines. Other trains were staying behind another week, waiting to see if this one made it.

Fee paid the ferry man for both wagons, then held her breath during the sloshing, rocking ride across the swollen river. She drove her wagon up the steep embankment and stopped, looking at the vast, flat expanse of land stretching before them. It was so far, farther than the eye could see or the mind imagine. Her courage faltered and she turned to look back, back at the land of her beginnings, back towards the last of her family.

Rising above the land in the distance she could see a black cloud of smoke. Perhaps some farmer was simply burning his field in preparation for spring planting, but to Fee's eyes, it was a Virginia farmhouse being destroyed by hate. A foreshadowing of the waste that would be laid across the land by the evil of war.

She turned, dried her eyes on the corner of her apron, and looked at the land stretched before her. She'd not look back again.

Chapter IV

Damned if he knew how or why, but Nathanial was beginning to look at Fee in a new light. Maybe it began when he saw her standing ramrod straight in the charred skeleton of her home, or on the trail to St. Louis when she stuck out her chin and defied the wilderness, fate, and even his wrath. Whenever it was, he was having trouble making his opinion of women accommodate his newly evolving view of Fee.

It wasn't that he hated women. They were fine—in their place—but up until now that place was limited to his bed and an occasional kitchen.

It was an opinion he'd formed early in life. His gentle, hard-working father tried to improve their lives, but Nathanial's whining, manipulative mother always thwarted him, claiming illness or frailty. When they could have moved to settle the new land in Ohio, she was too weak. When they could have sold the farm and moved to a settlement along the Mississippi, she was too sick. His father had abandoned his dreams because of what Nathanial saw as selfishness in his mother and what his father called weak English blood, which wasn't strong enough to keep up with his lusty Irish ways.

44

When he was fourteen, Nathanial was so filled with disgust at what he deemed his mother's selfishness and his father's weakness that he left home, never to return. Despite frostbite and hunger that first cold winter, Nathanial refused to give in. Shivering alone in a makeshift shack, he vowed he'd never be like his father, manipulated by a woman whose frailty was her strength.

This became the main tenet of his life. He wandered the wilderness, free and answering only to himself. By sixteen he'd discovered females of all races willing to gratify his growing physical needs without the bonds of marriage. With that discovery his life became complete—and he remained free.

Now, much to his chagrin, thoughts of Fionna Barry were circling around his mind, challenging his long-held beliefs, and entwining her in his life. And, confound it all, she was doing it while professing it was the last thing she wanted.

There was that incident at the Missouri River today, the place where he'd held out one last hope that she would give up and go back where she belonged. Preparation for a ferry crossing meant heavy labor. First the mule team had to be unhitched and tethered, then the wheels of the wagon had to be taken off and about a thousand pounds of goods unloaded from the wagon bed. Next the wagon had to be carried onto the flatboat and, finally, the goods piled back on the wagon and covered with heavy canvas or rubber sheets to protect the provisions from water damage. Certainly not the kind of thing a woman could do.

Deliberately, Nathanial left Fee on her own while he went to help the other wagons who were ahead of her in line. At the end of the day, figuring she'd be in tears because she couldn't possibly be ready when her wagon's turn came up, he returned, prepared to chide her and point out the foolishness of her decision to press on. Instead, he had to swallow his pride.

When Nathanial swam his horse ashore, having helped set up the campground on the other side, he saw that both of Fee's wagons had been loaded on the flatboats.

As they did with all wagons, the men had helped carry her wagons to the ferry. But all the rest was her own doing.

"You got some little woman there, Coughlin," Findley Hanna crowed as Nathanial got off his horse. "She got those wheels off in no time. Done it right, too."

"Strong, too," Jacob Teall put in. "Moved the goods off before we knew it. Didn't hesitate to put her back right in there when we carried the wagons to the ferry, either. You've got no worries there."

Nathanial stared at them, confused not only by Fee's obvious abilities but also by the fact that he was being complimented for them.

Grandpa Gibson spat over his shoulder and winked slyly at Nathanial before turning to help carry the next wagon to the shore. "Right pretty, too. She does you proud."

Nathanial turned back to watch in disbelief as Fee tied the ropes to the horns of her cattle, then sat tailor-fashion on the bottom of the raft, ready to guide her animals across the river. The animal feed was resting in a removable rack he hadn't noticed before, which had made the transfer simple. It indicated forethought he'd believed a woman incapable of.

The boat cast off, and she looked up. Seeing him, she waved cheerily, seemingly mindless of the danger of a river crossing. A frayed rope or a moment's carelessness on the ferryman's part could thrust her and her precious animals out into the torrent, leaving them at the mercy of the strong currents fed by melting snows.

He watched the raft bob and the murky waves slosh over the side. With what he considered an unnecessarily harsh bump, it finally made contact with the opposite shore about fifty yards downstream. The men worked the pulley, and the ropes slowly drew the raft safely back upstream from its downriver landing. Nathanial breathed a sigh of relief and realized that he'd actually been holding his breath, concerned for her safety.

Only a fool wouldn't feel some kind of admiration watching her going about setting up camp that night, managing to start a succulent stew bubbling before milking the cow. As Nathanial ate his dinner she busied herself delivering the milk to Mrs. Gould, visiting with other women in the train, setting beans to soak, and staking out the cattle, taking only a moment to grab a bite to eat before she washed the dishes and crawled into the wagon to sleep. She didn't even say good night.

Nathanial was hard put to explain why he felt a bit disappointed that she should be acting exactly as they'd agreed she should act. As did many of the men, he bedded down with the cattle lest they stray during the night. The hard, cold ground and the gentle warmth of the cow at his back did little to dispel his ill humor before morning. Somehow the whole situation galled him. These weren't even his cattle.

*   *   *

It rained the next morning, making the progress of the twenty-four-wagon train painfully slow as it slogged through the mud. Nathanial's mood was hardly improved by constantly having to go help one wagon or another get unstuck from the ruts in the road. Since they were still within the state of Kansas, which had scattered cabins and settlements, they were often able to find a fence post or extra mule to help pull the heavier wagons from the mire. However, it also meant that by the time they stopped for their noontime meal, people were wet, muddy, cold, and out of sorts—especially Nathanial.

Then to top it off, along came Fee with a cheerful smile as she handed him a bowl of warm beans and a hot cup of coffee.

"How come you're so damned chipper?" he asked with a growl as he took the bowl.

"Well, I figure I'm pretty lucky. Where most of the women have to walk because their wagons are so heavy and their husbands are driving, I've been able to drive my own wagon and keep dry. There's no one to tell me what to do. Where the other women have to put up with whatever their husbands decide is best, including this trip west, I only have to put up with what I decide. Besides, I've come to realize I can handle most anything that comes up, and that's a good feeling."

She paused, looking carefully at Nathanial. "I know that's not the way a woman's properly supposed to feel, but I don't think I'm going to be too concerned with that 'proper woman' stuff for a long time." She grinned mischievously. "And I intend to enjoy every minute of it." With that she pointed to her skirt. To his surprise he saw it was cut into two legs, like extra wide-cut pants. She was wearing some kind of bloomers— and it made sense.

Nathanial threw his head back and laughed the kind of laugh that bursts unbidden from the very center of the soul. "So that's what old sour-face Clyman was talking about this morning."

"Whatever are you talking about?"

"He came riding up to me stiff as a poker and said that he thought I should look to my woman. When I asked him what he was talking about, he said that you were setting an immodest example for the other womenfolk and God would blame me as much as He would blame you."

"Well, you can tell him for me that I think his attitude is an

47

unbecoming example to other human beings—and God will surely blame him for that!"

Her blatant defiance brought another howl of laughter from Nathanial's throat. "You know, Fionna Barry," he said finally, wiping the tears from the corners of his eyes, "I think you're right—you're going to be just fine."

Reaching for a pan biscuit, he chuckled and turned his attention to his beans, still grinning and shaking his head.

As Fee began gathering dishes and cleaning up, the sun came out, filling the air with a gentle warmth. He put his tin bowl down and stretched. "Looks like the sun might shine on us after all."

Fee smiled sweetly. "I think it was that laugh of yours. It could bring out the sun at midnight."

"It doesn't hurt to enjoy life," he said, looking at the slim girl who smiled as she cleaned up his dirty dishes.

He suddenly felt the need to be moving. "Well, stock needs watering. I'll go hitch the mules while you get things put together." He added awkwardly, "You make mighty good beans."

"Thank you." Then with a giggle, she added, "I'll remind you of your words when beans are all we have left to eat."

He laughed again.

With the sun, they were able to make better mileage by nightfall. They were twenty-five miles from Independence when they stopped that evening at Lone Elm campground, so named because of the elm tree that had once stood there, until the early migrants had used it—three-foot trunk and all—for their campfires.

That night for the first time, Ezekial had them camp in what would become their standard formation. Standing at the head of the train, he motioned the first wagon to circle around to the left and the second to circle around to the right. Alternating wagons went right and left until the circle was completed. The wagons were then locked into formation, rear hub chained to the front hub of the next wagon. The children bounded into the resultant corral formed by the wagons, the stock was hobbled, latrines dug, and cooking fires started.

By the time the sky was tinted a rosy glow, fires were burning, and cookpots bubbling. Sounds of quiet conversation and playing children drifted through the air. Fee and some of the women were down by the stream getting water and gossiping.

So far, the train was getting along admirably well. Ezekial had chosen carefully. Many of the train were in family groups. One family, the Gibsons, filled nine wagons with children, grandparents, uncles, and aunts. Five more wagons were their former neighbors. Other wagon groups were similarly close.

As on the night before, people living within five miles of the campground came out to visit with the migrants. It was the one way they could get news. One family didn't even know that Kansas was a state, admitted to the Union four months previously. But even the most isolated knew that there was big trouble brewing between the South and the North. One migrant passed a copy of Lincoln's inaugural address around the campfires. The evening's discussion was filled with speculation as to whether there was going to be a full-fledged civil war.

Grandpa Gibson had a fiddle and someone else had a Jew's harp. Soon war and politics were forgotten and the fire-lit circle filled with music. The travelers were well fed and there was a star-studded sky overhead, promising a clear day of traveling tomorrow. It was no wonder the camp quickly took on a party air.

Most of the locals joined in, but there was one family that stayed pretty much out of the light. Despite their caution, Nathanial could see that they were black. They were talking to Fee. Were they slaves or freemen, he wondered. Either way, their presence would stir up painful memories. He made a mental note to bring Fee into the circle of music when they left. It wouldn't do to have her dwelling on what she'd left behind.

Later he looked around to see where Fee had gone, but she wasn't anywhere to be seen. Feeling both irritation and concern, he got up to look for her. As he rounded the wagon, he found not only Fee but also Ezekial Edwards. They were head to head in a serious discussion, serious enough for them not even to notice when he came up.

"You're unreasonable." It was the first time since she'd buried her family that Nathanial had heard even a tremor in her voice. "These people are willing to pay their own way."

"You're not using your head, Mrs. Coughlin," Ezekial explained patiently. "We're twenty-five miles from the Missouri border. There's no way of knowing they're not runaway slaves."

"In my mind there's no such thing as slaves," Fee said stubbornly. "So I don't see what that matters. We're here in a free state and we're going to a free state. Why can't these people have a chance? We can help."

"No, we can't. The free state we're going to don't much care to have people of another color in it. The Free Negro Admission Article that was proposed for the Oregon Constitution failed. If you're going to get along with your new neighbors, you're going to have to go along with their standards."

"Perhaps they just need someone to explain right from wrong. Surely, Mr. Edwards," she said fervently, "you don't think these people should be put back under the whip."

Nathanial stepped forward to intervene but stopped when Ezekial bowed his head and put his hand on Fee's shoulder. "No, little lady," he said with a heavy sigh, "I don't believe in slavery any more'n you. But I know the evil fightin' it can cause. You see, last December back in Virginia my brother and his family were murdered for doin' just what you want to do here."

Fee gasped. "Edwards. Not in Wood County?"

"Why, yes. Why do you ask? Did you know them?"

"I slept there the night before they were killed . . ." Fee paused, trying to control her voice. "My father and brother were killed by the same people . . . our farm completely burned . . . that's why . . ." She could go no further.

Nathanial stepped forward and cradled her in his arms as she sobbed uncontrollably. "I'm mighty sorry to hear it was your brother and his family," he said to Ezekial. "When I heard the marauders were on their way, I tried to warn them. I was too late," he murmured softly. "All I could do was just keep on riding to warn Fee's family. I was too late for them, too. I could only stop her from riding in on the massacre."

"Ah," Ezekial murmured. "I didn't know, or I wouldn't have spoken so plain."

"I'm sorry I was so stubborn," Fee said through her sobs. "Dear little Della was your—"

"My beloved niece," he finished for her.

"Ezekial is right, Fee," Nathanial explained softly. "You simply can't try to save these people, too. You know what kind of fanatics are out there."

"But—but they say they're freemen."

"If you were escaping, what would you say?"

She didn't answer.

"You see, Mrs. Coughlin, we can't risk the same thing happening to this whole train of people as what happened to our families back home. It isn't the kind of decision we can make."

"You're right," she said. "But what about these poor people?" She pointed to the family huddled in the shadows, anxiously waiting to hear their fate. "We can't turn them over to the likes of them that killed our kin."

"What with the war talk in the States and all, they would be better off to keep going north to Canada," Ezekial said.

"It's a less traveled road and shorter," Nathanial added. "I've traveled most of it myself. I'll draw maps and write letters for them. Truly, Fee, I think this is better."

Fee nodded. "I'll give them some money."

"And so will I, Mrs. Coughlin," Ezekial added. "In memory of my brother and his family."

So it was that Nathanial once more became involved in the abolition movement. His earlier travels north had brought him into contact with many active abolitionists. Contact with these people had made him approach Donnell Barry and the other people in western Virginia to set up an alternate route on the Underground Railroad. His horror at what had happened because of his actions made him vow never again to do such a thing—yet here he was again, trying to help another human being live free.

Nathanial stood and watched until they melted into the darkness surrounding the wagon train. "Whatever will happen to that poor family?" he murmured to himself. "Whatever will happen to us all?"

But that wasn't Nathanial's last thought before falling asleep. It wasn't the tormenting dilemma of slavery or the liquid brown eyes of the frightened child peeking from behind his mother's calico skirt. It wasn't the shock of finding yet another person whose life was sorrowed by their efforts to aid escaping slaves. It wasn't even the growing horror of the impending war between the states. It was the soft feel of Fee in his arms as she cried, warming his chest with her tears.

Chapter V

The road ahead was relatively dry, and Ezekial set an ambitious goal for the day. They would noon by the creek off Coon Point at Blue Mound—and not before. Phineas Gibson was put in the lead, followed by Fee, because both had mule teams and would set a steady pace. Ezekial gave the call of "Wagons ho!," the white-topped circle unwound, and they were once more on their way.

Gesturing for Nathanial to follow, Ezekial galloped ahead, leaving the plodding train in his dust.

Ezekial was a taciturn man, but Nathanial knew what he had in mind. Ezekial wanted to get an idea of Nathanial's pathfinding abilities before he sent him out on his own when the trail got rougher and decisions had to be made based only on his information.

It was a cool, crisp spring morning, and Nathanial was in high spirits. When a covey of prairie hens flew up in front of him he bagged one without even stopping to aim. After picking it up, he grinned at Ezekial. "Looks like I should invite you to dinner tonight."

Ezekial's slow smile wreathed his face. "I'd be mighty grateful," he said. "Goes without saying that us single men have had occasion to hanker after the smells coming from your campfire."

As he tied the hen to the back of his saddle, Nathanial suddenly realized what a lonely, uncomfortable trip it would have been without Fee. He promised himself that he'd remember to invite Ezekial to dinner whenever there was fresh game. After last night, he had a feeling that Fee had a soft spot in her heart for their wagonmaster and wouldn't object. Maybe Ezekial'd be able to teach Fee something—if she'd listen.

From the occasional grunt of approval he knew that he was passing Ezekial's inspection. As Nathanial looked across the plains of greening grass, occasionally interspersed with a struggling farm, he noted they would soon leave the United States behind and enter Nebraska Territory.

Within a couple of miles of Blue Mound, they would have

to cross the Wakarusa River. There was nowhere to ford it where the banks weren't uncomfortably steep. They found the marked crossing, complete with an approach made of logs and a large dead tree on each bank, their trunks girdled by the many ropes used to let wagons down to the river.

While Ezekial checked the anchor tree and the log approach to see how they had fared the winter, Nathanial approached the swollen banks of the river.

His big bay Morgan horse, Seneca, stood fifteen hands high. He was strong, intuitive, and Nathanial's pride. Nathanial gave the horse his rein and took careful note of where he chose to go. Upon approaching the middle of the stream where the water swirled under his belly, Seneca took a sharp turn upstream, found firm footing, and crossed without incident.

Nathanial checked the anchor tree on the opposite side, found it still strong, and once more entered the water. Seneca again made the same veer, now downstream, as he approached the middle. Nathanial reported this to Ezekial; they would instruct the wagons to do likewise. They'd camp on the other side, because the crossing would take the better part of the afternoon.

They turned back to meet the train at midmorning. On the way back, Nathanial bagged two more prairie hens and Ezekial could barely keep his lips from smacking in anticipation.

Blue Mound was a mile-long bump in the middle of the plain that looked for all the world like a mud turtle sleeping in the middle of the prairie. Although it wasn't very high compared to what they would be seeing out West, it was high enough to afford a tempting view of the expanse of flowering plains.

The wagons had halted at the base of Blue Mound, and everyone seemed to have taken a holiday from their chores. Cattle, oxen, horses, and mules grazed contentedly on the grass, and emigrants were skylarking up the sides of Blue Mound or searching for wild strawberries in the meadow. None of this surprised Nathanial. What surprised him was Ezekial's reaction.

Suddenly spurring his horse, Ezekial charged into camp, scattering dogs and children in his approach. Then, taking a triangle-shaped metal pipe hung from a string, he began banging out a god-awful alarm.

The emigrants wasted no time running into the camp. Men

dashed to get their weapons, and mothers quickly gathered their children. Fee was one of the last to arrive, having been on top of Blue Mound when the alarm began. She leaned against the side of her wagon, listening to Ezekial's roar as she gasped for breath.

"What in tarnation are you thinking of?" he bellowed. The only response was the sound of people catching their breath and the whimper of a frightened child.

"Do you know what the Blue Mountains are?" he asked.

"They those mountains in Oregon?" Phineas Gibson asked.

"They're more mountain than you can imagine," Ezekial shouted angrily. "They're higher and pointier and meaner than what you greenhorns call mountains. And they have the bones of many a pioneer bleaching on their sides. If'n we don't get there before the first snowfall—and the snow comes early when you're that high—we might as well learn the funeral service by memory, 'cause that's all the words we'll be needing. And there won't be any neat little graveyard like the one back yonder. You'll have to leave your loved ones' bones scattered on some strange mountaintop, to be gnawed clean by wolves and panthers after their clothes and belongings have been robbed by Indians."

He paused, letting his words soak in. "Now," he said more quietly but with just as much anger, "how many more miles afore we get to the Blue Mountains?"

It was a rhetorical question, and the intervening pause was dramatic. Nathanial had to hand it to him, Ezekial was instinctively masterful when it came to building up the drama of a moment to emphasize his point. "It's one thousand seven hundred and forty-four miles from here!" he shouted, drawing out each numeral, making it sound as if it measured the space from here to eternity.

"Now, if you figure snow can fly on the Blue Mountains in mid-August, how many days you figure till we're frozen out?"

There was a long pause while some of the adults began counting on their fingers. Finally Grandpa Gibson said, "I calculate about a hundred and twenty-three days, Ezekial."

"Now some of you smart ones figure out how many miles we got to go each day between now and then," Ezekial said.

Another long pause ensued. " 'Bout fourteen," little Harley Gould chirped, having outfigured all the adults.

"That's right," Ezekial said. "An' there's a damned sight many of 'em that's much rougher than what we've seen so far. Days that'll get us no more'n about five miles. An'

54

that's not counting the times we stop to rest the weak animals or the times we've got to stop because of repairs or sickness or trying to find food for our stock or our folks.

"That's why you don't go off skylarking every time we stop. You take care of your chores, and then you hitch up and get ready to go again. Now let's get ourselves fed and get moving. I want those animals hitched and pulling wagons within the hour."

There was a brief silence, then a flurry of motion as everyone scurried to meet Ezekial's deadline. From the sober looks on their faces, Nathanial judged that from now on, the mere mention of the Blue Mountains would serve to add a few extra miles to each day's journey.

Although Ezekial told them this was not a major river crossing, the confusion of this first attempt was enough to discourage anyone. Animals were unnecessarily unhitched from wagons, children got lost, and no one seemed to listen to Ezekial's instructions.

Nathanial went across the river first, pulling a rope to fasten around the far anchor tree. Ezekial stationed himself at the tree on the beginning side of the river and directed the wagons' approach down the sharp decline.

Phineas was first. The rope was fastened to the back of his wagon, wrapped around the anchor tree, and the wagon was slowly let down the bank. Phineas cracked his whip and urged his mule team into the water. They balked. For all that team cared, the whole train could stay right there until the Wakarusa River froze solid. No matter what the command, holler, or threat, they would not budge past the water lapping at the lead mule's feet.

Judging that they'd have to do without dinner if this kept up, Nathanial rode Seneca back across and took the lead mule's harness in his hand. He turned his stalwart horse around, and the mules followed as meek as a herd of old milk cows.

They started to balk once more in midstream when Seneca turned to lead them upstream to avoid the hole in the middle, but a judicious crack of the whip soon had them up the opposite bank.

Nathanial felt that he should at least accompany Fee's team in the same manner. It had to be better than sitting on the shoreline holding his breath, as he had at the Missouri crossing.

Fee had good control of her team, and they didn't balk.

Nathanial rode up to join her when she got out to check how the wagon had withstood the crossing.

"Looks like all that time in Independence you calked and tarred this wagon was well spent."

She smiled proudly. "It's just what they told me . . ." She stopped, looking over his shoulder in horror. "Nathanial, look!" She pointed to Eustace Gibson's wagon, which now was about six feet out in the river.

Little Lucy Gibson had fallen from the back of the wagon and was being swept downstream. Her Aunt Patience and two older cousins were running along the bank, screaming and calling out to her. The frightened five-year old couldn't get footing even that close to shore. If someone didn't catch her soon, she would drown.

As Nathanial jumped on Seneca and dashed to the river's edge, Grandpa Gibson jumped on the back of a loose mule and plunged into the river after his little granddaughter.

The mule suddenly stumbled in a hidden hole. Grandpa Gibson was thrown off and was in as much danger of drowning as Lucy. The frightened mule lunged for the far shore, leaving the old man thrashing helplessly in the swift current.

Nathanial nudged Seneca into the river and headed straight for the child. Her apron caught on an overhanging branch, and she was held more under water than out. She was nearly drowned by the time he pulled her, spluttering, out of the water and threw her over his saddle.

He turned just in time to see Grandpa Gibson heading downstream, helplessly caught in the current. With a lunge Seneca headed back into midstream. Nathanial reached down and caught the old man by the suspenders as he was about to go by.

"There's no room for you up here!" Nathaniel shouted. "Hang on to the tail while I pull you in!"

Luckily, the old man still had strength enough to hang on until they reached the shore, where Nathanial handed Lucy over to her tearful mother and helped Grandpa Gibson sit down on a rock to catch his breath.

"I think it's time for a camp meeting to get a few rules laid down," Ezekial said. "You're not going to be around every time these people don't use their heads."

Nathanial nodded, accepting the implied compliment. He took a rope from Eustace, who was considerably paler than usual, and motioned for Jacob Teall to follow him to the water's edge.

Jacob had arranged with three other bachelors—Wesley Fleming, Victor Ainsley, and Cameron Gartner—to buy a wagon to carry their supplies. A fifth man, Granville Sears, earned his keep by driving the wagon, leaving the four others free to ride their horses and to act as guards and general helpers for the rest of the train. They hadn't been on the road two days before everyone saw the wisdom of having them along. Whenever a wagon was mired or in difficulty, one of the four was there to lend a hand. In Nathanial's opinion, Jacob was the best of the lot. There was something different and distant about him, but he sensed this darkly handsome man was one you could rely on.

"I'll tire out my horse crossing with every wagon. I'll take you across," he told Jacob as he handed him the rope, "show you where the hole is, and we'll take turns at it."

Jacob agreed, and Nathanial led the way. Once they reached the other side, Jacob suggested that Nathanial check on the camp setup and give his mount a rest after the scare. Nathanial was anxious to see that Fee was getting settled. After all, there were those prairie hens for dinner.

Fee looked up from plucking the hens as he approached. "Thank God you were able to rescue that poor child," she said. "Poor Grandpa Gibson, having to lose his dignity like that."

"Better to lose your dignity than your life." Nathanial climbed down from the saddle and dropped the reins so Seneca could graze on the grass. "Thought I'd let you know that I'd invited a couple of extra people to dinner tonight."

"I figured as much when I saw how many hens we had." He noted that she was carefully saving the feathers in an old flour sack, a beginning for a feather bed. "Who's coming?" she asked.

"Ezekial's been hankering for some good cooking, and since Jacob's helping with the crossing I thought this would be a nice way to thank him."

"I'll have enough for three hungry men, then."

As it turned out, that was an understatement. Lucy's grateful mother, Charity Gibson, had sent over a bucket of wild strawberries picked in the meadow by Blue Mound. Grandpa Gibson had sent his thanks in the form of butter and buttermilk. While the prairie hens roasted over the fire, Fee caught the drippings in a pan in which she baked some potatoes she'd brought from Independence. With the buttermilk she made light biscuits and with the butter and berries she made a cobbler topped with thick cream.

It was a feast to do a man proud. The looks on the faces of Ezekial and Jacob as they ate spoke volumes. Nathanial was hard put to pretend that he wasn't surprised.

It wasn't until they'd eaten the last crumb of the cobbler and drunk their last cup of steaming coffee that Nathanial noticed that Fee had eaten her meal with the men, instead of serving them first and eating the leftovers, as was the custom of the other women. Somehow, her magnetic presence and the tin cup filled with buttercups gave the impression that they were not only having a feast but also dining in the home of a great lady, instead of sitting by the mud-splattered wagon of a slip of a girl. She really was something else—just what he didn't know.

Ezekial called the company meeting to order just as he'd done at Blue Mound. The fact that they all assembled rapidly seemed a good indicator that discipline had been established. Nathanial and Fee sat together on a box they carried to the main campfire.

"Are we goin' to elect our captain, Ezekial?" one of the men called out.

"You can elect all the captains you want," Ezekial said with a growl, "just as long as you remember that I'm the general and I gets to choose all the majors."

There was a quiet murmur around the circle. This went against traditional wagon train procedure.

"See, I figured your agreement to accept me as your leader to get you across the plains to Oregon was a solemn oath of cooperation on your part."

He waited for his words to sink in. "I started goin' over this trail in '49. Instead of gold, I just got itchy feet. I spent the winter of '50 in the mountains with trappers. I was assistant to the captain of one-hundred- and two-hundred-wagon trains coming out in '51 and '52. Those were the bad cholera years, and I saw a lot of suffering. In '53 I led my first train by myself, and in spite of the fact that people in trains in front of us and behind us were dying like flies, we only lost five people, and those were the ones who didn't pay attention to what I told them to do. Every year since then I've brought a train out safe to Oregon. There's a spot of land in the Willamette Valley that I've staked out for myself, and I'm going to settle down after this. This'll be my last train, and I want it to be the best.

"Now, considering that record, I'm going to lay down a few

rules. Those who don't want to abide by them are welcome to leave now. Those staying are honor-bound to follow them."

"We don't get no say in it at all?" asked one of the Gibsons' neighbors.

"Nope. Those that die on the trail are usually the ones making bad decisions because of bickering or stupidity. We won't have none of that. Now, unless you've got the record of traipsin' across this vast wasteland that I have, you'll accept my word and we'll go on from here."

"Let's hear what you've got to say," Phineas Gibson said.

Ezekial nodded, his grizzled beard partially obscuring the wry twist to his mouth. "Fair 'nuff. First off, what I say is law. I've picked out a couple of good men to serve in my place if something happens. I had dinner with them tonight, and they've agreed. Nathanial Coughlin and Jacob Teall are crack shots, good woodsmen, and have shown uncommon sense. They'll serve as scouts and hunters with me. Any other men who can find time away from their wagons without slowing up any and who want to hunt for some fresh meat are to check with me. Most likely, they'll accompany one of my men here. If not, and if'n they don't go where I say and come back when I say—barring some accident—they'll be subject to discipline, which can go from bein' confined to the camp for a time to as far as being kicked out of the train lock, stock, and barrel.

"Now, for ordinary types of justice, we'll set up a jury of six men. I'll serve as judge.

"Each family unit is responsible for itself but still is a part of the whole train and answers to the rules of the train. I made sure that we didn't have any stray women to bog us down. Yet accidents do happen. Should the man of the family git kilt along the way, the women are expected to take over and continue on the same. We're too early for any trains to be going east; it'll soon be too dangerous to consider going back alone, so's you'll just have to make do even if widowed."

The shudder that filled the hearts of the women was more felt than seen, but it was real just the same. Nathanial could understand. Suddenly it seemed pretty lonely to consider doing this all on his own.

He stole a sidelong glance at Fee. Her chin was high and her jaw was set firm. It would take more than loneliness on the trail to intimidate her. For the second time that night he marveled at how different she was.

"Now, you will elect two captains each week who will be

in charge of guard duty. When we get to the Snake River country, we'll increase that number," Ezekial continued.

"That leads to Indians. They have different ways of doing things than we do. That don't mean that we have to try to change 'em or try to mow 'em down for being different. It means we have to try to understand them so's we don't go looking for a fight.

"Rule number one: You don't shoot them unless they try to kill you or yours. They'll try to steal you blind. If you catch 'em doing that, simply shoot the dirt at their feet, and they'll usually drop whatever they have pretty fast. Best as I can figure it, they have some kind of setup that doesn't quite understand property rights as we know 'em. That leads to some misunderstandings that can be pretty tragic. I helped bury most of a train once, thirty people. Wiped out by Indians because some hothead shot some brave for stealing a blanket."

Preacher Clyman was a long-faced man with an even longer beard. Nathanial had seldom seen either him or his pinch-faced wife smile since the start of the journey. Now he spoke up. "Army should've been called out and exterminated every last one of those heathens."

"And so we have a war that takes the lives of God knows how many people, and all over a lousy blanket? Better to have let them have the blanket."

"And have them steal whatever they want?"

"You're responsible for keeping track of your own belongings."

"What about them kidnapping women and children?" asked a timid female voice from the back of the circle.

"Only ones I've heard of them taking are the ones left on the trail or the ones who survive a battle. You can't believe the fantastic tales you've read. They're written to sell books, not tell the truth. However, one hothead shooting off his gun at the wrong time can get us all killed. For that reason anyone doing that is subject to immediate dismissal from the train, which can mean a sentence of death to him and his family."

"What are you? Some kind of heathen-lover?" asked Clyman with a sneer.

"I'm a survivor," Ezekial said flatly, ignoring the taunt in the man's voice. "Another thing. We're going to be crossing out of Kansas in the next few days, and we'll be in Indian territory. More and more we'll see Indians along the road, begging. They're not as clean as we're used to and they don't dress like us, but they're still people. The reason they beg, as best as I can figure it, is they figure we're crossing their land and using their game so's we should give them some kind of payment for it. Looking at it that way, I encourage each of you to give 'em some small amount of food. Remember, exchange of food is a sign of goodwill—another reason for acting in a neighborly way as we pass through their land. Those who understand this live longer than those that don't.

"Another thing about the Indians. They'll want to trade with you. Sometimes they want a gun or a dish or a pair of boots. Sometimes they even want your woman!" He paused. "What you've got to remember is that you can't out-trade an Indian. If you want something he has and are willing to make a fair trade, go ahead. However, don't expect to outsmart 'em. They've been doing this for centuries, and you're just too much of a greenhorn to get the best of 'em.

"Now, we'll start out early tomorrow morning. From now on we'll stop for ten minutes every hour to give the animals a rest. We'll noon for an hour to eat a bit and give our animals water and food if it's available. We'll stop at the first good campground we come to after four each evening.

"When we do stop, all latrines are to be at least fifty feet from any moving water. The only water you drink has to come from a flowing stream. I've never seen a case of cholera in someone who abided by those two simple rules.

"Oh, one more thing. We're lucky enough to have Dr. Samuel Breckenridge and his wife along with us. Most of you have met them. I don't think we want to bother him for medical help on little things. But it's good to know that he's along just in case something serious comes up. Any questions?"

Preacher Clyman stepped forward. "You were mistaken when you said that we'd start tomorrow morning. Tomorrow's the Sabbath. We don't travel on the Sabbath."

"We'll travel on the Sabbath unless it happens we can't travel because of sickness or repairs."

"You're not only a heathen-lover, you're a pagan yourself!" Clyman spat. Turning to the rest of the company, he shouted, "Let's show this squaw man that God-fearing folk won't travel on the Sabbath, and furthermore, we won't have the likes of him leading us to the Promised Land of Oregon!"

There was a long silence and then a quiet murmur as Clyman looked around the circle of wagons.

Nathanial stepped forward and stood beside Ezekial. "It's

best you and anyone else who's of the same mind stay here and wait until the next wagon train comes along," he said calmly. "For myself," he said, turning to the rest of the gathering, "I'm going with Ezekial Edwards here. He's none of those things you call him. He's got good sense, and he'll get us through alive."

The preacher spun around as Nathanial spoke. Clenching his rifle tightly in his fist, he started to say something, then snapped his mouth shut and glowered at Nathanial.

Nathanial looked at him levelly. "If you insist on stirring things up any more, you'll have me to deal with," he said, fully aware that he towered over every man there.

Jacob quickly stepped to his side, bringing his wagonmates with him. "We vote with common sense," Jacob said quietly, "and we promise to abide by the rules outlined by Mr. Edwards."

There was a general murmur of agreement. Only three men emerged from the shadows to join Clyman.

"The decision's made," Ezekial said. "This is the last night these four wagons will be with us. Now, how about some music?"

Young James Gould pulled out his harmonica and began playing "Rock of Ages." With even the separatist families joining in, the evening ended on a plaintive but not unfriendly note. It seemed to Nathanial that Ezekial had once again used his unfailing good sense. There was nothing like a bit of music to soothe the soul.

When the last hymn had been sung, Nathanial and Fee walked side by side back to their wagon. Fee's head barely reached Nathanial's shoulder but, alone in the dark, sharing a companionable silence, he was very much aware of her presence. The soft woman-scent of her was barely discernible, but it filled his mind with warm images. It had been a long time since he'd lain with a woman. Too long.

Nathanial recognized that he was a man of strong physical needs, something he'd learned to control through hard labor and sheer dint of will. If he couldn't control his body, it would control him and he would end up no better than his father.

He'd learned a hard lesson from Letitia, the sloe-eyed daughter of a French trapper and a Sioux Indian whom he'd met one September in St. Louis. With a skill she'd learned from her mother and an abandonment born of her nature, she had warmed his bed all that autumn. Her lithe arms and legs had nearly wound a steel trap around his life in the same delicious way they'd wound around his body, making him forget his freedom in her soft prison.

He'd have relinquished all claim to independence if he hadn't overheard her father telling a fellow trapper that he was about to have his daughter bred and cared for. Nathanial left St. Louis that afternoon. He later heard that she'd married a ferryboat captain the following spring and moved to New Orleans. It had been a near-miss—so near it made him sweat every time he thought about it. And yet the remembered pleasure of her arms still could make him moan in his sleep.

Was it these memories still haunting him, or the softness of Fionna walking near him that made that hungry burning spread through him tonight? He walked a little closer, enjoying her warmth as his own desire grew.

"Oh, I almost forgot," she said suddenly as they approached the wagon. "I still have to mix up the mush and biscuits for breakfast. Would you mind checking the animals?"

Her words startled him. "Sure," he said hoarsely. It took no more than a few minutes to check the stock and return to the wagon. He banked the coals of the campfire, prolonging the simple chore to watch her from the corner of his eye.

A lantern on the tableboards cast its glow on her every movement, and he watched from behind the firelight. Although she was a small woman, she was full-bodied enough for any man. Her breasts moved against her dress as she stirred the cornmeal into the bowl, and Nathanial felt his breath catch in his throat. Although her waist was uncommonly small, her hips were rounded, just right for a man to hold on to. He got up from the fire and quickly moved to the shadows of the wagon. His desire was much too obvious for him to remain in the light.

He stood by his bedroll, pretending to untie it from the side of the wagon, all the while watching Fee with hungry eyes, picturing her every curve, soft and naked, caressing her in his mind. If she had been any other woman he would have long ago taken her in his arms and overcome any resistance, taking her body for his own. But Fee was different. Something about her made him hesitate, something strong and exciting yet very nearly dangerous.

She covered the bowls, turned off the lantern, and walked toward him, seemingly oblivious of his emotions.

"It looks to be a cold night," she said.

He tugged at the rope holding his bedroll, swallowing the lump in his throat. Then he turned, putting his arm on the edge of the wagon above her shoulders, leaning uncommonly close to her. "Do you think you might get too cold sleeping alone in the wagon?"

She laughed. "I don't think I'll have time to get cold. The way I feel, I'll be asleep before my head hits the pillow. I'm more worried about you." Then she added, "But you've had a pretty big day yourself, haven't you? If I had the right, I'd say I was mighty proud of you."

"What for?"

"Why, you saved the lives of two people at the river today. Then just now at the campfire, I think you saved the whole wagon train. Who knows what those fools would have done if you hadn't stepped in? That idiot Clyman's blathering could have caused trouble for us all if you hadn't been there."

Nathanial let his arm drop, gently brushing her hair back from her face so he could see her more clearly in the moonlight. "And you did pretty well for yourself today," he said softly. "I could say I was a mite proud of you as well."

She smiled smugly at him. "I did do just fine, didn't I?" She paused. "If it weren't for Ezekial's silly notions about women traveling alone, I wouldn't be needing anybody."

Nathanial felt as if she'd slapped him. He dropped his hand to his side. "What do you mean?"

"I mean that I'm able to take care of myself and not be a burden to anyone. We've both kept our independence. That's something more important than heroics, isn't it?" When he nodded, she went on. "It's a good feeling to know that I don't need a man. It gives me the freedom to choose the one I want when I want. A lot of women come to sorrow because they don't have that choice," she added solemnly. Then she smiled. "I'm grateful you're so understanding. Not many men would be. I'm lucky to have you for my friend."

Nathanial was stung by her words, though he didn't know why.

"Well, if you think you'll be warm enough, I'm going to get some sleep. Morning'll come awfully early." With that she pulled herself up into the wagon. Nathanial watched in silence as her firm buttocks disappeared into the wagon.

Confound that woman! he thought as he tore at the knot holding his bedroll. Why did she have to be so all-fired independent all the time? Couldn't she just sometimes—

"Are you sure you'll be warm enough?" she asked softly

from above him. She'd unpinned her hair, and the dark cascade around her moonlit face as she peered out from the wagon cover was breathtaking. Nathanial looked up, longing to climb into the wagon and possess her. "Because if you get cold," she continued, "I have an extra blanket you can use."

"I'm fine," he said with a growl, ripping the bedroll from the rope and stomping off to the cattle. He heard her pulling the wagon cover tightly closed as he threw his blanket on the ground.

Damnation! Why must she be that way? What kind of woman would be so independent, so bold, so liberated from the need for a man? Who would want a prickly woman like that? What kind of man could possibly find something desirable in a woman who didn't need him?

He pulled the blanket around him with an angry jerk that made Daisy the cow—*her* cow!—flinch in her sleep.

Then as he looked at the crystal stars suspended overhead, he knew the answers to his own questions. He was that kind of man. He wanted her desperately. And he was filled with a pang of uncharacteristic doubt. Would she want him? Would he be enough man for her? And how in the hell could a little smart-assed snippet like her make him so uncertain of himself?

He rolled over with a soft moan, his loins aching with unfulfilled desire.

Chapter VI

Fee had never been so lonely. Somewhere she had crossed an invisible line. By the end of that day she was no longer in the United States of America. She was in Nebraska Territory, and it looked to be a lawless place. All her life she'd been cradled in her family's love. Now she was cast alone on this wild, empty land. And for the first time since she'd crossed the Missouri River, she felt her will trembling.

The vast greening prairie rolled out in front of her towards an endless horizon. Each day was a litany of creaking wagon wheels, bone-grinding jolts, and aching muscles.

Just after they crossed the Kansas-Nebraska line and started following the Little Blue River, two families joined them. They'd been homesteading in Kansas for three years, but the men had caught "Oregon Fever." They pulled up stakes and asked to join the first wagon train heading west. Ezekial put it to a vote, and it was unanimous.

Perhaps the vote wouldn't have been quite so solid had the train not passed out of the States. Everyone knew that from now until they reached Oregon the only law, the only protection they had was what they carried in this little band of wagons. More people and more guns suddenly seemed important.

Still, they seemed to be good enough people. The men appeared to be more taken with the idea of a Promised Land in Oregon than most. The women looked pretty gaunt, but they did their part and kept to themselves.

It was no wonder the women looked the way they did, Fee thought as she rode along. Out here for three years, struggling to scratch a living off the land . . .

Suddenly a thought stung her with surprising force. Would she look hollow-eyed and gaunt after working her own land for a few years? Would she be shrill-voiced and listless after she'd struggled against the elements for that long?

"Be cursed if I will," she muttered to herself, gripping the reins more tightly. "I won't. I'm going to be rich. I'll run my own life, be my own boss. I won't grow wasted and worn out by some man's decisions. I'm not going to . . ." She stopped in midthought.

It was one of Fee's strengths, if not one of her comforts, that she was mercilessly honest with herself. She would not hide from the facts once they were apparent to her. This was one of those times. If she became worn and ugly, how would any man ever notice her? For all her talk of independence, Fee had never once considered living her life alone, without the love of husband and family. Her girlhood dreams had always included a perfect, loving man who would worship her just like in the romantic novels she'd read.

She looked down at her hands, calloused by work and browned by the sun. Certainly no dainty lady would have hands like these—nor arms like these, not soft but tight with muscle born of cracking the whip, tugging the reins, and putting her shoulder to a wheel stuck in a muddy rut. Mud splattered the hem of her skirt and whitened her boots. Even her nose was sunburned.

"I'd give a penny for your thoughts, but you look so somber, I'd probably be wasting my money."

Fee laughed. Jacob had ridden up unnoticed. When there

was nothing else to do he often rode alongside her wagon and chatted about what it was like back home or favorite books they'd read—anything to pass the time of day. She looked forward to these shared times in spite of the rattling and creaking sounds they had to talk above.

"You caught me feeling sorry for myself," she admitted.

"That's a surprise. It's out of character."

"Oh, I'm just getting so dirty and ugly. No man could find me attractive." She normally wouldn't admit this, but Jacob was a trusted friend, and he'd caught her in a weak moment.

To her surprise Jacob threw his head back and shouted with laughter. "You are by far the funniest woman I've ever met," he said finally. "You'll never need to worry about that. Nathanial should worry that too many men find you attractive."

Fee gasped to think that she'd almost given away her secret. However, Jacob must have misunderstood her expression, for he added reassuringly, "And surely you know that he can hardly take his eyes off you himself."

Fee felt herself beginning to blush uncontrollably under her sunburn.

"Don't let it bother you," Jacob said with a smile. "He's a lucky man."

"Oh . . . well," Fee stammered, "I wouldn't have been so honest if I'd known it'd bring out such talk." She looked at his laughing brown eyes, then quickly away. "What do you think of the new people?" she asked, desperately trying to change the subject.

"Seem all right," he said hesitantly, then added, "Their wagons are a bit quarrelsome at night."

"Is that where that was coming from?"

Jacob nodded, and they rode in silence. Fee's mind was spinning. When Jacob started talking again, she couldn't concentrate on what he was saying. She was actually relieved when he had to ride ahead and help pull a wagon wheel from a prairie dog burrow.

Why did he have to go and say that, anyway, she thought impatiently. Just what did he mean—Nathanial could hardly take his eyes off her? It was hard enough dealing with that soft, warm feeling she got inside every time he was near, without Jacob adding to her confusion.

She'd been miserable ever since that night she'd cried and he'd held her so tightly. She hadn't known that Nathanial could be so tender and caring. Now it was hard for her to look at him and not yearn for a reason to begin crying just so he would hold her again.

She flipped the reins impatiently over the backs of the mules as they began to balk going up an incline. It was more than she could bear. She didn't need anything like this muddling up her plans.

Nathanial wasn't the man for her. She was certain of that. He was too full of wanderlust, too prone to take off and disappear for months at a time. She'd learned that much when he was hanging around her father, when she'd first noticed how tall and strong he was, how manly his face was beneath his coppery beard, how intelligent his bright gray eyes were . . . She stopped herself right there. It did no good to think that way. He was not for her. Certainly not what she needed in Oregon.

Besides, she thought, unconsciously setting her chin at a stubborn angle, she needed someone to help out after she had land in her own name, not some man putting her land in his name just because he was her husband. Fiddlesticks, if that was the way it was going to be she'd do just fine without any man.

"No wonder that team minds. A look like that would make Goliath tremble." Nathanial was laughing as he said it. She hadn't seen him ride up, and the thought that he'd intruded on her thoughts about him left her flustered and embarrassed.

"I just take my work seriously," she said finally. "That seems to be more than you do, coming up and scaring a body half out of her wits by laughing at her."

He looked at her solemnly. "I wouldn't laugh at you. I was enjoying that special determined look you have about you." When this embarrassed her even more, he quickly went on in a more casual tone. "Jacob and I are going on a hunt. Probably won't be back till after sundown. Could you hold out a bowl of beans or something?"

"Don't worry," she said, grateful to change the subject. "I'll stay up. If you have any luck, we can have a late supper. If not, there's still the beans."

He grinned and began to gallop off. "Good luck," she called after him. Without looking back he waved his hand in response. Jacob joined him from the front of the train. She watched as they became two specks, then disappeared behind a hill.

Why did she feel so confused when he was around, so alone when he was gone? Oh, it was all such a bother!

The ground became boggy in the afternoon. Even though they were spread out rather than moving in a single line, it was still difficult going, and tempers grew short before day's end. They pulled into camp late because of the many delays. Clouds were climbing the horizon and the sky was red before Fee had staked out the stock and built the fire.

Elsie and Lemuell Slead, two of the newcomers, were having trouble setting up their camp. This was the first evening they'd camped nearby, and Fee couldn't help but remember Jacob's words as she watched poor Elsie's difficulties. It all began when she got the reins tangled as she unharnessed the team. Lemuell shouted at her about that and hadn't let up since.

Then, as Fee put the pot of beans to simmer over the coals, she could see things getting worse. The four Slead children were tired, hungry, and fussy. Elsie bustled around the fire, holding the baby on one hip and stepping around a crying toddler clinging to her skirts. Lemuell sat on a barrel untangling the lines, angrily cursing Elsie's stupidity. Their six-year-old son tried to help his mother, anxiously keeping his eyes on his father.

Fee decided to do some mending while waiting for Nathanial and Jacob to return. She lit the lantern and sat on a box where she could watch the Sleads and not be obvious. She couldn't imagine that two people could possibly live like that. Somehow they had to make up, and she was hoping to see a happy ending to the evening's difficulties.

By the time Elsie finally got the children fed and quieted down, Lemuell had finished untangling the lines and coiling the ropes, something that Fee thought took an unusually long time, considering the simplicity of the chore. Elsie, who hadn't had a moment's rest or a bite to eat, scurried around to make sure that Lemuell had his meal set before him. Fee heard the spoon scrape the bottom of the pan as Elsie filled his plate and suddenly understood why Elsie was so thin. She probably did this most nights, feeding everyone else and then not having enough left over for herself.

"I guess it'd sort of make a woman lose her appetite, anyway," Fee muttered as she threaded her needle.

Just then Lemuell jumped up with a roar and threw his tin plate, food and all, at Elsie, splattering her skirt with hot potatoes. She flinched, then ducked behind the wagon. Their

69

six-year-old son cried out, "No, Daddy!" and ran to pick up his little sister, who was crying nearby.

Lemuell ignored his son and circled around the wagon, shouting at his wife. Fee heard what sounded like a series of slaps and cries. Throwing her sewing down, Fee ran to the wagon on the other side of her. Millard and Rachel Harris had come with the Sleads. Perhaps they could do something to stop it.

"Mr. Harris," Fee called as the couple were eating their dinner. "Do something. Your friend Mr. Slead is hitting his wife."

"Yup," he said, taking another bite, "he does that now and again."

"Stop him!" Fee demanded.

"Not my place."

"Well, it's something he'll have to stop," said Ezekial, coming up behind. "We're not going to put up with that every night."

At that Millard Harris stopped eating. "Howdy, Mr. Edwards," he said amiably, seemingly unaware of the ongoing crying and shouting. "Sorry you're bothered by it, but Lemuell there figures his wife's sort of like a mule—you got to hit her now and then to get her attention."

"Well, I don't see it that way. You're coming with me whilst I go tell him so." With that Ezekial stalked off towards Slead's wagon, Millard reluctantly following behind.

Rachel looked gratefully at Fee. "I'm glad you came over," she said quietly. "In Kansas they lived a mile away, and there were nights when I could hear him going on at her for hours. I'd go over next day 'n she'd be all beat up. I don't know what to do, and Mr. Harris, well, he just don't figure it's any of our business."

"Would it be your business if he killed her? You'd be willing to help bury her but not willing to help save her life," Fee said angrily. Then seeing the hurt on Rachel's face, she added more gently, "I'm sorry. I just think it's sinful to see something wrong being done and not do anything about it. It's the same as saying it's all right."

Rachel nodded. "I got to admire you, Miz Coughlin. You're so strong, and everybody looks up to you so. We can't all be that way, but we sure can admire it when we see it."

Fee was surprised by the woman's words. Rachel was no more than about five years older than herself, yet three children and a hard life made her look as if she were at least twenty years Fee's senior. "Thank you," Fee smiled. "I think we can all be strong if we stick together and help one another."

Fee went back to her wagon. The shouting had stopped. Millard came strolling by as if nothing had happened and shortly after was followed by Ezekial, who strode quickly to Fee's campfire. Fee poured him a cup of coffee, seeing that he was too angry to speak just yet.

"That Lemuell is a pitiful excuse for a human being," he said finally.

"Been my opinion all along. But what brought you to say it?" Nathanial said, coming around the back of the wagon.

"He's been pounding on his wife."

Nathanial's jaw clenched tightly as he threw down his gear. "What'd you do?"

"Told him it'd better not happen again."

Jacob came around the wagon, carrying a bloody flour sack. "How about frying us up some liver?"

"Oh, you got something," she said with delight. They hadn't had fresh meat for over a week.

"Two antelope," Jacob said. "One apiece."

Fee quickly took the sack and began washing and slicing the liver.

"Slead was at it again," Nathanial told Jacob.

"You talk to him?"

Ezekial nodded.

"Then all we can do is see if he pays attention this time."

"You mean it's happened before?" Fee asked, astonished.

"Two nights ago Jacob tried to reason with him and didn't get much thanks for his trouble," Nathanial explained as he sharpened his knife on a whetstone. "Come on, Ezekial. We field-dressed them, but we could use a hand cutting up the meat for sharing around the train."

Fee had trouble falling asleep that night. Thoughts about the new people on the train kept gnawing at her. How could anyone put up with that? Maybe if she got to know Elsie Slead better, she could help her.

However, what really kept her awake was what Jacob had said. Was it true that Nathanial could hardly take his eyes off her? Had he stopped thinking she was a pest? And if he did see her in "that way," how did she feel about it? Why had her heart leapt when she heard his voice tonight? Why did she find it hard to look at him for fear of blushing? She tossed and turned with each question, wishing she could talk to her sister, wishing she were not so alone.

A coyote howled in the distance. Then rain started pattering on the canvas cover overhead—big, wet drops that gradually became smaller and faster. She fell asleep to its gentle sound, only to dream strange dreams of Nathanial looking at her, dreams of Nathanial reaching out and taking her hand, dreams of Nathanial holding her in his arms, all while Jacob mournfully intoned, "You know that he can hardly take his eyes off you."

Rain made traveling slower the following day, but it was dry by afternoon. When they reached a small stream, Ezekial called an early halt and everyone used the time to take care of household chores that had been neglected for the past week. Fee took her bedding out to air. Then she gathered her mud-spattered clothes and went to the stream to do laundry. Mrs. Gould and Rachel Harris soon joined her. The men were mending wagons and tack, checking their animals, or hunting with Nathanial. Other women were caring for children, rearranging their wagons, cooking, or doing laundry farther downstream. It was a time for women-talk, something Fee had seldom known.

Rachel was doing double laundry because Elsie Slead's toddler was sickly. Mrs. Gould and Fee offered to do part to help out. It was Mrs. Gould who brought up the subject.

"What on earth is the matter with that man of hers?" she asked.

Rachel continued beating some diapers on a rock for a moment before she answered. "Well, Elsie figures it's her fault that he's the way he is."

"You said it was like this when they were in Kansas."

"Yes, but it'd let up pretty much until he took up with the idea of coming west. Elsie says he's driven and don't know what he's doing. She says it's because of her."

"What could she do to bring it on?" Mrs. Gould asked.

Rachel spoke hesitantly. "It's what she *doesn't* do."

Mrs. Gould nodded, but Fee was confused. "What's that?"

Rachel put down her soap and looked across the stream. "She's 'fraid of having more babies. She near died last time. I know, I tended her. She'd die for sure if she started carrying one now."

"Well, he's more the beast for not caring if she risks her

72

life," Fee said emphatically. "There's got to be something she could do."

"There are ways of preventing pregnancy," Mrs. Gould said quietly.

"There are? What?" Fee asked

Mrs. Gould smiled. "Don't you have no mother, girl?"

"She died when I was fourteen, so we didn't have much chance to talk about such things."

Mrs. Gould went on. "Well, I hear there are things you can get, order from magazines or big-city apothecaries. They're called female preventatives. Never seen one; they say you put them inside before lying with your man. But us common folk don't use those. The old ways are the ones I know best. One is a kind of moss you use in the same way. You find some and keep it handy. The most reliable one is mistletoe berries. You eat a couple soon's you miss your flow and it'll start right up. Makes you so sick you like to die. Just depends on how desperate you are, I guess." She looked along the banks of the stream and shook her head. There were a few straggly cottonwoods and some green bushes dragging their limbs in the water, but no oaks. Beyond the stream there wasn't a tree on the horizon. "Looks like we'll be hard put to find any mistletoe for a while, anyways."

"But if you see some of the moss, could you show us?" Rachel asked. "We could all get some, and that would surely help poor Elsie a bit."

"I surely will, but that'll only take away one reason for his hitting on her."

Somehow Fee knew that Mrs. Gould was right, and it made her sad. There had to be more between a man and a woman than that.

Chapter VII

As yet, Fee hadn't admitted to herself that the reason for her hopefulness about the relationships between men and women was her growing attraction to Nathanial.

There was seldom an hour that didn't pass without her puzzling over her feelings. No doubt about it, he was attractive, and she fairly ached to have him hold her. Sometimes when they harnessed the team, their hands brushed and she felt an inexplicable thrill. It was something mighty powerful, and she couldn't help but wonder if it was love. But how could it be? He wasn't right for her. Not now. Maybe not ever.

She watched married couples in the wagon train, trying to find some who acted as if they were in love. It was hard to tell under such circumstances, but real love seemed a rarity.

Maybe the Goulds were in love, but they were older, and it was hard to tell. Maybe what she saw pass between Charity and Eustace Gibson when they smiled over the heads of their children was love. And then she noticed Phineas self-consciously handing Patience a ragged bouquet of wildflowers. That fit more with her idea of romantic love—until she heard them arguing over something quite silly the next morning. It was surely more than she could understand.

One night Elsie Slead came over and asked Fee if she had anything to break a fever. Her four-year-old, Francis, was down. Fee wasn't sure what to do, but suggested maybe a cool bath and a tiny dose of laudanum might do it. She portioned out a small dose of her own precious supply and suggested that Elsie speak to Dr. Breckenridge if it persisted through the night. The poor woman seemed so grateful that Fee was certain she had no one to turn to.

Fee kept an eye on the Slead camp through the evening. The children played quietly and walked on tiptoe past the wagon, obviously trying to let their little brother sleep.

Everything changed when the hunters came back. Lemuell Slead had gone out with them. Although most of the men came back with some meat, Lemuell did not—and he took it out on Elsie. When he tried to shush him, pointing to the sleeping child, he exploded. Without warning, he knocked her down with a blow to the head. Then, grabbing a stick, he began beating her unmercifully. The children ran behind the wagon. Elsie gritted her teeth, trying not to cry out lest she awaken her sick child.

Hearing the ruckus, Nathanial dropped the rabbit he was skinning and ran to the Slead wagon. Ezekial and Jacob were close behind. The two younger men grabbed Lemuell and held him while Ezekial knelt beside Elsie. Lemuell struggled in Jacob and Nathanial's grip, bellowing that they were interfering in his private business.

Grabbing the man's shirtfront, Ezekial shook him into

74

silence. "You touch that woman of yours again and you'll be called to account for every time you've ever raised hand against her."

Lemuell glared but said nothing. Before letting him go, Jacob said clearly, "This is the third time."

Elsie leaned over her sick child, soothing him back to sleep. She said nothing when the men left, but her eyes held profound thanks. She would limp for days from Lemuell's blows.

"Why did you tell him it was the third time?" Fee asked as she fried the rabbits for their dinner. Jacob and Ezekial sat by the wagon, mending their tack while Nathanial cleaned his rifle.

Jacob was silent for a moment. "It's ancient Judaic law that a man may be forgiven his transgressions three times. After that he must face his punishment."

"Seems fair," Fee said. "How do you know that?" Jacob had spent many hours around their campfire, but she suddenly realized how much she didn't know about him.

Jacob exchanged looks with Ezekial, then put down the bridle he was mending. "Because," he said softly, "I'm Jewish. My grandfather, father, and uncles left Bavaria because of persecution and set up a business in New York. I'm the youngest son of the youngest brother, and my prospects looked better out West."

"Oh," Fee said, knocking the coals off the lid of the Dutch oven and taking out the browned biscuits. "If you bring the coffee over to the table, we can eat."

Ezekial chuckled as he pulled up a barrel to sit on. "See, Jacob, you don't have anything to worry about in this camp."

"What do you mean?" Fee asked.

"There's some're narrow-minded about a man's beginnings," Nathanial said as he slathered a biscuit with fresh butter.

"Oh, fiddlesticks," Fee said. "Better to be concerned with where a man's going than where he's been." She laughed and winked rakishly at Jacob. "It's easy to see that this one's going the same way we are."

Jacob grinned with relief. "It's something that's best left unsaid to the others. But I'm grateful for your friendship . . . all of you."

"Quit your fool blabbering and pass the stewed apples." Ezekial said with forced gruffness.

* * *

Because they were the first wagon train out of Independence that year, they hadn't seen any other people since they'd hit the Nebraska Territory. However, as they approached the sand hills that led to the Platte River, they encountered a band of Pawnee Indians.

Fee was fascinated by the Indians in their strange and dirty undress. The men wore the hair of their scalplocks stiffened and dyed red. Scarves were twisted around their heads. The women painted their scalps red in the middle where they parted their hair to pull it into two braids. They carried their children on their backs in cunning little packs that held the babies tightly bound and passive.

Some in the train were nervous about the Indians, but, trusting Ezekial's judgment and seeing the logic of what he'd said, Fee simply offered food to the women she saw. They stoically accepted the gifts as their due, and Fee went about her chores unhampered.

One young Indian woman was watching her intently. Though the Indian's dress was strange and soiled, she had a lovely face and fathomless brown eyes. Fee smiled. The Indian maiden gave her a shy smile in return. And in that smile, Fee felt the warmth of understanding.

As they were hitching the mules to the wagon, the young woman appeared once more. Pointing to Fee's worn and muddied boots, she held out a pair of beautifully crafted Indian boots. Then she pointed to Fee's shawl on the wagon seat.

"Nathanial," Fee said. "What does she want?"

"Looks like she wants to trade your shawl for those Indian boots."

"What do you think?"

"Do you need your shawl?"

"I have another."

"Indian boots are made for the plains. They wear well."

She grabbed her shawl and held it out to the girl. Gleefully, she handed Fee the high-topped moccasins and took the shawl. Holding the soft shawl to her face, she smiled and pointed to Fee's feet.

Leaving the harnessing to Nathanial, Fee sat down on the ground and put on the Indian moccasins. She walked experimentally in them, then smiled her approval. They were comfortable and offered a surprising amount of protection.

Fee showed the girl how to tie the shawl around her shoulders. In turn, she showed Fee how to tie the boots properly. They looked at one another approvingly. While this little drama was going on, they were unaware that they'd acquired an audience. However, when they both spun around to show off their new acquisitions, there came a rumble of laughter from the Indians and a spattering of applause from the emigrants who'd been enjoying the exchange.

Ezekial rode to the front of her wagon and called back, "You done enough good will for today, Fionna. That's the chief's favorite wife. Let's git while the gittin's good. Wagons ho!"

"Did he say 'wife'?" Fee asked as they rode out. "She was younger than I am."

" 'Bout fourteen-fifteen, I'd guess," Nathanial said. "That's about right."

Fee was quiet for a few minutes, then murmured, "I'll be eighteen day after tomorrow."

The undulating hills stayed on the horizon for the rest of that day. They hadn't reached them when they made camp that evening. Distances seemed so far out here, Fee thought. There was an awful lot of space between two places of nothing. She couldn't help but feel overwhelmed every time she contemplated what they were attempting.

Was it that same feeling of helplessness that made Lemuell act the way he did? It seemed that life was too much for him to handle. When one of their cows broke her hobble and wandered off, he sent their oldest son after her, then turned on his wife.

Elsie's pitiful cry of "No, Lem," caught Fee's attention. Silhouetted in the firelight, Lemuell was beating Elsie with a shovel as she raised her arm, trying to fend off his blows.

Impulsively, Fee dashed to the Sleads' camp.

"Stop it!" she commanded.

Lemuell spun around, his arm raised, only to freeze in mid-swing as he faced Fee's pistol.

Ezekial came running up, closely followed by Jacob. They grabbed Lemuell's arms and quickly tied his hands behind his back. He never took his eyes off Fee nor lost his astonished expression. Fee didn't lower the gun.

As Ezekial pushed Slead down on the ground, Nathanial came up behind and said quietly, "You can put the gun down now."

Still shocked, Fee looked at him and then suddenly dropped her gun. She knelt beside Elsie's unconscious form. "Someone get Dr. Breckenridge!"

She spent the rest of the evening helping the doctor and caring for the Slead children. Lemuell was kept under guard while Ezekial called a meeting of the wagon train. A jury would decide Lemuell's fate in the morning.

It was late when Fee returned to her wagon. Nathanial was waiting for her. He'd roasted a prairie hen on a spit and had dug out some of her cold biscuits.

"It's not as good as what you cook up," he said apologetically as he handed her a tin plate, "but it's filling."

Fee took it gratefully. "It's wonderful," she said between bites. "I'm starved."

"How's Mrs. Slead?"

"She's still unconscious. Doctor says she has a cracked skull. Her arm's broken. We're all going to have to help with the children and driving the wagon until she can get up and around. He says it'd be best if we don't travel tomorrow."

"Probably wouldn't get far anyway. Trial'll take a while." He leaned back against his saddle and poked at the fire with a stick. "It was pretty brave, you running in there like that. He's crazy enough to start hitting on you, too, you know."

"He's crazy, all right," she said as she poured them each another cup of coffee.

"How much you use that pistol?"

Fee looked sheepish. "Haven't. Why?"

"It wasn't loaded."

"I didn't have time. He would've killed her if I'd waited to load the thing."

"How did you know you wouldn't have to shoot it?"

"I didn't. But I figured only a coward would beat his woman all the time. He probably didn't have the courage to go up against a gun pointed at his head."

"Do you know how to use it?"

"No."

"Maybe we'd better have some lessons tomorrow."

His eyes twinkled and his smile was barely suppressed. Fee sat down on the blanket near him. "I'd appreciate it. Does anyone else know?"

"No. I picked up the gun." He leaned forward and banked the fire.

"Nathanial, why do people like that stick together?"

"Beats me."

"I can't figure out what marriage is for if it ties people together who don't get along."

".... "Me neither," he said, getting up. "We'd better get some sleep if we're to get anything done tomorrow."

She followed him to the back of the wagon. "Have you ever been in love?" she asked as he untied his bedroll.

"Don't know that I have," he said brusquely.

"Have you ever kissed a woman?"

He paused, then turned and looked at her curiously. "Yes."

"When I was ten-and-a-half Alvin Renward ran up at recess and kissed me on the cheek. If you don't count that, I haven't ever been kissed. What's it like?"

"Depends," he said, looking down at the ground.

"On what?"

"On who you're kissing."

"I'm going to be eighteen tomorrow. Will you kiss me?"

He looked into her eyes. Fee held her breath, afraid that she'd gone too far, that she'd been too bold. Slowly and carefully he placed his hands on her shoulders and leaned down, gently brushing her lips with his. Fee felt a shiver run through her body. She opened her eyes and saw him still leaning over her. Then, without warning, he pulled her tightly to him and kissed her long and hard. She felt consumed by his great size, smothered in his arms. His beard was both soft and harsh against her skin, and she found herself breathing the air he breathed, wanting whatever he wanted. His hand wandered down her back, pulling her even closer to him.

Then suddenly he pushed her away. "You little fool," he said hoarsely, "you don't know what you're asking." With that he grabbed his bedroll and disappeared into the night.

Fee leaned back against the wagon, trying to catch her breath. She didn't know why, but she was crying.

At dawn Fee was awakened by a commotion in the circle of wagons. She peeked outside and saw several men pushing three wagons together. Quickly, she brushed out her hair and got dressed, then climbed down from the wagon and joined the gathering crowd.

The tongues from the three wagons were tied together, and the wagons were pushed so as to force the tongues straight up in the center. She saw Jacob standing on the edge of the gathering and quickly joined him.

"What's happening?"

"Mrs. Slead still isn't conscious. They think she's dying."

"Poor Elsie. But what are they doing with those wagons?"

"Fixing to have a hanging," Nathanial said, coming over to

79

them. "Hanging from a wagon tongue serves the purpose when there's no tree handy."

Fee shuddered. "Where's Ezekial?"

Jacob nodded toward the center. Ezekial was just climbing on the back of one of the hanging wagons. The crowd quieted down. Mrs. Slead, he assured them, was now awake, with her children all around her. He took off his oversized hat, put a handful of papers in it, and passed it around. Every adult male had to take one. Those getting one of the six marked papers would make up the jury. Ezekial would act as judge.

Fee whispered, "Where's Slead?"

"Took him away. Too many hotheads," Nathanial said. "Soon's the trial's ready to start, I'll go get him. No need tempting fate until then."

Millard Harris got one of the marked papers. "Seein's how you came along with Slead, maybe you feel you're not a proper juror," Ezekial said kindly. "If you druther, you can put your paper back."

"Nope," Millard said after consideration. "Figure I can offer some balance."

The trial didn't take long. Most of the wagon train had seen Lemuell beating his wife at one time or another. Jacob and Nathanial reported their warnings to Lemuell. Fee was called to tell how she stopped him. The fact that she'd pointed a gun at his head caused a ripple of laughter to go through the crowd. Lemuell glared at her.

When it came time for him to speak, he stood up and said simply, "What goes on 'tween a man and his wife ain't no one's business 'cept theirs. No one's got no right to stop a man from hitting his mule or his wife." He looked around for approval; getting none, he sat down.

Ezekial explained that there being no other law, they had to make their own. However, he felt that they should act as much as possible as if they were under the laws of the United States. He pointed out to both the jury and to Lemuell Slead that the trouble in the Slead camp disrupted the train, which wasn't for the general good. He added that killing another person, which was just about what had happened last night, was against the law in most any land. Since the defendant had been warned repeatedly and had persisted in the beatings, some action had to be taken. That he left to the jury.

After several minutes of deliberation, the jurors asked Dr. Breckenridge whether Mrs. Slead would live. He said that she would have to stay bedridden for several days but had good promise of being able to recover.

With that the jurors went back into deliberation for another ten minutes. In the end it was Millard Harris who was elected to announce their decision.

"There's no doubt you been beating your wife somethin' bad, Lem," he said to Slead. "So's there's no choice but to declare you guilty of that. Now then, the big problem comes up in what to do with you. The others here, they seems to think you should be hung. Leastwise they did till I pointed out that could leave us with a passel of orphans to care for. Even if the missus gets well, it's going to be hard going. That's why we're going to recommend to Mr. Edwards here that you be treated like you done treated your wife. Maybe that will help you understand what's wrong with it."

He turned to Ezekial and solemnly declared, "We the jury find old Lem here guilty as hell and we recommend that he learn his lesson by being whipped twenty-five lashes with a horsewhip on the bare back. If'n he don't learn from that, well, there's still the wagon tongues." With that he sat down and wiped his brow with his handkerchief.

"Justice will be carried out at high noon on yonder hill," Ezekial said, pointing to a nearby sand hill. "That way the young'uns don't have to see it. Now let's use our time getting all those odd chores done. There's not much water around here, and we have to make the Platte by tomorrow evening."

"You cotton to seeing the whipping?" Nathanial asked.

Fee shuddered. "No."

"Then I'll meet you around eleven o'clock. We'll have that pistol-shooting lesson."

Fee was surprised that he would have anything to do with her after last night, and vowed she wouldn't make a fool of herself again. As they walked away from the campsite, she spoke only when spoken to and pretended interest only in learning to shoot her pistol.

They'd walked a mile and had put about three hills between themselves and the wagons before Nathanial stopped. Taking the powder, he proceeded to show her how to load the pistol. It was a cap and ball and worked differently from her old flintlock rifle in that she had a detonator cap to fit on the nipple instead of filling the flash-pan. It was a five step procedure and she was afraid she'd make a mistake because

81

she was having trouble concentrating. When Nathanial put the pistol in her hand and showed her how to aim it, putting his arms around her, holding her hand in his, Fee could barely keep from trembling.

"Are you afraid of guns?" he asked in her ear.

"No," she said, angry with herself for letting her feelings show. "I'm a fair shot with a rifle. This is just new to me." With that she pulled the trigger. A fountain of dirt spewed up about three feet to the left of her target.

"You're pulling to the left. Try again. This time you load."

Fee took the powder and, between remembering what Nathanial had showed her and recalling what she did with a rifle, she was able to load it. She closed her mind to Nathanial's nearness and concentrated on aiming the pistol. She pulled the trigger, and the rock that was her target split in two.

"I did it!" she crowed. "I did it!"

Nathanial's face showed unabashed pride, "You sure did. I'm right proud of you. You can stay by my side any day."

Fee blushed deeply, fidgeting with the pistol as she slipped it into its case. She looked up to find Nathanial watching her. His eyes held hers, and she was drawn to him as strongly as if he'd reached out and pulled her to him.

This time his lips met hers with certainty. He kissed her deeply and long. Holding her to him, enfolding her in his arms and burying his face in her hair, he murmured, "Ah, Fionna, what am I to do? I don't know how to court a woman, even if I wanted to. Yet here you are, more than the strongest man could resist. It isn't the way we had it planned, is it?"

Fee touched his cheek with her fingers, then rested her head on his chest and said, "I will belong to no man, Nathanial. But if what I'm feeling is love, I would like to share it with you."

"We have over a thousand miles to go," he said, brushing her forehead with his lips. "Let's see what happens."

Chapter VIII

They heard them just before daybreak. It was distant, but that bellowing snort when multiplied by thousands created a continuous drone that was unmistakable. As soon as the train had headed out, Nathanial, Jacob, and Ezekial rode ahead, looking for buffalo.

The rising sun burned the dew off the grass, and the wind was in their faces. Ezekial repeated the old buffalo hunters' principle: "Buffalo ain't dumb and they ain't harder of seeing than your ordinary cow. Just most things what gits 'em, they can smell. So that's what they count on." Coming in upwind, the hunters would be able to approach them undetected.

It was midmorning when they reached a small rise that gave way to a view that caused them to rein in their horses abruptly.

"Jesus, Mary, and Joseph," Nathanial exclaimed.

Jacob let out a low whistle and shook his head as if trying to clear his vision.

From their vantage point they could see a buffalo herd seemingly stretching almost to infinity. The black mass became distinguishable as individual buffalo only up close. Nathanial noted it was really a loose gathering of many small herds, each one made up of one hundred to two hundred buffalo. The two small herds he'd seen that had strayed into the northern Mississippi Valley hadn't prepared him for this.

"Yeah," Ezekial drawled, "it's more'n a man can fathom. There's so many buffalo in this country, they'll never git rid of 'em all." He spat and shifted in his saddle. "No problem, though. They're good to eat; they have tough, woolly hides to keep you warm, and they're using a patch of pretty worthless land."

"Well, let's get us some dinner," Jacob said, getting down off his horse.

"Don't like shooting what we can't use," Ezekial said. "'Gainst my principles. We could use about six if the women jerk the meat."

The three men took their stand and in less than an hour shot four cows and two bulls without disturbing the rest of the herd.

"That's it, boys!" Ezekial called, leading the way down to their kill and causing the herd to amble away from the intruders. "We've got ourselves a day's work. You got to clean 'em fast or they spoil on you."

They had been working in silence for about fifteen minutes when Ezekial said, "We'll have to hold out one of the tongues."

"Why?"

"We're being watched."

"How many?"

"Just enough to find out what manner of men they're dealing with. Don't leave a thing to waste."

Nathanial worked for a while longer, then asked, "They still there?"

"Yeah. They've got more patience than a cat at a mousehole." He spat over his shoulder and then added, "It's their land, you know. Don't figure there's going to be any problem long's we're not wasteful. Lived with the Sioux one winter. Indian's pretty reasonable if you understand his ways. If they see that we're taking just what we need, they'll allow us that. Crazy killing some people do just for the tongue or the shootin'—leaving the carcasses to rot—now, that makes 'em mad. They figure the buffalo is a gift from the Great Spirit to their people."

"What are you going to save the tongue for?"

"Well, when we see them Indians along the trail tomorrow— and I guarantee you we will—you have Fionna find that little squaw she traded with and give her the tongue as a gift. That'll git back to the chief and we'll be in fine shape. Ain't no one going to be put off by a gift of the best part of the whole animal. It'll show our respect and we'll pass clear to Fort Laramie with no problem 'tall."

That night they had a buffalo feast that became a real celebration when Grandpa Gibson played his fiddle and everyone danced. Then clouds covered the night sky and thunder rumbled across the prairie. Soon sheets of rain were soaking the campground sending everyone scrambling for shelter. The land was surrounded with a circle of celestial growling.

Morning brought sunlight streaming through broken clouds. Steam rose from the ground and within the hour there was little indication of the night's storm, save for a few lingering puddles.

As Fee was packing the wagon, the Indians appeared from nowhere. Ezekial came to get her, handing her a packet containing the buffalo tongue he'd saved.

"The chief's brought your little friend along," he said. "Her name's Morning Cloud. I want you to make her a gift of this."

Fee could tell from his tone of voice that this was an important gesture. "How about giving them the hides, too? We can't tan them out here, and the Indians use them all the time."

"Good idea. I'll get 'em. You go find Morning Cloud."

Fee walked towards the Indians who were waiting beside the river, watching them with open curiosity. Ezekial gathered the buffalo hides and quickly caught up with her.

Seated on a robe beside her husband, Morning Cloud was proudly wearing her new shawl. Fee was glad she was wearing her Indian boots. She waved and smiled. Morning Cloud's face brightened as she shyly raised her hand in greeting.

With his hands, Ezekial signed a greeting to the chief, but Fee instinctively went to Morning Cloud and proudly pointed to her boots. Morning Cloud smiled and wrapped her shawl more tightly around her shoulders, indicating that it even smelled good. Fee laughed. The Indians did carry a distinctive smell about with them, a combination of body odor, tanned leather, and other scents she couldn't identify. She imagined that the shawl, which until last week had been packed in lavender, was a pleasant change.

Ezekial presented the chief with four hides, and Fee followed suit by giving Morning Cloud the packet of buffalo tongue. The chief nodded and indifferently placed the hides behind him, with a gesture to an older woman, which Fee interpreted to mean "take these and get them cleaned and tanned properly."

Morning Cloud looked in the packet, and her eyes shone with approval. She stole a glance at Fee before handing it over to her husband. Even though the chief kept his face impassive as he looked in the packet, Fee thought she saw just a flicker of surprise cross his face. The present had done exactly what Ezekial hoped.

She turned to follow Ezekial, but not before waving goodbye to Morning Cloud. As if hiding the gesture from her people, Morning Cloud shyly wiggled her fingers from beneath her shawl and gave Fee just a flicker of a smile.

"How'd it go?" she asked as they returned to the wagons.

"The old chief was as tickled as a kid at Christmas," Ezekial gloated quietly. "Wished us a safe journey. Can't ask for more'n that. He's a pretty big chief with the Pawnees."

"I liked Morning Cloud."

"She liked you, too. You're an asset to have along, little lady. You got good instincts. Don't ever doubt 'em."

The white-topped circle of wagons was uncoiling like a snake in the morning sun when suddenly from behind, a series of blood-curdling whoops split the air. Fee's heart jumped in her throat and she turned to see what was happening.

Although she didn't expect any treachery from the Indians, the savage yell was unnerving. Several of the men began loading their guns, frantically preparing for the worst. Some tried to circle the wagons again, causing more confusion as they crossed the path of teams that were not circling. Men shouted, oxen bellowed, horses neighed, children cried, and a woman screamed.

In a cloud of dust, Ezekial dashed down the line of wagons calling, "Don't shoot!" at the top of his lungs.

Fee's mules bolted at all the noise and she suddenly had her hands full. Her own voice calling to her team added to the cacophony. Pulling on the reins, she looked over her shoulder to see which way to go.

Then, out of the dust clouds, a single rider came galloping. It was a lone man on an incredibly fast horse, with a red neckerchief and his hat brim turned back by the wind. He sat on his light saddle, waving his arm in greeting as he rode past. He looked for all the world as if he were having the time of his life and stirring up the wagon train was just one highlight of his day.

Fee calmed her mules down and looked behind to see what was chasing him. *Nothing.* Nathanial was laughing as he rode up.

"What on earth was that?" she asked.

"Don't you recognize the Pony Express when you see it?" he said. "Their route goes pretty much the same as ours from Alcove Springs on through South Pass. Surprised we haven't seen any before. Must've been a ways off the trail until the river."

The train was slowly untangling, and Fee took her place in line. Nathanial continued riding alongside her wagon, obviously enjoying her discomfort, despite her scolding. In fact, he was enjoying it entirely too much.

"The least you can do is warn a body that such surprises might be coming."

He tried to stifle his grin but lost the battle. "It was worth the confusion just to see everyone tuck their tails between their legs." Then seeing her frown, he added more contritely, "We might have to eat the dust of a cross-country stagecoach or two. A few of those run along the same route."

"What news do you think he was carrying?" she asked.

"War news," Nathanial said grimly. "We'll hear more when we get to the forts."

"How long does it take to go from the states to California?"

"Pony Express claims they can get letters and news from one side of the country to the other in ten days. Hard to imagine, isn't it?"

Fee shook her head in wonderment. "It's hard to believe when it's going to take us at least four months." Suddenly the road in front of her seemed so empty and the task facing her so large that she had to fight back the tears that loomed in her eyes.

Fort Kearny was a disappointment. It amounted to no more than a few low-slung, mud brick buildings by the Platte River, with the Oregon Trail running between. They had few supplies, and the only real advantage to reaching the fort was the blacksmith, who could repair some of the wagons that needed attention and shoe the animals, Fitz-James and Smokey, her lead mule, included.

The few men stationed there knew very little about what was going on in the States. But it was a feast for the news-hungry travelers. Fort Sumter had fallen to the South, and Lincoln had called up an army to bring the secessionists back into line. The soldiers expected it to be a summer campaign, ending in about three months, which was how long they figured it would take the rebels in the South to find out they didn't stand a chance.

Fee remembered what she'd left behind and felt the soldiers were wrong, dead wrong.

As they pulled out the next morning, Grandpa Gibson questioned if the Platte River even knew where its bottom was. Judging from some of the exposed sandspits dotting the mile-wide breadth of the water, some of that river bottom seemed to be floating on top of the water instead of beneath the surface where a proper river keeps its bed.

Ezekial laughed and quoted previous pioneers. "A mile wide and a foot deep. Just remember, no digging wells on the banks. Drink your water from the flow. If it's thick, let the sediment settle in the bucket, then use what's on top."

Nathanial joined in, quoting from a guidebook, "It's too thick to drink and too wet to plow, but it's all we got."

It was Fee who thought of a solution to the bathing problems. Sighting one of the many wooded islands off the shore of the riverbank one afternoon when they stopped to allow for wagon repairs, she gathered a few of the women with her, took off her boots and, carrying a shovel and a towel, waded to the other side of the island, finding the water level never went above her knees. With her shovel she dug a hole deep enough for the women to bathe in. They sat on the bank of the island, chatting, waiting for the mud to settle and the sun-warmed water to fill their outdoor "bathtub."

It was true luxury to be able to wash the trail dust from their bodies and rinse the dirt from their hair. Before long they were splashing one another, playing in the water in their camisoles and bloomers, like children.

Fee climbed out and began combing her hair. The sky was washed with a humid haze.

"Oh, look at them curls!" exclaimed Rachel Harris, sitting down beside her. "Let me brush your hair, then you brush mine," she suggested. "Miz Hinshall said she'd keep an eye on my little ones."

The other women began gathering their things, preparing to leave. Mrs. Gould already had her hair neatly coiled in its usual bun. Minnie, her eldest daughter, was sixteen and had just finished pulling her hair back in two sleek brown braids. "I'll go back with you, Mamma," she said quickly.

"You know why Minnie's so anxious to get back, don't you?" Rachel asked as soon as they were alone. "She's sweet on that Wesley Fleming. Every chance they get they're exchanging glances, and he's at their campfire practically every night."

"No, I hadn't noticed. What does her father think about it?"

"Oh, he don't notice much. But Miz Gould's a sharp one, she's keeping an eye out. Don't want to have no shotgun wedding. But I'll bet there'll be a wedding soon's we hit Oregon, if not before. They're too hot to wait long."

Fee was a little shocked at the boldness of Rachel's gossip, but she didn't mind. She'd never had a girlfriend to share confidences before, not since her sister had left home. Besides, a lot of the things Rachel said were most informative.

"Oh, look how I got your hair to curl down over your shoulder. I'll bet that just drives your man crazy when you let it fall over your bosom like that. Does he like to see you naked?"

"Well, he . . . uh," Fee stammered. "I . . ."

"Not that he needs anything to drive him crazy. You're so pretty. I can just tell he can hardly wait to get you alone sometimes." Rachel chattered on. She didn't even seem to notice Fee's discomfort. When Rachel had a subject on her mind she had a momentum all her own.

Rachel handed Fee the brush and sat down in front of her. "Oh, Lord, on a day like today I just fairly ache to have my man pleasure me. But then I go back to the wagon and there's three pair of eyes watching me and waiting for their dinner. Then I got to put them down to bed and I'm near beat. But I'll still slip off into his tent. Lord, don't them hard rocks on the ground bother you, though?" She giggled. "I swear, I'm afraid I'll be carrying another baby if we don't find some of that moss Miz Gould told us about. She said we're not likely to find any until we hit the forests. Wouldn't it be fine if it really works? I would have quit nursing the baby right when we started on the trail, but my mamma told me that keeps you from getting pregnant. I feed 'em as long as I don't dry up just to ward off another child."

Now, that was news to Fee. "I didn't know that."

" 'Course you wouldn't, your mamma being dead and you not having children yet. But it's something to keep in mind." She was quiet for a moment as Fee began braiding her hair. "You know, my mamma said that laying with your man is just the price a woman pays to have him take care of her and to get children. She never told me it could feel so good."

Fee wanted her to keep on talking. She'd never before heard so much she so badly needed to know, all in one sitting. She pinned Rachel's braids up on her head and began brushing her own hair again.

"Oh, here, let me pin back those curls real pretty," Rachel said, taking the brush and jumping up. "Lands, I'll bet you think I'm just the boldest thing, talking about a man and a woman like I do."

"Not really."

"Oh, maybe it's just the weather that sets me off. I just feel like laying out all lazylike and letting him have his way with me." She stopped brushing and giggled. "I guess those tents of ours'll have something to jiggle about tonight."

Fee was grateful Rachel couldn't see her blush. They put their dresses on and waded back to the riverbank.

A distant low rumble, more felt than heard, filled the air. "Did you hear something?" Rachel asked.

"Could have been thunder," Fee said as she laced her boots. "Don't see any thunderheads, though."

"Maybe that's why I'm so restless. Can't wait for nightfall," she said slyly. "Can you?"

Fee laughed with wonder and uncertainty and followed her new friend back to camp.

Big thunderheads rose out of the west, painted a violent pink by the setting sun. Nathanial told Fee he was hoping the impending storm would bring enough moisture to the land to make the dry twenty-two miles to Fort Laramie easier on the animals. They could carry enough water to take care of the people, but the animals would suffer.

A restless tension vibrated through the heavy air. Everything was washed in pink as she put the dinner on the table boards, trying hard to listen to Nathanial's conversation.

Fee needed time to think. She was all stirred up since her conversation with Rachel that afternoon. She didn't want to marry anyone; she wanted her own land in her own name in Oregon. And Nathanial had told her he needed his freedom. But what could she do about this terrible hunger growing inside her?

She sat in the shadows, gazing at his handsome face in the glow of the fire, and felt as if she would shatter if she had to live with this aching longing. She only had one person she could talk to about this dilemma, only one person who knew her secret—and that was Nathanial. How could she possibly confide in him when he was also her problem?

There was a long, low rumble that seemed to come from the very center of the earth. The sky was black overhead and a cool wind was starting to blow, bringing the smell of rain. Maybe that was it, she thought as she jumped up and started stowing the food. Maybe the rising storm was making her restless after Rachel's silly ramblings had left her mind in a turmoil. Then Nathanial was by her side, helping her put things away, and she wasn't so sure.

"I got a bell from Ezekial," he said.

"What for?"

"Well, mules will stick by a horse usually. I figured if we belled Fitz-James, then if they break their stakes and hobbles, they might stick together and we could find them just by listening."

"Do you really think there's a chance of losing them?" she asked, suddenly frightened by the thought that she might be stranded out here in the middle of nowhere.

"Storm like this one could spook anything. We don't want to take any chances." He slammed the lid of the box holding the cooking things and tied its leather thong. "Better hurry and stake them out right. I've still got my tent to put up."

The animals seemed as restless and skittish as Fee felt. The wind was picking up, and she had a difficult time convincing Mouse, her large wheeler mule, to hold still for the hobbles and staking. It would be awful to lose this strong animal before Windlass Hill and the other steep grades ahead.

The storm was suddenly upon them, and Fee dashed for her wagon. Nathanial crawled into his tent just as she pulled an oilcloth across the wagon flaps. With a crash of thunder they were thrust into the heart of the vicious storm. She huddled inside her wagon, shivering and alone, watching the canvas light up with increasing frequency from lightning flashes.

The wind buffeted the wagon until Fee thought she would be blown over. Men were shouting outside, trying to hold down their tents, their animals, and their wagons. Hailstones clattered to the ground. She could feel animals huddling against the wagon, threatening to tip it over should the wind suddenly change direction. So intense was the storm that the double walls of her wagon cover beaded with moisture and tiny rivulets began streaming down the sides.

The thunder was a continuous, deafening crack. She could hear water running under the wagon. A huge flash of lightning struck frighteningly near, accompanied by a bone-shaking crack of thunder. Suddenly she was overcome with fear. What about Nathanial, struggling in the tent? She looked out and saw the camp in chaos.

In a series of lightning flashes she could see Nathanial chasing his canvas as it blew away from him. His bedroll was in the middle of a tiny stream, soaked beyond use. Hailstones the size of walnuts piled up to the wheel hubs and cruelly battered everything left exposed.

"Nathanial!" she called. He couldn't stay out in this. It was too dangerous. Men were climbing into their wagons, under them, anywhere to seek shelter from the fierce hail. "Nathanial!"

The din of the storm swallowed the sound of her voice even as it left her mouth. She scrambled out of the wagon and picked up his soaking bedroll.

Pelting ice stung her flesh. Within seconds she was soaked and shivering. "Nathanial!" she called, running up to him as he rolled his tent into a manageable wad, "come into the wagon! You'll get killed out in this!"

"What are you doing out here?" he shouted above the thunder. "Get back in the wagon!"

"You, too!" she said, grabbing his arm and running.

A flash of lightning momentarily blinded her, and the thunder vibrated through every fiber of her body as she climbed into the wagon, followed by Nathanial.

"It's terrible," she exclaimed as they sat on the boxes at the end of the wagonbed. "Here—move over so I can get something to dry us off."

He was shivering uncontrollably, even more than her own chilled chattering. She pulled out some toweling and handed it to him. He was shaking so hard he couldn't hold it. She took it and began wiping his dripping hair and beard, then quickly pulled off his soaking jacket and shirt.

"Your boots and pants are drenched. Take them off while I get a blanket for you to wrap in," she ordered.

"Wh . . . why d . . . did y . . . you c . . . come get me?" he chattered between his teeth as he fumbled with his boots.

She grabbed the heel of his boot and pulled. "Because," she explained, holding a blanket out to him, "I didn't want anything to happen to you."

Lightning flashed, and in that instant, she saw the look in his eyes and knew that was all he'd ever needed to hear from her. "I don't want anything to happen to you, either," he gasped out between his shivers. "N . . . now you dry off." She saw his tightly muscled chest just before he wrapped the blanket around himself, and her breath caught in her throat.

Fee quickly took another towel and began drying her hair. Her dress was soaked, as were her boots and underclothes. She began to shiver more violently as the coldness settled into her body. She took off her boots and then hesitated.

"Better do the same thing I did," Nathanial told her. "You catch pneumonia, it'll be a lonely trail to Oregon for me."

Her heart was racing as she quickly stripped off her wet clothing and reached for a blanket. Lightning flashed, filling the wagon with light, while the thunder shook her to her very soul. Lightning flashed again and hailstones pelted the wagon cover with renewed ferocity.

In that second their eyes met. Suddenly Fee knew what Jacob and Rachel meant when they mentioned how he looked at her. When he reached out and pulled her to him, she went eagerly.

His kisses were rough and demanding as his hands caressed and explored her body possessively. The thunder was a continuous roar, and Fee felt as if she were reeling uncontrollably as they fell onto her feather mattress.

The heavens crashed around them but she didn't even hear her own cry as his body covered hers—nor did she realize how eagerly she mirrored his every motion despite her own fear at his near-savage possession of her. The lightning was still flashing, filling the wagon with sporadic blue light when he quieted his movements, kissing her throat but leaving her restless and unfulfilled.

Catching her breath, she ran her fingers through his hair, seeing his face in the pulsing light, feeling the thunder as well as Nathanial. "Is this what you meant when you said I didn't know what I was asking?"

He crooned in her ear, "This and more . . ." Running his hands over her body, he kissed her breasts and thighs so that she moaned with pleasure, involuntarily arching her back, receiving him once more. Instinctively, Fee echoed the timeless rhythms of love that Nathanial taught her. As the skies stilled and the storm moved across the plains, they shared the fulfillment of their love.

Thunder gave way to distant murmurs, replacing the tempest with a gentle pattering of rain on the canvas of the wagon. Entwined in each other's arms, together, they found their rightful place in the universe. Nathanial kissed Fee's face, gently caressing her and whispering in her ear, "I've loved you for so long, longer than even I knew."

She ran her hands down his back and held him tightly. "Tell me how long," she said mischievously.

"Ever since I heard you play the piano. It was your sixteenth birthday, and I think I came more to see you after that than to borrow your father's books."

"I remember. I came out of the kitchen and saw you sitting in front of the fireplace and you looked up at me and I felt so . . . I didn't know what it was then, but I do now. No wonder I blushed and ducked back in the kitchen."

He joined her laughter, then said quietly, "Are you sorry?"

"About what?"

"About this . . . us . . . together like this."

She thought for a moment before answering; she wanted above all else to be truthful with him. "No," she said finally, "I don't think I'm sorry. I'm not sure where this will take us, but I don't think I'm sorry."

He was quiet for a moment, then said softly, "I do love you."

"I know. I love you, too." She paused, then asked, "Do you think this was meant to be? Do you think maybe we don't have any choice in these kinds of things, that somehow they're all planned out for us ahead of time?"

He didn't answer. From his steady breathing, she knew he was asleep, still holding her tightly in his arms.

"Maybe so," she whispered, stroking his hair and answering her own question.

Chapter IX

When a buffalo has an itch, it has to scratch. And out in the middle of the prairie, where there's not even a sharp stick to rub against, that presents a buffalo-sized problem. That's why buffalo have been known to travel miles out of their way just to find a good itching post.

That night the storm separated a young buffalo bull from his herd. However, when the gray dawn revealed a tall, white-topped, sharp-edged object, all thoughts of finding his herd disappeared from his buffalo brain. That white thing could serve but one happy purpose: rubbing the last itchy shreds of his matted winter coat from his tough tide.

Fee didn't see it that way.

The violent rocking of the wagon was the last straw. She was not the screaming type, but her voice did rise an octave higher than usual as she grabbed her nightgown and threw it over her head, lest she be thrown out of the wagon stark naked. "Nathanial!" she cried, shaking him because he was blissfully sleeping through the seeming earthquake. "Nathanial! Wake up! Do something!"

Then a sharp crack accompanied the ferocious shaking. The wagon was falling apart.

A wild-manure smell filled the air. Then there was a thunderous snort. They were about to be eaten alive!

Holding on to the sideboards, Fee scrambled to the end of the wagon and peered out.

A great, black, shaggy head loomed right in front of her

face. The beast's eyes were closed as it blissfully sent splinters of wood flying, bringing the wagon closer to destruction with each lunging rub.

Glancing at Nathanial, who was hastily pulling on his pants, she shouted, "A buffalo! It's breaking the wagon!" She grabbed the shovel. Before her very eyes she was losing her sole means of transportation. All because some buffalo had an itch.

She leaned out the back of the wagon, raised the shovel over her head, and brought it crashing down on the buffalo's head. Her arm stung from the reverberations of the blow, but the buffalo acted as if this only enhanced his scratching. A second blow accomplished nothing more than cracking her shovel handle.

A large splinter of the wagonbed flew off, and the animal rubbed all the harder.

Nathanial nudged her aside and poked the rifle through the opening. He put the barrel to the buffalo's shoulder blade and pulled the trigger.

The roar of the blast nearly threw Fee back on her heels but the buffalo merely stopped scratching and shook its head, as if shaking off flies. Then, while Fee watched in openmouthed horror, it staggered in the lingering gunsmoke, stepped away from the wagon, and stood swaying.

The animal was barely bleeding from the wound, and it stood a good five and a half feet tall at its woolly shoulder. What if the shot had just made him mad? Would he charge? And how could she get out of the way if he did?

"Do something!" she cried. "Reload!"

Nathanial smiled. "Wait."

As she watched, the beast snorted a bucketful of blood, fell to its knees with a shudder, rolled on its side, and died.

"It's like Ezekial says," Nathanial explained. "Buffalo's powerful strong. Takes 'em a while to know they're dead." He grinned. "How about steak for breakfast?"

Fee was too shaken to find any humor in his question, but his laughter was contagious and she smiled weakly.

"It's a pretty lazy hunter who has the game come to his bedroom to get shot," she quipped as she scrambled to put her clothes on. "Let's just hope that the wagon isn't badly damaged."

"Doesn't look like it," he said with a yawn and reached over to give her a good-morning kiss.

"Nathanial, don't," she protested. "I hear people coming."

"Why let that bother you? We're an old married couple, remember?" he teased as he caught the shirt she threw at him.

They crossed the South Platte, then crossed a high plateau, an arid triangle of land, to the North Platte. They spread out in a fan shape to avoid the white alkali dust boiling under their wheels for twenty-two miles. As moisture left the wagon wheels, they creaked and squealed noisily. Spokes pulled out of wheels and one tongue snapped. Everyone's skin dried and cracked painfully.

By the end of the two days everyone was coated with a ghostly veil of white dust. Even food was permeated with the dusty alkali.

From the crest of Windlass Hill they looked down on a six-mile-long plain, Ash Hollow. There was nothing between the empty horizon and the hill except thin air and three hundred yards of steep, winding trail. It took Fee's breath away.

Since Fee had a strong team of mules, Ezekial decided her wagon should go first. People were directed to lock their brakes, chain the front wheels to the back, and walk beside the wagons rather than ride in them.

Mouse, a large, stolid gray mule, was a strong wheeler. Her dapple brown teammate, Sally, was equally strong although more skittish. These two animals bore the bulk of the wagon's weight through the breeching straps on their hindquarters, keeping the wagon from careening down the hill. The others could break the speed of the descent only by the pressure they kept against the tongue. Many an animal had died on this hill attempting the same thing.

Fee held her breath as they started down. Ezekial walked on one side of the team, Fee the other, giving verbal commands with just an occasional light tap with the whip when one seemed to be losing its concentration.

The mules took smaller and smaller steps, almost sitting back on their breeching straps, holding the weight in the summer's sun. The team needed no guidance. Smokey could easily see the deeply worn path and was following it. Fee and Ezekial went to the back of the wagon, and grabbed the rope trailing behind. The two of them helped hold back the load by dragging their feet the full three hundred yards down the hill.

When they reached the bottom, she could hear the others, at the top, cheer. Only twenty-one more wagons to go.

After Fee got the farm wagon down the track, she led the wagons across the plain, following Nathanial's directions to a spring about two hours ahead. She and some of the other women would set up camp while the rest of the wagons made the descent.

"I think we're about due for another freshwater bath, don't you?" Rachel said as her wagon came alongside Fee's.

"Sounds wonderful." Then she spotted Rachel's five-year-old son riding on the tongue of the wagon, a favorite occupation of small boys. They'd straddle the wagon tongue, resting their hands on the back of the oxen plodding alongside. Fee said with concern, "The Goulds won't let their boy ride like that anymore. He about fell off and got crushed under the wheels yesterday."

"Was he foolin' around?"

"No. The wagon just hit a bump."

Rachel shuddered and called, "Johnny, you git on up here now! Miz Coughlin says you could git yourself kilt doing that!" She pointed to the side of the trail and added, "Guess we don't need to add any more of those."

Fee turned and saw a lone gravestone. "Been a lot of them, haven't there?"

"I've counted two hundred and thirty-five since Independence, and probably missed some. It's the little ones that bother me the most."

"They say most people put their graves right in the middle of the trail so's the wagons pack 'em down good and the wolves and Indians can't get at 'em," Elsie Slead said, bringing her wagon alongside Rachel's. "That means we've been driving over the top of most of the dead and not even knowing it 'cause they don't have even a headstone."

"Oh, Elsie, don't let little Francis ride on the wagon tongue. Miz Coughlin says he might fall off and get run over."

"Well, Miz Coughlin can mind her own business," Lemuell Slead said, riding up from the other side. "No son of mine is going to listen to some busybody woman what's too big for her britches."

It was the first Fee'd heard him speak since the whipping, and his voice was shrill and bitter. She pulled her wagon ahead. Best not to tempt fate.

Six days later, they camped at the foot of Chimney Rock, a

funnel-shaped, sandstone tower that rose five hundred feet above the North Platte.

At sunset, Fee and Nathanial walked up the steep slope to the base of the natural obelisk and carved their names into the soft rock alongside hundreds of other pioneer names. Since no one else was around, Nathanial took Fee in his arms as they watched the sun set across the prairie, washing the sky in a rose tint.

What did it mean? Fee thought as she leaned against Nathanial's shoulder, listening to the beat of his heart. Their names were side by side on Chimney Rock, yet at the end of the trail, they'd agreed to go separate ways.

No need to worry before times, she quickly decided. *Enjoy what you have while you have it, and worry about the rest when it happens.*

"Race you back to camp," she dared him, breaking away and running down the trail.

Fee tried not to notice the graves they passed. The other women might choose to count them, but she refused to let them fill her mind. Instead, she averted her eyes and thought about what Ezekial said last night about seeing sign of Indians along the trail. They were probably heading towards Fort Laramie to do some trading. She hoped they were only interested in—

A woman's scream shattered the morning air. "No! Oh, my God, no! Someone help!"

"Get the doctor!" another voice cried.

Fee halted her wagon and jumped down, running in the direction of the screams.

It was Elsie. They ran to the Sleads' wagon.

Pushing through the crowd, Fee found Elsie on the ground behind her wagon, cradling her son Francis in her arms, his blood spreading over the bodice of her dress. His tiny head was crushed, his face an unrecognizable pulp.

Elsie looked up at Fee in disbelief. "He . . . he's dead!" Elsie cried. "He fell off the wagon tongue. Just like you—"

"You damn fool! Why the hell did you let him . . ." Lemuell began to shout, until Fee swung around and faced him. Seeing her standing in front of him, he swallowed his words, glared, then turned away, muttering about having to build a coffin.

The mournful burial in the middle of the prairie cast a pall over the train. The emigrants came face to face with their own mortality. For Fee, it brought back the painful memory of the graves she'd left behind. Even the view of Laramie Peak from Scott's Bluff, their first hint of the real mountains to come, was not enough to lift the unnatural chill she felt in the hot summer sun. How many more graves were ahead?

To Nathanial, the gloom was deepened by the naked hatred in Slead's eyes as he'd looked at Fee across his son's coffin. He acted as if it was her fault. Sure, it was Fionna, a woman, who'd actually stopped him from beating his wife. But didn't the fool realize that others were coming to stop him, too? Didn't he remember that six men, his friend Harris included, convicted him? Couldn't he admit he was the one who'd insisted his son be allowed to ride on the wagon tongue, despite Fee's warning?

Fee had made a deadly enemy in Lemuell Slead. Nathanial decided to keep an eye on the vicious, unhappy man.

Fort Laramie was larger than any of the stage stations, forts, or settlements they'd passed so far. The adobe stockade contained several buildings. The sutler's store was stocked with the basic trading items but, as Fee pointed out, was generally overpriced. Nathanial noticed with some amusement that she could not forgo the opportunity to stock up on some items "just in case." He told her later that she was suffering from a severe case of what he called "the winter squirrels," always hoarding something away against bad times.

Hundreds of Indians were encamped around the fort, come to trade or palaver with other tribes.

Nathanial accompanied Ezekiel to one of the encampments just outside the fort. They used a unique combination of sign language, mixed Indian tongues, and pidgin English, but Ezekial and the Indians seemed to find it a satisfactory means of communicating. Nathanial watched intently, determined to learn as much as he could.

"What was all that excited talk right before we left?" he asked as they walked back to the wagon train.

"Some young hotbloods going through here, heading towards the mines opening up in Washington Territory," Ezekial said grimly.

"Some left a week before us back in Independence. You tried to tell 'em it was still too muddy, but they wouldn't listen. What happened?"

"Hearsay is they grabbed one of the Blackfoot women west of here—kept her about a week.

"She get back to her people?"

"They threw her over a cliff when she tried to knife one of 'em in his sleep."

"Bastards. That mean trouble for us?"

"Could. Hard to tell."

"But keep our eyes open."

"And our mouths shut. Some nervous Nellies might start firing their guns at anything that moves. That's the real danger. There's those that think the Indian has to be exterminated and anything's an excuse to start the killing."

The land between Fort Laramie and Fort Casper was barren. They followed the milk chocolate colored North Platte, grateful for its turbid presence.

The sun beat down on Nathanial's back as he rode ahead of the train, sending up clouds of grasshoppers from the dry grass with each step of Seneca's hooves, filling his nostrils with an acrid, dusty smell. The wagons spread out to avoid eating one another's dust. He could follow their progress from great distances just from the cloud of red dust they stirred up. Even though it was dreary, flat land, Nathanial wasn't unhappy. He watched an antelope bounding across the plain and realized why. He was doing what he loved most, and each evening he had a wonderful meal and Fionna's soft body beside him when he slept.

They reached the great dome, Independence Rock, and the Sweetwater River by the end of June. There they stopped to put things in order before they crossed the Continental Divide and faced the scorching deserts beyond.

Seeing the damage caused their draft animals by the heavy loads, people finally gave up the last of their cherished heavy possessions. Anvils, plows, dishes, chairs, and dressers all joined crumbling piles of abandoned cargo from previous trains.

Nathanial had to laugh, watching Fee look at the mounting piles of booty. It was more than she could bear to see things that might prove useful later on being left behind.

Oxen were twisted to the ground and their split hooves repaired in anticipation of the road ahead. The searing iron filled the air with stench and the animals' bellows added to the cacophony.

The going was rough in the loose sand, but they still made satisfactory progress as they started out on the gradual incline towards South Pass.

Ahead of them lay the most dangerous part of the trip.

Ezekial grew increasingly edgy with each day's progress. They were heading right into a party of Sioux. Nathanial rode more closely to Ezekial. Although Nathanial was an excellent woodsman, it was Ezekial who could read Indian signs like no other man he had known. He was determined to learn everything he could from this crusty old mountain man.

Inevitably the time came when they stopped just downstream from the Sioux. Ezekial set up a tight camp and, with Nathanial, made a courtesy call on the Indians.

It was a hunting party, as Ezekial had suspected, with squaws along to preserve the meat. They accepted Ezekial's gift of tobacco, inviting the men to sit down and smoke a pipeful with them. Ezekial was more at ease as they made their way back to the camp.

However, the next morning, as they were preparing to pull out, Nathanial couldn't find Fee. Her wagon was in the lineup, unattended. Harley Gould said she'd gone to catch a stray cow.

Following Harley's direction, Nathanial turned Seneca upriver. As he passed the wagons, he noted there'd been some bartering with the Indians. A spotted Indian pony stood beside the Sleads' wagon, and the two older children were squabbling over who would get to ride it first. Minnie Gould was wearing a new pair of Indian boots, and even Grandpa Gibson had a buffalo robe across the seat of his wagon.

"Where you headed?" Ezekial asked, reining his horse beside Nathanial's.

"Fee's out chasing a cow. Thought I'd track her down."

"Figured we'd make near twenty miles today. It's an easy—" He put his hand on Nathanial's arm. "Look."

Behind a small rise he could see an Indian trying to carry Fee, but she was putting up a fight. Nathanial spurred Seneca, barely hearing Ezekial call after him, "Take it easy, now!"

Just as he rode up, Fee pulled away from the Indian. The brave had a knife, but as Fee spun around, she pulled out a small pistol and leveled it at the surprised Indian. He backed off. Five other Indians stepped forward, their guns raised.

Nathanial fired his pistol in the air as he jumped from the saddle. "Stop!" he called, making the hand motion he'd learned from Ezekial. "Don't do anything."

Fee refused to put her gun down. Never taking her eyes from the Indian, she glowered. "He was trying to kidnap me." Her dress was torn and her hair disheveled, but she looked better than the Indian, who was scratched and bleeding.

The Indian, never taking his eyes from Fee, spoke over his shoulder to his comrades.

"He says he bought her fair and square," Ezekial said from behind Nathanial.

"Well, I wasn't for sale," Fee said grimly. "You tell him that?"

Ezekial said something and the Indian answered. "Fee, put down the gun so he can talk," Ezekial said. "He's not going to do anything now."

"I'm not so sure," she said, slowly lowering the gun.

The leader of the group stepped forward and started talking to Ezekial; both men were doing their best to avert hostilities.

"This fellow claims he paid his best horse so he could have this white squaw. He can't be cheated out of his horse."

"How dare he—" Fee sputtered.

"With these folks, they buy their women same as their stock," Ezekial tried to explain. "So just calm down whilst I explain that's not our custom."

"Well, I'm not staying here—"

"If you don't behave, little lady, I just might let him keep you," Ezekial said, his eyes twinkling. "Now stand here and be quiet."

Fee could barely contain her wrath, but she stood still.

"If you can keep them talking for a minute," Nathanial said suddenly, "I think I can get to the bottom of this." He jumped on Seneca and headed back to the camp.

When he returned, the Indians pointed behind him in recognition. "Just as I thought," he said, pulling Slead down from the Indian pony. His jaw was cut and swollen from Nathanial's convincing argument. "You tell this Indian that Slead is giving back the pony with his apologies. The woman wasn't his to sell."

"I ain't apologizing to no red—" His words were cut short by Nathanial's quick twist of his arm.

Ezekial repressed a smile and gave a quick explanation, handing the pony to the offended Indian, who muttered something as he took the reins. The other Indians all nodded.

"What'd he say?" Slead asked, taking Ezekial's laughter as proof his offense wasn't too grievous. "Says she was over-priced anyways?"

Ezekial spun around, glaring at Slead. "He said he should have known better. A vulture could never own an eagle."

"What the hell does that mean?"

"It means even the Indians can tell that you're a worthless son-of-a-bitch," Ezekial said evenly. "Now let's all walk out of here while our scalps are still attached."

Once they were back in sight of the camp, Ezekial grabbed Slead by the collar and said, "Whatever Coughlin does to you ain't enough. If you even spit crooked from now till Oregon you're a dead man. I won't leave that family of your'n behind, but sure as shootin' you'll find yourself in the middle of the desert alone and on foot, buzzard bait!"

"I—" he stammered, "I's just makin' a joke. Miz smarty-pants here—"

"You ain't good enough for her to wipe her feet on," Nathanial said, grabbing Slead. "If I ever see you even lookin' in her direction again, I'll save you the agony of a slow death on the desert by blowing your brains out. That clear?"

"You hain't got no right," he whined. "It was jist a joke—"

It was more than Nathanial could endure. He hauled off and hit Slead on the jaw, knocking him off his feet with the blow. "That's just so you know I'm serious," he said, rubbing his knuckles. Then, taking Fee's arm, he walked back to camp.

"Thanks," she said softly.

"Ah, it just made me mad. You're worth at least three flea-bit Indian ponies." He caught her arm as she swung at him. "Just teasing." He laughed as he put his arm around her, then added soberly, "Gives me the chills to think what might have happened if I hadn't noticed you were missing."

She smiled sweetly. "I know. That Indian would have been dead."

Most people expected South Pass to be a notched ravine between two sharply rising mountain peaks. In actuality, it was a gradual incline that began when they picked up the Sweetwater River and continued on up a twenty-mile-wide valley. The summit was a broad saddle in the mountains almost thirty miles across, with the end of the Wind River range on the left and the Antelope Hills and Pacific Butte on the right. If Ezekial hadn't told them, they might have missed it. According to the odometer on Fee's wagon wheel, they were 956 miles from Independence. From now on all water would flow to the Pacific Ocean.

They camped at Pacific Springs then took the Lander Road cut-off which saved time and mileage. It did not save them the miserable desert heat nor the painfully long trek to Soda Springs.

It was just past Soda Springs when Ezekial took it upon himself to write a note on a board and nail it to a tree. He'd seen too many signs that the men preceding them on this trail had made trouble with the Indians. The trains following had to be alerted.

The day after Three Buttes came into view, Nathanial and Ezekial found a dead Indian. It was the first time Nathanial had seen a scalping, and the bloody bone exposed from the eyebrows to the back of the head turned his stomach.

"He sure made some Indian mad to have that done to him," he said, looking down from his horse as Ezekial knelt beside the body.

"Wasn't an Indian that did it."

"How can you tell?"

"Tracks around here are white man's boots. 'Sides, it's a botched job. Best reason's over there in the sage. It's the scalp."

"Think it's the same bastards as grabbed the squaw?"

Ezekial nodded. "Probably were gambling with him and he won. There's their camp. Looks like there was another Indian that got away. Fat's in the fire now. These are Bannocks, and they won't take kindly to this."

He started gathering rocks and placing them over the body. "Let's try to give him some kind of a burial. Maybe when his folks come to find him they'll see that we're not all like those hotheads."

Nathanial began piling rocks on the body, too. "Think they'll get the message?"

"Nope. They'll get even. Probably with us."

The train was a slow-moving, easy target. Ezekial had the men armed and ready. Children were not allowed to wander when they stopped, and the guards were doubled. A tense, waiting-quiet settled over the camp as night darkened around them.

A signal fire flared on a nearby hill. Indians. On the other side, another fire pierced the darkness with its ominous flame. They were surrounded.

Then they heard distant drums and chanting wafting through

104

the clear night air like a ghostly incantation, weaving with the howl of a coyote in a savage symphony of death.

"How 'bout riding out there and talking to them? Tell them we'll punish the bastards. Maybe they'll leave us alone," Phineas said as they sat around the fire waiting for their watch.

"Not a chance," Ezekial said. "First one to walk into their camp would end up skewered like meat over the fire. They don't give much time for talking when their dander's up."

"All the women are armed and ready," Grandpa Gibson said as he sat down. "But they're worried about the children."

"How much longer before they attack?" Nathanial asked. "Sounds like they're getting closer."

"Probably not till daybreak. Most tribes feel they don't go straight to Indian heaven if they're killed at night."

So they sat, quietly passing the time, cleaning guns, sharpening knives, and watching the Big Dipper turn overhead. They were preparing for an attack.

At first Nathanial thought it was a night bird singing. The fluid sound began tentatively, then rose more confidently. The song was plaintive, weaving a melody of home and sunshine. The liquid notes poured over the camp and out across the sage, singing first with the wonderment of a bird, then with the joy of a free heart.

The chanting stopped. The drums were silent. It was as if the whole earth were listening to this magical song.

"Look," Grandpa Gibson whispered, pointing across the camp. "It's your little lady."

Sure enough, there was Fee perched up on the seat of her wagon, playing a flute. Nathanial shook his head, thinking he was seeing an apparition. *Where did she get that? When did she learn to play it? And whatever was she doing playing it now?*

"Get out to the guards and tell them to hold their fire unless they're fired on first," Ezekial ordered.

Three men scattered, carrying the message to the guards. Each one had seen Indians skulking in closer since the music began. What did it mean?

With only a few brief rests, Fee continued playing throughout the early-morning hours. Finally, when the sun pinked the eastern sky, she put down the flute with a deep sigh and looked at Nathanial standing beside the wagon, his gun at the ready. "It was worth a try," she said simply as she pulled out

105

her guns and powder and climbed down to take her position beside him.

A lone horseman appeared on the horizon, riding slowly towards them. "This is it," Nathanial whispered. "Keep down."

"Hold your fire," Ezekial called. He watched for a minute, then mounted his horse and rode out to meet the Indian.

The rising sun warmed the sage, and a jackrabbit loped between two rocks. Somewhere in the distance a killdeer flew across the land, piercing the morning air with its sharp, mournful cry.

Ezekial returned to the train and stopped at their wagon. "You remember when I said you had good instincts?" he asked Fee.

"I remember. That's why I played last night."

"Well, you bring those instincts and your flute and come with me. They're wondering what kind of magic we have in this woman who holds the song of a bird in a stick."

Nathanial borrowed Jacob's black mare for Fee, and they followed Ezekial back to where the Indian waited, with five other braves.

"Did you tell him we didn't have anything to do with the murder?"

"Yup. It helped that we buried him. Helps even more that they can read tracks. Still, they think the white man should be taught a lesson."

"Where will it all end?" Nathanial muttered as they approached the waiting group. The Indians' eyes were all on Fee.

Ezekial gestured towards Fee and said, "Play something that sounds like a bird if you can."

Fee put the flute to her lips, closed her eyes, and the trill of a lark flying into the morning sun filled the air.

Nathanial had to admit that as she sat on the big black horse, her gray skirts spread over its flanks and her black hair curling over her shoulders, she was a beautiful picture. His chest ached with pride and longing. Would he ever hold her again?

There was silence when she stopped and then a respectful murmur from the Indians. The leader of the group spoke.

Ezekial turned to them and said with only the trace of a smile, "Whatever you do, don't laugh. They want to buy Fionna."

"You got a price?" Fee asked with a bemused smile.

"Five horses and two buffalo robes."

"Well, at least my value has gone up," she said wryly.

"Don't worry, little lady, I'll tell 'em you aren't for sale."

"No, wait," she said. "Tell them that just as you can't hold a bird's song in your hand, no one can hold me. Tell them that my magic soothes the spirit and I will share the music with them, but no one can own me."

"Good instincts," Ezekial muttered to Nathanial with a wink as he turned back to the Indians.

Fee sat gazing at the horizon, seemingly detached from the negotiations. Nathanial was about to explode with not knowing what was happening.

"Running Antelope here is the son of the chief of their tribe. Seems his father is feeling poorly. The murdered Indian was to be his future son-in-law. He understands that your medicine is soothing, and he buys your story of not being able to hold a bird's song. To smooth feelings all around, I've offered to give him some cloth and tobacco."

"I'll go round it up," Nathanial volunteered.

"Not so fast. I promised him something more," he said, glancing at Fee. "I promised that the little lady here would go to their village and play for the ailing chief to soothe things over. This hunting party of about twenty braves will accompany us down the trail for the next four days. We'll pass through their territory safely as far as the Snake River, then they'll turn us over to some of their friends, who'll probably escort us to Three Island Crossing if they can have a few concerts of their own."

"Tell them that she must be accompanied by me when she goes to the village."

"They already offered to take us both along. That agreeable to you?" Ezekial asked Fee.

"Of course." She smiled. The Indians murmured approvingly, and the tension was broken.

Thus it was that with the help of Fee's music, they traversed the dry, hostile lands of Idaho Territory. It wasn't until they reached Fort Boise that Nathanial even thought to ask where she'd got the flute.

Chapter X

The British had abandoned Fort Boise six years earlier. Subsequent Snake River flooding wiped out almost all remains of the old fort. However, the site was a convenient campground, and the ford, about a mile below the mouth of the Boise River, was a good one. They stopped and took an extra day to repair wagons and rest the animals before heading across the Oregon desert to the dreaded Blue Mountains.

The women washed their laundry in the waters of the broad river, hanging their clean garments to dry on the willows lining the banks. There Rachel asked Mrs. Gould about the subject foremost on Fee's mind.

"You find any of that moss you told us about?"

"Don't expect to until we reach some place that gets more rain," Mrs. Gould said with a gentle smile. " 'Sides, we have no way of knowing that familiar things grow in Oregon."

"Did you say mistletoe berries worked after your flow has stopped?" Elsie Slead asked quietly.

"If you catch it in the first month after you've missed it. But it makes you powerful sick, you near die. Some do."

"What happens if you take them after that?"

"I wouldn't dare try it, dear. How long has it been?"

" 'Bout two months."

"Looks to me you'd better plan for a baby around January."

Fee could stand it no longer, "How can she be sure that's what stopped her flow?"

"Lands, girl, I keep forgetting you lost your mother," Mrs. Gould said good-naturedly. "There are other signs, aren't there, Elsie?"

"Yes, I been tender in my breasts for some time now. And I don't feel like eating too much in the morning. Fact is, I been feeling downright sick."

"But couldn't that just be mountain fever?" Fee persisted.

The women laughed. "Not likely," Mrs. Gould said patiently. "Mountain fever knocks you down flat. Babies just keep you a bit off center for a while." She turned to Elsie and said, "Looks like we all might have to pitch in and help out a bit with the Slead children. I wouldn't mind having your little one ride along with me."

"And your other little girl is just about Sarah's age. They can play together in my wagon," Rachel offered.

"It's probably all for the best, Elsie," Mrs. Gould said. "This babe is a gift. A consolation in your grief."

Elsie smiled through her tears and turned back to her washing. "I'm grateful for your help," she said softly.

"Just make sure you're near a midwife come January," Mrs. Gould added.

Water dripped from the wagon after they crossed the Snake River, leaving a dark trail in the dust as they continued on. Fee walked beside the wagon, over the gentle hills, dragging her feet through the dry thistles and grass, smelling their sharp, sweet scent and trying not to think about the burning sun throbbing on her head. Grasshoppers flew up in front of her feet in clacking clouds. Step by step she was getting closer to the Blue Mountains. Step by step she was getting closer to her new home—wherever it may be. For now, she was in Oregon.

The trail wound through barren hills that rose sharply on both sides, then gave way to gentle, rolling land, only to go back into sharply rising hills once more. All along just when they would begin to fear that they'd never see water again, they caught glimpses of the Snake or some small nearly dry creekbed, something to reassure them and give them the courage to continue on through the oppressive, dry heat.

One night as Fee was dipping her bucket into the gravel of a stream to get water for dinner, Grandpa Gibson came by with Ezekial. The men had become fast friends, although Grandpa was the elder by about twenty years. She admired them both, finding a comfort in their company that eased the sorrowing ache left by her father's death.

"What're we heading into tomorrow?" she asked Ezekial as he splashed his face in the stream.

He snorted water, dried his face on his neckerchief, then tied it back around his neck. "There's Cow Hollar comin' up. Right up a long, steep draw, then down again. After that we got Farewell Bend, where we'll camp. Say good-bye to the old Snake."

"How long till the Blues?"

"Coupl'a weeks."

"Middle of August. Think we'll hit snow?"

He squinted at the rose-colored horizon, watching where the sun set. "Hard to imagine snow when the sun bakes you alive. Still, there's no telling."

Grandpa Gibson sat down on a rock and tamped his pipe. "I tell you," he said with a wink at Fee, "baking alive or no, I'm mighty glad to be here. I was afraid I might miss out on this one. Born too late for the Revolution, but my pa fought in it. Country's been burstin' at the seams ever since. We moved out West when west was t'other side'a Pennsylvania. Then that got too crowded for Pa and we moved to Kentucky. Then we headed on to the Ohio River Valley, and my pa died with his eyes looking west. I took up from there and followed the sun to Illinois and Missouri, each time breaking the land and leaving it better than I found it. Saw each one become a state."

He shook his head with a wistful smile. "Now, once we hit Missouri, Ma said she wasn't going to move no more. So we stayed there, raising our brood and making a good life. All the time I saw these young 'uns taking off and heading west, going to conquer the last frontier, and here I was sitting, missing the whole shebang. When she died two years ago, God rest her soul, it was Eustace what first brought up the subject. It helped me break the mourning. If these youngsters were willing to take up and go west and shoulder the burden of an old man with young dreams"—he paused here to puff on his pipe—"why, I'm mighty glad I made it to Oregon. This state here touches the Pacific Ocean. Don't know that I'll see it, but it's gratifying knowing that I've seen the country stretched from sea to sea and been part of it."

In spite of their barren appearance, the hills sustained herds of pronghorn antelope, elk, and mule deer as well as jackrabbits, quail, sage hens, and other small game. Nathanial got fresh meat for the train almost daily. That meant that their campfire usually rang with stories and laughter, because Ezekial and Jacob were not about to miss out on Fee's cooking.

These were times that Fee would always cherish. Ezekial would spin yarns about his years as a mountain man. When he paused for a breath, Jacob would talk of the books he'd read or dreams they shared. Fee's spirit was sustained by her three men.

In some ways Ezekial filled the void left by her father's death, and Jacob was a wonderful companion, a kindred spirit she could share ideas and dreams with. Their campfire was

110

never quiet, and Fee was grateful to have such good friends. Besides, Nathanial wasn't much for conversation.

It was Nathanial's reticence that was causing Fee the most grief. Everything would be just perfect if not for that. She had no idea how he really felt, aside from what he'd said the night of the storm. Why didn't he tell her again that he loved her? She felt he did, but never hearing him say the words worried her. Why didn't he tell her he wanted to stay with her forever? She could see the warmth in his eyes when he looked at her across the fire. But now she needed more.

When he was gone, as he often was, either scouting or hunting, she felt empty and frightened. When he rode into view, her heart leapt and her throat tightened. She loved to watch him working, his strong muscles moving beneath his shirt. She loved to see him laughing at one of Ezekial's jokes or intently listening to Jacob's well-reasoned arguments. Still, what she wanted most was to hear him tell her he needed her as much as she needed him. And he wasn't much for talking.

They had begun to catch glimpses of the Blue Mountains, looming in the distance like the purple shadows of sleeping giants. They strained to see if there was snow on the peaks, but they would have to wait until after Farewell Bend.

Ezekial was right about Cow Hollow. Although the trail wound around the shoulder and stayed in the lowest places, it was still a long pull up the incline. Since Nathanial was out hunting again, Phineas and Grandpa Gibson came and helped put their shoulders to Fee's wagon. Once on top, she went back down and returned the favor. Thus it was that their wagons were the last to start down the other side, another steep-sloping, long incline.

The air was hot and heavy and the sky a milky blue. As they stopped at the top to catch their breath before the descent, flies buzzed around their heads with sticky persistence. Fee noticed that they clung inside the wagon cover the same way they used to cling to the walls of her house before a storm.

"Might be picking up to rain," Grandpa Gibson said.

"Flies seem to think so," she agreed.

Phineas led the way down, with Patience and the children walking ahead. Fee waited, letting her eyes wander across the taffy-colored hills covered with grass and thistles and dotted with gray-green sagebrush. A hawk circled lazily in the sky. She started her team down the incline, watching carefully that the strain was not too much on the two wheeler mules.

Just then Phineas shouted. A wheel had caught in a badger hole, and his wagon was tipping over. She watched helplessly as the wagon slowly fell and Grandpa Gibson scrambled to get out of the way, only to stumble and fall. With a mournful creak and a crash the wagon toppled, crushing the old man under its load.

Fee shouted, turning her team off the trail, and stopping the wagon sideways on the slope. Then, quickly unhitching the team, she drove them down to the Gibson wagon. Phineas rigged a hitch to the toggle lines. Then Fee signaled her team and they pulled the wagon upright. Tying the reins, she left them standing and ran to see how Grandpa Gibson was.

Patience was cradling his head in her lap. A crimson thread of blood came from the corner of his mouth. His eyes were closed.

"Is he? . . ." Fee asked.

"No, he's still breathing."

Fee bit her lip to keep from crying. "Here comes Dr. Breckenridge."

The doctor checked Grandpa carefully, probing his body with gentle skill. Finally he turned to Phineas and said, "There's a broken leg, but that's not what worries me. He's hurt inside—bleeding—and there's not much I can do. He'll have to heal himself. Let me set the leg and we'll get him in the wagon, then see what happens when we make camp."

"Do you think he'll . . ." Patience started to cry softly before she could finish the question.

He shook his head. "Don't know. It's not good."

"Your wheel broke off when it went over," Fee said to Phineas. "I'll fix a bed in my wagon and bring it over for him."

Fee made the bed, and they placed Grandpa Gibson on it. Although he was unconscious, she went as slowly and as gently as she dared. Fee slept in the tent with Nathanial that night rather than move Grandpa Gibson.

"Do you think he'll die?" Fee asked, fighting back the tears as she and Nathanial lay on their bedroll.

"He's a tough old man. We can always hope," he said, putting his arm around her. With that Fee knew Nathanial held very little hope himself, and she tried hard to swallow the lump that was filling her throat.

The sky released slow, fat raindrops to plop heavily on the

canvas over their heads. The air smelled ginger fresh and Nathanial's breathing became steady beside her. She crawled out of the tent and went to keep watch over Grandpa Gibson.

The next day they went on, although he had not regained consciousness. Two hours away from Farewell Bend, Patience emerged from the wagon, crying. Grandpa had died.

Fee helped Charity and Patience lay out the body. "I never got to lay my own daddy out in a proper way. Maybe this will help make it up to him," Fee explained.

Using Nathanial's razor, she shaved him while Patience and Charity bathed his body. They used a strip of sheeting to tie his chin, placed a coin on each of his eyes, then carefully wrapped him in a quilt his wife had made. Ezekial and Nathanial carried the body from the wagon. Phineas made a coffin from the sideboards of their wagon, and Eustace chiseled Grandpa's name and dates on a rock. That night they sat around the coffin, singing Grandpa's favorite hymns. Fee played her flute because Phineas said that's what he would have liked.

The next morning they stood around the new grave and Ezekial spoke a few words about his friend. "It's hard to say good-bye," he said after much throat-clearing, "but if we've got to do it, 'spose a place called Farewell Bend is as good as any. Grandpa Gibson was a good man and we'll all miss him." He paused and looked across the bend of the river, squinting against the morning sun and his own tears. "But he died happy. Miz Coughlin here can attest to that. He told us, 'I made it to Oregon.'" He stopped and looked down at the ground, shaking his head. Phineas read a few verses from his Bible, and it was done.

Within half an hour Ezekial's clarion voice was calling, "Wagons ho!" As they pulled out, Fee turned in her wagon seat and looked back at the solitary rock standing on the knoll above the riverbank. The river wound gracefully through the land like a great silver serpent sleeping in the sunlight. A blue heron stood on its stilt legs, fishing in the backwaters while swallows executed their aerial dance overhead. It was a place Grandpa Gibson would have loved. "Farewell," she whispered, then turned and faced West.

The farther they traveled, the more frequently the train had to lay over for rest and repair. Now was one of those times.

Nathanial, Ezekial, and Jacob all had gone off hunting and

scouting the trail through the Blue Mountains. Left on her own while the others were busy with their families and various chores, Fee wandered along the tiny stream near the camp. Maybe it was just her sorrowing for her own family, but she wanted to be alone. She missed her father and Matthew. She missed her home.

They had camped in a relatively flat spot between the rolling hills, but after following the stream for about two miles Fee discovered a small, hidden canyon with rock walls rising abruptly on each side.

Foliage was sparse, offering little shade from the broiling sun. Sharp-scented sage brushed against her shoulder, and the scrubby rabbit brush with its thin, pale leaves scratched her ankles. Gnarled and twisted juniper trees, stunted by the harsh climate, leaned over the small trickle of water. A green-black magpie sat on top of a juniper and flipped its long tail as it gave a harsh call. From a tree across the stream came a single piping note, a solitary bird hidden in its branches. Enchanted by all the unexpected activity, Fee sat down on a rock in the shade of a juniper to watch.

The afternoon sun was so hot she untied her Indian boots, pulled up her skirt, and trailed her toes in the water. Gray-blue juniper berries hung from the branch over her head. She picked some, bit one, shuddered at its bitter turpentine taste, and threw the rest into the stream.

She looked down at the clear, cool water running over her feet. There was something shining in the water. Curious, she leaned down and picked it up. It was a rock about the size of a walnut, but much heavier. She held it up to the light, marveling that it gleamed like gold. Gold! Could it be? She bit it. Her teeth left marks. Did that mean anything? She kneeled down, moved the gravel around, and within an hour found three smaller nuggets and one larger one.

How could she find out if it really was gold? And if it was, what would she do? There wasn't enough here for everyone on the train. No, she'd have to keep it to herself.

Maybe Nathanial would know what to do. She glanced around at the sharply rising hills and barren rock. He'd want to stay and send her on ahead, insisting this was no place for a woman. He'd be half right about that. No, she couldn't tell Nathanial.

If only she could stay long enough to gather a few more nuggets. Added to her dwindling cache of funds from the sale of the farm, she could set herself up well in Oregon—buy the equipment she needed, maybe even make some investments. But was this really gold? She set to searching the gravel for more after she dropped the nuggets in one of her socks. If it *was* gold, she'd find out soon enough. For now, she would gather as many as she could find.

By dusk she had filled the bottom of her stocking with shiny rocks. She made her way back to camp, grateful that no one had noticed her absence. Tomorrow they would still be camped here, so she could go back upstream on the pretense of searching for some kind of plant or picking flowers—and she'd spend the day sifting through that streambed. She'd take her washpan along; maybe she could pan for gold, like they did in California. She went to sleep that night, her mind filled with plans for the gold—if it really was gold.

It was a good sign. The next morning she awakened to find that Penny had delivered a healthy heifer calf—just what Fee needed to carry out her plans. Beauty would drop her calf within the month. Fee smiled, watching the wobbly-legged calf nuzzle its mother for milk. Then she gathered dry grass to place in the bed of the farm wagon so the calf could ride the first few days and over the rough parts of the remainder of the trail.

She grabbed some cold venison, a piece of bread, and her small washbasin and headed out of the camp. She told Mrs. Gould she was going to look for wild berries.

The place in the stream where she'd found the nuggets was farther up the canyon than she'd remembered, but she had no trouble finding it. She spent the rest of the day sifting through the gravel and picking out shining rocks. Her only company was a shy doe that ventured down with her half-grown fawn to get a drink.

When the sunlight slanted through the juniper trees, telling her it was late afternoon, Fee stopped. The stocking was nearly full. Hefting it, she guessed she had nearly ten pounds of—whatever it was.

The men came back that night dirty and tired, carrying two fat deer. Over dinner they regaled Fee with their descriptions of the Blue Mountains. There was considerable argument as to whether the huckleberries would be ripe by the time they got there. Jacob had found some wild plums ripening along a ravine. They had high hopes of feasting before long.

115

"Columbia has people thick as fleas on a hound," Ezekial said. "We ran into a couple of fellows who were on their way there. Said there was a gold rush going on to the east, in Washington Territory."

"Like the one in California?" Fee asked, her interest suddenly piqued.

"Can't tell. Gold seekers'll take off at the first scent of gold. Could be a big one, or could be a bust. Whatever, there's a lot heading out to get their part of it."

Fee stole a glance at Nathanial but couldn't tell if he was interested in this or not. She was afraid his wanderlust would strike and he'd take off to find gold himself. "How do they know it's really gold?" she asked.

"Oh, they can take it into an assay office to make sure, but most—well, they knows."

"My great-uncle used to deal in gold," Jacob volunteered. "If I stumble on some, I won't have any trouble telling. And I wouldn't take it to any assay office, I can tell you," he added.

Nathanial nodded. "It'd bring out the ticks, all right."

"What do you mean?"

"Word spreads, and when it has to do with gold, it spreads instant," Ezekial said. "You'd never git back to your claim without a hundred claim jumpers clinging to your back."

"I imagine this is just a small run, gone in a few months," Nathanial said, spearing another piece of venison. "We'll know for sure when we hit the Columbia."

Fee remained silent for the rest of the meal, her mind spinning in a confusion of hope and fear. Should she ask Jacob if it was gold she'd found? She felt she could trust him. Of the three men, she felt that Jacob most of all shared her dreams and hopes for the future. But would he understand this? She'd have to confess her fears about Nathanial deciding to stay here without her. Would he keep her secret? Nathanial and he were awfully good friends.

She'd just finished cleaning up when one of the Gibson children came for Nathanial. They had an ox with a lame foot and needed someone to help throw him down while they fixed it. When he left, Fee seized her chance.

Looking around the circle of wagons, she found Jacob sitting alone, mending his bridle by lanternlight.

"Jacob, I need your advice," she began.

"Why, Fee, it'd be a privilege."

Relieved at his warm response and the friendship in his

eyes, she relaxed a bit. "You'll have to come back to my wagon. There's something I want to show you."

As they walked, she tried to explain about Nathanial's wanderlust and her worry about his taking off before she'd settled in. She didn't admit anything else, but Jacob seemed to understand and was sympathetic.

"That's why this has to be a secret just between you and me," she said stopping at the wagon. "Please sit down there by the lantern and try not to show any surprise when you look at this." She reached into the back of the wagon and pulled out her sock full of rocks.

Curiosity shone in Jacob's eyes as he took the sock. But when he looked in, his expression froze. Taking one of the rocks out, he turned his back to the camp, set the rock on the table, and examined it closely in the lanternlight. After scraping it with his knife, he looked up at her, "Where did you find this?"

"Is it what I think?"

"It is, if you think it's a nugget of pure gold."

"I found it not far from here. There's no time for me to get any more out. I suspect there's quite a bit more. But I don't dare tell Nathanial. He's just the kind to get gold fever and forget why we really came out here," she explained in a rush. "This kind of windfall doesn't set you up for life unless you use it to build on. You just can't abandon your plans for it."

"I admire your common sense." Jacob smiled. "How about a partner?"

"What do you mean?"

"Tomorrow morning you show me where you found these. I'll go on with the train through the Blue Mountains. Then I'll claim to have gotten bit by the gold bug, which is pretty much true," he added with a grin. "I'll outfit myself up at The Dalles and come back here, spend a year getting what I can from the claim. Since you found it, it's half yours. When I come out, I'll find you and pay you your half."

"How will you find me?"

"Two ways. I know where Ezekial's settling, and I'm sure he'll know where you are. Better yet, I have family funds that have been forwarded to the Ladd and Tilton Bank in Portland. You leave word there where I can find you. If they don't know where you are, I'll set up an account in your name and make a deposit. Within a year to a year and a half you can go to Portland and claim your account. How's that sound?"

Fee thought about it for a minute and then smiled at him.

"It's more than I'd get otherwise. I'll give you the largest of these nuggets to outfit with; the rest I'll use to set myself up in the Willamette Valley." She held her hand out to him. "It's a deal." She paused for a moment, then added, "Could you please put it in my maiden name, Fionna Barry?"

"Whatever you think is best. Would you like your new partner to sign something?"

Fee studied him for a moment. His dark brown eyes were clear and his angular face handsome. He was a good, smart man, and she instinctively trusted him. She smiled. "No need. Your word is good enough."

"I'll spend my life living up to that trust, Fionna," he promised.

According to the odometer attached to Fee's wagon wheel, they'd gone 1,627 miles from Independence, Missouri in the past four months. Now they were approaching one of the most dangerous parts of their trip and one of the last. Within another month Fee hoped to find herself in her new home, wherever it might be.

They stopped and rested at the top of Flagstaff Hill, taking time to catch their breath. Below them the hills opened to the lush Powder River valley bordered on the other side by the Blue Mountains. Fee saw snow on some of the peaks, and her heart sank.

"Don't worry none," Ezekial said when she pointed it out to him, "no trail goes that high. We keep low down."

The climb down was tortuous, but the Powder River ran through the valley like a welcome presence. They camped by it that night and the next morning set out across the valley. On their left were the ominous Blue Mountains and to their right a huge range of jagged sawtoothed peaks.

"Wallowas," Ezekial said when she asked about the other mountains. "Them's wild mountains, little lady. Hain't no one wants to go there." Fee nodded. The Blues with their sharp snow-streaked peaks looked inviting by comparison.

In the next few days the trail started to climb gradually, gently taking them along the foothills of the massive mountains. They continued up the canyon and camped that night. When she awoke the next morning, Fee found a crust of ice on her water bucket. It seemed an ominous sign. Still it was glorious to see trees again, pines, firs, alder, all kinds of trees. The higher they climbed, the more evergreens there were, towering tall and stately above them. Then the canyon walls got steeper and jagged rocks jutted overhead.

The weather was clear and the nights cold but Ezekial said they had time, so they didn't push the animals, choosing to camp along the river bank and take occasional rests rather than lose stock this close to the end.

When they finally reached the top they stopped to gaze at the spectacular view below—a rich, lush valley about twenty miles in diameter. The towering amethystine Blue Mountains circled the valley like a crown. A silver ribbon of river meandered through it. The Grande Ronde, the French trappers had called it. And grand it was.

Then, they slowly began the murderous, twisting descent into the valley. Trail-experienced, they made it with no mishap.

They rested in the valley and then headed out over the last range of the Blue Mountains to the Columbia River.

Once they left the mountains, the trail wandered over straw-colored hills for endless miles until Fee thought she would never see the Columbia River. When she did, it took her breath away.

It was not as large as the Missouri, but somehow more imposing. Its mighty waters flowed between the soaring gold-colored hills of the Washington Territory and the vast lands of Oregon. Rocks jutted into the surging waters, towering cliffs rose above the banks, and timbered islands dissected its flow. Even sea gulls flew above its great expanse. Fee was finally nearing her destination.

Just as impressive to the emigrants who'd been on the trail for more than four months was the amount of activity they saw. A steam-powered ferry churned upriver, puffing black clouds of smoke. Trappers paddled fur-laden canoes, entrepreneurs ferried goods on rough-hewn rafts, and Indians speared the waters for fish.

They stopped at The Dalles, a little hamlet that had grown at the point where emigrants either chose the water route down the Columbia River or the Barlow Toll Road around the shoulder of formidable Mount Hood. Either way had its hazards. The tolls for the road were cheaper, but it took much longer. The rates for the portages and ferryboats were exorbitant, but travelers would get to Portland within one to three days.

The Gibsons and several other families who had arrived with herds of livestock would be taking the road. Fee was loath to spend the extra money on the ferries until she knew how much her land was going to cost.

Before they all parted company there was one last celebration. Wesley Fleming found an itinerant preacher in The Dalles and obtained permission to marry Minnie Gould. Everyone pitched in, offering food from their meager stores for the wedding. Even townsfolk joined in, welcoming the chance for a party.

Fee watched the wedding plans with mixed feelings. She was happy for the young couple, yet torn by her own situation. Their sanctioned marriage suddenly made her "arrangement" with Nathanial seem dangerously temporary. How would he respond to the wedding of their two young friends? Would he see the advantages of marriage? On the other hand, what were they, really? It was all too confusing. She turned her attention to matters more easily resolved.

After Jacob announced he was leaving to search for gold, he and Fee made their plans. Fee gave him her two gentlest mules, went over his provisions, checked his map, and made him promise not to take unnecessary chances. When Jacob was all packed, they joined Ezekial and Nathanial at the wedding party.

Nathanial and Cameron Gartner, one of the four bachelors, were teasing Wesley. "It's your last chance," Cameron said. "In another hour you'll be a married man. You can still cut and run."

"Or say good-bye to freedom," Nathanial said with a laugh.

Fee swallowed hard and sat down beside Ezekial.

"You know they're just kidding around, don't you?" Ezekial asked. "He don't mean nothing by it. Leastwise not against you."

Fee forced a smile. "I know." She glanced at the sky. "She's a lucky bride, the sun's shining on her."

"We're all pretty lucky," Ezekial said. "I found old Milton Blakely here, wandering the streets like a lost dog. He's a fiddle player who has the spread next to my claim in the Willamette Valley."

Milton's face reminded Fee of a hound dog, with sorrowful brown eyes and long jowls. Even his hat brim drooped in a woebegone manner. "Why are you here instead of on your farm, Mr. Blakely?" she asked.

He shook his head mournfully, "Ah, farming's gone and lost its heart. Produce what used to get good money now cain't be given away. Politicians and newspapers say stick it out. I can't eat if 'n I do. I just walked off and left it. They say there's gold out there, and I'm going to find me some."

It turned out that Milton had a wealth of information about gold-mining and little else. He was stuck in The Dalles until he could scrape together enough money to get himself a grubstake and transportation to the mines.

Fee listened to them talking, considering the situation. "What's his farm like?" she quietly asked Ezekial.

"A good one. I wanted it but he'd already staked his claim." He took a stick and began to draw in the dirt at their feet, showing Fee the relationship between the two home-steads. "Problem is, they're both a long ways from Salem—twelve miles for Milton here and near seventeen for me. Some folks think that's a drawback. For me, I want my elbow room."

"But the roads are good enough for you to get your produce into town?"

"Sure, 'less the weather stops you by washing them out or flooding."

"And Salem's the state capital?"

" 'Tis now."

"Tell me more about your farm, Mr. Blakely," Fee said, turning to him.

It took some prodding because the man had long ago lost interest in farming, but she learned he had a cabin, three cleared fields, a small orchard that wouldn't produce for a while yet, and a shed for sheltering his livestock before he'd sold them all. There was a large wooded hill behind the orchard with a spring. He'd cleaned out the streambed that the spring flowed through and directed it so it ran near the cabin, providing water. A yearround creek flowed through the property about one hundred yards below the house. He'd planned on using the water to get a garden producing this summer but had lost heart.

"What are you going to do with it now that you're going prospecting?"

"Let it rot, for all I care. 'Cain't sell it. Farm prices so low, no one would look at a place so far from town."

"What price were you asking for it?"

"I asked twenty dollars an acre for the full three hundred and twenty acres. Would've taken ten. They wouldn't even bargain. Just laughed."

"I'll pay you ten dollars an acre," Fee said.

Nathanial and Ezekial both stared open-mouthed at her. "You want in on the bargaining?" Ezekial asked Nathanial.

Fee smiled sweetly. "Nathanial said I can do whatever will make me happy because this is my inheritance and dowry money."

Nathanial swallowed hard and nodded. "That's right. When you've got a smart horse, you give it the rein. Same with a smart woman." Fee had to give him credit; he was quick-thinking even when surprised.

Milton Blakely looked as if Fee had waved a magic wand in front of him. "Cash out?" he said, his voice cracking.

"Yes, if you're willing to draw up a document and have it witnessed, giving me full ownership of your property. It will be in government coin—and some gold. Is that all right?"

He barely took time to answer before running off to find a town official who could draw up the transfer.

"You think it's wise buying it sight unseen?" Nathanial asked quietly.

"It's right next to Ezekial's place. He says it's good land. I trust his judgment. From Mr. Blakely's description it'll fit my needs. Do you mind?" she added with sudden concern.

"It's your place, Fee. This is what you set out to do. I'm glad to see you do it."

Fee went back to her wagon and took her father's steel box and her treasure stocking from their hiding places. She would still have some gold left. Then a thought struck her. The deed must be drawn up in her name, not Nathanial's.

She found Milton Blakely talking to the storekeeper, who was writing laboriously as Milton dictated. "Oh, you're just in time," Milton said. "Who am I selling to?"

"The name is Fionna Barry," she said in a clear voice. "Will this gentleman be good enough to witness the signing and exchange of funds?"

"Sure will. He'll be getting a part of the money in exchange for the things I've had him lay by for my grubstake."

Moments later Fee was the proud owner of her own farm. To be extra secure, she took the deed and had Ezekial sign it as well. Luckily, Ezekial was checking the description of the property so carefully, he didn't even notice that Fee's name wasn't Coughlin.

They were in time to witness the wedding ceremony. Fee's heart beat in her throat as she watched Nathanial's taciturn face instead of the radiant bride's.

PART II

THE LAND

Chapter XI

It cost Fee a small fortune, over sixty dollars, to get passage for her livestock, two wagons, and herself plus pay the extra charges for portage around the rough Cascades on a tiny railroad pulled by mules. Nevertheless, in her mind, it was worth it. She was on her way to her new home. And Nathanial was still with her.

Lemuell Slead left the night before, leaving his family to go with the Goulds on the Barlow Toll Road while he went off to the Washington Territory to search for gold. Fee was shocked that any man would leave his small children and pregnant wife to chase after some rumor of gold, but she wasn't surprised that Lemuell Slead did. He was no man in her eyes.

They said good-bye to Jacob at the ferry landing. As the ferry pulled away from the bank they could see him at the top of the road with the two mules behind him. Would they ever see him again? It was dangerous in eastern Oregon at any time, deadly in the winter. Suddenly Fee wished she'd never told him about the gold.

Once on the ferry, after months of jostling and jolting, pervasive grime and dust, relentless clangor and jangle, all noise ceased. Suddenly they could hear only the swishing of the cool river around the raft. A strange lassitude overcame them. After months of struggle and fear, there was nothing to do but sit with numbed emotions and watch the beauty unfold around them.

They left the dry, pale-gold hills behind. The river flowed through canyons jutting with gray boulders and towering black symmetrical rock columns. Pines, willows, and thick green underbrush lined the banks. Silver waterfalls cascaded over fern-laced bluffs, and mammoth pine and fir trees seemed to touch the cloud-scudded sky. Cool, willow-spiced air caressed their faces and cleansed their dusty hearts with its sweetness.

Ezekial asked Fee to get out her flute. After finding it, she wearily blew a single lonely note, then softly played, as much for herself as for the other trail-worn travelers resting on the deck of the ferry. Soon her haunting melodies touched their hearts. Even the men's eyes filled with tears of homesickness and relief in the knowledge that they'd survived the hazardous journey.

Through her music Fee was able to express the inexpressible joy and sorrow that they all felt at the conclusion of their journey. The beauty of melodies from home nourished their starving souls and raised them above their mean situation.

Then she played happy tunes, and the passengers smiled and tapped their toes, looking with bright eyes at the wonders around them. Ezekial winked and whispered, "Good instincts," and Nathanial laughed out loud.

They pulled into the town of Portland as the sun was setting over the broad river, painting the water in a wash of ruby and amber, lavishly outlining the trees on Sauvie Island in gold.

The population of the town was over three thousand, and Fee was overwhelmed by the bustle. She'd forgotten there could be so many people in one place doing so many different things.

The first order of business was to find a stable for the stock and a hotel for themselves. That night Fee and Nathanial ate under a roof for the first time in four and a half months.

It was over dinner that they heard the war news. There'd been a big battle at Bull Run, Virginia. The government forces had been defeated terribly by the rebels. Lincoln was blockading all shipping to the Southern states. Eleven states had seceded, calling themselves the Confederate States of America, and had chosen Jefferson Davis as their president. It was going to be a long and bloody war.

The transcontinental telegraph would be completed within a month, and soon they would be hearing news from the East Coast that was no more than a week old. Nathanial and Fee felt as if they'd just entered a foreign country and were trying to learn everything about it in an evening.

They paid extra so they could each have a hot bath. Fee basked in the luxury of the sled-shaped copper tub until the water turned cold. The lamp was turned low, and Nathanial was already in bed when she tiptoed in. She slipped into bed and pulled the comforter up to her shoulders. The clean sheets were cool, but Nathanial felt warm to her touch. Careful not to awaken him, she gently kissed his forehead and turned out the lamp. A soft September rain brushed the windowpanes.

"Is that any way to celebrate our arrival?" he asked softly, then pulled her to him.

Fee's first stop the next morning was Ladd and Tilton Bank in downtown Portland. She deposited her gold with the banker, saying she'd brought it out from Virginia. Then, obtaining a letter of credit from the bank, she began her shopping. She wanted to have all the equipment she needed before setting out for her new home. Assured that she could get her dry goods and lumber in Salem, she was ready to leave by the end of the week.

Poor Fitz-James was shocked to find himself pulling a loaded wagon once more, but he threw his weight into it and they made the forty-mile journey to Salem, camping one night along the Williamette River and arriving in the afternoon of the second day. While Nathanial found a hotel room, Fee went to the authorities to register her purchase of Blakely's farm. Once that was accomplished, she breathed more easily and set about her last-minute shopping.

Farm prices were low, so stocking up for the coming winter months was inexpensive. However, dry goods were the going price. Fee bought bolts of material, thread, needles, and pins from a storekeeper who told her how to find Quail Hollow. With his written instructions carefully tucked under her pillow like a precious talisman, she and Nathanial spent their last night under someone else's roof.

Before departing, she left word for Dr. and Mrs. Breckenridge and for Minnie and Wesley Fleming. Both couples were planning to settle in Salem. Wesley might need work when he arrived, and Fee had it for him.

The Willamette River Valley was all she'd hoped it would be. The farms may have been suffering from temporarily depressed prices, but she knew that wouldn't always be the case.

Two mountain ranges, the Cascades and the Coast Range, bordered the long, lush valley on the east and the west. Roads dissected the rich land, and steamers and boats plied the Willamette between Salem and Portland. The flatlands were either cleared into neat, prosperous farms or thickly covered with brush, oak, and evergreen trees, harboring deer, raccoons, opossum, bear, and other wildlife. Creeks and brooks jumping with trout and salmon flowed into the Willamette.

As they drove down the road toward her new home, she watched fat cows grazing in green pastures and hawks circling lazily in the sky.

Yes, Fee thought, *I'm going to like it here.*

When it seemed they should be nearing the farm, they stopped at a small cabin to ask directions. A surly man put his shovel down and came to the fence.

"Can you tell us how far to the old Blakely place?" Nathanial asked.

" 'Bout five miles down yonder. Ain't no reason to go there, though. Blakely got the right idea and gave it up."

"He sold it to us. We're your new neighbors. I'm Nathanial Coughlin, and this here's Fionna."

The man's eyes showed new interest. "Bought it, eh? Been thinkin' of selling my spread. Got eighty acres, but only twelve broke. Know anyone who'd be interested?"

Fee cast a calculating eye over the tiny cabin and shabbily kept yard. "I paid ten dollars an acre for the Blakely place," she said. "In time I might consider adding to it. Keep me in mind if you decide to sell."

He eyed her and said, "Ten dollars is below market. I might dicker with you."

Fee looked him squarely in the eye. "I'm neither interested nor willing to make any decisions for some time yet, Mister—?"

"Lawton. Frank Lawton. That there's my woman, Velina," he said, pointing to a worn-looking woman in the doorway who was holding a baby to her breast.

Fee nodded in her direction, then said, "We better get going. It was nice meeting you folks."

Nathanial lingered behind, asking about the hunting. But Fee was so anxious she couldn't wait. She flicked the reins and started towards her new home. And her heart sang because Nathanial had said *we're* your new neighbors.

So many times she'd tried to picture what it would look like. From the map Ezekial had drawn in the dirt, she'd gotten a fairly clear picture of the lay of the land, but because she'd spoken only with men, no one told her what the house was like. She didn't expect anything like her father's home, but she hoped for more than one room . . . for a real floor instead of dirt . . . and for Nathanial to like it.

After climbing a slight rise she stopped to survey her land. A covey of quail scurried across the road in front of her. The place was aptly named. From the shelter of the blackberry vines the quail shot a single note of complaint at her intrusion. A stream flowed around the bottom of the knoll, complete with a sturdy log bridge. A split rail fence zigzagged around the front pasture. The grass was high. She'd have to mow it right away. Twelve small trees stood in neat rows behind the cabin. It was a log cabin, about twenty by fifteen feet, with real glass windows. A small log building with one side open to the elements stood to the west of the house. Obviously the barn and unsatisfactory. There'd be a good deal of work to do before winter set in, but it wasn't bad.

She flicked the reins and went down the hill to the house. A familiar rattle told her that Nathanial had caught up with her. She turned in the seat to wave and he stood up, waving his hat happily over his head. *If only he likes it as well as I do,* she thought nervously. *If only he wants to stay . . .*

They left the animals in their traces while they checked the yard and the side pasture. Nathanial agreed that they should mow the front pasture for hay, so they decided to put the stock in the side pasture for now.

The barn was badly in need of a floor, enlarging, enclosing, and general repair. Fee smiled as Nathanial started planning how it should be done.

She found the spring ditch that went by the house and tasted the water. It was clear and cool, sweeter than any water she'd ever tasted in her life—and it was hers. She had started towards the cabin when Nathanial called to her.

"Wait," he said, running up. "You can't go in like that." Laughing, he picked her up and carried her over the threshold into the house, then kissed her tenderly. "Now you've entered your home properly," he said as her feet touched the floor.

Fee rested her head against his shoulder as she looked around. Dust danced in the column of afternoon sunlight slanting through the windows. A large stone fireplace dominated the room. Built into the stone to one side was an oven, its rusty door left slightly ajar. Much to Fee's relief, she was standing on a puncheon floor made from twenty foot logs hewn in half. It was only one room, but large enough to be divided if she wanted. A bedstead made from peeled poles with tied rope for a mattress stood in one corner. A homemade table and chair were on the other side of the room. A washbasin hung on the wall next to a shelf holding a coffee pot, three plates, and two cups.

"Look, they're not tin," Fee exclaimed happily, blowing a spider out of one of the white cups.

"There's some wood cut out by the door," Nathanial said as he began cleaning out the fireplace and checking the chimney. "What do you say to a porch?"

"Oh, it'd be lovely, real homelike. Oh, Nathanial, tell me honestly, what do you think?"

"I think I've got me a pretty shrewd little woman. This looks to be a good bit of land. With a little fixing up, we'll have a nice place."

"'We'? Then you'll stay?" she asked almost breathlessly.

He stood up and looked at her for a moment, then nodded. "At least until we get this place in order. Just seeing those mountains makes my feet itch, but after we've come this far together and lived out of a wagon for so long, I know I'll want a place to come back to whenever I do leave."

Fee smiled so hard she thought she'd burst. "As long as I've a roof over my head, you'll have a place to come home to."

His gray eyes were soft and loving as he pulled her into his arms and held her. "Fionna," he finally whispered as he bent to kiss her ear, "I'm a lucky man to find a woman like you who understands."

A month later, Wesley Fleming rode up. "I got your letter, Miz Coughlin," he said, dropping his reins and walking over to where Fee was sweeping out the newly remodeled barn. "You got some work for me, I sure can use it. Minnie's got herself a job at the wool mill in Salem, but I can't find anything." His thin face was drawn with concern.

"It's wonderful to see you, Wesley," Fee said, wiping her hands on her apron before shaking his outstretched hand. "Nathanial's out in the field, but he'll come in when he spots your horse. Let's sit down over there and talk," she said, pointing to a fallen log beside the rail fence.

"Where are you living, Wesley?"

"Minnie's folks are renting a little farm outside Salem. We're boarding with them until we find something of our own. That's one reason I got to get a job. Another is . . . well"—he blushed profusely under his brown beard—"well, it's like this, Minnie's going to have a baby and she won't be able to keep working much after the first of the year."

Fee laughed. "Congratulations. You'll be a fine father."

"Not if I don't get a job. Do you have something?"

"I want to build a creamery over there. Nathanial laid it out, but we need someone to help build it. Then, if my plans work out, I'll need someone around to help out. It's more than one man can do and you know Nathanial's itchy feet."

"Sounds good. I been looking at the stores, and there's not much fresh dairy produce available. Even with bad prices you'd make a nice bit with your sweet butter."

"I'm thinking of cheese, Wesley. Did you see any in the stores?"

"Not that I can remember. But Miz Coughlin . . . there's, well, there's still a problem. It takes the better part of a day to get out here and, well, I can't just up and leave Minnie for very long. I mean, we've only been married a little while and—"

"I've thought of that, Wesley. We won't be ready to start the creamery for at least another two weeks. I'll commission you to round up the building materials in town. Once we start, I think I might be able to move you and Minnie out here."

Wesley's face lit up. "Oh, Miz Coughlin, if—howdy, Nathanial." He jumped up as Nathanial rode up on Seneca. "Your wife was just telling me your plans. I'd be mighty glad to be working with you folks again."

"It's hard times, Wesley. Friends got to stick together," Nathanial said. "Come on in for a cup of coffee."

Later, as Fee was drying the dishes, Nathanial asked her, "Do you think you can actually buy Lawton's place?"

"They looked desperate. It's a dry farm with no water. They'll starve if they winter there. Frost's already turned the trees. It's going to be a cold winter. I'll give them enough so they can get out and get a new start in town. It's better for them and a bargain for us." She hung up the dish towel and turned to him. "But I think you'd better deal with him. He's the kind of man who'd try to take advantage of a woman but will listen to another man. Tell him you know there'll be a job opening up at the wool mill," she said with a wink.

"I know," he said, "instincts."

Fee laughed. "I like knowing Ezekial's only a few miles away."

"I think he feels the same."

"Now all we have to do is find him some widow to take care of him."

"Do you ever stop scheming?"

131

*   *   *

Fee's instincts were right. Lawton was desperate to sell and relieved to talk to Nathanial about it. He agreed to sell for twelve dollars an acre for his improved acreage and five dollars an acre for the unimproved, the bargain prices Fee had hoped for. As Fee said, they'd live through the winter and get a new start in town. As Nathanial said, it gave her four hundred acres.

What Fee didn't say was that her funds were dangerously low. She had just enough to pay Wesley for three months' work. By that time she hoped to have some money coming from her cheese, but it was cutting it closer than she liked.

A late October rain was pattering on the roof one night as Fee took a bath in front of the fireplace. Nathanial had gone into Salem to get more nails for the creamery, and she didn't expect him for another hour or so. When she heard him ride up she quickly wrapped a towel around herself and stepped behind the curtain separating the bed from the rest of the room.

"I knew there was a reason for getting home as fast as I could," Nathanial said. He sat down and pulled off his boots. "I was talking to some fellows in town. They said you can get some real nice furs up in the Cascades from November on, so I bought a few traps. Thought I'd go off for a while. You seem to have everything under control here."

"That was our agreement in Independence, wasn't it?" she said softly from behind the curtain. "We're both free to come and go," she added, swallowing the lump in her throat.

"That's my Fee," he said. "Now stop hiding behind the curtains and come to me."

Fee stepped out in her flannel nightgown and wrapped her arms around his waist. "I'm glad you're home," she murmured. "Would you dump the water outside and then we'll go to bed."

She was standing in front of the fire when Nathanial came back in. He paused in the doorway, looking at her. Closing the door quietly behind him, he walked over to her and put his arms around her. "How long have you known?" he asked gently.

"Known what?" she said guiltily.

"I could see your silhouette when you stood in front of the fire. How many more months before the baby comes?"

"Oh, Nathanial," she said, fighting back tears. "I didn't

132

want to tell you. I was afraid you'd think I was trying to keep you here. It's not the way I'd planned it. I knew you'd be going out into the mountains. I figured I could get to Dr. Breckenridge in time if the roads stayed open. But lately, I've been so afraid. Everyone says it's going to be a hard winter. Ezekial says the woolly bear caterpillars have stripes . . ." She stopped and took a deep breath.

"I think I'll move into town by February," she said, hoping she sounded more confident than she felt. "The baby isn't due until April, but sometimes they come early. You don't have to worry. I can take care of myself."

"And what about my child? Will you take care of it, too?"

Fee looked up at Nathanial, scarcely daring to hope. "You mean . . ."

"It's my baby, too. The trapping can wait a year," he said, gently brushing away the tears on her cheeks.

The creamery had a flagstone floor, and the springwater ran through a channel right in the middle of it to keep it cool and moist all year round. The first four feet of the walls were brick, the rest lumber. Fee had purchased a cream separator, crocks, shining vats, wooden paddles, and even a wire cutter—called a cheese harp—when she was in Portland. Now it was in full operation, and her cheeses were in great demand.

That was why Fee was working so hard despite her backache. She wanted an extra supply of cheese for the upcoming Fourth of July celebrations—she couldn't ask for a better advertisement than that. She'd just started selling butter and two new kinds of cheese. The creamery was an overwhelming success. She'd had to buy five new milk cows and enlarge the barn. She'd barely had time in the evenings to make baby clothes.

Nathanial was doing the milking now; she was so large she couldn't lean over and grab the cows' teats. Fee stood up and rubbed the small of her back, hoping to alleviate some of the ache. Wesley would be coming in an hour with the wagon to pick up this week's shipment of cheese, buttermilk, and butter. She had to have it ready. She bent back over the butter paddle and deftly shaped another loaf, stamping it with her trademark, a fat quail with its jaunty topknot curling over its head.

Dr. Breckenridge had assured her that she wouldn't deliver for another two weeks. Perhaps she ought to stay with Mrs. Gould in town at the end of the week, just to be sure.

For now, she vowed, she'd never again have Mr. Gould's sausage for breakfast. She was sure that was what was causing her indigestion.

She stacked the last loaf of butter and wheel of cheese by the door of the creamery and headed towards the outhouse. What a time to be sick, what with the baby coming and all. She still had to finish quilting the little down comforter she was making to fit in the cradle Nathanial had built. It seemed as if there just weren't enough hours in the day.

"Fee! What's the matter?" Nathanial said, running up to her as she leaned against the doorpost of the creamery.

"I . . . I just don't feel well," she said. "Maybe it's the flu. I think I'll go lie down after I go to the outhouse."

"Is it the baby?"

She smiled weakly, feeling the perspiration on her forehead. "I don't know. I've never had one before. Dr. Breckenridge said it'd be another two weeks."

"I'm going to go get him."

"No! Don't leave me!" she cried, suddenly frightened. Her knees gave way. Nathanial caught her and carried her to the house, gently setting her down on the bed.

"I'm going to go for the doctor. I'll stop by and have Minnie come stay with you."

"No, she's just a silly girl. She'd never know what to do. Just help me to the outhouse. Don't go," she pleaded.

Nathanial carried her to the outhouse behind the house, but it didn't help. There was a vast flood of water, but no relief. Then he helped her back to her bed, insisting that he should go for the doctor as soon as he had her undressed and comfortably settled.

"Don't go!" she cried as he slipped her nightgown over her head. She clasped his arm tightly, taking a big breath. "There's no time. I think it's coming."

"What'll I do?"

Fee gasped and strained, then tried to smile. "Just pretend I'm a cow and you're helping me calve."

His normally ruddy face was chalk white as he moved to the end of the bed and raised the covers with shaking hands. "You're right. I . . . I can see the head. Push."

She pushed again, and again, and again.

"Again," he cried.

Fee thought she was going to split. She pushed, cried out, and suddenly felt a great release.

"Again, push again," Nathanial commanded, and she did.

She was panting for breath from the effort when he laid the tiny wet creature on her stomach and began patting it. "Isn't it supposed to cry?" he asked desperately.

"Hold it upside down and make sure its mouth is clear. Just like a calf," she said, raising up on her elbows. Suddenly a clear wail filled the air. She'd never heard a more beautiful sound. She took the baby in her arms.

"What about the cord?" he asked.

"Tie it off with a string."

Fee wiped the baby with a towel while Nathanial tied off the cord. She looked up. "It's a boy."

"I know." Tears ran down his cheeks, but he was smiling. "I know," he whispered.

"I think he has your red hair," she said, putting him to her breast. "What shall we name him?"

"How about Donnell, for your father?"

"I was hoping you'd say that. Welcome to our world, little Donnell," she said through tears of happiness.

Chapter XII

Donnell was lying on his quilt in a corner of the creamery chewing on his chubby fist while Fee separated the cream from the milk.

"Oh, Donnell," she said, laughing, "you look so serious. Is that a tasty fist?" She put the milk pail down and went to her baby. "You're such an enchanting little boy, I get half the work done that I did before."

He looked at his mother and stopped chewing, considering her for a moment. Then he broke into a dimpled grin and raised his tummy, begging to be picked up.

"Now, why should I stop what I'm doing just to hold and cuddle you?" she teased, chucking him gently under the chin.

He squealed with delight and then blew bubbles, his tiny rosebud mouth forming a perfect "O" as he tried to talk to her.

Fee couldn't resist. She picked him up and nuzzled his neck with kisses. "What am I going to do with you?" she asked. "You'll grow up so spoiled, and it will be all your own fault because you're so charming. Oh, I feel sorry for the girls. They won't stand a chance when you walk into the room."

"I thought I heard laughter in here," Nathanial said from the doorway.

"I was explaining to your son that he has inherited a devastating charm," she said, bringing Donnell to him. "But then I don't have to explain to you, do I? You're the one he got it from." She raised up on her toes and kissed his cheek. "Are you done clearing the south field?"

He dipped a tin cup into the cool buttermilk and sat down, pushing his hat back on his head. "Took long enough, didn't it? Well, I'll get it plowed and planted and we might get a crop of winter wheat out of it."

"That'll make it worth all the work. Next year I want to put another fifteen head of dairy cows in there."

Nathanial shook his head and smiled. "Nothing holds you back, Fionna. Who's going to milk them all?"

"I'll figure that out when the time comes. Will you take Donnell into the house and give the stew a stir? I have to finish washing out the milk cans, then I'll be right in."

Donnell was fussing by the time Fee got to the house.

"It would be a lot easier if you'd just tell me what's wrong instead of making that noise," Nathanial was saying as he paced the floor with his son. "There, there, shhh . . . Oh, good." His voice filled with relief as he saw Fee taking off her boots. "I'm glad you're here. I don't know what's the matter with him."

She laughed. "Two things, silly. His diaper's wet, and he's hungry. If only you'd learn how to change a diaper," she said, deftly replacing the soggy one with a dry one.

"I'm no good at that kind of thing."

"Put the dishes on the table while I give little Donnell his dinner, then," she said, unbuttoning the front of her dress. "He's like his father, doesn't like dinner to be late. Look at him, he's such a little pig."

Nathanial watched for a moment, smiling at his son. "You know," he said, taking down the dishes from the shelf, "I'm going to miss seeing him grow. He seems to change with each day."

"What do you mean?" Fee asked, forcing calm into her voice.

"When I leave in November. I want to set a trap line and check out some of the timber country. With that Homestead

136

Act they passed in May, I figure I might be able to claim some land with some good timber on it, log it, and then develop it. When this war is over, they're going to be needing all the lumber they can get. If I can get some logged, sawn, and shipped to the parts of the country that are rebuilding, it could set us up. They say the Union forces are doing well in the western campaigns."

Fee was looking down at Donnell, who was alternately nursing, then dozing, then nursing again. She'd always known this time would come. Now that it had, why was it causing such a lump in her throat? "Don't you have to live on a homestead to prove it up?" she asked slowly.

"For part of the year."

Fee was quiet, unable to look up at Nathanial. She'd been prepared for this, but now she wasn't sure she could bear it. There was so much to do, more than she could handle all on her own. Besides, the thought of being alone, without Nathanial by her side, without Nathanial to share her bed, without . . . She swallowed hard, forcing her mind from dwelling on the misery that lay ahead.

"Look, Fee, you're doing fine. I'll only be gone a few months during the winter, when things are slowest for you, and you've got Wesley to help out. It's not like I'll be leaving you alone."

Donnell was sound asleep. She gently removed her breast from his mouth, wiped his chin, and placed him in his cradle.

"You're right," she said, taking the Dutch oven from the coals. "We'll be just fine. We always said you could go your way and I could go mine."

Nathanial sighed and then continued explaining patiently. "I've helped you get your dreams started, Fee. Now I need to do what I want to do. I'm not deserting you and Donnell. I'm just doing what I've always done. Nothing's changed."

Fee studied him for a long time, accepting that this was all part of the man she loved. Then she kissed him and finished making dinner. "Of course, dear. You don't have to explain. I've known all along that you'd never be happy staying in one place. I won't tie you down. Now let's eat."

So it was that Fee was alone for the first time in her life, only now she had a baby to care for. She worked hard keeping the dairy and creamery going through the winter months. Wesley came over and helped with chores three times a week, but he couldn't come more often. He was trying to fix up the Lawton farm so he could begin making a profit from that while paying its rental by working for Fee.

Occasionally he brought Minnie and her baby girl along with him so Fee could have some "woman talk." The visits were pleasant enough, though Minnie was young and talked mostly about cooking and babies. Nevertheless, Fee preferred her frequent visits with Ezekial.

The single joy in her life was her son. She doted on him, rejoiced in each new skill, and cherished his every smile. Soon she was talking to him as if he could understand. He was a good baby, and his serious expression led her to wonder if he did understand more than ordinary babies. She didn't think she could have withstood the lonely days and nights without him. He was her companion and her comfort.

It was the last part of December, and Fee didn't expect to see anyone for another ten days. Wesley had taken Minnie and the baby in to spend the Christmas holidays with the Goulds. They wouldn't be back until after New Year's. Although Dr. and Mrs. Breckenridge had invited her into town to spend the holidays with them, she and Donnell had to stay on the farm to take care of the animals. But they wouldn't be alone. She'd invited Ezekial to come for dinner and share Donnell's first Christmas. Her time was filled with baking and making gifts.

The wind was howling around the chimney as the rain poured in a steady stream off the eaves. Donnell was asleep and Fee was sitting by the fire knitting a sweater for Ezekial when there was a knock on the door. She lifted the latch and then stared as if she'd seen a ghost.

"Well, aren't you going to invite me in?" Jacob laughed. "I'm soaked to the skin."

"Jacob!" she cried as she hugged him and pulled him inside. "How wonderful to see you! Here, let me take your things. How long have you been back? You don't know how many times I've thought of you and wondered if you were all right. Where did you come from?" she asked as she shook the rain from his coat and hat and hung them on the pegs behind the door.

"Whoa, one question at a time." He went to the fire to warm himself. "I got into Portland about a month and a half ago. I just came from Salem because I had to get directions to Quail Hollow . . . and what else was it you asked?"

"You're soaked to the skin. Let me get some of Nathanial's clothes. You can change behind the curtain there," she said as she opened a trunk. "They may be a bit too big, but maybe not; it looks like this past year has put some meat on your long bones."

Jacob's smile softened as he spotted Donnell's cradle. "And who is this?" he asked softly, peeking under the covers.

"Meet Donnell, the joy of my life. If you give him half a chance, he'll charm the socks right off you."

Jacob laughed and took the clothes and a towel that Fee handed him. "I'll certainly give him a chance."

"Can I convince you to stay through Christmas? Ezekial is coming for dinner."

"Where's Nathanial?" he asked, hanging his wet clothes over some wood Fee had stacked beside the fireplace.

"Oh, you know Nathanial," Fee said quietly, "itchy feet and adventurous soul."

"He didn't . . ." he said, his eyes flashing in sudden anger. Then he said more calmly, "I mean, when do you expect him back?"

"Probably in the spring. That's when he'll be done trapping anyway," she said with a brave smile. "I can't wait to show you my farm. I have a dairy herd, a creamery with customers waiting for my cheese, and . . . oh, have you eaten?" she asked, jumping up. "Some cold meat and bread?"

"I'm famished," he said, laughing. "As usual."

As he sat down to eat, Fee joined him with a cup of coffee. "So everything is going well?" he asked.

"Business is good enough to keep us in clothes and food—but it's not enough." She leaned forward earnestly. "Oh, Jacob, remember how we sat around the campfire on the way west and talked about our dreams? Ezekial wanted his cozy little farm, Nathanial wanted open skies and new horizons. But you and I—well, we wanted to build something more. Being alone, I've had lots of time to think. What I want is money, lots of it. I want to make investments with every penny I can scratch together. I want the comfort and, yes, the power that comes with money. I don't ever again want to face the world cold and alone like I did after Daddy and Matthew were murdered.

"Besides," she said, raising her chin, "I've thought about their murders. They wouldn't have been murdered if we'd been rich and powerful. No one would have dared. But we were just ordinary folk, and so they burned us out and killed my kin. If we'd been rich and powerful, that sheriff wouldn't have just shrugged it off like he did. He would have had the whole state out looking for those butchers. No," she concluded fervently, fighting back the tears, "I'm never going to be that vulnerable again. I'm going to surround myself—and my child—with the protection of being rich and powerful."

Jacob nodded. "I understand," he said as he poured himself another cup of coffee. "My grandfather brought his whole family out of Bavaria and escaped the pogroms because he had money. It took every last penny he had, but he did it—and then we started all over again. My father couldn't go to school, but he insisted that all of his children did. Two of my brothers are attorneys. The other two run the clothing manufacturing plant our family owns. We all grew up knowing that our only security is what we can put aside for our family. That's why they scraped together all they could and sent it with me to invest."

"So what are you going to do with their money? How are you going to invest it?"

"Oh, several things. But first things first. You haven't asked about our gold mine."

Fee shrugged. "If the news was good, I figured you'd tell me right away."

"Not necessarily," he said mysteriously, pulling a small black book out of his pocket. He put it on the table in front of her.

"What's this?"

"A record of your bank deposits."

Fee opened it and looked at the column of figures. There at the top was her first deposit, then all the subsequent withdrawals that brought her funds so dangerously low. At the bottom there was a new entry. "Twelve thousand dollars!" she exclaimed.

"Your half of a gold mine."

"I can't believe it!"

"Well, I worked it for a full year. Nearly died in one of the winter blizzards, but work it I did. Just kept panning on upstream until I hit some pretty rough places. We should keep that spot a secret. Once they develop better mining equipment we could go in there and take out the vein from those rocks."

"You got twenty-four thousand dollars out of it?"

"Closer to twenty-five, but I took the extra for myself, figuring I put in the time. Do you mind?"

Fee laughed. "Not at all. You earned it fair and square."

Jacob went to the pack he'd brought with him. "I also used

part of it for presents. If I'd known about Donnell I'd have brought something for him, too." He lifted a heavy box to the table. "Something we'd talked about. Consider it my Hanukkah gift."

Fee opened it to find a full set of books—novels, philosophy, science, enough to keep her reading for months. "Oh, Jacob, how . . ." She looked up with tears in her eyes. "How did you know what I pined for most?"

"There's a new book of Lincoln's speeches, Washington Irving's *A Tour of the Prairies,* Melville's *Moby Dick,* some Dickens, Thoreau, and Emerson, quite a selection," he said enthusiastically. "I hope you like my choices. I got duplicates of everything I got for myself. There's even one in there on investments."

"It's perfect! Thank you for remembering." She smiled at him affectionately and he grinned in satisfaction. "Now tell me about your investments. I seem to have come into some money I'd like to invest myself."

They talked long into the night. Jacob had purchased a printing press and was setting up a newspaper. "I'm calling it *The Occidential Journal* because I want it to cover the whole West, not just Portland. Influencing what people read is power, too," he said, and she nodded.

Portland, it seemed, was suffering from a shortage of homes and office buildings. Part of Jacob's money would build an office building to house his newspaper and other offices, as well as a store downstairs. Fee immediately told him she wanted to be a partner in the building, and he agreed.

Hours later, when they finally stopped talking and said good night, Fee had finished Ezekial's sweater. More importantly, Jacob had spilled his dreams alongside Fee's, and they matched marvelously well.

Jacob spread out his bedroll in front of the fire, and Fee disappeared behind the curtain. It was just a short time before Donnell woke her up for his early-morning feeding, but she was rested and happy nonetheless.

The next week was a holiday for Fee. Of course, she still had her chores—milking, caring for the animals, making the cheese and butter for her customers—but Jacob was by her side, pitching in to help wherever he could. When he wasn't helping with the chores he was playing with Donnell.

Their Christmas was wonderful. Jacob explained that they had the best of all possible worlds: two holidays to celebrate,

141

Christmas and Hanukkah. They promised to make it a tradition that they celebrate them together.

To the delight of everyone, Ezekial arrived on Christmas Eve with a Canada goose he'd shot out by the creek and a Christmas tree for them to decorate with paper ornaments they made while sitting around the fire.

The next morning, while the goose sizzled over the fire, they exchanged gifts, told stories, and sang songs.

Ezekial brought Donnell a little wooden rocking horse he'd made himself. Donnell couldn't ride it for at least half a year yet, but the horse's bright red paint caused squeals of delight. Donnell crawled to it as fast as his chubby arms and legs would go, plopped down on his diapered bottom, and rocked it enthusiastically.

Ezekial brought Fee a bottle of real French perfume he'd found in a shop in Portland.

Ezekial and Donnell were both happy with the matching blue sweaters Fee had made for them. She gave Jacob a walnut brown sweater she'd made for Nathanial just in case he came back for Christmas, but now, she explained, she'd have plenty of time to knit him another.

The dinner, with its roast goose, coal-baked yams dripping with butter, cheese bread, and rich pound cake, was a resounding success. Ezekial had brought a bottle of sherry, which they shared after dinner, while Fee read aloud from her volume of Thoreau. Best of all, Fee was surrounded by dear friends, whose laughter and conversation she treasured.

At Ezekial's insistence, Fee got out her flute and played it for the first time since she'd come to Quail Hollow. Little Donnell cooed, laughed, and slept. Fee was exhausted but happy when Ezekial finally kissed mother and son good-bye.

Jacob stayed to help her put things back in order. When he left the following afternoon, he took the wagon loaded with her order for the week. He would leave it with Wesley to deliver when he visited with the Goulds for a couple of days. Fee gave Jacob a letter authorizing him to use part of her money to build his office building in Portland. She was left with the knowledge that she now had some capital with which to do some further development at Quail Hollow come spring.

In all, she thought as she waved good-bye to him, things were looking very good. Still, she couldn't deny the fact that Jacob's departure left her with a new and aching loneliness.

*   *   *

Oregon winters are gray. Clouds hang low over the wooded hills, trailing a veil of rain behind them. Mud is a way of life, and boots and wet coats steaming by the fire are a constant from October through April. Still, Fee enjoyed the thick, velvety green moss that coated the rocks, and the delicate green ferns that grew along the stream. Juncos, little gray winter birds with black heads, hopped in and out of the bushes, and deer came to graze in the meadow with the cattle. The blackberry vines retained their amber, gold, and ruby leaves long into January, brightening the fence line with their color. Six cows were rounded with calves due in the spring.

Best of all, she had Donnell by her side. By the end of February he was tottering on his feet, standing up, and clinging to anything he could find. Ezekial made him a "walker." It was mounted on wheels and shaped like an open-ended square. When Donnell stood in the middle of it, he could push it around and, in effect, walk.

"Thanks a lot," Fee said, laughing when he brought it over, "now I will have to run around twice as fast."

Later, as Ezekial filled his pipe and sat by the fire reading Jacob's paper, he asked, "Did you hear about that Emancipation Proclamation of Lincoln's? Freed the slaves. Not all of 'em. Jist the ones in the states what's fighting the Union. But it's a start."

Fee looked at him and the smile they shared said more than their words ever could. "Do you ever wonder what happened to that family who came to our wagon train?" she asked.

"Yup. Do you ever wonder what happened to some of them you got out on the Underground Railroad?"

"They were people, Ezekial," she said, surprised by the tears burning her eyes. "I'd do the same today. Wouldn't you?"

Ezekial puffed on his pipe, watched the smoke, then said, "People like us, you and me, we got to do what we believe in, else we die inside."

Donnell was walking by the end of March, unsteadily at first. Then with growing confidence his sturdy little legs carried him wherever Fee was going. He was still trying to talk to her as she talked to him. His sounds were getting nearer and nearer to words. Already he could say "Mamma," and Ezekial was teaching him to say "Grandpa," or a close imitation of the sound.

Late one afternoon the first week in April, Fee was transplanting seedlings into little pots of soil sitting on the table. She'd spread a newspaper on the floor and had given Donnell his own pot and some pebbles to play with. Practical as always, she was trying to get her vegetable garden started. She'd also gotten some flower clippings from Mrs. Breckenridge's shrub, and she hoped to have the yard flowering, too.

Suddenly the door burst open. Nathanial bounded in and grabbed her in his arms, swinging her around and kissing her. Once over the shock, she enthusiastically returned his kisses. It wasn't until he held her tightly and kissed her long and hard that they heard the long shriek.

Donnell was sitting on the floor crying in abject terror. His face was as red as his hair, and tears streamed down his chubby cheeks. "Mama!" he cried, trembling in fear. "Mama!" Then he jumped up and began hitting Nathanial's knees, screaming, "No, no, no! Mama!"

Nathanial released Fee and looked down at his tiny attacker. "Well, what's this?" he asked, chuckling as he picked up his son. "You're quite a brave little man."

"No! Mama!" he shrieked, reaching desperately for Fee.

She took him from Nathanial, who looked hurt. "Shh," she said. "This is your daddy. He wouldn't hurt Mama or you. See? It's Daddy. Can you say Daddy?"

He buried his head on Fee's shoulder, sobbing softly.

"You can't blame him, Nathanial. He was just a tiny baby when you left. He doesn't remember you."

Donnell peeked tearfully at Nathanial and then hid his eyes once more, as if that would make the great bear of a man who had tried to bite his mother disappear. He was still hiccoughing a tremulous sob now and then.

Nathanial looked wounded. "I guess you're right," he conceded. "He'll just have to get used to me."

Still holding Donnell, Fee put her free arm around Nathanial. "I'm glad you're home," she said, kissing him through his beard. "How was your winter?"

"It's beautiful up in the Cascades, Fionna," he said, his eyes lighting up. "I made a good haul trapping. We have a little nest egg now, and I found a wonderful place to homestead off the Powder River. Wait'll you see it. Good timber, a river, good location for a mill."

"A mill?" she asked, putting Donnell back down to play. "Do you really want to build a sawmill in the Cascades?"

"No, in the Blue Mountains. Can't right away, but someday I plan to have a timber empire. This will be just the beginning."

"But when will you begin homesteading?"

"I'll have to put in six months before next April." He went back outside and quickly returned, carrying a bundle under his arm. "I've got something for you," he said, grinning. He untied it and revealed a pile of furs. "There's enough beaver here to make you a full cape, and even some ermine for trim. I tanned these rabbit skins myself to make sure they're nice and soft for Donnell. He'll have a lined coat to keep him warm next winter. And there should be enough left over to make you some warm gloves."

Donnell's curiosity overcame his fear. He toddled over to the pile of furs and fell on them, squealing at their softness as he patted them with both hands. Nathanial took out his knife and cut off a piece of rabbit fur and handed it to him. "Here, son. You can have a piece all your own to play with."

Donnell looked at him with gray eyes that matched his father's. Then he solemnly reached out and took the piece of fur, smiling shyly.

"He has two dimples, just like you," Nathanial exclaimed.

"I think it's the only thing he got from me," she said. "He's more like you every day."

The baby was so interested in his piece of fur that he didn't notice that Nathanial had taken him onto his lap. Nathanial watched his son in wonder for a few minutes, then looked up at Fee. "It's good to be home," he said simply.

Before the evening ended, Donnell had adjusted to Nathanial's presence, considering him another adult to charm and play with. He trustingly fell asleep in his father's arms as they sat by the fire after dinner.

Alone with Nathanial for the first time, Fee found herself suddenly shy. He was so much bigger than she remembered. His beard shone with an almost metallic copper glint that she'd forgotten, and his eyes had lines around them that crinkled when he laughed. He was such a handsome man, she thought. She was drawn inescapably to him as always, but this time it felt strange, new, like starting all over again.

He threw another log on the fire and banked the coals while she soaked cornmeal for the morning's mush. It seemed that he felt more awkward than usual, too. Could it be he felt the same way, she wondered as she set out the dishes for breakfast. He checked Donnell and added another coverlet to the cradle.

" 'Bout outgrown his cradle," Nathanial commented. "I'll have to make him another bed before the month's out."

"Yes, that would be nice." Just then the wind blew the rain against the window, startling her. "You'd think I'd be used to that by now. I guess I'm just a little jumpy tonight."

"I remember another storm," he said softly.

Fee blushed. "Yes, we've seen a few, haven't we?" she said with a smile.

"One in particular. Storms always make me think of you. And want you."

"Me, too."

He reached out and unpinned her hair, letting it fall around her shoulders. Then, unbuttoning her dress, he let it drop around her feet, leaving her standing in her chemise in front of the fire. "You're a beautiful woman, Fionna," he said, lifting her in his arms and carrying her to the bed.

His kisses were warm and caressing and Fee found herself returning them, her passions slowly growing, her demands more eager. She could see his muscled body over her, burnished in the firelight. The wind whistled around the chimney and blew the rain against the window, and she laughed for joy.

He fell asleep still holding her in his arms. As she closed her eyes she realized how much she'd missed him, how much she'd denied the pain of his absence.

From the angle of the moonlight coming in the window Fee knew that it must be long after midnight. The storm had blown over and the house was silent except for Donnell's even breathing. The coals in the fireplace glowed faintly, casting a pale rose tint into the corners where the moon's silver light didn't reach.

She rolled over and looked at Nathanial lying beside her. Just seeing him there caused her heart to leap. Her nightgown was still on the floor, but the feel of his bare skin against her breasts warmed her against the chill. She leaned over to kiss him.

"Don't waste it," he whispered.

"You're awake," she murmured.

"No healthy male could sleep with you beside him," he said, running his hands knowingly over her hips.

Nathanial was home.

Chapter XIII

"You're a wicked woman, Fionna Barry," Nathanial proclaimed one bright June morning.

"And what brings you to that conclusion?" Fee asked as she paused at the door with a milk bucket in her hand.

"Because any man with an ounce of sense would be packing right now. There's that land in the Blue Mountains, just waiting for me. Miners all over the place just begging for food. I can buy a herd of scrawny cattle with my fur money, drive them over there, let them graze all summer, fatten them up, then sell them for a tidy profit while proving up my claim. There's timber in the mountains and a stream for me to put my mill on. All while I raise cattle on the flatland. Why, it's a gold mine all its own."

"How does that make me a wicked woman?"

"Because you keep me here," he said, nuzzling her neck.

"There's no rope tying you to the doorpost," she retorted. "You're a free man, just like we agreed."

"Ah, but the thought of a cold winter without your warm body is more than I can bear."

She giggled at his feigned look of pain. "Then you'll have to raise your herd of scrawny cattle right here. I'm not about to go back on the trail again."

She turned and called to Donnell, "Let's go, my little helper. I've got twelve cows that need milking," she said, kissing Nathanial's cheek. "And I wickedly admit I'm proud that you're in such a dilemma." Taking Donnell's hand, she went out the door.

" 'Bye, Nada," the boy called, using the name he'd devised for Nathanial. Having heard him called Nathanial and told he should call him Daddy, he came up with a compromise, much to everyone's delight.

Nathanial stood in the doorway, watching them go out to the barn. Fee with her slender waist, neatly plaited black hair, and graceful walk was followed by their sturdy son, toddling two steps to each one of Fee's, his curly red hair shining in the sunlight like a crown. He carried a can to which Nathanial had attached a bale, so he could have a bucket of his own. Fee let him hold it while she shot a stream of milk into it. While she finished the milking, he would amuse himself by feeding the bucketful of warm, foamy milk to the two barn cats.

Nathanial thought about The Two, as he called them, while he was hitching the mules to the plow. Fee and their son were like a matched pair. She always devised something for Donnell to do while she worked.

When Nathanial was planting the garden or chopping wood, Donnell would sometimes join him, his baby voice chirruping with unintelligible questions. Fee seemed to understand the baby talk he used, and she always answered him. However, Nathanial couldn't make any sense out of it and was reduced to grunting noncommittal responses. Donnell knew the difference and soon left his father, seeking intelligent conversation with his mother.

What a pair. Nathanial's heart swelled with pride and love as he watched them through the open barn door. How could he ever leave such a loving woman, such a wonderful son? Maybe he'd have to learn to keep in one place after all.

Later that afternoon he found Fee hanging out the laundry. Curls of hair had escaped her hairpins and coiled down her white neck. When the weather was nice she liked to set her fire and laundry pot out nearer the creek so she could hear the water while she worked. Nathanial had built a clothesline there, and it did make the tedious job seem more pleasant just to be able to look over and see the sparkling water and the tree-lined banks. Birds flitted in and out of the trees, and their chatter combined with the rippling of the water to make a sound that Nathanial considered prettier than any symphony on earth.

"Where's Donnell?" he asked, coming up behind her and lifting the curls on her neck and kissing her nape.

"Over under the tree. It's his naptime. Poor little tyke tags after me all day long until he's done in."

A butterfly fluttered over the boy's head and landed on a bright yellow wildflower beside his blanket.

"How long does he sleep?"

"Oh, maybe another hour."

"Wesley take the produce into town?"

"Left right after lunch," she said, pinning the last diaper on the line. "Why all the questions?"

"Just figuring how much time I have to make love to you."

"Now? You must be crazy. We can't do anything like that out here in the open."

"Sure we could," he said, reaching up under her skirt and pulling her to him. "But the hay in the barn's a lot softer."

He could feel her yielding to his touch and felt his excitement grow. "Come on," he said huskily.

She glanced over at the sleeping baby, then laughed, pulling the pins from her hair and starting to unbutton her dress as she walked beside him.

Dust motes floated in the air as they went into the barn and the sweet barn smell filled his nose. The hay was stacked in the end nearest the door.

Within seconds, Fee had her dress over her head. She brushed her lips over his bare chest, kissing the well at his throat as she caressed his broad back. He slipped his hands under her chemise and felt her full breasts. Her nipples were hard to his touch. She pulled the white linen over her head and drew his mouth to her breast as he lowered her to the hay. She moaned with pleasure, pressing eagerly against his hardness.

"Mmm," she said, suddenly still. "Did you hear something?"

"No. You're just nervous 'cause we're not in bed." He reached down and felt her moistness, and she forgot everything but Nathanial.

He ached to possess her, and when he did he could tell she felt the same pleasurable relief. Returning his passion, she cried out in pleasure with his every move. There was no need to hold back. She reached her peak at the same time he did, and his release was complete, carrying him to new heights of pleasure.

"Oh, you're such a pagan." Fee giggled as she buttoned her dress. "I never thought it could be like this. Look at me. I'm all covered with hayseeds. What would people think if they saw me coming out of the barn like this?"

"They'd think, now, there's a comely lass." He grinned, pulling on his boots. "Is this when Donnell takes his nap every day? I should come around more often."

"Oh, the baby," she said, going out the door. "I'd better check on him. If he wakes up and doesn't see me, it might be quite a fright."

Nathanial stretched lazily and pulled his shirt on over his sunburned back. Time to get back to the fields. He'd left the plow in the middle of a furrow.

"Nathanial!" Fee's voice was filled with fear. "Nathanial, it's Donnell!" she cried as he ran out the barn door. "He's not on the blanket!"

He glanced quickly around the fields and saw no sign of movement. "He's probably back at the house, looking for you. You go look there, and I'll check the creamery. Those are the two most likely places—"

"The creek!" Her face was white with panic.

"No, he wouldn't look for you there. Go check the house. Don't worry. He's just wandered off. He's all right."

"The creek, what if he fell in?" Tiny lines of fear pulled at her mouth as she turned and ran to the water.

He let her go, thinking the creamery a far more logical choice. But he'd not gone far before he realized her fear was contagious. His heart was beating in his throat as he peeked in the dark creamery and saw nothing.

Her scream was long, rising in fear with a building crescendo, and Nathanial responded to it without thinking. His feet barely touched the ground as he sped across the field, following her voice through the brush and down the creekbank.

Fee was wading into the water, her skirt billowing around her like a great sodden sail. Donnell's tiny body was floating under some overhanging willow branches, face down.

Fee picked up his limp form, held him out of the water, and shook him, crying soundlessly.

"He's not breathing. You made him breathe when he was born. Do it again. Make him breathe again."

The blue color of his baby's face told Nathanial all he needed to know. His son was dead.

Her eyes were wide and unseeing, confused and tortured. Nathanial took his son's body and held him upside down and patted him just as he'd done when he'd helped at his birth. He knew it was too late. But he did it for Fee. Then, holding the limp baby in one arm, he led Fee out of the creek.

"He's drowned, Fee," he said, putting his arm around her. Sorrow swelled his throat and tears burned his eyes.

Without a word, she glared at him, snatched the tiny body from his arms, and held it tightly to her breast.

"We'll take him back to the house. You lay him out and" —the words choked in his throat—"and I'll go ask Ezekial to go into town and get Dr. Breckenridge."

It was damned unnatural, he thought as he saddled his horse. She hadn't cried nor shed a tear since he took her from the middle of that damned creek. He'd left her sitting in the rocking chair he'd bought her, holding Donnell's dead body. Maybe by the time he got back she would have accepted it. As for himself, he had five long miles in which to shed his own tears and face his own terrible grief.

Ezekial decided to stop by the house before going into town. He said he'd known grief of all kinds, and maybe a word from him would help. But when they went in the door and saw Fee still sitting in the rocking chair, holding her dead baby, crooning softly to him, Ezekial turned and went out without saying a word.

The doctor recorded the death and rode out with Ezekial the next morning to see if he could help Fee. He was as shaken as Ezekial had been by the sight.

Nathanial hadn't been able to take the now stiff body from her arms. She'd sat up the whole night crooning until she was hoarse, still rocking, still crooning. Nathanial hugged himself and thought if he had to sit through another hour of this he would go crazy himself.

Luckily, Dr. Breckenridge had a sedative to give Fee. Once she fell asleep, they pried the body from her arms. Then Nathanial carried her to bed.

Wesley came over to do the morning milking and gave his and Minnie's condolences. Nathanial poured his grief into building a tiny coffin. Guided by the doctor, the four men laid the body out and put it in the simple box with the lovingly carved lid.

When Fee woke up she was pale and drawn but seemed to know the baby was dead. When Dr. Breckenridge suggested that they take the coffin to Salem and bury it in the churchyard, she said, "No. Don't lay him down with strangers. Bury him at home."

On a knoll at the foot of the great hill behind their house Nathanial found a spot covered with green grass and wildflowers of blue and white. From there you could look down on the whole farm and see everything. He dug the grave and, with their friends, Ezekial, Wesley, Minnie, and Dr. Breckenridge, Nathanial and Fee buried their son.

Then Fee sat down by the grave and began picking the blue lupine that grew on the knoll. They watched silently as she began plaiting it into a wreath. The soft, sweet flower-smell mixed with the rich scent of the newly turned earth over Donnell's grave, and Nathanial wondered if he would ever again be able to plow the spring earth without seeing this pathetic scene.

Tearfully, Ezekial knelt beside her, coaxing her to go back to the house with him. She stopped weaving the flowers long enough to stare at him as if he were a complete stranger. Then, without a word, she turned back to her flowers, quietly humming the lullaby she used to sing while rocking Donnell to sleep.

Dr. Breckenridge spoke. "Maybe she's best left alone with her grief."

Then quietly, as they filed down the hillside towards the house, he said, "There's some that take their losses harder than others. You might want to give her two of these so she can sleep at night," he said, handing Nathanial a bottle of pills. His hands were shaking and his face pale and drawn as he climbed back into his wagon and drove off.

Numbly, Nathanial thanked Wesley and Minnie, trying not to look at the squirming little girl in Minnie's arms. The sight of the child who'd been Donnell's playmate caused him sharp pain.

"I think maybe I'd better be staying on with you tonight," Ezekial said quietly. "She don't look like she's going to be no good for a while, and you need someone to help you through the grief."

Nathanial thought for a moment, then said, "I'd be obliged."

Ezekial had been right. At dusk they'd gone back up the hillside to fetch Fee. When they tried to bring her down, she protested. "No, I can't leave him!" she cried. "He'll get cold out here alone!"

Without speaking, Ezekial sat down beside her and she went back to her crooning. Nathanial went back to the house for a cup of water and the pills. When he handed them to her she didn't even look up, just swallowed a pill and water. By dark, she'd fallen asleep. Ezekial held the lantern while Nathanial carried her down the hill to bed.

The next day she left the house before daybreak without even taking a drink of water. They found her up beside Donnell's grave, placing branches of dogwood where the withered lupine wreath lay. She drank the buttermilk Nathanial brought her, but except for that and some water, she took nothing. He thought he could see her wasting away before his eyes. This couldn't go on.

They got her to bed that night the same as the night before. They were hopeless in the face of a grief so large.

Finally, through frustration and fear more than anything,

Wesley took the matter in his own hands. "She's neglecting her business," he said as he stormed into the house.

"I can't get her to even look at me," Nathanial said listlessly.

"Well, something has to be done. You'd better take a hand in the creamery, then. That milk has to be made up into cheese. There's people waiting for it."

Nathanial sighed. The burden of it all seemed more than he could bear. He felt as if he were closed in and there was no escape. "I don't know how. Throw it out."

Wesley looked at him with surprise and some irritation, then turned and walked on up the hill. Ezekial went to stop him, but Nathanial said, "Let him go. We've done all we can. Maybe he can do something."

"Best follow just in case."

Nathanial forced himself to go once more up the hill, dreading the pitiful sight he would see when he got there.

"Miz Coughlin," Wesley was saying as he looked into Fee's eyes, "you got to git hold of yourself. You're sitting here neglecting your work. You got milk clabbering up in the creamery. Now, enough's enough. There's too much depending on you. You git on down there."

Fee stared at him wordlessly. Then, as if his words had slowly sunk into the part of her brain that still worked, she nodded, got up, and walked down the hill to the creamery.

Tears filled Nathanial's eyes.

Ezekial shook his head. "Guess you got more common sense in your little finger than the both of us have between us," he said to Wesley.

"I thank you," Nathanial murmured hoarsely.

"Well, somebody's got to git this place back on its feet," Wesley said with a shake of his head, then turned and stalked back down to the barn.

From the clattering coming from the creamery, they knew that Fee was back to work.

Ezekial blew his nose loudly into his red handkerchief. "Work's the most healing of all things," he said, wiping his eyes. "Guess I'd better git back to my place and start doing more than just milking the cow. Body can't curl up like a sow bug just 'cause life knocks him around."

What Ezekial didn't know was that Fee spent every minute she could beside Donnell's grave. She'd rush through her chores only to hurry on up the hill to sit plaiting flowers and

153

crooning lullabies. She would leave at night only when Nathanial went up to get her.

The burden of his growing guilt, his imagining that it would never have happened if he hadn't seduced her on that warm afternoon, was increasingly more than he could bear.

After a week, he was nearly frantic with his own grief at losing his son, and now he felt that it was his fault he was losing Fee to some insidious disease of the mind. Something in him broke. He grabbed her shoulders and shook her, crying out, "Fionna, you've got to stop this. Donnell's dead and you've got to accept it. We can't go on sorrowing until we're sick. You've got to get hold of yourself. I can't live with you like this."

She looked at him coldly, standing stiff under his hands. "How could you understand?" she said evenly. "You were never home. You didn't even know your son."

He stepped back as if he'd been slapped, stunned by the cruelty of her words. "I thought I should stay with you through your grief," he said helplessly, "but—maybe I just add to it."

Without another word, she turned and went to bed, closing the curtain after her. Once more, he went to sleep on the floor.

By morning his mind was made up. "I hear a man by the name of Bledsoe has some cattle for sale up out of Silverton. 'Less you want me to stay, I think I'll drive them over to the Powder River Valley and start proving up that homestead."

Fee continued washing the dishes.

"Well, what do you think?" he said finally.

"I think you'll do what you want."

"But if you need me, I'll stay around," he said hopefully.

"We—I've gotten on without you before."

"I'll stop by and ask Ezekial to look in on you," he said as he gathered up his pack and went out the door. Fee didn't even turn to see him go.

The next day Wesley told Ezekial that she was doing the same as ever, hurrying through her chores only to go up the hill to sit by the grave.

"I told that stubborn fool not to leave her, but no, he wouldn't listen to me. Had some tom-fool notion in his head that she blamed him for the death of the child. Said he was keeping her from healing just by being around."

"Well, I don't know," Wesley said. "I'm not going to be able to keep on coming over here more than usual. Can't keep two places going when there's just one of me. She's going to have to shoulder some more of the load, and I can't talk to her anymore. It's like she don't hear. 'Sides, she don't eat, and she's wasting away to nothin'. Won't be of no use to nobody if'n she's dead."

Ezekial nodded. "See if you can keep it up another week. I got me an idea of someone who might be able to help."

Fee could remember very little about Donnell's drowning and burial. There was a blur of pain and an overwhelming cold, black hole in her life. She couldn't cry, and the loss was welling up inside her like a great dry lump that was growing and consuming her very life with each passing day.

She was angry. Angry that her baby boy was snatched from her. Angry that Nathanial didn't seem to understand. Angry that Donnell had died because she'd wandered off into the barn to indulge her desires instead of watching over her son.

Now Nathanial was gone and she was alone. More alone than she'd ever been in her life. When her father and her brother had been killed, she'd cried herself to sleep for many nights. Then she'd had to take care of herself, and the work had helped fill the void. But now the sorrow just kept growing until there was no Fee left, just emptiness. And she felt guilty for not even shedding a tear over Donnell's grave. It was as if chains bound her tighter and tighter, keeping her from ever reaching out and loving again, keeping her from living.

She threw herself into her work, trying to remember why. Then, at the end of the day the memories of her laughing baby boy called to her, and she had to go back up the hill and talk to him as if he were still beside her, gabbling in his funny baby-talk that only she understood. She would sit in the shade of the tree and remember his dimpled smile, his bright eyes, his tousled red hair. And it was as if she could hear his laughter in the warble of the meadowlark, see his smile in the sunset, and she felt some easing of the pain. But then night would come and she would have to go back to her cold, empty cabin. She would find that the pain had increased and the emptiness had grown.

Even her body rebelled against her. She started her monthly flow and was made sick with stomach pains. She no longer wanted to go on.

Ezekial came over every night the week that Nathanial left. Then on Saturday he told her that he wasn't going to come so often. She would have to find her own consolation. She thought it a strange thing to say, knowing that the hurt and the cold emptiness would be with her always. But she was indifferent even to Ezekial's companionship.

Rain started falling on Sunday. It was a cool rain that persisted throughout the week, making it all Fee could do to wade through the mud in the barnyard to feed the animals and milk the cows twice a day, then hitch Smokey to a cart and carry the milk cans to the creamery. She went up the hill only once a day now because of the rain. The cheese wheels and butter loaves were piling up beside the door. Wesley came first thing Friday morning, loaded them up, and took them to the market. Then she was alone again.

Late Saturday night she was startled by a loud thumping at the door. "Who is it?" she called.

"Open up! I'm soaked to the skin."

Although she wanted more than anything to be left alone, there was something familiar in the voice that drew her to the door and made her lift the latch.

"Jacob!" she cried in surprise as he stomped into the room.

"Hope you don't mind. I already put my horse in the barn and gave it some oats," he said, handing her his coat and hat. Prying off his muddy boots on the bootjack beside the door, he added, "I came to stay awhile."

She looked at him, trying to understand.

"Ezekial wrote and told me," he said softly. "I came as soon as I got the letter. You needed me."

It was as if a dam broke inside her. To think that he would ride all the way from Portland just because . . . suddenly the tears she'd never shed burst forth in great, gasping sobs, and she fell against his chest.

"There," he said, lifting her up in his arms and carrying her to the fire, "that's what you need to do. Just cry it out. Grief stays inside and eats away until there's nothing left unless you wash it out with your tears."

And he held her and cried with her.

And when her sobs were dry, he took a cool, wet rag and washed her face. Then he took off his wet shirt, and held her in his lap. Her head rested on his bare shoulder and sleep blocked out the newly washed pain.

She awoke the next morning with the sun streaming across the floor. He'd carried her to the bed still dressed, and had lain down beside her. Feeling her stir, he opened his eyes

156

and looked at her soberly. "I didn't want you to be alone," he said. At that she began to cry once more, this time sadly and gratefully.

Tears were close to the surface for the rest of the day, but Fee could feel herself being pulled back into the world. She could feel Jacob willing her back to life.

That night after dinner as they sat by the fire, Jacob took one of the books down from the shelf and began reading aloud. It was the poetry of Emerson, and Fee felt the words of New England reason and passion soothe her soul and speak to her aching heart. Tears flowed freely down her cheeks as she listened to Jacob's soft voice, giving in to the words he spoke.

Putting the book down, he looked up and saw her tears. "Ah, Fee," he said, reaching out to her. "I didn't mean to make you cry."

"You didn't. . . . I just . . ."

He smoothed back her hair from her face and wiped her tears with his thumb. "It pains me to see you cry so," he whispered, kissing her forehead.

Suddenly, as if hearing the title of the poem once more, she whispered, "Give All to Love," and raised her face to his, needing to leave death behind and seize life once more with open arms.

He kissed her lips, gently at first, then longer and longer as if drinking from a goblet of narcotic, unable to stop. She returned his kisses, gasping for breath, clinging to him the way she was now clinging to life.

Spiraling in uncontrollable desire, they fell to the floor, plummeting through whorls of their inner chambers of passion. Within minutes, they lay, spent, with Fee holding him as she trembled with renewed joy.

"Fee," Jacob whispered, "I've loved you for so long. When I saw you slowly dying, I couldn't—"

"I know," she said, running her fingers lightly over his angular cheekbones and across his thick black moustache. "I know. It's wonderful. Don't say anything more. Come to bed with me."

Through Jacob's love Fee's spirit grew and flourished. When her sorrow surfaced, Jacob would hold her until the tears stopped. Although she knew she'd always carry the hurt with her, she learned it could no longer consume her. She was alive again. Jacob was more than a balm of healing for her wounded soul. He gave her a love she'd never believed possible.

She had never known such joy. For the next two weeks they worked side by side, talking, laughing, teasing, and planning once more. Often they would leave their work to find a shaded glen where they could make love, or hurry through dinner so they could eagerly tumble into bed, touching and loving and then falling asleep to the gentle chirping of the crickets outside.

One night they walked in the silvered meadow under the full moon and Jacob recited Shakespeare to her, quoting a fairy's speech from *A Midsummer Night's Dream.* Fee laughed, wondering at the friend and lover she'd found in Jacob.

"How could I have been so lucky?" she asked. "When I'm with you I feel as if I'm soaring above the earth, as if I'm pulled out of myself into some greater part of the universe, as if . . ." she stopped, embarrassed by her extravagance.

"I was afraid that you didn't feel the same way I did," Jacob said softly, "and now I find that you are my soulmate."

There in the soft moonlight on the tender grass, he took her to him, teaching her the depth of his love, uniting their bodies over and over until she knew they would never be apart. And she cried for joy and his tears joined hers on their cheeks as they lay together.

Silently, an owl flew overhead, then called from the pine tree.

Their days were like golden coins, cherished for the joy they bought. Then came the day they were in the creamery and Jacob was reading from Thoreau's essays while Fee was making her cheese. They were arguing over the meaning of a passage when Ezekial rode up.

"I knew it," he said, poking his head in the door. "You two ain't never been together without some kind of talk taking over. Now you got some fellow you ain't never met and you're arguing about what he has to say. Ain't your own ideas enough?"

Fee laughed. "Ezekial, you're just what we needed."

He smiled. "That laugh is the prettiest music on God's earth. I was afraid I'd never hear it again, little lady."

"You've been so good to me, Ezekial. I'm sorry if I worried you," Fee said, kissing his cheek.

"Wesley said he was mighty glad to see you when he came

by last Friday, Jacob. Said he hadn't seen you since you left off at the Columbia River. Thought you looked real good."

"I could say the same about him. Married life agrees with him," Jacob said. "Looks like a bear storing up for the winter, and he used to be skinny as a rail."

"Speaking of married life, I was wondering if I could ride along with you when you go up to Portland."

Fee laughed. "What does that have to do with married life, Ezekial? You're always running off to Portland every couple of months or so . . ." She paused, noticing how Ezekial was studying his feet. "Ezekial Edwards! Do you have a widow lady you've been courting in Portland?"

Ezekial shuffled around and ducked his head. "She's a right nice lady. Thought I'd ask her to git hitched."

"That's wonderful!" Jacob said.

"Well, hold on here," Ezekial said, "I haven't asked her yet."

"She couldn't refuse a prize like you," Fee said, tweaking his cheek. "How soon do you want to leave?"

"How about tomorrow?" he said with a grin.

Jacob looked at Fee for a moment. "Think you could get along without me for a while?"

"Of course," she said. "I can manage now."

Jacob left, and once again Fee was lonely, but it wasn't an empty, hungering loneliness like she'd known before he came to her. She knew that he'd come back. She spent the long nights reading the books he'd left, walking the paths they'd shared, and remembering the time they'd had together—knowing that she'd always have that no matter what happened.

Strangely enough, now that Jacob had come into her life, she was able to think once more of Nathanial and the life they had together. And the thoughts she had were good.

It was a difficult notion for her to resolve, but she had to accept the fact that she loved two men. It was as if the perfect companion for her had been split in two. The companion of her girlhood, of the earth where she was born, the man who shared her beginnings and stirred her longings, was Nathanial. But the companion of her soul, the one wedded with her mind and spirit, was Jacob. And both were inextricably woven through her dreams and plans.

She knew that if forced to choose, she would be tempted to choose Jacob. Yet the thought of losing Nathanial left a deep, lonely ache inside. Besides, Jacob was concerned that his being Jewish put them apart. She quickly pushed the thought from her mind. She loved them both.

It was unorthodox, unheard of, yet she had to have both men to complete her life. What could she do?

In many ways, her love for these two men was a gift, a gift that made her life more complete, yet that gift insured she could never be content. She would always be torn between the two loves, each by itself incomplete. Like listening to a divided orchestra playing in two different rooms, Fee could never hear the full symphony of love. Still, she knew she would accept it. There was an ominous threat of conflict, even tragedy, but she would deal with that when it happened—if it happened. In the meantime she would simply love these two men.

That September Ezekial went to Portland and brought home his bride, Pearl, a sweet, gray-haired woman with laughing blue eyes.

In November Jacob came back and Fee had to tell him: Their baby would be born in the spring.

At dinner the following night Ezekial made a comment that set them both to reeling.

"Yessirree," Ezekial crowed. "Old Nathanial is going to pop his eyes right out of his head when he comes back next spring and sees the filly I have in my corral."

Jacob was the first to recover. "I'm sure he'll be happy for you, Ezekial."

Fee feigned a slight laugh and said, "You sound like you know when he'll be coming back. If that's true, you know more than I do."

"Well, you probably just don't remember much from when he left," Ezekial said softly. Turning to Pearl, he explained, "That's when she was grieving so."

"Then he told you?" Fee asked carefully, looking down at her plate.

"Sure did. Said he'd be back soon's the snow melts in the passes. That's March, if weather keeps on the way it is and if'n he meant the low passes."

"Then he said he was coming back here—I mean straight back here, without stopping off someplace else first?"

"Sure, little lady, just like I said. You don't think he can keep away from the likes of you any longer, do you?" he added with a sharp look in Fee's direction.

* * *

They were quiet as they rode back to the cabin that night. It wasn't until they were inside and Jacob had built up the fire that he said something. "I have to go home and mind the paper tomorrow. I'll be back so we can celebrate our double holiday in December. I might be able to make it back down one more time after that before he comes back."

"It's your child I'm carrying," she said softly.

"I know that. You said that the time is close enough that it could be his."

"It could be, but it isn't."

"But Nathanial's your husband and he's the one you've set your life with."

Fee started to say something but Jacob held up his hand and came to her, pulling her into his arms. "Ah, Fionna, what we have can't be taken away. I don't know how we got ourselves into such a state, but here we are and we have to live it out."

"But—"

"Shh. You've opened your heart to me, now I have a secret I must tell you." He motioned for her to sit, then went on. "You know I'm Jewish and why that's a problem we must face."

"But—"

"There's more to it than that. Before I left home, my father arranged a betrothal. I've been promised. Fee, don't look that way. I've been engaged to be married since before I came out here, before I ever laid eyes on you. She's a lovely girl; her name is Ruth. She'll be a good wife. Her father is my father's partner, and they're all counting on me to marry her. I can't go back on my family, on my faith, on everything I knew before I met you."

Fee sat there staring at him, astounded. Finally she found the words to say, "You will never belong to her."

"I know. But I will be her husband, the same as you are Nathanial's wife."

The times they spent together that winter were gentle and sweet, filled with wonder at the miracle of their love. They both knew it was rare and indestructible. They knew their love would always live through the child Fee was carrying. Distance and other loves could not separate them even when they said good-bye.

There was a false spring in February, causing enough of the snow to melt for Nathanial to get through the pass. He arrived on the doorstep, weatherworn and worried-looking. When Fee opened the door and smiled, it was as if a cloudy sky had cleared. His eyes filled with tears as he embraced her.

"I never should have left you alone," he murmured. "When is it due?"

"Maybe the last of March."

"We're not going to have any birthing like last time," he said. "I'm not taking any chances. You'll go into town and stay with Mrs. Gould until it's born."

"But Nathanial, you've only just returned."

"I didn't mean right now," he said, turning her around like a top so he could admire her rounded shape. "We've got some plans to make."

"Plans?"

"Yes. I'm going to build a fine house for you and our baby. I made a tidy profit with the sale of that herd. And your cheese. I took a couple of wheels with me, and the miners paid for it in gold—an ounce for an ounce! I'm going to buy some sawmill machinery. There's a cabin on the ranch. I can take the machinery there when we've finished logging some of the back hillside here to build our own house. The war can't last much longer. Then there's going to be some big rebuilding."

The next few days were spent planning the house. Then Nathanial insisted that Fee pack up and go to the Goulds'. He'd come in and spend every Sunday with her, but she'd have to take it easy for the next month until her delivery.

She wrote out the instructions so Minnie could continue in the cheesemaking. To keep Nathanial happy, she went into town and stayed with Mrs. Gould. It was lucky she did. She became sick within a week and had to spend the following month in bed until she was delivered of a healthy baby boy.

When she looked at the baby, her heart nearly stopped. What could she say?

But when Nathanial looked at him he just grinned and said, "This one takes after your side, darlin'. He's got your brother's big brown eyes."

Fee breathed a sigh. "Then let's name him Matthew." In her worry, she'd forgotten that her brother, as well as Jacob, had brown eyes.

"Matthew it is," he said, beaming at Fee. "And Matthew is the beginning of a Coughlin dynasty in Oregon. We have the farm here in the valley and your creamery. We have the cattle ranch and the sawmill. Fact is, if I could figure out where to get the money, I would leave this sawmill here and get it going and build another one over in the Powder River Valley. There's going to be a lot of demand for lumber. The state's growing, Fee, and we're going to be part of it."

"Do you really want to start two sawmills?"

"Sure, but I can't afford the machinery just now."

"I still have some of my . . . ah, my legacy from home. Maybe I can help out."

So it was that Matthew and Fionna moved into their two-story white clapboard house that spring. And so it was that Nathanial set up his sawmill along the Willamette River, hired a foreman to run it, bought another herd of cattle to fatten on his range, and left to start his sawmill along the Powder River that fall. And so it was that Fee was once again alone in November when Jacob came to see her—and to see his son.

Once more they made love, once more they took joy in knowing that what they had could not be taken away, could never die. He stayed for a week and they reveled in the wonder of their son, rejoiced in their love, and tried not to think of the days to come when they could no longer be together.

"She's coming on the boat the fifteenth of the month," he said one stormy Tuesday night as they lay in bed.

"When will you be married?"

"I've arranged with the rabbi to be married in the temple right after the first of the year."

"I hope I like her."

"You will."

"Jacob? Do you think we'll ever—"

"Make love again?" he asked, turning over and wrapping his arms around her. "Yes, we will. In my heart, it will be every day of my life."

"But I mean—"

"Yes, I think that, too. Somehow I can't see us being apart, not always. We'll always be friends, we know that. But I also believe that there will be times when we'll be free to love again. It will be a blessing to us both."

She considered his words, then leaned over and kissed him gently.

He left early the next morning.

Chapter XIV

April 12, 1865

"Are you sure you're all right?" Nathanial asked anxiously as they entered the elegant lobby of Portland's Union Hotel.

"Of course I am," Fee snapped. "That dreadful cigar just made me ill for a moment—as it would anyone with a sensitive nose. Why they allow smoking in hotel corridors is beyond me." She was as exasperated with the cause of her discomfort as she was with Nathanial.

Even Fee's temper wasn't enough to forestall Nathanial's genuine concern. Any sign of weakness was unlike Fee. Something wasn't right, and he didn't know what to do.

"All the same, you sit here while I go see if the carriage has come," he said, helping her to a horsehair couch covered in rose-colored velvet. "You don't seem up to your usual self these days," he said with a shake of his head.

She watched irritably as he quickly covered the length of the plant-lined lobby with his long strides. "Usual self, my fanny," she muttered. It was all his fault she was feeling this way, anyway. She wouldn't be in this condition if he hadn't come back from eastern Oregon full of romantic notions. Nevertheless, she'd keep up the charade as long as she could. She didn't want him to know—not yet. After all, she could be wrong.

Fee had to admit that her dizziness could be caused by other things—nerves, or her tightly laced waist cincher. She also had to consider the fact that she'd been in a tizzy for over a month—ever since Nathanial had casually mentioned he'd seen Jacob when he stopped in Portland. Jacob had invited them to come to dinner and meet Ruth. Since Nathanial planned on returning to Portland to observe the operation of a newly completed steam-powered sawmill, he had accepted the invitation for this week in April.

The prospect of seeing Jacob again and meeting his new wife had brought on a severe case of vanity in Fee. Ruth was the woman from Boston that Jacob had married, someone who probably was dainty and cultured and fashionably dressed.

Fee suddenly felt dumpy. What if she'd unwittingly become like the weary homesteader women she'd pitied so long ago, worn-out and frumpy? Her ego couldn't handle the prospect of such a dreadful comparison in Jacob's eyes.

Fee had plunged into a whirlwind of activity, studying magazines Pearl loaned her, noting the latest fashions, and making detailed notes. She'd sent Mrs. Gould to purchase material and have stylish dresses made by the best dressmaker in Salem.

When they stopped there on their way to Portland, news of the fall of Richmond came over the telegraph, bells rang, and each citizen rushed to be first to predict the end of the war. In the midst of all that furor Fee spent her mornings in fittings and her afternoons arranging for the construction of a new creamery just outside of town. With the war ending and the gold rush in the eastern territories, now was the perfect time to expand. Luckily, she had the money set aside to do it. It had all happened so fast her head was still spinning.

The idea for expansion began last fall when Wesley asked her if she would buy some of his cow's surplus milk and cream. She'd quickly realized that many farmers would do likewise. Someone else could care for the animals, and she'd use their harvest in her growing dairy.

The end result of all the activity was that she'd fallen into bed exhausted each evening. Added to that, she was worried about making a good impression upon meeting Jacob's wife.

For dinner at Jacob's house (Fee refused to acknowledge that it also was his wife's house) she'd chosen a taffeta dress of sapphire blue, complete with a stiff crinoline that made the skirt billow around her like a shimmering sea. The deep neckline edged in delicate handkerchief lace emphasized her full breasts. "Like two ripe melons," Nathanial had said, trying to seduce her in their room before she'd pushed him away. She'd chosen this style especially for tonight, knowing how Jacob had loved to fondle her breasts, filling her with desire as he teased and nuzzled her nipples. Her face flushed at the memory. She wasn't about to be shown up by the woman Jacob had married.

She'd spent a full hour pulling her hair back in intricate coils and curls, fastened with matching taffeta ribbon to accent the blue of her eyes. A final look in her mirror told her that she'd achieved exactly what she'd wanted, a vivid reminder of the passionate woman Jacob left to marry the wife his family had chosen.

Nathanial's reaction had assured her, even as he complained about having to cinch her waist down to seventeen inches. As soon as she'd allowed him to tie the strings, his hands had wandered deliciously over her and his lips had been hot and demanding. But Fee had other things on her mind and put him off. Keeping him interested and unsated served her purpose. His looks during the evening would speak volumes, making Jacob jealous.

Fee couldn't help feeling bitter, as contradictory as she knew it was. She'd been alone all winter raising Jacob's son and aching for companionship while Nathanial was off across the state and Jacob was married to a woman he couldn't possibly love. She could accept the fact that she loved two men; she couldn't seem to accept the fact that one of those men could possibly love two women. She only knew that when she needed him, Jacob had left her to languish alone throughout the cold, lonely winter. She wanted him to know what he'd been missing.

"It's a good thing it's an early dinner," Nathanial said, coming up to her. "The whole town has gone wild. Lee surrendered and the war is over." He took her cloak and held it out for her. "We'd never get a carriage later on. The streets are filled."

The driver of the carriage held an umbrella to protect Fee from the fine rain. She raised her skirts and stepped into the cab, realizing the wires of the crinoline took concentration to maneuver gracefully. It was easy to see that this was a style for women with servants and not for those who worked.

Was that what she wanted from life, she mused as they began moving. She wanted the security and power that came with wealth, and if she had to wear the trappings to have that power, so be it.

The gray clouds had lowered in the sky, darkening the day even before the sun set. Gaslights lined the streets, casting their shimmering reflections across the wet cobblestones. Their carriage clattered up Yamill Street towards Jacob's address.

Fee could hardly concentrate on what Nathanial was saying. Her heart was beating in her throat and her stomach was turning over. *Oh, why do I have to be in this condition now—of all times?* she wailed inwardly.

"You're awfully quiet tonight." Nathanial's words intruded on Fee's thoughts. "Is something bothering you? If you don't feel well, maybe we'd better turn back. Jacob and his wife would understand."

Fee winced at the mention of Jacob's wife, then forced herself to smile. "I'm fine. I'm just worried about Ruth. What if she doesn't like us? Jacob's been such a dear friend, it'd be just awful if we couldn't continue being friends."

Nathanial laughed and patted her hand. "Don't worry about it. Jacob wouldn't tolerate a woman who didn't accept his friends. Besides, it would be impossible for anyone not to like you."

They left the business district and began climbing a small hill where the residences increased in sumptuousness with the altitude. Large evergreens, remnants of the lush forests found by the first settlers just fifty years earlier, wooded the spacious lawns leading up to the comfortable homes.

Nathanial felt a twinge of smugness as he looked around. This was the kind of neighborhood most women clamored for, making their men feel failures if they couldn't provide it. Thank God Fionna wasn't that kind. She was her own person—independent, strong, not affected by social vanities. Money to her was for investment, not show. He couldn't help feel a tug of pity for Jacob, who'd married a woman with all those female expectations and weaknesses. He looked over at Fee, her tiny jaw tilted in characteristic determination. With a flow of warm affection, he took her cold hand in his and tucked it under his arm.

The driver turned the horses between two large iron gate-posts, hung with lanterns casting warm yellow beams. Is this it, Fee asked herself in dismay as they drove up the long curved drive. Ahead, on a knoll overlooking the rest of the neighborhood and part of downtown Portland, was a spacious two-story house with a broad stair leading up to a porch that encircled the front of the dwelling.

As Nathanial helped her down from the carriage, her heart shrank with envy as she saw the golden light streaming through the leaded panes flanking each side of the large oaken door. Oh, how will I last the whole night here, she thought. It all seems so gracious and . . . she struggled for a word . . . imposing? No, more subtle. It had an implied sense of power in its lack of need to impress. Here she was struggling alone with her dairy farm while Jacob had given that power to the woman who'd usurped her rightful place in his life.

"Do they have any children?" she asked Nathanial as they walked up to the porch.

"Not that he mentioned. Missing Matthew?" They'd left their active toddler in the capable hands of Pearl and Ezekial. Fee had been both hurt and pleased when he cheerfully waved good-bye without a whimper.

"A little, I guess. We should bring him with us next time. Jacob would enjoy seeing him."

Nathanial turned the bell, and the door was answered by a heavy-set woman in a black dress with a white apron. "Yes?" she asked.

Nathanial took off his hat. "Mr. and Mrs. Coughlin to see Mr. and Mrs. Teall."

"Yes, they're expecting you. Please come in." She stepped back and let them in.

A maid? Good grief, Fee thought, this is going to be harder than I'd thought. She handed her cloak to the woman, looking around the foyer, impressed by the lamps hung with crystal drops, the rich wallpaper, and the curved staircase. In silence she followed the woman through the double paneled oak doors into the parlor. She was unaware that she was holding her breath—only that her heart was beating loudly in her ears.

Her first view was of Jacob as he stood up from his wing-backed chair in front of the fireplace. In that moment their eyes held and she knew that she'd never needed worry. Then he looked behind her and smiled a hearty greeting to Nathanial, rushing forward to greet them both.

"Nathanial, Fionna, how wonderful to see you," he exclaimed, chastely kissing Fee's cheek and shaking Nathanial's hand. "It's been too long. Come in, come in. You haven't met Ruth yet, have you?" In his energetic burst of greeting, Fee could see that he was as nervous about this meeting as she, and her heart went out to him.

For the first time Fee noticed the figure in the chair opposite where Jacob had been sitting. She was putting down her knitting and rising, a friendly smile on her face. Ruth was slightly taller than Fee and more rounded—softer-looking, with a delicate appearance. Her round face was framed with thick brown hair, neatly coiled at the nape of her neck. She was wearing a sedate, dove gray dress over medium crinolines. The scooped neck was edged in white linen, as were the full sleeves. Fee suddenly felt overdressed as she looked into Ruth's warm, hazel eyes.

"We need no introduction," Ruth was saying as she took Fee's hand. "I feel as if I've known Fionna and Nathanial as long as you have, Jacob. Welcome to our home," she said. "How lovely you look. Please, come sit beside me and tell me about little Matthew. Jacob has told me of your son, and I'm eager to hear about him from you."

Fee stifled a gasp. Had Jacob told her about their relationship and his fathering a son? She glanced in his direction, and he smiled tightly.

"Ezekial and Pearl have raved about Matthew so much we both look forward to meeting him," he explained.

"Of course. I'd love to tell you all about him. He's the joy of my life," she said, sitting down beside Ruth. "In fact, I have a miniature of him in my purse," she said, opening the drawstring. "It was taken at Christmas time, so he was only nine months old, but you can see the mischief in his eyes even in the photograph."

Jacob came over and looked over her shoulder at the picture of his son. "Why didn't you bring him with you?" he asked almost accusingly.

"I was afraid that he wouldn't behave properly when meeting new friends. He's a very active one-year-old. You must remember how Donnell was at that age, Jacob," she said, feeling a stab of pain at the thought of her lost son.

Jacob saw the pain in her eyes as clearly as he'd seen her nervousness and anguish as she'd come in the door, and his heart went out to her once more. He had to be strong from the outset if they were to survive this meeting. He could not reveal his love any more than he could deny it. He looked down at her soberly and nodded. "I do, but we will never again accept that as an excuse. Matthew, as well as his parents, is a part of this household." *He is my son and I love him as much as you do,* he added silently to himself.

"Oh, yes," Ruth agreed. "We want you always to feel welcome here. All of you. Jacob and I have talked of this many times. You're part of our Oregon family, and our door is always open to you."

"That's most kind," Fee said, swallowing the lump in her throat. "I'm touched—and grateful."

"Good. I hope you won't mind if we have an early dinner," Jacob said, his expression excited. "There's going to be a great illumination tonight celebrating the end of the war. We don't want to miss it. I've arranged for us to go downtown. We don't want our view blocked by the crowds, so we'll have to leave early."

Fee looked at Ruth, whose eyes sparkled with excitement. "I'm sure you'll love it, Fee. You don't mind if I call you that, do you?"

"Please do. I'm sure it'll be great fun." In spite of herself she couldn't help but be drawn to the gentle woman Jacob had married. She was so warm and accepting. How could she have ever thought Ruth would be an enemy?

The dining room was behind the parlor. Where the front of the house looked down on the lights of Portland, the back looked over the Columbia River. Jacob told them that on a clear day they could see Mount Hood. The oak table was covered with a lace cloth and set with sparkling china, silver, and crystal. Oak wainscoting was surmounted by a wallpaper of delicate rose. Brocaded draperies were drawn back from the bay window so they could enjoy the sunset on the river. Fee was enchanted with the gracious elegance of it all. This was how she wanted to live.

Throughout the meal, Fee avoided looking at Jacob. If their eyes met she feared that Nathanial and Ruth would suspect something. Still, she could feel his gaze on her and she felt her soul torn in two.

On one hand she felt a soaring joy simply being in the presence of the two men she loved most in the world. She'd never felt so complete. On the other, she was in agony for fear of hurting those she cared for.

What she couldn't know was Jacob's agony. Seeing Fionna again awakened all the longing and passion he'd forced himself to forget. The one thing he'd allowed himself to hope for was that she would bring his son. He ached to hold him in his arms, to admire his stumbling attempts at words and walking, all the things he remembered from watching Donnell and had hoped he'd be able to enjoy with his own son.

Just looking at Fee conjured up so many memories—visions of laughter in the moonlight, visions of a hollow-eyed woman who'd returned to life at his touch, visions of a brave young girl pointing her gun at a wretched man beating his wife, visions of an ethereal figure perched high on her wagon seat, serenading Indians with her flute. How could he not love her?

"Jacob, didn't you tell me you'd heard news about some of the people who came out with you?" Ruth's words broke into Jacob's memories as if she'd sensed what he was thinking.

He started guiltily. "I'm afraid it isn't too pleasant," he said. "I saw Millard Harris at the hardware store."

"Oh, how is Rachel?" Fee interrupted. "And the children?"

"Fine. They settled on a little farm outside Oregon City. They have another baby—a girl, I think," he said, anticipating Fee's question with a smile. "I asked him if he'd heard about anyone else and he told me about the Sleads. About two years ago Lemuell came crawling back with nothing more than the ragged shirt on his back. Elsie died birthing a son a few months after he'd left them."

"Oh, poor Elsie," Fee said, tears filling her eyes. "That's what she was afraid of. She had such a miserable life," she said to Ruth.

Ruth looked sympathetic. "What of the poor children?" she asked Jacob.

"Well, the Harrises had taken them in. Had a hard time struggling to feed them all, but Rachel was devoted to them. Even wet-nursed the baby. She was Elsie's best friend. Well, old Lemuell came back and without even a thank-you packed up his brood and carted them off to somewhere in eastern Oregon, where he was going to stake a claim. They figured he took one look at the kids and saw some strong backs he could put to work for him. 'Bout broke Rachel's heart to see them go."

"It's enough to make a saint spit," Fee said indignantly.

"Sounds like Lemuell," Nathanial said. "Never thought beyond himself a day in his life."

"Those poor children," Fee murmured. "I wonder what will come of them?"

"Also heard the Clymans settled in eastern Oregon," Jacob added. "Remember them?"

"Sure do," Nathanial said. "He was the coldhearted preacher with a poker up his . . . ah"—he caught himself as he saw Ruth's expression of genuine interest—"ah, a poker through his heart," he ended lamely, much to Fee and Jacob's ill-concealed amusement.

"He caused a good deal of grief," Fee explained to Ruth, controlling her laughter, "saying he was talking for God. If it wasn't for Jacob's and Nathanial's quick thinking, he would have mutinied against Ezekial."

"I've heard stories about the courage and resourcefulness both you and Nathanial exhibited on the trail, but this is the first I've heard that my own husband was a hero."

"Hardly a hero, Ruth," Jacob objected.

"He's too modest, I know," Ruth said, brushing his protest aside. "You'll have to tell me more sometime, Fee," she said with a mischievous smile. "When he's not here to interrupt." Then she added, "I hear stories about your trip west, and I'm envious. I wish that I'd insisted on going along. That way Jacob and I wouldn't have had to wait so long for each other."

"You wouldn't have made it," Jacob said tenderly. "Are you forgetting how frail you were when I left?"

From the concern in his eyes, Fee knew that it must have been a serious condition.

Ruth laughed lightly. "Ah, but you gave me something to live for, didn't you? Father said I gained in health with each of your letters. That's what convinced him I was up to the journey on the ship."

Suddenly Fee understood more completely why Jacob had left her. Ruth was a dear sweet person, one that Jacob least of all could abandon.

"Enough of all that," Ruth said, suddenly self-conscious. "We're going to be late for the illumination."

Great bonfires were beginning to flare around the city, heralding the start of the festivities. The streets were filled with carriages, wagons, and horses of all types, creating a clamor of rising intensity. Each person and each carriage carried at least one lighted torch. The whole city looked as if it were inhabited by thousands of giant fireflies.

Jacob's intention had been to listen to the speeches from the balcony of the office building he and Fee owned. The newspaper office was on the second floor. It overlooked the plaza, and they could watch from there. However, the stops and starts of the carriage and the shouts of the drivers indicated that they might not make it that far.

They had not gone five blocks in half an hour when bells rang from every church steeple and every place of business. Some proprietors had gone so far as to buy bells to ring; others had fashioned bells from pipes, pots, pans, and crockery. The clangor was deafening.

"That means it's seven-thirty," Jacob shouted, giving in to his impatience. "It's only a few more blocks. Would you mind walking?"

"Sounds exciting," Ruth agreed. "I'd love to. He never lets me do anything like this," she whispered to Fee. "I hope it's all right with you."

Fee forced a smile and pulled her cloak more tightly around

172

her shoulders. She'd been feeling weak all evening and had counted on the carriage ride to save her strength so she wouldn't spoil the evening for the others. Still, there seemed to be no choice; Jacob had already rapped on the roof to signal the driver, and Nathanial had opened the door and jumped to the street, holding his hand out to help her down.

Jacob led the way, and Fee leaned on Nathanial's arm for support. The crowd was growing thicker, and she was pushed and shoved as they all moved towards the center of the city, where the greatest illuminations were and where the speeches were scheduled to be given when the torchlight parade was completed.

She could hear a fiddle playing and laughter coming from up ahead. As they approached, they could see a young man with a wooden leg wearing a faded Union uniform and playing the fiddle while another man dressed in buckskins played the banjo. The people gathered around, cheering and clapping in time with the lively music.

The massa's run, ah ha!—the darkies stayed, oh ho!
Must be salvation's coming in the year of Jubilo!

The fiddler's voice was raw and untrained, but his enthusiasm carried the joy of the moment in words celebrating the end of the war.

"Year of Jubilo! That's what this is," proclaimed one reveler as he raised his hat overhead. "The massa's run!" and he did an unsteady jig before stopping to take a pull from his flask. "Son-a-bitchin' rebels done learned a real man don't run slaves."

Behind them, Fee heard a man with a strong southern accent murmur to his companion, "You'd think they'd find something other than the darkies' triumph to sing about."

Unfortunately, Fee wasn't the only one to overhear the remark. "You got cause to complain of the celebratin' here tonight?" a large hulk of a man demanded from a tavern doorway.

The Southerner rose to his full height and replied, "I have lived in this here state for six years, sir. It's a white man's state, and I have no complaints about what is here. I merely said that there should be something else to sing about other than the abolition of slavery."

"You're a goddamn Copperhead!" shouted a lanky man

nearby. "Bet you claim you're a Peace Democrat." He spat out the words.

The Southerner and his companion stopped in their tracks, hands sliding to their coat pockets. "We stand proud of our beliefs. No drunken northern abolitionist is going to frighten us into denying them. And not even a white-flag–waving General Lee is going to stop us from expressing them, much less the inebriated likes of you."

Fee's head was spinning. She kept picturing the missing leg of that poor Union soldier playing the fiddle and couldn't bear the thought that his celebration should be tarnished by bloodshed. "Please, sir," she said in her deepest Virginia drawl, "this is hardly the place or time for you to hold your pride above the safety of others. Perhaps if you moved away quickly . . ."

The crowd's attention turned from the musicians to the Southerners. Nathanial stepped closer to Fee and placed his hand on her shoulder, trying to guide her out of the mob.

The two Southerners looked around, suddenly realizing how tenuous their situation really was. One tried to slip away, only to be blocked by the two drunks from the tavern. As the other tipped his hat to Fee and stepped back, he was stopped also.

Nathanial's arm was holding her up as she leaned weakly against him. She didn't have the strength to get out of the ugly nightmare surrounding her.

Suddenly Jacob was standing on the top step of a nearby building. "Gentlemen," he cried out, "this is a time of celebration! No fighting! We finished with that in Appomattox."

"By Gaw, it's Jacob Teall the newspaperman," one of the men declared.

"You tell 'em, Mr. Teall," declared the large drunk from the doorway. "An' you put it in your paper, too!"

"Good idea," Jacob said with a smile. "Now, on with the music!" he added, tossing a gold coin into the musicians' fiddle case. "How about 'Camptown Races'?"

"Fee, you look pale," Nathanial said, holding her arm. "Can you make it?"

"It's only another block," Ruth said, taking her other arm. "You don't look well, dear."

The crowds and torches became a blur. Fee found herself at the side door of a large building. Jacob unlocked the door as her knees finally gave out on her. Somehow she was lifted in the air, and the last thing she remembered was the smell of Nathanial's coat.

Nathanial's mind was numbed by the shock of Fee's fainting. The thought of her ill sent chills through the center of his heart. Fee was too strong to be sick, too independent. . . . He gently laid her down on the chaise by the window of Jacob's office.

Luckily, Ruth was not immobilized by shock and panic. "Jacob, go get the doctor and a fast carriage. Nathanial, you stay here and help me loosen her clothing. Jacob," she cried sharply, "don't stand there! Move! Get Dr. Steinfeld. His office is just around the corner. He might still be there. Go!"

As Jacob went out the door she turned to Nathanial. "Take off her cloak and help me turn her over so I can loosen her stays. Is she pregnant?"

"Pregnant?" Nathanial stood frozen in place, the pieces finally falling into place for him. "I don't know . . ." he stammered. "She hasn't . . . she didn't tell me . . . but she's been so . . ."

"You should be more aware of your wife's cycles," she said with a gentle pat on his arm. "It helps you avoid such surprises. Now, don't be embarrassed. We can't afford the luxury of propriety in emergencies," she added. "Does she by any chance carry smelling salts in her bag?"

"Fee? Smelling salts?" Nathanial asked. He held her limp body while Ruth unlaced her clothing in the back. "She wouldn't even know what they were . . . until now," he added softly, looking down at her pale face. If only she'd be all right, he thought desperately, if only . . .

Ruth had Fee's dress slipped over her head and her waist cincher removed in no time. Nathanial was shocked to see a spreading red stain as Ruth untied her crinoline and slipped it down her legs. Her petticoat was soaked with blood.

"Oh, dear," Ruth said, then quickly smiled reassuringly at Nathanial. "Can you see if Jacob is coming with the doctor?"

In spite of Ruth's quick recovery, Nathanial had seen the fear on her face, and he was as shocked by that as he was by the sight of blood on Fee's garments.

"She's bleeding!" he exclaimed.

Ruth quickly covered Fee with her cloak, her face carefully noncommittal. "Yes, she seems to be," she said quietly.

Nathanial grabbed Ruth's arm and shook it. "Seems to be? My God, there's enough blood there to fill a calf. Do something! We can't just stand here and watch her bleed to death!"

Ruth's eyes quickly filled with tears. "I don't know what to do, Nathanial," she said. "I've never had any children, and I know nothing about these kinds of things."

Nathanial guiltily dropped her arm, "I'm sorry, I didn't—"

"I know," she whispered, "it's so frightening." She watched with silent tears while Nathanial knelt beside Fee, stroking her forehead. "There is one thing . . ." she said hesitantly. Nathanial quickly turned, his pale face hopeful. "It may sound unusual—"

"What? I'm willing to try anything," he said, standing up and putting his hands on Ruth's shoulders. "What is it?"

"Well, I know a woman who—" She was interrupted by the clomping of footsteps up the stairs. "Oh, I hope that's Jacob with the doctor."

Jacob came bursting in, followed by a puffing elderly gentleman with glasses. "How is she?" Jacob demanded.

"If you would slow down a bit, young man, I could catch my breath," complained Dr. Steinfeld. "Now, where's the patient?"

"She's over here, Doctor," Ruth said, "and she's still unconscious. There's considerable bleeding."

"Oh . . . yes, I see," he said, looking quickly under Fee's cloak. Turning to Nathanial and Jacob, he said, "I want you to go get me some water, preferably hot, and a basin and some towels. You should be able to get the tavern around the corner to give you some if you polish the barkeep's palm."

"Is she going to be all right?" Nathanial demanded.

"Not if you stand around here lollygagging, young man. Both of you get going because one can't carry it all. Now, go."

His voice was authoritative enough and his words frightening enough that neither Nathanial nor Jacob stood for a second longer but were gone.

"Now, then," he said, turning back to Ruth. "Tell me what happened."

By the time Ruth had spoken and he had checked Fee's eyes, pulse, and abdomen, the men were back with a steaming kettle of water, a bucket of cool water, three towels, and an enamel basin.

The doctor took them without a word and set up his bag on Jacob's desk. "You fellows wait outside," he said flatly.

Nathanial would have none of that. "No. I delivered her first child myself. I won't be shut out now."

Dr. Steinfeld looked at him, then nodded. "You can stay, but Jacob waits outside the door."

When Jacob paused, his eyes filled with pain, Ruth said softly, "Don't worry, dear, Nathanial and I will keep you posted."

Poor Jacob had no choice but to go outside and pace in the corridor of his own office building. The only person who could possibly have known the agony he was going through was Fee—and she wasn't even conscious.

It took the doctor only a cursory inspection to determine the cause of the problem. "She's miscarried, all right," he said, dropping some bloody matter into the basin, "but I can't do much about the bleeding. It's up to her."

"Goddamn it, man," Nathanial exploded, "what do you mean, it's up to her? She isn't even conscious. It's up to you, that's who it's up to!"

The stocky little man shook his head. "I'm sorry, young man. If that were her only hope, I'd not have much encouragement for you. But the human body is a wonderful thing. When the physician is incapable of doing anything more but the patient wants to live, miracles greater than this happen."

"Miracles? You mean she's—"

"I mean that she could stop bleeding a few minutes from now, or she could go on until there's no lifeblood left in her. It's not in my hands any longer." He turned to Ruth and said quietly, "She has had the benefit of my skill; now she'll have the benefit of my prayers."

"And mine," she whispered tearfully. "Thank you, Doctor."

"What else can we do?" Nathanial asked.

"She can't be moved until the bleeding stops. Keep her covered and warm. Give her plenty of liquids to drink when she's even partially conscious. And you might try talking to her even if she doesn't seem to hear you. I think they sometimes do. It might give her courage to fight."

His instructions were given as he stood in the open doorway, and Jacob's face behind him reflected the desperation he was seeing in Nathanial's face.

"How is she?" Jacob demanded.

"Your wife will explain, son. Best thing for you two young men is to use your energy rounding up some blankets and pillows to make her as comfortable as possible until you can move her. You could also find some good soup to offer her when she wakes up. I'll be at home if you need me." With that, he put his hat on and walked down the stairs.

"I was thinking earlier," Ruth said as Nathanial turned to her with unreasoning panic in his eyes, "there's one other thing we could try."

"Anything."

"Well, there's this woman I met in synagogue. We called them wise women in the old days. Well, some of the women have said Mrs. Hiram's skilled with herbs and folk remedies. I don't see that it would hurt to call her in to look at Fee."

"Where does she live?" Jacob asked, heading out the door.

"Just down from the synagogue, a block and a half on the right in that little yellow house with the vines in front."

Ruth caught Nathanial's arm before he could follow Jacob. "I need you to find those blankets and things the doctor was talking about. I'll stay here with Fee. You go to our house and get what we need to keep her warm and comfortable."

Having something to do eased Nathanial's anxiety as he spent his energy riding hard to the Tealls' house. He got blankets, pillows, and food from the housekeeper, whose concern was not only for Fee but also for the strain this might put on her mistress. "Now, you make sure she comes home and gets some rest," was her admonition to Nathanial as he hurried down the walk.

Her concern was not misplaced. Ruth was exhausted. She could feel her limited strength quickly ebbing. She pulled up a chair and took Fee's hand in hers as she sat down. The crowd outside cheered incongruously. Torchlight flickered on the dark wall, lighting it beyond the ring of warmth provided by the lamp. Ruth pulled the cloak tighter around Fee's pale face and huddled into her own coat.

The crowd cheered once more, and Ruth could hear the distant voice of a speaker intermittently interrupted by cheers and clapping.

"Oh," Fee moaned, turning restlessly.

Ruth was suddenly alert, reaching out and stroking her forehead, remembering what the doctor had said. "Yes, Fee dear, everything's all right," she crooned.

"Matthew . . ." Fee whispered, her eyes still closed. "Matthew," she called more intensely.

"Yes, dear. You must get well for Matthew. He needs you."

She moaned, tossing fretfully.

Ruth latched on to the idea that Fee was worried about her

178

son and tried to play on her mother's instinct, hoping to give Fee courage to live. "You must get well, Fee. You must get well for Matthew." She paused, watching Fee's pale face. "Get well for those who love you. Little Matthew needs you and loves you. Nathanial needs you and loves you." She added softly, "Jacob loves you—and even I love you."

"Matthew," Fee cried softly, a single tear rolling down her white cheek. "Oh, no . . . and Daddy . . ."

Chapter XV

Nathanial had just arrived and covered Fee with the blankets when they heard a clatter on the stairs. The door burst open and a hook-nosed woman with piercing black eyes stormed into the room. Jacob was still running up the stairs behind her.

"Where's the patient?" she demanded. Seeing Fee, she turned to Jacob, nearly knocking him over as she did so. "Take him on out with you," she commanded, pointing her thumb over her shoulder at Nathanial.

"I'm not leaving," Nathanial said stubbornly.

"She'll die if I don't get the bleeding stopped," she said sharply. "And I can't work with a man hanging over my shoulder wanting to know what I'm doing and getting ready to faint at the sight of it. Ruth can give me all the help I need. You'll know soon enough how she is." As she talked, she shoved Nathanial and Jacob out the door. Before she closed it, she added, "Besides, I need you to go down to the corner tavern and get me some hot water." With that she slammed the door and dashed to Fee, throwing her shawl and bag on the floor in her haste.

She pulled a bar of lye soap from her apron pocket and quickly lathered her hands and arms. "Not many do this, but they lose more patients than I do. I think it's worth taking the time." Wiping her hands on the towel Ruth handed her, she turned to the chaise.

"Let's see," she said, deftly examining Fee. Then, "Hellfire! He didn't even clean her out. Hand me the basin," she commanded Ruth. "Damned men," she muttered as she worked quickly, "they shouldn't be allowed near a woman. Don't know the first thing about them. A woman needs a woman doctor, but where are they?" she said as she quickly threw bloody tissue into the basin. Ruth felt her head begin to spin but forced herself to look away and take deep breaths.

"She's bleeding something awful," Mrs. Hiram explained. "But I got all the placenta out. Sorry, sweet one," she said to the unconscious Fee. "It's the only way." With that she shoved one fist up inside Fee and clamped the other over her abdomen and held it.

Even in her unconscious state, Fee's body reacted. Her back arched, and she gasped in pain. Ruth rushed to hold her head, wiping her forehead with her handkerchief. "Is she—?"

Mrs. Hiram shook her head. "Still breathing, but she won't be if the bleeding doesn't stop." After a few minutes she gently removed her hands and watched. "Maybe we stopped it," she said with a hopeful smile. "Get me that brown vial out of my bag."

"What is it?" Ruth asked as she handed it to her.

"Ergot," she said, lifting Fee's head. "Made from rye smut, and it stops bleeding real good. Got some teas to give her soon as she's conscious, but this has got to get in her fast."

Mrs. Hiram's large square hands were garden-rough, but her touch was gentle as she forced the bitter syrup down Fee's throat. A strand of gray hair escaped from her bun and fell over her weathered cheek.

"There you go, sweet one," she crooned, "just a bit more. There," she said gently, letting Fee's head back down on the pillow.

Fee's eyes fluttered open momentarily. Then she drifted off into her other world, as Ruth now thought of it.

"That's how she's been ever since we got here," Ruth said.

Mrs. Hiram nodded as if it was to be expected. "You can let those two men back in," she said brusquely. "On second thought, better let me look at you first," she said, making Ruth sit down. "You're too pale for a healthy person. How do you feel?"

"I am a bit tired," Ruth admitted.

"Here," Mrs. Hiram said, rummaging through her bag, "drink this. It'll help bolster you up a bit. You're too weakly." She quickly poured hot water over some dried leaves and handed the cup to Ruth, saying, "Let it steep for three minutes. Won't hurt to chew on the leaves at the bottom, either. Stay put. I'll get the men myself."

"You can come in," she said, opening the door, "if you tell me what smells so good in that basket over there."

"It's some soup their housekeeper sent along," Nathanial said, never taking his eyes from Fee. "How is she?"

"Too soon to tell," Mrs. Hiram replied honestly. "We'll just have to wait. While we are, you get that soup out. We got another lady here we don't want fainting on us, and you two don't look any too good, either."

Within moments, the two men were also under Mrs. Hiram's spell. Somehow her bustling around, her blunt honesty, and her motherly commands made them all take hope and relax.

"Fee was calling out when you were gone," Ruth said to Nathanial. "I thought she was concerned about your son because she kept crying 'Matthew,' but then she cried for her father as well. She seemed so upset, it didn't make much sense to me."

Nathanial nodded. "It does to me. Matthew was her brother's name, too. Little Matthew has brown eyes just like him." Then, pushing away his half-eaten bowlful of soup, he proceeded to tell Ruth and Mrs. Hiram the story of the massacre on Bear Creek Ridge, including the part about Ezekial's brother's family. When he finished, the others were silent for a moment. Then Ruth said softly, "Poor thing. In just five years she's lost her father, her brother, her home, and her firstborn child."

"And now this," Mrs. Hiram added.

"I never heard the story all the way through," Jacob said. "Did they ever get those men?"

Nathanial shook his head. "Not that I know of. Didn't even act like they were going to try." A cheer rose from the crowd outside the window, and the band started playing "Yankee Doodle."

An hour later, Mrs. Hiram checked Fee, then told Nathanial and Jacob to get a carriage.

"Can we move her?" Nathanial said, stopping his pacing.

"Her color looks better. I'll examine her after you're gone and find out for sure. Either way, you're going to need that carriage. She can't stay here any longer," she said with a nod to Ruth, who was dozing in a chair.

The sound of the men shutting the door behind them awakened Ruth. "What's happening?" she asked.

181

"Shush, don't worry," Mrs. Hiram said. "I'm going to check Fee. Then you're going home."

"The bleeding?"

"Bring that lamp closer," she said in answer. After a few moments she muttered something under her breath, then put the covers back.

"How is she?" Ruth asked anxiously.

"Looks like the bleeding's stanched. If you're real careful and don't jar her too much, she might be all right. I'll come by tomorrow and check on her."

"Ruth?" Fee's voice was faint but clear.

"Fee! You're awake. We've been so worried."

"What happened? Where's Nathanial?"

"You've been terribly sick," she answered softly.

Mrs. Hiram stepped forward and looked Fee in the eye. "Been tending you all evening, Mrs. Coughlin. You miscarried that baby you were carrying. You've been bleeding awful bad. I've got some tea I want you to drink down before we take you back to the Tealls'."

"Miscarried? Is it . . . what happened? I never should have—"

"Shush, stop your worrying," Mrs. Hiram said as she held the cup to Fee's mouth and raised her up to drink. "There's nothing can be done to stop a miscarriage like yours. Some babies just aren't right for being born. This one was like that. It's nature's way of taking care of mistakes . . . mistakes that are none of your doing," she added, wiping a tear from Fee's cheek.

"I was angry that I was pregnant again." She sobbed. "If I hadn't been angry—"

"Nonsense. You probably knew something wasn't right from the beginning. That's what made you not want it. You'll see. Soon's you're pregnant again, you'll be carrying a healthy baby and happy about it."

"You sound so sure," Fee said drowsily.

"I am. Now go to sleep. When you awaken, you'll be in Ruth and Jacob's house."

For Fee, the next two days were a collage woven through the lace-curtained light of the bedroom. Nathanial, pale and worried in the bright morning light—Ruth, gentle and calm in the warm afternoon light—Jacob, anxious in the filtered dusk of evening—Nathanial, in the pale lantern of night, all were seen in the blur of her waking, which often was indistinguishable from the haunting dreams that filled her mind.

"You must live for your loved ones," whispered Ruth's voice. "Don't die, Fee. I love you," pleaded Nathanial's voice. "Live, my Fionna. I love you," urged Jacob's voice.

Sometimes Jacob was Matthew, sometimes Mrs. Hiram's hands were her father's, sometimes Ruth's soft voice was Donnell calling her. The living and the dead swirled indiscriminately around her as she lay trembling between the two worlds.

Then on the third day she opened her eyes and looked at Nathanial with the clarity of one who has passed through shadowy dangers and survived. "How long have you been there?" she asked.

His eyes were soft with relief. "Three lifetimes."

"I'm sorry I've worried you. What's today?"

"Saturday."

"I've been sick that long?"

"Too long. How do you feel?"

"Tired . . . and hungry."

"Good. Miss Meisinger, the housekeeper, has chicken soup on the stove. I'll go get it."

"Where are Ruth and Jacob?"

"They've gone to synagogue. It's their Sabbath. First time they've left the house since you took ill."

"I'm such a bother," she said with a sigh.

"No, you're so loved," he said, kissing her on the cheek. She drifted off to sleep again until he returned.

A distant church bell rang as Nathanial spooned the soup into her mouth. Then it was joined by a closer one in a long and mournful drone, then another, more distant. Fee swallowed, then asked, "Didn't you say today was Saturday?"

"Yes," he said, getting up to pull the curtain back and look out the window. "Wonder what's going on?"

"What time is it? Maybe the churches chime the hour."

"Ten to one. That's strange . . . here come Jacob and Ruth. They couldn't be done yet, could they? They look upset."

There was a flurry of activity down below. Jacob shouted for Miss Meisinger, and it sounded as if Ruth were crying. "What's going on?" Nathanial called down the stairs. There was a muffled answer and he said, "Come on up. Fee's awake and eating."

"Thank God something good has happened," Ruth cried in a broken voice as she climbed the stairs.

"I've got to go. Just brought Ruth home first," Jacob was saying as he came in the door, his face flushed under his dark beard. "I can't believe it's happened. Thomas found me in the synagogue. It just came over the telegraph."

"It's so terrible," Ruth said and then started crying anew.

"What's happened?" Nathanial shouted above the confusion. Jacob glanced hesitantly towards Fee.

"Hearing can't be worse than imagining," she told him. He nodded resignedly. "It's Lincoln. He's been shot."

"What?" Nathanial exclaimed. "How?"

"Oh, dear God," Fee cried, sitting upright. "Is he—"

"He's dead." Jacob uttered the words in disbelief. "It happened at a play last night. He died this morning at twenty-two minutes after seven. They say it's treason. A plot from the South. God knows what this means, what kind of retribution the hotheads will want to extract from the South. It might mean that the war isn't even . . ." He stopped and looked at Fee, who had fallen back on her pillow, tears streaming down her cheeks. "I'm sorry. I never should have told you," he cried, taking her hand. "It's a miracle seeing you awake again. You're not strong enough for such a shock."

Fee was moved by the profound concern she saw in his eyes. "I'm all right, Jacob. Just a little weak, that's all." She patted his hand reassuringly. "The strength of this country comes from a well-informed citizenry." She forced calm into her voice. "You said that yourself, and now it's more true than ever. Go, exercise the free press," she said, ending with a melodramatic gesture.

Jacob broke into a laugh. "Ah, Fionna," he cried. "Whatever would we do without you?"

"Probably about as you do now," she said pithily.

"Oh, no," Ruth said, laughing. "We'd never do as well. I'm so glad you're better."

Nathanial began laughing with them. Although Fee was astounded at their near-hysteria, she knew it was merely a release from all the tensions they'd been living with. "If you will be so kind as to take your party elsewhere, I want to sleep." Then, as they started guiltily, she added with a smile, "Your laughter is more healing than any of Mrs. Hiram's herbs. Thank you for everything."

She was still weak and sleepy, but it was clear to Nathanial that she was going to get well. That night, for the first time since her miscarriage, he slept beside her in the bed instead of in the chair. She awakened to find him watching her in the early-morning light, and from his haggard face and the pain in his eyes, she knew how frightened he had been. Her heart filled with gratitude and love for this red bear of a man who was so tender, yet so incapable of expressing the depth of his emotions. He was devoted to her and a good father to Matthew. She felt very lucky. And she loved him deeply.

By Monday Nathanial had Mrs. Hiram's assurance that Fee was on the mend. Buoyed by the news, he asked Fee if she would mind if he went back down to Salem. He felt he should check not only the farm and the mill but also see that the new creamery was being built properly. The assassination of Lincoln had left everyone with an uneasy feeling, a feeling of impermanence, of lurking danger. Fights and riots were breaking out spontaneously around the nation as people irrationally took out their anger and sorrow on people they imagined were part of "the plot." Nathanial felt he should check to make sure that nothing had happened to their businesses. After all, they did come from Virginia, and many people knew it.

"I hate to leave when you're still sick," he told her. Then taking her hand between his two big hands, he added with endearing awkwardness, "I don't know what I'd do . . . what I'd do without you."

"Nor I without you," Fee said, kissing his head as he leaned against her shoulder. She knew he was trying to regain control, trying not to cry, not wanting her to see what he considered a weakness—and her eyes filled with tears, as much for herself as for him.

After a moment he got up, walked to the window, and stood there with his hands in his pockets, looking out. "I'm going to bring Matthew back with me," he said finally.

"But he's so young," Fee protested. "It's asking too much of the Tealls to bring him into their orderly household. I've already been such a burden to them."

Nathanial shook his head. "It was Jacob's suggestion. And Ruth agreed immediately. She even offered to ride down and help me bring him back up, but we decided you needed her here. We'll catch the morning stage and be here by night. He'll do just fine. Stop fretting."

"I do miss him," she admitted. "How long will you be?"

"Probably no more than four or five days. Jacob and Ruth have asked us to stay at least another two weeks. They insist that the house is big enough for us all. There are four bedrooms upstairs and one down, Fee. Stop protesting."

That evening Fee ate an early dinner in her room, and

slept through the night. She awakened when Nathanial kissed her good-bye, only to fall back asleep again until mid-morning.

"I've brought something to remind you that it's spring," Ruth said when she came in to check on her. She set a pot of hyacinths on the washtable where Fee could see it.

"It's lovely, Ruth," she said, smelling the sweet fragrance. "I'm so frustrated, Ruth," she admitted. "My arms are shaky if I even try to lift a hairbrush. I'm not used to being so helpless and dependent."

Ruth laughed as she sat down on the edge of the bed. "Please don't feel badly. I'm enjoying being the strong one. This'll be the only time in our friendship that I'll have that privilege," she added wistfully. "Now, it's such a warm day, let's get you down to the front porch, where you can soak up some of the afternoon sunshine. What do you think?"

"Oh, I'd love it," Fee cried.

"Now that you're not sleeping so much, I thought maybe you'd like to read a book. I have a few here that you might enjoy. And we can read aloud to one another," Ruth added. "I've always wanted a friend I could share these things with. When I was sick I would sit and imagine what it would be like to have a friend to read with and talk to . . . and now," she added as her bright smile erased the dreary memory, "I have that friend."

"I've never had a friend like that, either," Fee admitted. "Nathanial and Jacob and Ezekial are the closest, but there are some things they don't understand because they aren't women."

"They most certainly aren't that!" Ruth exclaimed.

"Tell me," Fee said when their laughter had subsided, "what's happening in the news? Has the assassination renewed hostilities? Who shot Lincoln?"

Ruth shrugged. "I'm afraid I don't know. You'll have to ask Jacob. I believe he did say that the peace is still on."

As much as she'd come to care for Ruth, Fee knew that she'd never be the companion for her that Jacob had been. What they had shared that golden summer had been a rare bonding of mind, soul, and body. Now it was gone, with only their son to prove it had ever existed. The thought suddenly overwhelmed her. It was Jacob who'd requested that Nathanial bring Matthew back up to Portland.

"Is something the matter?" Ruth asked anxiously.

"Oh, no," Fee said guiltily. "Do you think you could call Miss Meisinger to help me downstairs?"

"Of course," Ruth said, jumping up from her chair. "I'll put the chaise out on the protected south side of the porch."

Soon Fee was reclining on the porch, her eyes closed, in the soft warmth of the April sun. A pot of hot tea was on the table beside her elbow, and Ruth was reading from a popular book of poetry that Fee found rather insipid. She longed for the steady cadences of Wordsworth or the clear thoughts of Thoreau but didn't have the heart to tell Ruth. Jacob would understand.

She didn't know how long she'd been dozing. Ruth had left shortly after lunch, promising to return as quickly as possible. But it wasn't Ruth coming up the steps that had awakened her. When she opened her eyes, Fee saw Jacob standing by the porch pillar, gazing at her.

"You look lovely in the sunshine," he said softly.

"You startled me," she said with a smile. "What time is it?"

"Just three o'clock. How long have you been outside?"

"Probably too long. That breeze is beginning to feel a bit chilly. Could you get Ruth and Miss Meisinger to help me in?"

"Ruth is still shopping, and from the sounds of it, Miss Meisinger is doing the laundry out back. I can handle the job, if you don't object."

The thought of Jacob so near, of Jacob touching her, made her heart turn over, but she knew she couldn't let him know. She forced a casual smile. "If you don't mind," she said, holding out her hand and swinging her feet over the side of the chaise.

As he put his arm around her waist, she tried to concentrate on using all her strength to stand up on her own, telling herself that she was imagining the musty man-scent of him so near, that she was only remembering the strong warmth of his body, that it was her illness making her weak, not his nearness. Still, her legs would not hold her, and she faltered.

Instantly his arms lifted her, cradling her from harm. She looked into his eyes, and her heart soared like a butterfly.

"Thank goodness you caught her, Mr. Teall," Miss Meisinger exclaimed from the doorway. "I was coming to check on you, Mrs. Coughlin. I was just hanging out the clothes and thought to myself, that breeze seems a bit chilly. Here, can I help you get her upstairs, Mr. Teall?"

"She's as light as a feather, Miss Meisinger," he said, not taking his eyes from Fee's. "I'll manage just fine." Then, finally looking at the housekeeper, he added, "If you will be so kind as to prepare us tea and bring it up, perhaps I can induce Mrs. Coughlin to eat something."

"Thank you, Miss Meisinger," Fee called out, grateful that the woman had not seemed to notice anything strange. Yet how could she not be aware of the powerful currents flowing between them? How could she not hear the beating of Fee's heart nor see the love in Jacob's eyes?

In her weakened state it was more than Fee could bear. The world seemed to swirl around her, and she rested her head on Jacob's shoulder as he carried her up the stairs, giving in to the joy of being surrounded by him once more, yet weakened by it at the same time. *If I must die*, she thought, *let it be in his arms*.

The sunlight angled across her freshly made bed as he gently set her down on the comforter. Then, tenderly, he took her face in his hands and kissed her, tentatively at first, then deeply as she put her arms around him, holding her to him possessively and hungrily.

"Jacob, we can't . . . No, stop . . ." Fee pleaded with tears overflowing.

"You know we'll never stop loving one another," he whispered, trailing his lips across her cheek and down her neck. "That's the one constant in both our lives."

"I thought you would forget—"

"Forget my very soul? Forget my son? What kind of a fool do you think I am?"

"You never should have asked Nathanial to bring him up here."

"Damnit! He's my son. I've every right to see him. I love him. He's of our flesh, the one beautiful thing between us that we can hold on to. Don't keep him from me."

Defeated, Fee rested her cheek against his chest and whispered, "He looks like you."

"Nathanial said he has your brother's eyes."

"They're yours. Someday someone is sure to notice."

There was the rattling of china coming up the stairs. Jacob handed Fee his handkerchief and quickly went to the door. "I was just going to come down and see if you needed help carrying everything up," he said to the housekeeper.

"I'm just fine, Mr. Teall," she said briskly. "But I do need you to bring that table over nearer to Mrs. Coughlin if you will. I cut up some of that lovely cheese you brought, Mrs. Coughlin. Thought it might do you some good to taste your own." She set the tray down on the table and turned and looked at Fee.

"You look all washed out," she exclaimed. Then she turned to Jacob accusingly. "Don't go giving her any of your long stories, now. You get her to eat and then you leave her to sleep until dinnertime."

"I'll stay only long enough to make sure she cleans her plate," Jacob assured her with a smile. "If Mrs. Teall comes home, send her up to join us."

When she was gone, he handed Fee some buttered bread and a slice of cheese.

"What are we to do?" she asked.

"As we've been doing. We don't have any choice, do we?" he said, pouring the tea.

"Ruth needs you." It wasn't a question any longer but a statement born of understanding.

He nodded, then added, "But I need you."

"And I you."

"And what of Nathanial?"

"And Matthew? Oh, it's more than I can sort out, Jacob," she cried. "Is it possible to love two people at the same time in two such different ways? It seems that we're both bound in a web of love we wouldn't cast off if we could."

"I know." He was silent for a moment, then added, "I'm afraid it's going to be too much of a strain for you." He took her hand and pressed it to his lips. "I nearly revealed everything when I thought you were going to die. It was all I could do to keep from shoving everyone else out the door and holding you in my arms until you got well. Instead, I slipped in when the others were sleeping or busy elsewhere and watched you, held you . . ."

"I remember seeing your face sometimes. I didn't know if it was a dream or not."

"I was afraid that you'd say something in your delirium."

"I didn't?"

"Not that anyone else could understand."

Their eyes held for a moment, reading the bond they shared, exulting in the reaffirmation of their love. Then, for the sheer joy of the moment, Fee laughed, and Jacob joined her.

"It sounds like you two are having a party," Ruth said, coming into the room. "I was invited to join you, according to Miss Meisinger. Do you mind?"

"Oh, Ruth, come in," Fee said with a curious mixture of

189

guilt and relief. "Jacob is trying to fatten me up. You must help me."

Ruth smiled warmly as she untied her bonnet and pulled up a chair. "If he can do that as well as make you laugh, then he needs no help. It's wonderful to see you getting better. The sunshine must have helped. Your cheeks have some color."

Fee turned to Jacob and said with genuine happiness, "I've never thanked you for bringing me such a lovely friend as Ruth, Jacob, so I will now. I shall always cherish her."

"Oh, it is I who should be thanking him for you," Ruth exclaimed as her eyes filled with tears.

But it was Jacob who understood and was grateful.

Chapter XVI

Spring laced their Portland days with a silvery rain that enhanced rather than hindered their time together. The air was washed fresh and clean with each new dawning. Bright spring flowers flourished as did their friendship. Matthew toddled sassily from one adult to another, gathering love and attention from doting grownups until even his baby needs were sated. And they all basked in the glow of Fee's returning health.

With May came the warm sunshine and a quickening of the earth. It was time to return to Quail Hollow.

The five parted company early one morning. Fee cried at leaving, Ruth cried to see them go, and Jacob was loath to turn his son over to Nathanial's arms once more. Nathanial shook his friend's hand heartily and overlong. Then Fee, Nathanial, and Matthew climbed aboard the stage and they all turned back to the lives they had chosen.

Only Fee and Jacob knew the painful pull of other lives, other choices, and secretly mourned.

By June Fee was feeling quite herself and told Nathanial so, having quickly tired over the past month of his gentle and platonic affection.

"That's why I thought I should start sleeping in the other

bedroom," Nathanial said matter-of-factly as he methodically pulled clothes out of the drawers and piled them on the bed.

"Whatever are you talking about?" Fee exclaimed. She stopped brushing her hair and went to him. "I said, I'm just fine." She put her arms around his waist and leaned her head against his shoulder, enjoying the feel of his taut muscles through her cotton nightgown. "You can love me whenever you want," she whispered.

"I do love you—too much to risk losing you ever again," he said brusquely, turning from her, his fists clenched. "I will never again sit helplessly, watching your lifeblood draining from you, knowing that this is what comes of my loving you," he said hoarsely. Then he picked up his things and went out the door, letting it close behind him.

"You're a fool!" Fee cried, running to the door, calling after him. "What kind of a man would do this? What kind of a man would leave me to sleep alone?"

Nathanial stopped and looked back at her, the pale light from the bedroom lamp shadowing his face. "A man who loves you," he said sorrowfully. He went into the other bedroom and closed the door.

Fee threw her hairbrush against his wall, slammed the door, and fell upon the bed, sobbing in frustration and anger.

How could he do this to her? How dare he? First he'd taught her the joys of sexual love, made her yearn for his touch, then chosen to spend nearly half of each year away from her. And now . . . now, this. She felt rejected and unloved, and she cried herself to sleep, awakening in the morning with a cold hollow in the pit of her stomach as she looked at the empty pillow next to hers.

In spite of her anger, Fee knew that Nathanial still loved her. It was in his eyes when he looked at her and in his gentle touch as he held her and chastely kissed her good night outside her bedroom door. That was the irony of it all.

A few weeks later she was watching him chop wood, admiring the muscles rippling along his bare back as he swung the ax, and she felt her frustration and longing grow. Then she realized what power was hers to use. Here was a man whose very nature demanded that he wander free and unfettered, yet here he was, voluntarily committing himself to stay on the land with her. It certainly wasn't from any false sense of duty, nor was it because of any legal paper saying he was married and obligated to her. It was not only love but it was the sexual pull she had over him. That was what had first brought him into her wagon, that was what drew him back to her every spring. Now, if she didn't use that power, he might find that he no longer had any reason to return to her. In that moment Fee knew what she could do.

With a smug smile on her face, she turned back to hanging up her laundry. "Your daddy is going to have a run for his money," she said, lifting Matthew out of the empty laundry basket.

"Daddy run?" he asked with a quizzical look on his baby face.

"Oh, yes." Fee laughed as they headed towards the woodshed, "Daddy run." She walked with long, purposeful strides, feeling the power of her own body renewed with each step.

"When you're done with that," she said as she approached Nathanial, "will you please come on down to the water hole in the creek? I want you to help me with Matthew. It's so hot this afternoon, it's the perfect time for it, and we're long overdue," she added over her shoulder.

It was an idea she'd been thinking about for some time. Now it would serve two purposes. By the time Nathanial got to the stream's edge, she and Matthew were in the water, stark naked.

"What the hell you doing?" he asked.

"I'm not about to have another son drown. This boy is going to begin learning how to swim before he's two, the sooner the better. By the time he's four he'll no longer be scaring me with images of him slipping off to the creek and not being able to take care of himself."

"But why are you . . ." he stammered, never taking his eyes from her. "Do you have to be . . ."

Fee laughed, a feeling of exultation flowing through her. "I'm hot and dirty after working all day. I figured I could bathe while you teach him to swim." She looked at him appraisingly. "But you'd better strip down if you're going to join us."

"You're like a couple of little savages," he said with a growl, pulling his shirt over his head. "There's not an ounce of modesty between the two of you."

Fee chuckled inwardly, noticing that he chose not to take off his breeches and knowing the reason why. "And why should there be? It'd be false modesty," she said firmly, handing the squealing, splashing little boy to him. "There's not a soul to see us for miles around. Could you hand me that soap, please?" she asked, thoroughly enjoying the effect her nakedness was having on him.

While Nathanial splashed in the water with Matthew, trying valiantly to concentrate on teaching him to kick, Fee lathered herself from head to toe, then lay back in the cool water, letting her hair stream around her as she looked up at tufts of clouds floating overhead. When she finally rose from the water, her hair streaming down her back and over her breasts, she saw the hunger in Nathanial's eyes and knew that her days of forced celibacy were at an end.

That night after Matthew was asleep, she lit a candle and slipped into Nathanial's bedroom.

"Is something the matter?" Nathanial asked, rising up on his elbow as she placed the candlestick on his bedside table.

"I couldn't sleep," she said, unbuttoning her nightgown and letting it slip to the floor around her feet. "I thought maybe you could help me."

His eyes devoured every line of her nakedness as he helplessly watched her climb into his bed. She felt a surge of power warm her body. He would make love to her—even when he was afraid to, even when he didn't want to—because she could make him desire her.

"Fee, don't—" he said hoarsely.

"It's not your fault," she said, pulling back his covers and trailing kisses up his naked chest to his throat, savoring the man-smell of him, enjoying the hard lines of his tightly muscled body. "I'll take the responsibility. Just enjoy me."

She ran her hand down his side, along his thighs, and between his legs, finally caressing his hard erection with her fingers, delicately teasing him, then stroking him slowly. A long shiver ran the length of his body, and a low moan escaped his lips, a moan that built up to a growl of desire as he pulled her to him, and took her with a savagery she'd never experienced before. But she was ready for him, giving as much as he gave until they both cried out in release. Then they lay, still joined together, panting in surprise at the intensity of their lovemaking.

Nathanial looked down at her, gently brushing her hair from her eyes. "Did I hurt you?" he whispered.

"Not now. What hurt was when you refused me."

"I thought I could because I love you so much. But I can't. Are you sure you're willing to take the chance?"

"Willing? I demand the chance." She giggled. "I have no intention of letting Matthew grow up an only child. He's already too spoiled and hasn't the slightest idea of what it means to share."

"Is that the only reason?" he asked in mock hurt.

"Only a secondary one," she said, raising her hips as she felt him growing once more inside her.

This time he loved her gently and long, prolonging their enjoyment of one another, expertly teasing her until she cried out with pleasure.

Never again would they need two bedrooms. Never again would Fee discount her own power.

It seemed as if Fee's life were tied to the seasons, ebbing and flowing as the land flourished and waned with the changing months. Matthew toddled after her and Nathanial, growing sturdy and strong, tanned like ripe wheat in the summer sunlight. The cattle calved, the garden teemed with vegetables, the trees were heavy with fruit, and the fields buzzed with bees.

Fee watched her brother's namesake in the fullness of the summer sunlight and mourned that he had not lived to see that namesake's dark hair tangled with hayseeds or his dimpled knees covered with dirt. She mourned that her brother was gone and his murderers alive, that her brother, buried in the dark Virginia earth, would never sing to his nephew but that somewhere in the sunlight his murderers laughed.

The nights turned cool and the air bore a crisp feeling of expectancy. It was a time of waiting. Then one evening she saw the "V" of geese overhead, silhouetted against the golden clouds, calling their farewell. Frost turned the blackberry leaves along the fence amber and rust, and the animals' fur thickened in preparation for winter, and Fee, squirrel-like, canned, pickled, and dried the last of their harvest.

As she smoked and salted thick hams over the fire, she remembered her father and how he loved her ham and beans, and she mourned again. It seemed as if her lost father and brother were haunting her more often, surprising her with their memory in everyday things. Seeing her brother's smile on Matthew's face, imagining her father's laughter at the antics of a calf, her loneliness for her lost family grew. And the thought of their murder galled her. Now that she had her own home, the comfort and time to remember, it galled her.

By the time she was harvesting the pumpkins, Fee knew she was pregnant again. She didn't tell Nathanial lest he bother her with worrying. But he suspected something, because he returned from eastern Oregon in February. Having his suspicions confirmed, he hovered over her like a hawk.

Her new creamery was running smoothly. She made a trip into Salem about every two weeks to check on it and talk over decisions with her manager. Harley Gould was helping out regularly, and she knew he would soon be ready to take on more responsibility, something she was ready to give him.

In the meantime, she'd hired a man, Abner Winkle, who'd lost one leg in the Union Army fourteen months before the end of the war. As Abner told her when he came looking for a job, he'd cursed both the South and the North and headed west, where he intended to stay. Since he'd worked in a creamery when he was fifteen, Fee hired him on the spot. He had proved a worthy, hardworking, and loyal employee and she never had occasion to regret flying in the face of the advice of well-meaning, two-legged men.

However Abner was only the harbinger of a huge influx of manpower coming into the state. At the mill Nathanial was besieged by men looking for work. The roads were frequently occupied by strangers walking or riding weary Army mules, all trained in war and newly discharged, all looking for a meal, work, and a new life in the West.

In late March, Fee once again moved into Salem and stayed with Mrs. Gould. Fee was so large that she could no longer care for herself or do the chores around the farm and creamery. On the second day of April she gave birth to two strapping boys. The surprise brought a whoop of joy from Nathanial and a sigh of relief from Fee. As their sons cried lustily, she fell asleep. When she awakened, Nathanial and Mrs. Gould told her they wanted to name them Timothy and Daniel.

"Daniel for my brother who was killed by that bear, and Timothy for Mrs. Gould's father," Nathanial explained happily. Fee wearily agreed and went back to sleep.

As Fee and the twins gathered strength under Mrs. Gould's watchful eye, Fee once more took notice of the world around her. Salem was no longer the small town she'd seen at first. It was growing with each day, and part of that growth was due to the arrival of families and ex-soldiers, refugees from the Civil War, fleeing the ashes of their old lives. Amid the hard-working, wearied families were the stragglers, drifters still in their ragged uniforms. Fee would look at the twins and in their broad brows and blue eyes she would see her father, and she hated the soldiers.

It was these stragglers who kept Fee's anger riled. Some were clearly not Union soldiers. Their thick southern accents, empty defiance, butternut trousers, and ragged jackets said as much. It was these rebel soldiers whom Fee eyed suspiciously as she rode to town. It was these men, ragged and beaten, whom she hated without reason and blamed for the death of her father and brother. It was these men who were most puzzled by her icy reception when they applied for work at the creamery, especially in light of her soft Virginia accent.

One night when Pearl and Ezekial were over for dinner, Fee couldn't help expressing her rancor.

"T'ain't just rebels, it's Union, too," Ezekial said as he dandled one twin on each knee. "Lots of them finished soldiers are feelin' desperate times. 'At's why they come out here, lookin' for a new start." He paused and chucked Daniel under the chin. "We were looking for the same thing when we came," he added, with a sharp glance in Fee's direction.

"We were different," she protested.

"We just caught on earlier," Nathanial said with a grin.

"Well, there are some strange things happening," Pearl interjected. "I was talking to Mrs. Donnelson down at the store last time we were in town, Ezekial. She was telling me about a terrible thing some of them are doing to poor, unsuspecting women. They're just taking advantage of our good and open nature, that's what."

"What're you talking about, woman?" Ezekial asked impatiently.

"They call it the twenty-dollar-gold-piece trick. Lord knows not all folks got food to spare these days. Most aren't lucky like us. Well, Mrs. Donnelson says that there's these men goin' around to farms, asking to buy a meal. Well, no one is going to turn a hungry person away from their door, not good God-fearing folk like we got around here. When they give him a meal out of their own larder, he eats it right up and then offers to pay for it with a twenty-dollar gold piece, saying that's all he's got."

"So what's so bad about a man paying for his meal honest-like?" Ezekial demanded.

"Who's got change for a twenty-dollar gold piece lying around their house these days?" Pearl pointed out triumphantly. "It's here the story takes two different turns.

Most just say they don't have it, so the man goes off with a free meal in his belly and the farm wife sits stewing because she's been robbed and can't do anything about it."

"You said there were two things that can happen," Fee said encouragingly.

"This's the worst part. If the woman—and they always choose to go to a farmhouse when there's no man around— says she'll get the change and goes into a back room to get it, he follows her and robs her of all she's got at gunpoint."

"Sounds like a story made up to frighten naughty children," Nathanial said with a snort of disbelief.

"Well, Mrs. Donnelson says it's true. She's had people telling her that knows," Pearl replied defensively.

"Still it doesn't hurt to be a bit cautious these days," Fee said reflectively. "It's just the kind of thing those rebels would think of doing. They're too cowardly to do anything outright."

"Come on, Fee," Nathanial said, going out on the porch with Ezekial, "it wasn't the whole South that killed your father and brother."

"In a way it was," Ezekial said softly but not out of earshot. "It was the whole Southern system what did it, killed her kin and mine. Don't hurt none to keep your powder dry."

Chapter XVII

Nathanial left that autumn with a herd of two hundred cattle, including several from Fee's herd for breeding stock. His cattle ranch, including the rangeland, was growing, and he was hiring people to run it full-time, the same as he was hiring men to run his sawmills year-round.

While Nathanial's businesses prospered, so did Fee's, in spite of the postwar depression affecting the rest of the nation. Both of them were producing goods for which there was a high demand.

By February, Fee decided she needed to have a full-fledged delivery system. Harley Gould was sixteen and more than ready to take the responsibility. Fee knew she could have no one more faithful and conscientious. Besides, he idolized Abner Winkle, and the two of them made a good team.

By March she was beginning to think that she needed four more hands and was seriously considering another two, if only she could find the right ones. In the meantime, she was grateful for Pearl and Ezekial, who cared for the boys once a week, and Wesley Fleming who was still her hired hand.

When Harley rode out one evening, she knew something was wrong.

"What's the matter?" she asked as he hitched his horse.

"Well, Miz Coughlin, I hate to come talk to you about this, but I don't see no other way 'round it."

"Well, come on in and sit down, Harley. Tell me what's bothering you."

"It's Mr. Winkle," he blurted out. "He does more work than a man with two legs and it's still not enough. You just got to get yourself another person. There, I done said it. Mr. Winkle, he's goin' to be real mad at me 'cuz he'll be thinking it's because of his one leg, but that's just not the case."

"Slow down, Harley," Fee laughed. "I know it's getting out of hand. We'll hire someone when I come in Thursday. You keep an eye out and tell Abner to do the same. And you can tell Abner that it's my idea because it really is."

Harley's face fairly burst with a grin. "I just knew you'd understand."

The rose bush was gnarled and dry, but tiny red nubbins at the end of some of its branches told Fee it was time to prune and train its vines. By the end of May it would be covered with bright yellow blossoms and crinkled green leaves that were almost as fragrant as the flowers themselves. It was the same rosebush that had grown along her mother's garden fence, the same rosebush she'd nurtured so carefully over the Oregon Trail, and now it was growing as sturdy as a weed. She smiled as she nipped vagrant branches and secured it to the trellis she'd had Wesley build alongside the house.

As she stepped back to admire her handiwork, rain started falling again. Fee threw her hands up in surrender. She still had to get the children ready for Ezekial and Pearl. But first she stooped and picked some herbs from her garden. Remembering how Pearl loved lemon balm tea, she dug up two plants to take as a gift.

Every second week on Wednesday afternoon, Fee took the boys over to Pearl. Then early Thursday she drove into Salem, took care of business at the creamery, did her shopping, spent the night with the Goulds, then came back home on Friday. Sometimes if there was a lot of business to take care of, she would forewarn Pearl and stay over until Saturday. Considering Harley's request for more help, she knew that this trip would be one of those times.

She sniffed the pungent herbs as she went into the kitchen. She'd never regretted struggling to bring these plants along to Oregon. They provided something to remind her of home in this wilderness she was taming, something to make it more a home for her.

It was still raining when she was ready to leave, so she put on her slicker, bundled up the boys, set them under the spring seat of her wagon, then covered them with a tarp, warning them to stay still and not quarrel, so they would be able to play with Grandma Pearl and Grandpa Ezekial.

The patter of the rain on the tarp and her floppy-brimmed hat played an erratic rhythm to the songs she sang as she drove to Ezekial's farm. By the time they pulled into the yard Mathew's little voice was still piping along with hers but the twins were sound asleep on one another.

"Where's my boys?" Pearl called. "Did I hear one of my boys singing me a song?"

"I need a helper over here in the barn!" Ezekial said.

"Me, Grandpa! Me! I'll help!" Matthew called as he scrambled off the end of the wagon by himself.

"I've got some warm cookies just for my boys," Pearl told the twins, "and fresh milk. You'll come on in for some tea, won't you?" she called to Fee over one shoulder.

"Just for a minute," Fee said with a laugh as she hitched Fitz-James to the tree and followed Pearl into her warm, fragrant kitchen.

It was difficult for Fee to leave such a warm, loving place and head back to her empty house. So it was dusk by the time Fitz-James turned down their road. Although the rain had let up, it was getting colder, and the dark house looked bleak. Fee was glad that she'd banked the fire and put the pot of leftover stew on the hook in the fireplace before she'd left. At least she'd have a warm meal waiting.

She put the wagon in the shed and unharnessed Fitz-James, leading him into the barn, a little bothered that she'd forgotten to latch the door properly before she left. She lit the barn lantern and filled Fitz-James's manger with oats and hay and began drying him off and brushing him, humming softly to herself as she did, wondering why he seemed so jumpy.

"Here, stop that," she said, patting his shoulder and side-stepping his restless fidgeting. "What's the matter?"

"He probably smells me."

Fee gasped as she looked up and saw the face of a strange man watching her from the next stall. His wet hat shadowed his face, and a ragged black beard covered his gaunt cheeks. There was a hunted, defiant look to his dark eyes as he gazed at her unwaveringly. A grimy kerchief was knotted about his neck, and his tan jacket was too thin for the season.

"How did you get in here?" she asked, striving to regain her composure, only too aware of how alone she was.

"Just lifted the latch on the door," he said with a humorless grin. "I was hoping to find someone who'd let me buy a dinner off 'em. Let me sleep in their barn."

It was less a request than a demand. He knew that she was alone. Probably had plenty of time to scout the place out, she thought to herself. Still, the normal and right thing to do would be to invite him to eat—normal if she wasn't frightened by his appearance, normal if she didn't expect to remain alone until the snow melted from the mountain passes.

"I have some stew I've kept warm over the fire . . . waiting for my husband," she lied. "You're welcome to come in and have some." Without waiting for a response, she turned and headed out of the barn and up the walk to the house.

As she lit the lantern inside the door, she noticed that he was still wearing his muddy boots, dripping mud on her floor. "You may take your boots off where I did," she said pointedly. "The bootjack is beside the door." She paused and then added as naturally as she could, "But before you do, could you please bring in an armload of wood from off the wood-pile? Just leave it beside the door here."

While he was outside, she ran upstairs and got her pistol, checking to see that it was primed and loaded before bringing it down and putting it in the back bedroom, hoping that she wouldn't have call for it, but feeling better knowing that it was near.

She'd built up the fire by the time she heard him drop the load of wood on the front porch. She deliberately turned her back to take out a plate as he came in the door, hoping that would mislead him into thinking she wasn't frightened.

"There's a washbowl out on the back porch," she said with a nod. "Towel on the peg. Dinner'll be on the table soon's you're washed up."

Wordlessly, he followed her directions. She dished up the

stew, scraping the bottom of the pot to fill his bowl. She placed it on the table as he sat down and then turned to slice some bread.

"Where's yours?" he asked.

"I've already eaten," she lied. "I just came back from the neighbors and we had dinner there."

"Oh, I thought maybe you'd lied to me about expecting a husband back and this was all you had."

Her heart was in her throat but she forced herself to smile, saying, "Whatever would I do that for? There's more in the pantry. I'll warm it when he gets here."

"Why don't you go put it on the fire?" he asked pointedly.

Anger was beginning to overcome Fee's initial fear. Why was he trying to corner her? "As you can see, the stew you're eating is a bit burnt. Keeping it on the fire wasn't such a good idea after all. I'll warm it up fresh when he comes."

He nodded and grinned as if they were sharing some conspiracy. "That's a good idea," he said as he leaned over his bowl and began shoveling in the stew.

"There's a bit of Dixie in your speech," he said as he spread a generous amount of butter on his second piece of bread. "Where you from?"

"Virginia. You?"

"Same. You east or west?"

"West. Guess now it's a state in its own right."

"Yup. Damn nigger-lovers. Cut themselves off from their mother state just like a yellow dog. When you come out?"

"Left Virginia in '60."

"Smart. You missed the bad times. Nothin' worth havin' there now."

There was something about the man that bothered Fee, something that made her stomach knot in hatred, something more than just his arrogant attitude. His tan jacket bore telltale stitch-holes around less faded patches where his Confederate insignia had once been. But more than that was bothering her. She just couldn't put her finger on it, but her heart was beating furiously as she picked up her sewing and sat down by the fire.

"You from the east?" she asked, still probing, still trying to find out what was bothering her.

"Mountains. Been through the west part of Virginia, though. Right before the war. Probably just missed you," he added with a wink.

She looked down at her sewing, refusing to acknowledge his rude overture. "You go on business?"

"Might call it that." He smiled but his eyes were cold and calculating. "You make a mighty fine stew, ma'am, burnt or not," he said, scraping the legs of his chair on the wooden floor as he pushed back from the table and picked his teeth with the point of his knife. "I'm on my way to join up with one of my—ah, Virginia business partners," he added. "You know a Ransom Farron? We rode together. In his letter here," he said, fishing a grimy envelope from his shirt pocket and consulting its contents, "he says here that he's staked a claim in the Willamette Valley out near the head of Pudding Creek, outside a' Salem. You got any idea where that's at?"

Fee paused, studying his bent profile carefully. What was it? Why did the very sight of him chill her heart?

"I heard tell there's a man clearing some land about ten miles east of here. Don't know his name. Haven't met him, but he's said to be up in Dark Hollow off Pudding Creek. You just take the road out front here and follow it east until it branches. Take the right fork. It looks more like a track, but it'll get you to where they say someone's clearing a piece."

She spoke politely, automatically, her mind not quite on what she was saying as she stared at his face, mentally removing the rough beard, picturing him in another place—another time.

"Well, I'd like to pay you for your hospitality before I go bed down in your barn," he said with a sly grin.

She looked down at the twenty-dollar gold piece and knew. Her stomach was ice and her heart stood still as she took the coin in her stiff fingers and turned towards the back bedroom. "I'll get you change," she whispered.

There was a loose floorboard that creaked outside the bedroom door. But she didn't need that to know he'd followed her. She could see his long shadow bending and crawling up the wall as he stealthily came in behind her. She could feel her hate growing with his nearness.

He had no warning. She spun around and pulled the trigger as soon as the barrel touched his ribs. His knife dropped as he slumped to the floor with a surprised look on his face.

"You killed my father and brother!" she cried hoarsely, looking down as the life left his startled eyes and his blood trickled on her rag rug. "You killed them!" she shrieked, kicking his staring head.

She dropped the pistol and put her hands to her eyes. "And now I killed you," she said with a gasping sob. Peeking between her fingers she saw his hand touching her shoe.

Now what?

Slowly her mind began working, pushing away her racing emotions as she quickly analyzed the situation. "Can't let Wesley find you in the morning," she told the corpse as she rolled him up in the rug. "I'll put you in the wagon. Drop you off in the woods. They'll think you were robbed or shot yourself . . . or something." She pulled the rug to the door and left him on the front stoop while she went back in to get her raingear on.

She had no sense of how long it took to hitch Fitz-James to the wagon, bring it up to the porch, and get the body in the wagon. By the time she was done and Fitz-James was back in his warm stall, she was soaked to the skin and shivering uncontrollably. Then she went back to the shed to make sure the body wasn't visible in the rug. A spot of blood was seeping through on the side.

She paused, looking down at the still form. "I don't even know your name," she said derisively. "Butcher will do." She spat out the words as she closed the door.

She built up the fire and brewed herself a cup of tea, trying to quiet her shaking hands, trying to warm herself. She wrapped herself in a quilt and sat by the roaring fire. No matter what she did, her hands wouldn't warm, her stomach wouldn't stop turning. She knew that she'd not sleep that night.

Hours later she took her satchel out to the wagon and left the ranch, after leaving her customary note to Wesley. No one must suspect. How could she prove she was justified in killing him? The ultimate injustice would be that she should have to pay for killing the man who helped murder her brother and father. She couldn't let that happen now that she'd partially avenged their deaths. Not now.

Fitz-James slowly picked his way along the familiar road, knowing the way by feel and scent as much as by sight. Fee shivered uncontrollably, hearing footsteps in the dark woods and betrayal in the owl's call.

When she was several miles away from the farm, she stopped the wagon and got down, dragging the body in the rug into the bushes alongside the road. The first gray light of dawn was filtering over the horizon and she was fearful of being detected, so she worked quickly. Rolling him out of the rug, she tossed his pistol and boots on the ground beside his hand and quickly got back in the wagon, carefully tucking the rug under the wagon seat. Soon the rain would wash away all tracks.

"I hope the vultures pick your bones clean," she said as she flicked the reins and started once more for Salem.

Ransom Farron. The name kept circling in her brain. Pudding Creek. "One of my—ah, Virginia business partners," he'd said. Fee was certain that he'd been talking about one of the other marauders. Now that her memory was awakened, she could see the face of each of them as they had ridden past her hiding place seven years ago. Each one was clearly etched in her mind. If only she could see this Ransom . . . then she'd know. If only . . .

Her mind was not on her work, and both Abner and Harley asked if she were sick. They'd arranged for some people to talk to her about a job. It took her only ten minutes and half her concentration to decide to hire Uriah and Myrtle Collins from Ohio. By noon she had placed them in Abner's hands, and by evening she'd finished her work and shopping and had arrived exhausted and distracted at the Goulds'.

Mrs. Gould immediately decided that she was sick, fixed her a bowl of warm soup, and put her to bed. Fee fell asleep immediately, only to awaken in the cold morning hours to stare at the ceiling, thinking of Ransom Farron . . . out on Pudding Creek. Was he the one with the knife who slit her brother's throat, or was he the one who'd broken her father's neck? Or was he the one who laughed as he set the torch to their barn, burning the animals alive that were trapped inside? Was he the one who'd burnt out the Edwards family? Had he killed little Della?

Damnation! She pounded the pillow in frustration. When the government passed policies encouraging Civil War veterans to settle in the West, why didn't they assure us that none of them were marauders, killers, and murderers of innocent men, women, and children? She buried her head in the pillow—and still their faces filled her mind.

She got up before dawn. Mrs. Gould heard her stirring and came into the kitchen as she was fixing herself a cup of tea. "You look as bad as when I put you to bed," she said. "You should stay over and get well before going back to those boys of yours."

"I'm fine, Mrs. Gould, thank you," she said absently. "I've got to get back."

"Least you can do is take something to eat along with you," she said, knowing Fee's mind was made up. She pulled out some cold sidepork and handed it to Fee with some cornbread all wrapped in a napkin. Fee stared at it and then took it stiffly, tucking the napkin in her apron pocket.

"Thank you," she whispered and turned to go. How ironic, she thought numbly. Wasn't that what Mrs. Edwards had given her that cold morning seven years ago?

"You sure you're all right? I think Dr. Breckenridge should check you."

"No. No, I'm fine," Fee said with her hand on the doorknob. "I'll be just fine, Mrs. Gould. Thank you."

Fitz-James stoically accepted her early-morning departure and soon was plodding along the road back to Quail Hollow. But Fee's mind wasn't on the road. It was racing over the hills, towards Pudding Creek, so she was startled when the horse shied away from something at the side of the road. Only then did she realize she was passing the spot where she'd dumped the body the day before. The rippling sound of water running alongside the road and the curious chirr of a raccoon from the woods was all she heard as she passed on by. She felt oddly detached and lightheaded.

She put Fitz-James in the stall, noting that Wesley had already come and done the morning chores.

She had to go there. She had to know. If she timed it right, she'd be back before Wesley returned that evening.

Quickly, before she could think about it, she saddled Boots, the horse Nathanial had brought her last year. She primed and loaded her pistol. "Don't hurt none to keep your powder dry." How right Ezekial had been. Should she tell him? No, couldn't tell anyone. Might not understand. But she had to know. She had to know. Revenge must be hers. It would burn her, consume her until she had it.

It took four hours of riding through the rain, four hours she couldn't even remember. Once she started out, her brain stopped working. Her actions were automatic.

She saw the smoke from the chimney first, then followed the rough track off the trail towards the hollow. A pitiful excuse for a cabin was perched on one end of a partially cleared field. A hastily built shed leaned precariously against the encroaching woods on the near side of the clearing. From the sounds of hammering, someone was working in the shed. She nudged Boots forward.

Quietly she tied the horse to a tree and walked to the door. Daylight filtered between the slats as well as through the door. A man was bent over some poles, swearing and sucking his thumb. His shape was sharp and angular, and his clothes were like those of the man she'd shot last night. He looked up, an oath half uttered as he spotted her standing in the doorway. The scar across his cheek took her breath away.

"Are you Ransom Farron?" she asked.

"Yeah, that's me. Who're you?"

"I understand you're from Virginia."

"'At's right," he said, boldly appraising her and stepping closer. "You talk soft, like home," he said with a leer.

Fee forced herself to smile. "Might be we've met. You ever been to Wood County?"

"Just for a short visit," he said, his eyes puzzled. "Doubt we met there." He stepped closer, his sour breath making her want to gag. "I'd remember a pretty thing like you. You alone?" he asked, looking behind her and out the door.

"Yes. You just don't remember me." She braced herself as he took one more step and reached out and stroked her cheek. She felt the threat of his closeness and willed her feet to hold their place. "You remember Bear Creek Ridge off Green Valley?" she asked. His hand paused in midair as he stared at her, suddenly wary.

"Why you ask?"

"You remember a young boy whose throat you slashed with your hunting knife?" His eyes became calculating slits of cold blue. "You remember there was a sister you missed?"

He stepped back and for the first time she saw his rifle leaning against the wall. As he edged towards it, he whined, "I don't know what you're talking about."

"You do. That's why you're reaching for that gun," she said, pointing the pistol at his head. "I saw you ride away. I saw you wipe my brother's blood from your knife."

"Too bad we didn't find you." He leered. "We'd 'a had fun with a piece like you." He stepped towards the gun, grinning. "You don't have it in you to pull the trigger," he taunted. "But I'll show you what I can do with you—"

He didn't finish the threat or reach the gun. Fee pulled the trigger and saw half his head disappear in a splash of red and gray. His one remaining eye was still open, shocked at his sudden death. He fell to the floor, twitched, and was still.

Fee put the pistol back in her pocket and walked out the door. Then she leaned against the doorpost and vomited. She stood there for a moment, catching her breath, shaking convulsively. Then, using her last bit of strength, she walked over to Boots and climbed back into the saddle and urged her homeward.

Rain dripped desolately from the oak trees as she plodded down the muddy trail.

"You'd think butchering hogs would have prepared me . . ." she murmured. "So much blood . . ." She shivered violently, barely able to cling to the saddle horn and maintain her seat. With her eyes clenched tightly she tried to blot out the image, but open or closed, it was still all she could see.

Before, she'd been haunted by the death of her father and brother. Now she was haunted by the two men she'd killed.

She was numb by the time she got back to Quail Hollow. Boots stopped at the barn door and she fell out of the saddle, slipping in the cold mud as she tried to get her footing.

She put the mare in her stall and threw the saddle over the sawhorse in the corner, barely able to make her stiff fingers hold on to the wall for support.

Her knees were shaking so badly she was having trouble walking. She stopped as she went out the barn door, leaning against the doorpost. Taking a deep breath to gather her strength, she looked down. There, on her skirt front, was a piece of bone, bloodied on one side and matted with black hair on the other.

With a shriek, Fee threw it from her. Then, her head spinning, she vomited once more. But her stomach had long been empty, and her body was torn by dry heaves.

Gasping for breath, she staggered to the house. She dared not go in the back bedroom and she couldn't make it up the stairs, so she simply rolled herself in the quilt and lay down on the hard floor in front of the cold fireplace, shivering herself into an unconscious stupor.

She lay there, shivering, sleeping fitfully, only to start awake from nightmares filled with bloodied faces with staring eyes. Sometimes when she opened her eyes the faces were still there and she would sit up, turning away from their staring eyes, crying out in the darkness closing in around her.

Suddenly the room was light. Something brushed her forehead. She opened her eyes and saw a face staring down at her, leaning over, its eyes blinking. With a scream she sat up, covering her face to make the image go away, but when she looked again, it was still there. She screamed again and backed away, bumping into a chair.

"Hey, easy there, Miz Coughlin," Wesley said. "You're downright feverish. Whatever did you go riding back early in this storm for? You'll catch your death of cold doing that. Just look at you. Mud all over." As he talked he carefully laid a fire. "You too weak even to make it to bed?"

Fee was still catching her breath, trying to reconcile her hallucinations with the real image of Wesley before her eyes. "Yes," she whispered, "I guess so."

"Well, let me help you get into the back bedroom there."

"No!" she cried out, terrified to go into the room where she'd shot the first man. "I mean . . . I'd rather stay here by the fire. I'm so cold."

"Well, you got to get some dry clothes on and some food in you. I'll get some clothes for you and heat up the teapot."

When he came back downstairs with her dressing gown and some woolen socks, he also brought a bottle of Nathanial's whiskey. He poured her a glassful. "You drink this. Warm you up, stop that shivering some." Obediently she gulped the amber liquid, feeling it burn all the way down.

In minutes Wesley had her wrapped in a blanket in the rocking chair in front of the fire, sipping a hot cup of tea. He toasted some of her own cheese on a piece of bread and told her to eat it in spite of her protestations.

"You don't have to worry none about the little 'uns 'cuz they're not expecting you back till tomorrow anyhow. You just rest up real good. If'n you're still poorly tomorrow, I'll ride on over to Ezekial's and ask them to keep the boys. You're just pushing yourself too hard, Miz Coughlin," he said seriously. "You need a rest."

Fee closed her eyes and sipped the tea, grateful that she could close her eyes and not see the bloody images. By the time Wesley left, she was strong enough to stand and thank him.

"No, no, you stay put," he protested. "You have to change into your dry clothes soon's I'm gone—" He stopped, looking down at Fee's dress. "My God, Miz Coughlin. Your front there is all covered with blood. What happened?"

Fee looked down, seeing the mess, remembering its cause. "I . . . I . . . I had a bloody nose on the way home," she lied. "I just didn't realize it'd gotten all over. It looks much worse than it was . . . really," she reassured him.

"Well, don't worry none. I'll be back in the morning."

It took all of Fee's will not to call him back and beg him to spend the night. She stood, leaning against the rocking chair until she heard his horse ride off. Then she turned and picked up her dry dressing gown. Trying not to look at the bloodstained clothes she was taking off, she slowly and carefully dressed herself in warm, dry clothes, poured herself another cup of hot tea, then wrapped herself tightly in the blanket and quilt, and lay down on the chaise Wesley had pulled up to the fire.

She was unable to sleep more than a few minutes at a time without being awakened by nightmares, sounds that hallucinated into haunts, howling wind that screamed through her mind, flickering firelight that threw shadowy faces on the wall. Her terror at what she had done mixed with her anguish at finding out that revenge was anything but sweet. When the pale light of dawn crept across the floor, her mouth was dry with the bitter knowledge of empty vengeance.

She didn't know how she could carry on, but she had to. Offering her illness as an excuse, she quickly gathered the children from Ezekial and Pearl and brought them home, fearing that the blood on her hands might taint them.

The nightmares remained. Although she got through the days with only a few starts and shivers, once she lay down in her bed at night, she was alone with her secret horrors.

A week passed. The children had become withdrawn and quiet. Was she destroying them too? Would the blood on her hands destroy them all?

Then on the following Sunday help came from an unexpected source.

Wind was blowing rain around the eaves of the house, and the sky was dark. She'd just thrown another log on the fire and put the twins down to nap when the door suddenly burst open.

"Nathanial!" she cried in surprise and relief. Then, seeing the burden he was carrying, she said, "What is it? What's the matter?"

"Get some blankets and start heating water. She's near-frozen. Not even conscious. She's rattling something terrible inside."

"Who is she?" Fee asked as she wrapped the young girl in blankets and tucked her in the chair by the fire. "Where did you find her?"

"Came back early. Took one of the south passes. Lot of rivers are flooding. Heard from some folks on the other side that there was someone new clearing a place off Pudding Creek. Thought I'd stop by on my way home. Be neighborly, see if they needed anything what with all the high waters. Found this girl alone in a cold shack, about dead. Best I could get out of her was that her folks had married her off to this stranger who came through town last year so's he could claim a full section of land in her name as well as his. Must'a been a damn fool," he said, hardly noticing that Fee stood frozen in horror and shock. "He didn't even know how to build a shelter worth a damn. Mud floor, wind blowing through holes in the wall big enough to shoot through. Nothing but a squirrel ranch up there. Couldn't raise anything but rocks."

He paused in his recitation of the story and looked at her. "Here, help me get her boots off. Don't just stand there."

Fee jumped guiltily, then quickly began to help. "How did she get so sick?" she asked, hoping against hope that this had nothing to do with what she'd done.

"Her damn-fool husband hauled off and shot himself. Couldn't even use a gun right. She found him with his head blown off and spent most of a day and night digging a grave and burying him. Then she came down sick and can't remember much else. Couldn't leave her there, could I?"

"No—no, not at all. I'll fix the tea." She moved mechanically, dazed to think that her act of revenge almost caused the death of an innocent person. Still might, for that matter.

At that moment, Fee vowed that she would do everything within her power to redeem herself. She would help this young girl, she would heal her and take care of her the rest of her life if need be.

"What's her name?" she asked, stirring honey into the tea. "She looks too young to be off and married."

"Name's Nell. She is young. Fourteen."

"They're beasts to send her out that way," she muttered. "Don't know what her folks were thinking of."

"In all her rambling while I was bringing her here, I gathered that she's had a pretty rough life. Like as not they just wanted to get rid of her so they didn't have to feed her."

Fee looked down at the girl's pale, thin face, and her heart went out to her. Nell's hazel eyes fluttered open, looking at Fee with confusion. "It's all right, dear," Fee said softly, helping her to drink the tea. "You're safe now. I'm going to take care of you."

Chapter XVIII

As the mud, rain, and desolation of February turned into the wind, rain, and budding hope of March, Fee saw Nell begin to respond under her care. By April Nell's health was blooming like the flowers beside the kitchen door, and Fee rejoiced in spring and the young girl whose death she'd almost caused.

Every time Fee thought of the wretchedness of Nell's former life, she was angry. Every time she thought how close she'd come to being the instrument of Nell's death, she shuddered.

What Fee refused to recognize was that when she started caring for Nell, she had been ill herself. For almost two months she'd neglected her own health to the point of serious collapse. A deep cough ripped the lining of her chest with each rasping attack. She lost weight until she was dangerously thin and her complexion was sallow. Still she kept on, forcing herself to continue working her usual schedule, ignoring all the danger signs.

Then one day Fee became faint and nearly collapsed in the kitchen. Like a bantam hen to her chick, Nell rushed to Fee's side, scolding a bewildered and contrite Nathanial as he sat helplessly at the breakfast table. She then fiercely went about nursing Fee back to health. She insisted it was her right. "It's the least I kin do. Miz Coughlin saved me from the brink of death."

So it was that for two weeks Nell faithfully cared for Fee. By the end of their convalescences, the bond between Nell and Fionna was sealed.

Nell insisted upon working for her keep, a proposal Fee could hardly pass up. With Nell to watch over the children, Fee was able to go into Salem more frequently to tend to her business, and the creamery prospered as a result. With Nell there, life on the farm was less lonely. With Nell by her side, work was easier, and Fee counted her blessings. But Fee wasn't the only one to see the advantages of Nell's presence.

One morning in May, when the sun was particularly warm and the air exceptionally sweet, Nathanial returned from

Salem with a new travel bag for Fee and a mischievous look on his face.

"What's this for?" she asked, accepting his present and laughing at his little-boy expression.

"Fill it. I'm going to take you on an adventure. We'll load up the wagon, leave the kids with Nell, and travel into the wilderness, just like old times."

"Whatever are you talking about?"

"There's a beautiful place where Silver Creek falls over a high cliff in torrents of water and rainbows," he said, gesturing elaborately and making her laugh even more. "We'll camp there and celebrate your recovery and our good fortune." Then to make sure she understood he meant business, he picked her up by the waist and swung her around the kitchen to the delight of Matthew, who danced around them, clapping his chubby hands.

"Come on, Fionna, pack your things. I want to leave in an hour," he said, putting her down with a kiss.

"An hour? Oh, Nathanial, I can't. There's the laundry and the cheese and—"

"Forget it. I'm leaving the mill and the farm and everything else behind just for a few stolen days." He leaned down and held her face gently in his hands. "We need time together," he added softly.

"Nell," Fee called out to the back porch. "Nell, I need to talk to you . . ."

"I know, Miz Coughlin," she said, peeking around the corner of the kitchen, "you're going off with Mr. Coughlin. Don't you worry none. The boys and me'll do just fine. Wesley will be coming in the morning to help with the chores, and I'll keep the creamery going and do the laundry, too. You just go off and enjoy yourself. You need it."

Fee hugged the slim girl, once more grateful for her presence, and then went off to fill her new traveling bag, feeling like a young girl going courting.

"I'll pack you some food to take along," Nell called after her.

Within an hour, Fee and Nathanial were riding side by side on a wagon, driving a mule team along a strange wood-lined track. Nathanial had been right; it felt like old times.

"It's good to be with you," Fee declared, leaning her head against Nathanial's shoulder. "Now, tell me the real reason why we're going to Silver Creek. You planning on putting another mill in?"

"I told you why," Nathanial said, hurt in his voice. "I wanted some time with you—just the two of us."

"Why, Nathanial Coughlin," Fee declared with delight, "if you're not careful, you'll get romantic and write me a poem."

"Couldn't write anything prettier than you," he said, playfully planting a kiss on the end of her nose. "Now that the boys are getting older and Nell's with us, we can do this more often. Oregon's a beautiful place, Fee. I want to show it to you—piece by piece."

They stopped at the top of a hill to eat lunch. Feasting on bread and cheese, they sat side by side, drinking in the flower-sweet air. Then, lying back in the new grass, they watched birds with broad wings carve circles in the porcelain-blue sky.

"Red-tailed hawks," Nathanial said. "Probably have a nest somewhere around here. You ready to go?"

"Yes, if we have to. It seems like heaven here."

"Wait until you see the falls."

"Nathanial," Fee said after they were under way, "have you ever thought about other ways to sell your lumber?"

"What do you mean?"

"I mean you could sell in other places and make more money. You're selling it right out of the mill. If you could set up a lumber store in the cities, you'd be able to make a bigger profit because people could get just what they need and would be willing to pay a higher price not to have to drive out to the mills themselves. They might even pay you to deliver."

He was quiet for almost a mile, making no sound other than a clucking to urge the mules onward. Finally he said, "Might have possibilities. Don't feel I have the capital to set it up right now. I'll think about it."

"I have the capital. Would you let me do it?"

"Cheese doing that well?"

"Cheese—and other things. Would you let me set up a lumberyard inside the Salem city limits? I'd promise to sell only your lumber."

He looked at her in amazement then broke out laughing. "You are the most astounding woman to ever walk the face of the earth."

"But the lumberyard—"

"Of course, set one up. You have my blessing," he said. He turned his attention to driving the wagon, and Fee knew that her business proposition was already out of his mind. His heart was in the woods, not in business. But her mind was busily weaving new plans, always looking for new ways to gain the power and security she craved.

Silver Creek Falls were breathtaking, and Nathanial presented them to her as if handing her a diamond necklace—and she accepted them as if he had. Silver Creek plummeted over a series of cliffs, weaving rainbows of spray through the thick green lace of ferns as it cascaded into shimmering pools.

While Nathanial set up the tent, Fee wandered along the bank of the creek, marveling at the roaring towers of water high above her. She picked wildflowers for their dinner table, delicate lilylike lamb tongues with lavender petals curling back from a magenta stamen, and purple bird-bills pointing their beaklike blossoms toward the afternoon sun.

Later that evening, as she squinted her eyes against the stinging smoke of the campfire and heated the stew Nell had packed, she had no nostalgic longing for the discomforts of their westward trek along the Oregon Trail. Still, it had been a good time for them. After the meal, she put the dishes in the creek and scrubbed them with sand—just as she used to do—and she remembered the longing with which she used to watch Nathanial around the campfire.

"Your hair is hanging in curls around your face," he said, slipping his arms around her waist as she put the dishes away.

"It always does that when it's moist. It's the mist from the falls." She turned around and put her arms around him, nuzzling his neck as she said, "I was just thinking about how I longed for you on the trail. You were hardly aware of me."

"Aware of you!" he shouted. "I thought of little else. It's a wonder I wasn't scalped because I wandered so far afield just thinking of you."

"You did?"

"Of course." He kissed her, pulling her closer to him. "Come to bed with me and I'll show you what I was thinking about." He started unbuttoning her dress, and she could feel her desire rise with his touch.

"Nathanial," she protested as he slipped her dress down over her hips, "it's so cold. Let's go in the tent."

"Let me look at you first," he said, untying her camisole. In spite of her protests and her shivers, he didn't stop until he had her standing naked by the fire. "You're a very beauti-

214

ful woman, Fionna," he said. Then he picked her up and carried her to the tent.

He surprised her with the urgency of his lovemaking, leaving her unfulfilled and restless when he finished. She remembered the first time they made love and promised herself to awaken him in an hour.

"Nathanial?" she asked as he rolled over to go to sleep.

"Um-hum?"

"Do you love me?"

"Don't be foolish. Would I be here if I didn't?"

"I don't know. I guess I just need to hear you say so now and then."

"Well, I do."

"I'm going to have a baby."

"Another one?"

"Well, that's what comes from what you just did."

"You know so soon?"

"No." She laughed. "I think I'm about two months along. It happened right after you came back. Remember, you were so insistent even when I was taking care of Nell? Oh, Nathanial, I so hope it's a little girl this time."

He was quiet for a long time, and she thought he was going to say something else. But then his even breathing told her he'd fallen asleep.

It was strange, but Fee had to admit she wasn't the adventurer that Nathanial thought she was, surely not the one who tramped over two thousand miles on the Oregon Trail. She missed her soft feather bed, she didn't like cooking over an open fire, and she was cold. She got up, put her nightdress on, and banked the fire. Yet, she thought, Nathanial is in his element. He's happiest when he has the sky over his head and trees and animals around him instead of people. What a pair we make, she thought ruefully as she drifted off to sleep.

When Fee realized she was pregnant again, she was less frightened by the prospect of birth. Although Nathanial probably would be gone when the baby came, Nell would be there to help in case of an emergency. With her ready hands and near-worshipful devotion to Fee, she had become a vital part of Fee's work and life.

Fee had chosen to tell Nathanial about her pregnancy first. But the second person she told was Nell, who, unlike Nathanial, shared her excitement.

"Oh, Miz Coughlin, we'll have such a wonderful time. You think it'll be a girl this time? I know how to find out. Here, you lie down on the couch and I'll go get a rock and string."

Within minutes she was back, holding a rock tied to a string over Fee's belly, watching it intently. "You just watch it," she said in a whisper. "If'n it goes in a line back and forth, it's a boy; and if'n it goes in a circle, it'll be a girl."

Fee watched the string and then began to laugh. "What does it mean when it goes in a long circle back and forth?" she asked the astonished Nell.

"Ma'am, I never seen it do this afore. Why, my mamma used to have me do this every time her belly swelled, and it always worked. Guess we'll have to try it later on. You're not big enough for the rock to get a good sight on, anyhow."

She wound the string around the rock and sat down beside Fee. "You know, I think this is the best thing that could happen. I'll be able to have a baby to play with, and I don't have to do the hard part to get it. You know, I got to say that . . . promise you won't hold it against me if I talk honest to you?" she asked.

"Not at all, Nell."

"Well, I wasn't too sorry to see that man of mine dead. Maybe I'm evil, but if it weren't for the idea of starving, I would like to have clapped my hands in relief. I know it's powerful bad to think like that, but he used to hurt me something awful. And he made me do things"—she bit her lip and turned her head away—"he made me do things that I don't think were right. And he used me something terrible. I could hardly walk sometimes, he hurt me so."

"Oh, Nell darling," Fee said, putting her arm around her.

"That's why I don't ever want to leave here. I don't ever want another man to touch me. Your letting me have a baby to love and care for without all those terrible things is worth the world to me. I pray every night you won't never send me away. I promise to take care of you and the baby just like it was my own 'cause it's the only one I'll ever have." With that she broke down and sobbed.

"Oh, dear Nell. You're part of our family now," Fee said, trying to console Nell while her own mind filled with anger and guilt.

In October Nathanial left Quail Hollow Farm with a lighter heart than he'd had in a long time. Part of this was due to the presence of Nell. Another reason, he guiltily admitted, had to do with the fact that he felt it was time to get out into the open again and away from Fee. She was a wonderful woman and he loved her, but her vast energy and drive wore him out.

He shook his head in wonder as he remembered how quickly she'd set up the lumberyard in Salem. Before the end of June she had the property purchased and the lumberyard stocked. By fall, she'd shown a profit.

However, this latest pregnancy had sapped her energy, and she'd become weaker than ever before. Such limitations didn't set well with her nature, and she'd been as bitchy as an old she-bear these past few weeks.

Outside of Albany, twenty-three miles south of Salem, he bought breeding cattle along with some promising yearlings and a couple of cow ponies. Hiring two young men to help him, he set off across the Cascades, crossing before the first snow fell in the middle of October. Mining activity had slowed in eastern Oregon, but the cattle and farming business had continued growing. As a result there was still a demand for his lumber and beef.

It was a joy to sleep in the open once more and have no one to answer to but himself. The mountains rose in purple and blue before him. The sharp smell of sage filled his nostrils, and he felt as if he could soar like the goshawk circling above their rocky trail. By the time he'd reached the Powder River Valley he was a rejuvenated man.

There were several improvements needed on the ranch, including a new windmill to pump water for the livestock on the range and a shake roof added to the ranch house before the snows came. He talked with Button Hogberg, his ranch foreman, until late that night.

"Someone waiting to see you, Mr. Coughlin," Wilkens, his manager, said when he entered the mill the next morning.

"How'd anyone even know I was in town?"

" 'Spect he's been watching out for you."

Nathanial found a spindly boy of about thirteen hunkered in the corner of his office like a frightened pup. "What can I do for you, son?" he asked, trying to hide his surprise.

"Don't know if you 'member me or not, sir," he said, his voice cracking with nervousness. "Name's Thomas Slead."

"Slead?" Nathanial said in surprise as he shook the outstretched hand. "You're not any relation to Lemuell, are you?"

"Yes, sir," he said, his eyes betraying his fear. "His son. I 'member you from the wagon train. And I want to thank you for all you did for my ma," he added.

"Wish I could have done more, son. Sorry to hear about her passing." He watched the boy from the corner of his eye as he sat down at his desk.

"Thank you, sir. Just want you to know that I'm not like my pa," he said. "That's the first thing. I'm a hard worker. I've had to be." The truth of his words was obvious from his calluses and his youthful face already worn by the elements. "What I'm here for is a job. I know I'm young," he said quickly, anticipating Nathanial's response. "But I'm a good worker, like I said. I got to get some money. Need it bad, and I was hoping I'd be able to help out here."

"Does your father know you're here?" Nathanial asked.

Thomas looked down at the floor. "No, sir," he admitted. "And I'd be beholden to you if he didn't find out. I figured you'd be coming back to the mill pretty soon, so I took off. It's the only hope me an' my sisters got. Zenas, he's our brother born when Ma died, he's pretty much Pa's kid, spitting image. The rest of us, well, we're just somethin' for Pa to work. Food's in short supply. Pa spends most'a what he gets drinking. He hits on my sisters pretty bad when I can't stop him. Not too different from what you saw on the train. 'Cept . . . 'cept Ma's gone. He won't let us go to school. Just wants us to work his land."

"What's your plan, son?"

"I'm going to work for you as long as I can. I'll save every penny. Then in about a year, I'm going to have enough saved to take my sisters away from there. Figure we can find some kind of work in Portland—or Oregon City. Anything would be better than what we have now. He won't be so likely to come get us if it'll take some doing."

He stood waiting for Nathanial to decide, trying hard not to fidget. The boy was wiry but hard-muscled from long hours of hard work. It'd do Nathanial's heart good to get those kids away from that bastard. They were probably thinking of making their way back to the Harris farm. However, they were smart enough to know that would be the first place Slead would look. No, Thomas was right, he'd have to have some money put by to keep them for a while until their trail was cold.

Nathanial held out his hand. "You got yourself a job, son.

218

Go tell Wilkens to put you up in the bunkhouse. Then hustle yourself on back and I'll set you to stacking lumber."

"Gee, thanks, Mr. Coughlin," Thomas said, tears brimming in his eyes. "I . . . I don't know what to say . . ."

"You might ask how much I'll pay you."

"I know it'll be fair, sir. Fact, I was going to ask you to just keep accounts. That way, if the old man ever catches me, I won't have any money for him to grab. We'll still something to hope for, even if the worst happens."

Nathanial smiled tightly. "You've thought this through, haven't you?" Thomas nodded, watching Nathanial anxiously. "I'll help you and your sisters every way I can. Now get going and don't talk to too many people. And stay out of town. The fewer who know you're around, harder you'll be to find."

"Yes, sir!" he said, running out the door, pulling his hat over his ears. "And thanks again."

Nathanial stood, shaking his head. What had he gotten himself into this time? Still, he knew that he was doing the right thing.

Sally was in the kitchen roasting a hunk of beef with some onions and potatoes over the coals of the fire when Nathanial returned that evening.

Sally was a young Umatilla Indian woman. Widowed at the tender age of fifteen, her haughty attitude discouraged all would-be suitors. In frustration, her father gave in to her persistent request to attend the mission school. She'd never returned to her father's home. Instead, she'd learned to read and write and then took a job as the cook at the Bar C Ranch.

"Smells wonderful," he said, slipping his arms around her slim waist.

"You didn't come see me last night," she said, turning around and putting her arms around his neck. "I left my door unlocked."

"I didn't want to frighten you by waking you up," he said, kissing her firmly. "When's dinner?"

"Soon's you wash your hands I'll ring the bell."

Besides Sally, five hired hands, and Button lived on the place. Nathanial had built the small ranch house for himself and as a cookhouse and dining hall. A rectangular bunkhouse and two smaller cabins, one for the cook and one for Button, completed the living quarters.

Sally kept to her cabin when he was gone and discreetly slipped into the ranch house when he was there. None of the hands knew for sure if Sally was Nathanial's woman, and none were willing to try to find out in his absence. They'd all seen the Colt pocket pistol he'd given her when he left last time. She kept it in a holster around her waist.

Once Sally put the dinner on the table, there was no superfluous talk until the last bone was picked and the last crumb of cake finished. Then, while Sally cleared the table and went back into the kitchen to eat her dinner and wash the dishes, they leaned back in their chairs, picked their teeth, and told Nathanial what had happened in his absence. When most of the gossip and all the essentials had been taken care of, they lingered on.

"How's the beef market look?" Slim asked.

"Steady. Rumor has it there's a city being built on the other side of the Blues. Going to be a county seat. That'll open another market for us."

"What about railroads?"

Nathanial shook his head in wonder. "Getting closer each year. Give us about five more years and we'll be shipping beef and lumber from Portland to San Francisco."

"Those gold fields petering out don't bother us none?"

"Hell, no. Just gives us a more reliable market by having settled people instead of prospectors buying our beef." He paused and looked at them all, then asked, "Why you so anxious about things, Slim? You looking to settle down?"

The others laughed, slapping Slim on the back and teasing him. "I ain't the only one," he complained. "Old Button there, he took off last winter, you may remember, and came back with a mighty satisfied grin on his face. I'm betting he has a squaw over on t'other side of the river just waiting to hear that it's all right to move into that cabin of his."

"I'm not one to advise you on your private lives," Nathanial said. "But if any of you are wondering if I'm going to keep this spread running, the answer is yes. You want to take your off-time and build yourself a little place for your woman, just let me know and I'll point you to a spot, give you the lumber at cost, and take it out of your pay."

From the grin on Button's face, Nathanial knew he'd better start marking off the ground where the men could set up housekeeping. Couldn't expect to keep them happy if they weren't satisfied by a woman, he figured.

"Ain't just us worried about a steady job," Button said when the more raucous comments had died down. "Sally in there, she's got nowhere else to go, either. She whelped a cute little pup 'bout two months ago. Her old man came out here and spit at her feet. Looks to me like she's stuck this side of the river."

Nathanial kept his face composed, surprised to find out that he was a father. He immediately thought of Fee back home, pregnant. What if she found out? "Know who the father is?" he asked cautiously.

"She keeps to herself," Button said evenly.

"Well, she can raise it here. Any of you thinks he might be the father, better claim it and her right up front," he added, scooting his chair back. He knew his men wouldn't condemn him or cause trouble. Still it was best to play his cards close to his vest.

"For now," he added with a long yawn, "I want to get some shut-eye. If you're going to bring those strays down from the mountain this week, you'd better get to bed, too."

As they all filed out, Nathanial closed the door behind them, turned down one lantern in the dining room, then took the other and went into the front room, which served as his sitting room and bedroom.

He set the lantern on his washstand and sat down in his chair, opening the newspaper he'd brought with him. There wasn't a sound, but when he looked up, Sally was standing in front of him.

"Where's the baby?" he asked as she knelt and pulled off his boots.

She didn't flinch, but he knew she'd wanted to tell him herself in her own way. "Sleeping."

"You shouldn't leave him alone like that. Let me see him."

She went out the door and returned carrying a tightly wrapped bundle. Silently, she handed him to Nathanial.

"I'm his father?" he asked, looking down at the tiny baby. He was yawning, but it was clear to see that his dark hair and cheekbones spoke of his Indian mother.

"Look at his eyes," she said softly.

The baby opened his eyes and Nathanial found himself staring into soft gray eyes, replicas of his own. "Mmph," he grunted, returning the baby's solemn stare. His heart turned over as he looked into his son's eyes. The child wrapped his hand around Nathanial's finger and captured his heart.

"He's a good baby," Sally said anxiously.

"What'd you name him?"

"I wanted him to have a good white name. I call him John."

"And his Indian name?"

"Summerhawk. But no one around here knows that one."

"Bring his bed in so's he can sleep by the fire."

Quickly, Sally went out and brought in the wooden box she'd been using for the baby's bed. While Nathanial finished reading the paper, she nursed John, and when he was asleep laid him down on the soft blankets of his bed.

Nathanial put down the paper and looked up to find her standing before him, calmly watching his face. "Anybody been keeping you warm when I'm gone?" he asked, needing to clear all doubt of the baby's parentage.

"You're gone in warm months. I have no need for someone else."

"You satisfied with just me?" He knew he was pinning her down. Still, he had to know. Until now, he hadn't realized how essential a part of his life Sally had become.

"No one but you."

"You mean no one even tries?"

"Some tried. The gun discourages them."

Nathanial watched her and she returned his look, her black eyes unblinking, her pride unflinching. With a sigh of relief he accepted his second family. "Don't leave my son unattended like that. He should be with you while you work."

The fleeting smile that crossed her face was more than relief. Sally, his bride of the wilderness, his silent partner who understood the whisper of the wind and pull of the forest.

"You needn't worry about anything as long as I'm alive," he added, knowing that he was answering her greatest wish. "Now, how about turning down that lantern and welcoming me home?"

Chapter XIX

Fee's baby was born in early December, a full month early. Nell, who had delivered three brothers and one sister, knew what to do. The long and difficult labor left Fee with barely enough strength to raise her head and see her daughter before falling into an exhausted sleep.

The next morning Matthew and the twins solemnly looked at their little sister, then kissed Fee's cheek and went with Wesley to stay with the Flemings while Fee regained her strength.

Rosalind, as Fee named her, was frighteningly tiny. She was a fussy baby, who slept fitfully and had trouble nursing. When she did eat, she spit up half of her dinner within the next hour. Nell fretted and worried, saying that "her" baby was getting smaller rather than bigger. Fee was too weak to tell.

By Christmas Fee felt strong enough for the children to return home. However, when they burst into the room, her brittle nerves shattered like glass. Surely they hadn't always been that noisy. Rosalind wailed in protest at being so rudely awakened, and the three children stopped guiltily in the middle of the room, their happy smiles frozen on their startled faces.

Fee took a deep breath, gathering her patience around her like a protective cloak. "See, you mustn't be so noisy," she said, gently reprimanding them. "Your sister isn't very strong yet and she needs all the sleep she can get. Now, come give me a kiss and then go to your room and play quietly."

"What about the Christmas tree, Mama?" Matthew asked.

"And prethenth?" Timothy lisped anxiously.

"Don't worry about that now. Grandpa Ezekial said he'd take care of getting the tree. Now run along, all of you."

"I'm glad we're home," Matthew announced as he paused at the door. "Sarah was cranky and Obey went to bed with a headache. It wasn't any fun anymore."

"I'm glad you're home, too," Fee called as he ran up the stairs. "I hope they didn't have something catching," she murmured to Nell, who was holding the baby. "That's the last thing we need now, a houseful of colds."

The twins started coughing two days before Christmas. By morning Matthew had joined them and they all were miserable with watery eyes, coughing, and runny noses. Fee sent Nell over to Ezekial and Pearl's to warn them away. Christmas dinner would have to be postponed until everyone was well again. Christmas night all three children had a raging fever, and to Fee's terror, baby Rosalind began coughing.

Both Nell and Fee were up all night with the children, and by the morning after Christmas, Fee was desperate. She sent Nell to ask Wesley to get Dr. Breckenridge.

Nell returned, saying that he'd already gone to get the

doctor for his own children and would send him over as soon as he finished at their house.

That afternoon she paced in the boys' room while the doctor examined them, carefully pulling down their lower eyelids, peeking in their mouths, and probing their necks. He looked behind Matthew's ears and called Fee over to look for herself. Indefinite pink spots were spreading across his skin.

"What is it?"

"You got yourself a houseful of measles. Same as the Fleming children. Have you had them?"

"Yes, my mother said she was frantic when all three of us came down with them the first year we all were in school."

"Good. You don't usually get them twice. What about Nell?"

"I had something that made me all spotty 'bout three years afore I left home. We all did. Made us powerful sick."

"Let's hope that's it, because you're going to need all the help you can get, Fionna." He put his instruments back into his bag. "The thing to do is keep them down. Keep the fire going so they don't get chilled. Pull the shades. They won't feel like eating much, but try to get them to drink some soup and water. You know how to treat coughs as much as I do. Try some honey and brandy in one of your herb teas. If the fever isn't gone in about three days, come get me. The boys will probably bounce back within a week or so," he said, going out and closing the door behind them.

He stopped at the top of the stairs. "It's the baby I'm worried about," he confessed. "Nell says she's been weakly ever since she was born."

"She was a month early."

"Still not big enough to dent a feather pillow. Keep a close eye on her. Don't let her get chilled. Keep the blinds closed so you don't harm her eyes. If she starts coughing bad or her fever runs too long, come get me even if it's in the middle of the night."

He took off his glasses and wiped his forehead with a crumpled handkerchief. "I'd better be prepared for more. Measles spreads like wildfire once it gets going. Wesley said he and the wife took the children to church every Sunday starting last September. Looks to be where they might have gotten it. I had two other cases this morning. They were Methodists, too."

The doctor was right. Soon the boys were covered with a

virulent rash and wanted nothing more than to sleep. However, by the following day their fever broke, and Fee and Nell rejoiced.

Then Rosalind broke out in a rash that made her tiny body a red, swollen mass. She remained hot and restless, fretting and sleeping little, yet never fully awake. Fee couldn't get her to nurse for more than a few minutes. She knew that the baby had to be miserable, because where her hot little body rested against her, Fee was quickly soaked with moisture.

And then she was no longer wet, just frighteningly hot. She coughed, and each breath came with a wheeze, as if it were a great effort just to breathe. Suddenly Fee was frightened.

She sent for Dr. Breckenridge, who arrived shortly after midnight—just minutes after Rosalind stopped breathing.

Fee was numb. She could barely understand that the tiny body they were taking from her was no longer alive. How could she give up what had been a part of her for so long, a child she'd nurtured inside for almost nine months, a baby she'd fought to save these past weeks?

And then the tears came. Great gasping sobs wrenched her body, tearing at her heart, burning her loss into her soul. Not again—how could it happen again?

Still, when only dry, empty sobs were left, she knew. As she prepared Rosalind's frail little body for burial, she found herself admitting that this time she was not surprised. The pregnancy and birth had given her a sense of foreboding from the outset. She couldn't help wondering, is this my punishment? Is this what comes from shooting the two marauders?

She frantically invested her remaining energy in caring for the three boys, nursing them back to health. She was determined that the disease would not rob her of her other children as well. She vowed not to pay for the lives of the two men with two lives of her own flesh and blood.

Nell was devastated. Rosalind was the child she'd considered her own, and now she was gone. She couldn't look at the empty cradle without breaking into tears. The mere act of pouring milk would cause her to crumple in sobs.

They buried the baby on the hillside next to Donnell's grave. Fee stood alone in her own silent world, her mind swirling with painful memories. Nell cried loudly, making it difficult to hear the words Dr. Breckenridge was reading from his prayer book.

Because they were not well enough to go out, the three children clung together in sorrowful confusion, watching from the window of their upstairs bedroom, watching the adults huddled on the hillside, watching them bury their baby sister beside the grave of the brother they'd never known.

Grandma Pearl and Grandpa Ezekial stayed over that night. It was Pearl who rocked the twins to sleep and Ezekial who stayed up with Matthew, playing checkers and answering his little-boy questions.

Fee slept a dreamless sleep. But Nell couldn't sleep at all. She paced the night away, greeted everyone with red-rimmed eyes, and staggered through her days.

After a week of lonely grief Fee and Nell knew they couldn't continue this way. They worked together, struggling once more to forge a routine upon their lives.

Their grief would take longer. As Fee knew from Donnell's death, there would always be an empty place in their hearts.

Two weeks after Rosalind's death, Mr. Monroe, a freckle-faced Episcopal priest from Salem visited them. It was at Dr. Breckinridge's request, because he remembered Fee's extreme grief at Donnell's death. Touched by their concern, Fee didn't have the heart to turn him away. Besides, after his first awkward expression of sympathy, he was able to provide some of the most stimulating conversation she'd had in months. It was his story of a family of children orphaned on the Oregon Trail that led Fee to her first overt act of philanthropy.

"Please take this bank draft and use it to help these children," Fee said, impulsively going to her desk and writing. "And dairy products from my creamery and lumber from my lumberyard are available at cost to them."

"That's most kind of you," the priest stammered. Before he could say any more, Fee shooed him out the door, firmly refusing all offers to join St. Paul's congregation in Salem.

"Well, Miz Coughlin," Nell said with a shake of her head as she stood at the window watching him leave, "you sure did buy yourself a rung on the ladder to heaven with that one."

"Don't be silly, Nell. If there is a heaven, which I sincerely doubt, I'm sure you couldn't buy your way into it."

Maybe you don't buy your way into heaven, she thought to herself. But you sure do buy your way into things on earth. Through proper use of earthly goods you can buy prestige and power—and that's just what I should be doing. Then she smiled to herself. But the best part will be helping others for no other reason than doing what's right and feeling good about it.

If the rider hadn't been swearing at the mule so loudly, Nathanial wouldn't have looked up from his desk at the mill office that snowy February day—and he wouldn't have had any warning. As it was, he recognized Slead and was able to slip out the back door and signal to his sawyer, who was just going into the shed.

"Get young Thomas out of the yard and under a bed in the bunkhouse and do it quick," he said.

Charley didn't waste a movement but sped around the corner without a word. Nathanial didn't know if any of the other workers knew Thomas's plight, but judging from Charlie's response, he must have known.

There was shouting out front, but Nathanial took his time going to the front door. Wilkens was holding Slead at arm's length, trying to talk to him. Slead, roaring drunk, was swinging his arms harmlessly in Wilkens' direction.

"What's going on?" Nathanial asked innocently. Then he stopped. "Why, is that Lemuell Slead?" he asked, feigning surprise. "What're you doing in these parts, Lemuell? Last I saw you, you were heading up the Columbia to the Idaho gold fields."

Slead stopped swinging his arms and brushed Wilkens away, turning to face Nathanial. "You know damn well why I'm here, Coughlin," he said, staring up at him, swaying just slightly under the effects of the cheap booze Nathanial could smell only too well. "I'm here to get my son. You're the only damn fool in the country fool enough to hire a man's son right out of his own father's home."

"Why, now that you mention it, I think I do remember you having a second son, Lemuell," Nathanial said calmly. "Seems as if he might be about ten or so now."

"He's nigh on to fourteen and you know it!" Lemuell shouted, sounding a little less sure of himself. "He's finally grown to be a little use to his poor widowed father. Helpin' out on the farm, he should be," he whined.

"What is it you want, Slead?" Nathanial interrupted, more irritated with each sniveling word.

"I want my son, damn you!" he said. "I want you to give me back my son."

"I'm afraid I can't give back what isn't mine to give. Now

you go on into town and sober up." With a nod Nathanial turned and walked back towards his office.

"You ain't gettin' rid a' me that easy!"

"Nat! Look out!" called Wilkens.

Nathanial swung around in time to see Slead pulling his rifle out of his saddle holster. In three quick strides, Nathanial had him by the back of the neck and turned him around. He yanked the rifle from his hand and threw it into the mud.

"What kind of fool are you, Slead?" he asked with disgust.

Slead let out an incoherent shriek of anger and pulled a knife from his belt.

Enough was enough. Nathanial pushed him away, then hauled off and hit him square in the jaw. Slead staggered backward, lost his balance, and fell into the millpond.

Nathanial turned and walked back to his office without even watching to see if he came up out of the water. "Get him out of here," he said to Wilkens. He rubbed his knuckles. "He'll foul up the pond."

Wilkens came into the office about an hour later as Nathanial sat in front of the stove.

"He was madder'n a wet hen," he said as he closed the door behind him. Then he laughed and shook his head. "I wisht I coulda had a picture of him flying back'ards into that pond. Don't know where you met up with a son-of-a-bitch like that, but he ain't worth rat piss."

Nathanial laughed. "Thanks for cleaning up after me. I was afraid if I stuck around I'd kill him."

"Probably be doing the world a favor if you did. As it is, you'll see him again. Says his son is here. Says he'll be back with the sheriff outta Baker. Going to bring the law down on you for kidnapping."

Nathanial snorted in disgust. Wilkens was quiet for a moment, then added, "Don't think it's safe for the boy to stay here."

"I know. I'll wait till dark, then take him on out to the ranch."

"Hate to see him go. He's a hard worker. Could amount to something in the mill."

"Yeah, he'll amount to something just to get away from his father. He's got two little sisters he's trying to get out of that mess. Good reason to work hard."

"Me 'n a couple a' the boys were talking. Wouldn't do no harm if Slead had an accident on the way home."

Nathanial knew Wilkens was right. It would probably do

the country a service to rid it of vermin like Slead. Still, it wasn't right. He shook his head, looking grim. "Thanks just the same. I'll probably live to regret it, but it's not our place to be judge, jury, and hangman."

Fee had little cause for rejoicing when Nathanial returned that spring. Since Rosalind's death she'd been reflecting on her life more—and Nathanial had turned out to be more of a liability than an asset in her personal ledger. He'd been gone every time she needed him the most—except for that first time, when the marauders had murdered her family. When he returned to hear the tragic news of Rosalind's death, she saw his sorrow at the loss. But then he announced he was taking off for Washington and Montana Territories to look at sawmill equipment. Just when she needed him.

It wasn't that she hadn't known from the beginning. He'd always said he needed to be free to wander. If she ever expected anything else, she'd deceived herself.

Somehow she'd expected him to change just because they had a family. She should have known that a hawk doesn't give up meat just because you're raising chickens.

"You need anything before I go?" he asked, sticking his head in the door.

Fee sighed and looked at him. He was such a handsome man, tall and strong with clear gray eyes. His hair and beard were turning a deeper color with the passing of the years, like burnished copper aging in the elements. She did love him. She just couldn't count on him being there when she needed him.

"No," she said finally. "Nothing that you can give me."

He paused for a moment, then crossed the room and wrapped his arms around her. "I'll be back in a couple of months at the most." He kissed her on the forehead and turned to go.

After he left for Montana, Fee allowed herself one good cry, filled with the self-pity and frustration she'd squelched for years. Then, drying her eyes, she looked to the future—a future she'd build with her own hands.

The following week she went to Portland, leaving the children with Nell. It was time Fee started handling her own investments instead of leaving them up to Jacob.

Although she'd told herself this was a business trip, the moment she walked into Jacob's office Fee admitted that she'd had another reason for coming to Portland, one she had to face.

"I just got your letter day before yesterday," he said, crossing the room to take her hands in greeting. "It's wonderful to see you, Fee."

"Yes," she said, thrilling to his touch through her gloves, "it's good to see you, too." *How could I have forgotten his eyes?* she thought. Their deep liquid brown was warm with affection for her.

She hadn't prepared herself to face this—not now. Her thoughts had been so focused on business and family that she'd foolishly ignored the needs of her own heart. She was no longer a young girl unaware of her body's needs. She was a mature, sensual woman who knew how to respond to a man's touch. And now, seeing Jacob again, she was made breathless by the currents of desire suddenly surging through her.

"I hope my visit isn't inconvenient. I can stay at the St. Charles—"

"Not at all. And I won't hear of you staying anywhere but with us. It's just what Ruth needs. She's confined to her bed now," he said. "The baby is due in three months," he added. "I don't know if she wrote to you."

"No, I didn't know. She's so circumspect about such things. If she's not well, perhaps I shouldn't—"

"And break her heart? She's been excited ever since your letter arrived. She's eager to visit with you and exchange all the 'female' information she can. Don't disappoint her, Fee. Besides," he added, his gaze resting gently on her face, "I want you in my house."

He paused. "How are the children?"

"They're fine. They recovered from the measles with no aftereffects at all. Matthew is growing like a weed. He's not only handsome, he's also very smart," she added quietly. "I brought a picture of all three of them."

"You know how sorry I was to hear about your daughter."

"Yes. Thank you for writing."

He looked at the likeness of his son, then reluctantly handed the photograph back to Fee. He was quiet for a moment.

"I brought a copy of the photograph for you and Ruth. I'll give it to you both this evening. I wanted you to see it first, alone . . ."

230

His face lit up with pleasure. "How thoughtful. Now let's get down to business. Have you been to the bank yet?"

"No, I came here directly after checking my bags at the stage station."

"Then you don't know."

"Know what?"

"How well you're doing. Since I couldn't contact you, I made a decision without your knowledge about three years ago. There were two young miners who came to town, talking about going on to Montana. They came into the bank looking for someone to stake them—pay to have their equipment shipped upriver to the mines. They had some pretty sophisticated mining machinery that gets the last bit of gold out of abandoned claims. So I leased them our claim, dividing the proceeds with them. To insure that we would get our fair share, I hired Millard Harris to oversee the operation. He and Rachel were having tough times."

"Look here," he said, pointing to the numbers in one of the columns of his ledger.

"My goodness," Fee exclaimed. "Is that what we made from their operation?"

"No, that's what *you* made. My ledger shows an equal amount, and Millard was able to support his wife and children well enough to get another start with their farm."

Fee looked at him with amazement. "I should come to see you more often. Every time I do I find I'm wealthier than the last time."

Jacob laughed. "My family is impressed, too. They've sent out some more money from the East Coast, asking me to invest it. That's what I wanted to talk to you about. There's a chance we can buy into the bank."

"If you say it's a good idea, I'd like to do it."

"And this office building. I think we should sell it and build another, farther out of town."

"Why?"

"The city is growing, particularly in that direction. I found some land we can get cheap out by the new post office building. We can build again. I'll drive you by it on the way home."

They spent the rest of the afternoon going over the books and discussing possible ventures. It was as if their minds worked as one. Jacob would start an idea and Fee would finish the explanation in her own words. Fee would propose something and Jacob would proclaim it was his very idea.

When they did disagree, they found it soon led them to a compromise more reasonable than their original ideas. Fee couldn't have asked for a better business partner.

Yet she did ask for more. His hand brushed hers as they looked at the books, and she thrilled to his touch. Just being near him, she felt as if she were magnetically drawn closer. Then, as she stood in the doorway of their building waiting for him to bring the carriage around, she shamelessly admitted that she wanted him for her lover once more.

Ruth had miscarried three times, each one within the first three months. Now, as she told Fee about her problems, it was easier to understand why the doctor had ordered her to bed for the entire pregnancy. Since she was determined to carry this baby to full term and a healthy birth, she abided by his instructions to the letter. Jacob had moved to the bedroom down the hall, and she was confined to her bed, day and night.

It was Friday night and they had their dinner in Ruth's room. Since it was the beginning of the Jewish Sabbath, Fee was witness to the beautiful prayers and rituals, which Ruth insisted on carrying out from her bed. Watching Jacob's expression throughout the ceremony, Fee began to understand the ancient obligation and joy this was for them both. It was a bond that Fee could never share with Jacob, and she ached in the knowledge.

Ruth and Jacob were bound by the faith of their ancestors in a way that was beyond her understanding. Seeing Ruth's luminescent face over the candles, Fee's thoughts of the afternoon shamed her. How could she ever take Ruth's husband as a lover?

Feeling sure of her decision, she looked across at Jacob's strong face. She knew its lines and planes as only a lover could, knew the intimate touch of his skin and the sensations of his body. Shocked by her unbidden memories, she nearly gasped in the sudden certainty that she was helpless to refuse him if he should ever ask. In that moment he looked up, as if he'd heard her thoughts. She recognized a longing in his eyes that echoed her own and quickly forced herself to look away. It was more than she could face.

Jacob attended services alone the following day, so Fee stayed with Ruth, fetching her water and books as she needed them.

"How are Ezekial and Pearl?" Ruth asked toward the end of the afternoon.

"Well, they're not getting any younger," Fee answered truthfully. "I've needed a full-time hired hand for some time now, but I had no place for him to stay. I finally hired Sam this past year, and Ezekial and Pearl let him live at their place. It's best for everyone. This way Sam can help Ezekial out for his board and room, and I have someone, too."

"And the children," Ruth said, "do they still get to visit with Grandpa Ezekial and Grandma Pearl?"

"Oh, yes." Fee laughed. "Now that the boys are older, the problem is keeping them from wandering down there all the time, making pests of themselves. If I can't find them, they'll be either at Ezekial's or on their way."

"It sounds as if you have your hands full," Jacob said from the doorway.

"Jacob!" Fee said with a start. "How long have you been standing there eavesdropping?"

Ruth laughed. "Don't worry, he didn't hear anything embarrassing. I've been watching him from the corner of my eye."

"In that case," Fee said, reaching into her bag, "I have a present for you both. This is so you can see what my mischievous trio look like." She handed the photograph to Ruth, who exclaimed with pleasure.

"How thoughtful, Fee," she cried. "I can't wait until Jacob and I can give you photographs of our child. Look, Jacob, I couldn't be prouder if they were our own. They're so handsome."

Jacob looked down at the picture he'd seen earlier and smiled. "Let's put it downstairs on the mantel next to the fern."

"It's a lovely idea. But that's when I'm up and around to see it. For now, put it over there on my dressing table."

Fee watched Jacob place the picture of their son on his wife's dressing table. In seeing his loving gaze on Matthew's picture she felt a twist of remorse struggle with pride. What an odd turn of events fate had forced on them. Would it ever resolve itself? Or was this the resolution—quiet agony and longing?

Fee took the carriage the following week and looked at the site Jacob proposed for their new building. Everyone said it was too far out of town and would be inconvenient, but Fee could see that its location made the land a bargain. It would soon be the heart of town.

"You're right about the site for the office building," Fee told Jacob over dinner that night. "But I suggest that we go a bit to the south and buy the whole block."

"The whole block? We don't need that for the office."

"No, but people will be clamoring for shop space and offices within five years. If we have the whole block and have built the space, we'll be sitting pretty."

Jacob thought about it as he carved the roast. "You're right. I'll start negotiations for the land tomorrow. Do you want to talk to the architect with me?" He looked at her and she felt herself held in the embrace of his eyes. With great effort she forced herself to look away and answer.

"Yes. This is going to come as a shock, but I want it to be built out of brick."

"But you're a lumberman's wife," Ruth protested. "Won't you feel disloyal?"

"Not at all. Houses will always be made of wood out here. It's beautiful and plentiful. But I took a long time looking at the downtown area where our building is now, then drove around looking at other areas. I might not have thought of it if this was one of our typical rainy autumn days, but it's hot today. And I realized that we're sitting on top of a firetrap. All those buildings are wood. And, except for ours, they're of flimsy construction, thrown up in a hurry to meet the needs of the growing community. Why, some of those people don't even clean up. There are piles of junk waiting to be set off by a careless spark. And the Chinese section is even worse because no one will sell them decent material even if they can afford it. And their laundries have—well, you get the picture," she ended abruptly, seeing Ruth's dismay.

Ruth glanced anxiously out the window, as if she were expecting to see flames encroaching on them at that very moment. "Now that you say it, Fee, I can see you're right," she whispered.

"Well, you needn't worry about your house," Fee said reassuringly. "Since I was thinking about it, I observed on the way back that you're set apart from the rest of town. You have woods and streams between you and those flimsy buildings."

Ruth smiled gratefully. Jacob added his reassurance and then said, "We'll meet with the architect the end of this week, and there'll be work for some hungry masons. It's the kind of thing that my father and brothers are hoping to invest in. I'll see if they want to buy the adjacent block. What do you think?"

Fee laughed. "I think we might as well make it a family venture. That way we can control the kinds of businesses and the quality of the buildings. It's something we'd never regret."

The expansion of their business ventures kept Fee in Portland longer than she'd planned. She stayed nearly a month, meeting with architects, business owners, bankers, and others. Ruth expressed her pleasure at having Fee nearby, and Jacob agreed it was essential she be there for the planning stages. What neither one of them could have anticipated was the agony Fee suffered the whole time.

When she was near Jacob, she felt a pull that was as strong as life to her. She ached to touch him and longed to be with him. At the same time, she truly loved Ruth as a friend and didn't want to hurt her. How could Fee possibly still long for anything more than Jacob's friendship?

She found it more and more difficult to sleep. She would crawl into her bed in the downstairs bedroom, knowing that upstairs Jacob was alone in his bed, and tears would come to her eyes. She imagined what it would be like to crawl into bed beside him, to stretch out against him and simply hold him. It only made her more lonely, and she would toss and turn in frustration until the early morning hours were chimed away on the parlor clock.

Fee knew she would leave in seven more days. And she counted them as she listened to the night-quiet of the house, as she once again tossed restlessly on her bed. Finally, to keep her mind from dwelling on what she couldn't have, she got up and wandered down the hall to the parlor. Quietly, she set her candlestick on the table and lit the lamp. Maybe she could find a book to read. She ran her fingers over the titles, looking for one that would interest her.

"You can't sleep, either?" came the soft question from the wingback chair by the French doors.

Fee jumped, gasping in surprise.

"Shh," Jacob said, putting his finger to his mouth as he stood up and walked towards her. "Ruth is fast asleep. I'd hate to have her awakened by your screaming."

"You've never heard me scream," she whispered, looking into his eyes and finding her own longing reflected there.

"I know. You always seem to know how to handle every

235

situation. What is it Ezekial calls it? Good instincts?" He reached out and stroked her cheek with his hand.

Fee closed her eyes and rested her face against his palm. "I'm afraid that my instincts have failed me in this case. What am I to do?"

"What am I to do?" he answered, echoing her. "We're helpless, aren't we?"

"I thought you were just fine. That you weren't suffering. That you knew what was right, what you wanted, that everything would go on as it should, and I'd get over it."

He reached up and turned out the lamp, leaving just the candle glowing in the corner. "How could you think I was that cold? The one thing, the only thing that goes on is our love. Working beside you, watching you every minute I could steal a chance, starting with the moment you walked into my office looking more beautiful than even I remembered . . . then showing me the picture of our son, having his eyes, my eyes, looking out at me even when you aren't near. What the hell can I do?"

She stared at him, hearing the anguish in his voice, seeing the love in his eyes. And then there was no one else in the world. Only Jacob. He took the candle and silently led her to her bedroom. She felt her feet moving without her command. She was beside him, and that was all that mattered.

He quietly shut the door behind them, then pulled her to him, tasting her lips tentatively, tenderly, then eagerly, hungrily kissing her with all his pent-up passion.

She slipped her hands beneath his dressing gown, feeling the textures of his skin, the soft hair on his chest and his smooth muscled back, rediscovering the joy of his touch.

Jacob slipped her bedgown over her shoulders and, as it slithered over her hips to the floor, drew her close. His hands cupped her hips and she felt his hardness against her stomach and her knees gave way. Together they slipped to the floor.

Before either of them thought, before the rest of the world could have stopped them, their bodies were joined. They made love with a desperation and passion that had no bounds. Fee cried, sobbing in release and relief, yet fearful of what they'd once more begun. And she felt his tears join hers, mingling on both their cheeks.

Then, as they lay together, clinging to one another, afraid to let go lest the moment disappear, Fee whispered, "Is it possible that this is right?"

"I don't know," Jacob whispered. "But I do know we can

no more deny our love than we can deny ourselves. I've tried, Fee. God knows I've tried. I'm defeated and I'm glad the battle's over." He traced the line of her throat with his finger, looking at her in the moonlight. "I know that I must have you. Even if it must be in stolen times like this. I will have you."

With that he rolled over and once more entered her, loving her deeply and slowly, with full knowledge that he was possessing her as his very own. Finally, when she found herself swirling helplessly in the whirlpool of their passion, he filled her with his seed and stopped her cry of joy with his lips.

For the final week that Fee stayed in Portland, she never slept alone, except for the early-morning hours, when Jacob would slip out of bed and silently creep back to his own bedroom. She would feel him slip away from her, and feel the chill of the empty place beside her where he'd lain.

And then she would think, *is this my destiny in life? Always to long for what I can never keep? Always to have what* I cherish most slip away in the cool of the morning?

That last morning, as the sun traced the sky with the golden promise of another day, Fee got up and wandered into the garden. Overhead she heard a distant, lonely call.

Looking up, she saw a dark "V" etched against the dawn sky. Wild geese were flying overhead.

"They mate for life," she could hear Nathanial telling her last autumn. And silently she counted the number of figures in flight. Eleven. There was one up there like her, searching, alone, and yet flying with the flock. Somehow, there was solace in that.

Chapter XX

August 1875

"Oh, Fee," Ruth said warmly, "I'm so happy for you. When do you think it'll be born?"

"In the spring," Fee said with a laugh. "That's when they all come. About nine months after Nathanial goes over the mountains. About two months before he leaves he begins storing up for the winter like a squirrel."

Ruth's laughter joined hers, sharing their womanly joke. They were sitting on the Tealls' front porch, drinking tea and watching Jacob and Nathanial play baseball with the four boys. The seven-year-old twins were two copperheaded batters competing with one another, while dark-haired Matthew was patiently catching the balls Jacob pitched. When one of the twins did manage to hit a ball, Ruth's five-year-old Samuel, solemn and dark-eyed like Jacob, would scramble across the lawn to bring it back.

Fee watched the men and children playing, and her heart filled with love for them all.

She and the boys had traveled to Portland with Nathanial. They would stay at the Tealls' while Fee conducted her business and Nathanial left for the ranch. It was a common practice, one that pleased the Tealls as much as it did Fee.

"Watch me, Mother!" Timothy yelled lustily. "I'm going to hit it clear out of the yard."

"I'm watching, dear," Fee called. "I swear," she confided, "that child is determined to dominate every situation. It wears me out just watching him—him and his brother."

"Probably the making of a president," Ruth said proudly. "You have three wonderful sons, Fee. Don't you hope for a daughter this time?"

"With all my heart. Ever since Rosalind died, I've pined for a daughter. Frankly, I'd thought my child-bearing years were over because I hadn't conceived in so long."

"Does Nathanial know?"

"Not yet. He'd just worry. Ever since that incident up here—"

"Incident? My dear, you about died. It scared us all half to death."

"Well, you should talk," Fee said affectionately. "You were bedridden for nine months just to get Samuel. And you're lucky to have him. He's such a dear."

"I don't want him to be an only child."

"Ruth, you're not—"

"Not yet. But I'm hoping."

"What does Jacob say?"

"He'd have a fit. He thinks I'm still taking precautions."

"But you—"

Just then there was a crack as Timothy hit the ball. With a whoop of triumph he threw the bat and ran towards the pillow Jacob had designated as first base, unaware that the bat had hit Matthew in the head.

"Matthew!" Fee cried, jumping up from her chair and running down the steps.

Jacob ran to his son, getting there even before Nathanial, who was still watching Timothy running.

"Is he all right?" Fee asked breathlessly. Matthew was moaning by the time she got there.

"He was out for a minute there," Jacob said.

"He seems to be coming around," Nathanial told her.

"That's quite a knot," Jacob murmured. "Get some ice from the kitchen while I carry him up to the porch."

Nathanial turned to the three boys standing watching. "He'll be all right," he said reassuringly, "but you've got to remember not to throw the bat next time," he added before going on to the house.

Timothy looked sullen and stubbed his toe in the ground. "I had to hurry because Jacob made me think he was going to catch my home-run ball," he muttered defensively.

Fee knelt beside Matthew, wiping the blood trickling down his cheek. "There, darling," she murmured, "you're going to be fine. Jacob has you." She looked up and saw Jacob's eyes reflecting her own concern for their son. "He will be all right, won't he?" she whispered.

Jacob nodded, then stood up with Matthew in his arms. "Come on, son," he murmured, "we'll fix you up."

Matthew was fine, but the episode left Fee reeling. First the thought of their son hurt, then seeing that fear shared by Jacob was more than she could stand in the early stages of pregnancy. She excused herself and went to lay down.

Nathanial checked on her late that afternoon. "Are you all right?" he asked with concern.

"Yes, I'll be fine," she said, opening her eyes.

"The boys were asking about you. They're used to having you hovering over them all the time," he said as he sat down on the edge of the bed. "I think Timothy's a little jealous. Matthew's not only sporting an impressive knot on his head, but no one noticed his big hit."

Fee laughed. "I imagine that is disturbing. And Daniel probably is no consolation. If he saw it, he wouldn't admit it unless forced to."

"That about sums it up," he said, taking her hand. "Is anything the matter? Anything I should know about before I leave tomorrow morning?"

"Can't think of a thing," Fee said, sitting up to prove her health. "I should be done with my business here by the end of the week and we'll be on our way back home."

"Be sure to have Abner check the nuts on the hub of the right front wheel of the carriage before you drive out to the farm. It's been working loose lately."

Fee nodded. "The train gets into Salem too late to go directly to the farm, anyway. Do you think you'll be back by Easter?"

Nathanial kissed her on the forehead. "I'll be back way before then. Probably by late February, when the false spring melts the snow on the lower passes."

He left early in the pale gray of pre-dawn and Fee once more had an empty bed.

Later that day she met Jacob at the office. As he showed her in and closed the door, she sensed he had something on his mind. Before he began, she said softly, "It was quite a scare with Matthew yesterday, wasn't it?"

"The only other time I've been more frightened was that night in our old office when you nearly died."

She was held in the intensity of his gaze from across the room. Their shared secret gave his words more meaning, seeming to make the air tremble with their emotions. Fionna forced herself to turn away, uncertain of what she might do if she continued looking at him.

Jacob was silent for a moment. "Ruth says that you're with child," he said. "That the baby's due in the spring."

Suddenly Fee knew what he was thinking.

With beautiful clarity she remembered that week last June when she'd come up for a three-day business trip. Ruth had gone to a concert the last evening she was here. Fee had declined Ruth's invitation, choosing to pack and rest instead. Jacob had driven Ruth to the concert hall, then excused himself, saying he had to write the morning's editorial. Instead, he'd hurried back to the house, where Fee was alone in her bed. The surprise had been delightful and their love-making delicious. She smiled at the memory and at Jacob's unspoken question.

"The baby isn't due until May," she said. "It's Nathanial's child."

His back was still to her, but she saw his shoulders slump ever so slightly. "Oh. I see." He placed a ledger on the desk.

240

Then, looking up at her, he said, "What a strange and difficult life we lead—torn in two like this."

"Yes. If I could choose, I would want all my love in one place." She paused, looking down at her hands. Then, smiling faintly, she looked up at him and added, "But I can't give up what we have, either."

"Nor I. I must admit to being disappointed."

"I know. But we do have our Matthew."

"Yes," he said. "We have our Matthew."

Nathanial was as good as his word. He returned before the end of February. His delight at Fee's condition was enough to make up for his absence.

Fee's relief at seeing him was even more of a surprise to both of them. "I'm so glad you're here," she said when they were finally alone. "I'd heard some ugly rumors about problems with the Indians east of the mountains."

"Nothing to worry about. It's the Bannocks, the ones you charmed with your flute. They're unpredictable and fierce, but they're mostly in the eastern territories." He smiled. "It's good to know you worried, though."

Fee still wasn't convinced. "You're sure there's no problem?"

"Of course," he said, pulling her to him. "The only Indians around the ranch are Umatillas and they're gentle, helpful people. Even after mistreatment from idiots like the half-witted miners and land-grabbers, they're still our friends."

He ran his fingers through her hair and looked down at her. "Hey, what's the matter?" he asked, brushing a tear from her cheek.

"I'm just being silly." She forced a smile past her quivering lips. "I don't want anything to happen to you."

He wrapped his arms tightly around her, holding her to him. Slowly, all her fears melted away.

Three weeks later, Fee was in the parlor mending one of Nathanial's shirts. Matthew and the twins were at Ezekial and Pearl's farm, helping them plant their garden. Nathanial was chopping wood by the side of the house. Nell was out back doing the laundry. A teakettle whistled softly on the kitchen stove. Even a quail was chirping its contentment in the blackberry bushes. Her baby's movement fluttered across her swollen belly, and Fee was happy.

Then her happiness splintered into little pieces with the urgent clatter of a horse across the bridge. Fee leaned out the window as the rider pulled his lathered horse to a halt in front of Nathanial.

"Slim! What is it?" Nathanial exclaimed, taking the horse's bridle as the man climbed down.

"It's Sally and the boys," he said breathlessly. "They've been shot."

"What?"

"She got it in her mind to ride over and let the boys meet her father. We told her not to ride past Slead's place. He's been making all sorts of trouble. Well, Button heard shots from the east pasture and went and found them."

"Slead?"

"Saw the tracks. He's the only one around with a horse limping from a broken shoe. Too damn lazy to fix even that."

"How's Sally?"

"I'm sorry, Nat." Slim's face was filled with grief. "That's what I come to tell you. They're dead. Sally and the two boys."

Fee watched Nathanial as he closed his eyes and tilted his head back, a silent scream stretching the muscles in his neck. Then he raised the hatchet and slammed it through the chopping block, splitting it with the force of his blow.

She was at the door when he came in, followed by a very pale Slim. "Is there anything I can do?" she asked.

"Some problems at the ranch," he said curtly. "Got to go. Slim's been riding all night. Feed him and put him up before he goes back."

He was checking his rifle and ammunition when Fee went into the bedroom. "How long do you think you'll be gone?"

"Not long." He looked at her, his eyes red-rimmed and full of pain. "Not long." With that he picked up his pack, kissed her cheek, and headed out the door.

Fee's mind was reeling as she watched him gallop down the road. It was something she'd suspected, yet refused to acknowledge for some time now. But she had to know for sure. Somehow she had to get Slim to tell her more.

"Sit down and make yourself at home, Slim," she said as he came in and hung his hat on a peg by the door. "Mr. Coughlin's mighty lucky to have someone like you who'd come riding all that way," Fee said as she put food in front of him.

"Just doing my job, ma'am," he said, stabbing a slab of ham with his fork.

When he had eaten enough for two men, Fee filled his coffee cup and said, "Sure you won't have more?"

"Thanks, ma'am, but no."

"Would you like to smoke?" Fee asked. "I don't mind. I know that Mr. Coughlin likes his pipe after meals."

"Don't mind if I do," he grinned gratefully, pulling out his tobacco pouch and cigarette papers.

"I'd be grateful if you'd tell me what trouble Mr. Coughlin had," Fee began. "I can't help but worry. I heard part of what you said when you rode up. There's been a shooting?"

Slim was suddenly wary. "Yes'm. Our cook was shot in cold blood."

"That's terrible. Do you know who shot her?" Fee casually slipped in the "her" to let him think she knew all about the arrangements at the ranch.

"Slead. He's a real troublemaker."

"Lemuell Slead?"

"Same one."

"He's a terrible man. Came out on the same wagon train with us," she confided. "Beat his wife something awful until people put a stop to it. The kind of man who's not smart and knows it, so he's bitter and mean. Can't do a thing right because he's stupid and lazy. Then blames everyone else for his failings."

"That's him, all right."

"Why would he want to shoot that poor girl and her two children? There were only two, weren't there."

He nodded.

"Can't imagine she'd done anything to him."

"She hadn't. There's the evil of it," Slim said, his eyes flashing with indignation. "She wouldn't do no harm to no one. Not Sally. It was just 'cause she's"—he stopped himself and looked at Fee—"just 'cause she works for our ranch," he finished unconvincingly.

"Slead still has it in for our family, then?"

"That's right. She wouldn'ta been touched if'n she hadn't been . . . hadn't been working for Mr. Coughlin."

"I see," Fee said. "And her children? How could he hurt little children?"

"Pure hate, ma'am," he said, then stopped, not knowing how to explain further.

"I see," Fee said. And she did.

*　　*　　*

243

It had been like a shadowy presence in the back of her mind, one whose features she didn't see and therefore didn't have to recognize openly. But now she made herself look it squarely in the eye. Nathanial had another family at the ranch.

Fee paced the floor of her bedroom that night, trying to understand her feelings.

She'd probably always known something like this was coming. Nathanial was too lusty a man to be away from her as much as half of each year without having some . . . someone to fulfill his needs. That hurt but didn't surprise her. What troubled her was the idea of another family, more children. How many were there? What did they mean to him? How did that affect her and her relationship with Nathanial?

She knew that she was accepting this new knowledge with much more equanimity than Nathanial might ever have expected. They had agreed not to tie one another down. She'd never once extracted any promises from him. Perhaps it was easier for her to accept because she, too, had another love, and she believed that love did not diminish her love for Nathanial.

She sat by the window and looked out across the moonlit fields. Nathanial had not really been unfaithful, because faithfulness had never been part of their bargain. Still, she felt a deep grief.

Then, suddenly, she knew what was tearing at her heart. It *was* grief. Nathanial had lost two children and a woman he'd loved. He was grieving, and because she loved him and shared his life, she shared that grief as well. She wished she'd been able to see his two sons, and she suspected she would have liked Sally. A single tear rolled down her cheek, and she put her head in her hands and began to cry. Her tears were for them all.

The next morning Fee stood in the doorway watching Slim as he rode away. Just as he got to the bridge, he turned and waved his hat and she waved back. Standing on the porch, watching the early morning sunlight slant across the wooden steps, Fee had a very empty feeling. Then, slowly there was a tiny, insistent movement in her stomach. An uncomfortable lump rose up under her ribs and she looked down, stretching the material of her dress smoothly across her belly. She could see a tiny bulge, like a little foot or hand pushing out against her skin. Gently, she caressed the little bump until it slowly slid down the wall of her stomach and back into place. She figured she had another month before the baby came. And she would welcome its arrival.

Nathanial arrived late one night a week and a half later. Fee heard his horse and went out to the barn to meet him.

She hung her lantern on the hook beside the door and watched him stiffly climb down from the saddle.

"I'm glad you're home," she said simply.

He looked at her. "I'm glad to be home." Then he held her in his arms.

The smell of hay and horse sweat filled the air. Lantern light cast a golden glow over the stall and she remembered him in that other lantern light so long ago on the trail.

"Was it Slead?" she asked.

"Slead's horse tracks, his boot tracks, same caliber rifle. No doubt about it."

"What did you do?"

"Slead met with a little accident. He can't make any more trouble."

"It's not a good thing to say, but I feel as if the world's a better place because of it. What about his children?"

"The boy Thomas and the two girls lit out of there about a year ago. Just his young 'un, Zenas, left. Slead had a woman there with him. She insists she can care for the boy and that squirrel ranch on her own. Mean as an old sow hog. No one out there wants to argue with her."

"Did Thomas get the girls and go back to Oregon City?"

Nathanial hung the blanket over the stall and threw some oats into the manger for the horse. "Sure did. Stopped by and saw them on the way back."

He looked her up and down pridefully. "You look like you're about to pop. How you feel?" he asked as he put his arm around her shoulder and closed the door behind them.

Fee laughed softly. "I'm fine. Haven't felt the baby moving for about five days now. Seems as if they settle down real quiet right before they're ready to come. Maybe we'd better go into town tomorrow."

Fee was right. She went into labor just as they reached the outskirts of Salem. Their daughter was born within the hour. There were all sorts of suggestions for names for the tiny baby girl sleeping in her arms, but none of them seemed right. Much to Mrs. Gould's dismay, they went back to the farm four days later with the baby still unnamed. The children were elated to see them and perfectly charmed by their baby sister. Still, it puzzled them that there was nothing they could call her other than "little sister."

It rained during the night, but the sun broke through the clouds as Fee nursed the baby in her bedroom the next morning. She couldn't help feeling contented and proud as she examined her daughter's dainty hands and curled her dark reddish hair around her fingers. But what to name her?

She put the baby back in the cradle and began cleaning out some drawers to put the baby clothes in. She would sleep in Fee's room until she was weaned. Then she would move down the hall with Nell.

As Fee reached into the back of one drawer, her fingers brushed something hard and sharp-edged, and she pulled it out. It was the metal box she'd rescued from her father's farm almost fifteen years ago. It was nearly empty. She'd long ago used the coins he'd saved for her education. They'd helped pay for the first creamery.

The only thing left was a delicate old ring. Gold filigree set with seed pearls surrounded a deep red garnet. It was the ring her mother had brought with her from Ireland. Fee was supposed to wear it on her wedding day. There had been a matching brooch. Fee had sent it on to her sister Siobhan with the money from the farm. She couldn't help wondering if Siobhan had had a wedding, and had worn the brooch.

Fee's mind wandered back across the years to that little farm in western Virginia where they had played so happily. They had laughed, told secrets, made plans in such a wonderful sisterly fashion. Fee could still see the little nook down by the creek she and her sister had pretended was an imaginary fairyland.

Fee looked down at her sleeping baby girl and longed to share her happiness with her sister. But how could she possibly find her? Last she'd known she was still in school and planning to marry. She couldn't even remember the man's name. Then suddenly the idea struck her. Perhaps the people at the school knew where she was.

Taking pen in hand, Fee sat down and began writing. She told her sister of her life in the new land, of their farm, of Nathanial's businesses and her own. She described the children—Matthew's studied approach to everything, and the twins' tumbling, competitive romp through life. Then she wrote about her daughter—her tiny perfection, her clear blue eyes, and her graceful little fingers.

Suddenly she knew the baby's name: Hannah, because she'd once read that meant grace. Hannah Siobhan, named for grace and Fionna's sister. And technically, Siobhan was the first to know because Fee sealed the letter and handed it to Wesley to take into town before she ever told anyone else what she'd named the baby.

It was nearly six months later, when Fee had more than she could handle with the creamery, the farm, four lively children, her business investments, and her dairy herds that she heard from her sister. For a moment Fee just stood staring at the envelope, trying to think who could possibly be writing to her from Boston. Then she remembered her quiet moment of nostalgia last spring. Brushing her hair back from her face, she poured herself a cup of tea, asked Nell to take the children outside to pick apples, then sat down to read what Siobhan had written.

My dearest sister,

You can't imagine the tears of joy I shed upon receiving your letter. I'd thought you'd died along the trail when I didn't hear from you. Now I find that you're alive and doing so well. I even have a precious niece carrying my baptismal name. I should add right here that I no longer go by Siobhan because it was too difficult for most people to spell. Although Daddy would probably turn in his grave to hear it, I've taken the Anglican pronunciation and answer to Judith to all my friends in Boston. Still, I'm delighted that my niece bears my name.

I've fifteen years to tell you about and I must make it brief if the letter is to be delivered.

I married the young man I wrote about and my dowry, which you so thoughtfully provided, helped him to set up a successful textile mill and clothing manufactory. The War Between the States caused him to increase his production fivefold within as many years.

I'm afraid that my story is not as happy as yours. My beloved Aldrich was taken from me five years ago by a heart attack. Luckily, he'd provided for me very well. I inherited his entire estate and have been living comfortably. That is why the school was able to forward your letter. I made a donation to their scholarship fund last year.

We were not blessed with children, so you can imagine my joy when I find that I have a niece and nephews. I'm eager to see you all. I would like to come out for Christmas this very year. I've checked and I can take a train across the entire country now, arriving in San Francisco. From there I can take a steamer up to Portland. According to my map, you should be able to meet me there and take me to your home in Salem.

I long to hear from you soon.

> *Your loving sister,*
> *Judith*

Fee sat staring at the letter, her feelings racing from happiness to despair to panic.

Suddenly she was remembering her older sister not as the companion of her idyllic childhood but as the critical older sibling. She remembered how Siobhan (Judith, now) would come home from school and mock her country ways, her manners, and her clothes.

Fee looked around her kitchen, which was the original cabin on the farm. It was comfortable and homey, but seeing it through Judith's eyes, terribly inadequate. And there was no extra bedroom. And just the shabby front room that served as sitting room, parlor, and library with an old braided rag rug she'd made. How could she have lived this way and not noticed?

It wouldn't do. She'd have to act quickly. She began by writing a letter to Judith. The roads and weather were too unpredictable for a winter arrival, she said. As much as she hated to suggest it, would Judith please postpone her visit until the spring? She carried the letter to Wesley before he drove into town. It would be posted and on its way by nightfall.

Then she turned and looked around her house with new purpose. There was so much to get done in the intervening months.

Chapter XXI

September 1876

"They'll be starting the roundup this week," Nathanial said as he came into the bedroom.

"Figured it was about time. When are you leaving?" Fee was brushing her hair over the shoulder of her linen nightdress.

"Day after tomorrow," he said, tugging at the heel of his boot.

"I think while you're gone I'll do a little fixing up around the house. Hannah will be needing a room of her own—and we don't have any place to put guests now that our family's so big."

Nathanial raised one eyebrow. "What kind of guests are you talking about?" he asked with a grin.

Fee had to giggle at his look. "I got a letter from Siobhan today. When Hannah was born I tried to find her by writing to her old school. They sent it on and she wants to come out and visit."

"When's she coming?"

"I wrote and told her to wait until spring. She's a widow now and sounds like she's comfortably settled. She's not moving out, just visiting."

Nathanial's smile betrayed his relief. "Be nice to see her. Can't remember much except she seemed a bit of a pruneface compared to you."

"Oh, Nathanial," Fee said, leaning over and kissing his cheek, "you're such a flatterer."

He hung his pants on the bedpost and reached over to turn out the lantern. "You know," he said, pulling her closer to him, "when you have the carpenters out, you might have them cut another window in our bedroom. Right over there."

"That might be nice. Why there?"

"So the moonlight will fall across the bed and I can see you better on nights like this," he said, unbuttoning her gown.

Fee knew that Nathanial had no idea what he was agreeing

to before he left, but she was sure he'd approve when he returned in the spring and saw the results of her efforts.

She worked with the architect who'd designed the bank building she and Jacob had built in Salem. They decided that two complete wings should be added to the existing house. Carved decorative trim moldings would give unity to the entire structure, and a wraparound porch would make a grand entrance and tie the whole thing together. There would even be a ballroom built above the kitchen.

Her next feat was to secure enough carpenters who were willing to work through the winter to meet her schedule. Contrary to what she'd told her sister, the Oregon winters in the Willamette Valley were noted for their wetness rather than their severity. Once the building began, she contacted a family that was starting a nursery in the valley. She gave them a blanket order for landscaping her yard with trees, shrubs, and flowers as soon as the remodeling was finished.

One night after the children were in bed, Fee sat at her bedroom window, trying to understand what was still plaguing her about her sister's impending arrival.

It had to do with Judith's inheritance of her husband's estate. Not that Fee felt she had any worry in that area. She'd become a wealthy woman in her own right and didn't expect there would be much competition between them on that matter. The feeling came when she reread the line in Judith's letter that referred to her husband's death: "Luckily, he'd provided for me very well. I inherited his entire estate . . ."

There it was. Would she get the same if something should happen to Nathanial? They weren't married. They had four living children, yet there was nothing to prevent him from giving all he had amassed, with her help, to someone else.

Last spring she'd learned she wasn't the only one in his life. Nathanial had had a second family at the ranch. Did he have others? Where did that leave her and the children, his children?

There was something else, too. Judith was a married woman. She had probably even worn their mother's brooch on her wedding day. Fee had never worn their mother's ring because she'd never had a wedding day. She didn't even have a wedding ring. How could she face her sister knowing that she was unmarried?

By Christmas, Fee had found a solution. For the first time the children attended a church service in Salem, accompanied by Pearl. Afterwards, while Pearl and the children had tea with Dr. and Mrs. Breckenridge, Fee met with Mr. Monroe.

Fee smiled as she accepted a cup of tea from him. "May I assume that all I tell you here will be confidential, never to be told to another living soul?"

"Of course, Mrs. Coughlin," he assured her quickly.

"In that case, Mr. Monroe," she said, "I would like you to marry me to Nathanial Coughlin this coming spring."

"Marry you? But—"

"We came together after my family was murdered and burned out at the beginning of the War Between the States," she explained. "Nathanial very generously agreed to take me with him across the plains. We didn't have time for a wedding. When we got here—well, we were busy making ends meet, breaking the ground, and starting a family. We never got around to it. I don't feel right about it. It's a loose end I would like to tie up."

"Of course," he said with a smile. "You know, your story is not unusual. Many folks were caught by circumstances, and we just have a simple, very private ceremony to remedy the situation."

"But I want a full-fledged wedding held in our own parlor and attended by our friends and neighbors."

"But don't you think the community would find it—"

"I wasn't planning on letting the community know what they were witnessing," Fee said with a triumphant smile. "They'll think they are attending a renewal of our vows on our fifteenth wedding anniversary. Could you do that?"

Mr. Monroe threw his head back in a great, hearty laugh. "It's wonderful!" he exclaimed.

"Then I will have a wedding on June tenth."

The beauty of Fee's plan was that Nathanial was gone while she put it in order. Because of the snows that year, Nathanial didn't return until March. By that time, Fee had mailed out invitations to her friends in Portland and Salem—as well as to some of Nathanial's associates she knew by name in eastern Oregon.

Then came a windy March day with crisp white clouds scudding across the blue sky. She saw Nathanial ride up to the bridge and stop. She watched him, and when he didn't come forward, she ran out to greet him. "Welcome home," she called.

He was sitting astride his horse, staring at the busy scene in front of him. The house was essentially finished except for a few final details. Two men were busily digging, cleaning, and planting in the newly fenced yard. Fee followed the direction of his stare, looked back at him, then looked at her new home. It was quite lovely and impressive, but looking at it from Nathanial's view, it must have looked very different from the home he'd left five and a half months earlier.

"What the hell has happened?" he asked. "Am I lost?"

"No. I told you I was going to fix the place up, do some remodeling, remember?"

"You didn't say you were going to build a full-fledged country estate while I was away."

Fee's breath caught in her throat. "You don't like it?"

Nathanial looked down at her, and his face softened. "Just surprised," he said, getting out of his saddle. "Just surprised. But that's what I've come to expect from you, anyway," he added with a laugh. Then he kissed her and she knew everything was all right.

"It'll look better when they finish the painting and trim. We haven't gotten all the wallpaper up yet, and the curtains are still being hung. But most of the furniture and carpeting is in place. Oh, Nathanial," she said, leaning her head against his shoulder, "I do hope you'll like it."

"Are you going to live in it?"

"Yes, of course," she said, puzzled.

"Then I'll like it."

Fee went alone to Portland to meet her sister. When she saw the straight-backed elegant woman walking down the gangplank, Fionna clearly remembered all her childish insecurities. But when Judith saw her and waved, then ran to her, Fionna remembered her love for her childhood companion, her sister.

"You look the same—only more beautiful and elegant!" Judith proclaimed, holding her in her arms.

"And you . . . you look wonderful," Fee cried.

Then they stepped back and gazed at one another, Fee with her blue eyes and Judith with her hazel eyes, each struggling to fight back the tears. "I've missed my kin," Fee whispered.

"So have I," Judith said, tears of happiness rolling down her cheeks. "So have I."

The children and Nathanial were on their best behavior

when they arrived at the train station—much to Fee's relief, for she knew that four active children must be overwhelming to someone who lived alone. However, within a day, they were competing for their Aunt Judith's attention and approval. And she obviously loved every moment of it.

It wasn't until Judith had been there for three weeks that Fee told Nathanial of her plans for June tenth.

"A what?" he exclaimed in the privacy of their bedroom early one morning.

"A celebration of our fifteenth wedding anniversary. We'll make it a party and—"

"Anniversary?"

"I've invited all our friends and neighbors. Even some people you work with in eastern Oregon. Thought you might like to have—"

"How can you have an anniversary for something you never had?"

"Well," Fee said, smiling as sweetly as she could and feeling more frightened of him than she had felt since they were on the Oregon Trail, "everyone will think it's an anniversary celebration. In truth it will be our wedding. I've talked to the minister at St. Paul's—"

"Wedding!"

"—and he knows the truth and has agreed to marry us in this way."

"Marry?" Nathanial looked for all the world like a cat that just spotted a pack of dogs.

Fee had to laugh, "Yes, darling, our wedding. Don't you think after six children, it's time?"

"Why bother?" he asked lamely. "It's an awful lot of fuss for something that we've been living all along."

Fee sighed and started brushing her hair. "I suppose we could just continue on, if you insisted. But I got to thinking when Judith wrote to me about how she'd inherited all her husband's estate. There could be a problem with our children inheriting your ranch, the sawmills, and properties if anything happens to you. All sorts of people could come forward and claim—"

"I'm not going to die for some time yet, and who the hell would cause problems like that, anyway?"

"You know full well there are all sorts of people out there—"

Nathanial looked her in the eye, holding her with the intensity of his gaze. "Not anymore there aren't," he said evenly.

253

Fee knew what he was telling her, and she met his look. Maybe there weren't any other women now, but she had no guarantee for the next time, no promise for the future. "You never know what kind of people are out there," she said finally. "I think you should consider your children."

He was silent for a moment, then pulled on his boots and turned and went out the door without saying a word.

Fee felt as if she were walking on eggs all day long. Every time Nathanial came into view she was tongue-tied.

That night as he came in the bedroom, she put down her brush, leaving her hair loose over her shoulders. "Nathanial, I won't force you to go through with this, but I have to know so I can have time to call it off."

"Mmph," he said as he threw his pants over the bedpost.

Fee reached over and turned down the light. "Did you notice how I had them arrange the windows?" she asked.

"How's that?"

"The moonlight falling over the bed." She slipped the nightdress over her shoulders and let it slide down to her feet.

Nathanial looked at her, then looked at the window, then back at her. Slowly, he smiled for the first time that day.

The next morning he rolled over in bed and kissed her awake. "I've been thinking," he said, running his hands through her hair. "Can't see what is going to be changed in my lifetime by a few words and a piece of paper. If it makes you happy, we'll have your wedding."

So it was that Fee was wed. She and Nathanial were married in their new parlor, with her long-lost sister as her attendant, their children and friends as witnesses, and her mother's ring on her finger.

At the end of the ceremony, Nathanial called to some men to help him bring in a present for his wife. Then he presented Fee with a beautiful teakwood piano. At Nathanial's insistence, Fee sat down and played for him, just as she had as a girl. And the look in his eyes as he watched her told her that the man she'd married truly loved her.

PART III

THE CHILDREN

Chapter XXII

May 1888

Being the youngest was no fun at all—especially if you were a girl, a girl with three big brothers. Hannah knew. When they weren't tormenting her they were telling her to leave them alone. The next worst thing was being twelve and having everyone treat her like a baby. And the next worse thing, Hannah thought as she raced up the stairs to her secret hiding place, was having the only brother who even came close to understanding her go clear across the country to go to Harvard College. She just knew that he was sent far away because he took her side so often. Mother was jealous that Hannah was Matthew's favorite, because Matthew was Mother's favorite.

By the time she opened the trapdoor to the attic, Hannah had worked herself into a good pout. In fact, she had such a whopping case of self-pity she almost decided to stay up there all night and give everyone a scare—if they even noticed she was missing!

No one ever came up to the attic, except Nell when she was doing the spring cleaning. And it was full of unexplored corners and boxes and trunks. What Hannah liked best, though, was sitting by the big round window that overlooked the front yard. Dusty sunlight filtered in as she sat in the shadows, watching the comings and goings of Quail Hollow unobserved.

She could hear her mother calling her from downstairs as she curled up in the nest of old draperies she'd piled beside the window. She smiled smugly as she watched her mother step off the front porch and call her name, then give up and go back into the house. She was supposed to be practicing the piano, but Mother couldn't make her do it if she couldn't find her.

After ages of no one coming or going, except Daniel and Timothy returning from their Saturday trip to town, Hannah tired of her secret perch and turned her attention to the contents of the attic.

She'd never really explored the part of the attic tucked away on the back side of the house. Two chimneys intersected the attic, bringing warmth from eight fireplaces. They also divided the attic into sections, creating dark corners and cubbyholes on their back sides.

Much to her delight she found an old wooden chest, with a leather-banded lid, cracked with age and neglect. She wiggled the rusty lock, and it gave way. Opening the lid released years of dust. She quickly covered her nose and mouth with both hands to silence her sneezes.

It was lucky that she did, because before she could even move the old newspapers covering the contents of the chest, she heard voices coming from right under her feet. She stood and listened, frightened that she might be discovered.

"You don't understand," Daniel was saying.

"Come on," Timothy wheedled, "we always share everything. Don't stop now with the most important."

The door slammed just to the left of the chimney, and Hannah realized that she must be right over the top of her brothers' bedroom. Being twins, they got the largest bedroom after her parents. Without hesitation, she put her ear to the rough wooden floor of the attic and listened.

"Mary Catherine's just a friend. We like to talk," Daniel explained patiently.

"You mean you were alone with her, her with her ripe, full breasts, and all you did was talk? I tell you, Dan—"

"Cut it out!" Daniel's voice interrupted. "Keep your dirty thoughts to yourself. She's a nice girl."

Timothy laughed heartily. "Nice girls don't come from that neighborhood. Nice girls come from good families. Pleasure girls come from that side of the tracks."

"Damnit! I told you . . ." Daniel's steps quickly crossed the room to where Timothy's voice came from.

"Oh, come on," Timothy pleaded, suddenly conciliatory. "I didn't mean anything by it. Have all the friends you want from wherever you want. Now let go."

"Will you give up that kind of talk about Mary Catherine?"

"Sure, sure. Don't get so excited."

There was a rustle below and Hannah knew that her brothers were separating, another fight just barely averted. She heard footsteps cross the room and the door open. "Just make sure that when you do stick it to her I get to hear the details," Timothy's voice taunted, and then the door closed quickly.

Hannah heard a thud that sounded like Daniel must have thrown something heavy at the door. "Damn!" he said hoarsely, and something else slammed down on the floor. She heard nothing more until the door opened again and she knew Daniel was gone, too.

Hannah sat back on her heels and thought about what she'd heard. Not only did she now know that her brother Daniel had a girlfriend named Mary Catherine, she also knew that Timothy didn't consider her the "right kind" of girl. Timothy was always so right and proper, she knew that Daniel must have been trying to hide it from his twin for some time now. She smiled, wondering just how she could make use of this information.

She also remembered what Timothy had said about this Mary Catherine. Something about her breasts. Hannah looked down and moved from side to side, wondering if her budding breasts would ever sway under her dress.

Then something else struck her. She'd just made a wonderful discovery. She could come up here anytime her brothers were in their room and spy on them. She'd know more about them than even Mother. She'd hear all their secrets.

She turned with renewed interest to the chest. There was just enough daylight left for her to see if it held any treasures.

There were several dusty journals, a couple of smaller boxes, some shoes and a woolen coat, and a long, leather-covered box with a silver latch. Curious, she lifted that out of the chest and took it to the window so she could see better.

There was a neat, solid click as she pushed the latch open. The box was lined with blue velvet and a rich, secret scent filled her nose as she opened the lid. She gasped with surprise. A long black wooden flute with silver keys was resting on the velvet.

Very carefully, she lifted it from the case, felt the satiny smooth finish of the wood, and fitted her fingers carefully into the curves of the silver keys. She'd seen flutes played when she'd gone to concerts with her mother and the Tealls in Portland. They'd always fascinated her, sounding like the voices of birds.

She placed her lower lip on the cool silver mouthpiece and blew gently. A soft, haunting tone filled her secret hiding place. She blew once more, this time lifting her fingers from the keys one at a time. Her heart turned over with joy to hear the tones change. It was the most beautiful sound she'd ever made.

Granted, the piano was lovely and she lost herself in it when she was playing. Sure, Mother and everyone else said that she was truly gifted. But it was boring. This was new and exciting. She quickly put the flute back in its case and took it downstairs. She had to learn how to play it.

Her mother was in the parlor. She'd just turned on the lamp, and the blue shadows of oncoming dusk gave way to a circle of golden warmth around Fee's desk.

"I'm going to quit my piano lessons," Hannah announced breathlessly as she came into the room. "I'm going to play this."

Her mother turned and looked with surprise at the flute Hannah was holding in her hand.

"Where on earth did you find that?"

"Upstairs in a chest. Listen." She put the flute to her lips and blew the prettiest note yet. "I haven't figured out where to put all my fingers. That's why I want lessons."

"That's very good, dear," her mother said with a smile. "But to develop your musical talent, you'll have to continue on with the piano."

"I hate the piano," Hannah said, stamping her foot. "All I do is play scales, dumb scales. And my music teacher is—"

"Hannah, that will be quite enough. In fact," she added as Hannah threw herself into a chair and folded her arms angrily, "I was just sitting here thinking about you. I got a letter from Aunt Judith today." She held up the blue sheets of paper she'd been reading when Hannah came in.

"Aunt Judith says perhaps you've outgrown your piano teacher. She proposes that you come to Boston and live with her. You would have all sorts of musical opportunities there . . ."

Hannah's heart suddenly chilled with fear. "Leave Quail Hollow? Leave Oregon?" She sat up, tears filling her eyes as she looked at her mother in genuine terror.

"Well, not forever, dear. But you would be away from home for the better part of the year." She smiled. "My only hesitation is selfish. I don't know that I want to be separated from you so soon."

"Oh, no, Mama, please, no," Hannah pleaded. "Don't send me away. I'll put the flute back. I'll keep on with my piano lessons here. I won't make any more trouble." The stream of promises poured forth without a thought before them. Ever since Matthew left home, Hannah had been haunted with dreams of being sent away, too. Now her worst nightmare was coming true, and she had to do something, promise anything, to avert it.

Her mother reached out and took her in her arms, quieting her tears with her warmth and soft mother-scent. "I'll tell you what," she said as she handed her handkerchief to Hannah. "Why don't I go into Salem and see if they have any music professors at the university who'll take you?"

Hannah blew her nose and managed a smile.

"Is that a better idea?" her mother asked. Hannah nodded her head. "Now run along and put the flute back where you got it. You can play it when you've mastered the piano, not before."

"Thank you, Mama," Hannah said with relief. She gave her mother a quick hug and ran up the stairs.

The man Fionna found for Hannah was a young professor at Willamette University who was supposed to be something of a wonder. He wanted to hear her play first. If she was good enough, he would accept her as a student. Hannah was stricken with renewed fear. If he didn't accept her, she was certain to be sent away to Aunt Judith.

She practiced with a frenzy for the next month, filling every moment she could find with flurried scales and the two pieces she'd chosen to impress this important teacher. When the day finally came, she thought she'd spoil everything by throwing up or bursting into tears. But once she started to play, she forgot everything but her music. She floated into that secret world that held her heart's song and she played as she'd never played before.

When the last note hung in the air she was jarred back to reality. Professor Raines was standing beside her, his fair hair falling across his forehead. She held her breath until he spoke.

"That was lovely," he said quietly. He sat down beside her on the bench, "Let's see if we can put more line in that last phrase." His long fingers stretched across the keys and he played the same section she'd just finished, only it came alive under his hand, with newly revealed beauty.

"That's lovely," she said, and then was immediately embarrassed that she'd repeated his praise.

"Let's hear you do it."

Her hands shook as she put them on the keys. Then she was lost in imitating the graceful flow the professor had given the last phrase.

"Perfect," he exclaimed even before she'd finished. Turning to Fee, he said, "She's what every music teacher dreams of—and I was lucky enough to have her walk in my door. You'll have no reason to be disappointed." He stood up. "We'll begin lessons next Friday at four," he said as they walked out the door.

Anxiously, Hannah watched her mother's face as they went down the stairs. Finally, as they emerged into the spring sunshine, Hannah could wait no longer. "Does this mean I can stay at Quail Hollow?" she blurted out.

"Oh, good heavens, yes," Fee said, putting her arm around Hannah's shoulder. "You'd think I'd threatened you with exile the way you talk. I think we can rest assured that you'll have proper instruction for the next few years."

Hannah gave a little skip of happiness, then ran back and hugged her mother. "I love you, Mother," she exclaimed before running ahead to unhitch the horse so they could drive the carriage home—home to Quail Hollow.

Hannah's interest in the piano was renewed with her lessons with Professor Raines. He taught her music along with the theory represented by the hated scales. She played until she thought her heart would burst. The flute was forgotten.

However, once she settled into the routine of practice and lessons once more, she noticed that her brothers were fighting worse than ever.

She watched them come home from school the week before graduation and remembered her secret place in the attic. She'd heard her mother talking to her father the night before, wondering what was going on between them. Even they didn't have an answer, but Hannah knew how to find out. Maybe if she knew what the problem was she could help.

Dust danced in the sunlight as she quietly let down the trapdoor and crept across the floor of bare, wide boards to the back of the house. Heavy footsteps ran up the stairs as she put her ear to the floor. Then the door to the twins' room opened and closed. Another set of footsteps came up, and the door opened again.

"Stop hounding me," Daniel said. "You have a twisted sense of values. I don't need to hear anymore. You don't flinch at having me do your homework, but you look down your nose at—"

"I have every right to hound you. What you do reflects on me and the rest of the family. There are two kinds of people, those who run our society and those who are the workers, the drones. It's not right for the two classes—"

"If you want any help with that geometry test, you'll stop right there. I don't need to hear that garbage."

There was a long silence. "Listen," Timothy began, "I understand what she offers. She looks up to you, and rightfully so. But you can do much better. Just promise me," he said quickly, "just promise that you won't do anything rash. We're not leaving for another two months."

"You'll be the first to know when I plan anything rash, Tim."

There was a laugh of relief from both of them as they pulled out their chairs and settled in to study. Hannah was just about to get up when she heard Timothy speak once more.

"I've got to admit you got an eye on you."

"What do you mean?"

"I mean, her breasts are like ripe cantaloupes, and her hips . . . I'd give a lot if you'd share a go under those skirts—"

There was a sudden crack of flesh hitting flesh. "Hey!" Timothy cried in surprise as a chair fell against the floor. "What the hell—" His words were cut off by the door slamming.

"Jesus Christ," he murmured under his breath. Then Hannah heard him pour water into his washbowl. There was a sharp intake of breath after he wrung out a washrag in the bowl. Daniel must have given him a good one. Hannah slipped over to her spot by the window and tried to think. Maybe she was learning more than she wanted to know.

In June, after school was out, Hannah overheard a conversation between her mother and Timothy. Hannah was heading into the parlor when she heard their voices coming from the drawing room.

"Helen Winston?" Fee was saying incredulously. "The bank president's daughter?"

"Yes," Timothy answered stiffly. "She's the logical choice. Although her family's not as wealthy as ours, they are comfortable . . ."

"But do you find her appealing?" Hannah stopped beside the door and quietly stood listening. "I've seen her only a few times," her mother said, "but she didn't seem like the kind of girl who would . . . well, who would attract a young man's eye."

"She's nice enough," Timothy continued. "A good head on her shoulders and a nice laugh. She's a bit plain, but that's what I should have. Remember, Mother, I'm going into politics, and a plain, dutiful wife with the right background is exactly what I need."

"I hardly think it's the criteria for a lasting marriage," Fee protested. "Don't you think you should consider the importance of love?"

"A man with my ambitions can't be ruled by his passions," Timothy said indignantly. "I plan on making my intentions clear before I leave for school this August. She has to finish school, so I'll wait to propose marriage."

"Oh, by all means," Fee said, "do wait until she's a bit older."

As her mother rose to leave the room, Hannah quickly raced down the hall. She didn't know what to think anymore.

The twins' graduation came in a flurry of speeches, white-dressed girls, and stiff-collared boys—and a temporary truce from the twins' hostilities. Even Hannah got a new dress for the festivities. Graduation morning she watched as her mother and father presented the twins with identical gold pocket watches, inscribed with their names and graduation dates, a gift that came as no surprise to her because she knew her parents tried not to play favorites and that was the identical gift Matthew had received four years earlier.

The rest of the month was spent in dewy morning garden work, warm afternoon creek-wading to catch pollywogs, and occasional forays into the cool darkness of the creamery to help Mother with her specialty cheeses. Best of all, summer meant that Matthew would be coming home. At least he said he'd try. Professor Raines had taken a summer leave of absence so she didn't even have piano lessons to worry about, just enough practicing to keep her fingers agile.

Fee left in early July to go to Portland on business. While she was gone, the twins' battles erupted with renewed violence. Hannah listened from her secret place and wrote a long, pleading letter to Matthew, begging him to come home just to see her.

Perhaps her mother knew something wasn't quite right

when she got back. Two days after she got back from Portland, she made an announcement at the dinner table.

"I've got a surprise for you boys," Fee said brightly. "I was told by several men in Portland who are Harvard graduates that you should arrive there early to have time to settle in. I've booked tickets for you to leave on the train the third of August. We'll have a going-away party Saturday, July thirtieth, so you can say good-bye to all your friends."

"But I didn't expect to leave until September," Daniel blurted out.

"I know, but it's better this way, dear, believe me."

"I'm sure it is," Timothy agreed quickly. "Give us time to get the lay of the land."

Daniel glowered at him. Hannah figured it was because Daniel didn't want to leave Mary Catherine but Timothy wanted to avoid the August haying.

Late that night she heard the twins talking in their room. Hannah opened her door and quietly slipped into Matthew's room. She reassured herself that Matthew wouldn't mind just this once. Then the voices from the next room drew her to the wall, and she forgot all else.

"You're a goddamned fool!" Timothy said with a growl. "You're going to ruin us all!"

"The only thing that can ruin us"—Daniel was on the other side of the room and Hannah had to press her ear hard against the wall to catch his words—"would be for the rest of the world to find out what a prig you are. A prig and a bigot!"

"I'm going to do everything I can to stop you!"

"It'll take more than the likes of you!"

"It's not just you, you selfish—"

There was the sound of scuffling, and she knew that the twins were once more at one another. It was getting loud enough that even her parents would hear. Quickly, she slipped back down the hall. She'd just closed her door when she heard her father grumbling as he went to break up the fight.

That was two nights before the party. The boys seemed to bring their anger under control for the festivities, much to Hannah's relief. She wasn't allowed on the hayride that picked everyone up and brought them out to Quail Hollow. But she was helping with the ice cream freezers when she heard the wagon come over the bridge. They were singing and laughing and Hannah couldn't wait until she was grown up like that. Maybe some boys would be fighting over her by then, she thought with a secret thrill.

Much to Hannah's disappointment, she saw that Mary Catherine was very pretty, but her shape—although quite lovely—wasn't in the least like fruit. What was exciting was to hear how she laughed when Daniel whispered in her ear and to see the way they looked into one another's eyes. Surely that was the true love she'd read about.

On the other hand, although Helen Winston seemed to be doe-eyed around Timothy, the feelings certainly weren't mutual. Timothy treated her in a courtly manner, all the while looking around the room, watching everyone else. Now, if it were true love, Hannah thought, he wouldn't be able to take his eyes away from her—like Daniel and Mary Catherine.

Maybe that was it! Timothy was jealous that Daniel had found true love. Hannah felt terribly grownup, having figured it all out.

The next three days were a flurry of activity. The twins seemed to have called a truce.

Then, the day before they were to leave, it all boiled to the surface. The trouble began the previous morning, when Nathanial called them all into the parlor. Self-consciously, Father handed each of the twins a package, saying, "This is for you to take with you back East—from your mother and me."

"Whew!" Timothy whistled, holding up a gold watch chain. "It's wonderful, Dad."

"I'll wear it with pride," Daniel said, holding his up to the light. "Let me see yours, Tim. Terrific. They're just alike."

"Look at the clasp," Hannah said, stealing a closer look. "It's a bird. Put them on. They're for your graduation watches."

"We'll be the envy of Harvard, eh, Dan?" Timothy said carefully.

"Ah, yes, I imagine so," Daniel answered stiffly.

Hannah watched Timothy ride off that afternoon to run errands. This time Daniel stayed home, nervously packing and repacking, searching through his belongings for particular keepsakes and favorite items of clothing. Hannah tried to help but gave up, watching solemnly from his bedroom door. "You'd think you were leaving forever," she murmured.

"It just seems that way, pumpkin," he said, rumpling her hair affectionately. "It'll be for the best. Just wait and see."

Hannah looked at him, trying to figure out what was different, what was wrong. "Are you nervous?"

"I guess so. But I know I'm doing the right thing. Just remember that, okay?"

Hannah nodded, even though she didn't understand.

"Now run and get a collar button from Father for me. I seem to have lost mine."

That night Hannah heard Timothy ride in late. She peeked out the window and watched him go into the barn. The lantern light shone through the slats of the door, then the circle of light swayed its way toward the house. Daniel had been in bed for over an hour. Timothy was quiet, so there were no arguments.

The next morning a rider crossed the bridge before Hannah had finished brushing out her hair. Daniel came out to meet him. A young boy, dressed in a flour sack shirt and overlarge trousers held up with big black suspenders, handed Daniel an envelope, then pushed his bare heels against the horse's side and quickly rode back across the bridge. Within five minutes, Daniel was riding after him.

Hannah was just going down the stairs when she met Timothy. "Last day, Hannah-girl. From now on the house is yours to command."

"It'll be pretty quiet," she said, looking up at his freshly shaved face.

"Ah, not when you start bringing your beaux around," he joked, tugging one of her curls. "You know where Daniel is?"

"I just saw him riding out."

"Oh? Which way?"

"Towards town, I think."

"I wonder why," he murmured, more to himself than to her.

"Maybe it had something to do with the letter he got?"

"What letter?"

"A boy just rode up and gave him one."

"A boy? What'd he look like?" he demanded, glaring at her.

"I don't know. Maybe ten. Rode a pinto—"

"Scruffy little kid—dressed like trash?"

"Well, I guess so."

Timothy looked around as if searching for something, then dashed into the parlor. Hannah peeked in and saw him throw a paper into the fireplace.

"How long ago did you say he left?" he said, bumping into her as he ran into the hall.

"About ten minutes ago."

"Tell Mother I had to go into town and tell someone good-bye . . . someone I forgot. One of my teachers. I'll be back by afternoon." Without another word, he was out the door and soon riding across the bridge.

Hannah watched him leave and then quickly went into the parlor. She fished around in the cold ashes until she found the wadded-up piece of paper. Its message was brief:

All is undone. The bridge. 11:30 A.M. *M.C.*

Hannah puzzled over the words, then put the paper back in the fireplace.

The day was hot. The hours moved as slowly as the droning fly on the screen of her bedroom window. Hannah spent most of the time sitting by her window, leafing through a book and restlessly watching the road.

Finally, around three Timothy came riding back down the road. Hannah threw her book down and ran downstairs to meet him.

"I'm glad you're back," she said as he came in the door.

"Oh? Why's that?" he said as he hung his hat on the hall tree.

"Just am. Where's Daniel?"

Timothy looked at her sharply. "How should I know? He left before me."

"Just thought you might have seen him."

"No." He turned and went back to the kitchen, saying, "Is Nell back here? I'm starved."

Hannah was on the stairs when he came back, balancing a sandwich and glass of milk as he stepped over her. "Don't block the stairs, Hannah," he complained with his mouth full.

She heard her mother going into his room. Hannah scurried up the stairs and listened from the hall in front of her door.

"Did you see Daniel in town?" Fee asked.

"No, I didn't expect to. He'll be back in time for dinner. Train doesn't leave until eight." Hannah heard the sides of his trunk sliding together and the lock clicking. "Now, if you will excuse me, Mother, I have to finish packing."

With a shrug, Fee came out of the room, then turned back and said, "Dinner will be early so we'll have plenty of time to make the train. Figure on eating around five." Then, spotting Hannah, she added, "That means that you probably have just enough time to get some practicing in, little one."

"Yes, Mother," she said reluctantly.

The heavy heat of the afternoon rumbled across the sky ahead of growing clouds. A murmur of thunder added a bass line to the polonaise that Hannah was playing. She practiced for an hour, trying to push away the growing uneasiness, as the thunder was pushing the clouds down the mountains. For once the music didn't absorb her. She kept glancing out the window, hoping to see Daniel coming even before she heard him.

From the restless murmur in the drawing room, she knew that her parents were also waiting, and that knowledge didn't calm her vague fears.

Then her heart leapt to her throat. The sound of a horse's hooves clomped across the bridge as great fat drops of rain began thumping against the windowpane.

"There's Daniel, I'll bet," she heard Father say as he got up to go look out the door.

Mother was right behind him and Hannah behind her. "That's not his horse, is it?" Fee asked.

"Doesn't look like it," Nathanial said, stepping out on the porch and emptying his pipe against his heel.

They all stood there watching as the sheriff got off his horse, dropped the reins over the gatepost, and came up the walk. His face was strained and pale.

"Mr. and Mrs. Coughlin?" he began, although he knew them full well.

"Yes, what is it, Stanley?" Father asked.

"It's your son. Daniel, I think he is . . ." he stammered, twisting his hat in his hand. "He's fallen off the old South Fork Bridge. Broke his neck. I—I'm sorry. He's dead."

"Oh, dear God," Fee cried, burying her head on Nathanial's shoulder.

"Oh, no." Nathanial was like a great tree ready to fall.

The words spun around Hannah's head like bees around a hive. "Bridge?" she whispered. "Not really dead—"

"If he's dead, he's been murdered!" Timothy roared from the top of the stairs. "Get his murderer! My brother's been killed! It wasn't an accident!"

"No, Mr. Timothy. Warn't no murder. That old bridge's been a nuisance for some time now. Been rotting away since '42. Seems your brother just leaned against the rail and it gave way."

"What was he doing there?" Nathanial asked no one in particular.

"Seems he went to meet his little gal, you know, little Mary Ranahan. They was on the bridge when it happened."

"She killed him!" Timothy cried. "Or her father. It was her

269

father. He killed my brother. You get that son-of-a-bitch and you'll have my brother's murderer."

Fee gasped. "Timothy, how can you say that?"

Hannah watched her brother's twisted face through her tears. "It's . . . it's obvious," he cried, his body trembling, tears on his cheeks. "Everyone knows old man Ranahan didn't approve of his daughter seeing anyone who wasn't a goddamned Catholic."

The sheriff shook his head. "Ain't that way 'tall, Mr. Coughlin," he told Nathanial. "Pretty clear accident, judging from the evidence. Little Mary's right hysterical about it all." He paused and then said, "I . . . I'm right sorry I had to bring you the bad news. If there's anything I can do to help . . ." With that he put his hat on and walked back down the walk.

"You can hang the murdering Catholic son-of-a-bitch that killed my brother," Timothy called after him. "That's what you can do," he added, leaning against the porch railing, choked with tears.

"Come on inside, son," Nathanial said softly. "It's natural to want to find someone to blame when you're hurting so bad." He put one arm around Timothy and the other around Fee. Fee reached out and pulled Hannah into the family embrace. Together they went into the house to share their grief.

The next day they buried Daniel alongside Donnell and Rosalind.

A week later, Timothy left on the train for college—alone. And Hannah was left to wonder what had really been undone on the bridge.

Chapter XXIII

Daniel's death was not the last blow to hit Fee that year.

The day of the funeral she received a letter from Matthew. He was working as a purser on board a ship sailing out of Boston to the West Indies. He wouldn't be home this year. He'd never received her telegram.

Fee's loss was magnified by a sense of growing isolation. Nathanial once again threw himself into his work, just when Fee needed him most. Jacob had become withdrawn over the years. Even more puzzling was Fee's increasing estrangement from her only daughter. In an outburst just before school began, Hannah accused Fee of somehow engineering Matthew's long absence from the family.

It was ironic. Fee had worked long and hard to become successful, and now that she was a wealthy woman in her own right, powerful in her state and influential in her community, she felt more lonely than ever before.

And then like the encroaching dusk, it all began.

On a gray afternoon when everyone else was away, Wesley arrived with the mail pouch, assuring her with a wink that it included a letter from Matthew.

Fee took the letter into her corner office and quickly tore open the envelope, then sat alone, reading the very words she'd feared for twenty-two years.

Dearest Mother,

This is a difficult letter to write. I've put it off for too long. Still, I want you to know from the beginning that it is filled with love for you. Don't be angry with me or yourself.

First, I must tell you that I'm not going back to school this fall. I know we had planned my life in Oregon's universities. But now that can't be.

I've always felt I was special in your eyes. I thank you for that. I've also felt somehow different from the rest of the family. Now I've come to understand why. I'm enclosing a photograph that helps explain it, even though it doesn't show quite as clearly as it would in person.

As you can see, I've decided to grow a mustache, a simple decision that young men often make. However, for me it has made all the difference. A month ago, I looked in the mirror and saw not myself but Uncle Jacob. And then I understood.

If I should come back now, everyone else would understand, too.

Now I know why I've always been his favorite. Why he helped pay for my studies, why he asked his family to help me get settled when I first arrived here. Now I know why I've always felt such a special bond with him.

I'm also sure that Father—I still must call him that because he's always been that to me—loves me and has never thought any less of me nor suspected I'm not his

271

child. But if I should come home now, grown-up, with the face of my real father imprinted on my face, it would cause much pain.

I got a job this summer working on a ship. While we docked in Havana, Cuba, I had the opportunity to meet some of the people who live there. They, especially the Creoles, live under terrible oppression from the Spanish government and have been trying to get the United States to give them aid in overthrowing their oppressors. So far they've been ignored, but I'm sure that America will eventually come to its senses and help free its neighbors. But until then there are some of us who won't wait. I've joined a group that is smuggling supplies from Florida to the Freedom Fighters. We're not going to make great profits from our endeavors, but we will be doing what's right. And that's what my parents—all three of them—have taught me to do.

Please understand that this is the right decision for us all. If you wish, you may show this letter to my blood father. Tell him that I've grown up enough to know that I must have been born because of a deep love, one that I now realize I've always seen but never before recognized. I don't know the circumstances, but I think I can understand. I also know that he has loved me as his son.

But please don't cause any pain by showing this letter or the photograph to Father. I think this should arrive around the time he leaves for eastern Oregon for the roundups, so it shouldn't be any problem for you.

I send you my love and abiding respect,

Your son,
Matthew

P.S. I'm using the money you sent me to buy the first shipment of supplies for the Freedom Fighters. I thought you would approve.

He'd miscalculated; his letter arrived a week before Nathanial was to leave for eastern Oregon. Luckily, he and everyone else were gone. Otherwise they would have heard the cry of anguish as Fee looked at the photo of Jacob's son.

She looked at the young face staring solemnly out from the picture. It was so like the face of the young Jacob she'd first loved so long ago. Then, she cried for them all. Her son had been taken away from her by the very love that had brought him into the world. He was the one remaining bond between her and Jacob, their one sharing. Now he could never come home again.

She slipped the photograph back into the envelope as she heard the rattle of a wagon over the bridge and knew that Nathanial had returned from the sawmill. She quickly dried her eyes and ran upstairs to splash her face with water.

Nathanial burst into their bedroom with an expectant look, just as she was just patting some powder on her tear-stained cheeks.

"Wesley said we got a letter from Matthew."

Fee froze. "Wesley was wrong," she lied desperately. Her mind spun through all the possibilities. She looked in the mirror, composed her face, and adjusted a comb in her hair. "It was an honest mistake. I saw the envelope and thought it was Matthew's handwriting, too. But it was one of my new tenants in Portland whose hand is very much like Matthew's. There are some problems with his building."

"Oh. I see." Then, looking at her, he added sympathetically, "You must be as disappointed as I am."

Fee's eyes filled with tears at his surprising kindness. "Yes," she admitted. "But I'm sure we'll hear from him soon. His job must have made writing letters impossible."

Nathanial leaned down and kissed her cheek. "Children don't know the agony they put their parents through, do they?"

Fee smiled and shook her head. "Not in the least." She blew her nose, then added, "That letter does mean I will have to go up to Portland. Are you going through there when you leave in a couple of days?"

"No, I'm going over McKenzie Pass and checking out some timber on the way."

"Then you won't mind if I take the afternoon train up tomorrow."

"No, we'll say good-bye tonight."

She sat with a heavy heart, watching the landscape rush by the train window. How could she tell Jacob? He'd always been an introspective person, keeping his thoughts private except in those rare moments of love when he shared his deepest feelings with her. Then, with the passing of years, she'd seen him withdraw, not just from her, but also from the world. It had puzzled her at first, then pained her, as if she were

273

watching the slow withering of a vital being. She wondered if Ruth saw it, too.

Fee met Jacob behind the closed doors of his office. She handed him the letter and held back her tears long enough to lock the door. Then she turned and saw him crumpled over his desk, shaken with deep, quiet sobs. She held him in her arms then, feeling his sorrow and loss, shocked at how shattered he was.

When their tears had subsided, they walked along the riverbank, quietly discussing their son and his decision. It was the most intimate they'd been in a long time, and Fee silently thanked Matthew for that. Together, they concluded that Matthew had made the only sensible choice.

"As soon as you receive any kind of address from him," Jacob said, squeezing her hand so tightly she almost cried out, "you must promise to give it to me."

Startled, Fee looked into his deep brown eyes, clouded with sorrow, and could read no explanation there. "Of course. But why is it so important? You've seldom written before."

"For over a year now," Jacob said, "my brothers have been asking me to come back East to see them. One is quite ill. This is the time to go. And I will stop and see my son—to acknowledge him, to hold him at least once as my son."

His voice was husky with emotion. Neither spoke as they rode home in the carriage. Fee felt once more that here was something she could not share nor experience, and she felt all the more lonely.

On the way back to Salem, she watched the flow of the Willamette River, which nurtured their huge valley of fertile farms, and she thought about how so many of her dreams had slipped away from her.

She'd hoped that through her encouragement and their natural excellence her children would become leaders in the state. Her family would someday inherit and take the responsibility for their land in all ways, and through that leadership they would have the security she'd never had. Now she would have to rethink her plans. Daniel, her hope to take over the family business, was gone. Now Matthew, her brilliant son, who was to have led a great university, could never return.

She'd always believed that even though one man had not given her the total love she needed, she'd be able to find it in two men, and that would be enough. But it had always left her unfulfilled. Now she felt both men slipping away, one to the land and one to some unknown inner torment. She'd have to reshape the dreams that had nourished her for so long.

The human soul does not tolerate emptiness well. Once faced with it, the natural thing is to fill it up as quickly as possible. And that is what Fee did. She threw herself into her work with a vengeance, expanding her creamery, opening a new lumberyard, reinvesting profits in new ventures and stocks. When she had a moment of spare time, she gave it to the community, establishing a scholarship in Daniel's name, encouraging cultural events, anonymously donating to struggling families, and building her own empire of influence.

As usual, Nathanial was often gone. As Hannah grew into a lovely young woman, a slender reed with fine features and a crowning glory of cascading auburn hair, she became more interested in her own friends and activities. The next four years seemed to fly by in a blur of bustle and flurry. Before she knew it, Timothy was ready to graduate from college.

Neither Fee nor Nathanial attended the ceremony, only Fee's sister, who'd offered Timothy a job at her textile mill for the summer. Part of his letter to them gave Fee some concern.

I'll finish in Boston in September. Then I will travel down to Georgia. You may remember my mentioning a young lady by the name of Geraldine Franklin. Her father has a large operation in Georgia, cotton plantation and sawmill. He's offered to show me how he runs the place. I think the combination of information from Mr. Franklin's and Aunt Judith's businesses will serve me well when I return to Oregon.

Nell sniffed when Fee finished reading the letter aloud. "Sounds like he's going to bring back more than fancy business ideas." Without waiting for a response, she pulled herself up out of the chair, took another cookie, and went back out to the kitchen.

"Interesting," Fee mused. "Timothy never had much of a head for that kind of thing. Between you and me, I think business is the farthest thing from his mind."

"What do you mean?" Nathanial asked, looking at her sharply over his glasses.

"I mean Nell's right. That southern belle Geraldine is what's on his mind. I'm willing to bet that we'll be having a wedding in this family before the year's out. By the way," she added, "who's that good-looking young man who waved to me from the front field?"

"Might be the one we've been looking for. Name's Ephraim Balfour. Hard worker. I'd like to keep him on, give him responsibility."

"Well," Fee said, "if he works as good as he looks, he'll be here a long time."

In November, when Timothy's next letter arrived, Fionna was in the midst of preparing for a holiday piano concert Hannah was presenting at the university.

Dear Mother and Father,

I've learned a great deal here at the Franklin plantation, but I have something else I'll be doing before going home.

Geraldine has been touring the Continent these past two months, and her letters convince me that I should follow her example. As you know, a young man's education is not considered complete in this day and age unless he's traveled to Europe.

I'll leave on the boat for London on December 1. I plan to spend Christmas in England with some friends of the Franklins. From there, I'll probably travel to the Continent. You may expect me home no later than spring.

Your obedient son,
Timothy

"What did I tell you?" Fee asked Nathanial, trying to hide her disappointment. "Now he's chasing clear aross the Atlantic after her. We'll be hearing wedding bells by summer."

She put down the letter and looked out the window. Hannah was just getting ready to leave for her piano lesson. "Do you think the roads are too muddy for her?"

"I asked Ephraim to drive her. He has to pick up some supplies from the hardware store anyway."

"Do you think that's wise?"

"Why not?"

"Well, just look at her. And he's a very handsome, virile young man. There's no sense in throwing temptation in her path like that. She has all her schooling ahead of her."

"Ah, Fee," he said, taking her into his arms, "she'll be fine. You worry too much. Ephraim's a perfect gentleman."

"But he's human," she protested. "And have you noticed Hannah recently? She's a bundle of raw nerves."

"It's just the recital. She'll be fine after she's the toast of the Willamette Valley. Once she tastes the wine of applause, she'll not be content with the farm foreman."

"Why, Nathanial Coughlin," Fee said, laughing. "I do believe you have more poetry in your soul than I suspected."

"Ah," he said, a gleam in his eye, "if you'll come upstairs with me, you'll see what kind of poetry I have in me."

Hannah's concert was a smashing success. Readers of Jacob's *Occidential Journal* learned they had a rising musical star in their own Willamette Valley.

Professor Raines was beside himself with pride. Pulling Fee aside at the champagne reception, he told her he was doing his best to get Hannah admitted to his alma mater next fall.

Fee stood beside her daughter in the reception line and accepted compliments from over two hundred people. That night the lights shone a little brighter, and in their glow Fee could see her dreams unfolding.

Then in January they received a cryptic wire from Timothy.

GERALDINE MARRIED ITALIAN COUNT. ARRIVING HOME JANUARY 30. EVENING TRAIN. TIMOTHY

"I guess we won't be having a southern belle for a daughter-in-law after all," Fee said with a stunned look.

"An Italian count?" Hannah asked, looking at the telegram again. "How romantic! I wonder if he and Timothy dueled? Or maybe Timothy chased them across the Continent trying to rescue his true love from this wicked count, only to have lost because—"

"Hannah, for heaven's sake!" Fee exclaimed. "I doubt it was anything that silly. And when he gets here, you should mind your tongue. I doubt your brother wants to hear any of your romantic fantasies."

They were never to know the story. Timothy was atypically silent on the subject, refusing to talk to Fee or answer his sister's persistent questions. He was home less than a week when he sought out Helen Winston, and from then on they were constant companions.

He threw himself into the business operations, working by Nathanial's side during the day and attending political meetings at night. Fee assured herself that her son was settling down, beginning to realize the dreams they'd spun together. Yet there was a cold edge to him that she hadn't seen before, an unforgiving nature she hoped would disappear when his wounds had healed.

A cold February rain was dripping from the eaves as Wesley came up the walk with the mail pouch.

"Afternoon, Wesley," Fee said as she opened the door. "How're Minnie and the children?"

Wesley took off his hat and stepped inside. "Minnie's got some sniffles," he said as he wiped the rain from his face. "Other than that, we're happy as hogs in a waller."

"How about little Mary? It's hard to imagine she's going to be a mother herself soon."

Wesley shook his head in wonder. "She right appreciated that cradle you sent her. Planned on having the baby sleep in a dresser drawer till that came along." He looked sympathetically at Fee. "Your Donnell would be giving you grandbabies by now had he lived."

Wesley's long face was lined by sun and work, his hair thinned by the years, but his pale blue eyes were still those of a man who would work hard and do the best he could with integrity.

Fee smiled wistfully. "That's why I sent the cradle to your Mary," she said.

"You're mighty generous with a lot of young folk. Our young Lowell sure appreciates the help you've given him with college."

"Nonsense," Fee said, brushing aside his thanks. "It's good sense. An investment in the future. Lowell works hard for me each summer, and I take care of him in the winter."

"Just the same, you're a good woman, Miz Coughlin."

"That's a mighty fine compliment, coming from you. Nell's got the coffee pot on the stove."

She took the mail and went into the sitting room. A fire crackled in the fireplace. That and the rain on the porch roof were the only sounds in the house. Hannah was in school, Nathanial was in Portland, and Nell was in the kitchen baking bread.

The mail rested in her lap as she gazed pensively into the fire. Mary, Donnell's childhood companion, was about to become a mother. Donnell, her red-haired firstborn, Nathanial's son. How would things have been different had he lived,

278

she wondered. Would she ever have loved Jacob? Would she have had Matthew, the son of her other love? Would her marriage with Nathanial have been different, more complete, even though it never held what her relationship with Jacob had?

She shook her head, dispelling the cobwebs of doubt, silently upbraiding herself for such a waste of time and energy.

Fee quickly sorted through the mail, hoping for a letter from Matthew. With the exception of one envelope with a Miami postmark, the mail was all business. She put the business mail aside and turned her curiosity to the Miami letter. The clock on the mantel chimed two-thirty as she opened the flap and began to read.

Dear Mr. and Mrs. Coughlin,

You don't know me, but I have been Matthew's best friend for the past five years. Matthew and I promised to do this for one another if the time ever came.

We've been shipping arms and supplies to the Cuban Freedom Fighters for the past four years. I have come to think of Matthew as my brother. Danger does that to friendships, I understand. I can hardly write because of my tears. Matthew was killed last night.

We were taking a boatload of supplies, ammunition, guns, and medicine to the Freedom Fighters. Our rendezvous was to be in an isolated area on the northern side of Cuba. Matthew and another man took a small boat ashore shortly after midnight. I was watching through the glasses. I don't know what happened, but suddenly his boat blew up. Perhaps they were spotted and shot from the shore. Just as likely, they hit a reef and it set the explosives off. Against the protests of the captain, I took the dory and paddled out. I found only small pieces of the boat and flotsam. I knew that no one could have survived. I went back to the ship and we returned to the mainland, our mission a failure and your son a martyr to the cause.

We all share in your loss. Please accept my condolences. That doesn't seem to be enough to say, but it's all I've been taught.

Matthew and I spent considerable time on Cuba. There is terrible oppression going on there. The people need help. Your son was the first casualty in what one day will be a war for a cause the United States can no longer ignore. You can be proud of your son.

> *With deepest respect,*
> *John Brooks*

Fee's world whirled around her. A high-pitched whine filled her ears. Numb with shock, she picked up the envelope. There was no return address, no way to find out more.

Barely breathing, she stumbled upstairs, then stood in her bedroom, looking out at the rain. With tears streaming down her cheeks, she quickly packed a valise and went back downstairs.

Stopping by her chair, she picked up the letter and shoved it into her coat pocket. Then she went to the kitchen, barely seeing the familiar objects she touched, only vaguely aware of the aroma of baking bread. Nell was alone at the kitchen table.

"Nell, I'm going to Portland."

"Miz Coughlin! What's the matter? You're white as a ghost," she said, jumping up from her chair.

Fee shook her head, trying to dispel the haze that was surrounding her. "It's Matthew," she whispered. "He's dead. I just got a letter . . ." Then tears began once again to flow down her cheeks, and her voice caught in her throat.

"No! Not my Matthew!" Nell cried.

"I've got to talk to his father."

"How? What happened?"

"An . . . an accident at sea. Not even his body . . ."

Nell quickly put her arms around Fee, holding her as they wept. "Don't you worry none," she said brokenly. "I'll take care of everything here. I'll tell little Hannah. Yes, you go to Mr. Coughlin."

"I must tell Jacob."

"Yes, the Tealls, too," Nell said. "Hannah and I will go to Ezekial and Pearl."

Fee nodded and walked woodenly out the door to the carriage. *If I hurry,* she thought with strange detachment, *I'll be able to catch the evening train.*

She didn't remember the ride up to Portland, nor did she remember how she managed to get to the Tealls' house. She just knew suddenly she was standing on the porch and Jacob was answering the door.

"Fee!" he exclaimed. "We didn't expect . . . what's happened?" His look of surprise was replaced by genuine concern as he pulled her inside.

She handed him the crumpled letter and watched while he leaned on the banister under the hall lamp and read it.

When he was finished, he looked up in disbelief, his eyes filled with tears. "Our son."

She leaned against him then and cried—deep, soul-tearing sobs that only Jacob could share. Together they went into the parlor and sat on the chaise, holding one another and mourning their loss.

Finally Jacob said hoarsely, "Nathanial's having dinner with some ranchers from Pendleton."

"And Ruth?" Fee asked.

"She's at a ladies' meeting at the synagogue."

They looked at one another for a long moment. Fee said softly, "He was our son."

"He was our blessing—and our love was his curse. If only—"

"He brought us great joy."

"Yes, we can't forget that." Then their tears began to flow again.

Shortly, there was the clatter of a carriage pulling into the drive. Hearing Nathanial's voice, they looked up and saw him holding the door open for Ruth.

"Look who came by and offered me a ride," Ruth said as she came in. Then, seeing Fee, she stopped and said, "Fee, what a surprise . . . What's the matter?" she cried, rushing over to them.

"It's . . ." But Fionna couldn't finish her words as grief once more conquered her.

Jacob struggled to hold back his tears but could only choke out, "Matthew . . ." as he handed Nathanial the letter.

Ruth read over Nathanial's shoulder, quietly weeping. Then, as Fee cried on Nathanial's chest, Ruth put her arms around them both and Jacob rested his hand on Nathanial's shaking back. Their circle of grief was complete.

The next day they left to arrange for a memorial service in Salem. Fee's heart was filled with grief not only for her lost son but for Jacob as well. In the eyes of the world, he was only a grieving friend of the family, not the grieving father. And she knew that the pain must have been doubled.

Through it all, Fee was grateful for Nathanial. Even though it had been a source of contention between them in the past, not once did he remind her that she could have persuaded

Matthew to come home instead of allowing him to wander with strangers. Instead, he held her while she wept.

Later that month, when Nathanial had gone to eastern Oregon, Fee finally had some time alone with Jacob. They rode in his carriage out along the Willamette River, then stopped along a wayside, next to a gray clump of river willows.

"It's finally over, Fionna," Jacob said as he looked across the murky winter waters.

"What is?" Fee asked, her heart turning over at the gloom of his voice.

"Us. It died with Matthew."

"What are you talking about?"

"For years you and I have been trying to live with two spouses, two loves, two commitments—to live two separate lives. It was wrong. It has destroyed me, Fee. It's eaten me up. My spirit is hollow."

"I don't understand."

He sighed. "I was afraid you wouldn't." He was silent for a moment. "We couldn't find everything we needed in one person," he said in a voice of careful instruction, not the familiar voice of lover and friend. "So what we did instead was try to piece that complete love together out of two people. It doesn't work. It's against all the teachings of my people, against the laws of society, against the teachings of your church. For good reason. It has torn me in two."

Fee's senses whirled and her heart twisted in pain. Deep down she knew the truth of his words. "You mean that when you were with me you thought about Ruth, and when you were with Ruth you wished she were me?"

He looked at her for the first time that day. "Was it the same with you?"

"Yes. I've been torn by my love for two men. Yet each one answered such a deep need, I thought I must withstand it."

Jacob nodded. "I don't believe that I can bear the burden of guilt any longer. I had two families and I had two loyalties. Now, at least, there is only one family—and I know where my loyalty must be placed."

"But we have so much," Fee couldn't help pleading softly. "Can you bear the thought of never sharing what we had again?"

"What I can't bear is the thought of ruining the lives of so many other people. So much possible hurt."

Fee was silent.

"I will miss you," he admitted in a whisper. "You have so much of my mind, my spirit." He paused. "And I'm straw without it, hollow and useless."

Fee was shaken by his words. "No, you're not. I give it back to you freely and lovingly."

He looked at her, his dark eyes black with pain. "You can't. Once given, it's gone forever."

"Jacob, dearest," she said, hiding her fear, "you're depressed because of Matthew's death. Time will—"

"Matthew's death has freed me," he interrupted. "Don't you see? Now I can turn away from all this . . . this sordid mess. Now I can try to piece together the parts of me that have been so long separated. I'm telling you, Fionna, I can no longer see you as a lover, or even as an intimate friend. We must restrict our contact to those times when it is unavoidable. I'm instructing our accountant to handle our business correspondence. And you must not come up here and stay with us. I couldn't bear it."

Fee felt a part of herself die in the anguish of his voice. "Very well," she whispered. "We will both try to put all the pieces in their rightful place in our lives."

Chapter XXIV

Matthew's death was a shock to the entire family, but it was Hannah who felt as if she'd been robbed of her last friend.

She mourned the loss of her brother, losing herself in hours of musical retreat that ended only when her mother entrated her to come to dinner. Reluctantly, she would get up from the piano stool, muscles aching, only, return within half an hour to play again until sleep forced her to quit.

After two weeks of this, with the resilience of youth, she began to come out of her shock. Although she still missed Matthew deeply, she saw the greening of spring and her soul began to lift. She felt a frustration with the dreariness of her life. Timothy's mysterious European adventures held all the romance Hannah felt she was missing.

Perhaps it was the strange "seeking," a word her mother

used in describing her father and Matthew. Suddenly Hannah was overwhelmed with longing, a need to find that "something" that mattered passionately.

As the youngest and only girl in the family, she'd always been pampered. Matthew had protected her like a precious jewel. Even the twins with all their antics and rambunctious energy were careful around her. She'd grown up feeling special—but with no other purpose. Until she sat down at the piano.

Through music she entered another world, a world teeming with beauty, colors, and passion, a world that transcended ordinary life. Music gave her a voice to speak, to touch other's hearts and to raise them above everyday life and sorrows. And she knew the power of music to speak to the human spirit.

Professor Raines had expanded her horizons from their very first meeting. He sat down beside her and played a difficult movement and she was enchanted. She watched a wisp of hair fall over his forehead and saw a beautiful soul. His playing was crisp and clear where hers had been vague, uncertain. She heard different voices passionately calling to one another, first in the bass, then the treble, voices she'd never known were there. How could she have missed so much? She immediately threw herself into his instruction, eager to please him. While her body was maturing with startling beauty, Hannah was going through a metamorphosis of an intensity unusual even to young girls.

Once each week she was with a man who understood her, a man who touched her soul because his own spirit sailed the same course as hers.

For at least one hour each week, Hannah knew someone who shared her most intimate thoughts and dreams. She watched him as his pale golden hair fell over his long, ascetic's face. He would lean into his music, concentrating on the score in front of him. He would close his sky-blue eyes, listening to the voices within him, making them harmonize with the pure tones of the piano.

Within a year she was able to play duets with him, keeping up as best she could. When his long, graceful fingers ran over the keyboard and brushed hers, he touched her more intimately than if he'd made love to her.

Was it no wonder, then, that at eighteen Hannah found the young men clamoring around her door vacuous and boring?

And no wonder that the only man she could envision ever loving was Professor Edmund Raines?

The Saturday after her eighteenth birthday, she decided to take matters into her own hands. She wasn't getting any younger. And all this talk about sending her back East to a conservatory after graduation sent a cold chill down her spine.

She stood before the mirror in her bedroom, studying her reflection. Everything had to be perfect for today—for Edmund, as she'd begun to call him in her fantasies. She put her hands on her hips and stepped back, studying her figure. Her breasts were firm and full, and when she moved, they swayed gently beneath her thin cotton camisole. Her waist was naturally tiny, but her hips were round and full, just right for the popular Gibson Girl look.

Her thick, curly auburn hair was a bit difficult to handle, she thought as she began brushing it up and tucking it in with combs. The back looked too nice to hide in a bun, so she let it fall loosely down her back in luxurious curls, curls that Edmund could run his fingers through.

Just then she heard her mother and Nell coming up the stairs. She quickly stepped into her petticoat with the small built-in bustle and tied it on.

"Here you go, honey," Nell said, opening the door without knocking. "You'll look as pretty as a June bug in this." She held out the pale green linen dress. Hannah put her arms into the blouse, then backed up so Nell could button it. It was a two-piece dress with Belgian lace inserts in the top that showed soft pink skin delicately peeking through the embroidered flowers. The stays in the lace collar emphasized her graceful neck, and she loved the way the blouse draped over her breasts, emphasizing them. The thought of Edmund seeing her in this made it impossible for her to concentrate on what her mother was saying.

". . . And so," Fee continued, "if—I should say when— you're accepted by the New England Conservatory of Music, we'll make our plans in earnest."

Hannah smiled absently into the mirror while Nell buttoned the tiny buttons all the way down her back. "We'll see, Mother." She stepped into the skirt, and Nell hooked the stiff, wide belt.

"My, my," Nell clucked as she tied a green ribbon in Hannah's hair. She caught Hannah's eye in the mirror and winked. "Some young man is going to be mighty lucky."

Hannah blushed with pleasure. It was just what she needed to hear.

That afternoon she barely remembered leaving for town, except for the look she got from Ephraim, the farm foreman, as he brought the carriage around. It reassured her that she was as stunning as she'd hoped.

At Edmund's studio she played Chopin's *Fantasy Impromptu* with all the yearning and fervor in her soul. She played for Edmund, seducing him with her music. He couldn't help but feel all the love and passion she was pouring out for him. Soon she would no longer be just his student. She would be his lover.

When the last note hung suspended in the air like a tremulous plea between them, Hannah sat back, exhausted and exultant. She had bared her heart. She felt as if she were standing naked before him, awaiting his first touch. And then she felt his hand resting on her shoulder, his warmth penetrating her thin dress.

"That was truly moving, Hannah," he said softly.

"I . . . I played it for you," she whispered, standing up and facing him, feeling his breath on her face, seeing his eyes gazing into her soul. "I wanted you to know—"

"You've been an inspiring student, Hannah," he went on, smiling shyly.

Don't hesitate, my love, she thought. *Don't be afraid.* She stepped forward anxiously.

"I've got some good news." His voice trembled with excitement. "I'm recommending you for the New England Conservatory of Music. Since I'm a graduate of some note," he added modestly, "they will admit you on that. Of course, you will have to play an audition when you arrive in Boston, but if you play the way you did today—"

"Boston!" Hannah's mind spun in confusion. "You're sending me to Boston?"

"Yes, I understand you have an aunt who lives there, so . . ." His face reflected mild puzzlement.

"How can you send me away? Don't you understand? I don't want some old conversatory. I want you."

The shock in his eyes stabbed her heart with her first doubt. Was it possible he didn't know, didn't feel? . . .

"How could you have thought? . . ." He stopped and shook his head. "If I've done anything to mislead you—"

"No, you've been perfectly discreet," Hannah quickly admitted. "But you taught my soul to sing. Through you I've come to know the meaning of love. Surely that means—"

"It means I've taught you the meaning of music."

Hannah stopped, suddenly realizing that he was trying to remain professional. She quickly gathered her composure. "I don't want to compromise you. I know you're a teacher and I'm your student, that you have a position and reputation to maintain here at the university. But I'll stop taking lessons. We'll wait a proper amount of time, see one another secretly, maybe," she explained. "I should be here—in your arms—not in Boston."

With that she hurried out the door. She had to get away before she ruined everything by begging, or crying. When he had time to think about it, it would be all right. He'd say yes.

She left in such a flurry that she nearly knocked over a clumsy young man who was coming up the stairs, another student of Edmund's. She'd heard him play and didn't consider him worth her attention, much less Edmund's. She didn't even pause to apologize, dashing out to her carriage before he could speak.

She reached the end of the street before she remembered that she'd forgotten her music. Reluctantly, she turned around and walked back up the stairs to Edmund's studio.

Feeling a bit foolish after her declaration and dramatic exit, she tiptoed, hoping to slip in and retrieve her music without being noticed.

The student's halting rendition of Beethoven's *Für Elise* made her wince as she quietly opened the door. Why did Edmund even bother with the likes of him? Then she stopped as she saw Edmund standing intimately close to the student, nodding approvingly and tenderly stroking his hair as he played. As he finished the piece, the young man leaned his head back against Edmund's arm, as a lover would lean back, awaiting a kiss.

Edmund must have heard Hannah's gasp because he jumped back guiltily. "Oh!" he exclaimed. Then regaining his composure, added, "I was wondering if you'd remember, Miss Coughlin. Same time next week?"

Hannah murmured something in her confusion and closed the door behind her.

It didn't make any sense. How could he be so affectionate with that boy and so cold with her? Was she lacking in some kind of essential feminine appeal? She wept half the way

287

home, feeling that she'd somehow made a fool of herself to the only man she could ever love.

By the time she reached Evans Crossing she dried her tears and began trying to understand what she'd witnessed. Maybe she wasn't appealing. Maybe no man would ever look at her, find her attractive. She'd seen her mother and father together enough to know that there was something special that happened between men and women. Fee had explained to Hannah where babies came from in very practical and honest terms, but from what she'd seen, Hannah believed that men and women "did it" more often than their number of children indicated. The idea intrigued her. But if that were the case, why had Edmund rejected her?

She was still turning the situation over in her mind when she arrived home. Ephraim Balfour came out of the barn and offered to put the horse and carriage away. She accepted, then followed him into the carriage house, reluctant to go in the house just yet. As he hung up the harness in the tack room, she was suddenly aware of his masculinity. Although a quiet man, he was muscular and strong, roughly handsome, with dark curly hair and a shy smile. She watched him—and wondered.

He led the horse into the stall, and her heart beat in her throat as she took a currybrush down from the wall and joined him. Here was a man she could test.

"I'm glad we have you here, Ephraim," she said softly, watching him out of the corner of her eye as he toweled the horse's back.

"Glad to be of help, Miss Coughlin."

She handed him the brush, holding it long enough for his hand to rest against hers for a tantalizing moment. "I mean, with Father gone so much, I feel—well, safer with you here."

His eyes rested on her in surprise. The swift look of appraisal and glint of interest were not wasted.

"You're the kind of lady any man would be pleased to look after." Then he turned back to grooming the horse. But it was enough. Hannah went into the house reassured. She did have the power over men she'd hoped for. After all, Ephraim was older, experienced . . . almost thirty. Edmund would reconsider by next week. He'd realize what he was missing.

"Hannah, is that you?" her mother called from her office corner in the sitting room.

"Yes, Mother."

"Come in, dear. Did Professor Raines say anything about the New England Conservatory?"

Hannah stopped reluctantly. "Yes, he did say something about recommending me."

"Darling, that's wonderful," Fee exclaimed. "It's a dream come true. Aren't you excited?"

"I'm not sure, Mother," Hannah said quietly, tracing the design of the carved sofa back with her finger. "Maybe something better will happen."

"I can't imagine what that could be. Don't throw away the possible by waiting for the impossible," she warned.

"Don't worry, Mother, I won't," Hannah said, giving her a peck on the cheek and escaping the lecture Hannah knew was lurking on her mother's tongue.

Somehow the following week passed, although Hannah felt as if the days were twice as long as usual. She filled the hours until she saw Edmund, with visions of what might happen when she finally did. When she saw Ephraim around the farm she went out of her way to smile beguilingly at him, finding reassurance in his growing interest in her. If she could make Ephraim respond like that just by smiling and saying a few nice words, surely Edmund would be hers when she returned to his studio.

Saturday finally arrived, and she spent the whole morning getting ready. Everything had to be just right. She settled on a dress of pale blue silk that shimmered sensuously in the light when she moved and felt like it was hardly there when she touched it. She even sneaked a dab of French perfume from her mother's dresser just before slipping out the door.

All the way into Salem she fantasized how Edmund would declare his love. Would he shyly admit it, or would he give full rein to his passions, pull her into his embrace, smothering her with long-denied kisses? She didn't think they had time for a summer wedding, but a holiday wedding would be lovely. Then again, she had promised to wait. Maybe they'd have to meet in secret until the holidays. Then they'd plan a wedding for next spring. Secret rendezvous for almost a whole year was such a delicious thought that it held her all the way onto the university campus.

In her eagerness to get to him, Hannah ran up the stairs, not realizing she was a full half hour early. She opened the door and then stopped dead. Edmund was holding the boy student in a passionate embrace, the embrace he was supposed to be sharing with her. They didn't even hear her come in. She turned and ran out, leaving the door partially open.

What had she seen? She stopped at the bottom of the stairs, holding on to the polished rail for support. Then, stumbling over to the window seat, she sat down. Hot tears fell as she leaned her head against the cool glass windowpane and tried to understand. How could this happen? It didn't make any sense. Men didn't love men, they loved women.

Finally the tears stopped and a cold, desperate anger took over. She was being made a fool. But why?

Just then the student came down the stairs. "Oh, there you are," he said. "You're late. He made me leave because you were coming. Don't waste his time."

"I could hardly waste it any more than you've just been doing," she snapped.

His eyes widened, then he looked at her calculatingly. "Did you come up earlier?" he asked.

She nodded.

"Then you were the one who left the door ajar. What did you see?"

"Enough to be very confused."

"I imagine so," he said softly. "May I?" He sat down beside her. "He told me about what you said last week."

"How dare he!"

"Shh," he cautioned. "He wanted to know what to do. That's when he declared his love to me." He paused. "You see, some men can't love women. I'm one of them. Lucky for me, Edmund is another."

"I . . . I don't understand."

"It's hard to explain. It isn't a choice. We're trapped in what we are. Edmund, I mean Professor Raines, is so proud of you. You're a brilliant musician. Edmund says someday he'll be proud to say you were his student. You'll be one of his great achievements. Creating great musicians is what he can do. What he can't do is love women as other men do. Neither can I. That's why I'm not his favorite student. I'm his lover." Seeing the shock on her face, he quickly added, "Please don't say anything about this to anyone. It would ruin us."

"You're wrong," she exclaimed, standing up. "Men don't love men! They can't. You'll see, he can love a woman."

The young man looked helpless. "I didn't want you to get hurt." He reached up and grabbed her arm. "Maybe I shouldn't have talked to you at all. If you care for him, you won't tell anyone about this," he pleaded.

"Who would believe me if I did?" she asked derisively. "I love him, so I won't say anything about your foolish delusions." She grabbed her books and ran up the stairs, hoping her voice had been calm enough to be convincing.

Just outside the studio she stopped and tried to compose herself. Taking a deep breath, she opened the door and stepped inside.

"Ah, there you are," Edmund said with a genuine smile. "I've been waiting for you. I just got a telegram from Boston this morning. You've been admitted. If your audition goes well, and I think it will, it will be with honors. Congratulations." His face glowed with pride as he took her hand, and Hannah knew that this was her one chance.

"Oh, Edmund," she cried, throwing herself into his arms. "Please don't send me away from you. Surely you know that—"

Gently but firmly he pushed her away. "What I know is that I have nothing to offer you here. For your sake, you must go to Boston and realize your full potential."

"Potential!" She spat out the word. "What could you know about my potential? You can't even . . ." Her voice failed her at that point, and she turned and ran down the stairs and out of the building.

How could it be? Sobbing hysterically, she unhitched the horse and drove out of town.

Finally, she stopped alongside the woods at Dead Reb Flat. There she sat alone, watching birds flit among the trees, trying to understand.

Why was it that the men she loved most always left her? Father was gone most of the time. Matthew had left, refusing to return, and then he was killed. Even Daniel, her favorite of the twins, had been torn from her. Now the man she wanted most in the world, the only man she could ever love, found it impossible to love her—or any woman.

It was more than she could accept. She leaned her face against the side of the carriage hood and wept. Then, when the sunshine still shone and the leaves of the trees still whispered of new life, she dried her eyes, then flicked the reins.

Ephraim was in the carriage house when she returned. Suddenly his handsome face, his strong arms, his open, eager smile seemed irresistible. She had no pride left. Going up to him, she rested her hands on his chest, leaned against his hard-muscled body, and raised her face to his. His honest virility, his hesitant, then eager response to her kisses, salved her wounds and made her feel wanted. His touch and the feel of his body against hers fired her frustrated passions, and she knew what it really meant to want a man.

While Fionna was busily sending letters and making arrangements for Hannah to go to Boston, Hannah was spending the summer sneaking out and following Ephraim around, enticing him into more and more passionate interludes. In his arms she felt powerful, needed. In his eyes, she saw she was charming and appealing. They could laugh together and tease one another. With Ephraim she was accepted for the person she was, not for her "potential."

Only when she sat down at the piano did she feel the loss of what she was leaving behind. Only when she was lost in the spells of her music did she long to have someone else with whom she could share it. And she shed private tears for Edmund Raines.

When her anguish became too much to bear, all Hannah had to do was slip out of the house and find Ephraim, and she did so often. She would wait until everyone else had gone to sleep and then tiptoe out the door to the small house Nathanial had built for Ephraim the year he came to Quail Hollow. There, in the darkness, Hannah could smother all dreams of Edmund Raines in Ephraim's muscular arms, forgetting her lost love at the touch of Ephraim's work-roughened hands.

Fee had convinced herself that Hannah's sudden withdrawal from the family was because of her very natural nervousness at leaving home for the first time. Still, it didn't hurt to keep an eye on her daughter.

"Hannah, come into the sitting room, please," Fee called to her early one June afternoon.

She could hear Hannah's weary sigh as she got up from the piano and came back down the hall. Timothy was lounging on the chaise, but Fee didn't ask him to leave, thinking his presence might help the conversation along.

"Yes?" Hannah said guardedly.

"I want you to begin sorting your clothes so Nell can start packing."

"I told you, I'm not certain I want to go," Hannah said sullenly. It seemed that her daughter wasn't sure about anything these days, Fee thought.

"Don't be silly," Fee said reassuringly. "You're just caught up in the end-of-school, long-summer blues. Have you decided who you're going to the church box social with?"

"I don't know. They're all so . . . so boring," Hannah said as she flopped down into a chair.

"What about young George Winston, Helen's brother?"

"His ears stick out and he stammers when he talks to me," she protested.

"It's because he's wild about you," Timothy teased. "He can't think straight when he's around you."

"Shut up!"

"Children," Fee warned. "You don't have to make up your mind right away. Didn't you say that Tom Helms asked you, too?"

"Oh, he's all right. I just don't—"

There was a sudden clatter and shouting in the yard. They rushed to the porch to find Wesley yelling from astride his horse. "There's smoke comin' from Ezekial's place! Looks bad!"

Nathanial rushed out from the kitchen, pulling on his boots. Ephraim ran out of the stable leading Nathanial's horse, already saddled, then ran back in for others.

Hannah and Timothy harnessed the horses to the wagon as Fee dashed into the kitchen. "Fire at Ezekial's!" she yelled to Nell.

The men galloped down the road while Fee threw shovels and buckets into the wagon bed, and they raced towards the fire.

The men had formed a bucket brigade from the creek by the time the women arrived. Fee took the buckets from the back and added Nell and Hannah to the line. Then she went to Pearl and tried to calm her sobbing friend.

"My home," she was crying. "My home . . ."

"At least you're both all right," Fee said, rocking her in her arms. "At least you and Ezekial got out all right. We can always build you another—"

Just then Ezekial dropped his bucket, grabbed his arm, and toppled to the ground.

"Ezekial!" Pearl screamed, running toward him.

"Grandpa!" Hannah cried. "Daddy, help!"

Nathanial was beside him before his head touched the ground. "Ezekial, what is it?"

He didn't answer. Nathanial put his head down on his friend's chest and listened. Then he looked up at Pearl and

293

Fee. "His heart . . ." he said, choking on the words. "It . . . it's stopped."

"No!" Pearl cried, tearing herself from Fee. She fell sobbing to the ground, cradling Ezekial in her arms.

"He isn't . . ." Fee asked, staring in disbelief.

Nathanial looked up at her, the light from the fire flickering across his sorrowing, dirt-streaked face. "Yes," he whispered.

Weeping quietly, Fee put her arms around Pearl and helped her up.

Then Nathanial gently closed Ezekial's eyes, and carefully carried his friend's body back to the wagon. "Take Pearl to our house," he said quietly. "We'll see to the place."

Fee turned to find Hannah and saw her crying on Ephraim's shoulder. He was holding her in his arms, soothing her. Suddenly Fee remembered that night so long ago on the Oregon Trail when she and Ezekial had argued and Nathanial had first held her when she cried.

She wiped her hands across her eyes, as if to brush away the dusty memories. "Hannah," she called, "come with us. I need your help."

The next day they buried Ezekial on the knoll behind the house, beside Fee's children and next to Matthew's memorial stone. It was where Pearl said he'd always wanted to be buried.

It was because of another of Ezekial's wishes that Pearl finally stirred from the depths of her grieving.

"Ezekial had a paper," she said one morning. "It was lost in the fire, but it was all legal. Told what he wanted done with things after he was gone. I remember what it said, and I want to put it down legal again."

Fee took Pearl's hands in hers. "Timothy, will you please stop by Arnold Hannover's office on the way into town and ask him to come out here? It will help Pearl rest more easily."

Pearl had moved into Matthew's bedroom the night of the fire, and Fee insisted that this was now her home. Without Ezekial, Pearl seemed a shell of her former self, but Fee hoped that when her mourning diminished, she could be happy in their home.

Hannah grew increasingly volatile. She'd break into tears for no reason. Fee could find no explanation for her distress. She did notice that Hannah was spending more time than usual talking to Ephraim. But then things happened so fast she didn't have time to do anything about it.

Pearl went into a fast decline only days after going over her papers with the lawyer. It was as if she'd lost all will to live. Before the flowers on Ezekial's grave had wilted they were burying Pearl beside her husband.

As the last of the mourners drove off across the bridge, Fee stood on the porch and looked at the double wreath on their door. They'd had enough of sorrowing in this house. Fiercely, she wiped away her tears and vowed to put it all behind them. She would do everything within her power to protect her family from any more tragedy.

The following night Hannah announced that Ephraim was taking her to the box social. Fee looked sharply at Nathanial, and from his look of surprise, she knew that he'd had nothing to do with this. This could ruin her plans for Hannah. Still, Fee had sense enough to know better than to object to her headstrong daughter's decision.

Much to her chagrin, she found Hannah spending more and more time around the farm that summer, helping in the stables and tagging after Ephraim under any pretense. Worse, her practicing suffered.

How long could that young man hold out in the face of such temptation, Fee wondered. How long could Hannah, who was very much her mother's daughter, keep from responding to any young man, much less one as handsome and available as Ephraim?

The only solution was to have Hannah leave early for the New England Conservatory of Music. Fee brought the trunks down from the attic and began packing. It wasn't until the week of her scheduled departure that Hannah protested.

"I'm not going," she said flatly, sitting on her bed with her arms folded, watching Fee sort through her undergarments.

"Of course you are," Fee said, holding up a petticoat to see if it needed mending. "This is what we've both worked for all along. You can't give it all up just because of some silly fears you may have at the idea of leaving home."

"It's not just a silly fear of leaving home, Mother. I am leaving home, but it's not going to be for the conservatory. I'm going to get married."

Fee stopped and stared at her. "What on earth are you talking about?"

"I'm going to marry Ephraim," she said with her chin sticking out stubbornly. "And you can't stop me."

"Of course not, dear," Fee said reasonably, hiding her shock. "I wouldn't dream of it. Still, you would want to wait until you've at least tried the conservatory for a year."

"No, I want to get married right away."

"Listen, Hannah," Fee said, sitting down beside her on the bed. "I know what it's like to have . . . well, to have desires. Still, they can be controlled. If Ephraim really loves you, he'll wait for you to finish at least a year. Give yourself to your music for a year. You'll never regret it."

Hannah's eyes filled with tears. "No."

"Well, what about waiting until Christmas? If you want, you can have a holiday wedding when you come home then. It would be lovely with greenery and all the—"

"I . . . I can't." Hannah's tears began to trickle slowly down her cheeks. "I have to marry him now."

"But why such a rush?"

"I . . . I let him . . . we . . . were together . . ." she said brokenly, as the sobs came rushing out.

"Ah," Fee said, suddenly understanding. "Well, sometimes those things happen. Not that they're right, but it doesn't mean that you have to rush off to the altar. You can wait—"

"Mother," Hannah blurted out, "I'm pregnant. I haven't had my monthly flow."

"Oh. I see." And another dream died.

Giving Ezekial and Pearl's deaths as an excuse Fee planned a small wedding. Ephraim and Hannah were married in the church before the month was out. For a wedding present, Fee and Nathanial gave them an ocean voyage to the Hawaiian Islands.

Hannah had a surprise when they returned. She was not pregnant after all. She and her mother looked at one another for a long time before Fee dared to speak.

"Well." She turned and walked to the window. "How do you think Ephraim would feel about you going away for a few months' schooling?"

There was a long silence. Then Hannah whispered, "I don't know."

"Why don't you find an opportunity to bring up the subject?"

Hannah was looking down at her folded hands. "I'll try."

It was only a fleeting hope. The day Timothy announced that he and Helen would be married in the spring, Hannah came and told her she was pregnant. This time she was certain.

Though disappointed at Hannah's abandoned musical career, Fee found joy in the happy, strong baby boy Hannah gave birth to. They named him Emmett, and Nathanial and Fee felt new hope.

Then Timothy married Helen and the entire countryside witnessed their beautiful wedding. Fee thought it was a strange alliance, but when they came back from their honeymoon, they appeared settled with one another, content. Perhaps things were working out for the best after all.

Chapter XXV

May 1896

"I'm going to build a house in Portland," Fee announced one evening.

"What the hell for?" Nathanial asked, looking up from his paper.

"It's the only sensible thing to do. That's where most of the people are. Nearly all of my business is up there now. Besides, we gave Timothy and Helen that lovely town house in Salem for a wedding present. Hannah and Ephraim are still living in the foreman's cottage," she explained.

"Well, build them another house. We don't have to leave this one. I hate living in the city."

Fee sighed. "You spend at least half your time over in eastern Oregon anyway. You can always come back and stay here when you want to. There'll be plenty of room, even after little Emmett has brothers and sisters." Nathanial glowered and didn't say anything, so she continued. "Besides, Sam has been boarding with Wesley and Minnie ever since Ezekial's place burned down. Now that we're going to be developing that land, we need him closer. We can't expect Ephraim to handle it all by himself, what with you gone half the time. Sam can stay in the cottage."

Nathanial snapped the paper back up and grumbled, "When do you start construction?"

"Next week. I'd like to move in just before you leave for the roundup this fall."

In Fee's mind it was the most logical move for her. Her retail stores were in Portland, as were her banker, her property investments, one creamery, and three companies in which she was a major, if silent, stockholder. She was also concerned that Hannah and Ephraim not feel second-rate next to Timothy and Helen, especially with all Timothy's talk of society parties and political connections.

She purchased ten acres on the top of a wooded hill about a mile from the Tealls' lovely home. Fee wanted her home to be just as gracious and have plenty of room for the entertaining she planned, as well as for the entire family, grandchildren and all, to come and stay for the holidays.

Most of all, she missed visiting with her friend Ruth. Ever since her agreement with Jacob seven years ago, she'd had little opportunity to be with Ruth, her single best friend. She hoped that once she was in her new home, Ruth would visit frequently, without Fee violating her agreement with Jacob.

She also missed the companionship she'd known with Jacob, the intimate sharing and the intellectual stimulation. Only on the darkest and loneliest of nights could she admit to herself she was also hoping the Portland house would help assuage this aching loss.

However, when she had moved into her comfortable new home and Nathanial was once more spending the winter on the cattle ranches, and gray November had settled softly over the hillsides, she had a compelling reason to talk to Jacob in private.

The letter had come one rainy afternoon. She spent that night in restless sleep. By the following morning she knew she had no other choice. She sent a message to Jacob, asking for an afternoon appointment.

Nervously, she went into his office, where he greeted her in a carefully guarded tone.

"This letter came yesterday," she said simply. "Since it concerns you as well, I thought you should see it."

Jacob looked at her questioningly as he took the envelope from her and read the letter in silence. For a long time he stared at the end of the second page. Then, finally, he said, "Do you think it's true?"

"I don't know."

"Well, if Matthew actually married this Cuban woman, it could probably be traced through church registries."

"They're Roman Catholic down there. If the boy is Matthew's, the baptismal records would say so," Fee added.

"They could lie. But if the dates match . . ."

"That's what I thought," Fee agreed quickly. "If the dates and everything else does, too, well . . ."

"I'd hate to deny help to our grandson."

Fee was quiet for a moment, then added carefully, "I've been thinking about nothing else ever since the letter arrived. Then something occurred to me this morning, something even more to the point for me. This is a child who needs help with his care and schooling. His mother is ill and can't do it. I don't think I can turn him down even if he isn't my own."

Jacob paused, then turned to Fee. "I agree. But for my own peace of mind I need to know if this is a child of my blood."

Fee nodded and he went on, "I'll get a lawyer to investigate this. I know a good one back East, a man who'll be most discreet."

"I will pay half the fees."

"And I will pay half the child's support." He allowed a small smile to flit across his face before adding, "Even if he isn't ours."

With that, an uneasy contact was once more established between the families. But it could never be as close as it had been before Jacob's conscience filled him with cold guilt.

In the eight months before the lawyer reported back, Fee began sending regular support checks for the child.

She knew Jacob must have the lawyer's report even before she walked into his office. Why else would he have set up an appointment?

Wordlessly, he handed her a letter as she sat down in the chair. She read it quickly, grasping its intent and absorbing the details. Then she read it once more to be certain.

"He feels it's likely Matthew was the father of the child," she said finally. "But no one except the mother can know for sure."

Jacob had formed a triangle with his hands, resting his fingers and thumbs against each other. He nodded solemnly, peering over his hands with doleful eyes. "The dates match perfectly. Matthew's ship had been in Cuba a month before he was killed. They were married the year before. The child was born eight months after Matthew's death." His voice was thin and brittle.

"Then we have a grandson—even if we no longer have a son. I would like to see him someday."

Jacob nodded wistfully. "That would be the final test. To look in his eyes and see Matthew. But his mother requested that we not try to see him. Because of the political situation, she's fearful it would be dangerous for them all."

"Why do you think she hasn't told him about us?"

"Probably thinks it's less painful for all concerned." He looked down at his hands and added almost inaudibly, "Little does she know the pain . . ." He seemed to be a dry hull of the vital man Fee'd first known.

"You thought you'd put it all behind you, didn't you?" He nodded. "Didn't you know it could never be put aside?" she asked softly.

Jacob was silent, lost in thought. Fee waited patiently, hoping that he would say something, anything to ease the mounting fear she felt in the face of his despondent silence. Finally, when it seemed that he was no longer aware of her, she said quietly, "I will write to her."

He didn't respond, didn't even turn his eyes to Fee as she walked out of his office.

Three weeks later Fee heard a loud shouting and pounding as she sat at her desk. She reached the door before Nell and opened it to the frightened face of Simon, the Tealls' young gardener. "Miz Coughlin," he cried, "you got to come quick! It's Mr. Teall!"

"What is it, Simon?" Fee said, taking her coat from the hall tree and hurrying down the steps to the buggy. "What happened?"

"A horse," he said. "Kicked him in the head just as Mr. Teall was going around to—"

"Did you get a doctor?"

"He was there when I left. Mr. Teall was bleeding something awful."

"Kicked him in the head?" Fee asked, grabbing the side of the buggy as they careened down the drive and into the street.

"And stomped him bad. Don't know what the doctor said, but Miz Teall says she needs you something bad."

Fee settled back in her seat, trying to curtail the hot tears that were rushing to her eyes. She'd have to be strong for Ruth's sake, but she didn't know if she could. Despite all that had happened, Jacob was still her love. He had to live.

"Fee!" Ruth cried the minute she opened the door. She fell into Fee's arms, sobbing. "Thank goodness you're here."

"Ruth, where's Jacob? What did the doctor say? Please stop crying," she added quickly. "We've got to be strong."

"That's why I wanted you here," Ruth said. "You always know how to take care of things. He's in the downstairs bedroom. He's unconscious. The doctor says he's got a bad head injury and he's hurt inside the chest and stomach. Bleeding inside."

They were walking quickly down the hall toward the room where Fee used to stay, the room where she and Jacob had made love. "What did he say about his recovery?" Fee pressed.

Ruth began to cry again. "He said it was up to Jacob. If he was strong and he wanted to live, he would."

"Well, that's good news," Fee said, softening. "You shouldn't be crying about that. Jacob's strong and—"

"You haven't seen him recently. He's been so . . . so withdrawn these past few weeks. He's spent hours at the synagogue. I don't know what it is, but he's been depressed. Sometimes he'd just look at me and his eyes would fill with tears, and he'd go and walk for hours. I think that's why he was so preoccupied he walked behind that skittish horse. Jacob just wasn't paying attention. Oh Fee," she said, giving in to sobs, "I told them to take the horse and shoot it."

Fee held Ruth, trying to understand what she'd heard. Ruth hadn't described the man Fee loved. Then she thought back to her last meeting with Jacob and realized that Ruth was describing the guilt-tormented man they both loved.

With a sinking feeling, Fee went into the library and sat down on a chair.

"Fee! What's the matter?" Ruth cried. "Get up. You must come to Jacob."

"I can't. Not just now, Ruth. I think it's the ride over, the scare. I'll just sit a bit."

Ruth looked at her. Her face was a smooth mask, the tears suddenly dried hard on her cheeks. "I won't have this, Fionna," she said finally. "You've got to help me."

"I will help," Fee said pitifully. "I'll help take care of everything so you can be with Jacob."

Ruth knelt by Fee's chair and looked intently into Fee's eyes. "No, I need you to help with Jacob. Remember when you nearly died, right here in this very house; Mrs. Hiram said that it helped to talk to people even if they didn't seem to hear you. And we all did. Nathanial talked to you, I talked to you, and Jacob talked to you. You told me yourself that you sort of remembered our voices coming in and out of your other world. That's what we're going to do with Jacob. Everyone who is dear to him is going to take shifts, and we are going to talk to him. Samuel and his wife, Elizabeth, are coming over to take their turns, too. They'll tell him about the grandson who'll be coming in the spring. Maybe that will give him something to hope for, to live for."

Fee was pinned by Ruth's soft hazel eyes, her intense gaze, her fierce determination. When Fee heard that Samuel was going to have a child, a grandchild for Jacob, hot tears filled her eyes and spilled down her cheeks.

"I don't know what's happened between you and Jacob. But it's not the way it used to be. You were the only one he could talk to about books, politics, all his ideas. But something's come between you in the past few years—"

"Not really," Fee protested. "It's just that—"

"I can't do it alone. You're coming in with me and talking to Jacob." She stood up and waited by the door. Fee got up and followed. Where her will had failed, Ruth miraculously supplied her with renewed strength.

Still, she hesitated at the bedroom door. The bedroom filled with beautiful memories suddenly was made vile by the sunken face of the man on the bed.

She took a deep breath and stepped closer to him, a knot of fear swelling in her chest. Jacob's eyes, though closed, were circled with dark hollows, his mouth taut, his thick steel gray hair lank and matted with blood.

"Jacob!" she whispered as she rushed to his bed. "Oh, my God, no . . ." She grabbed his hand, but it rested limply in her own. Then she turned and looked at Ruth.

"You see," she said simply, "we must talk to him. All the time."

Fee nodded, then looked once more at his battered face resting on the pillow. "Starting now?"

"Starting now."

"Maybe I'll begin by reading poetry to him."

Ruth smiled with faint hope. "He always liked that Wordsworth book," she said, pointing to the blue leather-bound book sitting on a bedside shelf. Fee immediately recognized it as the twin to her own, the one he'd brought her so long ago. With numb fingers she took it down and began to read.

There was a time when meadow, grove, and stream,
The earth, and every common sight,
To me did seem Apparelled in celestial light.

There was no stir of recognition, no flicker of life except the steady, shallow breathing. Yet still she read on until finally her voice was hoarse from speaking around the knot in her throat. She finished with the lines,

Thanks to the human heart by which we live,
Thanks to its tenderness, its joys, and fears,
To me the meanest flower that blows can give,
Thoughts that do often lie too deep for tears.

She looked up and saw Ruth's approval. "That's what he loves to hear," she said softly. "Samuel's here. He'll stay with his father while we have a cup of tea. Elizabeth will take over after that, and then it's my turn again. That will give you time to go home and get some of your things. You will stay in the guest room upstairs." Then, when Fee began to protest, she added firmly, "Because I need you and Jacob needs you."

Fee quietly complied.

The following forty-eight hours were a blur in Fee's mind. She willed herself to do the best she could, willed herself to give Ruth strength and support, willed herself to take her regular turn with Jacob's ghostly still figure.

Carefully and gently, she and Ruth raised his head and tried to get some small sips of water and scant spoonfuls of broth down his throat. Together she and Ruth bemoaned the fact that Mrs. Hiram had died and they knew no one to take her place. And alone, Fee sat holding Jacob's hand in the dark hours of night, softly urging him to live.

By the second day, they found hope in the small response, the soft groan he murmured when they talked to him. That afternoon, Samuel insisted that Jacob actually fluttered his eyelids when he talked about the baby.

"I told him he'd better be there for his grandson's Bar Mitzvah," he added. "I think that inspired him more than anything."

Ruth smiled at that, as did Elizabeth. But Fee felt a rising dread. His other grandson would never have a Bar Mitzvah.

Early the next morning, Fee was sitting with him, bathing his forehead, when she knew what she must do. "Jacob," she

303

whispered urgently, "listen to me. I know you can. I heard you when I was sick. Now you hear me. You must live. You must live for your family—your real family. I promise you, Jacob, you do that for me and I'll never, never again trouble your life. You'll be free of me. I promise you." A hot tear rolled down her cheek and splashed on his lips.

Then his eyes fluttered open, just for a moment, and Fee saw into the depth of his eyes. "Fionna," he whispered, "my Fionna." Then he breathed a sigh, as one who'd labored long and now was finished. And there was not another breath in him.

Chapter XXVI

As a man grows older the wheel of time spins faster and faster, robbing him of his days and leaving him with only a lifetime memory of whirling, flashing images. At sixty-four, Nathanial was feeling his mortality, and he was determined to hold those images. Maybe he missed out on much of his children's youth, but he wasn't about to miss his grandchildren's.

He looked at Emmett, Hannah's son, and he remembered Donnell, his chubby, red-haired, firstborn son, and the day so long ago when Nathanial had come home, burst in the door, and kissed Fee. Donnell had been terrified that some strange creature was biting his mother's face. And Nathanial decided he'd never be a strange creature to his grandson.

The following year, Timothy and Helen had a son, Andrew. Nathanial held the fair-haired child and marveled as baby fingers wrapped around his big thumb. And he remembered the twins, tumbling around his feet as he milked the cows, as unruly as a pair of wild bear cubs. Daniel was gone now, the same as Donnell. And Nathanial vowed to treasure every one of the precious days he had with his grandsons.

Emmett was two and a half and Andrew was one when Nathanial looked up from his newspaper and glanced out the window of their Portland home. The cold rain of February cast a gray curtain across the lawn.

"It's happened, Fee," he said quietly. "We're at war with Spain. They say they're going to liberate the Cubans. 'Remember the *Maine*, to hell with Spain!' That's the battle cry."

Fee was silent for a moment. "Matthew was right. He was a hero of the Spanish-American War." She paused, swallowing the lump that filled her throat. "But war heroes are most often dead," she added bitterly.

Nathanial nodded, looking across the long grassy yard that led down the tree-lined street. Matthew had never known this home. His mind turned once more to his grandsons and the joy they brought him. Could he save them from ever going to war?

The boys were just four and five when he took them over to the ranch—without their mothers. This was going to be a time for the Coughlin "men." The boys were beside themselves with excitement.

His main intent had been to teach the boys to ride horses so they could accompany him when he attended to the farm and the ranches. He couldn't have had a more enthusiastic pupil in Emmett. Little Andrew was a bit more hesitant.

Looking all the way up the horse's leg to its shoulder, neck, and head, Andrew's lip quivered. "Does it bite little boys?"

Nathanial patted old Topsy and laughed. "No, she doesn't even bite big boys. Want to watch Emmett give it a try?"

Andrew looked as if he'd just been granted a reprieve from the gallows. "Yes, Gramps, that's good. An' give Emmett a long turn," he added generously.

Emmett, sensing his cousin's discomfort, went to great pains to reassure him how easy this horseback riding was. "It's fun up there high," he said enthusiastically. "Just try it. You'll like it." He paused. His sales pitch wasn't working. Then looking at Nathanial, he added cagily, "But I might like it more if Gramps was riding with me—at least the first time."

Nathanial caught the hint. "Think you'd like that, Andrew?"

"Uh-huh," he said with new hope shining in his eyes.

For the next three days, Emmett followed on Topsy while Nathanial rode Seneca IV with Andrew growing increasingly confident as his passenger.

Finally, on the fourth day, as they were saddling up, Andrew announced, "I can ride that little horse over there by myself. It stands real still."

"You're sure?" Nathanial checked the cinch on Topsy after Emmett pulled it.

"Is it an easy horse?"

"That little mare? Yeah, she's a real pussycat."

"I'll ride Pussycat."

Nathanial laughed and asked Button to bring her over. "Just one problem," he said as he got another saddle out. "Her name's Boots."

"Like Puss 'n' Boots!"

"Yes, like Puss 'n' Boots."

For the next two weeks, they were a happy trio, riding the fence line, going to the sawmill, and taking care of business.

"We're saddle pals!" Emmett announced when he returned home. "An' we're goin' again real soon. Gramps says so."

Ephraim laughed and tousled his son's head. "I'm glad you had a good time, son. Now, your mother and I have a surprise for you." He smiled at Nathanial. "Come in and see her."

"Her?" Nathanial exclaimed. "Well, I'll be—"

Emmett raced to the doorway of his mother's bedroom and saw the tiny bundle Hannah was holding. "The baby!" he exclaimed, running to the bed, "The baby came. Can I play with it?"

"You'll have to wait awhile to play with her. You have a little sister," Hannah said, folding down the blanket so Emmett could see. "Her name's Josephine."

"Jose-a-bean?" Emmett asked.

"No, Josephine."

Emmett studied the name and turned it silently over his tongue while he gingerly touched Josephine's hand. She opened her clear blue eyes and curled her fingers around his outstretched finger. "Josie!" Emmett announced. "I like Josie."

Hannah started to correct him, but the men were laughing. "Sounds like she's got herself a pretty little nickname to go with a beautiful grown-up name," Nathanial said tactfully.

"She looks like a Josie," Ephraim agreed.

"Look! She's smiling at me!" Emmett exclaimed.

Hannah had to smile. "I don't think she stands a chance with you three around. Now go on out so I can feed her."

Nathanial paused and looked at his auburn-haired daughter with the face so much like Fee's. He could remember her as a tiny child, begging him to take her along with him. He never had. Then he looked at the tiny dark-haired baby, with the face so much like her mother's. *If she ever wants to go with me, she will,* he promised himself.

* * *

As far as Nathanial was concerned, his two children were not going to fulfill any big dreams. In the months following Josie's arrival Hannah had rapidly become more and more withdrawn—even bitter. And Timothy could hardly be in the same room for twenty minutes without saying something that made Nathanial furious. No, if he had to place his hopes and dreams somewhere, it was in the hands of his grandchildren.

On the other hand, Fee still had hope for Hannah and Timothy. "Remember, she has two small children holding her down," Fee said as she unpinned her hair one evening and began brushing. "Get her past this child-rearing stage and I'll bet she comes bouncing right back. She has too much musical ability to deny that part of herself."

Nathanial snorted his disbelief and pulled back the covers of the bed. "And Timothy. Why, I can hardly stand to listen to him and his elitist ideas. You'd think he was an English duke or some such."

"You know," Fee said as she climbed into bed beside him, "I think it all began when he spent so much time at that Georgia plantation. Those landowners always did take on airs. Give him time and he'll put all that behind him. People around here won't put up with such blather."

"Don't be so sure. He had some of that before he ever left home. And remember, a lot of rebels settled right here in Oregon. He's telling them what they want to hear. How do you think he got elected to the county board? I heard talk the other day in the mill that some are touting him for mayor of Salem."

Fee sighed and turned out the lamp. "He's our son," she murmured in the dark. "We must keep hoping."

"I am." Nathanial growled sleepily. "I hope for those grandkids of ours."

Nathanial stood on the front porch of the Bar C Ranch and watched cloud shadows race across the sage-mottled hills. The warm autumn air whistled through the wind-twisted pines sheltering the ranch house, and he shivered at its eerie song. Everything around him seemed to be singing the swift passage of time. Emmett, Andrew, and Josie were racing their horses in the front field. And in that sight, his heart rose once more.

Although the other two couldn't see it, Emmett was holding his mount back, just enough to ensure that they would have not only a close race but maybe a tie. The compassion

Emmett had for others had not gone unnoticed by his grand-father. Nor had it been wasted on his cousin. To Nathanial's delight, Emmett's good influence on Andrew seemed to out-weigh Timothy's poor example. And Josie's robust independence gave those two a healthy respect for girls.

"Hey, Gramps!" Emmett called as they approached the front yard. "Did you see our race?"

Nathanial waved. "You're some riders," he said.

"Can we go with Tiny?" Andrew asked. "He said his grand-father is going to teach him how to follow a rabbit trail." Andrew was fascinated by the Indian lore that Button taught them, and both boys were good friends with his grandson, Tiny.

"It's fine with me. But if you end up out at the Indian reservation, you behave yourself. Be real careful to do things the way they do. Understand?"

"Yes, Gramps," they chorused.

"You can learn a lot from these people if you respect their ways and keep your mouths shut and your eyes open."

"We will, Gramps," Emmett promised.

"We've gone before and done everything right," Andrew assured him.

"I helped make baskets," Josie said eagerly.

"Then have a good time. We've got to head back over the mountains tomorrow."

"Ah, Gramps," Emmett complained. "So soon?"

"C'mon," Andrew said, turning his horse around. "We're wasting time." Josie was ahead of them both.

Time. There it was again. Nathanial smiled as he watched his grandchildren disappear around the corner of the bunk-house. Where had the time gone?

He'd spent his life pushing forward, exploring his world. Now he knew there'd always be something new and he'd never be able to see it all.

Railroads crisscrossed the country, covering in days the same ground he and Fee had taken months to cross in a covered wagon. Telephones and electric lights were common-place. There were Kinetoscopes, moving pictures, that showed people moving in a picture on the wall. Last year a man had driven an automobile all the way from San Francisco to New York. And now the Wright Brothers were experimenting with a machine that was heavier than air but could fly. It was an exciting time to be alive, and he didn't want to miss a minute of it. Nor did he want his grandchildren to miss anything.

"Hannah!" he called into the house at Quail Hollow the following week. "Hannah, where are the kids?"

"The boys are out in the barn with Ephraim. Andrew's spending the weekend."

"Where's Josie?"

"She's in town visiting with one of her friends."

"Well, I'll have to take just the boys then. We don't have much time," he said, heading out the door.

"Where are you going?" she said, chasing after him.

"Taking them on a real adventure."

"Oh, Dad," she said with disgust.

"Don't be so stuffy," he called over his shoulder.

Emmett was jumping from the rafters into the piled hay when Nathanial walked into the barn.

"Hey, Gramps!" Emmett called.

"Came to get you two. Feel like an adventure?"

"Yay!" Emmett cheered, swinging down on a rope.

"Me, too," Andrew said as he clambered over the edge of the hayloft.

"Why'd you bring the wagon, Gramps?" Andrew asked as they walked outside. "I liked riding in your automobile when I was in Portland."

"Don't worry, it's sitting in your daddy's driveway just waiting for us."

"Oh, boy. Is that our adventure?" Emmett asked.

"Not all of it. We have to take the automobile to get there."

Both boys could hardly contain their enthusiasm.

Once they arrived at the Salem house, Nathanial had the boys take the horse and wagon to the carriage house while he started the automobile.

They were back and sitting in the seat, wearing goggles and sharing a large dust cover, before he was even ready to start cranking. He laughed, looking over the hood, and seeing their two happy faces beaming at him. Emmett had his left arm in the left sleeve, and Andrew had his right arm in the right sleeve. After they buttoned it up, they looked like a two-headed midget.

The boys sat expectantly as they rode out of town. Their anticipation was a palpable presence in the car, and Nathanial found it contagious.

"What's that?" Andrew cried as a large field came in view.

"It's a balloon!" Emmett cried. "Can we stop, Gramps? Please? Just to look?"

Nathanial laughed. "We'll do more than that, son. This is the adventure!"

"Oh, boy!" he cried, unbuttoning the dust cover before Nathanial had even pulled on the brake. He was climbing over Andrew and out of the car before Nathanial could stop laughing.

"Do we get to watch it go up?" Andrew asked.

"Better." Nathanial paused for dramatic effect.

"We'll go up."

Andrew's eyes widened and he didn't say a word, just silently turned and looked at the balloon hovering over the large wicker basket.

Emmett stood at the balloonist's side, asking questions about every movement he made. Finally the man, who called himself Marvelous Morris, gave in to Emmett's enthusiasm and let him help, carefully explaining every detail and caution.

Andrew was content to stand beside Nathanial and watch, absorbing the whole scene. Marvelous Morris pulled the cord to release some of the hydrogen, explaining to Emmett how hydrogen was lighter than air. Andrew jumped at the hissing sound, then turned to Nathanial and whispered, "It sounds like a dragon."

Nathanial laughed. "How do you know what a dragon sounds like?"

"If I ever hear one, it'll sound just like that," Andrew said assuredly, his eyes never leaving the vibrant colors of the balloon panels.

When everything was checked out, Marvelous Morris invited them into his basket with a flourish.

Emmett leapt in like an otter to water, but Nathanial noticed Andrew's grip tightening on his hand as they approached the basket. "Would you rather help his assistant Hank chase the balloon from the ground?" Nathanial asked quietly.

Andrew looked at Hank. "Is he going to drive your automobile?"

"They have their own automobile over there under the tree. The one with the wagon tied on behind."

Andrew hesitated for a moment, looking at Emmett and then at the new automobile. Finally he said, "Their automobile is different from any I've seen. I want to watch from the ground and ride in the new automobile. If it's all right with you," he added quickly.

"You're sure you won't be sorry you missed the ride?"

"I'm sure. I get butterflies in my stomach just looking down from the hayloft," he confided. "Besides, I love automobiles better'n anything. Mother says it's my passion."

"Well, one must indulge one's passions," Nathanial agreed.

Emmett hardly noticed his cousin wasn't along. He was busy helping toss sandbags over the side. As they slowly lifted off the ground, his face glowed with the ecstatic expression of a soul approaching heaven.

"It's the wave of the future," Marvelous Morris proclaimed with a wave of his hand. "You read about those Wright Brothers? They'll have us all flying before the decade is out."

His claim seemed extravagant to Nathanial, but he didn't have the heart to argue when he saw how enthralled Emmett was. "And I'll be a flier," the boy murmured. "I'll fly above the earth—just like this."

"Do you think it will be anything more than just an amusing pastime?" Nathanial asked.

"Not balloons. They're for fun and dreaming," Morris said, checking a gauge. "But they did use them for reconnaissance during the War Between the States. Here," he said to Emmett, "throw out another bag so we can catch a better air current up higher." Then he turned back to Nathanial, "Those lighter-than-air-machines. Those are our future. Think of all we can do, carrying people—even things—around in them."

Nathanial glanced at Emmett and decided he'd better offer the voice of reason. "It's a little farfetched to say that they're going to be able to carry cargo as well as people on those contraptions."

Morris wasn't intimidated. "You mark my words. This grandson of yours will look back on today and remember all we've said, and know he witnessed true prophecy."

Silence surrounded them as Morris's words echoed in their minds. Nathanial looked down and carefully gauged where they were. The Willamette River snaked lazily through the lush green valley that spread out for miles on all sides. Neat squares of farmland quilted the earth. In the far distance blue and purple mountains marked the east and west valley boundaries. "Look," he said, pointing to the north, "you can see Mount Hood."

"And Mount Jefferson," Emmett said, pointing farther south.

311

"Gee, the snow is lower already," he added with an experienced eye. "Think it'll be an early winter?"

"Could be."

"See," Morris said triumphantly, "already we're using this to predict the weather. See those clouds, working their way in from the coast? Bet we'll have rain by night from the looks of them."

"And there's new snow 'top the Coast Range, too," Emmett said. "Better tell Dad to get the hay in before morning."

Nathanial shook his head in wonder. He'd lost this argument. Following the trail of Branch Creek, he found the farm. "Look, over there," he said. "Can you tell what that is?"

"It's Quail Hollow," Emmett said. "I was just trying to see Dad, but it's too far away."

The rest of the ride left Nathanial breathless. Whether he was watching Andrew and Hank in the automobile below or listening to Morris and Emmett, he felt the younger generation spinning away ahead of him. There was a whole world out there to explore, but he wasn't the one who was going to do it. As much as he wanted to, he would not be the one crossing new frontiers; it would be his grandsons bringing the new frontiers to him. Strangely, he found the prospect pleasing.

Finding what he considered a good landing site, Morris pulled the cord, and with a long hiss of hydrogen, they slowly descended. By the time they touched ground, Nathanial knew that Emmett was hooked on finding a way to be in the sky for the rest of his life.

There was still another surprise awaiting them. As they approached the automobile and trailer, Andrew came running up. "Guess what?" he called, "Hank taught me how to drive the automobile. He says I'm a natural!"

"Great!" Emmett cried. "Morris says I'm a natural flier. Says I have a sense 'bout air and currents." They both stopped, looked at one another, then broke into hearty laughs, slapping each other on the back. Their enthusiasm was more than they could contain. While the men folded up the balloon and loaded it on the trailer, the boys were running and wrestling their way around the pasture.

Nathanial watched their antics and felt as if he'd caught a glimpse into the future. Through their eyes he saw new trails, through their words he understood new ideas, and through their ears he heard the call of the new century.

*　　*　　*

Fionna was particularly pleased with her growing family. And she was equally pleased with the time she spent with Nathanial. So in the spring of 1906, when Nathanial came to her with an idea for a trip together, she jumped at the chance even before knowing what he had in mind.

"I was thinking of a train trip," he began.

"I'd love one," she exclaimed.

Nathanial laughed. "Maybe go clear across the states. All the way back to West Virginia."

She was touched by the thought. "That's a lovely idea," she murmured. "Back to our beginnings. How did you know?"

"Know what?"

"That I've been remembering what it was like when I was a girl. Wondering if it's still the same. I long to see my homeland."

"Um-hum," Nathanial agreed, puffing on his pipe. "See what the old trail covers now."

The thought of Nathanial holding sentimental feelings for the places they'd been at the beginnings of their love brought quick tears to Fee's eyes. She leaned her head on his shoulder to keep him from seeing what a sentimental old fool she'd become. His sturdy grip on her shoulder told her he understood.

They left that May. For the first time, Fee noticed the slowness with which Nathanial moved, but she attributed it to the confusing bustle of the train stations. He was still an impressive figure of a man, tall and ramrod straight, carrying himself with an earned authority. She was proud to be with him.

The train followed the Columbia River, then crossed the high deserts of Oregon and Idaho, clacking rhythmically through river canyons and across greening valleys. The tracks wound around the sharp, majestic peaks of the Rockies, and Fee and Nathanial were spellbound, realizing that somehow they had come through this sharp backbone of their country with only a mule team and a creaking, covered wagon. Now they were traversing it behind a puffing steam engine of iron.

Fee sat holding hands with Nathanial, looking out the windows at the furrowed expanse that was once a forbidding prairie boiling with their dust. The wild, desolate land they'd crossed was now plowed and green. And her untamed man was now a loving and devoted husband.

Later, as they crossed the Platte River, Fee gazed at its

slow, murky waters and marveled how it had sustained them for so many miles and days.

She turned to point out the willowed islands scattered in the river when Nathanial gasped, throwing his head back in pain.

"Nathanial!" she cried, "what is it? Say something!" But his eyes were closed, his face the color of clay, and his breathing harsh and labored. Fee reached up and pulled frantically at the cord, all the while patting Nathanial's face, hoping to bring him back.

"It looks like a stroke," said an old woman from across the aisle. "Put his feet up." A man jumped up and helped Fee to do just that while someone hurried over with a flask of brandy, offering it for medicinal purposes.

"Yes, ma'am? Is something wrong?" asked the conductor as he strode into the car.

"It's my husband. Is there a doctor on board?"

"I think there's one in the next car."

"Hurry," she pleaded, trying to force the brandy between Nathanial's blue lips.

Within a minute the doctor was by her side, bag in hand. He quickly examined Nathanial, who was still unconscious, although his breathing seemed steadier.

"I'm afraid it's a stroke," the doctor said gently. "The prognosis is not good."

"What should I do?"

"We're coming into Lincoln, Nebraska, in about an hour. I suggest you get off there and have him checked into the hospital."

Fee looked out the window at the landscape streaming by. It was all so strange, so flat and monotonous. "How long will he have to stay there?" she asked. "He'll be so miserable in a strange city."

The doctor was silent for what seemed an interminable time. Then he spoke. "If you are financially able, get a private car, hire a nurse, and take him home. I doubt he'll recover, and he'll be happier in familiar surroundings with his loved ones around him."

Fee looked at him in shock. What was he saying? How could he ever think that a strong man like Nathanial wouldn't recover? Her head swam, every part of her mind screaming denial, refusing to recognize what was happening.

"My wife and I will be visiting our daughter in Lincoln. I'll make the arrangements if you'd like," he offered.

"That would be most kind," she whispered, "most kind." All she could think of was getting Nathanial back home, back to where he belonged so he could get well. She accepted the conductor's offer of a blanket to cover Nathanial, then sat beside her husband, tightly holding his limp hand.

When they arrived in Lincoln, the doctor arranged for Nathanial to be taken on a stretcher directly to a private car waiting on a side track. Fee stayed with him while the doctor hired a nurse to accompany them back to Portland.

With a jolt and a crash, their car hooked on to the train heading back West. Nathanial lay on a bed beside the window, still unconscious, with Fee by his side talking softly to him. The nurse stoked the fire in the stove, checked Nathanial, gave him medication, and tried to get Fee to rest.

Throughout the days and nights, Fee sat holding his hand, watching the landscape pass by the window. The vast wasteland that had throbbed with the drums of the Indians now passed with the throbbing of her frightened heart. The plains and mountains it had taken them four months to cross whipped by her eyes in a matter of days. And she told him about it all, reminding him of the times they'd had together, of everything they shared, praying he could hear her.

She wired ahead and Timothy met them at the station, accompanied by Ruth, who insisted that Nathanial go to her house, where she could take care of Fee while the nurse took care of Nathanial. Dazed from shock and lack of sleep, Fee agreed, putting herself into their hands. Timothy saw them settled in and then went back to Salem, promising to return with Hannah and the children.

The first doctor who examined Nathanial said he'd never recover. Fee brought in another who said he'd recover but would never walk again. She brought in still another who said that both were right. Nathanial's legs were paralyzed by the stroke, which he believed was caused by a blood clot. That blood clot, and others like it, were still in his system, like hidden bombs, ready to strike again at any time—which would be fatal. Until that happened, Nathanial could be made comfortable and might even recover enough to enjoy being with his family and friends. But his time was measured in days and weeks.

The first week, Fee slept in snatches, only when the nurse insisted she lay down on the cot next to Nathanial's bed. But by the weekend, when Timothy, Hannah, and the children arrived, she could see that he was beginning to respond to their care and she began to hope—and to sleep when Hannah promised to stay by her father's side.

Finally he began to respond, awakening occasionally and even murmuring some words. Although he couldn't move his legs, Fee's hopes soared. While Ruth went about her regular schedule and Timothy attended to his and his parents' businesses, Fee sat at Nathanial's bedside, holding his hand and talking to him, hoping her words might penetrate the thick fog that enveloped him.

One afternoon as she sat reading aloud from a book, he suddenly whispered hoarsely, "Will you put down that book and listen to me?"

"You're awake!" she exclaimed, tears filling her eyes. "How do you feel?"

"Lousy. But I want to talk."

"That's all I've been doing for the past three weeks, talking to you."

"I know. Heard you sometimes. It kept me trying. But now . . . listen. We've done a lot. A lot to protect." His speech was slow and labored and slightly slurred. It frightened her to see him struggling so.

"I know, dear, but that can wait. Don't strain yourself."

"Got to . . . not time," he said, closing his eyes and catching his breath.

"Don't—"

"Shh, listen." He lay with his eyes closed and, for a moment, she thought he'd gone back to sleep. But he was just gathering his thoughts. "I brought you out here, not even realizing what was happening myself. You always knew. Fought for what we believed in," he said hoarsely and with effort. "I know you worked as hard as I did to build what we have . . . and I know you did it because of what happened back in Virginia. . . . You were right, Fee. Money brings power, power for good and for evil. You wanted it to protect yourself— and to do good upon the land," he said with a faint smile. Fee could read the love in his eyes and accepted his rare accolade with a tearful smile. "Make sure what we've done stays done," he added weakly.

"We will," she murmured, holding his hand against her cheek. "We will—together."

"No. Not together. Everything's in your name. Did it before we left on the trip. Sort of a premonition, I guess. Won't be any problem with the estate. The will is clear."

"Nathanial . . . don't—"

He raised his hand, closing his eyes with the strain. "I'm passing everything on to you—moral as well as material . . ."

"Nathanial, please don't talk . . ." She stopped, frightened by his closed eyes and shallow breathing. "Nathanial!"

He opened his eyes and looked at her. "Through it all—I've loved you—my Fionna," he whispered with a sigh.

"And I love you," she said, leaning over and resting her cheek next to his, holding him in her arms, willing her strength into his failing body.

With tears streaming down her face, she crawled onto the bed and lay next to him, holding his still body. "And I've always loved you," she whispered.

But it was no use. He'd left her for the last time.

Chapter XXVII

August 1906

Fionna was alone. At the age of sixty-three she felt unreasonably deserted. Nathanial was three months in the grave; Jacob, ten years. Aside from her children and grandchildren, she had only Ruth. Fionna fought the oppressive sense of desolation with every ounce of her will, determined not to let it get her down. But it was a losing battle.

She looked across the green grass and watched the leaves of the great oak tree in front of her house move lazily in the hot August air. Perhaps her loneliness was merely accented by the letter she held in her lap. Nevertheless, she had to make this decision by herself.

Taking up her pen, she dipped it in the inkwell and quickly wrote a telegram.

SEND BOY IMMEDIATELY. AWAITING NOTICE OF ARRIVAL.

Placing the paper into an envelope, she stepped to the front door and called to her groundskeeper.

"Joe, when you go downtown to pick up the mail, please take this to the telegraph office."

"Yes, ma'am," he said, leaving the fence he was mending. "Do you want it done before lunch?"

"Please. You may take the automobile, if you promise not to drive so fast you scare Mrs. Campbell down the street."

"She won't even know I've gone by," he promised. He was a young man who worked for her full-time during the summers and part-time the rest of the year, earning money to attend college. Fee and Nathanial had long ago begun helping promising young people earn their education.

She sighed and went back inside. It was partly these same ideals that made her send the telegram. But she admitted to herself that idealism was just one of the reasons. There was much more than that—but she didn't want to think about it, at least not until she saw the boy.

Two months later, she impatiently paced as the large steamer dropped anchor in Portland Harbor. The smell of tar and seaweed filled her nostrils, and the scent of foreign lands seemed to drift from the hold of the boat.

As the gangplank lowered, she walked through the milling crowd towards the landing. How would she know him, she thought nervously. How would he react to her?

Her eyes searched the railing above, looking anxiously for any sign of him. Then she saw a figure, slim and tall, hovering back in the shadow of the bridge. As he stepped hesitantly into the light, Fee could see the youthfulness of his face. She raised her hand in greeting. His hand raised in tentative response, and slowly he made his way to the gangplank.

"Excuse me," he said, setting down his battered leather valise. "Are you Mrs. Coughlin—or perhaps her representative?"

His voice had the fresh, uncertain sound of having just matured in the past few months, and his words had a lilt, although his English was perfect. But it was his eyes that held Fee. Liquid brown and intense, they filled her heart with love for this child-man of fourteen.

"I am Mrs. Coughlin," she said, smiling. "You must be Mateo."

"Yes, ma'am." His hand was cold as he hesitantly returned her handshake. "My mother, before she died," he said, swallowing hard, "she said to tell you how much I appreciate the opportunity to come here."

"I consider it my good fortune," Fee said. "Do you have other luggage?"

"No, ma'am. We are not wealthy people in Cuba—at least not my people."

"Wealth is not always measured by material goods. I imagine that I have one of Cuba's greatest treasures standing by my side right now."

He looked surprised, then smiled brilliantly. "*Gracias*—I mean, thank you, ma'am. You pay me a great compliment." He picked up his suitcase. "If you will allow me," he added slowly, pushing his dark hair back from his eyes, "I must return it. I did not expect such a lovely lady to greet me. I thought I would be going to the home of a very old woman who would be wrinkled and smell of . . ." He stopped himself, blushing at his own confession.

Fee laughed as she put her arm around him in a hug of genuine affection. "I can tell you and I are going to get along just fine, Mateo," she said. "Now, there's a train leaving for eastern Oregon at noon. We'll stop by the house and have an early lunch, then catch that train. I'll take you over there now because it is time to find out how the roundup went and go over the books. It will be a good introduction for you before I have to leave."

"You don't live on the ranch?"

"No, I spend most of my time here in Portland. I go over to the ranch from time to time to check the sawmill and ranch operations. And sometimes I stay with my daughter in Salem, which is about forty miles south of here." She paused. "Now that you're going to be living on the ranch, I'll be finding excuses to go over there more often. And of course you will come over here for visits if you wish."

He raised his gaze from the pavement to look her in the eye. "I thank you for your kindness," he said softly.

Mateo watched in awe as she started to climb into the driver's seat of the automobile. "Let me show you how to turn the crank," Fee said, guessing that he'd never ridden in an automobile before.

Given something constructive to do, Mateo's reticence disappeared. When the engine finally caught, he let out a triumphant whoop and jumped into the car with a happy grin, as if afraid it would run away without him.

Over lunch Fee tried to break through his reserve with conversation.

"Tell me what it's like in Cuba," she urged.

He looked far away, beyond the room or the view from the

dining room window. "It is warmer there," he said finally. "And the plants are different."

"And the people?"

"It's too soon to say." He drank from his glass of milk, then set it down thoughtfully. "I've never known anyone who treated me like you."

"Does that bother you?"

He shrugged his shoulders and glanced away. "I don't know what to do," he admitted quietly.

"Just be yourself," she said, patting his hand. "You will be welcome on the ranch. It's like a new family."

She wasn't sure if she should have added the last part. His dark eyes revealed a brief flash of pain before he smiled softly and said, "I will work very hard for you."

"No more is expected of you than from anyone else. Just remember that. Now, if you'll take that piece of chocolate cake with you, we'd better get down to the railroad station."

He was increasingly quiet as they got on the train and rode along the Columbia Gorge. Sitting with his eyes glued to the window, he barely took notice of her comments throughout the entire trip. Finally, as they were pulling into the Baker station, Fee said, "This is our stop, Mateo."

He turned and looked at her, his eyes wide with wonder. "Ah, *señora*, I've never seen a place so big. The mountains so high. America is much bigger than Cuba."

Fee laughed. "Quite a bit bigger. You're still in the state of Oregon. There are forty-five states in the United States."

He looked out the window once more. "So much land," he murmured.

"And Mateo?"

"Yes, ma'am?"

"Please call me Fee. Everyone who is a close friend does, and I consider you my friend."

He looked at her a long time, as if considering. Then with a nod and one of his rare, brilliant smiles, he said, "Yes, Fee. Thank you." Then he jumped up self-consciously and pulled his suitcase from beneath the seat.

Button and his grandson Tiny were waiting at the station with a wagon. At the sight of the boy, Mateo lit up. Fee smiled and introduced them.

"Button, this is Mateo. He is moving here from Cuba and will be working with you on the ranch. He has no family left there and I said we would welcome him into our family."

320

Button grinned. "Been needing 'nother hand around to keep Tiny company. Welcome to the Bar C."

"It's a pleasure to meet you," Mateo said to Button, then turning to Tiny, added, "I didn't expect to find a boy out here."

Tiny nodded. "There're several kids on the ranch. Lots of families. You won't be alone." The lantern light shone on the child's open, friendly face.

With that Mateo seemed to be more at ease. He even dozed off on the wagon ride to the ranch.

That night as they all sat around the large table in the ranch house, he was silent but smiling, taking everything in and seeming to find his new home acceptable.

The next morning Button took him out to the corral. Mateo and Tiny soon came riding up, leading Fee's mount. "Fee," Mateo called. "Look! Button says he is my horse. I got to choose him myself. Button says my eye is good for horseskin."

"Horseflesh." Fee laughed as she swung into her saddle. "All of us have our own horses. You will learn to work together. Do you want to name him?"

He thought for a moment. "Yes. I will call him Neuvo Amigo. That means new friend, and that's what I have found here."

"Can I call him Amigo?" Tiny asked. "The rest twists around my tongue something awful."

Mateo laughed. "Yes—and you may call me that, too."

With that, Fee relaxed and began to feel that she need worry no longer. Mateo had a home.

Josephine was not quite fourteen when Andrew and young Jacob Teall were ready to leave for college. Since Emmett was returning to school at the same time, Fee invited all her children and grandchildren to a grand going-away dinner. Ruth, Jacob, and his parents, Samuel and Elizabeth, were the first to arrive. The sight of the young man, dressed in his best suit with his serious grown-up look, took Fee's breath away.

"Why, Ruth, he's the spitting image of his grandfather," she couldn't help exclaiming.

Ruth smiled warmly at her grandson. "Yes, that's just what I've been telling him." She smiled at Samuel and added, "We Tealls may not do much in quantity, but we do produce quality."

Fee laughed as she led them into the parlor. "Tell me,

Jacob," she said as she poured them each a snifter of brandy, "are you going to follow in your father's footsteps as a journalist?"

Jacob looked at his father and cleared his throat. "No," he said quietly. "I've decided to study law."

"Law?" Fee said. "Why, that's wonderful. We've needed a lawyer in our families for years. Fact is, we need more than one." She looked at Samuel. "I hope I haven't stepped on any toes here," she added quickly.

Samuel shook his head. "Not really. Naturally, every father dreams of having his son take over his business, but *The Occidental Journal* has grown. The owner will always have influence, but it's no longer a one-man operation like it was with Father or even a one-editor operation like when I took over."

Jacob broke into a smile of relief. "I was afraid you were unhappy."

The doorbell rang. Nell answered it amid a chatter of greetings. "Sounds as if our Salem contingent has arrived," Fee said with pleasure.

Timothy was the first to burst into the room, shaking hands with everyone and giving his mother a perfunctory kiss on the cheek. He was followed by Helen, who quietly said hello and took a chair by the empty fireplace. Andrew and Emmett came bounding into the room, happily greeting Jacob and heading straight for the brandy. Ephraim escorted Hannah into the room and gratefully handed her over to her mother. "You've taken on quite a crowd, Fee. Hannah is certain we'll never fit around the table."

"Don't know what you're thinking of, Hannah," Fee said. "We have this many and more at Christmas. Where's my granddaughter?"

"Right behind us," Hannah said.

Fee looked and saw Josephine standing shyly in the doorway. She was wearing a dress of pale violet linen that showed off her blossoming figure to fine advantage. Her shiny black curls were pulled back with a dark violet ribbon that hung down her back and matched the satin sash around her tiny waist. "Josie, you're absolutely beautiful," Fee exclaimed. Josie blushed under the compliment, making her delicate face even more beautiful. Inexplicably, Fee glanced at young Jacob and found in his eyes a confirmation of her words.

Ever since Josie was small, she'd always tagged after her brother and her cousin. Whenever Jacob was around, however, he made a point to include her. Whether it was because he felt left out himself or because he appreciated the quick wit and intelligence of the young girl, Fee didn't know.

Now that Josie was growing into a lovely young woman, it didn't surprise Fee that Jacob continued his practice. That evening, whenever she looked around the room, she found that he was never far from Josie, bringing her into the conversation or simply including her through his presence. It was precisely the gentle attention that a young girl needed, and Fee was grateful to Jacob for his sensitivity. Then, looking at them sitting beside one another at the table, she couldn't help wondering if Jacob was acting out of compassion or just plain passion. They did make a lovely couple.

Then, realizing that Jacob was going away for a long time, she pushed the thought from her mind. She knew she was merely remembering how it had been with Jacob's grandfather and herself.

"Grandmother," Emmett said, interrupting her thoughts, "what do you think? Will the United States be pulled into the European conflict with Germany?"

"Germany?" she said, embarrassed at being caught woolgathering. "You mean what the papers have been talking about? Well, the Germans do seem to want to rule Europe. Maybe it's in their nature, but it isn't right."

"Well, when I was in Europe," Timothy put in, "I found the Germans had a much superior culture to other countries. Next to the English, I'd say the Germans understood best what civilization really means. They were reserved and proper, not uncontrolled and passionate, like the Italians. It's just like those Italian dogs to deny their alliance with Austria."

Fee was surprised to hear the reference to Italy. Timothy hardly ever referred to that time in his life. "Did they seem to be pressing for conquest, then?" she asked.

"The Germans? The aspirations of a country's leadership is hardly a topic for the drawing room, Mother," Timothy said quickly. "But when I'm elected representative this fall, I'll have something to say about Oregon's trade with European countries, I can tell you that. We have to look out for our own."

Timothy was running for a seat in the Oregon House of Representatives. Fee knew that it wouldn't take long for him to bring the conversation around to his campaign. She was proud that he was active in politics, but she wasn't comfortable with all his views.

Fee changed the subject. "You haven't changed your mind about your fields of study, have you, boys?" she asked Emmett and Andrew.

Emmett shook his head. "Nope. Still going to study engineering. I want to be one of the first to work with the real airplanes. They're making some wonderful designs. Got one that takes off and lands on water. Roosevelt established an aviation section of the Army and they're building airplanes for them now. No telling where this will take us. First chance I get, though, I'm going to climb in one and take off into the clouds."

Andrew laughed at his cousin. Then he said, "No blue skies for me. I think I'll stick with accounting and business. You've always said this family needs someone with good business sense; besides, I think it's fascinating. Sort of like Emmett's fascination with airplanes, just not as glamorous."

"Well, between you and Jacob we'll have the family businesses covered. And Emmett will lead us to new frontiers." She turned to Josie then. "That leaves you, dear. What do you want to do?"

Josie was quiet for a moment, looking down at her plate. Then she looked Fee straight in the eye, as if defying any challenge. "I want to be a lawyer, too."

"Are you crazy?" Emmett exclaimed. "Girls don't—"

"Emmett!" Fee wasn't about to let him stifle this dream. "Josephine can do anything she chooses to do—the same as you—and she will have my blessing."

"It'll be rough," Jacob said softly. "You'll need all the support you can get—and you have mine."

Josie smiled gratefully at her grandmother and Jacob.

"You shouldn't encourage such dreams, Mother," Hannah said tightly. "Dreams can only lead to disillusionment."

There was an awkward silence. Ephraim looked down at his plate, and for a moment Josie looked as if she might cry.

Fee said quietly, "Dreams can be attained if we have the courage to do so. I believe that I'm a prime example of that." Then, smiling at Josie, she added, "Let's drink a toast. To our dreams and their fulfillment through hard work and determination."

For all their talk of dreams that night, it was the talk of war that came to fruition first. From 1914 on Fee found she could not escape reading about the bloody battles being fought on the Eastern and Western fronts of Europe.

Emmett's letters held an effective counterpoint. He ached to leave school and join the Royal Flying Corps in England. "That's where real aviation is, Grandmother," he wrote. "The United States is years behind England in aviation development." He seemed unaware of the fact that people were dying. Fee wrote back to him, sometimes daily, trying to convince him to stay in school, telling him that war was a fruitless exercise in spilling the blood of fellow human beings.

As it was, Emmett finished school two months after the United States declared war on Germany. He enlisted in the Army aviation division the following day. To Fee's despair, Andrew felt compelled to follow his cousin's example. He decided to postpone his last year of schooling in favor of joining the Army. Her only consolation was that young Jacob promised Fee and his mother to finish law school before signing up.

When Fee received a letter from Mateo telling her that he was following his friend Emmett's example and signing up, she was horrified. She stopped him by threatening to block his citizenship papers if he should defy her. With great reluctance and grumbling, Mateo settled back down to helping Button run the ranches.

Suddenly her routine revolved around the times the wire service was open. Once more she became a frequent visitor to the newspaper offices, hanging over Samuel's shoulder, reading the war dispatches as they came in. She learned European names she'd never heard before, hung a map of Europe in her office with pins denoting where the Allies and Germans were fighting. Strange-sounding names such as Ypres, Beersheba, Versailles, Aleppo, and Zeebrugge circled around her brain like vultures. Letters with strange postage stamps filled her mailbox, and she read them ravenously, trying to understand what her grandchildren were doing and praying they would be kept safe.

Then the dreaded wire came. Andrew was wounded. In March at the Ypres-San Quentin offensive, he inhaled deadly mustard gas. Fee immediately went to Salem, where, together with Timothy and Helen, she awaited further news.

"I've read about this mustard gas, Mother," Timothy said. "It probably isn't so bad. They said that twenty-six percent of our casualties are due to its effects, but only about two percent actually die from it."

Helen wept quietly as he spoke. Fee got up and paced, hating the feeling of helplessness.

"Seems it affects the breathing system," he went on. "Burns the lining of the nose and throat and stuff. Probably like a burn on the hand. You get some blisters, discomfort, but after a few days it can heal."

"Timothy!" Fee said in exasperation. "What's the matter with you? Here your son is in some hospital in a place we can't even pronounce, his body damaged by a chemical we'd never heard of a year ago, and you're trying to make it sound like a household accident. We should contact the government and find out if we can go over there. Use your influence as a state representative. I'll pay for it. And I'll go with you. But that boy should have his family by his side."

Her tirade was interrupted by the doorbell. Fee looked at Helen, who was crying openly now. "I'm sorry, dear. I just can't stand waiting around doing nothing. Really, Timothy, don't you think—"

The housekeeper came into the room and handed Timothy a telegram. His face paled, and he looked at his mother without opening it. Then he carefully slit open the envelope with his pocket knife and pulled out the single sheet of paper.

"Oh, no," Helen said softly.

"It . . . it's Andrew," he said. Then he covered his face with his hands and sobbed.

"No!" Fee cried, snatching the telegram from his hand.

". . . regret to inform you," she began reading as Helen cried hysterically, "your son Andrew Coughlin died this morning . . ."

She could go no further. It couldn't be. Once more a war had robbed her of her most beloved, her best-held dreams. Once more she cried with those who shared her loss.

For the first time in her life Helen stood up to Timothy. She insisted she was going to meet the boat that brought Andrew's body home, and travel one last time with her son.

Timothy protested, explaining that he couldn't go with her because the Oregon House was in session. Helen told him she would go alone—and did.

Then, on a rainy night on the other side of the continent, a bridge went out. The train that Helen was riding, the train that carried her son's body, crashed. Helen was killed.

A week later Timothy and Fee met another train and received two coffins, mother and son. After the funerals were over, Timothy had a fountain placed in one of the city parks, a fountain he had dedicated to his wife and son. Fee quietly established a scholarship fund in Andrew's name.

The war ended November 11, 1918. While the rest of the country celebrated the defeat of the Hun, Fee celebrated only because one grandson had survived the war. Emmett was coming home.

Josie was a freshman at the newly established Reed College in Portland, so she was able to join the family for the holidays. However, young Jacob was in his last year of law school at Harvard and wouldn't be coming. It wasn't until Emmett returned that Fee realized what a loss it was to have Jacob gone.

Unlike his normal, ebullient self, Emmett was withdrawn and silent. He refused to answer questions about the war, putting them off with cynical and bitter responses. Fee longed to hear the laughter and roughhousing that "her boys" had always created during the holidays. Now with Andrew dead and Jacob away at school, Emmett was alone, and the silence was unbearable. Only Josie could bring a faint smile to her brother's face, and she tried valiantly the entire holiday.

"You know, Grandmother," she said wearily the night before classes began again, "I hate to admit it, but I'm glad this vacation is over."

Fee smiled. "I know what you mean, dear."

"I think it would have been different if Jacob had been here," she added softly.

Fee looked at her granddaughter, so lovely in her dress of royal blue wool crepe. She wore her hair pulled back with a matching ribbon and, just like her grandmother before her, the curls persisted in escaping in tendrils around her face.

How would it have been with Jacob here, Fee wondered. Better for Emmett? Certainly. And for Josephine? She looked once more at Josie, the child of her heart. Yes, she believed, Jacob's presence would have been good for Josie.

Things did get better when Jacob came home. He immediately set about spending time with Emmett, accompanying him to the speakeasies that were springing up as a result of the Prohibition amendment, enticing him to go out with girls. Jacob encouraged him to use his college education now, find something he wanted to accomplish. And he was successful.

Emmett began to care about living again. Only now, Fee noticed, he seemed to be filled with a seeking drive, the same drive that had made Nathanial want to see the other side of just one more mountain.

When Josie decided to transfer to Leland Stanford College in California, Fee felt it was a good idea, even though she would be away from her family and friends for the first time. However, when Emmett came and told her his plans, she was overwhelmed.

He was using his savings to buy a Jenny airplane, one of the Army training planes now being sold as surplus. He wanted to start a business using his skill as a pilot, maybe doing air exhibitions around the country to earn money and to educate the public about the potential of airplanes— barnstorming, they called it.

As much as it left her aghast, Fee knew better than to try to stop him. Like his grandfather before him, he had to get it out of his system before he could settle down. Fee just hoped it would happen sooner for Emmett than it had for Nathanial.

Over the next three years her only consolation came from the fact that Emmett occasionally used his engineering skills. He flew to their ranches and mills around the state and checked on the operations. Within a short time, Fee began receiving reports from her mill foremen telling how Emmett had shown them new methods to make the machinery run more effectively. In two cases he'd taken the time to invent new equipment—once a molding knife and once a new line for the greenchain. Hearing that kept her hopes up.

Although she tried not to influence Josie's decision, Fee was greatly relieved to hear that she was going to enter law school at Willamette University in Salem. It was a fine school and, even more appealing, it was close to home. Fee wanted to hear all about it, and Josie happily accepted her invitation for the weekend.

"Guess what, Grams," she said, bursting in the door one crisp October afternoon.

"With you, I can never guess." Fee laughed as she took off her reading glasses. "You'll have to tell me."

"I had my first class, and you'll never believe who the lecturer was. Jacob! Did you know he was lecturing part-time?"

"No, I didn't. I knew that he had an office in Salem as well as in Portland, in order to keep up with my businesses. I wonder where he finds the time to lecture at the university?"

"Oh, Grams," she exclaimed, kissing her cheek, "you can't think that your business fills all his time."

"It should for what I pay him. And he's going to need some help. So don't dally around with your studies."

Josie laughed as she sat down in the chair opposite Fee's. "I think he was as surprised as I was, but he tried to cover it up and pretend I was just another student. We talked after class, though. He said he was looking forward to challenging my mind." She giggled. "I couldn't resist. I told him I was looking forward to challenging his."

"Impertinence," Fee exclaimed. "It will come back to haunt you."

"Or him. Got any cookies?"

"Go ask Nell."

Fee leaned back in her chair, listening to the chatter from the kitchen. So Jacob was now Josie's teacher, she thought. They'd both learn from this. Then a chill of foreboding went through her soul. *And maybe I have a lot to learn myself,* she thought.

For the rest of the year, Fee always tried to spend some time in private with Josie, so she could assess how her schooling was going. It saddened her that she felt closer to her granddaughter than she'd ever felt to Hannah. And from Josie's response, the feeling was mutual.

Josie's relationship with Jacob was taking on new and puzzling dimensions. She tried to explain it to Fee at the end of first semester, just before the Tealls arrived for a traditional holiday dinner.

"He . . . opens my mind," she began. "I just don't know how to respond to him in this situation, though. It makes me sort of nervous when we've been arguing and exploring ideas all term long and now I'm supposed to slip back into my usual little-girl role for the holidays."

"I doubt that Jacob would expect you to do that," Fee said.

"I don't know that I can keep from it. It's like when I'm with Mother. I feel thirteen again and she makes me angry with everything she says. It's hard to maintain your grown-up roles when people still think of you as a child."

"Do you think Jacob thinks of you as a child?"

Josie's eyes took on a faraway look, a look that told Fee more clearly what Josie felt than her words. "I don't know," she murmured. "I don't think Jacob knows, either."

The holidays managed to go just fine, in spite of Josie's misgivings. Jacob treated her much the same as he treated all the others—except for the look in his eyes. And Fee knew.

At least she thought she knew. It was late spring when Josie came up to Portland unexpectedly.

Fee looked up as she heard the door slam and saw Josie enter the house. "Well, what a welcome surprise," Fee exclaimed. "With final examinations coming, I didn't expect to see you for another two weeks."

"I just . . . just wanted to get away," Josie explained awkwardly. "I need a quiet place to look at my books."

Fee kissed her cheek and said, "Your room is always ready. Go on up and we'll call you when dinner's ready."

It was over dinner that Fee could tell something was seriously wrong. She tried to find out what it was as Josie picked listlessly at Nell's chicken pie.

"How do you think you'll do on your final tests this year?" Fee asked.

"My grades have been good all along. I don't think it'll be too hard," Josie said quietly.

"Do you still like your classes?"

"Of course," she said. "I love law. It's what gives order and defines our very civilization."

"I was just wondering if you were disillusioned about something. Is anything new going on at school?"

"Not much."

"Do you still have Jacob as a teacher?"

From Josie's involuntary wince, Fee knew she'd found the source of the problem. "Yes, for now," Josie murmured.

"Is he quitting?"

"He wanted to tell you himself," Josie blurted out.

"Tell me what?"

"That he's taking a sabbatical from the university because he's going back to Boston to work in his uncles' law offices. He says he needs to broaden his experience." Her voice was sharp with pain, and Fee was puzzled by what was happening between them.

"Is that the only reason he gave? What did he say?"

"Grams, I'm not sure. You'll just have to ask him. Now, if you'll excuse me, I have to finish reading this case if I'm going to be ready for the test on Monday."

Fee knew it was all she was going to get from Josie. Maybe Jacob would tell her more. Instead, she was disappointed. He repeated almost word for word what Josie had said, ending with the reassurance, "Ben and Charles Bradford have agreed to take care of you while I'm gone."

"But why? Don't you think you get enough experience here?"

"I'll come back a better lawyer for having worked with my

uncles. It's an old, established firm and they handle many different kinds of clients, criminal as well as civil. I need that experience."

"That's all you need?"

"Professionally, yes."

His voice was guarded and Fee could hear the same reticence she'd known in his grandfather when he was troubled. She couldn't find out what was really happening. A cold chill touched her heart.

Chapter XXVIII

January 6, 1924

She knew she was going to die. She couldn't complain. Eighty-one was a ripe old age. It was time.

Dr. McAllister had told her before Christmas. She replayed the scene as if it were captured in one of those moving pictures.

"Fionna," he'd said, taking off his glasses and wiping them nervously, "I don't know that I'd tell any other patient this, especially straight out, but with you, there's no way around it. And," he added with a sigh of resignation, "you'd have it no other way. The truth is, your heart's giving out on you. You're going to die. Probably within the next few months. And you'll keep having these spells. Better prepare for it."

His words had not surprised her. The growing weakness, the dizziness and breathlessness, had all given her warning.

Still, there were some things left undone—and some things she ought not to have done. More importantly, there were things she'd done she would not allow to be undone, not if it were within her power to prevent it. That was why she wouldn't die—not yet. She willed herself to live until she'd done everything to ensure her proper legacy to the world.

After her conversation with the doctor, she had watched her family around the Christmas dinner table in a new light. She studied them, her children and grandchildren, as they were. Each one was at a point in life where he or she could ruin it or make it all Fionna hoped—and knew—it could be.

Any one of them could destroy what Fee had spent her life building—or could redeem it all.

That was why she was so glad young Jacob came back last week and was teaching again. She needed a good lawyer, but more than that, she needed someone she could trust. Besides, he was part of her plan.

She looked at her watch. She had half an hour before she expected him to arrive, and there still were some papers to go over.

As she reached into her top desk drawer, her hand brushed against a piece of metal, like the corner of a picture frame. Curious, she pulled it out. After all, she was going to have to put all this in order. . . . Her breath caught in her throat as she found herself gazing into Jacob's intense eyes, his young face captured by that long-ago photographer.

He had been such a handsome man. It was easy to see how she could have been so swept away by passion for him. What the photographer couldn't capture was his intelligence, his quick wit and wry sense of irony, or his intuitive business sense, all of which had charmed her for so many years.

But it eventually took its toll. Fee had constantly had to watch her monthly cycle, fearful yet hopeful all at once. She knew now that the liaison had torn Jacob apart. After going through the Seder ceremony with Jacob and Ruth during one Passover, Fee understood that the difference in their religions had been a large part of his inner turmoil. Once she'd joked that his ancestors were worshiping the one Lord God just the way they did today when her ancestors were still making sacrifices to oak trees. But the truth of her words struck deep, and she realized once more that Jacob and Ruth shared a history that she could never share. And she mourned. She mourned his loss and, moreover, she mourned what it had done to Jacob. That it had hastened his death was one of her heaviest burdens.

The doorbell rang, ending her recollections, and she quickly gathered her notes. She wanted to be sure young Jacob had all the information he would need in the next few months.

Maybe it was because the memories were so close to the surface, but as he walked into the parlor, so full of life, a smile lighting his handsome face, Fee almost felt as if she were greeting his grandfather once again.

"Fionna," he declared, crossing to her and taking her hand, "you get more beautiful each day." He kissed her lightly on the cheek, and she laughed like a schoolgirl.

"Jacob, you should bottle that flattery and sell it to gardeners," she said, wagging her finger. "It would fertilize the flower bed very nicely. Still, I thank you."

He sat down in the chair she indicated. "It's true, you know," she said. "I find it hard to believe the doctor. I keep hoping he's wrong," he added softly.

"Well, he isn't. And you've promised not to tell anyone else. Now let's get down to business. Would you like some brandy?" she asked, remembering her hospitality. "I have some over there in the cupboard. If the Prohibitionists should ask, I keep it for medicinal purposes."

"It's a cold evening," he said with a wink. "I think some preventative medicine is called for. How about you?"

"Of course." She paused for a moment.

"What have you found out about Timothy?" she asked as he handed her a glass.

"Well, you were right about those people he's hanging around with. They're a pretty powerful crew."

"But what do they stand for?"

"This is a pretty conservative state," he said with a shake of his head.

"Red-necked, you mean. Too many Southerners poured in here after the Civil War. Been throwing a bigoted monkey wrench into the works ever since. You know, I think this state is destined to be—what does Freud call it?—a split personality? We're forward- and backward-thinking at the same time. I just want to make sure that Timothy goes forward and not backward to the Civil War instead."

"Well, I'm not so sure he's going to get mixed in with the Ku Klux Klan—"

"Don't you be so sure," she interrupted. "The KKK is one of the most powerful forces in this state, and Timothy is enthralled with power. Anything to have his own way. They say even Walter Pierce, the governor, is one of them. I'm afraid that son of mine might not know the difference between power put to good use and power used for evil. Either way, it's like a narcotic to him. And he's vulnerable to corruption."

"Well, you've done all you can. Time will tell."

"That's what I don't have. I can't wait and see. That's why we're writing my will this way. I'm counting on you to see that it is carried out after I'm gone." She stopped, sorry that she'd snapped at him. "Enough of that. What about Hannah? Is she still determined to throw her life away? When Ephraim

333

died, I thought she might change, but . . ." Her voice trailed off wistfully.

"She's still seeing Duke DeCarlo, that man from Chicago who's leasing some of your farmland."

"Have you found out anything more about him?"

Jacob shook his head. "That's a hard nut to crack. Nothing yet. And I haven't been able to find out much about his company. They're not on the Chicago Stock Exchange. They're in the phone directory, but they don't answer the phone."

"Well, keep trying. I smell something fishy. Have since the first time I laid eyes on him. If Hannah is ever to take control of her life, she's got to harness her weakness for men."

She reached into her folder of papers and pulled out an old, yellowed letter. "We've talked about the contingency provisions for the others, but I have a couple of straight bequests I want to make. The first is for Nell," she said, lowering her voice lest the housekeeper hear her. "I want her to have the boardinghouse in Corvallis. That way she'll have something to live on. Since she doesn't have any heirs, you can attach a covenant saying that it reverts to the estate after her death."

She paused, looking at the envelope in her hand. "Now, I want the original ranch claim along the Powder River, and the attached five hundred acres, to go directly to Mateo. He's been running it for twelve years and deserves it. The other rangeland will be split off and put under the other ranch books. Mateo will have first option for leasing those lands adjacent to his property at the price of fifty dollars a year for the rest of his life. And he gets the small amount of railroad stock I have."

She caught the surprised look on Jacob's face. With a sigh she added, "If there is any question in your mind as to the propriety of this bequest, I'm leaving this explanatory letter in the file marked 'Mateo.' You may read it upon my death, knowing that what it states is true and explains my precise intention." She placed the file in the file drawer, slammed it shut, and looked at him defiantly.

Jacob shook his head, smiling. "It's your will, Fee," he said. "You can do as you wish."

"Within reason," she said, taking her cane and walking to the chair opposite Jacob's in front of the fireplace. "Which leads us to my next problem. There's something in my past that might negate the entire will, throwing my estate to the whims of the state of Oregon."

"Good grief, I can't imagine what would do that."

"Well, sit back and listen, because I want to make sure that all I've built is not going to be gobbled up by some bureaucrats I didn't even vote for—a vote, incidentally, that I worked long and hard to be able to make. Did you know I was a suffragette?"

"I saw photos of you and Grandmother carrying placards down the streets of Portland one Fourth of July," he said. "Surely that isn't what you think may cause a problem with the will?"

"I'm not that silly." She drained her brandy snifter and held it out to Jacob for a refill. "Hannah and Timothy are illegitimate."

Jacob stood, glass in hand, frozen in astonishment. "Go on," she commanded. "Don't just stand there. Fill my glass and throw another log on the fire. We have a long story ahead of us. What I want to know is if that could get the will contested."

"Well . . . I . . . uh," Jacob stammered. "I suppose it depends upon the circumstances."

"Then I'd better start from the beginning. Quit poking at that fire and settle back in your chair."

Fee proceeded to tell the story of her trek west, how Nathanial had rescued her, and how she fell in love with her rescuer.

"You see, when Hannah was born in 1876," she continued, "we were unmarried. We were doing fairly well by then, what with the creameries, sawmills, lumberyards, and my investments. Your grandfather and I had sold our first building two years before the big Portland fire wiped it out. By then we'd put up the two blocks that still are standing down by the post office, and along with the bank building they were bringing in a comfortable income as well. Things were going well, I was secure, and I had the daughter I'd always dreamed of having."

Much to Jacob's delight, Fee told him the entire story of her successful scheme to marry Nathanial. "He looked like a badger in a hole," she said with a wink. "But I was able to convince him of the practicality of this legal linking, as he called it. We were married in Quail Hollow." She laughed, looking at Nathanial's picture on her desk. "Yes, he was quite a man, my Nathanial." She remembered how he'd looked at her on their wedding day.

"So I want an answer. I told you my children were illegitimate. I want to know if that can have an adverse effect on my will."

Jacob chuckled. "No," he said, "I see no problem arising from that. In fact, since you did marry their father, that negates the illegitimacy. Your children and your legacy are quite safe—along with your secret. I won't tell anyone—although it's a damn good story."

"Hmm, that it is," Fee said, murmuring more to herself than to him. "However, I would prefer keeping my image intact. There's just one other person who probably should know this, and then only at the right time."

"Who's that?"

"Josie. I'll have to trust you to tell her, because I feel that the right time will be after I'm gone. There's going to come a time when Josie is trying to decide who to marry, what to make of her life. You'll know when, don't worry."

It did not escape Fee's sharp eyes that Jacob had immediately looked away at the mention of her granddaughter. Yes, there was something there, and it was too painful for him to face just yet.

"She's already decided," Jacob said slowly. "She's engaged to Ron West."

"Engaged isn't married," Fee snapped. "You'll see. Now, when you see Josie doing what she thinks society says and not what she knows is best for her, I want you to tell her my story. Tell her that her grandmother married for love and the right reasons only when she was ready—not when society expected it."

Jacob looked at her, puzzlement and fleeting pain in his eyes. "I'm afraid I'm not sure when you mean—"

"You don't know now, but you will. Now, it's time for me to get some sleep. You're keeping me up entirely too late, young man. Besides, you have work to do. I want to hear from you in two weeks."

Jacob quickly jumped up, taking her hand. "Please don't see me to the door," he said, giving her his arm as they walked to the stairs. "I can see myself out." With that he kissed her good-bye.

She patted him on the cheek, saying, "You're so like your grandfather. Don't stay away too long."

* * *

Fee had not told Jacob the whole story, just enough to find out if she was on sound legal ground with her will. But as she climbed between her cool sheets she recalled the rest of the story, which had been the deciding factor in her decision to marry Nathanial—his other family. How could anyone understand? She and Nathanial. She and Jacob. Jacob and Ruth. Nathanial and Sally. Why couldn't they all have found what they needed in just one person? It would have made life simpler and easier to live. Why couldn't she have found just one man from the same background, one who beguiled her mind and enchanted her spirit, who filled her with consuming passion? Why had she always been split between two loves?

That was why she had to make Josie understand, she told herself. One love who offered everything. Before it was too late. Hannah seemed lost, Timothy didn't seem to need love, but Josie . . . With Josie she could break the chain of torturous loves, completing the circle with one perfect link.

It was several hours before her mind stopped spinning and plotting, before she could drift into sleep.

Chapter XXIX

It had the potential of being a good evening, Hannah told herself as she looked in the mirror, then sniffed in disgust. Potential. She had always hated that word. Why was she using it about herself? Life had always disappointed her. There was no reason to think it wouldn't again.

Still, she didn't look too bad. She'd bobbed her hair just like Duke had suggested. The short cut with deep waves softened the lines of her face and accented the coppery highlights of her dark auburn hair much more dramatically than the bun she'd worn at the nape of her neck. She looked younger, more vital. She smiled at her image and was pleased with herself for once. Maybe this was her chance. Maybe tonight did have great potential.

A long time ago Hannah had convinced herself that marriage held great potential. The passion Ephraim brought out in her had felt so deliciously good. Still, she had mourned the loss of her music, the chance to go to Boston and see the world. After the wedding, when she found that she wasn't really pregnant, she'd begun to dream of picking up her plans again, going to the Conservatory of Music. Then, suddenly, she really was pregnant. She spent the whole nine months crying over what she'd lost, and playing the piano. Then, after Emmett was born, things improved with Ephraim. Somehow, having produced a son and heir gave Ephraim more self-confidence. He pampered his wife and doted on his baby son.

By the time Josephine was born, Hannah had begun to feel that her life was being consumed by others. She didn't have time for her music, and she felt hollow inside. Ephraim was just as passionate as ever, and she still enjoyed their lovemaking. But she felt trapped. She'd get pregnant again and again and never have time for herself or her music. Ephraim simply was a nice man who was very boring. Hannah began to blame him for all that was wrong in her life, pushing him away, finally relegating him to a separate bedroom.

She *was* trapped. Granted, it was a gilded cage, a cage of her own making, but that changed nothing. Even after Ephraim died of a heart attack she saw no way out—until she got her idea.

If only—if only she could get enough money together, not what she received from the family businesses, but money of her own, enough to let her do what she wanted, then she'd be able to escape. She couldn't admit how wrong she'd been. She couldn't go to her mother at this late date and expect her to finance a new dream. Somehow she'd get her own money. Her plans were vague, but she knew money was the key.

Then she met Duke DeCarlo. She had accompanied her mother to a charity dinner in Portland. He was by far the most handsome man there, and he'd spent most of the evening asking her questions about herself and the farms and ranching operations she managed. She'd gone home feeling as if she had some worth after all, a new feeling for her. When he called the following week, asking her to show him the farm, because he'd been raised in Chicago and had no idea of what it all took, Hannah had been flattered by his attention.

Then one day a few weeks later Duke gave her the answer to her wishes. He told her how his company in Chicago was developing a new kind of feed that would make hogs grow to market size in two months. But they needed a place that was private, a place where they didn't have to worry about rivals stealing their formulas and getting the jump on them. He wanted to lease that unused acreage off Big Rock Hill, the rocky land with the spring.

It seemed to be a prudent way to make some useless land earn money, and it sounded exciting to be involved in some kind of industrial intrigue. But what would the rest of the family say? When Hannah hesitated, saying she'd talk it over with the rest of the family, he asked, "Don't you run this place?"

"Yes, I do. I suppose I could make the decision myself, it's just that—"

"Well, I can make it particularly appealing to you." He'd smiled ingratiatingly. "Since I know that you're the one living here and you'll have to put up with the extra traffic going in and out on the road we'll put in, I've been authorized to pay you an—ah, inconvenience fee, something for you to keep for yourself beyond what you'll pay into the farm receipts, which I understand belong to the whole family."

Hannah had been overwhelmed by the idea of money suddenly falling into her lap.

"And," he'd added, "when we have big shipments coming in and going out, you'll get an extra bonus as part of company profit sharing. Cast your eyes on this agreement," he said, placing two sheets of paper on the coffee table. The first was a standard land leasing agreement and offered the family the going rate for the use of the land. The second was the agreement between Hannah and Duke. She couldn't believe that she'd be receiving so much all for herself.

Possibly it was not quite right that she alone should be making all that money above the amount of the lease agreement, but she figured that the family owed her something. After all, hadn't she managed the whole farming operation ever since Ephraim died? Timothy put in very little and took out quite a bit. The lumberyards hadn't shown a profit since he'd taken them over, but because Fee encouraged his political aspirations they all ignored it. Well, Hannah had aspirations, too. They could at least contribute as much to hers, she reasoned.

Still, there were times when Hannah saw beat-up trucks and strange men driving down the new-cut road and she was filled with misgivings. They were not like the local farmers she'd grown up with. Then there were the phone messages she took for Duke that didn't make much sense to her. What would people listening in on the party line think?

Whenever Duke was around, though, he stuck to her like

glue. He acted smitten, and she felt it was wonderful to have that kind of attention again. Maybe he was a fast mover, but she imagined big-city men were all like that. She glowed in his attention—even though she sensed she had to be careful. Duke might want more than she was willing to give. She didn't want to marry again, and it would be a shame to break his heart, after all he'd done for her. He was such a sexy man, with his dark mustache and hair and his deep brown eyes. He had a catlike way of moving that thrilled her.

Recently Duke had been urging Hannah to get her daughter married off quickly, saying that she and her boyfriend were around too much and might suspect something. He'd even hinted that he wanted more privacy with Hannah. Whenever she mentioned setting the wedding date, Josie stubbornly refused to talk about it.

Hannah frowned at herself in the mirror. Life just kept getting more and more complicated.

She patted her nose with a powder puff and scrutinized her image once more. The violet silk chemise dress she'd chosen to wear tonight slipped over her body in a sensuous way. With the new flapper styles, her thin figure had finally come into its own. She straightened the fabric rose resting on her hip and went downstairs. She had to get the ice out of the icebox before Duke arrived. He always wanted his "cocktail" before they went out.

She heard the rumble of his Duesenberg coming down the drive just as she finished setting out the crackers.

"Boy, babe, have I got an evening for us," he called as he came up the walk, his wiry frame springing with each step. She could see by the porch light that he was carrying a large rectangular box under his arm. His dark hair gleamed in the light, and his pencil mustache looked particularly natty tonight.

"Here, gimme a kiss," he said, pulling her to him as soon as he reached the door. "You're the bee's knees, kid." Hannah laughed whenever he used the current slang. His kiss warmed her, and she led him into the parlor.

She dodged playfully as he reached to pat her derriere. "What have you got?"

"Here, open it. It's for you. I'll pour the drinks," he said, taking a bottle from the pocket of his overcoat. Even in the midst of Prohibition, Duke always came up with the smoothest whiskey made.

Hannah excitedly untied the big satin bow and lifted the lid. "Oh!" she exclaimed breathlessly. "It's . . . it's beautiful."

"Genuine fox. Full-length, too." He grinned. "Put it on. Thought that white coat would be just the thing to go with your good looks. Want to show you off to my friends."

"Oh, but Duke, how could I . . . I mean, something like this, I just couldn't accept—"

"Hey, it's beautiful on you. What's to accept? You turning down my adoration? C'mere and kiss me."

He grabbed her and held her possessively, his kiss harsh and overwhelming. She was shocked to feel his tongue slip between her lips and suddenly felt as if she were being used. She pulled back, frightened.

"What's the matter? You teasin' me?"

"No, Duke, I'm not teasing you. You just surprise me sometimes. I mean, I'm not—"

"You're not grateful? For all I've done for you? Come on, babe. There's plenty we can do for one another." As he spoke he stepped toward her and put his arms around her, his hands sliding down her back, caressing her buttocks, pulling her against his erection, which was all too apparent beneath his trousers. She felt her long-pent-up passion begin to respond and she was afraid, afraid that once more she would lose control of her life.

"Duke, I'm grateful for all you've done, but . . ." Hannah gasped out, pushing him away. She picked up the glass of whiskey he'd poured for her and took a big swallow.

"But what? Either you're grateful or you're not. And if you are, you have a way of showing it."

"But . . ." She hesitated, then took another swallow from the glass, stalling while she looked for the right words. There was something so menacing about Duke sometimes.

He sat back on the sofa and took a cigarette out of his gold case and lit it. "But what? Maybe you don't want to receive any more bonus payments from me? Maybe you don't think you have a good deal worked out with old Duke here?" he said, his voice rising threateningly. "Maybe I should be giving all that extra money to the family fund instead of that nice little bank account you set up for yourself?"

He leaned forward. "Is that daughter of yours causing trouble? I told you to marry her off before she caught on." He stopped, caught by an unpleasant thought. "Or is it that you're going to double-deal me?" As fast as a striking snake, his hand reached up and grabbed Hannah's arm, twisting it painfully. "Is that it?" he asked.

"Duke, no—"

"What's going on here?" Ron West stood in the kitchen doorway. "Let go of her arm . . . like the gentleman you aren't."

Duke spun around at Ron's words. "Who the hell do you think you are, barging in—?"

"Mother, what's happening?" Josie asked, following her fiancé into the room.

Ron stopped in front of Duke. "I'm her future son-in-law, that's who I am. And I have every intention of making sure she's at the wedding in one piece."

"You'd better watch what you're doing, sonny."

Ron glowered. "I know what I'm doing. I'm kicking you out of here."

"You can't do that," he said menacingly.

"I can and I am," Ron said, reaching out for him.

Duke spun around, his hand reaching into his coat. "Think twice before crossing me, farmer-boy. There's more where I come from—"

"Stop it! Both of you!" Josie cried, stepping between them. "This has gone far enough. Mother and I want you both to leave, don't we, Mother?"

Hannah nodded, her eyes round with fear.

"Ron," Josie continued, "you go out the back door to your car, and Duke, you leave by the front."

"Josie—" Ron protested.

"I mean it, Ron," she said, trying to hide the tremor in her voice.

"And I mean it, too," Hannah said, stepping to her daughter's side. "Duke, when you leave, I want to see your taillights turn to the right and continue on. Ron, I want to see yours turning left. Now both of you, please leave. Now."

Duke glanced at Ron, then at Hannah. Straightening his coat, he grabbed his hat and went out the front door. Ron reluctantly followed his example and left through the back.

Josie and her mother waited until they heard the two car doors slam, then walked to the front window and watched as two pairs of red lights drove down the road and turned in the proper directions. Josie didn't leave the window until Duke's lights were out of sight.

"Now, Mother," she said, turning to Hannah. "Will you please explain what he was talking about when we came in? Why is that slick thug trying to get rid of me before I cause trouble?"

"He's not a thug, and I don't have to answer to you."

"You do when slime like that is telling you to get me out of my own home. Did you see him? He was going for a gun. How can you associate with—"

"Nonsense. I would have felt . . ." Hannah stopped, wondering if she *had* felt a bulge at the back of his coat.

Josie looked her mother in the eye. "Are you skimming profits from all the operations, or just the farm?"

"I'm meticulous with the family books. This is a private arrangement between Duke and me."

Josie wasn't fooled. "Are you really holding money back from the family? You know if you'd only ask for what you need I'm sure Grandmother would approve it. What's going on?"

"How can you possibly understand? Your grandmother is just as likely to leave everything to Nell or some charity as she is to look out for her own kin. I have to take care of myself. I have no way of supporting myself," Hannah said, pouring herself another tumbler of whiskey. "You're still young. You're doing what you want to do. You're not trapped."

"Mother, what are you talking about?"

"I'm talking about looking in the mirror and seeing wrinkles and knowing that I'll never know love. I'll never know what it's like to reach my potential, to live my dreams. My chance is gone unless I grab it now." She took a deep drink from the glass. "You'd never understand. You've been spoiled and coddled all your life. You've gone to school and made something of yourself—unless you throw it all away. That seems to run in the family, too."

"Mother, what are you talking about? Are you drunk?"

"If I'm not now, I soon will be." She buried her face in her hands for a moment, then started pacing across the room, touching the wall like a caged tiger before turning back to face Josie once more, her face twisted with emotion. "I'm trapped! Trapped!" she screamed, throwing her empty glass against the hearth. "Can't you see?"

"Mother, stop it," Josie said, trying to take Hannah's arm. "Let's not talk about it now. Wait until morning and then—"

Her words were cut off as Hannah slapped her across the cheek. "Don't patronize me!" she shrieked.

Words stuck in Hannah's throat. Her hands were shaking uncontrollably.

Josie stood there, her face stinging from the blow. "May I help you to bed?" she asked.

"I can take care of myself." Hannah walked uncertainly to

343

the stairs, then paused. "Are you going to tell the others about this?" Her old defiance was edging back into her voice. "I doubt they'd believe you. They know how we've been fighting lately."

Josie shook her head in disbelief. "I don't know, Mother. I don't want to fight with you. I'd just like to understand you."

"You always favored your father because he spoiled you."

"That's not it at all, Mother. You cut me off like you did Dad. I can't imagine being married to a man and not sharing the same bedroom with him for all those years. I can't imagine resenting my own mother for the fortune she'd rightfully earned. I can't imagine driving everyone who loves me away with my bitter ways. And"—she bit her lip and walked to the window—"I can't imagine staying here any longer. I'm leaving."

"Sure, leave!" Hannah cried after her. "*You* can!"

Josie backed her car out of the carriage house, which had been converted into a garage. She knew where she was going, and she wouldn't need to take anything with her. She was going to her grandmother's in Portland, where she always went when she was unhappy and confused. The two-hour drive would do her good. She needed to think.

Fee had given her a Stutz Bearcat sports car upon graduation from law school. It was the talk of the town and Josie's joy. She loved to drive it wide open down the highway, her hair blowing in the wind, the trees spinning away on either side. Now, in the cool of the late winter, she had the top on and the window flaps down, but the countryside still passed in a blur. Lit by the pale glow from the instrument panel, she was in her own world, able to think.

She'd been shocked by her mother. She'd tried all her life to understand the unhappy, distant woman who'd raised her, but Hannah had never let her own daughter get close to her. Tonight, for the first time, she'd seen what was behind her mother's façade.

She had so many decisions to make—decisions that would affect so many people, that would determine how the rest of her life would go.

Should she tell Fee of Hannah's apparent treachery? To whom did she owe her loyalty? Or was it just a simple matter of justice? Her law classes had taught her to report misdoings. That was what she was bound to do as an officer of the court. And yet her law classes hadn't considered what happened when your heart was torn. Besides, she still hadn't passed the bar. Maybe that gave her some moral leeway, Josie thought.

Who was she kidding? She knew she'd have to do something to make her mother put things right, or she'd have to report her.

That was what brought her to think about Ron. He was such a dear and would make a wonderful husband. But still, he wasn't . . . She shook her head and concentrated once more upon the highway. It didn't pay to think about that anymore.

But she had to. She couldn't help remembering Jacob. She'd known him all her life, but he'd been away at school while she was becoming a woman. Then she'd walked into his class at Willamette School of Law, and what began as a strong attraction soon became a deep, compelling love, a forbidden love for her professor.

Not only was he the only one who truly challenged her mentally, teaching her to think on her feet like no other, but their thoughts were so often in unison that soon it became a joke between them.

She'd known, after that first term when he became her adviser, that she wouldn't be able to resist if he should ever make any kind of advance. And she'd thought he felt the same powerful attraction. Until he'd left.

She'd found him in his office at the end of her first year in law school, packing his books.

"What're you doing?" she'd asked.

"Leaving." It caused her pain even to remember the finality in his voice.

"How can you?" she'd cried, running impulsively to him. "I don't think I could . . . do very well without you."

"You'll do much better." There'd been pain in his eyes as he'd sat down, motioning for her to sit in the chair opposite him. "Josie, you know I'm Jewish, the same as my grandfather and father before me. The same as all my ancestors for thousands of years."

"What does that have to do with—"

"A lot. It sets up barriers. Personal ones. This may be 1924, but people don't approve of 'mixed couples.' Not here." He paused and she held her breath, hopeful, yet dreading what he might say next. "Then there's the family back East. My father thinks it would help me a great deal if I went back there and worked in my uncles' law firm, helped out with the family businesses. He's right. It would be good experience. I'm taking a sabbatical from teaching for two years."

"But—I'll be gone by the time you come back," she'd blurted out.

"I know."

That was all the indication she'd had. Looking back on it, she knew in her heart that he'd loved her as deeply as she'd loved him. But he'd made his decision without her. And it was final. She'd been angry with him, angry and hurt. Then she'd come to accept the inevitability of it. Maybe he'd been right after all.

Even now, she could clearly picture her mentor, for that was what she'd convinced herself he was. But could he have been the love she'd once fantasized? In the dark of the night she could see his deep brown eyes looking at her, and her heart turned over with the remembered feeling of being engulfed in their depths. She remembered his lean athletic figure as he wrote on the blackboard, his dark hair, which tended to be a bit rumpled, and the intense way he looked as he cut through her arguments and suggested a new thesis. The memory sent shivers down her spine, and she forced her attention back to the road. She was going too fast again.

It was simply a schoolgirl crush, she reasoned. A crush at twenty-three, but a crush nevertheless.

There was no hope, so she'd had to force it from her mind. Besides, now there was Ron.

She remembered sitting as a shy teenager, watching Ron race her brother at the Fourth of July picnic. He was always there, part of her way of life, her community. Ron represented security and comfort to Josie. He was gentle and kind, ruggedly handsome with his broad, open face and sun-streaked hair.

He had became owner of his father's farm five years ago after a wagon accident had killed both his parents. Point West Farm joined the Barry-Balfour farm on the other side of what had once been Ezekial Edwards' old place. It would make a wonderful addition to the family lands. And all she had to do was marry it.

He was just what her mother said she should have. But Grandmother disagreed. She'd been petulant ever since Hannah had announced the engagement, insisting that Josie shouldn't marry someone who was so reasonable a match, as she'd described it. She kept telling Josie to find her soulmate, her one love. Who'd ever have thought Grandmother would be such a romantic?

She sighed with relief as Grandmother's driveway appeared in the column of light from her headlamps. The house was dark as she pulled into the driveway. She couldn't wait to be in her own room.

Josie crept around to the side of the house and rapped on Nell's bedroom window.

"I'm sorry to wake you," she said softly as Nell opened the door.

"Don't you worry about it, honey. Your mama on the rampage again?"

"Something like that. I'll just go on up to my room."

"Don't worry about getting up early for breakfast. We were up late tonight, too. Young Mr. Teall left just a coupla hours ago," Nell said as Josie started up the stairs.

Josie turned. "Jacob's back?"

"Big as life and twice as handsome." She smiled affectionately. "You sleep tight, now."

Suddenly all of Josie's problems seemed smaller. Jacob was back.

She pulled on her nightgown and crawled under the quilt of her bed, the same bed she'd slept in at Grandmother's house ever since she was a baby. It was her room, and she belonged here. Jacob was back. The pillow was soft and she was glad to be here. She was also glad she hadn't set a wedding date with Ron. Grandmother would understand. Jacob was back.

Chapter XXX

When he was flying he was free. With the wind in his face and the earth below, he was away from family squabbles and expectations, he was free from cloying females and demanding customers; he was his own man. And the frightening, exhilarating, confusing Great War was long ago and far away.

Emmett looked down, seeing the richness of the land passing in patchwork glory. His goggles, tinted to ease the glare of the sun, gave the already green landscape an emerald hue. First the rugged mountains and now the rich farm and ranchlands enchanted him on his flight to Pendleton in the northeastern corner of Oregon.

He felt so lucky to live here—to be here at all. Andrew hadn't been so lucky. He'd died a prolonged, painful death in a French hospital—and Emmett had watched helplessly. His best friend, his own cousin, had died while Emmett soared over enemy troops, grimly seeking revenge. Ever since then his longing for new horizons, which always had been part of his nature, had become a longing for escape. Flying gave him that escape.

That was why he took these jobs, making deliveries for "businessmen." They never told him what was in the boxes they loaded in the cargo compartment of his biplane, but it had to be bootleg liquor from Canada. That was the reason he was paid so well. Only danger would garner these wages, even for a pilot.

He spotted the dark rectangle cut between two greening hills of wheat. A truck was waiting. He buzzed it, received the white-flag all-clear signal, banked the plane, then set his wheels down on the makeshift landing strip.

Emmett climbed down from the cockpit as Mr. Smith and his associate Mr. Jones quickly unloaded the crates into the back of an old Ford farm truck.

When Emmett came back to the plane after stretching his legs, Jones handed him a thick envelope. "Making good time these days," he said while Emmett counted his pay. "Any problems?"

"Nope," Emmett said, tucking the envelope into an inside pocket of his flight jacket. He tied his silk scarf around his neck and climbed into the plane.

"By the way," Smith said, "we're going to have a big order come in end of August, first of September. Probably about five flights. Keep your schedule open."

"No problem," Emmett said with a wave as he gestured for him to turn the prop. Jones stood by to remove the wheel blocks.

Fools, Emmett thought. *There's always a big shipment come time for the Pendleton Round-Up. You bet I'll keep that open.*

"Let 'er buck!" he called as Jones pulled the blocks. He grinned as he lifted off. They smiled and returned his jaunty wave.

It was too late in the day to go back across the mountains, but that was the way he'd planned it. He banked and cut across the undulating wheat fields, greening with their new crop of gold. Neat farmhouses and outbuildings were tucked into every other corner of each section of land. People out here dealt with vast amounts of land and wide-open spaces. It made for good agriculture and easy bootlegging.

Somewhere just beyond the Blue Mountains he could look down and see where the family land began. First there were the rolling wheat farms, then the more rugged cattle range, then the fenced ranchland, the neatly arranged buildings, bunkhouse, barns, and ranch house, all laid out by Grandfather over sixty years ago. To the west and south, as far as the California border, there were three other cattle ranches, but this, the first, was Emmett's favorite.

He buzzed the farmhouse and then, seeing small figures come out the door of the bunkhouse, he sighted on the macadam road five miles away, banked, and headed straight for it.

There was no traffic, and he was able to land on the first pass. A gravel pull-off intersected the road, just for his purposes. He taxied about half a mile from the highway before cutting the engine and climbing down from the cockpit.

The heavy silence following the roar of the engine was broken only by the bawling of a distant cow. He shoved blocks under the wheels, ran a couple of tie lines from the plane to two juniper trees, then sauntered over to a rock to sit and wait.

Picking a twig from a sagebush, he crushed the leaves between his fingers, smelling the acrid spice of their fragrance. Somewhere around here his grandparents had come through with their wagon train. Near here his beginnings were laid.

He breathed deeply, listening to the piercing cry of a Townsend Solitaire from a nearby juniper tree. Watching patiently, he caught a flip of the secretive bird's tail. He whistled an answer to its call.

As dusk came, he heard the distant cry of a coyote just as he spotted headlights coming down the road. He got up and walked towards the highway.

"Hey! Emmett!" the tall man called, jumping down from the truck and running to him. "You should let me know ahead of time and I'll have someone waiting for you!" He grabbed Emmett in an enthusiastic bear hug and Emmett, laughing, returned it.

"And give you time to prepare some kind of surprise?

Never. It's better to catch you off guard. That way you won't bushwhack me for that last poker game."

Mateo's face filled with sudden chagrin. "Emmett, I would never do anything like that. If I'm going to give you what you deserve, it will be when I can watch." He smiled, pleased with his joke. "Come, I brought the tarp this time. You see, I'm learning."

"It's good to see you, Mateo. How're things going?" he asked as he took one side of the canvas and climbed on the wing to help spread it over the plane.

His back was turned so he couldn't see Mateo's face, but he knew his friend well enough to sense something wasn't quite right when he heard him speak with false bravado. "Things are fine, my friend, just fine."

Emmett looked at him sharply as he crawled down from the wing and joined him at the truck. One of the most handsome men Emmett had ever met—a true "tall, dark, and handsome"—Mateo was also the most unassuming and ingenuous. Lying was not his forte.

"So what's going on?" he asked as Mateo turned the truck around and they headed back to the ranch. "Anything of interest?"

"Not really. Calving time. Some old bossies keep trying to go off and find a secret corner to drop their calves. Of course, those usually are the ones with complications. Most of the hands are worn out from chasing them down. I tell you, my friend, you've not lived until you've wallowed in the cold mud and reached inside a cow to try and turn around a stubborn young bull that's too big for his mother in the first place."

"When you driving them up to the summer range?"

"Probably the first part of June. You coming?"

"Wouldn't miss it."

It was apparent that Mateo wasn't going to tell Emmett outright what was bothering him. He'd just keep his eyes open.

It didn't take long. As they were driving up to the ranch house, the headlights of the truck caught on what looked like a burnt fence post in the middle of the yard.

"What the hell's that?" he asked.

"I'd hoped you wouldn't see," Mateo admitted. "It's nothing, really."

"Nothing? Then why did you hope I wouldn't see it?"

"Because it would upset you far more than it does me."

He sighed. "We had some night visitors last night. They left a small entertainment for us, a burning cross."

"Damn! Why is the Klan coming all the way out here?"

"I offer a perfect target for them," he said simply. "First, in case you've forgotten, I'm a foreigner. They say that foreigners are ruining the country, and they aim to drive them away. And I'm the worst kind. They don't even know where the hell Cuba is," he added. "Second, as the local newspaper says, it's mainly a religious organization." His voice was emotionless as he stated the facts. "And out here where there are few other targets, it's a fair definition. They are all for white, male Protestants. Unfortunately, I was raised to be Catholic, and I continue practicing my religion. A foreign Catholic—the combination is unforgivable, as a crusty old preacher by the name of Clyman keeps telling them. Says he's the son of pure pioneers and no one else has a right to be here."

He opened the door and gestured for Emmett to follow him in. "Smells like dinner's ready. You always seem to time your arrivals perfectly."

"I'm no fool."

Later, as the dinner dishes were cleared and they sat lingering over their coffee, Emmett leaned back in his chair, grinning impishly. "You have any idea why Grandmother gave you this job?"

Mateo gestured expansively. "Because I'm the best ranch foreman in the Western Hemisphere."

"I know that, but I doubt that she did when she brought you out of Cuba when you were fourteen. What was the real reason?"

"I'm not sure," he answered quietly. "It was something my mother arranged."

"How did she know my grandmother?"

"It was never clear to me. My mother was ill most of my life. Tuberculosis. Somehow she managed to send me to the best boarding schools in Cuba. As a result I didn't know her well—only saw her on vacations. Then, right before she died, she told me there was this wonderful woman who wanted me to come to the United States and work for her. She said I was never to question her generosity, just to trust." He shrugged. "That's all I know. Why?"

"I just think that it sounds—well, sort of mysterious. I'll bet there's more to it than that. I'll bet that our families have some kind of fascinating history."

Mateo laughed. "You've been reading too many dime novels. But, if you must know, I've been curious myself. And if you want to think that we're somehow connected, it's fine with me. Now, come, my *compadre*, I have something to show you in the barn."

Just then he noticed a young, dark-eyed woman standing shyly to the side of the door. "Are you ready to go home, Louisa?" Mateo asked.

"Yes, sir."

"Then get Tiny Hogberg. He'll escort you tonight."

As she left the room, Emmett asked, "What's that about?"

"Louisa has the same liabilities I do. Her family emigrated from Italy six years ago, and they've hardly two pennies to rub together because they can't get work in town. I've hired her on as cook. Heard about her through the priest at church."

"I see. KKK strikes again?"

"They might."

"I think I would like to take a ride with Tiny."

"Come on, Emmett. Don't go looking for—"

"I'm not, Mateo. I just think that having one of the owners along on the ride might give a certain authority to—"

"All right, all right," Mateo interrupted. "Maybe you're right. Maybe I am, but I know you well enough to know that no matter what I say I won't change your mind."

There was a clumping of boots on the front porch and Tiny ducked his head and came in the door. Emmett knew why Mateo had chosen him as Louisa's escort. He was as big as two regular men put together, stretching up to almost six feet, eight inches tall. His frame matched his height, and his Indian grandmother had given him a dark, glowering visage.

"Tiny," Emmett said, getting up and extending his hand, "I think you've grown another foot since I've seen you last. Old Button must be proud of you."

"Good to see you, Em," he said, enclosing Emmett's hand in his.

"Mind if I tag along tonight?"

"Nope. Truck's out by the barn." Louisa emerged from the kitchen and followed them out the door.

As they reached the truck, Tiny pulled a pistol and holster out from behind the seat and handed it to Emmett. "Might want to strap this on," he said.

"Oh, come on, Tiny. Surely you don't think—"

Tiny turned and looked at him. Emmett strapped on the gun.

Tiny drove in silence, while Louisa nervously fidgeted with the strings of her apron. After a few brief attempts at conversation, Emmett lapsed into longer silences, staring out the window at the night-shadowed landscape.

"You have any trouble before—taking her home?" he asked.

"Not yet."

"My pa," Louisa whispered, "some's been talking bad to him. Saying he should go back to Torino and take me with him."

Emmett nodded. He could see stars over the Blue Mountains. The headlights caught the lines of fence posts as they bounced along the road. Then, as they came out of a ravine about five miles out of town, there was a car parked across the road.

"What's that?" Emmett asked.

"What we've been trying to avoid," Tiny said, pulling on the brake. "What's the matter, fellas?" he asked, opening the door and standing on the running board. "Road out?"

"It is for you," came a voice from behind the headlights. Then five armed, white-robed, hooded figures stepped forward. "We're not after you, Tiny," he said. "We just think you should go back to your own and help us keep our country white and free. Leastwise, not escorting foreigners around at night."

Emmett stepped out of the truck and walked in front of the lights. "Hey, fellas, what put a burr under your saddle?" he asked. "I go away for a while and now my old friends won't even show their faces to me."

"Howdy, Emmett," one of the figures said. "Didn't know you were around. This ain't your problem. Just let us take care of our business and all will be fine."

" 'Fraid it is my problem, men. See, these people here work for my family," he explained, resting his foot on the front bumper. "I feel an obligation to take care of my own. You can understand that. Now, if you'll be good enough to show me your faces, maybe we can talk man to man. That is, unless you're afraid."

Two of the men stepped back hesitantly, but one stepped forward. "I'm not afraid to show my face to the likes of you. You got Coughlin blood tainting your veins like all the rest." He reached up and pulled off his hood, revealing the sagging face of a bitter, middle-aged man.

"Thought it might be you, Zenas Slead," Emmett said. "Glad to see you. Saves me the effort of riding over to your

353

place tomorrow. Seems you've been letting your sheep stray on to our range, fouling up the springs. You fellows know sheep and cattle don't mix. I'm thinking it's just because you've been so busy going around wearing sheets that you didn't notice. Guess now you know about it, you'll take care of it."

Emmett paused, then added, "You know, I don't have much taste for mutton myself. But I happen to know that the children at the Indian School just love it, and they're pretty hungry lots of the time. They can put the wool to good use, too. Just want you to know, your sheep get on our land again, you've just given a donation to the Indian School. Every last one that sets hoof over my line. Now, don't you worry none. I'll make sure that they send you a right nice letter of thanks."

The other men chuckled, but Zenas Slead bristled with hatred. "You do that and I'll have your hide," he said with a snarl.

"You and who else?" Emmett asked with a pleasant smile. He nodded to the others and said, "Now, fellas, if you've finished with your costume parade, maybe you'll move your car so we can go on about our business."

"You quit taking up with foreigners and Pope-worshipers!" Slead yelled. "It's unpatriotic! We got to rid ourselves . . ."

Emmett stepped forward until he was looking Slead in the eye and then said with deadly quiet, "Don't talk to me about patriotism. While you were here raking in war profits, I was fighting the Hun. While you were sitting on your fat butt smoking cigars, my cousin was dying because he defended your right to do just that. Now, I want that car moved and I don't want to see or hear any more of this again. Is that clear?"

Slead stepped back, blustering and fuming. "You can't come here and bully me . . ." he said, reaching into his car window.

There was a click, and his hand froze. He looked back at Tiny. The big man had raised the shotgun he'd been carrying at his side. It was leveled at Slead's head.

Slead climbed into his car and slammed the door. "Let's get out of here," he told the others. They needed no further urging. The car doors slammed, and Slead ground the gears as he turned around in the road. "I'll get you for this," he said with a growl.

Tiny grunted his approval as Emmett walked back to the truck.

354

"Nice seeing you again, Em," one of the men called amiably. "You all come round before you leave."

"Thanks, Jack," Emmett called back, recognizing his voice. Louisa was crying softly. "Don't worry," he said as Tiny pushed the starter, "they won't bother you anymore. I'll go into town tomorrow, and that should be the end of it." He swallowed hard to make the bile stay down. It was the same anger he'd felt after Andrew had died. And he'd killed because of it.

"Slead teethed on hate," Tiny said.

"Yeah, something to do with our grandfathers and his father. You'd think he could let it all go."

"Not his kind. We'll have to take care of him before this is all over."

Emmett nodded. " 'Fraid so, Tiny. One way or the other."

Hannah had already talked to Sam about the spring plantings, gone over the farm accounts, and listened to the farm market report on the radio. It was only nine in the morning, and here she was watching dust motes float in the sunlight streaming between the lace curtains. Surely there was more to life than this, but just now she couldn't think of what it could possibly be.

Ever since Josie had steamed out of the house four days ago, it had seemed even more lonely. Despite the fact that she had trouble getting along with her daughter, at least she brought some life to the house. Hannah sat down at the piano and morosely picked out a tune. Then, her attention caught, she pulled out some sheet music and began to lose herself in Beethoven's *Sonata Pathétique in C Minor,* wallowing in the plaintive melodic line and completely underplaying the more hopeful and persistent counter-melody.

She was just finishing the first movement when her concentration was interrupted by footsteps on the porch. She hadn't even heard a car drive up. Duke's figure was silhouetted against the frosted glass window in the door, and she felt a dichotomous twinge of dread and pleasure.

"Hey, baby," he said as she opened the door. "Miss me?" He put his arm around her waist and kissed her firmly on the mouth.

"I'd about given up on you," she said, taking his hat. "Did you go out of town?"

"Yeah, and I've got some great news. Got some coffee? I've been up half the night just to get back."

Hannah poured him a cup of coffee and offered him some homemade nutbread. He slurped the hot coffee, then leaned back on the sofa. "You know how you're always complaining about not having any money of your own so's you can clear outta this place?"

Hannah nodded.

"Well, I got a way out for you. My company's authorized me to buy that worthless bit of land. And," he added, anticipating her protest, "they authorized me to give you a finder's fee for coming up with it. Your family will be rid of a hunk of land they don't use. My company'll have a place they can keep on using for their experiments, and you'll have your getaway money. How's that sound?"

"Well, I don't know. I'll have to talk to everyone, of course, especially Mother."

"Come on, you can handle the old lady. And the others. You've got it made if you put your mind to it." He pulled her closer to him, kissing her ear and letting his hand wander down her blouse. " 'Sides, you be nice to me, I'll be nice to you. How about it? We'll do the world together, babe."

Hannah's breath caught in her throat, and she couldn't help stiffening. Her desire was rising, taking over her better sense. And she felt the walls closing in on her once more.

Luckily, she was saved by the sound of a car crunching the gravel outside the house. "It sounds like someone is here," she said with relief.

"Damn," he cursed under his breath. "I made sure your brat was still in Portland. Who is it this time?"

"My brother Timothy," she said, looking out the window.

"Good. Talk to him about my offer. He's always looking out for a fast buck. He'll go for it. I'll go so's you can talk to him straight," he said, getting up from the sofa.

"Tell you what, babe," he added as he took his hat, "I'll come back Saturday night and we'll do the town. Take you to hear a great band playing in Portland. Make a night of it, so wear something glamorous with that coat I gave you." He gave her a quick kiss on the cheek, threw his coat over his shoulder, and opened the door to Timothy. "How're you doing, Tim, old boy?" he said jovially as he brushed past him and down the steps.

"Still seeing him?" Timothy said with mild interest as he came in. "Be a good kid and get me some coffee, will you?"

"What brings you out here?"

"Oh, figured I'd better check in on my little sis. I don't get to see you much anymore."

"What's the real reason?"

"Don't be such a cynic. It's not becoming in a woman."

Hannah laughed dryly. "I'm a realist. You never come out here unless you want something."

"Well, you're right," he admitted, "I did happen to have something on my mind—a little proposition for you.

"You know how Mother is so tightfisted about supporting my political campaign?" He shook his head in disgust. "She says she expects great leadership from her son, great things," he said, waving his arm expansively. "Then she won't even cough up the dough to support her dreams. Says I have to earn it myself. Ha!" It was an old complaint, and Hannah nodded automatically.

"Well, now I've figured out how to do it. A timber firm approached me, asking to buy Old Round Top. Remember, that worthless mountain Father bought way back when? Well, these folks are foolish enough to want to try to log it. Let them try. We can turn a pretty penny and the whole family will be a bit fatter in the pocketbook. What do you say? Back me up when I tell Mother about it?"

"You're crazy, Timothy. You know Mother's sentimental about that. Father used to go up there all the time, said it was the only place left in the West where he could find the old wilderness. He took you up there once, didn't he?"

"Yes, and I came home filthy dirty and covered with mosquito bites, scratches, and scrapes from climbing around like a heathen. You can't sleep on rocks and sticks, but that's what our father thought he should do half his life. He was snoring away like a babe and I was waiting to be eaten alive. I swear, he didn't hear a single one of those sounds the wild beasts made that night."

"You weren't his best disciple for the great outdoors, were you?" Hannah said, laughing. She paused, enjoying her brother's discomfort. "It's so steep," she mused. "Besides, any firm offering to buy it has to be a direct competitor with our logging firm. Who's your buyer?"

"S&R Logging."

"You must be crazy! All the owners are members of the KKK. You know how Mother feels about them. They may have great political clout, but don't think you can hand over Mother's favorite piece of land to them."

"Ah, come on, Hannah, they aren't that bad."

"Maybe you're forgetting the Tealls. They've been our friends since the beginning, and they're Jewish. Remember the burning of the synagogue in Portland, the marches, the threats? KKK isn't just a political group, Timothy, they're bigots, and that's one thing Mother won't tolerate."

"I don't know why you're so fussy. Hanging out with the likes of Duke DeCarlo."

"I hardly think there's any comparison. A man who's running a legitimate feed business, and people who wear masks and ride around—"

"Ha! That's a good one, Sis. Great act. But it doesn't work with me. Your old Duke has some pretty powerful connections of his own. I was even thinking of talking to him, lining up support from his kind, too."

"I don't know what you're talking about."

"Sure you don't," he said, still laughing at her as he got up. "When you think about it, you'll help me convince Mother to sell the timberland. The money is too good to turn down."

"I doubt that we can get Mother even to listen to any offers. Besides, I think it's sort of nice to save a piece of land like that. Romantic."

"I'll bet what you could do with the money would be more romantic," he said, knowing Hannah's weakness.

"No matter what I could do with it, " she snapped, "Mother won't hear of it. You might as well put it out of your mind."

"Well, it would be nice if I could get a little help from you," he said, his voice raising in anger.

"She'll know you're just trying to finance your political ambitions. Why don't you just come out and ask her?"

"The same reason why you don't ask her for money for your schemes," he said with a growl. "She doesn't approve of some of my goals any more than she approves of some of your company. She'd hit the roof if she knew you were shacking up with that Duke."

"I'm not—"

"You should consider the consequences if you don't help me out in this little thing. She pays attention to your opinion, feels you have a level head on your shoulders. Don't want to ruin your image, do you?" he said maliciously.

"Timothy, you're awful. You'd have been better off just reminding me of what I could do with the extra money without threatening to blackmail me."

"I'll come back and talk about it tomorrow. We're supposed to meet with Mother on Monday," he said, closing the door behind him.

Hannah sat on the sofa, listening to the car drive down the road. She tried to recall what he'd said, sensing that there was something she didn't understand. What had he been referring to? Why did his words sound so ominous?

"Damnit!" she exclaimed suddenly. "Why now? Why me?"

It seemed as if everyone was pressuring her, trying to get her to do something she wasn't sure of, tempting her.

She went back to the piano. Sometimes things sorted themselves out while she played. She had to play from memory because tears blinded her vision.

Ron had been perfectly willing to meet Josie for dinner at a nice restaurant, but when she suggested they go to a roadhouse to the east of Portland, he rebelled.

"It's not right for you to frequent places like that."

"What do you mean, not right for me? Half of Portland does. Besides, I hear there's a terrific jazz band playing. From St. Louis. They're only here for a week. Everyone's talking about them."

Although he continued grumbling, Ron gave in. They were driving her roadster; she'd insisted that he leave his truck at the restaurant and take the car—it'd be more fun. Josie ignored his complaining and told herself she'd have fun whether Ron wanted her to or not.

They hadn't been in the dark, smoky roadhouse for more than five minutes when the band—four black men playing piano, drums, clarinet, and trumpet—stopped for a break. However, Josie was sold. She clapped loudly and appreciatively, then ordered a drink.

"Hey, Sis, what're you doing here?" Emmett said as he pulled up a chair.

"Emmett! You're back in town. See, Ron, I told you everyone would be here. Are you alone?"

"Nah, there's a gang over there in the corner."

"Let me guess. Your date's the blonde with the bee-sting lips."

"How'd you know?"

Josie laughed delightedly at his surprised expression. "I know my brother," she exclaimed. "The band isn't finished, is it? They're great."

"No, they have a couple more sets to do. Here," he said, motioning behind them, "when you like something, tell them."

359

The short black trumpeter came over to their table. "Augustine Jackson, I want you to meet one of your fans—my sister, Josephine. Josie, Augustine. Known as Gus to his friends."

"Gus, I'm glad to meet you," Josie said, extending her hand. "You were just great up there. I was afraid I came too late, but Emmett says no."

"It's a pleasure to meet you, ma'am," Gus said in a deep voice. "Anyone who's related to Em here has to be good folks. I'll play something special just for you when we start up."

"Boy, when he says that—" Emmett's comment was interrupted by a loud buzzer sounding over the bar. "Uh-oh."

"Feds!" yelled the bartender. "Everyone stay calm," he said as a woman screamed. "We got everything covered. Just stay where you are and the crew will take care of it." As he spoke, he began cranking a handle beside the back bar. Josie could hear a sliding behind the wall.

"This is great," Emmett said. "They got this whole back wall that just slides back. Watch this." As he spoke, the waitresses quickly took the glasses of liquor from the tables and replaced them with empty glasses, bottles of soda pop, and plates of stale cookies.

Josie shushed Ron's urging that they run out the back door and watched in fascination.

The bar swiveled on a central pivot, momentarily revealing a glimpse out-of-doors exposed by the sliding wall. When the turning stopped, the bar and its contents were hidden from view and its back side was facing the room. It was now a breakfront with cups and saucers and a two-burner hot plate complete with teapot and coffeepot. The bartender plugged in the hot plate, rolled the outside wall back in place, and turned to inspect the room. Everyone was sitting at the tables, sipping soda, ready to listen to the band. He smiled, and the room broke into spontaneous applause at the rapid transformation. It had taken less than three minutes.

Just then the door opened and a man burst in, gasping for breath. "It's not the Feds," he shouted. "It's the Klan! Get the niggers out of here fast or we'll have a necktie party!"

Confusion took over. Two women screamed. Chairs scraped and fell to the floor as people stood up, looking out the window.

"I got room for the drums and two of 'em in the back of my truck," one man called out, rushing to the stage. "Who'll take the other two?"

360

"I'll put one under the seat of my sedan," said a man nearby. Three band members followed them out the back door.

"I'll take the other," Josie said, pushing Ron's arm away as he tried to quiet her.

"Good going, Sis," Emmett said. "Gus, go out and get in the rumble seat of that cream-colored Stutz Bearcat." He looked out the window. "They're coming up the hill now. Josie and I'll create a diversion to give you time to get in and close it behind you."

"Are you crazy?" Ron protested.

"Ron, there's no time for arguing. Just follow our lead," Josie said, getting up. Gus dashed for the back door, and Emmett, ignoring Ron's protests, quickly gave Josie his idea.

They went to the door and stood there listening.

"Sophie," the bartender said to one of the waitresses, "go over there and play the piano."

"I ain't played nowhere 'cept in church," she protested.

"Good. Give us a hymn."

As she began playing the first chords, Emmett opened the door and stepped out. "What the—?" he exclaimed.

Josie was right behind him. As soon as she spotted the hooded figures, she let out a bloodcurdling scream and feigned a faint into Ron's arms.

"Omigod! Josie!" Emmett cried, patting her face. "What the hell's going on here?" he demanded over his shoulder. "What kind of fools are you, scaring the daylights out of my sister?" He turned and faced the men. "You all ought to be horsewhipped for this," he shouted, picking up Josie's limp figure.

"Sorry about the lady," one voice said.

"We got more important work tonight," said another with a growl. "Outta the way. If you weren't out here where you shouldn't be, she wouldn't'a been scared anyway."

They brushed on past them and Emmett turned, shouting, "Hooligans! Scaring decent citizens out of their wits when they meet together to sing hymns." The hooded figures stopped in the doorway as the first tremulous voices joined the piano.

Emmett set Josie down when they got around the corner. "Good job. Now let's get rolling," he whispered.

Josie knocked at the rumble seat and got a reassuring rap in response, then sat on Ron's lap.

"You're both a couple of goddamn fools and I won't allow

this to happen again," Ron said as Emmett took off down the road.

"Shut up, West," Emmett said. "And keep an eye on the rearview mirror for me."

"There's no reason why you should take a risk like this—"

"This is the second time this week I've had to deal with those bastards," Emmett said, ignoring Ron. "What'll we do with Gus back there?"

"Let's take him to Grandmother's. She won't mind, and there's no place safer. Are those headlights following us, Ron?"

"Yes. Your adventuring is going to get your sister—"

"It's just the other two cars," Emmett said. "There were five Klan cars, and only two are following us."

"Damn!" Ron exclaimed, hitting his hand against the dashboard. "I don't want any wife of mine gallivanting—"

"Then you're lucky you don't have a wife," Josie said coldly. They rode in silence the rest of the way to Portland.

Josie directed Emmett to the restaurant where Ron had left his truck, and they let him off. "Josie," he said, leaning in the window, "we'd better talk about this. We need an understanding—"

"Only if there's a future for us to understand," Josie said. "You're sadly mistaken if you think you're engaged to a meek little woman who's going to stay at home in your kitchen all day and mend your shirts and chase after your children."

"Now is not the time to talk about this," he said.

"You're right," she answered, and closed the window.

Emmett laughed as he turned the car around and drove towards their grandmother's house. "You know, Sis, you got more going for you than all the rest of the women in the whole state—with the possible exception of Grandmother."

"Thanks," she said. "Best compliment I could get."

They were still laughing as they helped Gus out of the rumble seat and walked up the front porch steps.

"You sure your granny don't mind chocolate-flavored guests?"

"Don't be silly, Gus," Josie said, opening the door. She stopped. Her breath caught in her throat. She was face to face with Jacob Teall.

"Well, hello," he said. "I didn't expect to see you here."

"Hello, Jacob," she said softly. "I heard you were back."

"Jacob!" shouted Emmett, "you old SOB! What nerve you have, coming back to town and not calling your best friend."

362

"False accusation," Jacob said. "I tried, but you've been out of town ever since I arrived. I think it was planned."

Josie stood, listening to their exchange. How could any man be so strikingly handsome, she thought. How could she have forgotten the power he had over her? She caught sight of her grandmother coming around the corner to witness the reunion and realized that she was bracing herself against the doorjamb like a cornered cat.

"Grandmother," she said, forcing a smile, "you may have had a surprise for us, but we have a surprise for you, too. This is Augustine Jackson. He's our houseguest for the night."

"If that is acceptable with you, ma'am," he said softly.

"I'm pleased to meet you, Mr. Jackson," Fee said, extending her hand. "Of course you're welcome. All my children's friends are. Please come in. You know, I haven't seen a five dollar gold-piece like that in years," she said, noting Gus's watch fob.

"That's my good luck piece, ma'am. My grandpappy was given that by what he called our angel. He was escapin' the slavers with his family and this lady on a wagon train gave him money. This was all they had left when they got to Canada."

Fee looked at him in silence, then quietly asked, "Do you know if that was about twenty-five miles into Kansas?"

Gus looked surprised. "Sure was. The first free state they'd hit. But how'd you? . . ."

Fee smiled. "I'm just glad to hear a happy ending to the story. Mr. Coughlin would have been pleased."

Then before Gus recovered, she turned and said, "Jacob, you can't go now that the party is just beginning. Put your hat and coat away and come join us."

Jacob glanced at Josie, then smiled at Fee. "I'm afraid I'll have to take a rain check," he said. "You've given me enough work to keep me busy until late next week."

With that he turned and left, nodding good-bye to Josie and exchanging friendly insults with Emmett.

Josie stood in the entryway while the others moved to the parlor. Why was her heart beating so loudly, she wondered as she watched Jacob's car leave the drive.

"Is something the matter, dear?" Fee asked.

"Oh, she had a spat with Ron," Emmett said. "He doesn't approve of headstrong women."

"Then he's got his hands full," Fee said with a knowing
363

smile. "We'll talk about it later, dear," she said to Josie. "Now come on in and tell me why Mr. Jackson says you're a heroine."

Chapter XXXI

It was the first warm day of spring, and the air was lilac-sweet. Restless, Josie got a basket and shears from Nell and went into the garden. She was retreating from everyone these days, even avoiding talking to Grandmother. She wasn't even on good terms with herself.

Overnight the dogwood had suspended delicate white blossoms the entire length of its spreading limbs. She paused under its branches, listened to the drone of a honey bee, then reached up and clipped three sprigs.

"Josie?"

Ron was standing hesitantly behind her. "Oh, Ron," she said, putting the basket down on the grass, "I feel miserable . . ."

"Me too," he said, kissing her gently.

She rested her head on his chest. "Why does everything have to be so complicated?" she murmured.

"It isn't unless we make it that way."

She could hear his voice rumbling deep in his chest, the same voice she'd heard as a schoolgirl, and she felt safe and protected.

"Josie, let's set the date. Then I can hold you all night, every night. We'll be together always. Besides," he said, "your grandmother deserves to see her great-grandchildren. If you wait too long, she won't even be at the wedding. You know, she seems weaker each time I see her."

He made sense. It sounded so simple—so tempting. That did seem to be the way it should be. All Josie's school chums were married. And most had at least one child, a fact that had effectively isolated her from almost all female company, with the exception of her mother and grandmother.

"Maybe we should talk," she murmured.

"That's my girl," he said, visibly relieved. "We'll talk to your mother tomorrow morning. Together." He took her hand, and they strolled up the expansive lawn.

"You know," he said, "I'm going to talk to your mother

about that Duke. I don't trust the guy. Something strange is going on, something your mother has no idea about."

"You and me both, but I won't interfere with my mother's life any more than I let her interfere with mine."

"Even if it's dangerous? That creep is just too slick."

"It seems that the Barry-Coughlin women always have had difficulties with their men."

"Until now, you mean."

She smiled. "Maybe."

"What difficulties? We're getting married, aren't we?"

"I said we'd talk about it."

"Damnit, Josie!" he exclaimed. "I wish you'd make up your mind. You keep running hot and cold with me. I need to get my life in order. Settle down, start a family—and I want to do it with you. We're not getting any younger, you know."

"I know. But I'm not sure if settling down, as you call it, is right for me. I may hurt you badly if I'm not careful."

He grinned. "I'll take my chances. Now let me see that pretty smile of yours. You've been too gloomy ever since last night. And that's another thing—"

"I don't think we should talk about it now, Ron."

"That's what you said then. I say we talk about it now."

"Very well, then," she said, sitting down on a patio chair, "but I don't think you'll like what you hear."

"And you probably won't like what I say," he admitted as he sat down on the marble bench. "I'm putting my foot down. I won't have you going places like last night and taking the chances you did."

"And I'm saying you have no right to tell me what to do, either now or after we're married. I'm an independent person with a mind of my own, and I won't be ruled by you or anyone else. I'm capable of making my own decisions—and my own mistakes. And when I'm acting on principle, out of conviction for what I believe, I *will* take chances. Either you accept that or you don't accept me."

He stood up, indignant. "I refuse to accept any ultimatums from you. Josie, I care for you too much to let you risk—"

"If you really care for me—instead of caring for what you imagine me to be—you won't carry this conversation any further. Now, let's go in the house and see Grandmother."

"This is not settled, Josie," he said, holding her by the arm. "It's too important a matter to be settled by your stubborn whims."

"Whims?" She spun around, facing him. "Is that what you think it was last night? It just goes to show how little you know me." She moved to leave, but his hand stopped her.

"Wait," he said. His voice was conciliatory. "We'll talk more later. I've got to go. See you tonight?"

"I don't know," she whispered. "I really don't know."

"We just need time together."

"No, I need time to think—alone."

He looked at her as if trying to understand a puzzle. "I love you, Josie," he said finally, then turned and left.

Josie took the dogwood branches into the kitchen and arranged them in a large black and pink Chinese vase.

Fee looked up from her newspaper as Josie came into the parlor. "Has Ron left?"

"Yes. He had to get back to the farm."

"Josie, you seem at loose ends these days. Are you studying for your bar exams yet?" Fee asked, casting a concerned look at her granddaughter.

Josie shook her head. "Oh, Grams. Ron and Mother think we should get married before I try to pass the bar."

"Nonsense."

"Well, Ron says that if I keep postponing the wedding, you'll never get to see us married—much less see your great-grandchildren."

"I hope I never live to see the day you marry Ron West."

"Grandmother!" Josie exclaimed, shocked.

"Well, it's true. If you marry him, you'll be making the biggest mistake of your life. You'll never fulfill your real potential. And you'll never practice law."

"Ron says I won't ever need to."

"Need! What does he know about need? I swear, that young man sounds as if he got his upbringing at Queen Victoria's knee. This is the twentieth century! He simply can't face the fact that women won't be locked in a house anymore—not that some of us ever were. You marry that man and you'll live to regret it the rest of your life. You'll end up just like your mother," she said.

"Oh, Grams," Josie said with tear-filled eyes. "I don't know what to do. I really do care for Ron. It's not like Mother was with Daddy. Ron's the only man I know that I feel so—so comfortable with, so at-home—"

"And that's what you want to be all your life? At home?"

"I don't know. I'd like to have children. A bright kitchen, chintz curtains, a soft baby, it all sounds so good. But I don't

366

know . . ." she admitted. "And time seems to be passing by so quickly."

"There, there," Fee said, reaching over and taking her hand. "Don't cry. You just take your time. Nothing's going to pass you by. Don't let anyone push you. But while you're making up your mind," she added, "why don't you fill your time with something constructive? That always helps. At least study for the exams."

Josie laughed through her tears. "Oh, Grams, that's what I love about you. You never give up."

"And don't you," Fee said, cradling her granddaughter's head on her shoulder. "Don't you."

Timothy waited impatiently for the lumberyard manager to close up. Why didn't the man stop stalling and leave?

"All closed up, Mr. Coughlin," the manager said finally, sticking his head in the doorway. "Can I help you with anything?"

"No, no," Timothy said with a wave of his hand. "You go on home to your family, Hemmings. I'll finish what I'm doing and lock the door behind me."

"If you're sure. Good night, sir."

"Good night, Hemmings," Timothy said.

As soon as he heard the door close, Timothy took out the account books. It was a damn pain, but he had to do it this way. If Mother only realized how much money it took to get into office. If she only realized you couldn't do it on your own. She was the one who filled his mind with these ideas in the first place. You'd think the least she could do was help out when the time came.

He wrote out a check to himself, recording it in the register as "fence repairs" for the Albany outlet. Now he'd get it cashed and be on his way. He locked the back door, cut through an alley, and walked two blocks to the bank, getting there just before they closed their doors.

"Ah, Mr. Coughlin," said the pinch-nosed man behind the cage. "Another check to cash?"

Just who Timothy didn't want to see, the assistant manager who thought he was guardian of the funds. "Yes, and I'm late, so don't take too long, Shaw," he said, shoving the check across the counter.

"It is a bit unusual," the banker said. "This account is set up with you as manager, but it is also part of the family—"

"And I'm authorized to write and cash the checks. Now, will you get on with it?"

"It's just that I have to answer the questions your mother and her accountants ask each quarter, and—"

"So do I," Timothy said, looking him square in the eye. That did it. The man backed down and carefully counted the bills into Timothy's hand.

Damn nosey Catholic, Timothy thought as he went out the door. He could remember when that wimp played on the Catholic boys' school basketball team in the state tournament, and Timothy's team beat the socks off them. Served them right. That simpering, holier-than-thou attitude needed to be flushed down the sewer. That's what it needed.

The Oregon legislature had passed a law two years ago requiring all school-age children to attend public schools. That would close down the damn Pope-worshipers. They were fighting it all the way to the U.S. Supreme Court, but the way Timothy saw it, states had the right to govern their education the way they saw fit—and Oregonians saw fit to get rid of its Catholic schools.

About time, too, he thought as he climbed into his car and headed out to the house.

As he pulled up in front of his house with the broad neoclassical porch supported by Greek columns, he remembered that today was the housekeeper's day off—but he wouldn't be needing her, anyway. Since Helen's death he'd had no one to act as hostess at meetings like the one planned for tonight. He'd had to arrange for a private dining room at the hotel.

He showered and changed his clothes, taking extra care deciding what to wear. He had to look like the prosperous success he was while still appearing to be within reach, a man of the people. A tricky balance, he thought as he changed his tie one last time before leaving.

Timothy had gone over the menu and table arrangements with the hotel, and the results were perfect. He'd wanted to achieve just the right feeling of opulence, yet maintain a comfortable ambience to put these power brokers at ease and in his corner. The chairs were upholstered and the crystal and china sparkling. The roast beef had been flown in especially from the Bar-C Ranch by his nephew.

By the time the evening was halfway over, Timothy felt he could lean back in his chair and relax. Things were going just fine. The waiter poured the French brandy that had been

368

muggled in from Canada for the occasion, and Timothy passed around a box of Cuban cigars. As smoke billowed above the candelabra, he knew he owned the support of every man there. And with their support, his party's nomination was a cinch. That ought to please Mother, he gloated.

Marshall Ranford, the owner of five Willamette Valley hardware stores, was one of the kingpins of the group. He seemed to think Timothy's grooming was his personal assignment. "I tell you, Coughlin," he said, blowing a smoke ring above his head, "we knew you could pull in the granges and the men's lodges, but come this weekend, you'll be hooked up with the power that runs this state." He leaned forward and pointed at Timothy with his cigar. "Most powerful men in this whole damn country," he said with emphasis. He looked around the table, and the others nodded their solemn affirmation. "To prove my point, I got a little proposition. How 'bout you coming with us tonight on a little assignment? That way you can see how we work."

The others echoed their approval. Timothy nodded.

"On one condition," said Burris Martin, the city councilman. "You're sworn to secrecy. If it's found out we brought you along—"

"Now, Burris," Marshall said, "just because we're jumping the gun a couple of days—"

"Marshall's right," chimed in Wilmer Smith, the long-faced doctor. "Tim here's good as in. He just needs to see how things work, get the hang of it early on, so to speak."

"Well, fellas," Timothy said, "I'm in your hands. You know I'm a man of my word. And," he added with a laugh, "to get that Senate seat, I'd make a secret trip to hell and back."

"Then it's settled," said Marshall. "We'll take my car."

They trooped out through the drizzling rain to Marshall's new Lafayette eight-cylinder roadster, the envy of the town. The rain began coming down in earnest as soon as they left the city limits. The farther they went, the more silent everyone became.

Soon they were riding through the dark, wet countryside in complete silence, a silence that became ominous with the passing miles because Marshall's new car had only one headlamp. As they approached Martin's Hill, they were joined by other cars—cars that were also missing one headlamp.

They stopped at the top in a clearing where others were waiting. The six men sat in the car, listening to the rain drum on the roof, watching while hooded figures gathered in the circle of light created by the parked car lights. Flickering torches appeared and shadows danced in the gloom.

When the circle was complete, Marshall got out and pulled a bundle from his trunk. He handed out six white sheets and hoods, saying, "This here's yours, Burris, recognize your wife's embroidered rosettes. Yours is the one with the purple and gold trim, Wilmer. And here, Tim, I got you one too."

Silently they donned their robes, then walked through the mud to the hooded circle, shadowed by the light of sputtering torches.

A speaker was already addressing the group on the topic of the danger of labor unions. "Loyal, patriotic Americans must defend the American way of doing business," he was saying. "We must keep foreign ideas and troublemakers from coming in and ruining our economic system—our very freedom."

Timothy moved closer, his interest piqued. There were rumors of unions coming into his lumberyards. That could cut deeply into his own pocket because they were sure to bring up the fact that he was not paying the wages his mother thought he was. That was one of the ways he was financing his campaign, by skimming funds.

The speaker turned to another hooded figure standing behind him. "We've got to nip this in the bud before it becomes a dangerous canker in our lives—and here's the man who can tell us how!"

The second speaker's voice was filled with indignation and controlled anger. "Unions are run by Jews and Catholics. That's a fact. Those are our enemies. Know your enemies and you can eliminate them.

"Now, Jews, as you know, have no homeland, no loyalty to country. They've wandered the earth since they killed Jesus. They control the money wherever they go. And they control the money with unions. Where there's money, there's a Jew.

"But they're not the immediate problem. Not yet. First we take care of the organizers. And the organizers are Catholic. They're the first problem we've got to take care of. They're the ones trying to take over Oregon.

"Catholics take a secret vow of loyalty to the Italian Pope," he declared, elongating the word "Italian" and spitting out the word "Pope." "It's disloyal. It's unpatriotic. And it's treasonous. What's worse, they breed like rabbits," he said.

370

lowering his voice dramatically, "and that's dangerous. They'll take over by sheer numbers if we don't stop 'em."

As he stepped aside the crowd cheered lustily, and Timothy joined in. The righteousness of his own hatred was being confirmed.

In the midst of the cheering, a third speaker stepped forward. "Here's our plan, men. We can do something—starting tonight. The biggest union organizer in the state is setting his claws in—right here in the tender heart of our own city. Tonight we show that damned Catholic his dirty work won't be tolerated any longer. Tonight he'll see the power and the wrath of avenging Americans!" With that cry he raised a wooden cross, wrapped in cloth, ready for burning. "Follow me!" he shouted above the mob's bedlam.

The crowd surged forward, climbing into their cars, their voices rumbling with righteous hatred.

Timothy's emotions churned as he accompanied his silent companions in the caravan of one-eyed cars. They stopped outside the house of the union-organizing Catholic. Sheeted figures surged through the midnight rain, past the white picket fence, to pound the cross into the ground.

Hooded men gathered around. Kerosene soaked the cloth. The whisk of a match, and it burst into a spectacular blaze. Timothy thought he heard a woman crying in the distance, then decided it was a cat. Suddenly, someone threw a rock through the front window. The spell was broken.

Quickly, like cockroaches at dawn, they scurried to their cars, and within minutes only the burning cross remained to show that they had been there.

Timothy could see its flickering reflection in the rearview mirror until they took a turn in the road. Then only a faint illumination on the dark horizon could be seen.

They were quiet on the ride back to the hotel. As they got out of Marshall's Lafayette and headed to their own cars, Wilmer put his hand on Timothy's shoulder. "You see, buddy, we got the numbers and we got the power."

Timothy shook his hand. "And you've got me," he said before closing the car door. "See you at the initiation in Portland tomorrow night."

Sleep didn't come to Timothy that night. In the dark early-morning hours he paced the floor, smoking a cigar, thinking.

He paused at the window. Silver streams of rain streaked across the panes. But it wasn't rain he was seeing. He was looking across the years at a brown-haired girl with laughing blue eyes. Mary Catherine Ranahan, who had committed the sin of being born Catholic and then compounded it by loving his brother, Daniel.

Timothy had tried everything to abort the romance. But still Daniel was determined to marry her. Timothy was distraught. How could he possibly make it through college without his brother, his twin, beside him?

"You just want to have me there to help with your assignments," Daniel had said with a laugh when Timothy protested. "Time to grow up, brother."

Time to grow up, hell. Timothy was appalled that Daniel would marry a girl from the wrong side of town, one from a whole brood of Catholic brothers and sisters. As he pointed out to Daniel, fecundity ran in her family. She'd be pregnant within the year. Daniel'd never get to go to school, another argument that failed. What Timothy didn't explain was how all those little nieces and nephews were bound to cloud the inheritance scene when the time came. Timothy had already decided he didn't want a mob of squalling kids in his life. But if his brother had . . . well, it was more injustice than a man could endure.

But old habits died hard. In spite of all of Timothy's objections, it was to him that Daniel turned and confided his plans. Timothy had convinced him that his marriage would be forbidden by their parents, so Daniel felt he had to elope.

The day Daniel and Timothy were to leave for college, Daniel had planned to run off with Mary Catherine. The fact that the twins were supposed to be traveling by train clear across the United States would give Daniel plenty of time to complete the deed before discovery. He swore Timothy to secrecy and made him promise not to wire their parents about Daniel's absence until he arrived in Boston. Timothy gave his word, then immediately set about trying to foil the plan before he left.

His first plot had salacious appeal to him, and he immediately put it into effect. Forging his brother's handwriting, he sent a letter to Mary Catherine, telling her to meet him that night. Then, using Daniel's carriage, he drove to the park and waited. Mary Catherine eagerly got into the carriage and they were on their way before she realized that she was with Timothy.

"Where are we going?" she'd asked tremulously.

"Daniel asked me to bring you to him. There's been a

change in plans," he'd explained reasonably as he drove out to the countryside. They rode in silence until he stopped the carriage alongside the river.

"Where's Daniel?" she asked, looking around.

"You didn't really expect to see him, did you?" Timothy asked, pulling her towards him, pressing his lips against hers.

"What are you doing?" she cried, pushing him away.

Her trembling, her softness, and her tearful pleas proved to be strange stimuli, more powerful than any he'd known. Timothy couldn't stop himself. Throwing her down on the seat, he tore her dress open, fondling her most private parts while she cried, begging him to stop. Then, when he'd started to press his advantage, just as he'd pulled his erect penis from his pants she'd started screaming, screams that finally pierced his panting desire. What if someone heard? What if he were discovered? There were farmhouses nearby.

He quickly adjusted his clothes and picked up the reins. He'd proven his point. She wasn't worthy of his brother.

Mary Catherine cried hysterically at first, then sobbed softly all the way home. Timothy took her back to the park and told her to get out. "Don't try to trap my brother in marriage. Remember what I can tell him. I've had privileges even he hasn't enjoyed. He won't want you now. Not with what I can claim. So don't be stupid. Find one of your own kind."

Then Mary Catherine looked up at him, her eyes clear in the moonlight. "He will marry me," she'd said in a strong voice. "Daniel loves me and I love him. He won't believe you. He'll believe me. He knows you're no good. He'll believe my truth over your lies any day."

Even now, thirty-five years later, her words stung. Timothy knew she'd been telling the truth.

He'd had no other choice. He had to act to keep his brother from making the biggest mistake of his life. And to save his own hide. As repulsive as it was, he'd gone to Mary Catherine's father.

He knew Catholics had some kind of rule about not marrying outside the Church. That was Timothy's trump card. He'd decided to stir up her old man so he'd go out and take care of it himself. It'd humiliate Daniel, but he deserved it.

Timothy was an impressive figure as he walked through the Ranahans' tiny yard to their little house. He'd worn a new suit, one he'd gotten for college, and the gold watch chain his father had given him, identical to the one his brother was wearing with what he thought was his wedding suit.

He'd enjoyed the deference with which Ranahan greeted him. It had given him all the more confidence. Smugly he refused to sit down, choosing to stand and tell Mary Catherine's parents of her planned deception. He didn't want to stay any longer than he had to.

Mr. Ranahan's reaction was better than Timothy had hoped for. He'd turned angry red, trembling even as he spoke. "What has your brother done to my daughter? Where are they?"

"I'm sure he's done nothing—yet," Timothy said. "They're meeting outside of town, by the Old South Fork." He took out his watch and looked at it. "Ought to be there in about half an hour. It'll take a strong man to do it. I was hoping that perhaps you could do something to discourage this rash—"

"Damn right I will!" he'd shouted, grabbing his coat and heading out the door. The screen door slammed behind him and Timothy was left standing in the middle of the little parlor that smelled of woodsmoke and bacon, watching Mrs. Ranahan sob quietly. Without a word, he'd turned and left.

He'd gone home to his room to finish packing, whistling as he went up the stairs. He knew that his brother would be joining him on the train, his tail between his legs. The avenging fool of a father would take care of everything. He'd get there before Mary Catherine could tell Daniel anything, and Timothy would have won. He was sure that once Daniel met some of the cultured Boston women, he'd soon forget his cheap little slip of a Catholic.

Then the sheriff came. Daniel was dead.

Timothy couldn't let his brother's death go unavenged. He'd tried to tell his mother it was murder, not an accident, but she'd shushed him before he could get the words out, telling him that she'd known Daniel was seeing Mary Catherine, telling him that they all were grieving and that he shouldn't bring up his objections to an alliance that now could never be.

He'd gone to his father. But Nathanial told him that in grief sometimes a man looked for something to blame. It was only natural. But this was an accident. "It couldn't have been prevented, could it?" Nathanial had asked.

At that question, Timothy flinched. He knew that it had been his fault. He could have prevented it by keeping his brother's trust. He retreated into bitter silence.

After all these years, he still grieved for the loss of his brother. But now he turned his guilt into unreasoning hatred, a hatred that blanketed all those who call themselves Catholic.

As if his brother's death weren't enough, he had one other burning reason for hating all Catholics. He'd chased that bit of Georgia fluff, Geraldine, clear to Europe. Her letters to her family indicated she was smitten with some foreigner, and her father had understandably been upset. He'd even paid for Timothy's trip.

When Timothy arrived in London, he found Geraldine starry-eyed over an Italian count.

"He's so romantic," she'd said, telling Timothy about Count Michael Binelli. "I feel like such a . . . such a lady when I'm with him."

"He can't even speak good English," Timothy had protested.

"I don't care. I don't know that it's forever . . . I just know that it's for now," she'd said as she walked off in a daze.

Timothy was shocked. Then, on Christmas Eve, Geraldine refused to go with her hosts to Anglican services. Instead, she was going to the Catholic church with Michael.

"It sounds like this is getting serious," Timothy heard someone say and his brain blistered with fury. He could think of nothing else. He'd have to talk some sense into her.

That night he stayed up waiting, waiting for her to return. Then, as the clock struck one-thirty Christmas morning, the carriage pulled up to the door. He slipped into her room and waited.

Geraldine was startled to see him. It was that look, the look of fear and the soft yielding of her tender flesh that did it. Somehow she became mixed up with Mary Catherine in his mind. He even made the mistake of calling her that. He tried to reason with her, but she struggled and he couldn't help himself. Holding his hand over her mouth he forced himself on her, forced himself into her. From the blood on the bed, he knew that she'd been a virgin.

She was sobbing uncontrollably afterward, lying helplessly on the bed. Triumphant, he knew he could make her see reason. She had no other choice. She would have to marry him now, he told her. She was his. He even said he loved her, but she cried all the harder. The Italian count wouldn't consider her, he'd said. No Catholic wanted a spoiled woman. He left her in tears, telling her that they'd be leaving on the next boat departing for the United States. They'd marry on board. He'd be saving her reputation and doing something "romantic." It was her father's wish.

He'd thought she had no other choice. But like Mary Catherine before her, she defied him. She left that very night and ran away to that count, that damned Catholic count. And the bastard had taken her.

Timothy knocked the long gray ash off his cigar, took a puff, then tamped it out. "Goddamned Pope-lovers," he swore as he grabbed his coat and headed out the door. Tonight's initiation was just the first step on his way to revenge his brother's death, revenge his loss of Geraldine, revenge for the disaster that had been wreaked on his life. The Oregon bill closing parochial schools would be just the beginning when he become senator.

It was a dreary afternoon, and Hannah wished it would hurry by. She knew she should be excited about tonight, but she couldn't muster the energy. Instead, she was dreading going to Portland with Duke. Even though he'd promised to take her to a wonderful restaurant before the concert, she couldn't find anything to be happy about. She was more and more repulsed by Duke's demands. Hearing other musicians would depress her—and she didn't even look forward to wearing her new dress and white fox coat. She dreaded that especially. Somehow the coat had come to symbolize that she was being bought—in every way.

The phone rang, sharply intruding on her thoughts.

"Mother?" Josie's voice came uncertainly through the lines, distant and tremulous.

"Yes, Josephine. Where are you?"

"In Portland. Mother . . . it's Grams. She's . . . she's had a stroke. I think you should come up right away."

"Did you call the doctor?"

"Yes, he's here now."

"How bad is it?"

"It's too early to tell. Can you come?"

"I'll be there before dark. And . . . Josie?"

"Yes, Mama?"

"Thank you for calling." She ran up the stairs and threw a few toiletries, a change of underwear, and a dress into her overnight case. She paused before shutting the lid. Then, reluctantly, she took her good black suit out of the closet—just in case.

She made sure all the lights were turned off, locked the

door, then loaded her suitcase in the back of the sedan. Sam came and cranked the car for her.

As she drove down the drive, she remembered her date with Duke. Instead of turning right to go to Portland, she turned left and went down the highway to the newly cut road leading to Duke's experimental station.

She hadn't gone halfway down the road before Duke's big Duesenberg came speeding toward her. She pulled over and waited for him.

"What're you doing?" he shouted through his open window.

"Looking for you."

"What for? You're going to see me tonight. I told you never to come out here."

"This was an emergency, Duke. Mother's had a stroke. I'm on my way to Portland."

"Well, give me a call when you get back."

"I will," she said, putting the car into gear.

"Hey!" he yelled. "Where are you going?"

"Up there to turn around."

He jumped out of his car and opened her door. "Here, you're wasting time," he said, gesturing for her to move over. "I'll turn this heap around so you don't have to go all the way up there."

"Duke," she protested as he ground the gears and started backing it around, going forward, then backing it again until it was crossways in the road, "this is going to take longer than just driving up there would."

"Shut up, I know what I'm doing," he said sharply as he cramped the wheel and finally managed to turn the car around. "Now give me a kiss and call when you get back, okay?"

"Sure, Duke," she said, giving him a peck on the cheek.

"What kind of a smooch is that?" He grabbed her roughly by the back of the head and kissed her hard. "There, something for you to think about on your drive up to Portland." He winked.

Hannah tried to straighten her hair before she slid back into the driver's seat.

"Don't stay away long," Duke said, shutting the door.

By the time she'd reached the highway she was certain that something wasn't right, but she just couldn't put her finger on it. So once more she turned left instead of turning right towards Portland.

She hadn't gone more than fifty feet when Duke pulled alongside her, honking his horn. She stopped and opened her window. "Where the hell you going?" he demanded. "Portland's the other way."

"I've got to stop by Ron's place and tell him. After all, he's almost part of the family."

"Yeah? Well, tell the bastard to marry your daughter and get her off your hands, why don't you? Then maybe he'll have something to do so he'll leave us alone."

"I've got to go, Duke, there's a truck coming," she said, grateful for the oncoming vehicle.

"Yeah, yeah," he said, flooring the throttle of his car and spinning his wheels as he pulled away from her.

Ron was out by the barn, hooking the plow to his tractor when Hannah drove up. He saw her car and came up to the house, wiping his hands on a rag as she got out.

"To what do I owe this visit?" he asked. "Your daughter doesn't live here yet."

"I know," Hannah said, smiling tightly. "I just talked to Josie on the phone. Mother's had a stroke and I'm on my way up there now. I thought you should know."

"How bad is it?"

"I don't know. I'll have Josie call you."

"Want me to do anything while you're gone?"

"No, thank you. Sam has everything under control."

"What about that Duke character?" he asked. "Shouldn't I watch out so he doesn't rob you blind?"

"I doubt he'd do anything of the kind, Ron."

"Just the same, if you don't mind, I'm going to find out what kind of racket he's running over there."

"Really, Ron, I do mind. Duke has a pretty short temper, and there're lots of men working for him up there. You'd be way outnumbered. Besides, I've seen the hogs he's taken to market, and they're very fat. I'm sure he's just doing what he says, making hogfeed."

"I doubt it."

"Just the same, I don't want you taking any chances. Josie would never forgive me if something happened to you."

"And I would never forgive myself if I let something happen to either you or Josie. Give Mrs. Coughlin my wishes for a fast recovery."

"I will."

He waved as she drove off, this time headed in the right direction for Portland.

She was worried that Ron wouldn't heed her warning. She

378

could see his figure in the rearview mirror as he rode his tractor out to the field. A shiver ran down her spine, and she quickly turned her mind to what was waiting for her at the end of her drive.

PART IV

THE WILL

Chapter XXXII

March 19, 1924

"Enough!" Fee exclaimed, interrupting Dr. McAllister's instructions. "I've ignored you for years now and done just fine."

"Now, now, Mrs. Coughlin," he said in his best bedside manner, "we mustn't take this so lightly. After all—"

Fee stopped him with an impatient wave of her hand. "Don't patronize me, Alf McAllister. I'm not senile, just dying. Hush, Nell," she responded to Nell's cry. Then she turned back to the red-faced doctor. "And I don't need to pay your extravagant bills to find that out. Now, if you'll leave and not return until it's time to say my heart has stopped and I have indeed left my corporal body, I will be able to finish my work."

"Well, Mrs. Coughlin, perhaps if you—" he began.

"Perhaps you didn't understand. My mind isn't sick. It's my heart. I can't waste energy on the likes of you."

The doctor indignantly snapped his case shut. "Very well."

"Nell will see you out."

Fee leaned back against her pillow, grateful for the few moments of solitude.

It had been wonderful these past two weeks, having Josie and Hannah near. There had been a terrible rift between her daughter and granddaughter, but being together with Fee since her stroke was helping it heal. Fee was certain it would eventually work itself out, at least if her plans went the way she intended.

Still, having them hovering over her all the time grew wearisome. Those tickets to the chamber concert in Salem had been a godsend. When they'd arrived with an invitation from the governor, Fee gave them to Hannah and Josie. They should get out of the house, she explained over their protests, and they needed at least a day to catch up on their affairs in Salem. What Fee didn't say was that she also needed some time to herself.

She reached into her bedside drawer and pulled out a cigar

box full of photos. She'd had a good, long life, and this box contained remembrances of some of the best parts. She'd had six children, two still living, and four grandchildren, three who lived. On these five people rested all her hopes and dreams.

She pulled out a photo of Andrew, his fair hair and innocent young face peering from under that dreadful Army cap. Tucked in the back of the photograph frame was a yellowing letter. She opened the envelope with the faded French stamps and pulled out the sheet of paper with his slanting scrawl. It was as if she could still hear his young voice over the years, earnest and cracking with excitement.

Dear Grandma,
Everything is so different over here. But I know that what we're doing is important. It's like you and Grandpa always said, when there is wrong being done, it's everyone's duty and responsibility to set it right. You should see the kinds of things they do just because someone's Jewish. I always think about the Tealls and how much we love them.

I keep remembering the walks I used to take with Grandpa. And sitting in the kitchen stealing Nell's cookies. And listening to you tell us stories around the fire when it was too rainy for us to go outside. You and Grandpa have given me some of the best days of my life. I'm getting strength from them now. I just wanted you to know that.

I saw Emmett last week. We had a beer in what they call a bistro. He cuts a sharp figure in his uniform. It's the same as home, all the mademoiselles making eyes at him. He's flying like crazy. Whenever I'm in the trenches and there's a plane overhead, I pretend it's Emmett. And it might be.

Gotta go now. We're moving out tonight. Don't worry about me. You've made me strong.

Love, Andrew

It was the last letter he wrote. A corpsman found it in his pocket when he was taking him to the hospital.

Fee looked at the picture once more and sighed. There was so much potential in that eager young face. She knew she mourned his death even more than his father did, but then

Fee had hoped that Andrew would succeed where his father had failed.

She slipped the letter into the envelope. It was as if Andy had known he was going to die. His letter had been a great comfort to her the past six years.

She rang her bell, and Nell came running up the stairs, panting from the exertion. "Would you please telephone and ask Mr. Teall to come over this evening? He's staying at his father's place."

"Yes, Miz Coughlin."

"Oh, and please hand me the files labeled 'Matthew' and 'Mateo.'"

Nell grumbled as she reached into the file cabinet. "You know what the doctor said. You need your rest."

"I'll have plenty of rest soon enough. Stop fussing."

"Well, you can't get a straight furrow with a broken plow."

Smiling and shaking her head, Fee turned her attention to the files. They had to be in order when Jacob came. She rummaged through the box until she found the photo she wanted. She paused, her heart in her throat as she looked at Matthew's face.

The photographer had been most perceptive. He'd put him against one of those painted backgrounds that looked like he was standing on a mountaintop. Just like his father, always trying to find new frontiers . . . just like both his fathers.

She reached into his file and pulled out the letters that belonged with the photo. They were ragged with age, torn in the creases because they had been read so often. He'd written as he'd spoken—carefully and precisely. Like his father.

Even now his words caused tears of love and pain to well in her eyes. He was all she'd ever hoped for. He was the one visible bond between her and Jacob.

There was still another chapter in Matthew's story. She took the letter from Mateo's mother, Teresa, in her convent-school handwriting that told Fee of her grandchild, and put it in Mateo's file. There were two others, from the mother superior at the boarding school. The final letter to go into that file was the last one she'd received from Teresa. It was short and her handwriting was hard to read, the lines trembling and crooked.

Dear Mrs. Coughlin,
Your kindness over the years has been a blessing. Now I regret that I must ask one more thing. I am dying. My

greatest fear is that my son will become a poor peasant in spite of his schooling.

Please, let him come to America to be with you. Matthew told me of the cattle ranches you have. Mateo is very good with animals. I'm sure he would be able to work for you. I implore you, don't abandon your grandson. Ease his dying mother's heart. I am going to join his father in heaven.

Yours in Christ,
Teresa Ortega Coughlin

Fee had never regretted her response to that letter. Her visits to the ranch always filled her with joy at seeing Mateo, with his brilliant smile and his grandfather's eyes.

Now Fee wanted the whole story available should there ever be any question about Mateo's birthright. It wasn't that she wanted the story known, she just didn't want it kept secret if it should cause an injustice. Besides, she was proud of her grandson by her dear beloved Jacob.

She placed the letters and photos in the correct files, then added the documentation proving beyond a doubt that Mateo was her grandson, documentation she had paid for dearly these past five years in order to protect Mateo when she was gone.

She set the files aside and checked once more to make sure that she'd written the final copy of each of her letters. Then she leaned her head against the pillow.

"Miz Coughlin? You asleep?"

"No, Nell, I just closed my eyes."

"I took the liberty of asking Mr. Teall to have dinner with us. Hope you don't mind."

"Of course not, Nell. That's what I would have wanted. When's he coming?"

" 'Bout an hour and a half."

"Good, I have time for a nap."

" 'Bout time you did what the doctor ordered."

Smiling at Nell's adamant mothering, Fee drifted off to sleep.

Of the base elements in her life, Nathanial had been her earth and air, sustaining and essential. In spite of his frequent wanderings and his taciturn tendencies, Nathanial had always had Fee's love.

He'd remained a handsome man, strong and sturdy as a

386

oak, his coppery hair and beard slowly darkening with the years. By the time he was fifty-five, he'd become silvered like a proud eagle.

When he'd first bought Round Top Mountain, he'd been hesitant to show it to her. Then finally he took her there. They'd ridden their horses through firs rising hundreds of feet, like columns in a gigantic cathedral. Fee had watched the sunlight filtering through the branches in bright shafts of color, lighting the emerald-velvet moss and amber bracken, capturing a warbling bird in its beam, revealing a jewel of a butterfly suspended over her head—and she knew why Nathanial purchased the seemingly worthless land.

"It's too steep to log," he said.

"With the knowledge we have today. Who knows about tomorrow?" she said. "Still, who'd want to fell these monuments? It'd be a sin."

He agreed with visible relief. "This kind of forest should be preserved—for everyone to enjoy and learn from."

They'd followed a well-worn animal trail until Nathanial stopped and pointed to a mountain valley just below them. "This is ours, too," he said proudly.

Nestled between thickly wooded slopes of the mountain was a sapphire-blue lake. Thick fir and pine greened its shores. The lake drained into a small creek, bounded by reeds and willows. A doe and fawn were drinking at its edge.

"Oh, Nathanial, it's the most beautiful place on earth."

That hot summer afternoon they'd made camp beside the lake. On joyful impulse Fee had stripped off her dusty clothing and plunged into the lake's icy waters. With a whoop, Nathanial joined her, and they splashed like children. That night they made love under the stars. As Fee lay in his arms, listening to the lapping waters, watching the moon's reflection spinning a path across the lake, they made a covenant between them and the generations to follow. They promised to keep this wondrous piece of land in its pristine beauty.

When the children were grown, Fee and Nathanial were able to spend more time traveling. Nathanial wanted to go to the "last frontier," as he called Alaska, so Fee went, fearful that he would catch gold fever up there since he had missed it down here. Fee wanted to go to Europe and, reluctantly, Nathanial accompanied her.

Afterward, Fee always found great glee in remembering Nathanial wearing a tuxedo, towering like a giant and graciously trying to be polite to an adoring Viennese matron in Vienna's Town Hall. And Nathanial would always counter with his cherished image of Fionna shrieking in surprise as she discovered that she was bathing in an Alaskan lake that a bull moose considered his dinner plate.

When he'd suggested that train ride back to West Virginia, Fee had jumped at the chance. It was the fateful trip.

"Through it all—I've loved you—my Fionna."

"And I love you, Nathanial. I'm keeping our covenant."

Fee awakened from her nap to find a warm tear coursing down her cheek. Nathanial had seemed so close to her in the dream. It was the awakening that had caused the tear.

Slowly she got up from her bed and began dressing. She was sitting in front of her mirror, combing her hair, when Nell came in.

"What on earth do you think you're doing?" she asked, putting down the tablecloth she had over her arm.

"Getting ready for dinner."

"Well, get right back into that bed. I'm setting the table so you can have your dinner with Mr. Teall in here."

"Don't be silly. I will have one last dinner in my dining room."

"You're too weak for that, Miz Coughlin. You can't—"

"Nell, I'll be fine. After all these years, you should know better than to argue with me."

With a sigh, Nell agreed. "Miz Coughlin, you're more stubborn than a Missouri mule. Your kick's just as bad, too."

Fee laughed. It was a long, slow walk down the stairs, but Fee was determined. By leaning heavily on the rail and with Nell's arm around her waist, she made it. At the bottom of the stairs, she paused to catch her breath, then took the ivory-handled cane Emmett had given her and slowly walked into the parlor.

The French doors were open, letting in the cool spring air. She could hear the crickets bowing their single note of joy and the fragrance of lilacs filled the room.

"I'll sit in the chair by the fireplace, Nell," she said. "Will you please bring my shawl? And light the fire to cut the chill, won't you?"

Fee chuckled as Nell grumbled, lighting the fire, wrapping a shawl around Fee's shoulders and tucking a lap robe around her legs. "No, don't close them," she said as Nell stomped toward the French doors. "It smells so good and sounds so beautiful. I know it's silly, but I'd like to sit in front of the fire and feel the cool air. The best of all worlds."

"Miz Coughlin, sometimes I think you've taken leave of your senses—and then you explain and I think I've taken leave of my senses because I understand."

Fee laughed. "That's why you're so dear to me, Nell," she said. "You keep me practical while indulging my fancies."

She watched a moth fall through the amber dusk. As nighttime slowly crept into the room, she felt closer to her loved ones who'd died than with the people living around her.

She could almost reach out and touch little Donnell's red curls as he toddled beside her. There was her precious Matthew, solemn and wise, teasing and gentle—and young Daniel, so pragmatic and joyful, the bright side of her twins—and even tiny Rosalind, vainly struggling for life—all seemed to touch her in the flickering firelight.

And Jacob—her beloved Jacob. Yes, he even more than the others seemed a presence by her side. If Nathanial was her earth and air, Jacob was her fire and water, exciting and nourishing her spirit.

"I always loved you, my companion-spirit."

"And I loved you, my soul's rejoicing."

"What are you doing down here? I would have gone upstairs to find you," Jacob said as he came in through the French doors, a smile lighting his face.

Fee half stood, she was so shocked to see him. "I knew you would . . ." she stammered, "but—"

"Don't stand up," he said, hurrying across the carpet. He looked so real, so alive. Fee's heart was tremulous.

"Am I late?" he asked as he set down his briefcase.

"I . . . I—"

"Fee, are you all right?" he said, taking her hand. Only then did Fee realize that this was Jacob's grandson.

"I . . . I'm sorry." She sat back down, still shaken. "I must have been daydreaming. When I looked up . . . well," she said with a smile, "you looked so like your grandfather it quite took my breath away."

Jacob threw his head back and laughed heartily—the same laugh, the same gesture as his grandfather—and Fee's heart turned over. "Now you're seeing ghosts in the shadows. Best not sit by the fire in the dark, Fee. Here, let me turn on a lamp."

"Better yet," she said, gathering her wits about her, "go in
389

and tell Nell that you're here and we both need a dose of medicinal brandy—there's some Napoleon I've had tucked away in the cellar just for such moments."

As he left on his errand, Fee sat looking through the open doors, breathing deeply of the cool spring air to get her heart back to normal and her mind cleared before he returned.

"Now," Jacob said as he decanted the brandy and poured it into two snifters, "what's on your mind?"

"I've finished the letters."

"Already? You've been busy. What would the doctor say?"

"Fiddlesticks. The doctor is worthless—and understands less about human nature than he does about the body. That's beside the point. I want to go over some last details, and then I'll sign the papers tonight. You did bring them, didn't you?"

"Yes," he said with an indulgent smile. "I'd hate to be accused of underestimating my client the way McAllister underestimates his patient."

"Good. Let's start now. We can stop when Nell calls us to dinner and finish up after dessert. Does that meet with your approval?"

"With you, Fee, my approval would only be superfluous."

She smiled. "It's good you understand me so well, Jacob."

Carefully she began outlining the possibilities for each of her beneficiaries, each possible choice they would be facing, each potential turn they might take. For each heir she gave Jacob a packet of clearly marked envelopes. Then she had him repeat the instructions back to her.

"Dinner's ready, Miz Coughlin."

"Thank you, Nell," she said, holding her arm out to Jacob. "Jacob will help me into the dining room."

It was a slow walk, but neither of them minded. To Fee, it was almost as if she were walking once more with her beloved Jacob. And looking in Fee's eyes, Jacob saw the genesis of her granddaughter's spirit.

By the end of the evening—and the end of the bottle of brandy— Jacob had a clear vision of what Fee intended. She and Nathanial had carved a vast fortune from the raw land. She was determined her imprint would be written upon the land and its people for all time. It would be done by her heirs—her best bequest, her one hope for immortality.

Jacob brought the lap desk over to Fee, the one she'd used while crossing the plains in a covered wagon. She carefully read each page of the document. As he watched her silvered head bent over the papers, he was suddenly struck with the premonition that this was her last act, and his heart twisted with grief.

Unable to face his thoughts any longer, he went to the door. "I'm going to get Mr. Sanders from across the street to witness."

Within minutes, kindly Mr. Sanders was watching Fee's frail hand sign the will and initial each page. After Jacob, he cosigned the will, commenting that he didn't anticipate being called upon to confirm its authenticity for many years to come. When he left, Fee smiled at Jacob.

"I'm glad you didn't ask what was in the letters."

"You made it clear it was between you and your inheritors. I respect your privacy."

"I know. That's just one of the many nice things about you. Still, you must be curious."

"I'm human," he admitted with a smile.

"Well, I'm sure that you will learn the contents of one of them before the time is out, and that pleases me."

"Oh? Which one?"

"You'll see. Incidentally, I've placed the box of artifacts, as you so quaintly call them, in the bank. Just ask the chief officer of the bank to give it to you. Now, any questions?"

"Just one. You've been pretty explicit about everyone— except one. You've told me little of what I can expect from Josephine and what you want for her."

"Oh, Josie," she said, holding her hand out for him to help her up from the chair. "For Josie, there's only one choice, and I'm sure she'll make it. I've taken extra precautions that she will." They began walking slowly towards the front door.

"And that choice?"

"Ah, that choice is the one that will make the circle complete."

"Fionna, you're being mysterious again."

"And that's the way it will remain. At least until the time comes for you to see what I mean."

"I'm afraid that's the one I may mishandle."

"You can't mishandle that one—though God knows you've tried."

Jacob laughed. "You mean to tell me I've already fumbled and you still trust me?"

"Of course. That's *why* I trust you. You've fumbled already, and now there's nowhere for you to move but the right way. Now, if you'll excuse me, I'm tired." She paused by the door, leaning on her cane. "Kiss me good-bye, dear."

Jacob dutifully kissed her cheek, then leaned down and kissed her once more. "Good-bye, Fee. I love you. I'll do the best I can—even if you do insist on your mysteries."

"I do—and I love you, too," she said, patting his hand.

He turned and walked down the steps.

"Happiness will finally come when the circle is complete."

He turned to ask what she meant, but the door was closed. Had he imagined her saying it?

Jacob worked on the final arrangements through the night. When the phone rang the next morning, he was expecting it.

Fee was dead.

Chapter XXXIII

March 20, 1924

Hannah and Josie were at the farm when Jacob called.

"Why did she send us away last night?" Hannah cried into the receiver.

Josie took the receiver from her. "It's Grams, isn't it?" she asked.

"Yes. I'm so sorry."

"I know."

"Nell is pretty shaken. She asked that I call."

"We'll be up before noon to make the arrangements."

Josie hung up the receiver and rested her head against the oaken phone box, hot tears flowing down her cheeks. "Gram's gone." Her voice was hollow. Josie put her arms around her mother and together they mourned the loss of the indomitable Fee.

Finally, Josie straightened up and searched her pockets for a handkerchief. "I'll pack and then I'd better go tell Ron."

"I'll be ready to go when you get back," Hannah said.

After Josie was gone, Hannah realized that she, too, had some calls to make. Emmett would have to be sought out once she reached Portland, but she should call Timothy before leaving Salem. She cranked the phone, then waited, listening to the phone ring on the other end, wondering why her brother was never around when she needed him.

Maybe he was at the lumberyard. Hannah decided it wouldn't be right to tell him over the phone that his mother had died. He needed privacy for his grief as much as she did.

She closed her suitcase, carried it out to the car, and placed it in the trunk beside Josie's. She felt at such a loss—so alone. Then she realized she'd better tell Duke.

"Sam," she called to the foreman, "saddle Blaze for me, please." Spring rains had made the farm roads practically impassable for her sedan. It'd be a lot easier to ride to the experimental station.

When she got out to the barn, Sam looked at her question-ingly. *Dear God*, she thought, *I forgot about Sam.* Hannah put her hand on his shoulder. "Yes, Sam. She's gone. I'll let you know when the funeral is as soon as I know."

She saw his eyes fill with tears and felt her fragile shell of reserve begin to crack. Biting her lip, she quickly swung into the saddle.

The sky was gray with broken clouds. As she rode across the pasture and through the fields, faint warmth from the sun caressed her back. A meadowlark flew out of the grass in front of her, trying its age-old broken wing trick to lure her away from its nest. She followed the stream, which flowed from the spring up by the experimental station. A kildeer rose from a backwater and pierced the air with its warning call.

Noting the color of the water and the thick clots of algae, she realized that Ron had been right. Whatever Duke was doing up there, he was fouling the water, and since this spring runoff fed directly into Quail Creek, it was affecting Ron's water source as well. She'd better talk to Duke about it. The thought wasn't a pleasant one. Duke was becoming more and more difficult, and any discussion about his project seemed to guarantee a confrontation. Her back cooled notice-bly as dark clouds slid over the sun.

The air, which had been meadow-sweet, was taking on a distinctly sour smell. She sniffed, sampling the scent, trying to figure out what it was. Probably something Duke was trying with the hogfeed, she thought as she rode up to the building, past the hog pens. Whatever he was feeding the pigs had to be responsible for the smell.

She dismounted and tied the reins around a fence post and

started around the side of the building, concentrating on where she stepped, avoiding the largest mud puddles.

Duke's car was in front. She heard his voice coming from inside the building, so she walked around to the back door.

Another voice, harsh and guttural, was talking. As she got closer, she could hear what they were saying.

"You catch that goody-goody snooping around here again, you shoot him on the spot." It was Duke's voice. "He's been a thorn in my side ever since I laid eyes on him."

"You know the boss don't like no bodies scattered around."

"You do your part. I'll take care of the stiff."

Hannah could hardly believe what she was hearing. Who was he talking about? The smell—suddenly things started falling into place. Still, she had to know for sure. The door was left ajar. She peered in. A vast array of copper tubing, vats, and wooden barrels filled the large building.

"Hold it right there." Before she could turn around, a man's arm was across her neck and she could feel his gun. "What the hell you doing snooping around here?"

Hannah struggled helplessly against his hold. "It . . . It's my property!" she choked out. "Let go of me!"

"Let her go," Duke ordered.

The guard shoved her into the building but didn't lower his gun. "I told you you was courtin' trouble," he said with a snarl at Duke. "Now she knows everything."

Hannah's mind spun. Sour mash. Copper tubes and vats. It was obvious what was going on, and she'd have to talk fast to get out of this alive. The look in Duke's eyes said as much. For the first time in her life, Hannah became an actress.

"What do you mean, now I know everything?" she asked. "I've suspected all along. It's just that I see my Duke has a bigger operation than I'd anticipated." She smiled at him. "I'm more impressed than ever."

"You mean you knew?" he said, surprised.

"I'm no fool, Duke," she cooed. "But you do amaze me with the size of the still. You're no small potatoes, are you? You must be making booze for half the West Coast." She smiled winningly. "You're quite an operator."

Duke puffed up under her admiration. "Yeah, biggest still this side of the Rockies." He couldn't resist bragging. "Good stuff too. No cheap rotgut here."

"Nothing but the best for the Chicago boys, um?"

At the mention of Chicago he was suddenly on guard.

She'd gone too far. "What'd you come here for?" His expression was hard and calculating.

"I had to talk to you," she said, walking nonchalantly towards the door. The guard stepped forward, blocking her escape, but she turned, pretending not to notice. She took a deep breath. "Mother died this morning. I'm going up to Portland to take care of things. You'll be dealing with me directly from now on. We'll have to renegotiate the deal. Now that I see all this, I realize how much I've been underpaid."

Duke grabbed her arm. "What if the old lady gave the place to your brats? What if I have to deal with West?"

"Don't worry about it," she said, pulling her arm away. "You have me and only me to deal with." She ran her hand up his chest to his chin. "And I thought we had an—understanding."

"Yeah," he said hesitantly, looking at her as if he were trying to figure out what was going on. This was a side of Hannah he'd missed seeing before.

He grinned suddenly. "Yeah, we have an understanding." He put his arm around her waist and walked her out to her horse.

As she put her foot in the stirrup, he stopped her, his hand squeezing her arm tightly. "You'd better make sure it goes our way," he said. "People I work for don't like surprises. Moving costs money."

"Sure, Duke," she said. "You know me. I look out for myself."

He ran his hand down her arm, brushing her breast and then her hips. "Yeah, that's what we got in common, baby. But remember—I'm watching you." His eyes were like glittering pieces of onyx, and it was everything Hannah could do to keep from shivering as she looked at him. Instead, she forced herself to lean forward and kiss him quickly on the lips before pulling herself up into the saddle.

She rode off slowly, struggling to keep from looking back. The skin on the back of her neck prickled. She could feel their eyes on her. Blaze shied, sensing her tension, but she kept her back straight and her seat in the saddle relaxed. A show of confidence seemed her best defense.

"Shoot him," he'd said. Just like that. Shoot who? Oh, Mother, I've been such a fool, she thought with tears in her eyes.

* * *

The church was filled to overflowing. Mateo and people from the ranches had came over. Neighbors, friends, loggers, cattlemen—it seemed that half the state was there. Sam and Nell sat together, openly shedding tears for their employer and friend. People from everywhere came to pay their respects to Fionna Barry Coughlin, beloved "Empress of Oregon."

Through the crowd, Hannah saw Duke sitting at the back of the church beside three large men with harsh faces and coats that didn't fit. Then at the cemetery, behind tombstones of forgotten men, she noticed them again, waiting and watching. She knew they had not come out of respect for her mother.

As the family filed back to the limousine, Timothy asked Jacob to have the reading of the will the following day. Jacob looked surprised, but he said it could be arranged if the others agreed. Hannah remained silent. Josie and Emmett indicated that they were willing, if that was what Uncle Timothy and their mother wanted.

"Then I'll see you all in my office at one o'clock tomorrow," Jacob said as he climbed into his car.

Hannah glanced at the men waiting in the big black sedan just outside the cemetery fence. She didn't want to spend the next twenty-four hours alone. "Let's the four of us go on over to the farm for the night. I think Mother would have liked that. Sort of a wake. You, too, Mateo," she said, realizing that he had nowhere to go.

When they got into the car, she heard the rumble of the Duesenberg's engine starting up. As Duke drove off, Hannah breathed a sigh of relief. At least tonight she wasn't alone.

Timothy left early in the morning to take Mateo to the train station. Josie went over to see Ron before noon, telling Hannah that she'd meet her in Jacob's office. Shortly after Josie left, a young woman drove up in a roadster, and Emmett ran out the door, promising to be at the lawyer's by one o'clock.

Hannah had just reached into the closet for her coat when she heard Duke's car pull into the driveway. Quickly she picked up her pocketbook and left through the back door, locking it behind her.

"I came just in time," Duke said as he stepped around the corner of the house.

"Duke," she said, feigning surprise. "What brings you here?"

"I came to drive you to the lawyer's office. Like you, I watch out for myself."

"Oh, you needn't bother," she said, walking towards her sedan.

"No bother. Just business." He took her arm and steered her to his car. "Get in."

She looked around. None of the hired hands was in sight, not even Sam. Reluctantly, she got in the car. Her heart sank as Duke closed the door behind her.

Hannah watched his face as he started the engine. "How did you know the reading of the will was today?" she asked, forcing her voice to sound casual.

"Your brother's a fool. He spread it all over town that this afternoon he's getting his inheritance, his mother's fortune, he says. Making like the bigshot."

"I see."

"He'd better not be right," he said, glancing sideways at her as he pulled onto the highway.

"Don't be silly, Duke. I'll get the farm. My husband ran t before he died, and I've run it for over five years on my own. It couldn't go anywhere else."

"Except your brat. She's marrying West, who owns the adjoining land. A perfect joining of assets, you might say. Or what if your brother's right? He thinks he's getting the bulk of the estate because he's the only male heir."

"Well, he's forgetting his nephew. And you know full well Emmett isn't concerned about violating the Prohibition Laws. No, you needn't worry," she said, settling herself comfortably into the corner of the big car.

"I talked to the big boys last night," he said after a few minutes.

"Oh?" His tone made her instantly alert.

"Told them you knew. They're not too happy about it. Said now they want to buy the land, cheap. Get you out of the middle." He patted her knee. "Actually, babe, it makes sense," he reasoned. "You're in where you could do time if this thing comes down."

"I've been in all along—as an accomplice. Now I'd just like to get paid for it. And I don't know if the land's for sale. Especially not cheap."

"Figured you might say that," he said. "They said get —one way or the other."

Hannah looked at the road ahead. They were coming into

Salem. Just a few more minutes. Her heart was beating in her throat.

"Spent last night figuring the angles. Logical thing is for you to inherit the farm—which you say you will—and then marry me."

"Marry you?"

"Yeah. Then I have control of the land. You know you've been leading up to it anyway. Why not go ahead? Makes sense. And no wife can testify against her husband. Besides, you got a big name around here, a reputation. We're not so likely to get raided."

"Those are hardly reasons for marriage," she said stiffly. "We'd better keep this as a business—"

Duke slammed on the brakes as he stopped in front of Jacob's office building. "Now, listen here," he said, turning to her. "You're in too far to start playing coy with me. You just get your skinny little butt up those steps and come back telling me you own the farm. With that in your pocket, things will go just fine. We'll get a justice of the peace this afternoon."

"You must be kidding." The look in his eyes told her he was deadly serious. "Duke, we don't know how this reading of the will is going to come out—"

"For your sake, it'd better come out right."

"But what if . . ."

"You'll do as I say. It's easy to forge a corpse's signature. Now get up there."

"I'll ride home with my daughter. You needn't wait."

"Like hell I won't. I'll be sitting right here until you come out." He reached across her lap and opened the door. "Get going," he said roughly.

Without a word, Hannah ran up the steps and in the door.

It seemed her heart would burst with fear. She was trapped. She paused on the landing to catch her breath. Where could she go? Duke was part of a powerful syndicate, and everyone knew how they handled anyone who crossed them. What was she to do?

There seemed to be no choice. She took out her compact, powdered her nose, then walked up the stairs into Jacob's office. Maybe something would come to her.

Not only was Fee's will a surprise, it also was a curve that Hannah was afraid Duke wouldn't accept. From Jacob's office window she could see him sitting in his car, smoking and waiting throughout the entire reading.

The shock she'd received with the gift of the flute shattered what little reserve she had left. It seemed to say she'd made so many wrong decisions and her mother knew it. It also told her that Fee had loved her anyway.

When the reading was over, she panicked and asked Josie to drive her up to Portland. She couldn't face Duke with the news that she wouldn't know what she had inherited for several months yet. He didn't like being put off—and he wouldn't believe her anyway.

She stood waiting for Josie at the bottom of the back stairs. What was taking so long? Duke would suspect something soon. She heard a car approaching and ducked back into the doorway. The long nose of Josie's roadster pulled up, and Hannah jumped in the door before it even stopped.

"Let's go out the alley," Hannah said, pointing toward the back of the block.

Josie followed her directions and as they pulled out on Liberty Street and headed toward Portland, she looked at Hannah and said, "Mother, what's going on? That Duke creep was waiting outside like a vulture over a dying calf. What's this all about?"

Hannah looked at her daughter. Josie, with her determined chin and flashing eyes, looked so much like Fionna, capable, confident, and beautiful. Maybe she'd better tell her. If she knew, she'd at least be prepared for whatever was coming. Hannah sighed in resignation and poured out the whole story.

"So, I'm in an awful position," she concluded. "If I make the wrong move, they'll kill me and forge the land sale. I'm trapped. To save my life, I'll have to marry Duke—and that's the best choice I have. I've probably angered him already just by running out like this. By now he's figured out—"

"Right you are," Josie said, looking in her rearview mirror. "He's figured it out and he's on our tail. Pull the side curtains down, Mother. I'm going to step on it."

Hannah gasped. "You can't outrun him," she said. "They'll find us eventually."

"Eventually will give us time to figure something out." She set her jaw and pushed down the throttle. Hannah watched the landscape swirl past the window, the roar of the powerful engine filling her ears, lulling her fear into a numb chill.

As they approached the outskirts of the city, Josie watched in her mirror. "He's still back there. We can't go to the house. That's where he'll look for us. So we'll make him think that's where we're going, and go somewhere else," she said, turning the wheel and taking the road that would lead to Fee's mansion.

Although Portland was a large city, it was nestled amid many rolling, forested hills. When houses were built, people merely cleared a space for their homes, leaving most of the natural trees, rhododendron bushes, and green underbrush growing on the hillsides. The terrain and vegetation made for many winding residential streets. Josie's roadster could take the turns faster than Duke's large Duesenberg so she was able to keep out of his sight most of the time. As they approached a neighborhood grocery store, Josie glanced in the mirror, and seeing that Duke was out of sight, quickly pulled behind the store and out of view of the road. Hannah watched in silence, her eyes watering from looking so hard, until finally the long, black Duesenberg roared by.

Josie leaned back in the seat. "He's heading straight for the house. Let's go check into a hotel."

"A hotel?"

"Yes. Even if he thinks of looking for us in hotels, he'll have to spend a lot of time going to all of them. And, if he finally finds us, we'll be surrounded by people. Rather hard to make trouble then, don't you think?"

"Then let's go to one of the big ones, one that would intimidate a gangster."

"Benson Hotel, here we come," Josie said with a flourish. She put the car in gear and turned around, heading back towards the city center. "It's not the biggest, but I like its feeling of luxury."

As they walked under the red awnings, Hannah couldn't help looking nervously over her shoulder. While Josie registered, Hannah paced the carpeted lobby, watching the street through the arched windows, expecting to see the black car at any time.

At Hannah's insistence, Josie put her car in a garage even before going up to her room. After she'd settled into her adjoining room, Josie came into Hannah's suite to figure out their next move.

"I think we should call the police," Josie said, sitting down in one of the overstuffed chairs.

"And what would we tell them?" Hannah asked. "That some man is trying to make me marry him? That's not a crime. Or better yet, tell them I have the largest illegal still on the West Coast sitting on my farm. That ought to put me
400

away—but not far enough away that Duke's Chicago bosses couldn't find me."

"You're right," Josie admitted. "It either sounds like the delusions of a frightened widow or a suicidal confession."

"So where does that leave us, counselor?" Hannah asked with a touch of despair.

"How about dinner? Let's call room service and eat while we decide."

Hannah had to laugh. "Josephine, you amaze me."

Within half an hour they were seated at the table in Hannah's room, eating duck à l'orange and discarding options. Finally Hannah put down her fork. "Well, we can't stay in the hotel forever, but maybe we should sit it out for a couple more days."

"Makes sense. Maybe by then we'll have something to take to the police."

"And the way your Uncle Timothy talks, Duke will have heard that the inheritance still is not settled."

Josie looked out the window for a moment. "I know what is settled."

"What's that, dear?"

"I'm not going to marry Ron West."

"What are you talking about? It's already been announced in the papers."

"I've been thinking about it a lot—especially since Gram died. Ron wants a farm wife, someone who'll stay home and raise his children, share the running of the farm. But I want more than that. Mother, please try to understand. I don't want to keep repeating the mistakes you and Grandmother made."

"What do you mean?" Hannah asked defensively.

"You know. Grandmother had a marriage that was practical—even compatible—but there was something missing. Like it was only half a marriage. And you and Dad, well . . . you didn't even have that much. I know you must have thought you were doing the right thing when you got married, but it obviously wasn't for the right reasons. I want someone who can share my interests, respect my intelligence, not just my body—someone with . . . everything."

"Do you have some Greek god in mind?" Hannah asked cynically.

"No. I just know it isn't Ron. I care for him very much—too much to give him half a wife. I'm not sure what it is I'd be

401

missing, but I don't want to be the third generation to miss it."

Hannah looked at Josie and saw the confusion and determination in her eyes. *If only I'd been able to see so clearly so young*, she thought. With a smile she reached out and took her daughter's hand. "I wish I'd had you around about twenty-seven years ago."

"But then I'd never have been born!" Josie laughed. And Hannah laughed with her.

Suddenly something occurred to her. "You know," she murmured, "I wonder if it was Ron. Remember, how I told you Duke ordered his guard to shoot 'that goody-goody' if he snooped around the still again?"

Josie's reaction was instant. "Of course it was. He said he was going to find out what Duke was up to. Oh, dear God," she exclaimed, jumping up. "If he goes over there tonight, he'll be killed. I've got to warn him."

"But if you go down in the lobby, you could be seen," Hannah protested.

"So what if I am? Do you think they'd carry me off in the middle of the lobby of the Benson Hotel?" Her face softened. "Okay, I'll wear your hat with the veil and I'll go straight to the phone booth and sit with my back to the room. Don't worry," she said, donning the hat. "See? You can't even tell it's me."

Hannah relented. "Be careful."

"You'll stay here?"

"Where else?" She smiled. "I think I'll read your Grandmother's letter."

Josie leaned down and kissed Hannah's cheek. "Better try to get some rest," she said. "It's been a long day. And Mother, I think we should tell Jacob tomorrow morning."

Josie closed the door behind her, and Hannah was left alone in the silence of her room.

The flute was lying on the bed. She lifted the latch of the leather case and looked at the beautiful instrument once more, caressing its satiny wood, fingering its silver keys. Why had Fee chosen to give it to her now?

Hesitantly, she brought the mouthpiece up to her lips and gently blew into it. A long, mournful note, as pure as the call of a dove, came out. Something long forgotten stirred inside her. She carefully put the flute back in its case, then took the bulky envelope out of her purse. It was addressed in Fee's hand. As she opened it, she gasped. Along with a handwrit ten letter, there were two open tickets for a luxury steamer trip to Europe, accompanied by prepaid reservations for a month's stay each in hotels in five major cities.

Tears filling her eyes, Hannah turned to the letter. The firm voice of her mother reached out past the barrier of death and spoke to her.

My beloved daughter,

This flute has given me joy, solace, courage, and even protection. Perhaps now it will do the same for you.

Years ago when you were young and rebellious you asked about the flute and I foolishly didn't tell you its story. Perhaps things would have gone differently if I had. Now, hoping it's not too late, I'll tell you.

I bought it on impulse when I was a frightened young woman facing the long trek west. While waiting for the roads to dry, we stayed in Independence, provisioning our wagons and generally being very practical. Then I saw the flute. I bought it out of my precious savings from the sale of your grandfather's farm—unbeknownst to your father. I even taught myself to play it, stealing hours of practice in the stable. When we started on the trail, I put it away, a frivolity in time of dire necessity.

Then one night, almost three months later, we were camped in the middle of the desert, surrounded by Indians, Indians made murderous by the acts of ruthless outlaws who'd preceded us. Men who were not on double guard duty sat around the campfires, cleaning their weapons and counting their ammunition, wondering how long they could hold out. We were outnumbered, and there was no one to rescue us.

The women and children were supposed to be sleeping. I doubt that any were. I couldn't stand the thought of these two peoples killing one another—all over a misunderstanding started by others. Earlier in the journey I exchanged a shawl for some boots with a lovely Indian maid. I'd looked into her eyes and seen a woman like myself dwelling inside her Indian skin and customs. I saw the Indians as people, not as animals nor as treacherous heathens, as many of the pioneers thought of them. As I sat listening to the Indian drums, I tried to think of a way to prevent the killing.

It was then that I remembered how your Grandfather Barry always asked me to play the piano when any of us were fighting. He would insist that we all curtail our anger long enough to listen, even sing along. The result was always a cooling of tempers, a soothing of hurt spirits. So, while everyone else was sitting around the campfire wondering if they were going to die at sunup, I dug into the bottom of my trunk for my flute.

If it didn't soothe the Indians, it might at least calm the frightened migrants. If it didn't calm the nerves of my fellow travelers, it would at least quiet mine. I played all the tunes I could remember, pulling them from my heart. The drums were silent with listening. The crying of children waned, and men set down their rifles.

When morning came, the Indians brought not arrows and bullets but a flag of truce and an offer. The chief wanted to buy me and my magic stick! I should have been honored that he offered such a high price, but instead I was frightened that your grandfather might accept it. After all, the lives of the entire wagon train might depend on it.

They worked out a compromise. Accompanied by your father, Jacob Teall, and Grandpa Ezekial, I went with the Indians to their village and played music for a dying chief, who proclaimed it had extended his life because it soothed his pain and made his spirit soar once more. The Indians then escorted us safely to the Snake River.

After that, I often played the flute for the people on the train. Sometimes I was joined by a fiddle, a harmonica, and a Jew's harp, an odd musical ensemble but effective enough to put smiles on weary faces and set toes to tapping.

When we finally reached the Columbia River, we knew that we were among the survivors, the ones lucky enough to be Oregonians. We had left our old lives behind forever. We had said good-bye to our relatives and friends in the East and buried our loved ones along the trail. The price for the journey was much higher than we'd anticipated. It was a bittersweet moment when we pushed off from the shore and leaned back against the rail of the raft ferrying us to Portland.

I looked around at my fellow travelers and knew they no longer had the will to even lift their heads up and see the beauty we were passing. Their spirits were finally broken. And I felt that mine was as well.

Once more I took out my flute. This time it was to

express the deep sorrow I felt. I wanted to say farewell to all I'd left behind, to mourn those we had buried.

When I played, grown men cried.

The music healed our wounds, and soon I was playing songs of promise, songs that had carried us to this new frontier. Soon these trailworn people were humming along. By the time we reached Portland, we were renewed.

The first winter in Oregon was the worst in remembered history. Your father and I were barely able to keep ourselves from freezing, much less our livestock. We managed somehow. And those long, lonely nights, the times when we were most discouraged, were lightened by the music of this flute.

When Donnell, the brother you never knew, was born, your father began his travels. We were left alone during the long winters. However, when Donnell cried and I ached with loneliness, I would bring out the flute and we were soothed.

Such are the gifts of music. Such is the gift I give you, reminding you of what you have put aside for too long. You were, and are, the most talented of all my children.

We are all faced with turnings in the road, and the choices we make in our life are often irreversible. But, my darling daughter, I'm trying to take you back to a turning in your road, back so you can choose once more which way your life will take. You have the rare chance to retrieve what you once so recklessly threw away.

The steamer tickets need only be confirmed with the company for a time convenient to you. I bought two so you could take another person with you, if you wished. However, you may also sell one or both of the tickets and use the money for something else. The choice is up to you.

Remember, music can drive away your loneliness and calm the wild demons who dance inside your heart and outside your door. Remember that I loved you.

Mother

Hannah set the letter down on the lamp table, hid her face in her hands, and sobbed. Her mother really understood after all. How could she have known?

Then, with the tears still on her cheeks, she looked once more at the tickets. The point of departure was Boston. Shaking her head, Hannah smiled. It was so typical of Mother.

Now she could ask her cousin Rose, Aunt Judith's niece, to accompany her. And Mother had left the transcontinental passage from Oregon to Boston up to Hannah. She'd have to pay for her own train ticket. How typical—Fee was afraid of spoiling her daughter, even after her death.

There was a sharp knock on the door. Hannah quickly wiped her eyes and called out, "Who is it?"

"Josie."

She unlocked the door and saw her daughter's worried face. "Mother, he doesn't answer the phone."

Hannah checked her watch. "Well, he still could be doing chores. Why don't you wait an hour and call again?"

"But what if he still doesn't answer?"

"I'm sure he will, dear." Hannah tried to make her voice sound reassuring. "Just wait and see."

She locked her door and stood there listening until she heard Josie's door shut and the lock turn. And what if he doesn't answer, she asked herself. What then?

Chapter XXXIV

Damn! Timothy thought as he slammed his car door. What the hell had his mother been thinking? How dare she force him to toady up to that damned Jew lawyer to get his just inheritance. And the nerve of Hannah—refusing to go along with him on the Round Top deal.

Trembling with rage, he drove back to his house much faster than normal, stopping in the driveway with a screech of brakes and a scatter of gravel.

Mrs. Burack, his housekeeper, met him at the door. "Dinner'll be ready in an hour, Mr. Coughlin."

"I won't be eating," he said with a growl as he went up the stairs to his room and slammed the door.

He pulled the envelope out of his pocket, and the watch chain snaked through his fingers as if it were alive. Daniel's watch chain. Stunned, he crawled onto his bed.

His mind spun as he lay looking up at the ceiling. Each breath was labored, as if a heavy weight sat on his chest.

The phone and doorbell rang throughout the late afternoon and evening. After he refused to answer her knock on his bedroom door, he heard Mrs. Burack telling callers that Mr. Coughlin was prostrate with grief over his mother's death. But that wasn't it.

He was numb with fear. He knew the watch chain with the broken latch was his dead brother's, the one he'd thought was lost in the river. Now it had returned to haunt him.

Why did his mother have it? How had she gotten it?

He was afraid to open her letter, afraid to find out what it said. Had she known all along of his betrayal of his twin—that Timothy was indirectly responsible for his own brother's death? Had she borne him hatred and loathing all these years?

More importantly, he was frightened that she'd put some malevolent bequest in her will, one that would reveal his misdeeds, and cut him off from his rightful inheritance. He couldn't wait the long months Teall said it'd take. What would this do to his political career? His mind paced like a caged animal, probing each corner, each possibility for escape.

It was seven-thirty before hunger finally pulled him out of his frightened torpor. He rang for Mrs. Burack, only to realize that she'd left. Grumbling, he got up and went downstairs to the kitchen. Just as he was about to make a sandwich, the phone rang.

"Timothy? Arney. I've been trying to get you all day."

"Yeah—well, I haven't been feeling well," he said to his campaign manager. After the painful afternoon Arney's voice just underlined Timothy's bleak prospects.

"Well, the great state of Oregon is going to miss Fionna Coughlin," Arney said, lowering his voice sympathetically. "But it still has her son. There's a big meeting tonight. Did you forget?"

"Oh. I guess I did—"

"Can't miss it, Timothy, not if you want to win the election. You need these people behind you one hundred percent. I've been nosing around. Sounds like it's going to fall your way tonight. You get yourself together. I'll be over in fifteen minutes."

Timothy's spirits rose after Arney's upbeat call. If the man was right, he'd be kissing babies and making speeches for the next six months. He'd have his senate seat. As he dressed, he smiled at himself in the mirror. Portly enough to be distinguished, he thought smugly, admiring his image. Then his eyes fell on the envelope. Maybe he'd better take a quick glimpse at it after all.

Just then Arney's horn sounded in the driveway. Time

enough later on for his mother's ramblings. Timothy grabbed his coat and hat and went out the door.

"Well, Timothy," Marshall Ranford said as they all sat down, "we've been discussing the political platform we'll be running on. Got anything you want to contribute?"

Timothy lit a cigar. "First thing is we've got to get this state's economy back on track. Too many jobs going to outsiders. Got to take care of our own first. And then I'll work to keep the Oregon school law from being struck down by those damn Supreme Court liberals. The Constitution gives the states authority over the education of their own. Don't need any court telling us we have to accept the Pope's teachings for our school kids." He flicked his cigar ash in the crystal ashtray by his elbow.

Reverend Cook nodded. "That's right. America is God's chosen land. The Good Lord didn't intend that we have our children exposed to foreign influences, in school or in the workplace. And, I must add, God didn't intend for women to have the vote. That's where most of these problems have come from."

Timothy cleared his throat. "Well, Reverend, I agree with you. But I can't see that we're going to have much luck trying to repeal the Nineteenth Amendment while they have the vote."

Reverend Cook's voice took on sonorous tones. "I'm only pleading God's case. We must vow to protect our fair sex from further exposure to the sordid life of public affairs. That's the battlefield for the strong, the men. We cannot allow the liberals, the misguided, the tawdry smut brokers, the moneyed Jews, and the Pope-worshiping Catholics to pull our delicate women from their rightful place in the home and the pedestals of our hearts." There was a respectful murmur and a couple of spontaneous "amens."

"I can assure you, Reverend," Timothy said, "that I will protect the American family and the women who are its cornerstone with every moral fiber in my body and soul." He lowered his voice dramatically. "Only a man who has been deprived of his family could understand so deeply its value."

There was a respectful pause before Howard Schultz, whose construction company built most of the state's highways, added his comments. "I believe, gentlemen," he began, "that we can assure Timothy here the full support of the organizations we represent. Am I correct?"

Nods and murmurs of "Absolutely," "Hear, hear," and "All the way to Washington" filled the room.

The rest of the evening was spent planning the strategy for Timothy's campaign, county by county and speech by speech.

"You haven't had much to say tonight, J.W.," Arney said later. J.W. Maloney was a big man with an equally big nose and dark hair sleeked back from his boney brow, the kind of man who didn't have to speak because others did it for him. There had been much speculation about J.W. ever since he'd moved into the state about two years ago, speculation ranging from how he made his money to why he was missing the first joint on three fingers of his left hand.

"I haven't been here long enough to know what works," he said, pleasing the ego of the old-timers in the room. "I just know it's every American's duty to support the best man. That's why I'm here." He paused dramatically, reaching into his coat pocket. "That's why I want to make a little contribution to your campaign," he said, handing a check to Timothy. "You don't have much worry in the primary, but I think you could use this in the general election. That Democrat is talking like he wants to give you a run for your—ah, your—money."

Everyone laughed at his joke. "Why, that's generous of you, J.W.," Timothy said, then as he glanced at the amount, "most generous of you!"

Arney looked over his shoulder. "Gentlemen, here's a man who puts his money where his mouth is. J.W. here has just donated two thousand dollars to the Coughlin for Senator campaign."

There was a brief round of applause. Then Marshall reached into his pocket and pulled out his checkbook. "Gentlemen, this magnanimous newcomer had to teach us where our duty is. I'm writing a check this very moment, one I'm sure will be accompanied by your own contributions. And this is just the beginning. We represent some of the most influential organizations in this state, and Timothy Coughlin is guaranteed their financial support as well."

Before the evening was over, Arney had over five thousand dollars to deposit in Timothy's campaign account. The party broke up with a feeling of euphoria. "Our boy's a winner!" called one man as they left the house.

As they walked towards his car, Arney slapped Timothy on the back. "A few more nights like this and you won't have to worry about that inheritance."

J.W. put his arm possessively around Timothy's shoulder "Tell you what, Coughlin," he said, "come over to my car. got something else for you."

"Sure, J.W. Wait for me, Arney?"

"No problem."

"Grain business must be treating you good," Timothy said as he followed J.W. to his car.

"Good enough," he replied. "I thought you might need this for some of your personal expenses during the campaign," he said, holding out a check. Timothy could see it in the dashboard light. "It pays to take care of our own."

"Well, I'm mighty proud to be considered your own," Timothy said, looking at the check. "Good God, man, this is a twin to the other one."

"The beginning of a good relationship." J.W. smiled. " was talking to my associate, Duke, the other day. Seems we might have a union in the works. Doesn't hurt to work closely with your own kind. Here," he said, reaching into the side pocket of his car, "take this along with you. Man needs to relax now and then." He shoved a paper-wrapped bottle into his hand.

Timothy looked grateful. "You sure know how to make man happy. We'll keep in touch."

"No doubt about it," J.W. said, sliding behind the wheel "There's more where that came from."

Timothy looked up as he walked over to Arney's car. The stars were like bright, sharp pins in the sky.

Back in his room Timothy decided to treat himself an open the bottle of smooth corn whiskey J.W. had given him It'd been a memorable evening, and he wanted to celebrate

He took a sip of the amber liquid and sat back in his eas chair, feeling the whiskey warm a path down his throat. The the white envelope on the dresser caught his eye. He reache over and picked it up, studying his mother's strong, precis handwriting. Might as well read what she scribbled in he dotage, he thought, tearing open the seal.

He glanced over the first three pages and realized that sh was telling him the story of her father and brother's murder way back at the beginning of the Civil War. It was a familia family story and he couldn't help wondering why on earth sh was repeating it. He glanced over the pages, preparing t toss them aside, when her words caught his attention.

Revenge was my only thought. You see, although I was thousands of miles and years away from the crime, I was still haunted by it. Many were the nights when I awakened screaming, frightened by the sight of my father's twisted neck or my brother's bloodied body. Then I would lie awake in the dark, contemplating how I would someday, somehow, revenge their deaths.

My chance came when I least expected it. One evening when you and Daniel were still small and your father was away from home, I received a visit from a stranger. You children were visiting Grandpa Ezekial. As was the custom in those days, I obliged him with directions and a meal. When he offered to pay for the meal, I realized why he frightened me. He was one of the men I saw ride by after the massacre. I took his money and went to get change. He followed me into the bedroom. Perhaps he intended to rob me. I didn't give him a chance. I shot him dead.

Then I became obsessed. His blood didn't slake my thirst for further revenge. I remembered the claim he said he was looking for, the farm of an old friend of his. I couldn't get it from my mind that the friend must also be one of the murderers.

The next morning I rode to the stump farm he'd asked about. I approached the man who was working there and instantly recognized him as one of my father's and brother's murderers. His protests when he saw my gun quickly changed to admission that he was only following his friends. He was lying. His actions that day were indelibly imprinted in my memory. I could still see him wiping my brother's blood from his knife. I shot him in the face, wiping out his lies as I wiped out his life.

I rode home, numb, not even knowing when I finally arrived. I was miserable. I'd found out what only the unfortunate in life know: revenge begets revenge. I was haunted by their faces. My hands were stained with their blood.

Two days later, your father returned home. He carried in the half-dead body of a young girl. She was nearly frozen, starving and sick with pneumonia that she'd acquired while burying her husband, who had "accidentally shot himself." She was the girl-wife of the murderer I had murdered. She was Nell.

I took her in and nursed her back to health, hoping to

buy my own peace of mind with her life, hoping to retrieve my own sanity through her.

Nell has never known the true story. She lived as one of our family, serving us faithfully throughout all her life. Nell is my responsibility, the legacy of my revenge. And now I am passing this secret and this legacy on to you.

You are to see that Nell is always cared for. Before my death I transferred ownership of a small bit of property in Corvallis into Nell's name. It is your responsibility to manage that property in such a manner that she never wants for anything. Should the property ever prove to be insufficient for her care, you are to care for her out of your own pocket.

You must know that your father and I always believed that no human being should be enslaved, physically or mentally, by another human being. We helped a family of escaping Negroes on the trail. After arriving in Oregon, we continually helped those less fortunate, including the Indians and the Chinese. That became my atonement for my useless acts of revenge. And now it is yours.

I am also giving you your brother's watch chain, the one that matches yours, given with fatherly pride and in the hope of your brilliant futures. Alas, that pride and hope were cut in half when your brother was killed like a spring flower in a late frost.

You may wonder how I happen to have his watch chain when all these years everyone else has thought it was lost in his fall from the bridge. You speculated that it was stolen and asked the police to investigate, remember?

However, I stopped any investigation after a visit from Mr. Ranahan, the grief-stricken father of Mary Catherine, Daniel's sweetheart.

It seems that Daniel was planning on running away to marry Mary Catherine instead of going east to school with you. Through unfortunate circumstances, Mr. Ranahan learned of the time and place of their proposed rendezvous. He went to stop them.

He got to the bridge before Mary Catherine did and tried to talk to Daniel, reasoning with him, pleading with him. Daniel wouldn't listen. In fact, he was much angered that the man knew where to find him, asking him over and over again how he found out.

412

*When Mary Catherine arrived, Mr. Ranahan reached
out to grab Daniel. Daniel pushed him aside. Mr. Ranahan,
in frustration, lunged for Daniel and Daniel sidestepped,
only to lose his balance and fall against the rotten railing
of the old bridge. Mr. Ranahan reached out to catch him
but grasped only his watch chain, which broke off in his
hand.*

*Mary Catherine watched her beloved Daniel fall to his
death. The tragedy was too much for her sensitive nature. Her parents placed her in the care of a holy order
of sisters—but even they were unable to help. She died
within the year.*

*Mr. Ranahan came to me a broken man. He confessed
his part in Daniel's death, asking me to turn him over to
the authorities so that he could be punished.*

*I had already learned my lesson on revenge. I assured
him that it was an unfortunate accident and to deprive
his wife and family of his presence would only add to
what was already a tragedy. I took the watch chain and
promised that his story would go no further. Mr. Ranahan
served me faithfully throughout the years.*

*Since we are now both dead and no harm can come of
this knowledge, I believe that it should be passed on to
you. Perhaps you can learn from it.*

*The ultimate tragedy was that there was no opposition
to the marriage. Had we known, we might have encouraged the youngsters to wait until Daniel finished school,
but we would not have opposed the union. Mr. Ranahan
thought that we wouldn't approve of Daniel marrying a
Catholic girl, because he didn't approve of her marrying
out of the Church. However, that was never the case.
Had we known, we would have welcomed Mary Catherine into our family. If only we had known.*

*Please, my son, take these bits of family history and
profit from them, knowing that you needn't continue the
unfortunate legacy of revenge, knowing that you have a
personal obligation to carry on our best intentions and
avoid our worst mistakes.*

> *I give you my love and hope,*
> *Mother*

Timothy sat staring at the pages in front of him. What the
hell had she told him all this crap for? Was she saying she

knew he'd betrayed his brother? If so, why didn't she just come out and say he was disinherited? That was what mattered.

He looked back over the pages once more. There was no mention of his inheritance. She'd been an old woman. Maybe her mind had been more addled than they'd thought it was.

With a disgusted snort he walked over to his desk. He threw the letter down and took out a pen and paper. There was no more time to waste speculating on such drivel. He had to prepare a speech for the Grange meeting in Roseburg.

Chewing on his pen, he glared at the sheets of paper with his mother's firm handwriting. He should order some signs. Damn. If he only knew how much money he had to work with.

He turned to the speech, dipping his pen in the inkwell. The boys at the meeting had pretty well laid out what he should say. Hit hard on the American way. Exclusion of foreigners. The danger of unions taking over the free market, and Jews taking over the state's banking and universities. He wrote furiously, venting his frustration in the written word.

The hall clock chimed as he put down the pen. It was 5:00 A.M. The thin gray of dawn outlined the branches of the oak tree outside his upstairs window. Time to get some rest. Tonight there was a Klan meeting in Portland.

Chapter XXXV

Josie waited half an hour and then went downstairs to call again. When Ron still didn't answer she paced her room for fifteen minutes, then tried once more. Finally, at eleven o'clock, she could stand it no longer.

Her mother's lights were off. There was no need to awaken her; she'd be back before morning, anyway. Quietly Josie slipped out the back door of the hotel and to her roadster. She must warn Ron. She had to make sure he was all right.

All the way through the darkened countryside, she thought of reasons why he wasn't answering the phone. A cow calving—or maybe the tractor broke down and he was working on it—or maybe the phone was out. The last idea made the most sense. A strong wind was blowing black clouds across the moon.

Still, her heart beat anxiously. She wouldn't rest until she knew. The usual hour-and-a-half drive took sixty-five minutes.

When she was almost there, rain began pouring down in sheets across the highway. The range of her headlamps was not great, and the heavy rain made her speed even more dangerous. Still, she kept going.

No lights were on in the house or the barn as she drove down the long driveway. Josie began to feel foolish. The telephone lines probably were down, and Ron was sleeping peacefully. She considered turning around and going back to Portland, but she didn't.

Parking the car by the front porch, she ran up the steps and rang the doorbell. Wind whipped the rain under the porch roof and she stood shivering, waiting for him to answer. A strange sound, a steady whap-whap, whap-whap, came from out back. She rang again. Still no answer.

With the rain running down her neck, she ran to the back of the house, splashing cold water in her shoes and up her legs. The pounding got louder as she rounded the corner. The back door was open, banging in the wind. Why didn't Ron hear it?

She ran up the steps, slipping on the wet laundry room floor as she went in.

"Ron! Are you here?" She reached for a light switch but nothing happened. The power was out.

"Ron!" she called as she fumbled in the kitchen drawer for a candle. "Ron!" Her voice quaked as she felt her way to the stove to find the matchbox. Then her foot bumped something soft and she heard a low moan. Trembling, she lit the candle.

"Oh, dear God."

Ron was lying on the floor, his blood seeping into his mother's rag rug. "Ron, what happened?"

He moaned, then his eyes fluttered open. "Duke . . . till . . ."

"Yes, I know. Your chest—you're shot. Shh, don't try to talk. I've got to get you to the doctor." She blew out the candle and tried to lift him, her heart pounding in her throat.

As she draped his arm around her shoulder and staggered up with him, she glanced out the back door. Two wobbling pinpoints of light were coming up the field behind the barn.

"They're coming!" she cried. "Help me, Ron! We've got to get you to the car and out of here!"

He groaned, and she could feel him moving with her. His feet wouldn't stay under him, but he struggled, trying to walk. Between them, she got him through the living room to the front door. As she fumbled with the doorknob, she heard voices coming up behind the house.

"Leave me . . . save yourself . . ." he said, moaning.

"Don't be a fool," she snapped as she pushed the door open with her hip.

He had gone limp by the time she reached the steps. Luckily, the car was close by. She dragged him down the steps. He moaned, straightened up and tried to help her as she sat him in the seat and pushed his legs in. She heard a shout as she slammed the door and ran around to the driver's side.

She said a silent prayer as she pushed the starter. The engine turned over the first time.

"Hey!" a man shouted from the front steps. "Hold it! Stop right there!"

She slammed it into gear and stepped on the accelerator, turning on the lights as the car leaped forward.

There was a blast of gunfire. The glass on her side wing shattered, and she ducked behind the steering wheel. They fired again and again. It sounded as if the soft top of her roadster tore, and there was a thunk against the dashboard. At the same time she saw headlights turning down the driveway.

Josie was trapped.

Pushing her roadster as fast as she could on the gravel, she headed straight at the bigger car. If she timed it right, she might be able to make it. The headlights got bigger and she knew he was deliberately coming at her head-on.

Suddenly, just before they hit, she veered to the left. The Duesenberg just scraped her front fender. Her wheels caught on firm gravel, and she was past them. Ron had a pull-off that he'd built so cars and farm equipment could pass one another on the drive. Josie had found it in the dark.

She knew she'd bought only a brief head start with that trick. It wouldn't take them long to turn around and be hot on her tail. She reached the highway and floored the throttle.

She was driving faster than her headlamps or the rain safely allowed, but she was counting on her familiarity with the road, along with her smaller car's ability to take curves, to give her an advantage over Duke's large and powerful Duesenberg. It was her only hope.

She wasn't even sure she knew where she was going. The hospital? They couldn't protect them from gangsters. The police? How could she explain it all?

416

"Hang on, Ron," she said, "this is going to be one ride we'll never forget."

From the silence she knew Ron was unconscious. *At least he isn't feeling any pain*, she thought.

The headlights of the car were behind her, coming closer on the straight stretches, falling behind on the curves. She neared Salem. The river ahead. Down through the little gully, across the covered bridge, and up the hill. Town four miles from there.

Looking in her rearview mirror, she saw the big car gaining on her. She barely lifted her foot as she went down the hill and around the curve into the gully before the bridge. The turn was sharp, but she knew it was coming and maintained control. It was the only place she could hope to get far enough ahead to make it.

She heard her tires squeal on the pavement as she turned the corner approaching the bridge. With a quick shift down and a firm grip on the wheel, she was able to make it onto the bridge. The wooden floor rumbled under her wheels and then she pushed the accelerator down as she headed out of the bridge and up the hill.

She watched in the mirror as she approached the hill and saw the big car swerving around the corner to the bridge, its headlights careening off the treetops. It was out of control. Then, as it came to the bridge, its headlights suddenly dimmed. There was a flash of light and an explosion. She slammed on her brakes and stopped at the top of the hill. The bridge was burning.

With a whistle she let out the breath she'd been holding. "I think we're safe, Ron," she said in a shaky voice.

There was no answer. She glanced at him, shadowed in the light from the dashboard. His head was on his chest. She had a horrid foreboding that she quickly pushed from her mind.

The rest of the trip into Salem was a blur of swirling thoughts, jumbled and confused. She talked frantically to Ron, filling the ominous silence with a flurry of words.

"Don't worry. I know they're gone. No one could ever make it through that explosion and fire. You were right, you know. Right about Duke. Mother said so. I know you didn't like him."

She began crying as she drove, her tears blurring her view of the road in front of her. "I know you wanted me to be with you. I'm sorry, so sorry, Ron."

417

Before she realized what she was doing, she stopped in front of Jacob's house and ran up the steps.

Sobbing, she rang the bell. Time spun an eternity before he answered the door.

He turned on the porch light, and she saw him standing there in his bathrobe, his hair tousled. "Josie," he said, blinking in the light. "What's the matter?"

She had no breath to talk. She simply pointed to the car. Jacob ran out to look while she collapsed against the doorjamb, sobbing silently.

Jacob looked up at her from the bottom of the steps. "He's dead. Shot in the chest and head. Josie, what happened? Oh, Josie . . . stop now. Come on in. You can't sit out here like this." He lifted her up and helped her into the house.

In bits and pieces Josie told Jacob the story. He called the doctor and the police. When they arrived, Josie tried to answer their questions as best she could. Then she took the doctor's medicine and could remember no more.

The next morning she awakened to find herself in Jacob's spare bedroom, wearing a pair of his pajamas. She saw the bright sunlight streaming through the window. The clock said eleven o'clock. Then it all came back in a bitter rush that made her eyes fill with tears and her throat tighten.

Jacob's bathrobe was on the end of her bed. She put it on and went downstairs to the kitchen. Jacob was sitting at the table reading the paper, and his housekeeper, Old Miss Wyman, was at the sink peeling potatoes.

"Ah, you're finally awake," he said, looking up. "How're you feeling?"

"A little rocky. Was last night a nightmare?"

"Afraid not."

"What happened?" Josie said. "I remember getting here. You said Ron was dead?"

"Yes. I'm sorry. He was shot in the back of the head, died instantly. There are five bullet holes in your car. You're lucky you weren't killed," he said, concern in his eyes. "The police surmised you drove out of West's yard in a hail of gunfire and one of the bullets hit him. He might have survived the chest wound, but not the head wound."

"I see," she whispered. "Then he was dead all the way in. He never knew—"

"The police went back to the bridge," Jacob explained. "They said it was burned out. They found the remains of the Duesenberg along with three bodies. They don't have a posi

418

tive I.D. but the gold tooth in one indicates it was Duke. We should tell your mother. Do you know where she is?"

"Mother? Oh, yes," Josie said, looking up. "I drove her up to Portland yesterday." She wiped her hand across her eyes, as if trying to clear her vision. "At least I think it was yesterday."

Josie told him about the chase to Portland, Hannah's discovery of the still, and Duke's ultimatum and threat. "Mother's been terrified ever since. She couldn't go to the police because they'd think she was an accessory; the still was on her property. Oh, the still," she exclaimed, suddenly remembering. "We've got to tell the authorities."

"I told them what you said last night. The Feds are probably out there right now axing the place."

Josie shuddered. The phone rang, interrupting what she was going to say.

Jacob answered it. "It's Emmett. Says he couldn't find you or his mother and was worried. I told him what happened. Feel like talking to him?"

"I'd better." She went out to the hall and picked up the receiver. "Oh, Emmett."

"Josie, are you all right? My God, I can't believe what's happened. You're lucky you weren't killed."

"I know."

"I'm sorry about Ron. You must be a mess."

"You might say that. More confused than anything, though. Emmett, I feel so guilty. I told Mother last night that I was going to break off my engagement to Ron and now . . ." She swallowed hard, trying not to cry.

"Ah, Sis, don't worry. He never knew."

"I guess so," she said hesitantly. "Why were you trying to call me?"

"I wanted to read you Gram's letter. It's just crackerjack. Feel up to hearing it?"

"I'd love to," Josie said, sitting down, and he began.

My dearest Emmett,
It seems as if our brightest and best belong to the third generation. It is to you that I turn with the dreams your grandfather and I held together. Of all our progeny, you most of all will appreciate hearing about your grandfather's last trip to eastern Oregon. He asked me to accompany him, and it was one of the most memorable months of my life.

We took the train to the Bar C Ranch. From there I followed him as he checked the summer rangeland and the logging operations. Because of erosion due to overgrazing he had Button plan on taking the cattle to another range the following summer, even though it was not the most convenient grazing land for the ranch. He also called the foreman of the logging operation on the carpet for taking the easy way of harvesting the trees and tearing up the land. Before we left, we had a new foreman.

From there we rode the train to the other three ranches. It was the first time I had seen two of them, and I was impressed with the grandeur and beauty of the land as much as I was with the ranches.

When we got to Big Valley Ranch outside of Lakeview, we had a most unusual experience. The ranch foreman, Shy, had a half-grown bobcat following him around the ranch. When he went in at night, he would put her in a cage. She even answered to her name, Tawny. I was delighted by her grace, her intelligent yellow eyes, and paws that seemed too big for the rest of her.

Your grandfather didn't seem as enthralled. He immediately asked Shy why he still had her. He'd told him to put her back in the wilds when he first found her. Shy explained that he was afraid she wouldn't be able to fend for herself.

"So now what have you done?" your grandfather asked. "She's not where she's supposed to be. She's away from her own kind and can't take care of herself. She'll get a taste for chickens or run up to some stranger and end up getting shot. She should be out running free."

Shy had no answer because he knew it was the truth.

The next day, your grandfather and I took off for the mountains, leading two packhorses. We camped by a high mountain lake, miles from any trace of other humans. And while we camped, your grandfather taught Tawny to fend for herself.

To my delight and his disgust, she slept in our tent the first night, purring. But by the second night he had her interested enough in hunting that she was out wandering. The fact that she wasn't interested in our breakfast fish gave us our first hope. We spent that day looking for a likely home for her. By late afternoon, your grand-

420

father found a small cave under a rock ledge that didn't have any sign of use by other animals.

He shot a squirrel and threw it into the dark cave. Tawny raced after it with a hungry growl, and your grandfather smiled. We rode back to camp alone. Tawny didn't come around camp until late the following afternoon. She wasn't hungry, and her skittishness indicated she was adapting to the wild. When she left at dusk, we knew she was where she belonged. We broke camp and rode back to the ranch the following day. The whole operation had taken nine days' time and effort on your grandfather's part. And he had willingly spent it to return a wild creature to the land where she belonged.

Your grandfather was a man of the land, always learning, observing, and exploring. He taught you that as a small boy. Now I have given you his journals, and he will continue teaching you.

Read them, for this is the best legacy your grandparents can give to you.

Know that our love and hopes are always with you,
Grandmother

"That's a wonderful story," Josie said softly.

"Sounds like something he would have done," Emmett
id.

"Have you looked at the journals yet?" she asked.

"That's what I wanted to tell you. I'm going up to Round
p to read them. I think that's what he'd want. I'm going to
ad them straight from 1861—that's when Grandma gave
m his first journal when they started out on the trail west—
ar up until June 1905, right before he died."

"Sounds great, Em. When do you think you'll come back?"

"Do you know when Ron's funeral will be?"

"Probably Monday. Is three days long enough?"

"If it isn't, I'll come on down anyway. What about your
ter?"

"I'm ashamed to admit it, but I haven't had a chance to
ad it. I think I'll take some time off to read it this weekend,
."

"Just what the doctor ordered. See you Monday. And, Sis?"

"Yes?"

"I love you."

"I love you, too," she said softly.

She stood for a moment with her hand on the receiver. Then she knew what she was going to do, what she had to do.

"Jacob, do you think I'll be needed here?"

"Probably not. I can make the funeral arrangements. There's no reason for you to stick around. Why?"

"Would you call Mother for me? I'm going to take the next three days and go over to the coast. I don't want anyone to know where I am. I need time to think, to be by myself, and to talk to Grams. I still have to read her letter."

The drive to the Oregon coast felt like an escape—so much so that, for the first stretch, Josie kept checking her rearview mirror to see if she were being followed.

However, as the towering trees of the Coast Range began enclosing the highway, her fears slowly dissipated. By the time the winding road took her over the thickly wooded summit and followed the cascading streams to the ocean, her spirits were lifted. She felt as if she were where she belonged.

Driving down the coast highway, she could see the off-shore cloud bank move inland. The setting sun gilded the great purple mounds of clouds and cast a golden path across the shimmering water.

She headed straight for a little motor inn with small, slant-roofed cabins. By nightfall she was sitting in a cafe, eating clam chowder and sipping tea.

That night she opened her window so she could hear the ocean's roar and smell the sea mist. Then she sat down in front of a crackling fire and opened her grandmother's letter. As she read the words, she heard Fionna's voice and knew she wasn't alone.

My darling Josephine,

Your letter is the most difficult to write. I think it's because it's the one I want to write to the most. There is so much I want you to know, so much I want for you, yet I can't seem to find the right words. I guess the best thing for me to do is to talk to you as if you were sitting here, holding my hand, and tell you stories about my life that might most help you with yours. You have so much ahead of you. I want you to be able to avoid the pitfalls that caused me the most pain.

We can accomplish more in life if we have the right bonds of love—and we can be kept from accomplishments if we form the wrong bonds. I'm afraid that I must admit to having known both the advantages and disadvantages of loving the right and wrong men. Many men can provide part of what we need in our lives. However, there are very few who can provide all. Let me explain.

Your grandfather, Nathanial Coughlin, was my connection to my homeland, my security, and a wonderful man. I admired him tremendously. However, as I think you may have guessed, he never was everything to me. And because of that, I felt I was a little less than I could have been. Although we had a physical attraction and a common ground that went back to Virginia, your grandfather couldn't understand many of the things that were important to me—like music and art and investing for future generations. And I must admit that I didn't share his love of exploring, his need always to be on the move, much less his understanding of the wilderness.

What your grandfather didn't provide I found elsewhere. I had another man in my life, a man who was my intellectual companion, who shared his books and his love with me, who encouraged me in my investments—in fact, helped me immeasurably. He was exciting, passionate, and forbidden. He was the father of your Uncle Matthew. He was Jacob Teall, young Jacob's grandfather.

You see, I spent my life torn between two loves, never fulfilled with either one, always feeling as if I was missing something, always longing for what I didn't have right there with me. I don't want that for you. I want you to find the one man who can be your intellectual, spiritual, and physical lover, a man who shares your beginnings and holds the promise for your future, one who won't hold you down but will be your partner in life, one who will share all your dreams.

That's why I've chosen these gifts for you. The ring is from your great-grandmother's dowry, the one she brought over from Ireland with her. There is a matching brooch she gave my sister, your Aunt Judith, for her wedding day. This ring was for mine. It represents your beginnings, your roots.

The other gift is one I could seldom use. It is a pair of earrings made from two gold nuggets I found in eastern Oregon on our way out here. That find was the beginning of a gold mine and a partnership with Jacob Teall that lasted the rest of our lives. He saved these two *nuggets, refusing to sell them even when we both could have used the money they would have brought. Then, years later, when he was able, he had them made into earrings and set with emeralds. It was his gift of love to me, an extravagant gift and one I always cherished.*

Keep these two gifts from me, and know that through them I am reminding you of the love you must seek. Do not settle for less. I was a broken circle, incomplete, because all my life I was torn between two men. But you, you can complete that circle. You can live the life that could have been mine.

My love will always be with you.
Grandmother

Josie finished reading the letter, then, with tears slidin down her cheeks, looked out the window. It had taken s much love for Fionna to tell her this. She put on the earring and ring and felt closer to her grandmother.

Josie spent the next three days walking the beach, cros hatching the wet sand with her footprints, watching the s gulls skim the wavetops. Breakers veined the rocks with the white foam, and she felt at one with the elements.

She spent Sunday sitting on a pile of driftwood, watchi the fog move back and forth between the land and se Spindly-legged sandpipers poked the shoreline with the long bills, touching their reflections on the wet sand. It w then that she knew her grandmother was right. She unde stood, at least in part, what Fee would have her do. Th afternoon, she packed her things and drove back to Salem.

It was late that night when she rang Jacob's bell. "I do want to make this a habit," she said when he opened t door, once more in his bathrobe, "but I wanted to talk you."

"Josie." He smiled and invited her in. "I just got a c from Emmett. He's on his way over."

"Seems as if you're cursed with us."

"Not at all. I wasn't even in bed yet, just reading. Besid I can't think of anyone I'd rather see anytime, day or nig Any two people," he finished hastily.

"Well, it's good of you to say so," she said. "I've be thinking, and somehow it seemed that you should be the fi person to tell."

"Tell what?"

"I'm going to spend the next few months preparing for the bar examinations this fall."

"That's wonderful!" His smile seemed to light the room, and Josie knew in that moment that she was doing the right thing. "Fionna would be so pleased," he added softly.

"I know. I think she's the one who decided for me—so long ago. I just had to come around."

Jacob looked at her, his dark eyes warm with pride and affection. Josie swallowed hard and looked away, unable to face his intensity.

Just then the doorbell rang. Emmett came in, fairly bursting with pent-up energy. "I've just spent the most fantastic three days up on Round Top. It's like I've been talking to Grandpa the whole time. Got a better understanding of myself, too. I can tell you, I needed it."

Josie had to laugh. "I know what you mean. I feel as if I've been talking to Grandmother these past three days."

"But where's Mom?" he said, looking around. "We need her to make this complete. Besides, she needs to hear what I have to say."

"Oh, she's still at the hotel," Jacob said. "She's been out shopping all weekend. Seems Fionna gave her a trip to Europe with her letter."

"How perfect," Josie said.

"Well, she feels it's the solution to all her problems," Jacob said. "She doesn't want anyone else to know where she is, though. She's worried about retaliation for Duke's death, but she'll feel safe overseas. She said she'd write to us as soon as she arrives—"

"Speaking of Duke," Emmett interrupted, "that's what I wanted to tell you. We all may have a problem there."

"How's that?" Jacob asked.

"Josie, remember that trumpeter, Gus? Well, he was up in Seattle. I had to make a rum run from Victoria for a roadhouse up there. I know, I know," he said, holding up his hands before Jacob could protest.

He walked over and pulled the window shade all the way down. "Gus told me there's a price on my head—on all our heads. Seems this gang of Duke's is pretty big stuff. They had Oregon and Washington sewed up with that operation on the farm. Now it's gone, they feel they have to teach us a lesson—as a warning to anyone else who might double-cross them. That's what they're calling it, a double cross. They're looking for Mother and for us, too."

"What does it mean?" Josie asked. "Should we hide? Shoul we talk to the police or the Bureau of Investigation?"

"Hard to get protection based on a warning from a travel ing musician," Jacob pointed out. "Did he give you an names? Times? Anything specific to go on?"

Emmett shook his head. "Not really. Referred to one a Fingers—whatever that means. No last name. Said they wer very powerful. He was playing a gig where they met an overheard them talking when he was cleaning up. They sa him and shut up. He played dumb, whistling and putting h instruments away. Said he didn't dare stay to hear more. Bu he did hear them mention our names—called Mom 'th Balfour dame' and us 'her brats.' This Fingers guy told th other two to take care of us—permanently. That's when the saw Gus."

"Any description of the other two?" Josie asked.

"Too dark. He said one was short, heavyset, dark hai Other one was tall, light-haired, and walked with a lim That's it."

"Where do they come up with these names?" Josie sai shaking her head. "It's hard to take anyone named Finge seriously."

"Nicknames make it hard to trace them," Emmett e plained. "Jacob Teall is a lot easier to find than Finger Often their own people don't even know their real names."

"Don't tell me how you know all this," Josie said with shudder.

"I'll check with the authorities tomorrow," Jacob sai "Ask them if they have anything on the syndicate running th still, or someone called Fingers. You'd better stay here tonight

Ron's funeral was scheduled for 10:00 A.M. in the churc followed by a graveside service.

As Josie sat in the front pew, listening to the minister ta about Ron's many fine qualities, she felt tears of regret we up in her eyes. It wasn't until the end of the service that sh noticed Emmett was fidgeting. "What's the matter?" sh whispered.

"There are two strangers at the back of the church. One tall and blond, other's short and dark."

"Do you think—?"

"I don't know. Just watch them. We're supposed to go o first, then everyone else files out. If they leave before th rest of the congregation—and the tall one limps—we'll know

426

Josie didn't hear a word of the rest of the service. She just felt the hair on the back of her neck prickling.

As they got up to leave, Josie glanced back. The two strangers were putting on their hats and going out. She clasped Emmett's hand tightly and whispered, "They just left. And he limped."

As soon as they were in the sanctuary, Josie looked back through the door and gestured for Jacob.

"What's going on?" he asked.

"There're two strangers who answer Gus's descriptions," Emmett explained. "Here are the keys to my car. Go around back and bring it to the side door just off the chapel. The procession is forming on the other side of the church. You drive us to the barn where I have my plane. We'll fly over to the Bar C. You can call us there when things look better."

Within minutes they were in Emmett's car, crouching on the floor, with Jacob at the wheel. "I'd love to see their faces when they realize we're not at the cemetery," Jacob said as they headed out of Salem.

When they arrived, Jacob pulled the car around to the back of the barn. Emmett jumped out and lifted the trunk lid. "Here," he said, handing Josie a pair of goggles and a scarf, "put these on and get in the passenger seat. Jacob, help me push it out the door."

Josie climbed into the passenger seat, her heart pounding. She couldn't take her eyes from the road they had come in on. Was that a plume of dust?

"Hurry!" she called. "I think someone's coming."

Emmett jumped into the pilot's seat and told Jacob how to turn the propeller. When the engine caught, Jacob stepped back out of the way. Josie held her breath while the plane bumped across the field like a clumsy bird, then gracefully lifted into the air.

Emmett circled around once to see that Jacob was leaving safely and then headed towards the mountains and the high desert country. Josie turned and watched until she could see Jacob no longer.

A whirlwind blew the plume of dust across the field. Was that what all this was? Was she frightened by a whirlwind of dust, or was she really in danger?

Chapter XXXVI

"Emmett! And is that Josie?" Mateo cried as he jumped out of his truck. "How wonderful to—" He stopped. "What's the matter?"

"Tell you later," Emmett called down. "That hay barn out by Coyote Gulch empty?"

"This time of year? You bet. Why?"

"Meet us there. Give the prop a turn, will you?"

Mateo turned the prop, then stepped back with a puzzled expression on his face as Emmett took off.

They flew out over the range, circled back, came in low through a canyon, then up Coyote Gulch. The plane bounced violently, landing on the range. Josie gritted her teeth and clenched the seat edge with both hands.

As they coasted up to the old hay barn, Emmett cut the engine and jumped out. "Come on, let's get this thing in there before someone spots it."

Josie climbed down, careful not to let her heels tear the wing covering. She put her shoulder to the plane and they both pushed it through the open doorway.

"How did you know it would fit?" Josie asked, leaning against the barn to catch her breath.

"It's a standard opening. Jenny here fits in most barns."

"You've had reason to hide her before." It was a statement not a question, and Emmett acted as if he needn't reply as he shoved the doors shut.

It made Josie's heart turn over just thinking that her brother had put himself in so many precarious situations. Still, that was part of Emmett. She could remember him walking on the barn beams at Quail Hollow, scaring her to death as he balanced forty feet overhead, whistling and cracking jokes while she pleaded with him to come down.

"You think it's necessary to hide over here?" she asked.

"People over here are just as thirsty as people in Portland. I make deliveries to Pendleton. I assume they've got a network set up. No telling if they're associated or not. Best no gamble."

"I suppose you're right. What about the ranch hands?"

"We'll see what Mateo says. Personally, I think there's no problem with the ones who live on the place. The ones going back and forth to town might unwittingly let something slip."

"It might be a good idea—" She stopped, listening. "Is that Mateo's truck?"

Emmett was peeping through a crack in the door. "Yeah." He opened the side door, and Josie followed him out.

"Why all the secrecy? What's going on?" Mateo asked as he jumped out of the truck. "Are you two in trouble?"

"You might say that," Josie said with a laugh as she returned his hug. "It's good to see you."

"And you, even if you come with the family scallywag," he added, slapping Emmett on the back.

"I couldn't get rid of him. He insisted the plane wouldn't fly without him."

"Can you imagine?" Mateo said. "Now come, my friends. I'll take you back to the house—or do you have some hiding place picked out?" he said half-jokingly to Emmett.

"The ranch house is our hideout. Hope you don't mind."

"My pleasure. Get in the truck and tell me what this is all about."

When they'd finished, he pulled the truck off to the side of the road, coasted to a stop, and looked at them, shaking his head.

"Mother of God," he said softly. "I can't believe it. You really think these"—he paused, looking for a word—"these gangsters are out to kill you?"

"It didn't seem prudent to wait around and find out."

"I guess not. Now what?"

Josie sat between the two men, feeling the sun beat down on her black skirt, smelling the farm dust of the truck, and suddenly wishing she were alone so she could cry.

Instead, she took a deep breath and said, "The question is whether or not you think it's safe for us to stay here."

Mateo thought a bit, then said carefully, "It might be better if you wait to go in after dark. Let's go over to the ravine where Skillet Creek goes through the cottonwood land. Creek hasn't dried up yet and it's a nice place to spend the afternoon."

When they reached the cottonwood grove, Josie rolled her stockings off and walked barefoot on the soft new grass along the creek while the men forked some hay for them to lie on underneath the trees.

As Mateo threw his pitchfork back in the truck with a

whistle of relief, Josie asked, "Do you really think we couldn
trust the ranch hands?"

"They're not my concern."

"What is?" Emmett demanded.

"Well, I wasn't going to tell you," he said reluctantly. "Yo
got enough troubles." He looked at Emmett. "But if you insist o
knowing. You have gangsters. We have night riders. Th
KKK's still giving us trouble. Our cook, Louisa, is the onl
source of income for her family, but things have gotten s
rough she stays on the ranch and just sends them money."

"Have they been out here again?" Emmett asked.

"Few times. So far we've never been able to keep them at
respectful distance. But you never know. Everyone's a b
edgy because of it. And it seems that we have more visitor
than usual these days. Maybe it's my imagination," he sai
with a characteristic shrug, "but it does mean that what goe
on at the Bar C is pretty much common knowledge. Now tha
it's getting time for the cattle drives, they're probably to
busy to bother us for a while. Haven't come in about tw
weeks."

Mateo climbed into the truck. "But don't worry about tha
Take a nice long nap and I'll be back at dusk. The ranc
hands are loyal. Just be careful of strangers."

Josie stood watching while he drove off. "What's this busi
ness about the Klan?" she asked.

Emmett gave her a brief report on what had happene
when he was here before, including the run-in with Slead.

"Bastards."

"That they are," Emmett agreed cheerfully. "Slead's th
worst of the lot, too. You should hear what Grandpa's jou
nals said about him and his father. To use his words, the
aren't worth piss in the sand."

"Goes way back, huh?"

"Does it ever." Emmett leaned back and entertained Jos
with the stories about the Sleads on the Oregon Trail. "H
wife died in childbirth—Zenas Slead, who was with the Kla
harassing Mateo, was that baby," he concluded.

"The other kids took the name of the people who too
them in when their mother died—Harris. Didn't want an
one to ever associate them with their father."

"But Zenas Slead was raised by his father?"

"Apparently. Guess his father taught him to hate—a
specifically, to hate Coughlins. I tell you, Sis, reading Gramp
journals made sense out of a lot of things."

Josie leaned back and looked up at the leaves dancing against the robin-egg sky. "It's sort of spooky—knowing that hatred can be passed on from generation to generation," she murmured sleepily. "Wonder what's been passed on to us."

She awakened two hours later when she heard Emmett splashing in the creek.

"Gee, I'm thirsty," she exclaimed, going upstream from him and drinking. "I must have slept with my mouth open."

"Snored, too," Emmett said, drying his face on his kerchief.

"Did not!" Josie laughed, splashing him with water.

"Shh," Emmett said. "Someone's coming. Get behind those rocks."

Emmett watched for a moment. "It's okay. It's Mateo." As the truck lurched to a stop, he called out, "You're early."

"I've got it all figured out," Mateo said. "You're going on the cattle drive. We'll be gone for two weeks, and the only people you'll see will be our hands. What do you say to that?"

"Great!" Emmett exclaimed. "I was planning on coming anyway."

"I'd love it," Josie said. "But can we leave this soon?"

"You'll have to stay under wraps in the ranch house for about three days until we're ready, but it's close enough to the regular time. Word is, the snow's melting fast."

"Do you think black crepe de Chine is suitable for a trail ride?" Josie asked, looking down at her dusty dress.

Mateo laughed. "I've thought of that, too. I'll send Tiny and his wife into town tomorrow. You'll have to give them your sizes. They'll be getting supplies for the rest of us, so it won't look suspicious."

"You've taken care of everything," Josie said. "But that doesn't explain why you came out here before sundown."

"Ah, that." He pulled a basket from the cab of the truck. "I told Louisa she'd have two extra mouths to feed. When she heard the story, she insisted that I take this out to you now to hold you over." He pulled out a jug of lemonade rattling with ice, a warm loaf of fresh-baked bread, and a fat round of homemade butter with water beads still on it.

"I'm going to like Louisa," Josie said.

By the time they arrived at the ranch house it was after dark. The tempting smell of steak and onions floated from Louisa's kitchen, and Chicago gangsters seemed distant and harmless.

* * *

Each summer cattle are taken from the winter range in the lowlands and driven up into the mountains, where they graze at higher elevations, fattening up on the new growth of grass and avoiding the blistering heat of the valley floor. Then in the fall, they're rounded up and driven back to the flatland which, because it's been undisturbed, has a thick growth of grass for the winter. Beef cattle are separated from the herd and sold. Breeding cattle winter over on lower pastures where the weather isn't as severe and where the ranchers can watch over them and give them supplemental feed.

Cattle drives were one of Josie's favorite childhood memories. As a four-year-old she was forced to ride in the chuck wagon. But as she got older and she'd proven herself as a rider, she'd been allowed to drive the cattle along with the adults.

There was something reassuring about swinging into her saddle, hearing the creak of the leather and feeling the reins between her fingers. She fit her boots in the stirrups and headed out, listening to the cattle-murmur. It was a slow process, moving at the pace cattle comfortably travel. The smell of horse sweat, leather, dust, and fresh manure filled the air. Josie tipped her hat to shade her face from the hot sun and settled back in the saddle.

She plodded comfortably along, keeping an eye on a restless steer at the back of the herd and enjoying the view of the flat expanse of straw-colored land dotted with gray-green brush and edged by the jagged horizon of the Blue Mountains. The sharp, acrid smell of sagebrush penetrated the dust as the cattle trampled the plants along the side of the road.

Each stop along the way was planned—meal stops, watering holes, and overnight campsites. Smaller ranches combined their herds, and the cattle drives were done as a community affair. The Bar C was such a large spread, they moved to the mountains alone. They nooned alongside Skeleton Creek, and Josie was grateful for the thin shade she found under the cottonwood saplings. It was getting hot.

Louisa's beans and fresh bread tasted like a feast after the morning's work. Listening to the men talking about the horses, the cows, and the weather, Josie leaned back against a rock and soon drifted off to sleep. Within minutes she was awakened by Mateo's call of "Head 'em out!" The short rest had refreshed her. She caught her horse and was back behind the herd.

On the fifth day they finally came to the summer range

osie loved the pine and fir scent and couldn't wait to take er boots off and wade in the river. Since they would spend he night, she had the rest of the afternoon simply to wander long the stream, watching animals and enjoying her solitude. It was a healing time for her. When the smell of voodsmoke and dinner brought her back to camp, she knew hat Mateo's idea had been the perfect solution.

That night she crawled into her bedroll and looked up at he stars peeping through the pine trees. Someone was playing harmonica on the other side of the camp and the frogs along he river were singing a symphony. A cool breeze whispered hrough the pine needles and she snuggled down under her lankets and slept a deep, peaceful sleep.

It wasn't until they were almost back to the ranch that her houghts turned to what she was going to do next. They were nely thoughts. Mateo was riding alongside the chuck wagon, lking to Louisa.

Emmett caught her eye, grinned, then joined her. "Penny r your thoughts."

Josie smiled. "I was just noticing that Mateo's protectionist olicies might have more than humanitarian reasons."

"They don't seem to have eyes for anyone else."

"What a comeuppance for you, little brother."

"Oh, come on now," Emmett protested with a wounded ok, "you don't think that I always—"

"Yup," she said with a laugh. "We're almost there. I'll race ou the last mile," she said, kicking her horse into a run.

"Hey! No fair!" he called after her. "You got a head start!"

They were both laughing and breathless when they reached le ranch house. Then, as they walked the horses to the arn, they saw the charred remains of the chicken house and black scorched spot etched into the side of the barn.

Old Button Hogberg hobbled across the yard towards them. Others coming?" he asked.

"Yeah, we ran ahead. What happened?" Emmett asked.

"Damned night riders. 'Bout three of 'em comes riding up out one o'clock in the morning day afore yesterday. Godamned cowards. Bedsheets covering their faces. Just me and couple of the hands left to run the place, and they knowed . They throws torches on the chicken house and barn and en rides off like coons afore the dogs. I think I winged one 'em with my rifle, though," he said with a wink. "Took all e had to save the barn. Lost every last one of the chickens ept that old biddy Louisa let set under the house."

"Damn! We've got to do something. You call the sheriff?" Emmett asked.

"Didn't figure it'd do no good." Button spat his chaw on the ground and then looked out across the field. "He's one of 'em. Most folks around here are. Bar C stands out like a wart on a pretty girl's face far's they're concerned. We ain' got a single Knight of the Empire among us. Don't believe it. None of us."

Mateo arrived and reluctantly agreed to notify the authorities when Emmett and Josie insisted.

When he came back from the phone he said, "I hope it puts your mind at ease. The sheriff says to let him know when the next fire happens and then he'll drive the seventeen miles and see if he can catch the people who started it."

"Oh, brother," Josie said with disgust. "Button was right. We'll just have to set up watches and a system of alarms."

"We've two thousand acres here. I don't see how we can watch them all," Mateo protested.

"Yes, but we can watch the herds and the buildings and equipment." Emmett's voice was calm and reasonable.

"It'll tax the men something hard," Mateo warned.

"I'm sure they'll agree when we explain it to them."

The phone rang just then. Mateo answered it, then handed it to Emmett. "It's Jacob Teall."

Emmett spoke briefly and then turned to Josie. "Jacob wants us to come back to Salem and talk to a Bureau of Investigation agent. There's a field outside of Woodburn where we can meet them at one o'clock tomorrow. All right with you?"

"Don't see we have any choice. At least maybe something will be done."

Once they were in the air the next morning, Josie pushed her worries from her mind, letting the wind blow in her face and watching the land pass beneath them as they raced their own shadow toward the west. It wasn't until they flew over the Cascades and down into the Willamette Valley that she once more thought about her problems.

Emmett circled the small farm outside of Woodburn. Then, seeing only one vehicle, he made a bumpy landing in the pasture.

"Who owns this place?" Josie asked, climbing down from the plane. "How do you know he won't shoot us for trespassing?"

"It's Thomas Harris's place. Zenas Slead's big brother. He

said I could land here anytime I wanted. It's far away from the main roads. Perfect." They walked towards the car parked alongside the country road.

Jacob was leaning against the fender of a Buick touring car beside a heavyset man. He introduced him as Agent Carter of the Bureau of Investigation.

"I wanted to talk to you about the man you told your lawyer about. Guy called Fingers," he said abruptly. "You think he's trying to kill you?"

"We think he's hired two men to kill us," Emmett said. "They think we double-crossed them."

"What does he look like, this Fingers?"

"I don't know."

"Well, how do you know he's trying to kill you?" the agent asked impatiently.

Emmett and Josie exchanged glances. They knew it sounded farfetched, but it was all they had to go on.

"We admit it's hearsay," Josie said. "But we don't think we should ignore it, considering what's happened recently."

Emmett quickly explained how Gus had overheard the conversation of the three gangsters in the roadhouse that night.

"This Gus," Carter asked. "Where can I find him?"

"He's on the road playing with a group called Canada Parker and the Maple Leaf Five. They'd be heading towards San Francisco. But I don't think he'll be much help. I asked him for any kind of description, but he said they were in the back of the room when he was putting his instruments away up on the stage. This Fingers had his back to him and was wearing a hat. The other two were in shadows. All he could see was that one was tall, light-haired and walked with a limp, the other, short and dark."

"If they're the same ones who showed up at Ron's funeral," Josie said, "I can tell you more. The short one has a pointed face, like a weasel, a pencil-mustache, and dark hair. The tall one has blond hair, and a square face with a nose that looked like it'd been broken."

"That's good," said Carter, writing rapidly on a pad. "Now, about that Fingers."

"I told you, Gus didn't see him," Emmett said.

"Figures. No one has. He's the number-two man in the Chicago mob. Came out here to sew up the West Coast. Pretty much had the hootch market in his pocket until Miss Balfour here threw him a curve a couple of weeks ago. It fits

435

that he's out to teach you a lesson. He has a reputation fo revenge. It's how he keeps his hold—terror. Problem is, he' like the wind. Everyone knows he's there, but no one see him. No description, no real name—not even a clue as t why he's called Fingers. We assume he started as a safe-ma and that's where the tag came from. Still, we need description."

"Wouldn't it be easier to catch the two hoods he hired an ask them?" Emmett asked.

"We'll try. In the meantime, you're wise to lay low. It's safe bet that you have a price on your heads."

"What are your plans?" Jacob asked.

"Head back to the ranch for a while, I guess," Emmet said.

"Not me," Josie interrupted. "I've been thinking. This ma take a long time, and my bar exams are this fall. I can't stud out in the middle of nowhere."

"So what are you going to do?" Jacob asked. "You're no planning on going back home?"

"No. But last time I was in your building, I saw a sign for small third-floor office for rent. Is it still available?"

"Yes."

"I'm going to rent it from you. I'll take a hot plate to coo my meals, and put a cot in there, along with a desk and couple of chairs. I can use the books in your office for study ing, and you can bring anything else I need from the univer sity. There's a bathroom down the hall. I'd have to impose o you to buy my food. What do you think?"

Jacob shrugged. "You'll go stir-crazy in about a week, bu we can work something out. Slip out after dark, maybe." H thought for a moment, then smiled. "I think it's a terrifi idea. I'll feel better knowing where you are. Are you going t stay at the ranch the full summer then?" he asked Emmett.

"For a while at least," he said. "I've got a few things up m sleeve. I'll let you know."

"Well, if that's all," Carter said, "we'd better get going."

"Would you mind giving me a lift into town?" Josie asked

He looked at her appraisingly, then said, "If you ride in th back seat on the floor and let me take you to Teall's house. I' stay there with you until after dark. That'll give him time t fix up the office and you'll be protected."

"Sounds like a movie plot." She grinned. Then when h didn't smile back, she added demurely, "I'll be very coopera tive."

Quickly, Josie kissed Emmett's cheek. "Be careful," she cautioned. "Don't do anything foolish. And give Mateo and Louisa my love and thanks."

They watched the biplane taxi down the length of the pasture and lift off. He banked and circled over their heads, waving jauntily before he leveled his wings and headed east.

That night Carter kept watch from Jacob's office, which was directly below Josie's new hideout. He wanted to make sure no one suspected she was there. When nothing happened, he satisfied himself with standing guard outside the following night. Then, seeing nothing, he agreed that his time was better spent elsewhere—but only after he'd fitted her window with a black shade to keep the light from showing at night.

For Josie, the privacy and isolation were just what she needed. She threw herself into her books, pushing everything else from her mind. Everything, that is, until Jacob brought her dinner one Sunday afternoon.

"I was remembering," he said as he came in carrying a basket, "how we used to gather on hot July afternoons on our grandparents' back lawn and eat my grandmother's fried chicken and your grandmother's Irish soda bread."

"And you would always win at croquet," Josie said. "There wasn't a trace of chivalry in you. You wouldn't even try to lose—even to a determined six-year-old."

"And you've been trying to get even with me ever since," he said. "Well, this fried chicken isn't near as good as Grandmother's, and Old Miss Wyman hasn't the faintest idea what Irish soda bread is, but it'll have to do."

"I'm sure our grandmothers would understand," she said. "Is nostalgia all you brought?"

"That, and compassion. You've been locked up two weeks now. Don't you want company? Don't you want to escape?"

Josie laughed. "What I really want is to take a hot bath instead of the sponge baths I've been getting down the hall. And to wash my clothes. And a newspaper. I'd love to read a paper."

"Your wish is my command. How about sneaking out tonight and coming over to my house? There you can wallow decadently in the bath, do your laundry, and read today's newspaper, even the comics."

"It sounds wonderful. And that chicken smells wonderful. I get the drumstick."

"I'm ahead of you. I made sure there were two."

"Remember that Thanksgiving you insisted on having a whole turkey drumstick all your own?" she asked.

"Remember? I still have nightmares about it. Do you realize how big a turkey drumstick can look to a ten-year-old? How can you remember? You must have been no more than four."

"Oh, I remember a lot." She smiled. "You were one of my heroes. All you big kids."

Jacob looked at her solemnly. "And you were the prettiest little girl I'd ever seen."

Josie blushed. "I didn't think little boys ever thought girls were pretty."

"They aren't blind," Jacob protested.

Josie laughed, and the awkwardness of the moment passed. Still, there was a hesitancy in the air. She could feel his dark eyes upon her, just the way she used to feel them burning into her during class, and she had to fight to keep her composure. That was one of the things that was so disarming about Jacob, she thought, his intensity. A disturbing thought cropped up in the back of her mind. Was he this intense with everyone else?

She quickly looked at her books. "Do you really think *Hill* v. *State of Oregon* was a landmark decision?"

He leaned back in his chair and gave her his considered opinion, carefully outlining the facts of the case and its ramifications, noting times it had been cited in other cases.

The rest of the afternoon was devoted to tutoring. Still, whenever he showed her a passage in one of the books and their heads were close together or when he reached across the desk and their hands touched, Josie couldn't help feeling the electricity of his presence. She would hold her breath, concentrating on his words until the moment passed, willing it to pass quickly while wanting it to last forever.

When it was dark, Jacob brought his car around to the alley, and Josie slipped in the door.

"Lie down on the seat," he ordered. Then, once he pulled out into the street and finished shifting, his hand rested not on the steering wheel but on her shoulder. Josie suddenly felt safe and cared for. She lay very still.

Jacob parked in the back of his house, unlocking the back door before letting her get out of the car.

"I feel like an escaped convict," she said, hurrying inside

438

Do you really think all this cops-and-robbers stuff is
cessary?"

"I talked to Agent Carter yesterday. He has a couple of hot
ads on the two hoods we saw at the funeral. They have a
cord as long as your arm—and they're connected with the
hicago mob. They were in Salem this week. Now what do
u think?"

Josie shuddered. "I think I'll go take a nice, long bath."

"Jacob," Josie said, coming down the stairs an hour later,
found this newspaper in your room when I was dressing.
hy didn't you tell me about this?"

Her dark bobbed hair hung in waves and ringlets from the
eam of the bath, she smelled of soap, and she'd borrowed
s bathrobe.

"What?" he asked, glancing up from his reading. "Oh, that
tter to the editor. I didn't think it was worth mentioning."

"Jacob, this demands the university fire all Jews, and it
mes you in particular. Listen: 'It seems to this reader that
behooves the people of this beautiful state to protect the
gile young minds of our youth from such tainted influence.
e require all children to attend state schools; now we must
ke sure that their higher education is equally pure and
e from foreign influence. . . .' And then he goes on to
y—"

"Josie, I know full well what it says," Jacob interrupted.
"Well, what are you going to do about it?"

"Nothing. There's been a series of similar letters to the
ard of Regents and major donors. It's the Ku Klux Klan.
ey were behind the school bill."

"How can you sit there so calmly?" she cried, kneeling
side his chair. "I don't understand you. This must be
pped in the bud."

"Josie," Jacob said softly, "you really don't understand, do
u? I appreciate your concern, but this is something that
mes with being Jewish. It's part of a heritage you can't
derstand. It'll go away."

"Only if we stop it," she said, tears coming to her eyes. "I
n't stand any kind of injustice, but this is terrible—why, it
uld lead to all sorts of things—"

"Shh," he said, stroking her cheek gently. "You shouldn't
rry. But I do appreciate your concern."

osie impulsively grabbed his hand and held it. "But I do
439

worry," she whispered. "I don't want anything to happen
you."

She looked into his eyes and saw in their liquid depths h
own reflection, and knew that she was being held by hi
And then he leaned down and gently kissed her lips.

She felt suspended above their two worlds, cradled in ł
presence. As if she were being pulled by a powerful magne
she reached out and touched his cheek, then pulled his he
toward her until his lips were touching hers once more.

Tentatively, gently at first, they kissed. Then, when ł
arms wound around his neck, he lifted her up on his la
pulling her to him, holding her and kissing her deep
possessively.

"Josie, my Josie," he whispered as hē kissed her neck a
looked at her tenderly. He started to say something, but s
pulled his head down and kissed him again, this time fe
ciously and desperately, fearing his words, fearing his leavi
her again. She held him tightly, clinging desperately, archi
her body against his.

He pulled back from her embrace and looked at h
brushing her hair from her face and gently caressing ł
cheek. "I can't," he murmured. "I can't do this to you."

Panic raced through her. "What do you mean you can'
she demanded, tears in her eyes. "You've looked at me this w
before, and I've felt the same way before, but you ran away. Y
made me feel that I'd imagined it all. That this could ne
be. I'm not going to let you do it again."

"But it can't ever be. . . ."

She got up and walked to the fireplace, trying to und
stand her own feelings as well as what he was saying. Fina
she said, "I don't know what you mean. I don't even thi
you know." She ran her fingers through her hair and turn
to face him. "But I do know that what we have is importa
We *can* have that. At least for now we can have one anothe

He smiled as he walked over and took her face in
hands. "You're an enchantress," he said softly. "You've cas
spell over me all your life. The first day you walked into
class I knew. Then you questioned, you argued, you learne
and you bewitched my mind. The spunky little kid, t
pretty young lady, and now the beautiful and brilliant wom
You're everything I've ever wanted."

"And you, you're all I've ever wanted!" she cried. "Do
leave me again. I was so confused. But I'm not now. I l
you, Jacob."

Jacob sighed and wrapped his arms around her, holding her so tightly she could hear his heart beating. "And I love you, my Josie, so very much. You'll never know the agony that has given me."

"But it doesn't have to. Why should anything so wonderful cause pain? Why did you run away? Why did I feel compelled to say I'd marry someone I didn't really love simply because you'd told me to love my own kind? My own kind is you."

He looked down at her, shaking his head. "You read the letter to the editor."

"What does that have to do with us?"

He kissed her lightly once more, then released her. "I want you to think about it tonight. I'll wake you up before dawn so I can get you back to the office while it's still dark. We'll talk about it in the morning. Now you'd better get some rest."

"I don't need to think about it," she said as they went up the stairs. "I already know. I'm just waiting for you to come to the same conclusion."

He stopped outside her bedroom door and looked at her, a sad smile on his face. "Ah, Josie, it would be wonderful to be so sure. But you don't understand."

Josie looked at him in exasperation. "I do understand. And I don't think things like this should come between us. Our love can overcome any troubles we may have because you're Jewish. The same as it can overcome any troubles we may have because I'm a Coughlin or Episcopalian." With that she went in and closed the door behind her.

It was more than she could bear. She threw off the bathrobe, pulled on her nightgown, and climbed into bed, tears of frustration sliding down her cheeks. She had lost Jacob before, but she'd been younger then and uncertain of his feelings. Now she knew he felt the same as she did. Now she knew their love had begun when they were children—maybe even before they were born. But what could she do to convince him? What could she do to keep him from leaving her again?

There was a knock on her door. "Yes?"

Jacob stuck his head in. "May I come in?"

Josie quickly wiped the tears from her cheeks. "Of course."

"I've been thinking about what you were saying," he said quietly. He was wearing a long burgundy velvet dressing gown, and Josie could see dark, curling hair in the "V" at

441

his neck. The sight of him standing beside her bed, looking down at her with an expression that was no longer guarded but openly loving, made her heart beat in her throat.

"What did you think about it?" she whispered.

"I think that maybe you're right," he said, sitting down beside her on the bed. "I would be a fool to go on denying my very soul. But you don't realize what you would be getting yourself into—what kinds of things you would be subjected to."

"I should be the one to worry about that," Josie said leaning forward until his breath was her breath, until his lips were nearly touching her lips. "As you said, I'm not stupid."

He kissed her then, deeply, holding her in his arms, running his hands possessively down her back.

Her nightgown slipped off her shoulder and he kissed her throat. Breathlessly, she slipped her hands inside his dressing gown, feeling the texture of his skin, the hard muscles of his chest and back.

Then he was lying beside her, pulling the gown over her head and kissing her breasts, caressing her, filling her with desire.

"Oh, Jacob," she pleaded. "Now that we have one another love me now."

"My beloved Josephine," he murmured. "Now," he whispered, and covered her with his body.

Slowly and gently at first, he loved her, possessing her with his body. Then, as their passion flamed and consumed them, their love was unleashed and it made the universe spin, until with a cry, their bodies arched together and they were one. Josie cried with joy as their worlds collided, then joined. The scent of the honeysuckle vine blew over them and the earth was theirs.

Jacob kissed her tenderly, holding her to him. "You're crying," he said. "Did I hurt you?"

"I'm just . . . just wonderful," she said, wiping her cheek with the back of her hand. "I'm just happy . . . so happy." She kissed him then, tasting him with her tongue, holding him as her own.

"I love you more than life itself," he whispered.

"It's time we both stopped running away. I want to feel your arms around me through the night—every night."

"You can't stay here. You might be seen."

"I can stay tomorrow. Stay with me. We'll have all tomorrow and part of tomorrow night. I want to sleep in your arms—and love you. Tomorrow is soon enough for talking."

442

Chapter XXXVII

Emmett's face was lean and drawn beneath his summer tan. "You look terrible," he said to Josie as she opened the door.

Josie laughed and hugged him. "So do you. I'm glad you're here. What brought you?"

"Quite a bit. Where's Jacob? I stopped downstairs before I came up."

Josie's face, which had been animated, was suddenly non-committal. "Jacob? Oh, he's up in Portland for a few days."

"On business?"

"No, I believe it's personal."

Emmett watched his sister for a moment, then said, "Come on, I know you better than that. What's going on?"

"What do you mean?"

"Something's wrong. What's between you and Jacob?"

Josie looked out the window. "Nothing," she whispered.

"But you wish there was?"

She looked at him with tears in her eyes and then quickly looked away.

"Hey, you can tell your brother," he said. "Should I go bash his head in?"

Josie shook her head no, then put her face in her hands. "It's just . . . just . . ." she said, but the words wouldn't come.

"Ah, Josie," he said, putting his arm around her. "Is it that bad?"

Sobbing, Josie nodded her head. Emmett offered her his handkerchief. "Here, you'd better tell me all about it. Come on, let's go sit down." He took her over to the cot.

"I've realized these past weeks that I've loved Jacob almost all my life. When I was in law school I thought he felt the same way. But then he left—ran away, actually, back East."

"Is that when you got engaged to Ron?"

"Yes. Before Jacob left he gave me this long lecture about his being different and how I couldn't understand because he's Jewish and my professor and all. Anyway, I was confused. Ron came along and he was everything familiar and . . . comforting." Tears filled her eyes again.

"But you knew that was a mistake before Ron was killed."

Josie nodded. "It's more confusing than that," she said with a quivering smile.

"Does Jacob know how you feel?"

"Yes."

"How did he respond?"

"He loves me, too."

"That's great. Then what's the problem?"

"The same thing. He says that his being Jewish is a barrier between us. He doesn't want to make his cultural burden my burden. And he won't abandon his heritage for me. I told him he wouldn't have to, that we could continue in our own faiths—that we could respect one another and be the richer for it. But he won't accept that, and he says society won't accept it, either."

"So what's he doing?"

"He's in Portland. His father is giving a dinner for some friends of theirs, friends who have this beautiful Jewish daughter that Samuel thinks Jacob should marry," she said, her voice trailing off into a sob.

"You're kidding. That's medieval. Can't he use his own mind, his own heart?"

"I don't know. . . . Maybe he's right. I just don't understand."

Emmett sat pensively with his arm around Josie until her tears stopped.

Finally Josie sat up and looked at her brother with a weak smile. "Enough of my problems," she said. "Tell me why you look so terrible. Something brought you here."

Emmett nodded, looking down at his boots. "Sort of see through one another, don't we?"

"That's what brothers and sisters are for. What's up?"

"I wanted to talk to Jacob, for one thing. I was wondering what he's heard about the two goons."

"He told me before he left last night. He'd talked to Agent Carter. They figure we're pretty safe. Seems the people involved with that moonshine operation have moved on down to southern Oregon. The authorities think that they're setting up a big still down there, but it's hard to find it in all those hills and backwoods. They assume they've given up the revenge thing and moved on. They said we can come out of hiding and resume our normal lives."

444

"How do you feel about that?"

"It's nice to hear, but I don't trust it. Duke didn't run around with people who give up easily. Not so soon. Not when their honor and their 'business' were involved. I still want to keep out of sight."

"I agree."

"That isn't all that's bothering you."

Emmett shook his head. "The KKK struck again last night. This time they came in about three A.M. shooting their guns in the air, waving torches. We all ran out, tried to stop them. Poor old Button got knocked down. Hit his head on a post."

"Oh, no. How is he?"

"It . . . it killed him."

"No!" she cried.

"And Louisa ran out, trying to save her chickens from burning. Someone threw a rock and hit her in the head."

"Is she—"

"No. She's unconscious. We took her to the hospital in La Grande. Figured she's safer far away from it all."

"What about Mateo?"

"He flew over here with me. I gave him the keys to my car so he could drive up to Portland. He has her medical reports and he's going to consult with the doctors up there."

"Oh, dear God," she said putting her face in her hands. "Poor old Button."

"You know, he was ninety-five years old."

"And Louisa . . . she's got to get well. Did you tell the authorities?"

"The sheriff said they were accidents. Said he couldn't prosecute anyone for arson because we have no description. They were all hooded. Josie, he's one of them. We won't get justice out there."

They sat in silence.

"You know," Josie said finally, "we could go see Uncle Timothy. Tell him the ranch is having problems, property's being destroyed, and people hurt."

"He'd say we should fire Mateo and Louisa. That's a simple solution in his mind."

"We can't. Grandmother's will stipulates everything is to continue operating as it has been. Nothing is to change. Besides, I think Uncle Timothy is working hand in glove with the KKK in this state. Maybe he could call them off our backs

445

just by passing word down through the Grand Dragon or whatever they call their leader."

"You might have something there." Emmett stood up. "What're we waiting for? If we tell Uncle Timothy it's costing him money, he'll probably jump right on it." He held the door open for her. "Hope you don't mind, but I borrowed your car. I found it parked in Jacob's garage."

"He's been storing it for me. It's a pretty obvious announcement that we're back in town, you know, just driving that car down the streets of Salem."

"Well, maybe we'll smoke out some goons in the process. As far as I'm concerned, most anything is better than spending my life in hiding."

"I agree with you," Josie said, feeling defiant as she crawled into her car. "But aren't we acting like the mouse in that song, drinking the liquor on the barroom floor?"

Emmett laughed as he started the engine. "Let's see if I can remember it. 'Oh, the whiskey was spilled on the barroom floor and the bar was closed for the night.' "

Josie giggled and joined in.

" 'A little gray mouse came out of his hole to dance in the pale moonlight. He lapped up the whiskey on the barroom floor and back on his haunches he sat. And all through the night you could hear him roar,' " they sang raucously, holding the last note as they pulled into Timothy's drive, " 'bring on the goddamn cat!' "

They were gasping with laughter by the time Emmett turned off the motor. "That's it," Josie cried. "That's what I mean."

Emmett jumped out of the car, and with a bow gallantly held the door open for Josie. "You bet. Bring on the goddamn cat!"

Timothy was sitting in his parlor, talking to one of his political cronies.

"Emmett, Josephine," he exclaimed in surprise as Mrs Burack showed them in. "How are my favorite niece and nephew?"

"We're your only niece and nephew, Uncle Timothy," Josie said with a laugh as she kissed his cheek. "And we're just fine. Hope we're not interrupting anything."

"Oh, no, no," he assured them. "Come on in and meet one of my advisers. J.W. Maloney, Josephine and Emmett Bal four. Kids, this is J.W. You ever need anything, he can get it."

A large, meticulously dressed man rose from his chair and shook hands with them both.

"You'll have to excuse us," Josie said. "We've both been working and just wanted to take a few minutes to talk to Uncle Timothy about some family business."

"We can come back another time," Emmett began.

"No, no," Timothy said. "Whatever you have to say you can certainly say in front of J.W. here. He's my right-hand man. Don't know how I would have gotten along without him these past few weeks. So what's up?"

"It's about the ranch, Uncle Timothy. It seems that the KKK has been causing trouble over there, destroying buildings and livestock. Last night they raided the ranch again. Button was killed and the cook is still in a coma. Burnt down the chicken coop we'd just replaced from the last time. Seems they don't like Grandmother's choice of hired help."

"Well, why are you telling me?" Timothy said huffily. "Mateo should be talking to the sheriff."

"You know full well the sheriff is one of them."

"Well, that's what Mother gets for hiring foreigners. It's a family embarrassment."

"We can't change anything because of the will. Mateo will have to stay on until everything is settled," Josie explained. "So we're going to have to handle the problem in another way—or else we stand to lose this year's profits."

Timothy exchanged glances with J.W.

"We were hoping that you could use some of your connections," Emmett added. "Maybe pass the word to let this go for the time being. . . ."

Timothy lit his cigar, which had gone out. "Yes," he said, "maybe I can do that, until things are sorted out and I can take action on my own."

"Thanks, Uncle Timothy," Josie said. "We were hoping you'd help. Nice meeting you, Mr. Maloney," she said. "We won't take any more of your time."

"Oh, I was just getting ready to leave myself," J.W. said. "May I offer you a ride somewhere?"

"Thanks," Emmett said. "We have our car. See you, Uncle Timothy."

"Do you think he'll do it?" Josie asked, following Emmett out.

"Time will tell," Emmett said, slamming the car door and starting the engine. "Get in. We've got to talk."

447

As he backed out, Emmett asked, "What did you think of Uncle Timothy's friend?"

"He's as greasy and slippery as all those politicians," Josie said with disgust. "Except he has a better tailor and he wasn't as loud."

"Nope, real quiet type. See how he looked at you?"

Josie was quiet for a moment. "Like a cat. You know how a barn cat watches a mouse from across the room, just waiting because the mouse would get away if he jumped too soon."

"You're right," he said finally, the muscle along his jaw tensing. "Bring on the goddamn cat!"

"You mean—"

"He's mixed up with this whole mess. I thought he looked like he wanted to pounce when Uncle Timothy called out our names, but he settled back by the time we came into the room. Then when we shook hands—did you notice?"

"Well, it felt sort of funny—"

"He was missing the tops of three of his fingers."

"Fingers! Surely you don't think—"

"Why else would he be following us? I've doubled back twice and he's still on our tail. Has been ever since we pulled out onto Capitol. Don't look back," he ordered quickly. "Hang on to your hat, Sis. We're going for a ride—all the way to Portland."

Emmett was right. J.W. followed them for the full hour-and-a-half ride to Portland, carefully keeping his distance but never letting them out of his sight.

"You can probably lose him on the turn-off," Josie suggested. "That's what I did with Duke. This car goes a lot faster on the curves than those big things."

"I don't want to lose him."

"You what?"

"I don't want to lose him."

Josie looked at her brother in astonishment. "Do you think he's been hanging around Uncle Timothy just trying to find us?"

"Nah, that was just an added bonus. Uncle Timothy will probably win the election. His opponent is a weak fish. Old Fingers there would like to have a U.S. senator in his pocket. I'll bet you he has ties with the KKK as well as his mob friends and the moonshiners. As Carter said, he's virtually invisible—like the wind. Just everywhere. Keeps everything covered that way."

"So you're going to take him on?"

448

"No, just lead him on a merry chase—right down a dead end."

"Emmett," Josie said softly as she looked in the rearview mirror, "I just remembered the last verse to that song. 'Then a black cat came from behind the bar and gobbled up the little gray mouse.'" She paused. "I think it ends, 'So the moral of this story is clear to see: Never take a drink on the house.'"

Emmett laughed wryly. "You would remember that."

He pulled into the driveway of Fionna's mansion. "Good. My car's here. I'm going to let you off. You go on inside and tell Mateo to meet me—here." He quickly pulled out a piece of paper and wrote something down. "He'll understand."

"But what about—"

"Fingers? He'll follow me. Wants to know where he can find us both. It'll take a while for him to call out his goons. Soon's Mateo leaves, you call Jacob and tell him to come over and pick you up. Have Nell go visit someone, too. Don't leave anyone in the house, understand?"

"I'm beginning to. Will you please be careful?"

"You know I always am. Get going."

Josie ran up the steps and inside. She watched from behind the curtain as Emmett drove around the circular drive and out onto the street. As she watched, the long nose of J.W.'s car slowly pulled out from behind the hedge and followed.

"Josie, honey, when did you get here?" Nell exclaimed.

"Oh, Nell," Josie said, turning around. "I'm glad you're here. Where's Mateo?"

"Right here," he said. "I heard the car door slam. What's going on?"

"Oh, Mateo," Josie said, giving him a hug, "I'm so sorry about what's happened."

"It's not quite as grim as it was," he said. "Called the hospital. They said Louisa regained consciousness."

"Thank God," she said. "Give her my love when you see her. Emmett said to give you this, you've got to get there right away." As she talked she went over to the phone in the hallway and cranked the handle.

"What's going on?" Nell demanded.

"Nell, do you have a friend you can visit?" Josie asked.

"Yes."

"Well, call her soon as I'm done here. We've got to get out of here before those men come."

"What men?" Mateo and Nell chorused.

"I think they're the ones who've been after us ever since the accident with Duke and the still. . . . Hello, Jacob?" she said. "This is Josie. Can you come over to Grandmother's and get me? I'll explain when you get here. Please hurry!"

"I'm on my way," Mateo said. "Emmett's got something up his sleeve."

Mateo got to the roadhouse at dusk and found Emmett sitting alone at a table at the back of the room. Three empty glasses and one full one were lined up on the table in front of him. "What's up?" he asked as he pulled up a chair.

"I come out of hiding so you can make a nest egg and what do you do but screw me up already," Emmett said with a growl.

Mateo looked around the room anxiously. "Talk quietly, my friend," he whispered, trying to shush Emmett.

"Quiet, hell," Emmett said, downing his drink. "I've had it with you. First you steal my girl, but I'm a gentleman about it. Even try to help you out by cutting you in. Then what do you do?"

Mateo put his hand firmly on Emmett's arm. "Let's talk about it on the way home," he suggested quietly. Glancing around the room, Mateo leaned forward, talking softly to Emmett.

Their exchange hadn't gone unnoticed. Two men seated at a side table were watching everything. They exchanged glances, and the short one nodded to the tall one.

"Goddamn it!" Emmett exploded, shoving Mateo's arm away. "You Cuban son-of-a-bitch. You're not going to tie me down anymore."

Mateo jumped up and grabbed Emmett by the shoulder. "You can't—" Emmett hit him in the jaw, sending him staggering across the room.

Instantly, the bartender was over the bar and grabbed Mateo to keep him from striking back, but it was unnecessary. Emmett was out the door before Mateo had caught his balance.

"You all right, fella?" the bartender asked him.

"Yeah," he said, rubbing his chin. "Bring me a whiskey."

Mateo picked up his chair and sat back down at the table. He gulped down the first drink, then quickly ordered another, his face clouded in anger.

"Mind if I join you?" The stranger was slight and inoffen-

450

sive. Mateo shrugged. "Your friend is a bit hot-tempered," the man said.

"Might say that."

"I've seen him around. Isn't he a hotshot rumrunner?"

"Might be."

"You work with him?"

"Not anymore."

"Don't look like he had any right to treat you that way," he said. Mateo was silent, and the man signaled for a drink to be brought to him. "You looking for work?"

"Maybe."

"We might be able to work something out," he ventured. "Interested?"

"Depends."

"Money in it for you, plenty of it. Maybe even a little revenge."

Mateo looked up at him for the first time. "How?"

"Seems a man like you should be treated with respect—you know, given responsibility and paid properly for it, not kicked around like a stray dog. What do you say?"

"Go on."

"Well, the way I see it, that horse's ass that just left is supplying my competition. From what he was saying, you now about some kind of run he's planning on making. You give me time and place. I give you money and revenge. What do you say?"

Mateo looked away guiltily. "I . . . I don't know," he said hesitantly. "I'd have to think about it."

"You feel your jaw and you have to think about it?"

Mateo rubbed his swelling jawline. "How soon you want to now? I don't have all the details, but I can get them." The man's face broke into a toothy smile. "How much money are ve talking about?" Mateo asked suspiciously. "I need quite a bit for . . . for medical expenses. Not for me," he added quickly.

"How does two hundred now, two hundred on delivery sound?"

He thought for a moment. "Make it two hundred now and three hundred on delivery."

"You drive a hard bargain," the man said. "Hope you're worth it."

"I will be."

The man looked up as another man walked in the door and

451

nodded his head. "How about if we meet here again? When's good?"

"I'll need time. Delivery isn't until the end of August. We got two weeks. How about I come back in ten days, same time?"

"Great. Ollie," he said, looking up at the big man, "give him two big ones. We got a new partner."

The man reached into his bulky jacket pocket, pulled out a thick wallet, and counted out two one-hundred dollar bills. "You say so, boss. We sure he's on the up-and-up?"

"He will be," the first man said softly. "Won't you?"

"You bet," Mateo answered, pocketing the money. "I got two big reasons for doing this, and they're not going away."

Josie was quiet the entire ride back to Salem. Once she explained, Jacob excused himself from his family dinner and offered to drive her back to the office. She accepted, then sat in misery the whole trip. Occasionally she would steal a glimpse at him, but his expression revealed nothing.

They'd had that one night together, but more vitriolic letters to the editor had come out the following day, and Jacob was filled with remorse, telling her their relationship would only incense the bigots. He couldn't subject her to that, not if he loved her. She felt as if she'd swallowed a lump of cold lead.

"I have to swing by the university to pick up some papers," he said as they pulled into town. "It's late enough that I don't think it would be any problem. Do you mind?"

"No," she said quietly, then asked, "Have you heard any more about the complaints?"

"The KKK letters? Not much. I think the administration is going to ignore them. There are only three of us on the faculty, anyway.

"Why do people believe that stuff?" Josie asked.

"I was reading something a while back," Jacob said. "It said that bigotry surfaces in difficult economic times and times of change. What with the post-war depression and the social changes caused by more women entering the work force and women's suffrage, a lot of men feel threatened. It's easier to blame their troubles on scapegoats—and they choose those who aren't able to fight back—other races, religions, nationalities, and the 'weaker' sex. Maybe when things stabilize a bit their heads'll clear."

"I wouldn't bet on it."

"Want to come in?" he asked as he parked the car.

"I'd feel better." She followed him, feeling awkward in his presence. The result was that she was quiet and withdrawn, choosing to be distant rather than hurt by rejection. She waited patiently while he looked through his desk, collected the papers and books he needed, turned out the light, and walked back outside.

Suddenly, as they came around the corner of the building, Jacob pushed her back behind a bush. Before she could protest, a rock crashed through the front window of the administration building. Then a cross burst into flames on the front lawn. About fifteen white-hooded figures were standing in a group just beyond the shrubbery.

Jacob stepped back farther, pulling Josie with him. But something inside her snapped. White-hot anger wiped away all fear. This was what had ruined their love. Bigotry had robbed her of the most important thing in her life. Surrounded by bullies, she suddenly knew that she had to fight back. She would run away no longer.

Grabbing a rake leaning against the building, she started towards the gathering.

"Josie!" Jacob called to her. "It's not your fight—"

"Like hell it isn't," she said over her shoulder, pushing him back. "Stay out of sight."

Before any of the Klan had spotted her she was in their midst, swinging the rake and knocking over the flaming cross, scattering their group with the sparks.

"What a slimy bunch of cowards you all are," she cried. "You think you can skirt the law and force the rest of us to conform to your warped standards. Well, it won't work."

"Hey! Get out of here, little lady!" one man cried. "You ain't got no right . . ."

"It's the Balfour kid," someone said. "Coughlin's grandkid."

"You're all mocking the Constitution you say you love. If you really believed in God and country, you'd know that this kind of anarchy is forbidden. Go slink back under a rock where you belong!" she yelled, swinging the rake again and backing the men back up farther. "Go home to your wives and children." She stopped her tirade, noticing something familiar about one of the hooded figures. "Or if you don't have a family, maybe you'd better go home and think about your political future."

"Ah, get out of here," someone called as they started towards her.

453

Josie swung the rake once more, sending pieces of burning cross into the crowd. "You're not even man enough to show your faces!" she shouted. "But I can identify you. Walk down the street tomorrow and I'll point you out."

They scattered, trying to brush smoldering embers from their robes. Part of the cross still burned on the lawn, sending flickering shadows across Josie's angry face. She was like an avenging angel, and they feared her righteous anger.

"Hey, this isn't your fight, Miz Balfour," one voice whined. "We're just trying to rid the school of Jews. Ain't no skin off your nose."

"Like hell it isn't," she said, glaring down at them. "Every time you tear down a group of people just to make yourself feel better, you tear down the entire human race. If we don't stop this here and now, we'll all be back in the middle of the Spanish Inquisition. Go home and look at yourselves in the mirror. See if you see a man or a sniveling coward."

Swinging the rake a final time, she sent the last piece of the burning cross away from her feet and into the crowd.

"Let's get outta here!" one man shouted, and the others scattered, stepping over the burning pieces at their feet to get away from her fury.

"We'll be back!" one taunted over his shoulder.

"And I'll have others with me!" she shouted after them.

As the cars started up, she hit the smoldering embers of the broken cross with the rake, violently trying to smash the one remaining symbol of her frustration and hurt. A rock crashed through another window behind her.

"Damn," she cried, sitting down on the steps of the sidewalk, "Damn, damn, damn . . ." She put her head on her arms and sobbed uncontrollably in the flickering dark.

"Josie," Jacob said, gently taking her arm. "Come on. We've got to go before they decide to come back." He lifted her up and led her, sobbing, back to the car. "Come on, let's go home."

"What home?" she cried. "I don't have a home. They've ruined it all."

Eastern Oregon is hot and dry in August. Heat distorts the landscape. Cattle and men alike seek protection from the midday sun in the scattered shade of scraggling juniper, sagebrush, and gray-weathered buildings.

Waves of heat rose from the hood of the ranch truck, warping the shape of the road as Emmett drove into town.

He stopped in front of the general store and got out. The street was dusty, and the gas tank of the truck whistled its complaint. Pulling a truck tire down from the back, he bounced it on the wooden sidewalk and rolled it through the front doorway.

"Hey, Hiram," he said amiably. "Damn fool foreman rushed the tire to the other truck. Can you fix it?"

Hiram ambled out from behind the counter and studied the torn rubber. "Don't look likely, Emmett. This here's clean split out. What'd he do?"

"Damned if I know. He doesn't have the sense to pour piss out of a boot with the instructions written on the heel. Wish I could get rid of him. You got another one?"

"Not here. Can order one down from Pendleton or La Grande, probably."

"I need it in five days. Pay extra if I have to."

Hiram nodded, walked behind the counter, pulled out a book, and thumbed through the pages. "Might be able to get in a week. Not five days."

"Hell, man, I can't wait that long. Can't you call up there and get something moving?"

Hiram sent a graceful arch of tobacco juice into the spittoon and shook his head doubtfully. "Maybe I could. What's the rush?"

"Never mind. You just do it. I need it no later than Friday afternoon. That truck has to be loaded and on its way that night. I'll come back Thursday." He turned and went out the door, only to run into Mateo coming in.

"What the hell you doing in town?" Emmett demanded, grabbing his arm. "I told you to get those fence posts dug by nightfall, you lazy son-of-a-bitch."

Mateo pushed him away, "You have no right to treat me this way," he said evenly.

"I have every right, you damned Cuban," Emmett cried. "If I could, I'd send you back where you belong—"

Before he could complete his threat, Mateo's fist lashed out and knocked him against the wall. As Emmett staggered against the pile of feed, Mateo turned and left the store.

Hiram came over and helped Emmett stand up. "You all right?"

"Yeah, I guess so," Emmett said, shaking his head.

"I thought you fellas were pretty good friends."

"Not likely. He doesn't even think like a normal man. His

455

kind's got a mean streak bred right into 'em. There's n
trusting him or talking to him."

"What's going on here?" Sheriff Red Sterett said from th
doorway. "That Spaniard of yours took off mighty fast."

"He's no Spaniard of mine," Emmett said bitterly. "I'
send him down with the *Maine* faster than you could blink a
eye, if I had my way. Sneaky bastard."

"I heard your grandma did you a dirty turn on that one,
the sheriff said sympathetically.

"Yeah, we can't change a thing until the lawyers and th
state get done chewing things over."

"Maybe we could help him out a bit, Sheriff," Hira
suggested quietly. "Zenas would—"

"Maybe we could—" Red said.

"How?"

"Well, you tell us where to find him sometime when it
sort of private and we might convince him it's time to go bac
where he came from—all on his own. Or else. Ain't r
stopping that in the will, is there?"

Emmett was quiet for a moment, squinting against th
glare of the summer sun. "You wouldn't do anything bad—"

"Just send him on his way." The sheriff exchanged lool
with Hiram, and they both smiled.

"I'd like that," Emmett said slowly. "But there's a problem.
"What's that?"

"The time you can find him alone . . . well, he's going
be doing some work for me that I don't want to be gener
knowledge, if you know what I mean."

The men smiled broadly. "We know what you mean, Er
mett. The Pendleton Round-Up wouldn't be worth dog shit
you didn't help moisten it up," Red said. "Everyone arour
here knows you're making a big delivery. Ain't no one goir
to let on, though."

"You just send that foreign bastard out there and we'll ta
care of him," Hiram added. "If'n he ain't done what you ne
done by that time, well, maybe we can find a strong back
help out."

Emmett was quiet for a moment, sitting down on a bag
feed. "You know, you got something there," he said final
"If I work it right, I can get him to do my work before
leaves."

He stood up. "You got to promise me you'll stick to r
time schedule. He gets wind of it, he'll turn on us all. Sor
of the hands out there, well, they think he's all right. Th
456

might stick up for him if he goes back with his tail in the air. And be careful. He's sneaky—and he carries a gun. Might catch on before you know it. He just might have one of the cook's brothers helping him. I think he's been skimming lunch money to pay them on the side."

"Don't worry. We can handle that," Hiram said, moving his chaw to the other side of his mouth.

"You just tell us where and when and we'll take care of everything," Red assured him.

Emmett took a piece of paper from the counter. "Here's the road east," he began. "You take the north fork out by Badger Rock." The two men moved in closer, looking at his directions. Sheriff Red Sterett rested his hand on Emmett's shoulder affectionately.

Emmett pulled out his pocket watch, checked it in the dusky twilight, then rode his horse on down the fence line. He'd told the boys back at the ranch that he'd be checking the fences and coming in late.

By the time he reached the top of the rise, he could look back down on the lights of the ranch buildings, glowing like a colony of fireflies on the plain below. As he watched, he saw the lights of the truck start up, turn down the road, and head out the highway. At least Mateo was leaving on time. *Damn*, he thought, *I hope he gets it all loaded before they come down on him.* So much tonight depended on timing.

He turned his horse and headed down the ridge. He had some hard riding to do if he was going to make it.

A half moon had come up over the mountains by the time he reached Badger Rock. Taking time to let the horse pick his way down through the gulch, he made his way around the ledge they called Duck Breast. As he came out on the far ridge of the ridge, he could see two tiny pinpoints of light, indicating a vehicle was making its way towards the loading place. He would just have time to circle around the outcropping of rocks.

He tied his horse to a juniper tree and began working his way around a large escarpment of basalt thrust from the bowels of the earth a millennia ago. Emmett looked up and sighted on the crooked juniper hanging over the edge. Feeling with his hands, he groped along the edge of the rocky hill until he came to an opening. Taking a match out of his pocket, he scratched it on his boot, lit the end of a branch of greasewood, then entered the cave.

457

The inside of the escarpment was honeycombed with tun nels and caves. That was where he'd hidden all those ship ments of whiskey, flight after flight, saving them until tonigh when they would be loaded onto the truck, then taken to th prearranged meeting place in the Blue Mountains.

He'd gone through the tunnels on his last delivery to th cache and marked the passageway he needed tonight. Th black arrow pointed to the right, and he wedged his bod through the opening and followed the snaking tunnel until h could see starlight peeping through an opening above.

Stomping on the smoldering branch, he climbed up th tunnel shaft and took a deep breath of fresh air. Just off to h right, Mateo was loading a box into the truck. He could se the three figures of the sheriff and his two henchmen comir up from the far right. They should reach Mateo in fi minutes.

Straining his eyes, Emmett searched the rest of the te rain. Then a movement caught his eye. There was a dark bu parked off the road about a mile beyond the turn-off. Tv figures were moving through the sagebrush towards him fro the left. As they got closer, Emmett saw they were wearir regular city hats, not cowboy hats like the locals. Just in tim

Holding his breath, Emmett watched as, unaware, the tv groups of men approached from opposite sides. Mateo wer in and out of the cave, loading the boxes of illegal whiske seemingly oblivious to what was coming.

The two city men on his left came up and watched fro behind a large clump of sagebrush. Then, unseen to them b visible to Emmett, the sheriff and his accomplices crept and looked over the rocks.

Emmett leaned forward and a tiny pebble fell to the grou at Mateo's feet. But he didn't seem to notice. He simply we back into the cave to get his next load. Emmett slipped dov the rocks he was hiding behind and crept on his belly towar the bushes where the two strangers were hiding, counti slowly in his mind to two hundred.

He was just parallel with the two men when he saw a lo figure step out to the left of the rocks. Emmett pulled out gun and waited. A shot blasted over his head and someo shouted, "He's getting away!"

Emmett returned the shot, aiming above the figure by t rocks.

"It's a setup!" shouted one of the strangers near Emme

mmediately they began shooting. The sheriff and his accomplices returned fire.

Emmett slipped back around the rocks to the back of the ave. He could still hear the gunfire popping in the distance s he crept along, feeling his way through the tunnel. Sudenly there was a glimmering of light ahead. He stopped and aited.

Mateo's face looked drawn and anxious in the flickering ght, shadowed by the small torch he was carrying. But when e saw Emmett standing there, he broke into a grin.

"It worked, didn't it, my friend?"

Emmett clapped him on the back. "What the hell took you long? I was certain one of 'em would get you before you t away from that truck."

"Couldn't look like I knew they were there, could I?"

"All we have to do now is wait for them to take care of one ther."

"If they do—"

"Shh. Do you hear anything?"

"No."

"Me either."

"Shall we go out and see what's left?"

"Quietly. Just in case some are still hanging around."

Slowly they worked their way back out the tunnel and ound the side of the rocks. There was no sound.

Coming up on the stand of sagebrush, they could see no ovement. They worked their way around until they saw two ures lying on the ground. Mateo started to go over to eck them but Emmett stopped him. There was a sound m the other side. Signaling for Mateo to stay there, Emett made his way back up to the top of the escarpment.

The moon was overhead now, casting its brightest light on land below. He could see the two figures in the sagebrush, ll in the same place. Over to his right he could see one ure sprawled across the top of the rocks and another lying wn below. Where was the third?

Then he heard the horse. Someone was slowly riding across desert. He recognized the horse by the distinctive white ze on its left rump. The rider was hunched over in his ldle, letting the horse pick his way through the sagebrush. met watched as the horse slowed down, then stopped. e rider slid from his saddle and fell to the ground. The rse waited, but when his rider didn't get up, he lowered

his head and began to graze. Emmett climbed down th
ridge.

Mateo heard him coming and walked on over to the tw
men lying on the ground. He kicked their guns from the
hands and felt their pulses. "Chicago city slickers shoul
know better than to take on country hicks. What about th
others?"

"The third one just fell out of his saddle about a quarter
a mile from the road. It was Slead's horse. Somebody wi
find them by morning."

"I'll take the truck on out to the road," Mateo said.

"Meet you there. I'll drag some brush behind my horse
cover the tire tracks."

"Funny," Mateo said as he turned to go, "I thought r
venge would feel good."

"Never does. I feel like I cleaned out a snake pit, that's a
But maybe we pulled the teeth of the local KKK for a while

"At least Louisa can breathe a little easier in her sickbed-
and you and Josie won't have to be watching over yo
shoulders anymore, either."

Emmett was quiet for a moment, looking across the dese
Then he put his arm on Mateo's shoulder as they walk
towards the truck. "Yeah, maybe you're right. Maybe
letting the snakes bite one another, we bought some peace

Chapter XXXVIII

Josie looked up from her book and saw Jacob standing
the doorway, watching her. As their eyes met, her hea
turned over and it seemed as if she would drown in his gaz

She took a deep breath. "Hi," she said, hoping her voi
wouldn't betray her. "I thought you were in Portland."

"Just got back. How's the studying going?"

"Fairly well. I have a good grasp of the material. Now I
going over specific cases."

He nodded. "Bar exams are the first week of Novembe
he said, more to himself than to her. He slapped the newspa
he was carrying against his leg and turned to her, forcing
smile. "You'll do just fine."

"Thanks for the vote of confidence."

"Well-deserved. Here," he said, tossing the newspaper on
e desk in front of her, "thought you'd like to see it. Just
me out. Read the front page."

Josie picked up the newspaper and glanced at it. " 'Shoot-
t on Oregon High Desert,' " she read. " 'Bootleg liquor
stined for the Pendleton Round-Up was reportedly the
use of a bloody shoot-out in a desolate stretch of the Ore-
n high desert country. A local resident found the bodies of
eriff Red Sterett and two of his deputies, Hiram Mulder
d Zenas Slead.' " Josie stopped and looked up, her eyes
ed with fright.

"Go on," Jacob urged with a grim smile.

' 'Not far from their bodies were the bodies of two men
m Chicago, identified by authorities as Milfred Companillo
d Oliver Schultz. All five men died of gunshot wounds. It
speculated that the sheriff and his deputies came upon the
o men hiding the contraband booze in caves located off
ick Breast Ridge. One case of whiskey was found in the
ve and another was in a car parked two miles away on the
inty road.' "

osie put the newspaper down, shaking her head in won-
r. "All of them at one fell swoop." Seeing Jacob's expres-
n, she blurted out, "Do you think Emmett had something
do with this?"

'Well, he did call Friday and tell you that you didn't have
hide out anymore. How else would he know?"

'Are you going to report him?"

'What's to report? Mere speculation. Besides, we both
ow that whatever happened out there was an act of divine
tice." He smiled at her. "No, it's just good to know you
't have to worry anymore."

acob turned back to the window. "I think that was what
de me realize even more how I felt about you," he said
ly. "The thought of never being able to see you again."
looked at her, his eyes full of pain.

Oh, Jacob," Josie said, fighting back tears. "I just don't
lerstand you. No matter how you explain it. You say
igs like that and still say we will never . . ." She shook her
d, unable to finish. "I thought after your weekend in
tland you would come back—"

Ie sighed. "Afraid not. I'm going to take off before classes
t. Go over to the coast, maybe. It seemed to do you a
at deal of good."

But I had Grandmother's letter . . ."

"You didn't tell me what she said."

"It just helped put things in perspective," she said ev
sively. "What do you have?"

"I don't know. I just know that I have to get away and
alone. Now that I know you'll be all right . . ."

"Of course," she said with a show of independence. "I'll
just fine. I don't have time for interruptions, anyway. Not
I'm going to commit these cases and their relevant laws
memory."

"Good. Here's my office key. Use my books." He avoid
her look. "If my family asks, you don't know where I am."

"That'll be the truth," she said. Then, once the door clos
and the sound of his footsteps had faded, she whispere
"Hurry back."

Emmett wrote saying that he was staying at the ranch wi
Mateo, helping with the roundup and the cattle sale. It'd
November before he came back to the Willamette Valley.
wished her luck on her bar exams. With that, Josie was alo
once more.

She threw herself into her studies, spending long ho
over her books until she could no longer keep her eyes op
It was the only way she could keep her mind from dwelli
on her misery. For once her strong will and discipline serv
her well.

It was Halloween Eve when she stopped her roadster
the farm mailbox. A haywagon full of trick-or-treaters pass
and she was glad that she'd remembered to stop at
grocery store for a bag of apples and candy. She found t
bills and an envelope addressed in her mother's handwrit
and covered with foreign stamps.

As soon as she got in the house, she opened a soda pop
sat down at the kitchen table to see what her mother had
say. Josie enjoyed her mother's letters. They were full
enthusiasm and anecdotes about people and places. Josie
discovering a new friend in place of the sour, bitter mot
she'd known.

Hannah's letter described the wonderful Viennese m
cians, then gave the date she was coming home. She'd sp
a week in Boston and then arrive in Portland on Novem
tenth. She was full of plans for establishing a Portland m
conservatory. She was even importing European teach
They'd arrive in the spring, giving her time, she hoped
set up the physical facility and screen prospective student

Josie turned and looked at the calendar. In one week she'd [b]e done with her bar exams. In less than two weeks she'd [h]ave her mother back. Best of all, Emmett had called last [ni]ght to tell her he and Mateo were coming over for the [A]rmistice Day parade in Portland. Soon all her loved ones [w]ould be with her—all except Jacob. She hadn't heard a [w]ord since he'd left three weeks ago.

His father wasn't very pleased when he'd called two weeks [ag]o and demanded to know where Jacob was. When she said [sh]e hadn't the faintest idea, he was even more upset. Jacob [ha]d promised to come home for Yom Kippur, Samuel explained. [It] was unlike him to be away on such a solemn holiday.

She couldn't help worrying about Jacob. But it was out of [he]r hands. He'd made it clear that they were to live separate [liv]es. She felt as if she were only half alive, but she accepted [it] as inevitable. And she wore Grandmother's earrings every [da]y.

Josie was taking one last look at her notes when she heard [fo]otsteps on the stairs outside her office door.

"Good, I caught you," Jacob said as he burst through the [d]oorway. "I've got my car running downstairs. I figured I'd [giv]e you a ride up to Portland, wish you luck, talk to my [pa]rents, and then take you out to dinner afterward. What do [yo]u say?"

"Jacob!" she exclaimed in surprise. "You're certainly in [go]od spirits. Do you know that your father has been frantic?"

"Ever since I missed Yom Kippur, I suppose. No matter. [W]e'll talk about that later. Let's get going."

Swept up in his enthusiasm, Josie cheerfully answered his [gri]lling for her exams all the way to Portland. When he let [he]r out, she realized she hadn't even found out where he'd [be]en, much less what he'd been doing.

He was waiting impatiently outside the door when she [fin]ished the exams. "How'd it go?" he asked anxiously.

"I'm exhausted," she said. "They're nothing if not thor[ou]gh." Then, seeing his concerned look, she smiled. "But I'm [th]orough, too. I was well prepared. Thanks. You've been a [go]od teacher."

He looked relieved. "Great. Then let's go eat. I'm starved. [T]hought you'd never get out of there. Figured you were [ei]ther stumped or dawdling."

"Not quite," she protested as he held the car door open. "I [wa]sn't the first out the door, nor the last. That's a good sign."

He'd made reservations at Jake's, a favorite restaurant wit quiet atmosphere and good food. Once they were seated, h turned to her, taking her hand excitedly and asking, "No what?"

Josie suddenly felt cornered, forced to face what she' dreaded the most. "What do you mean?" she asked, pullin back.

"I mean, what are you planning next? Professionally?"

"Oh, professionally," she said, laughing with relief. "Han out my shingle, of course. What I'd really like," she sai seriously, "is to join an office here in Portland. I'd like benefit from the experience of one of our better law firm you know . . . the same dream every new lawyer has. Excep I'm realistic enough to know that there are precious fe attorneys in this town willing to take on a young fema lawyer," she added soberly.

"What would you say if I told you I know one lawyer wh might take you on?"

"I'd jump for joy—then ask if he was on the up-and-up."

Jacob smiled. "Oh, yes, he's one of the best. But," he sai raising his hand to stop her questions, "I'll have to do son research before I tell you more. Let's just say that I haver been idle waiting for my prize student to flounder around the wilderness by herself."

"Oh, Jacob, do you really think so? Can you give me a litt hint?"

"Not a breath of a hint. Go ahead and eat your dinner. M lips are sealed on the subject."

"I'm losing my appetite, I'm so curious."

"I'm not. So what do you think about your Uncle Timothy"

"What about him?"

Jacob looked at her and shook his head in disbelief. "Do tell me you forgot to vote yesterday."

"Omigosh, the elections!" she exclaimed. "I forgot con pletely."

"Well, your Uncle Timothy is now Oregon's new U. senator."

"If you tell me it was by one vote, I'll never forgi myself."

"No," he said, laughing. "By a landslide. Here." He hand her a copy of his father's newspaper. "*The Occidental* tells all. Look at the picture."

There on page one was Uncle Timothy standing on t capitol steps arm-in-arm with Governor Walter Pierce, w ng one hand over his head, and grinning triumphantly. "Well, here it is," she said grimly. "Timothy Coughlin, elected by he KKK, standing with the governor, who was also elected courtesy of the boys in white hoods. What does it bode for our poor state?"

"Ah, the Klan's on its way out, if you ask me," Jacob said. The Supreme Court decision knocking down the public-chool law took the wind out of their sails. People'll soon have other things to keep their minds busy."

"Until times get rough again and they need scapegoats," he said cynically.

"Maybe. But we'll be ready for them next time. And it tarts with better education and a more vocal press."

Josie thought for a moment, then changed the subject. "I have some news about a new wrinkle in the state's educa-ional system," she volunteered and then proceeded to tell im all about her mother's plans for a musical conservatory.

"Great. That means your mother and your brother will both e back here in a week. I'll contact Timothy and then we can ave the final reading of the will. How about November fteenth? Does that meet with your busy schedule?"

"I'm free, unless that mystery lawyer of yours comes riding p on a white charger demanding I go fight for law and rder."

"You're safe. He doesn't know what's happening yet. I'll all with a time to come in for the reading, okay?"

"I guess it'll have to be," she said. "It's enough to have hose exams over with and to see you in such good spirits. I'll njoy what I have now and not court trouble by thinking bout tomorrow."

Emmett whistled. "Will you take a look at that?"

Josie could hardly believe that the beautiful auburn-haired oman descending from the train was their mother. "Maybe hat I need is a few months in Europe," she murmured.

"Oh, darlings," Hannah exclaimed, hugging them both. t's wonderful to see you. Emmett, will you please help the orter?"

"You look beautiful, Mother," Josie said and then had to mother a giggle. "They're going back in for another load of ggage. Mother, did you buy up half of Europe?"

Hannah smiled brightly. "You wouldn't believe the bar-ins they have over there. I had the best time in Paris."

"Mother, all those trunks and suitcases and boxes—why,

they won't all fit into Emmett's car and leave any room for us."

"Probably not." Hannah signaled for a redcap. "Will you please hail a cab for us?" she asked him sweetly as he came up. "Have it wait at the Sixth Street entrance." She tipped him and turned to Josie, adjusting her fur stole.

"Mother, you seem like a new person. You look beautiful but it's more than that. It's from the inside."

"I'm happier," Hannah said, "and more comfortable with myself than I've ever been in my life. Mother was right—as usual. But you, dear, you look miserable. What's wrong? Did you take your exams?"

"Mother," Emmett said as he pushed an overloaded cart up to them, "I don't know what you think you're going to do with all this—"

"She's ahead of you," Josie said. "There's a cab waiting by the Sixth Street entrance, just for her luggage."

With the cab following behind Emmett's car, they made their way back to Fionna's mansion.

Hannah was full of ideas for the conservatory and wanted to tell them about the teachers she was bringing over as well as about the schools she'd visited in Europe. She even took them into the parlor and played the piano for them, just to prove that her time had not been wasted on sightseeing and plans for others.

As Josie listened to the crystal clear lines of Bach and reveled in the passion of Beethoven, she realized how much her mother's talent had been smothered by unhappiness. Like a caged bird, she'd needed to be set free before she could sing.

As they sat in front of the fire, sipping Fionna's brandy in celebration of their reunion, Emmett also announced some plans. "You know, I think the plane's the transportation of the future. I've given up rumrunning, Mother," he added quickly, "but I haven't given up planes. I talked to some of the people at the hospital here. There's a need for someone who can get medicine, supplies, even doctors to other places in the state in a hurry. It isn't a full-time job by any means, but I'll be using my plane for a sort of emergency service."

"Emmett," Josie said proudly, "that's brilliant. It's a wonderful idea."

"That isn't all. That's just one part of it. We're going to find wonderful uses for the plane in agriculture, too. I'm working with the college."

466

"Speed plowing?" Josie teased. "Or maybe cattle drives?"

"Not quite. Planes could be used to spray crops from the air with everything from insecticides to fertilizer. Think of the time it would save, not to mention money. And there's airmail delivery, even to out-of-the-way places—not just from New York to San Francisco. Just this July a guy flew a transcontinental flight—dawn to dusk, they called it—in less than twenty-two hours. I tell you, Mother, you'll be flying to Europe one day."

"Across the ocean? Oh, Emmett, you *are* a dreamer." Then, as she studied his face, she added, "But it's the dreamers who help us grow beyond ourselves. Don't ever stop."

Under his mother's praise, Emmett grinned his wide-open, boyish grin. "And what about your daughter? Josie's going to set up a law practice and keep the whole state honest."

Hannah looked at her proudly and with just a trace of sadness. "I know she will," she said. "Josie has always been our great hope—especially your grandmother's."

Later that evening, as she went to bed, Josie couldn't help feeling that Fionna was still with them—and that she was smiling.

"Josephine," Hannah called down the hallway the following morning, "are you dressed yet?"

"Almost, Mother."

"Well, throw on a dressing gown and come down here. I want to show you something."

What Hannah had to show her daughter were three beautiful dresses she'd purchased for her in Paris. "They're the latest thing," Hannah said proudly. "Two of them are the mannish-styled suits that are all the rage. I thought they'd be perfect for your law practice. And look at this," she said, as she held up a wool crepe dress. "You've got to try it on."

Josie slipped the soft, violet-colored dress over her head and fastened the tiny covered buttons at the shoulder. The drop waist flowed into a graceful bias-cut skirt that swirled gracefully around her knees. The simplicity of the dress was elegant and flattering.

"Look at you," Hannah exclaimed. "I just knew it would show off your dark hair and those wonderful eyes of your grandmother's. It's perfect. The designer must have had you in mind when she made it."

Emmett looked in then. "Hey, that's terrific. Wear that and you'll have to fight the guys off."

Josie blushed under the barrage of compliments. "Is that why you came in here?" she asked with a grin.

"Oh, I almost forgot in the face of such dazzling beauty. You have a phone call. It's Jacob."

Josie's breath caught in her throat. She'd prepared herself for seeing him tomorrow at the final reading of the will, but not before. She quickly left the room to take the call, ignoring the looks her brother and mother exchanged at her reaction.

"Josie?"

She could see his face in the inflections of his voice. She closed her eyes and felt his words wash over her. "Hello, Jacob."

"Do you have any big plans for this afternoon?"

"No, I guess not. Why?"

"Would you mind coming down to Salem a day early? I'd like to talk to you about some business."

"Yes, I suppose so. Mother and Emmett aren't going that soon, but I have my car, and I can stay out at the farm. Is there anything you want me to bring?" she asked, wondering if she needed a résumé or examples of her work for a potential employer.

"Just you. See you about five o'clock at my house. If it takes very long, I'll take you out to dinner." There was a certain tension in his voice. What if the lawyer he'd told her about had reservations about taking on a woman? Or maybe he had refused. A dozen thoughts flooded her mind, all o them bad.

Back in Hannah's room, Josie confessed her mounting fears "I'm afraid that it's going to be pretty hard to break into a profession that's been a male bastion since its inception. Maybe this whole thing has been a mistake—"

"Oh, cut it out," Emmett interrupted good-heartedly. "One thing I can't stand is a whining woman. You graduated at the top of your class. Someone out there will want the best—and you're it. What are you going to wear to meet this guy?"

"I don't even know if he'll be there," she said listlessly "Oh, I don't know. I don't know what to wear or say o anything."

"Since you're working yourself into such a full-blown case of the blues, I suggest wearing something that makes you fee good," Hannah said. "How about that dress?"

"You don't think it's too—"

"It's perfect," Emmett interrupted. "In fact, I'm hopin that you'll both do me the favor of going out to lunch wit me. If I'm seen with the two most beautiful women in the world, my image as a connoisseur of women will soar."

"Just like your planes." Hannah laughed. "You have a date."

Josie's spirits were in much better condition by the time she left her mother and brother. It was impossible not to be optimistic in the face of their enthusiasm.

Still, by the time she was halfway to Salem, her stomach started tightening. Was it because she was scared about her professional future? Or was it because she didn't want to face her personal loss? Jacob was the one love of her life, but the one that could never be.

Try as she would, she'd found it next to impossible to be at ease around him. It was like being around a cat that you wanted desperately to like you but knew it never would, being a cat and all, so you simply tried very hard not to offend or scare it so that it would at least tolerate your presence.

She hadn't succeeded in calming her stomach by the time she pulled into Jacob's driveway. There was simply too much tied up in all this, she thought as she got out of the car.

Her nervousness made her distracted, and she had to force herself to sit still in the chair Jacob offered her. Seeing that no one else was there, she allowed a few moments for small talk and then came straight to the point.

"Is anyone else coming?" she asked.

"No. Why?" For the first time, she sensed that Jacob, too, was uneasy about something.

"Well, I thought you might know something—or have someone . . . I mean," she admitted, "I was hoping that you'd have news about that lawyer friend of yours."

"Ah, well, he's not quite a friend," he said hesitantly. "I just thought—"

"Did you find out whether I could have a job or not?" Josie could bear the suspense no longer.

"Well, it depends," Jacob said, getting up and walking to the window. "He's interested in a partner," he said, turning nervously to Josie, "but there's a contingency, a kind of—"

"Oh, I'm willing to work my way into the business," Josie broke in. "As long as he's willing to give me a chance. Is it someone well established?"

"I like to think he's one of the better judicial minds in the state," he said wryly. Jacob paced back to the fireplace, stopped to poke the fire, then absently moved back to the window. "But it would work out only if you could see your way clear—"

"Why are you stalling? What is this contingency?"

Jacob cleared his throat. "You'd have to marry him."

"What? What old goat would . . . who is this so-called legal mind? Who would ever require that—" Josie sputtered angrily.

"Whoa," Jacob said, laughing. "Don't you even want to hear who it is? On the off-chance you might be interested?"

"I'd never accept something—"

"It's me."

"What did you say?" she said, rising in surprise.

"I said, it's me," he said softly, his eyes resting on her for the first time that day. "I want you to marry me."

"But I thought—"

"You thought, but I didn't. Josie, I love you more than life itself. I can't live without you. Fionna told me a story before she died, telling me that I would know when I should tell it to you. I realize now that she told me more for myself than for you. She told me that she wasn't married to your grandfather until she felt it was necessary to clarify inheritance rights. She didn't think that marriage was a convention to be adhered to because of the traditions of society—but because of love and practical necessities."

He began walking slowly toward her. "She was right. I've been bound by traditions that didn't apply to me. I've just been fooling myself, saying that everything I'd been taught was irrefutable. Traditions don't apply to everyone."

"But what about your family? What about our differences?"

"They don't matter anymore. They're nothing in the face of our love. When I was walking on the beach, I tried to picture what it would be like living without you. I can't." He looked at her, then turned away. "I'd understand if you decided you never wanted to see me again. I've tried to run away from you two times. Each time it's been a disaster."

"What about your teaching job?"

"I've handed in my resignation, effective January first. It's time I set up my own practice instead of hiding in an ivory tower. I've been running away from reality for too long."

"Just make sure it won't happen again," she said with tears in her eyes. "I couldn't bear it if I lost you again."

"Does that mean yes?"

"Yes!" she cried, going to him. "Yes, yes!" Joyfully sh
470

kissed him, then kissed him again, touching his face, feeling his arms encircle her.

Looking into his eyes, she knew she was where she belonged.

Later, as she lay in his arms, she told him the story of the earrings Fionna had willed to her, the story of the love her grandmother and his grandfather had shared so many years ago.

Jacob listened in silence, then murmured, "Somehow, I'm not surprised. This is the way it was meant to be a very long time ago." He pulled her to him, proclaiming their love with every touch. The circle was complete.

Chapter XXXIX

The reading of Fee's will was set for one o'clock. Josie didn't care how it went. Now that her life was the way it was meant to be, she would be happy no matter what happened.

However, that was not quite the way the others approached their lawyer's office that afternoon.

Hannah came full of hope that she would have a bit of the family fortune to start her musical conservatory.

Emmett came concerned about the land that his grandfather had written about and his uncle was determined to sell. He had grown up considerably in the past few months and was beginning to take his responsibilities seriously.

Timothy came confident that, as the only son, he would inherit the lion's share of the family fortune. He was anxious to have it settled before he moved to Washington, D.C.

Nell and Mateo were coming also. They both approached the reading with curiosity, expecting little more than kind words and perhaps a small remembrance from their former employer and friend.

Jacob was busily sorting through the final instructions that Fionna had left him. He knew most of what was going to transpire this afternoon, but there was one thing that Jacob was in the dark about. Fionna loved mysteries and surprises and she'd managed to arrange one for Jacob a full eight months after her death. It was as if his old friend were back in his office, laughing in her irresistible way.

Josie was the first to arrive. Jacob had barely closed the

door behind her before she was in his arms. "Tell me I wasn't dreaming last night," she whispered between kisses.

"I hope you weren't," he said, smiling down at her, "because I'm building my entire future on it."

"Now about our business arrangement," Josie teased. "I think since I have to pay such a high price up front, I should be granted at least a full partnership from the beginning."

Jacob bowed gallantly. "You drive a hard bargain, but I accept your terms."

"And vacations?"

"Only in the company of your partner."

"What about maternity leave?"

"Already?"

Josie laughed. "Silly, I just wanted to see how you felt about it."

"I think we should create a dynasty, one that will guide this great state of ours to new heights of glory, one that—"

Josie cut off his dramatic display with another kiss. "I do love you," she said.

"And I you. When should we tell your family?"

"How about tonight over dinner? We can invite everyone." She paused, then added, "I wish Grandmother could be with us."

Just then Hannah arrived, a silver fox stole draped over the shoulder of her emerald green suit. "Jacob," she exclaimed "how wonderful to see you again. You had something to do with Mother getting those tickets for me, and I want to thank—"

"Not at all," he protested. "I didn't have the faintest idea what was in that envelope until you told me. It was all her doing."

"I hope it was all her doing." Timothy's cigar smoke preceded him through the doorway. "Mother was eccentric enough. She didn't need you to help her in that way, Teall."

"Uncle Timothy," Emmett said, following him in, "that's your Maxwell out front, isn't it? You're in a no-parking zone."

"It doesn't matter," Timothy said with a wave of his hand "I won't be in here that long, and the police know my car. Looks like we're all here. Let's get on with it, Teall."

"Just a minute, Timothy," Jacob said, nodding toward the door where Nell and Mateo were entering.

"What the hell are they doing here?" Timothy said, growling

"It was stipulated in the will," Jacob told him. Timothy glowered but said no more.

472

"Fionna has left you each a second letter," Jacob began. "Only this one you are to read aloud to the rest of the group. That way everyone will know, through Fee's own words, that the disbursement of the entire estate is. Hannah, you go first."

With an air of anticipation, Hannah took the letter and broke the seal. The room became still as she began reading.

> *My darling daughter,*
>
> *As you read this you are starting on a new and brighter stage of your life, one that will lead you to fulfill the potential I have always known you had. It may not be the way that we'd originally envisioned it, but it will be uniquely your own. I wish you luck in your new venture.*

Hannah stopped reading and looked up at Jacob. "How did she know?"

"She left a choice of sealed letters. Instructions were attached to each one, depending on what had transpired in the last few months. Please go on."

> *To complete your plans, you will need access to funds as well as stable income. For that purpose, I've arranged for you to have a selection of stocks and bonds, which you can cash upon need. Jacob has the key to a safety deposit box in which they are kept. You also will have the house in Portland and the downtown office buildings, which will provide you with a comfortable income, and there is a large estate of investments left to me by my sister, Judith, with the covenant that they be passed on to you, her namesake.*
>
> *I want to set up a trust over which you will have control. It is to be maintained by the profits from your father's patent on mill machinery and the Roseburg sawmill. You are to administer this trust to finance educational and artistic ventures within the state of Oregon. The details of this trust are specified in a separate document I have left with Jacob Teall. You are to study all applicants carefully and choose the ones you deem worthy of support. These grants will be made in the name of the entire family.*
>
> *I know that I am leaving all this in capable, deserving hands. I pass on to you, my daughter, not only a legacy of material value but also a legacy of responsibility for*

473

furthering the cultural and educational growth of our state, the state that has been so good to our family. I give you this legacy with confidence and my love.

Your loving mother

The room was quiet when Hannah finished reading. Sh looked up from the letter and smiled tearfully. "How lovely, she whispered, holding the letter to her breast. "She knew a along. I guess I should have known, too."

"Your mother was quite a remarkable woman," Jacob agreed "Timothy, would you read yours next?"

"I'd like to read it and get on out of here," he said impa tiently. "Do I have to sit here and listen to everyone's sent mental little note?"

"It was your mother's wish," Jacob replied.

Timothy sighed as he ripped the envelope open and bega to read.

Timothy, my son,
If you are reading this letter, it means that you have achieved one of the greatest compliments the people of this state can confer. You have won the United States Senate seat. I offer you my congratulations and best wishes.

Timothy paused, looking around the room proudly. "Sh really had everything figured out, didn't she? I guess it worth staying to hear her rate of accuracy," he added with laugh.

I also offer you my plea for justice and common sense. However, I don't think that plea will land on a willing heart. If you have won this election, you have done so using the influence of those you should be working to eradicate rather than condoning through your association. For this reason, I must sadly conclude that you will never change from the selfish opportunist you've always been.

I can see now that you really were the one behind your brother Daniel's death so many years ago. Mr. Ranahan told me you were the one who betrayed Daniel's trust. All this time I've tried to convince myself that you did it out of misplaced concern for your brother's welfare. Now I know differently.

474

Timothy threw down the pages. "What kind of tripe is ~~th~~is?" he demanded. "Do I have to sit here and be insulted ~~b~~y a dead woman?"

"If you want to know what your inheritance is, you do," ~~Ja~~cob said. Timothy glared at him, then turned back to the ~~le~~tter, reading more hesitantly this time.

> *You betrayed a trust then and you have betrayed many others since then. For that reason, I am leaving you with a different kind of trust, one that you cannot betray but that might help you to become a better person in spite of yourself.*
>
> *The profits from the lumberyards and a few specified stocks are set aside for this purpose. But these are not for your personal use. You will administer this trust for others less fortunate than yourself. No doubt your political salaries and the gifts of grateful "friends" and good investments will maintain you very well. This trust, which is detailed specifically in an attached document, is to be distributed by you after careful study of the applying agencies. The qualifying agencies are: the Indian Orphans Fund, the Jewish Widows and Orphans Fund, the Catholic Fund for the Poor, Scholarships for Emigrants, and the National Association for the Advancement of Colored People. If you wish to donate one cent of this fund to any other agency, it can be done only with the unanimous approval of all other living beneficiaries of this will.*
>
> *In order that you understand this is your full and complete inheritance, I am leaving you your father's gold watch as well.*
>
> *In high hopes that you may someday rise above your baser instincts, I remain*
>
> *Your loving mother*

Timothy threw the letter to the floor. "This is pure, un~~ad~~ulterated trash!" he declared. "I'll hear no more of it. It ~~wo~~n't hold up in court—"

"Please, Timothy," Hannah said, "let's hear the rest of ~~wh~~at Mother has to say before you do anything rash."

Timothy muttered, "I'll listen, but it's not the last you'll ~~he~~ar from me. She was addled in her old age. Senile."

"Emmett, you're next," Jacob said, handing a letter to ~~hi~~m."

Emmett grinned. "I don't know what you're doing, Grams," he said, "but as usual, it's with style."

My dearest grandson,
If you are reading this letter, you've indicated that you are beginning to take your responsibilities seriously. I would like to think that reading your grandfather's journals had something to do with that. Either way, you are beginning to find your niche in the world, whatever it may be.
To you I'm giving what you will understand is one of the most precious trusts of the Coughlin estate. You are to be the owner of the wilderness and timberlands your grandfather so carefully acquired throughout his life. I believe you are the only one who will handle the land with the respect and care your grandfather wished.
Along with the lands, you will have the logging operations and the Strawberry Mountain, Bear Flat, and Big Valley ranches.
Under the influence of your enthusiasm I have invested in stock in a plant making airplanes. It is most appropriate that you receive that as well.
So to you, my grandson, I bequeath the legacy of responsibility for the land. I know it is in good hands. Care for it with the courage you were given by your grandfather.
                                         Your loving grandmother

Emmett shook his head as he carefully folded the letter and replaced it in its envelope. "She knew us all so well," murmured.

"It's a bunch of nonsense," Timothy complained. "The wilderness area is worthless. It would be better off sold, like proposed. I even have people willing to take it off our hands."

Jacob ignored his comments and turned to Josie. "Here your letter, Josephine. Let's hear what Fionna has in store her favorite granddaughter."

"I'm her only granddaughter, silly," Josie said as she to the envelope and opened it. She was smiling as she began read.

My dearest granddaughter,
I have so much to say for which there are no words Let me begin by saying that where your brother, uncle

476

*and mother had more than one potential letter, you have
only one. I cannot bring myself to envision that you
could possibly make more than one choice. Therefore,
let me announce that you have completed your bar exams
successfully and are now planning your marriage to
Jacob Teall.*

Josie gasped as she read the last sentence. Her eyes met
Jacob's as the others murmured in surprise.

Then Jacob threw his head back and laughed. He came
over and put his arms around Josie. "We should have known
better. We were going to make the announcement over dinner tonight. But Fee would have her one last surprise."

"How did she know?" Josie marveled. She turned to her
mother. "We didn't decide until last night."

"That's great!" Emmett said. "It's about time you two came
to your senses."

"I'm flabbergasted," Hannah said. "Josie, is this something
you've agreed to without your grandmother's pressure?" she
asked with concern.

Josie nodded. "Grandmother didn't make me fall in love
with him. That happened long ago, before she knew I was
ready to fall in love."

"Then I'm happy for you," Hannah said, hugging her.

Timothy was looking at them all with astonishment. "Do
you think this is the kind of thing to go rushing into?" he
asked. "What will people think? You two are hardly from
similar backgrounds—"

"Oh, Uncle Timothy, Jacob and I have talked about his
Judaism and it doesn't change a thing."

"Besides, we've all grown up together," Emmett said. "Our
families have been the best of friends for three generations.
That's a lot in common. And they're both lawyers. What
more could you ask? Put your bigotry away for a change. Are
you worried about what your hooded friends will do?"

Timothy snorted. "I don't know what you're all so happy
about. This will won't stand up in court, anyway. Get on with
your letter, Josephine."

*I have several real-estate investments in Salem and
Portland that I am leaving you, as well as the sawmills in
Eugene, Salem, Baker, and Klamath Falls. My shipping
stocks are yours as well as my savings account.
I know that the land and investments, when combined*

477

with the newspaper business that Jacob is destined to inherit, will provide you both with powerful leverage in this state. With your legal backgrounds, you two will help guide the destiny of Oregon very capably. Because of your unique viewpoints, diverse yet similar, I know that you will ensure that others are treated with justice both under the law and in employment.

That is your legacy, my granddaughter, the legacy of justice. Your real inheritance I've given you since childhood: my belief in equality for everyone under the law. I know that the power I have vested in you will be used with wisdom and love for the benefit of others.

I remain with you in love and faith,

Grandmother

Josie couldn't speak for a moment. Then she murmured "That's lovely."

"It's ridiculous," Timothy protested.

"Mateo," Jacob said before Timothy could begin again "you also have a letter to read."

Mateo came forward, his handsome face filled with curiosity and surprise. He sat on the edge of the desk and began reading aloud.

My dear Mateo,

I'm not certain how much your mother told you before she died. I never had the courage to ask. I know that you were still young. However, now that I am dying, I want to make sure you know your true rights.

You need not worry about becoming an American citizen, as we talked about before the Great War. I'm afraid that I was not quite truthful with you. Nor do you need worry about ever having a job again.

You are my grandson. Your father was Matthew, whom you were named for. I have spent a good deal of money investigating this claim, although I never really doubted it from the beginning. The results of that investigation are in a file Jacob Teall has, just in case this is disputed. You were born in Cuba six months after Matthew was killed delivering arms to the rebels there and a year after he married your mother in a secret ceremony.

I brought you to this country when your mother died, hoping that you would prove your father's son in action as well as blood. You have done more than that. You *have managed the Bar C Ranch with integrity and in a profitable manner. That is good, because it is now your ranch. You also have the first option of purchasing the other ranches should Emmett ever decide to sell them. Along with the ranch goes all equipment, livestock, buildings, and vehicles. I know you will run it with wisdom and care. There is also a portfolio of railroad stock I have set aside in your name, as well as the farmlands in Salem.*

So you see, Mateo, as a member of this family, you also have a legacy. It is a legacy of trust. You are given the first and largest Coughlin ranch and my original farm. Into your hands I have placed a part of the land and the lives of people who have been dependent upon our family for three generations. I know that you will treat them all with fairness and understanding.

> *I give you my love, my grandson,*
> *Grandmother*

Mateo put down the letter and looked around the room. "I . . I don't know what to say."

"It's wonderful," Josie exclaimed.

"I always said we had ties going way back, didn't I, cousin?" mmett said, slapping Mateo on the back.

"I have never heard of—" Timothy began.

"It's all well documented," Jacob interrupted. "I will be appy to show you as soon as we're finished. Nell, Fee left a pecial trust for you, too. She is giving you the rooming ouse in Corvallis and an office building downtown. The venue from these will provide a comfortable living for you ways, but she hopes you will remain with Hannah, whom e believes will benefit from your common sense, as she ways did."

Nell wiped tears from her cheeks and nodded. "Of course. e don't have to do anything and here she even thinks of me ith all she had on her mind."

"There's one other thing," Jacob said. "She has established trust fund for her great-grandchildren with some of her ersonal stocks and bonds. She even has a letter for them to ad when they come of age."

"It seems she thought of everything, except her son and ir," Timothy said, standing up. "I can assure you, Teall, u won't get away with this. I'm going to challenge this will the way to the U.S. Supreme Court if necessary. It won't

479

work, I tell you," he said, pounding his fist on Jacob's desk "You can't disinherit a son and give the family fortune awa' to a foreigner and a . . . a . . . charwoman!"

"That's your right, Timothy," Jacob acknowledged. "How ever," he added before Timothy had put on his coat, "I thin you should consider a couple of facts before you decide t take any action. You should recognize that the trust Fionn has set up will make you one of the most respected an well-loved men in this state. Why, you'll be in charge of on of the biggest charitable trusts this state has ever seen. It' be to you people will turn when they need help. And it wi be your name that they will remember when they vote You'll always be thought of as the benefactor of the poor an needy."

Timothy put his coat back down on his chair. "Go on," h said.

"Likewise, your mother was right when she said you' become wealthy in your own right. Your bank account rigl now has a sizable amount in it just from the profits you'v received over the past six months. It's enough to set you u in Washington. From then on you'll be able to use you political connections to make some fine investments."

"But that's not now," Timothy said. "And that's not m birthright. These lands and monies are mine—from birtl I've earned them."

"Well, go ahead and challenge the will then," Jacob saic walking behind his desk. "Remember that if you do, tha letter, which is part and parcel of the legal document, wi become public knowledge. It did say something about betrayir your twin brother, didn't it? Something about causing Da iel's death? Do you want that to come out in the papers?"

Timothy deflated like a leaking balloon in front of the very eyes. He could never allow that letter to be mac public, not if he wanted to run for office again.

He walked over to the window and looked down at tl street. "Mother certainly did me in on this one, didn't she' he asked with grudging admiration in his voice.

"What do you mean?" Josie asked.

"I mean, with that charitable trust, I'm guaranteed tl admiration of ninety percent of the voters of this state. At tl same time, I'm automatically cut off from the people wl elected me in the first place. My hooded friends, as Emme so colorfully calls them, will have nothing to do with me tl minute word of this gets out. So, you see, Mother has fin gled the situation so that I'm going to represent the views she held whether I like it or not.

"At the same time, that trust Hannah will administer will be in the family name. I'm going to come across to the voters as one magnanimous benefactor of the state. And they'll expect me to vote along those lines, too." He put on his coat. "And Mother arranged to get me some awfully good press coverage, something no politician can resist."

He shook his head. "She always got her way, one way or another," he muttered as he headed out the door.

Jacob watched as Timothy closed the door behind him. "You know," he said, "I can't shake the feeling that Fionna's somewhere laughing right now."

"I know she is," Josie agreed.

"I think she's right here," Hannah said, joining in. "Now, I get to take everyone out to dinner tonight. My mother announced my daughter's engagement today."

Postlude

"Where's Uncle Timothy?" Josie asked as she walked out the French doors of Fionna's mansion. "They're ready to start taking the pictures."

"I think he's in the den with the newspaper reporters," Emmett said. "Ever since he announced the Timothy Coughlin Foundation Grant, he's been front-page news. Want me to go get him?"

"Listen and see if the interviews are winding down. I'd hate to deprive him of that after everything that's happened—not that he didn't deserve it," she added hastily. "But I want everyone to be as happy as I am today."

Emmett kissed her cheek. "That would be hard to do, Sis. You're glowing—and a beautiful bride, too. In fact, you come pretty close to female perfection. Probably ruined it for me," he added with a dramatic shrug. "I'll never be able to find a woman as lovely as my sister. I'm doomed to wander the earth searching— "

"Oh, stop it," she said, laughing. "Just go check on Uncle Timothy, will you? And then you and Mateo come into the parlor."

Emmett started towards the door, then stopped, looking up at the enamel blue sky. "Tell me," he said, "how did you arrange for sunshine on a January day?"

Josie giggled. "I think it was part of Gram's will."

"What's all this frivolity out on the patio?" Jacob asked, coming out to them. "Don't you know that this is a solemn occasion?"

"If that's the case, wipe that silly grin off your face," Emmett challenged. "You're happier than a clam at high tide and you know it."

"Happy, indeed," he said, kissing Josie. "But I realize what it took to get us here."

"And what's that?" Emmett asked.

"Two generations of foolishness. And one generation of near-misses. Come on, you two." He smiled as he put his arm around Josie's waist. "There's a wedding party waiting for us."

The parlor looked like springtime. The florist had forced tulips, daffodils, hyacinths, and forsythia into bloom and filled the room with armloads of fragrant blossoms. Josie and Jacob stood patiently under the canopy, smiling and exchanging quips with friends and family while the photographer snapped away. Then, once the pictures were finished, they moved to the punch bowl.

Holding his glass of lemonade aloft, Emmett turned to the bride and groom. "It's my privilege, as best man and best brother, to make the first toast. Let's drink to my sister, the bride, and my friend, the groom. To Josephine Barry Coughlin Teall and Jacob Abraham Teall, the inheritors of a legacy of integrity, justice, and love."

Josie's eyes filled with tears as she raised her glass to accept her brother's toast. She leaned her head against Jacob's shoulder, and he kissed the top of her head affectionately.

"I, too, have a toast," Jacob said, raising his glass. "If I had three, I would toast first my beloved bride, and second her beautiful mother—but since I only have one . . ." Here he had to pause because of general laughter. With a smile, he continued, "since I only have one, I wish to toast our invisible hostess and most honored guest: To the woman whose wisdom will see us through the good times as well as the bad. To Fionna Barry Coughlin. She has truly left her mark on the land and its people. God bless you, Fee."

ABOUT THE AUTHOR

LANA McGRAW BOLDT was born a fourth-generation Oregonian. She attended the University of Oregon, earning a degree in English literature, and did postgraduate work in applied psychology at the University of Washington. With her husband, Darrell, she served in the Peace Corps in Micronesia. The Marshall Islands Cultural Museum is a result of some of her work there.

She has traveled in Asia, the Middle East, and Europe and has worked as a teacher, a magazine correspondent, and a resource writer for the Oregon Shakespearean Festival. Currently at work on her third novel, she resides in Oregon with her husband and two daughters.